THE RING
OF THE LÖWENSKÖLDS

THE RING
OF THE LÖWENSKÖLDS

INCLUDING

THE GENERAL'S RING
CHARLOTTE LÖWENSKÖLD
ANNA SVÄRD

BY

SELMA LAGERLÖF

LITERARY GUILD
NEW YORK
1931

PRINTED AT THE *Country Life Press*, GARDEN CITY, N. Y., U. S. A.

CONTENTS

THE GENERAL'S RING

I

I KNOW that in former days there were plenty of people who knew not the meaning of the word "fear." I have heard of folk who loved to skate on the thinnest of ice, of others who knew no greater joy than to drive unbroken horses. There have, indeed, been even a few who would play cards with Colour Sergeant Ahlegard, although he had every trick at his fingers' ends and always managed to win. Then there are intrepid souls who have had the courage to start travelling on a Friday and to sit down thirteen to table.

But I wonder whether any even of such would have had courage to wear the fearsome ring that had belonged to old General Löwensköld of Hedeby.

It was this same old General who had won fame, property, and a title for the Löwenskölds; and so long as there was one of the family living at Hedeby, his portrait hung in the big upper drawing room, between the windows. It was a large picture, reaching from the floor to the ceiling. On glancing at it casually, you might have mistaken it for Charles the Twelfth himself, standing there firmly planted on the tessellated floor, in his blue coat, chamois leather gloves, and enormous jack boots. But, on a closer glance, you realized that it was an entirely different person.

A broad, rough peasant face rose above the coat collar. The man looked born to follow the plough all the days of his life; but, in spite of his plainness, he gave the impression of being a wise, reliable, even great, man. Had he been born in these days, he would, at least, have been on a jury, or the chairman of a Municipal Council; but living, as he did, in the reign of the great hero king, he went out and fought as a poor soldier and returned as the rich General Löwensköld, receiving as the reward of the Crown for all his service the estate of Hedeby, in the parish of Bro.

As a matter of fact, the longer you looked at the picture, the more reconciled to it you became. You seemed to realize that it was men such as this who had, under the leadership of King Charles the Twelfth, ploughed the furrow between Poland and Russia. His army had not been composed wholly of adventurers and courtiers; there had been simple, earnest men, such as the one in this picture, who had loved him, and found him a King worth living and dying for.

While studying the picture, there was generally one of the family at hand to point out that not vanity alone had prompted the General to remove the glove from his left hand, so as to display the great signet ring which he wore on his forefinger. This was the ring he had received from the King—there was only one King for him—and it was shown in the picture as a sign that

Bengt Löwensköld was his faithful servant. He had been forced to listen to much bitter censure of his sovereign; there were those who even ventured to assert that, by his imprudence and recklessness, he had brought his kingdom to the verge of ruin; but the General was loyal to him through everything. The King was a man whose like had never been seen, and those who lived with him, had come to realize that there are nobler and higher causes for which to fight than merely worldly honour and success.

The same reason that caused Bengt Löwensköld to display his ring in his portrait made him wish to have it buried in his grave with him. And here, too, there was no question of vanity. He had no wish, certainly, to boast of wearing a great King's jewel on his finger when he appeared in the presence of Our Lord and the Archangels, but he hoped that, when he entered the hall where Charles the Twelfth would be sitting, surrounded by his trusty swordsmen, the ring might win him recognition, so that he would spend eternity close to the man whom he had served and honoured all his life.

When the General's coffin was placed in the walled vault which he had had prepared for himself in Bro churchyard, the ring was safe on the forefinger of his left hand. Many of those present regretted that so great a treasure should go with the dead man to his grave, for the General's ring was almost as well known as the General himself, and as famous. It was said to be of sufficient value to buy a vast estate, and that the red cornelian, engraved with the King's signature, was no less valuable. People were universally agreed that it was generous of his sons not to oppose his wish, but to bury his treasure with him.

If the General's ring really resembled that represented in the picture, it must certainly have been a clumsy thing which hardly anyone nowadays could wear; but a few hundred years ago it would have been greatly valued. We must remember that all jewels and vessels of precious metals, with very few exceptions, had to be handed over to the Crown; that the nation had to struggle against "Gortz's Tokens" and national bankruptcy, so that, to many people, gold was a thing only spoken of, never seen. This is why folk could not forget the ring, so uselessly buried under the coffin lid. Its burial there was almost an injustice. It might have been taken to some foreign country, sold for a great sum to be used in procuring food for the many who now had nothing to eat save straw and the bark of trees.

Yet, though there were many who longed to possess the great treasure, there was not one who thought seriously of appropriating it. The ring lay in the coffin, with the lid screwed down, in a walled-up grave, under a heavy gravestone, out of reach of the most daring thief, and there they believed it would lie till the end of the world.

II

GENERAL Bengt Löwensköld died in the month of March, 1741, and a few months later in the same year, it happened that his eldest son, George Löwensköld, who lived generally at Hedeby, lost his little daughter from dysentery. She was buried on a Sunday immediately after the service; the whole congregation joined in the procession to the grave of the Löwenskölds, where the gravestones were standing up on end. The vault underneath had been opened by a mason in order that the dead child's little coffin might lie beside her grandfather's.

While the people were gathered round the grave listening to the burial service, it is possible that many of them remembered the royal ring and regretted that it should be lying hidden and useless in that grave, of no benefit to anyone. Perhaps here and there one whispered to his neighbour that it would not be difficult to get the ring, since the grave would not probably be closed again before the next day.

In the crowd there stood a countryman named Bard Bardsson, who lived at Mellomstuga in the village of Olsby. He, however, was not one of those who had worried themselves gray over the ring. On the contrary, when people began talking about it, he always declared that he had a good enough farm, so had no need to envy the General for taking a bushel of gold with him to his grave.

Now, as he stood in the churchyard, it occurred to him, as to so many others, how strange it was that the grave should have been opened. It did not please him, it made him uneasy. He thought to himself: "The Captain ought to have it closed this afternoon, there are many people longing for that ring."

Although it was no concern of his, nevertheless, he kept on thinking how dangerous it would be to leave the grave open all night. It was the month of August; the nights were dark, and if the grave was not shut that very day, a thief might easily creep in and carry off the treasure. He was seized with such acute anxiety that he even contemplated going himself to warn the Captain, but he knew that people considered him foolish, and he did not want to make himself a laughing stock. "You are quite right about this," he thought to himself, "but if you are too officious you will only be laughed at. The Captain, who is such a sensible man, has certainly arranged for the grave to be shut up again."

He was so absorbed with his thoughts that he did not notice that the funeral was over, but stood still beside the grave, and might have stood much longer had not his wife pulled him by the sleeve.

"What is the matter with you?" she said. "You are

standing staring at one spot like a cat watching a rat hole."

The man turned round and, looking up, saw that he and his wife were alone in the churchyard.

"There's nothing the matter," he said. "I was only just wondering . . ."

He would have liked to tell his wife what he was wondering, but he knew that she was much sharper than himself. She would only think that he was worrying himself unnecessarily. She would say that if the grave were shut or not was a question that concerned nobody but Captain Löwensköld.

They turned to go home, and, as soon as Bard Bardsson had turned his back on the churchyard, he hoped he would forget the matter. But he did not, for his wife talked of nothing but the funeral, of the coffin, of the bearers, of the procession, and of the sermon; and he put in a word here and there—although he heard scarcely a word that she said—so that she should not know he was not listening. But presently her voice seemed to be reaching him from the far distance, and his brain went back to the worrying thoughts.

"This is Sunday," he thought, "perhaps the mason won't work on a day of rest. In that case, if the Captain gave him a rix-dollar, he could do it in the night. If only he could think of that!"

Presently he began to talk to himself aloud. "I ought to go to the Captain in any case. I ought not to mind whether folk laugh at me or not."

He had quite forgotten that his wife was walking beside him, but he pulled himself up when she stopped and stared at him.

"It's nothing," he said, "it's only what I was thinking of before." And so they continued their journey and soon reached their own door.

He hoped now that his troublesome thoughts would leave him; and so they might had he set about some work, but it was Sunday, and on that day the people at Mellomstuga all went to their own quarters after dinner. He remained by himself in the cottage, and immediately the same doubts recurred to his mind.

At last he got up from his seat, and, going out, began to saddle his horse, intending to ride to Hedeby and speak to the Captain.

"If I don't," he thought, "the ring will be stolen tonight."

Nevertheless, he could not bring himself to take the matter so seriously. He was too shy. He went, instead, to the farm of one of his neighbours, intending to tell the man about his anxiety; but, as the man was not alone, he again felt too shy to speak, and ended by riding home without having said a word about the matter.

As soon as the sun set, he went to bed determining to sleep till morning; but there was no sleep for him. All his restlessness came back, and he lay tossing and turning the whole night. His wife, naturally, could not sleep either, and after a time she asked him why he was so restless.

"It is nothing," he answered as usual. "Only something I am thinking about."

"You have said that several times already to-day," answered his wife, "but I think it is time now for you to tell me what you *are* thinking about. You can't have anything so dangerous in your mind that you can't tell me about it, surely."

Bard persuaded himself, on hearing his wife speak thus, that, if he told her his trouble, he would get to sleep.

"I am only wondering whether the old General's vault has been closed up," he said, "or whether it will stay open all night."

His wife laughed. "I've been thinking of that too," she said, "and I expect that everybody in church to-day was thinking the same. But you needn't let a thing like that rob you of your sleep."

Bard was glad that his wife took the matter so easily. He felt relieved and certain that now he would sleep.

But hardly had he settled himself before it all started again. He saw shadows come stealing out of every cottage, every quarter, all going on the same errand, all turning their steps toward the churchyard with the open vault. He tried to lie still so that his wife might sleep, but his head ached and his body sweated. He was forced to toss and turn. At last his wife lost all patience and blurted out, half in jest:

"Dear husband, I really think you had better go to the churchyard and see after the grave yourself, instead of tossing from side to side and never closing your eyes."

The words were hardly out of her mouth before her husband jumped out of bed and began to dress himself. He thought his wife was right. It was not more than half an hour's walk from Olsby to Bro church; he would be back within an hour, and then could have a good night's rest. But scarcely was he outside the door before it occurred to his wife that it would be a dreadful thing to let him go all alone to the churchyard; so she sprang up hastily, and she too put on her clothes.

She caught up to her husband on the slope, just below Olsby. Bard laughed as he heard her coming up behind.

"Have you come to see that I don't steal the General's ring?" he asked.

"Good gracious!" she said. "I know that you wouldn't think of such a thing. I only came to help you in case you met a ghoul or a hellhound."

They went forward at a brisk pace. Night had fallen, and it was quite dark except for a narrow streak of light in the western sky, but they were quite sure of the road. They chatted together and were in high spirits. They were only going to the churchyard to see whether the grave was still open, so that Bard could stop worrying and go to sleep.

"I can't believe that the family at Hedeby can be so rash as not to have had the ring fastened up again," said Bard.

"Well, we shall soon know," said his wife. "I believe that's the churchyard wall just close to us now."

The man stopped. He wondered why his wife's voice sounded so cheerful. Surely she could have no other reason than his own for coming on this journey.

"Before we go into the churchyard," said Bard, "we must come to some agreement as to what to do in case the grave is open."

"Whether it is open or not, I don't see that there is anything we can do, except go home and get into bed."

"No, you are right," said Bard, and went on. After a little, he said again, "I suppose we can hardly expect to find the churchyard gate unlocked at this hour."

"No, it's shut. We shall have to climb over the wall, if we want to pay a visit to the General and see how he is."

Again the man was astonished. He heard a slight rattle of falling stones, and his wife's form was outlined against the strip of bright sky toward the west. She had climbed to the top of the wall, which, after all, was not a great feat, as it was only a couple of feet high; but it was strange that she should be so eager to get in before him.

"Here," she said, "give me your hand, I will help you up."

They soon left the wall and went forward silently and carefully between the little mounds. Once Bard stumbled over a grave and nearly fell; it seemed to him as if someone had tripped him up. He was so terrified that he trembled, but he said in a loud voice, so that the dead might understand how benevolent he was:

"I should not be walking here if there was any harm in my errand."

"You may well say that!" said his wife. "You are quite right. But, do you see, there is the grave over there."

He could just see the gravestone standing on end, outlined against the dark sky. They soon reached the grave, and found it still open. The opening into the vault had not been walled up.

"I think this is dreadfully careless," said the man. "I believe it is only done to expose all the people, who know how great a treasure lies hidden here, to the greatest temptation."

"They rely on the idea that no one will dare to rob the dead," said his wife.

"It wouldn't be very pleasant, either, to go into that vault," said the man. "Getting down wouldn't be so difficult, but once in, one would stop there like a fox in a trap."

"I noticed, this afternoon, that there was a little ladder into the vault," said the woman, "but it has probably been taken away."

"I must just look and see," said the man, groping his way toward the opening. "Now, would you believe it!" he burst out, "this beats everything! The ladder is still here."

"That is very careless," chimed in his wife, "but, after all, he who dwells down there can very well protect his own property. It doesn't matter."

"If only I could be sure of that," said her husband. "Perhaps I ought at least to move the ladder away."

"I don't think we ought to move anything here. It is better that the grave should be found, to-morrow, exactly as they left it."

They stood irresolute and at a loss what to do, staring down into the vault. They ought, indeed, to have gone home now, but something mysterious, which neither of them dared to allude to, kept them rooted to the spot.

"I should let the ladder remain," said Bard, "if I were only certain that the General has the power to keep off thieves."

"You had better go down into the vault, and then you can see what power he has," said his wife.

It seemed as though Bard had been waiting for this order from his wife, for immediately he climbed down the ladder into the vault. But scarcely had he reached the floor of the death chamber when he heard a step on the ladder, and his wife stood beside him.

"So you have come down too," he said.

"I dared not let you be here alone with the dead."

"Oh, I don't believe he is so dangerous, after all," said the man. "There is no cold hand that will squeeze the life out of me."

"You see, he won't do anything to us, because he knows that we don't intend to steal the ring. But, suppose, just for fun, we were to begin to unscrew the coffin lid!"

Immediately the man approached the General's coffin, and began fumbling along the lid. He came upon a screw which had a little cross on the top.

"Everything here seems to have been prepared for a thief," said he, and began carefully and dexterously to unscrew the lid.

"Do you feel anything?" asked the wife. "Don't you feel something moving under the lid?"

"He lies as still as the grave," answered the man.

"He knows, of course, that we don't intend to remove the thing he values most," said the woman. "It would be quite a different thing if we took off the lid."

"Well, you'd better help me to do it," said the husband.

They raised the lid, and then it was impossible to restrain their longing for the treasure. They took the ring off the withered finger, replaced the lid on the coffin, and stole out of the vault in dead silence. They held each other by the hand while crossing the churchyard, and it was not until they had reclimbed the stone wall and reached the road that they dared to speak a word.

"Now I begin to think," said the woman, "that he has willed this. He understands that it isn't right of a dead man to keep such a firm death grip on a thing, and he has given it to us of his own free will."

Her husband laughed loudly. "I like that!" he said. "You will never make me believe that he let us take it willingly; we took it because he hadn't power to prevent us."

"Do you know," said his wife, "you have been very brave to-night. There aren't many people who would have ventured into the General's grave."

"I don't think I could have done it, if I were doing anything wrong, for I have never taken so much as a rix-dollar from a living man. But what harm can there be in taking something from a dead man that he does not want?"

They felt proud and happy as they walked along. They wondered why more people had not had the same thought as theirs. Bard said he intended to go to Norway and sell the ring as soon as he could see an opportunity. They believed that they would get enough money for it to keep them from want for the rest of their lives.

Suddenly the woman stood still. "What is that light I see over there, away to the east? Is the day beginning to dawn already?"

"No, it can't be the sun rising already," said the peasant. "It must be a fire—it seems to be in the direction of Olsby. Can it possibly be——"

He broke off, on hearing a wild shriek from his wife.

"It is our cottage burning," she screamed. "It is Mellomstuga burning—the General has set fire to it. . . ."

On Monday morning the sexton went hurrying to Hedeby, which lay not far from the church, to announce that when the mason and he had gone to the grave to wall up the vault, they both noticed that the coffin lid was crooked and that the stars and shields, with which it was ornamented, had been stolen.

An investigation was immediately set on foot. There was evidence of great disorder in the grave, and they found that the screws in the lid of the coffin were loose. As soon as the lid was lifted, they saw, at one glance, that the General's ring was no longer in its place on his forefinger!

III

I OFTEN think about King Charles the Twelfth and try to understand why people so loved and feared him.

I have heard that, one day toward the close of his life, he went to Karlstad church while the service was going on. He had ridden, alone and unexpectedly, into the town and, hearing that service was proceeding, he left his horse outside the gate and entered the church through the porch, in the same way as anybody else.

As soon as he got inside the door, he saw that the clergyman was in the pulpit, and, in order not to disturb anyone, he stood still and, without trying to find a seat, remained leaning against the doorpost, listening to the sermon.

But although he had entered so quietly, and although he stood in the dark, under the gallery, there was one in the last pew who recognized the King. It was probably some old soldier; he had lost an arm or a leg during the campaign, and had been sent home before the battle of Poltava, and he knew that the man with the upcombed hair and hooked nose could be no other

17

than the King. On recognizing him, the man immediately stood up.

His neighbours in the pew wondered what he was doing, so he whispered to them that the King was in church. And positively every man in the pew immediately stood and remained standing, as is the custom when God's Word is read from the altar or the pulpit. The news spread swiftly from seat to seat, till, finally, every person present—young and old, rich and poor, strong and weak—was standing.

As already said, this happened during the latter years of Charles's life, when trouble and opposition had begun; there was, in that church, probably hardly a man who had not been bereft of his kinsmen, or lost his possessions, in the King's cause. Even if they had nothing personal to lament, there was much food for reflection over the country, which lay impoverished, over the provinces lost, and the many enemies encompassing the land.

But, always and everywhere, it was the same, and now it was enough for the whisper to go round that this man, whom they had so often cursed, stood among them in God's House, to make every person present to rise to his feet. And so they continued to stand. There was not a man among them that would have thought of sitting. They could not. There stood the King near the door, and so long as he stood, so long would they all stand. To sit would have been to dishonour the King.

It would probably be a long sermon, but they must

be patient. They must not fail the man standing there at the door.

He was a soldier-king, and was accustomed to see his soldiers go willingly to death for him. But here, in the church, he was surrounded by simple peasants and arti-zans, by ordinary Swedish men and women, who had never aspired to sacrifice. Yet, he had but to show him-self, and they were immediately under his dominion. They would go anywhere, do anything, for him, for they believed in him and worshipped him. In the whole church, there was not a person who did not that day thank God for the marvellous man who was Sweden's King.

I have tried, as I have said, to understand how this love for King Charles could fill a man's whole soul, how it could fix itself so firmly in the heart of an old, harsh, rugged man that people all expected to find it there even after death. . . .

Indeed, the thing that most astonished the people of Bro, when it was discovered that the ring had been stolen, was that anyone had had the courage to carry out the project. It was known that loving women had had their betrothal rings stolen from their coffins, and the robber had escaped scot free; a mother had been buried with a lock of her child's hair clasped in her hands; this, too, had been fearlessly reft from her. Again, a pastor had lain in his grave with a Bible for his pillow; this could have been stolen without harm to the criminal. But to steal Charles the Twelfth's ring from the finger of the dead General at Hedeby, was a crime that they could not believe any man born of woman would dare to commit.

A thorough search was carried out, but not the faintest clue could be found by which to identify the thief. He had come and gone during the dark night, without leaving any trace which could help the seekers.

Here, again, people were surprised, for they had often heard of ghosts walking night after night in order to point out the doers of far lighter crimes. No one was the least astonished, therefore, when, at last, it was found that the General had by no means left his ring to its fate, but had fought to reclaim it with the same bitter mercilessness that he would have shown had the ring been stolen from him during his lifetime.

Nor did they show any doubt about the fact, for it was exactly what they had expected.

IV

MANY years had passed since the disappearance of the General's ring when it happened, one beautiful morning, that the rector of Bro was called to see a poor peasant, Bard Bardsson, who lived in the Olsby district. He was dying, and it was necessary that he should speak to the rector himself before he died.

The rector was an old man, and when he heard that it was a question of visiting a sick parishioner, living miles away in the trackless forest, it occurred to him that his curate might very well go in his stead. The message, however, had been brought by the dying man's young daughter, who, on hearing this decision, answered firmly that the rector himself must come and no one else. Father had told her to say that he wanted to tell the rector something that no one else in the world must hear.

The rector tried to throw his memory back into the past. Bard Bardsson had been a quiet man—certainly he had been rather foolish, but that was not a thing to cause a man uneasiness on his deathbed. Judged from a purely human standpoint, the rector thought he might have been one to find favour with God. During the last seven years, the man had met with every kind of misfortune. His farmhouse had been burned down; his cattle had died of disease or had been carried off by wild animals; his fields had been ruined by frost, so that he was now as poor as Job. Finally, his wife had been so distracted by all these troubles that she had drowned herself in a lake, and then Bard had gone to live at a small outlying farm, the only thing left to him now. Since that time, neither he nor his two children had ever been to church, and they had often wondered, at the Rectory, what had become of the family.

"If I judge rightly about your father, I don't think he can have done anything that he cannot confess to the curate," said the rector, looking with a friendly smile at Bardsson's daughter.

She was a girl of fourteen, tall and strong for her age. She had a broad face with rather coarse features, a somewhat foolish expression, like her father; but childish innocence and candour brightened up her face.

"Perhaps you are afraid of Strong Bengt, sir, and that is why you don't want to come to us," she said.

"What do you say, child?" returned the rector. "Who is this Strong Bengt you are talking about?"

"Oh, sir, he is the person who has made everything go wrong with us."

"Well, well," said the rector, "so there is a person called Strong Bengt, is there?"

"Don't you know it was he who burned down Mellon.stuga?"

"No, I never heard that before," said the rector; at the same time getting up from his chair, he began to take out a prayer book and a little wooden chalice, which he always carried with him on his sick calls.

"He haunted my mother into the lake," continued the girl.

"Ah, that was very dreadful, poor child," said the rector. "Is this Strong Bengt still alive? Have you ever seen him?"

"No, sir, I have never seen him," said the child, "but he is still alive. It was because of him that we had to go and live in the forest on the wild fell. We have had peace from him since we went there until last week, and then Father cut his foot."

"Do you think that was Strong Bengt's fault?" asked the rector in his gentle voice, at the same time opening the door and calling his servant. He told the man to saddle his horse.

"Father says that Strong Bengt bewitched the ax, or he would never have cut himself. It wasn't a bad wound at first, but to-day Father says that mortification has set up in his foot. He says he's got to die because Strong Bengt has done for him, so he sent me to the Rectory to beg you to come yourself, sir, as quickly as you can."

"I will come," said the rector. While the girl was speaking, he had put on his hat and riding cloak. He went on:

"I can't think why this Strong Bengt should be so

horrid to your father. Bard must have done something to him."

"Father doesn't deny that," said the child. "But he will never tell either me or my brother what it is. I think that is what he wants to tell you now."

"If that is the case, we cannot get there soon enough." He drew on his riding gloves and, mounting his horse, took the child on the saddle in front of him.

The rector scarcely uttered a word during the long ride to the farm. He sat pondering on the extraordinary things the girl had told him. He remembered having just met a man whom people called Strong Bengt; but it was possible that she was alluding to someone quite different.

A young man came out to meet him, as he rode into the yard; it was Ingilbert, Bard Bardsson's son. He was some years older than his sister, well grown, too, and somewhat resembling her in features, but he had deep-set eyes and lacked her candid, good-natured expression.

"You have had a long ride, sir," he said as he helped him off his horse.

"Yes," answered the old man, "but we came along faster than I expected."

"I ought to have come and fetched you," said Ingilbert, "but I was out all night fishing, and only heard when I came home just now that Father's foot was bad and that he had sent for you."

"Martha has been as good as a boy," said the rector, "and we got along famously. But how is Bard now?"

"He is very bad, but he is prepared. He was glad when I told him that you had appeared at the edge of the clearing."

The rector went straight in to Bard, and the brother and sister sat on a broad stone slab outside the cottage, to wait. They felt in a solemn mood, and talked about their dying father. They said how good he had always been to them; but he had never been happy since the fire at Mellomstuga, so perhaps it was better that he was going. Suddenly, the girl exclaimed that she was sure Father must have had something weighing on his conscience.

"He!" said her brother. "What could he have? I have never seen him lift his hand to a man or an animal."

"But there is something he wants to talk to the rector about—only to him."

"Did he tell you that? Did he say he wanted to speak to him before he died? I thought he only wanted him to give him Holy Communion."

"When he sent me off, this morning, he said I was to beg the rector himself to come, as he was the only man in the world to whom he could confess his heavy sin."

Ingilbert sat thinking for a moment. "How curious," he said. "I wonder if it is something he has imagined all the time he has been here alone. All that he has told us about Strong Bengt—I don't believe it is anything but imagination either."

"It is just about Strong Bengt that he wants to talk to the rector," said the girl.

"You can bet the whole thing is only a lie," said Ingilbert.

He got up and went to a small shutter, that stood open to let a little light and air into the windowless cottage. The sick man's bed stood so near the opening that Ingilbert could hear every word his father said; and the son stood and listened without the slightest twinge of conscience. Perhaps he had never even heard how very wrong it was to listen to a confession. Anyway, he did not believe that his father could have any very dangerous secret to confess.

After he had stood near the opening for a time, he returned to his sister.

"What did I tell you?" he began. "There is Father telling the rector that he and Mother stole the ring from old General Löwensköld."

"God be merciful to us!" cried his sister. "Do let us tell the rector that it is all a lie, that he has imagined it all."

"We can't do anything now," said Ingilbert. "Father must say what he likes, and we will tell the rector afterward."

He stole back to the opening to listen; but it was not long before he returned to his sister.

"He says now that the same night they had been to the grave, Mellomstuga was burned down. He says he believes it was the General himself who burned the house."

"You can hear it is all an invention," said his sister. "He has told us a hundred times that it was Strong Bengt who set fire to Mellomstuga."

Ingilbert was back at his post under the shutter before she had finished speaking. He stood a long time listening, and when he came back to his sister his face was ashen.

"He says it was the General who sent all his misfortunes to force him to put the ring back. He says that Mother was frightened and wanted him to go with her to the Captain at Hedeby and give him back the ring; Father wanted to obey her, but dared not go, because he thought they would both be hanged if they acknowledged that they had stolen from the dead. But Mother could bear no more, so she went and drowned herself."

It was the sister's turn to grow ashen white.

"But," she began, "Father always said it was——"

"Yes, yes, I know. He had just been explaining that he never dared to tell anyone who had brought all these misfortunes on him. Only to us, children who didn't understand, he had said it was Strong Bengt who pursued him. He says the country people always called the General Strong Bengt."

Martha crouched down where she sat on the stone slab.

"It must be true after all," she whispered, so low that it might have been her dying sigh. She gazed around in every direction. The farm stood near the edge of a forest tarn, and the tree-clad mountain ridges rose darkly on every side. There was no human dwelling within sight—there was not a soul to whom she could turn for help. Nothing reigned there but a great helpless solitude. And she thought she could see the dead man lying in wait under the gloomy trees, ready to send more misfortune.

She was still too much of a child to realize fully the shame and dishonour brought on her by her parents; but, as far as she could understand, it was a ghost, an implacable, all-powerful creature from the other world, who haunted them. She expected that she might see him at any moment, and her terror was so great that her teeth chattered. She thought how her father had lived for seven years with this same terror in his soul. She knew that seven years had passed since the fire at Mellomstuga, and all that time her father had known that he was being pursued by a dead man. Surely it was best that he should die.

Ingilbert had been listening again at the shutter, and when he returned to her, she said, making a last effort to escape from her terror:

"You don't believe it, Ingilbert, do you?" But as she looked at him, she saw that his hands shook and his eyes were wide with fear. He was as frightened as she was.

"What can I think?" whispered Ingilbert. "Father says that he tried several times to go to Norway to sell the ring, but he could never succeed. Once he fell ill, another time his horse fell and broke his leg, just as he was riding out of the gate."

"What did the rector say?" asked the girl.

"He asked why he had kept the ring all that time when he knew how dangerous it was to have it in his possession. Father said he thought the Captain would have had him hanged if he had acknowledged his crime. He had no choice but to keep it. But now that he is dying, he wants to give the ring to the rector, so that he may put it back in the General's grave, and then we children will be freed from the curse and will be able to go back to the village."

"I am glad the rector is here," said his sister, "I don't know what I shall do when he goes away. I am so frightened I believe I can see the General standing there under the pine trees. Think! he has been here every day, watching us. Perhaps Father has even seen him!"

"I am sure Father has seen him," said Ingilbert.

He went off to listen again, and when he came back he had a different expression in his eyes.

"I have seen the ring," he said. "Father has given it to the rector; it shone like a flame of fire. All red and yellow! It sparkled! The rector looked hard at it and said he recognized it as the General's ring. Go to the opening yourself—you will see it."

"I would rather hold a snake in my hand than look

at that ring!" said Martha. "You surely can't think it is beautiful to look at?"

Ingilbert looked away from her. "I know very well that it has ruined us, but all the same I admire it."

Just as he pronounced these words, the rector's voice reached them; they could hear him speaking loud and clear. Hitherto, he had allowed the sick man to speak, but now it was his turn. Evidently, he did not hold with all the wild talk about the dead man's hauntings. He tried to point out to the peasant that the judgment of God had struck him for committing so gruesome a crime as to rob the dead. He absolutely refused to admit that the General had power to burn houses or to send sickness either on men or on cattle. No, the misfortunes which had ruined Bard were God's method of forcing him to repent, and to restore the ring while he was still alive, so that his sin might be forgiven, for only so could he die a blessed death.

Old Bard Bardsson lay still and listened to the rector without any apparent objection. But it did not seem to make any impression on him. He had lived through too many awful hours for him to believe that they came from God. But the two young people sitting outside and shivering with terror began to take heart.

"You hear! You hear!" said Ingilbert. "The rector says it wasn't the General."

"Yes, I hear," said his sister. She sat with her hands clasped together, drinking in every word, deep down in her soul, that the rector was saying.

Ingilbert got up. He drew a deep breath, and stretched himself up. He was free from all his terror. He looked like a new man. He walked forward quickly, opened the door of the cottage, and went in.

"What do you want?" asked the clergyman.

"I want to say a few words to Father."

"Go away! It is for me to speak to your father now!" the rector spoke sternly.

He turned again to Bard, speaking now severely, now gently and reassuringly. Ingilbert returned to his seat on the stone slab outside; but a great unrest had now seized him. He buried his face in his hands, and sat for a little, but again he returned to his father's room, and again he was sent away.

.   .   .   .   .   .

When all was over, Ingilbert was to return with the rector, to show him a way through the forest. For a time all went well, and then they came to a place in the wood where the bog was spanned by a narrow log bridge. The rector could not recollect passing over this bridge on his former journey, and he began to wonder whether Ingilbert was leading him astray. On asking him, however, Ingilbert assured him that, if they could once cross the bog, it would be a considerable short cut.

The rector cast a sharp glance at the young man. He had an impression that Ingilbert, like his father, was possessed by a love of money. He remembered how he had come to his father's room, more than once, to prevent him from parting with the ring.

"This is a very narrow, dangerous road, Ingilbert," he said. "I am afraid that the horse may fall on these slippery logs."

"I will lead the horse, sir, so that you need not be afraid." So saying, Ingilbert seized the horse by the reins.

When they reached the middle of the little bridge and were surrounded on all sides by the bog, he began to force the horse backward. It seemed as though he wanted to push it off the log bridge.

The horse reared, and the rector, who could with difficulty remain in the saddle, shouted to him, for God's sake, to let go the reins.

But Ingilbert appeared not to hear. The rector could see him, with angry face and tight-clenched teeth, struggling to force the horse over into the bog. Certain death awaited both the man and the animal, if he should succeed.

Then the rector thrust his hand into his pocket and, drawing out a little goatskin bag, he hurled it in Ingilbert's face. The latter let go the reins in order to catch the bag, and the horse, being free, galloped madly along the path.

Ingilbert remained standing where he was and made no effort to overtake them.

V

I T IS not to be wondered at that, after so violent
a ride, the rector should feel a little giddy and light
in the head; and evening had fallen before he
reached the village. Neither is it to be wondered at that
he did not leave the forest by the Olsby road, but went
a long way round to the south and came out quite close
to Hedeby.

While trying to find his way through the forest, he
made up his mind that as soon as he reached home
he would send a message to Carelius, the sheriff, begging
him to go at once and get the ring from Ingilbert. But
when he found that he was riding so near to Hedeby,
he reasoned with himself whether it would not be ad-
visable to go up to the house, see the Captain himself,
and tell him who had stolen the ring from the vault.

One can hardly think that the rector need have hesitated long over so natural a course; but the fact was
that no very good feeling had existed between the Captain and his father. The Captain was a man of peace;
his father had certainly been a man of strife. As soon
as peace had been concluded with Russia, the Captain
had left the army and had used all the energies he pos-

sessed to further the well-being of his country, which had been brought to the verge of ruin during the long years of war. He was opposed to all despotism and cared little for military honours; indeed, he had even been heard to speak ill of Charles himself, and of many others whom the old man had esteemed highly. What was even worse, the Captain had taken a lively share in the parliamentary discussions on the war, but always as an adherent of the Peace Party. It may thus be seen that there was no lack of subjects for dispute between father and son.

When the General's ring had disappeared, seven years previously, the rector, together with many others, had remarked that the Captain did not greatly trouble himself to recover it. As this fact recurred to his mind now, he said to himself: "It is no good troubling to dismount at Hedeby. The Captain won't care whether Ingilbert or his father wears the ring. I had much better go straight back and let Carelius know at once about the theft."

Just as the rector had reached this conclusion, he saw that the gate leading to the Hedeby estate, swung slowly back on its hinges and remained standing open.

It struck him as curious, yet he reflected that gates often swung open if not properly fastened, and so thought no more about it. Nevertheless, he took it as a sign that he should go up to Hedeby and see the Captain.

The Captain received him more warmly than was his wont.

"It is friendly of you to come in," he said. "I wanted to see you; indeed, I decided to go to the Rectory, to-day, and speak to you about a very strange occurrence."

"You would have had your journey for nothing, Captain Löwensköld," said the rector. "I had to go, early in the forenoon, to a sick call in the Oldsby district. I am only now on my way home. It has been a most exciting day for me, old friend."

"I can say the same, although I have hardly been out of my chair. I can assure you, rector, that though I am getting on for fifty and have had my fair share of adventures during the years of war, I have met with nothing so strange as my adventure of to-day."

"That being so," said the parson, "you shall begin. But I, too, have a most strange story to tell you—indeed, I think one of the strangest I have ever come across."

"Well, in that case, perhaps you won't find my story so wonderful. But I will begin by asking you one thing. Have you ever heard of Gatenhielm?"

"You mean that gruesome pirate, that senseless privateer, who was created an admiral by King Charles the Twelfth? Who hasn't heard of him?"

"While we were at dinner to-day," continued the Captain, "the conversation turned on the old war days. My sons and their tutor asked me to tell them something about the war—young people always like to hear these things. I daresay you have noticed that they prefer to hear all about those fatal wars rather than to

know something of the hard, troublous years through
which we Swedes had to struggle after Charles's death,
or of what we suffered through bankruptcy and loss. My
God! do they think it was an easy task to rebuild burned
towns, to restart manufactories and workshops, to cut
down forests and reclaim the lands? I believe that my
sons are ashamed of me and my contemporaries because
we tried to put an end to military expeditions and to the
devastation of foreign countries. They seem to think
that we are worse men than our fathers, and that the
Swedish strength has gone out of us."

"You are perfectly right, my friend," said the rector.
"These young people's love of warlike things is greatly
to be deplored."

"Anyhow, I satisfied their wishes," said the Captain,
"and, as they wanted to hear about a great warrior,
I told them about Gatenhielm and his cruel treatment
of merchants and peaceful travellers, hoping to rouse
their horror and disgust. When I had succeeded in
doing so, I bade them remember that this Gatenhielm
was a true son of the warlike days in which he lived, and
I asked them whether they would like to see the world
peopled by such infernal monsters.

"But before my sons had time to answer, their tutor
took up the parable, and asked my permission to tell
yet another story about Gatenhielm. As he assured me
that the adventure he was about to relate would only
confirm what I had said about Gatenhielm's wildness
and cruelty, I allowed him to proceed.

"He then began by telling us that, when Gatenhielm was dead and his body laid in Onsala church, in a marble sarcophagus that he had stolen from the Danish king, there were so many ghostly happenings in the church that the parishioners of Onsala could not endure them. They decided, therefore, that there was no other course but to lift the corpse out of the tomb and inter it on a bare rock, far out to sea.

"After that was done, peace reigned in the church; but the fishermen, whose duty took them past Gatenhielm's new resting place, described how they heard noises of all kinds and saw the foam dashing high over the unlucky rock. The fishermen believed that all the sailors and traders whom Gatenhielm had thrown overboard from the captured vessels, were now rising from their watery graves, to torment and ill-treat him; they were, therefore, very careful not to go too near the rock.

"One night, however, one of the fishermen, who had sailed rather near, found himself swept into a whirlpool; the foam lashed his face, and a voice roared at him: 'Go to Gata in Onsala, and tell my wife to send me seven hazel sticks and two cudgels!'"

So far, the rector had listened patiently and silently to the Captain; but when he perceived that his friend had nothing better than an ordinary ghost story to relate, he could scarcely restrain a movement of impatience. The Captain, however, paid no attention to him but continued his tale.

"You can understand that there was nothing for it but to obey the command. Gatenhielm's wife also obeyed. The toughest hazel sticks and thickest cudgels were prepared, and a servant from Onsala rowed out to the rock with them."

At this point the rector made so marked an effort to interrupt him that the Captain noticed his impatience.

"I know what you are thinking, rector," he said. "Indeed, I thought the same myself when I listened to the story at dinner, but I must beg you to hear me to the end. I must say, I think that servant from Onsala must have had a stout heart and great devotion to his master, otherwise he would never have dared to carry out such an order. As he approached the burying place, the waves dashed over it as in a raging storm, and there was noise and uproar all around. But the man rowed as near as he could, and succeeded in throwing the sticks and cudgels on to the rock. Thereupon he hurried off, rowing with swift strokes to get away from the dreadful place."

"My dear Captain," began the rector, but the Captain was firm.

"He did not row very far, however, before he rested on his oars and watched to see whether anything extraordinary would happen. He had not long to wait. Suddenly the waves dashed sky-high over the rock; the noise was as the roar of guns on the battlefield; gruesome cries of distress went out across the sea. The uproar continued for a time, but with diminishing vigour, and eventually the waves ceased to rage over Gatenhielm's grave, and left the rock lying calm and peaceful like any other.

"The servant plied his oars again on his homeward journey, when suddenly he heard a loud, triumphant voice calling out: 'Go to Gata in Onsala and tell my wife that Lasse Gatenhielm triumphs over his enemies, both in life and in death!'"

The rector had been listening with bowed head, but now that the story was finished, he looked up inquiringly at the Captain.

"As the tutor said the last words," said the Captain, "I could see that my sons sympathized with that scoundrel, Gatenhielm, and enjoyed hearing about his arrogance. I recognized that the story was well constructed, but it could be nothing but a lie. I said to myself: 'If a rough pirate like Gatenhielm possessed power to assert himself, even after death, how can I explain the fact that my father, who was as great a swashbuckler as Gatenhielm but also a good and honourable man, should have let himself be robbed of his dearest possession, without doing anything to hinder the theft, or to molest the guilty person in any way since?'"

On hearing these words, the rector looked up with unwonted animation. "That is exactly my idea," he said.

"Yes, but listen to what happened next," said the Captain. "I had scarcely said these words when I heard a deep sigh just behind my chair. It was so like the tired sigh my poor old father used to give when he was suffering from the infirmities of his old age that I thought he was really there, and I got up from my chair. Of course, I saw nothing, but I was so certain that I had heard him that, instead of going back to the dinner table, I came in here, and have been sitting alone ever since, pondering over the matter.

"I should much like to hear your opinion of this, my dear old friend; was it my father whom I heard? Was he sighing over his lost treasure? If I believed that, ever since, he has been longing for it, I should go from farm to farm myself to search for the ring, rather than he should have to bear the bitter sorrow contained in that sigh."

"This is the second time to-day that I have had to answer this question—whether the dead General is still mourning over his lost ring and wishes to recover it," said the rector. "With your permission, I will now tell you my story, and we must come to some conclusion."

Therewith the rector began his story, and he soon saw that he need have no fear that the Captain would not energetically espouse his father's cause. He had never imagined that so gentle and peaceful a soul as that of the Captain could contain so much of the old Adam. But they tell us that even the little pigs grunt when the old boar suffers. He saw the veins swelling in the Captain's forehead, and he clenched his fist so that the knuckles showed white. He was seized with furious anger.

The rector, naturally, represented the case from his own point of view. He said how God's wrath had been visited on the evildoer, and would not admit that there had been any interference from the dead man.

Captain Löwensköld, however, interpreted all that he heard in quite a different way. He understood, now, that his father had been unable to rest in his grave because the ring had been removed from his finger. He felt anguish and remorse because he had hitherto taken the matter so lightly. He felt it as a pricking, aching wound in his heart.

When the rector saw how upset he was, he was almost afraid to tell him how the ring had been taken from himself by Ingilbert; however, he accepted the fact with a sort of bitter satisfaction.

"It is well that one of the pack of thieves still remains and that he is as great a scoundrel as the rest of them. The General has punished them and has hit hard; now it is my turn."

The rector noticed a merciless harshness in the Captain's voice. He grew more and more uneasy and began to fear lest the angry man should strangle Ingilbert with his own hands, or perhaps whip him to death.

"I felt it my duty to tell you of the dead man's confession, Captain," he said, "but I hope that you will not do anything hasty. I propose now to inform the sheriff about the theft of the ring from myself."

"You may do as you like about that," said the Captain. "But I will only say that you will give yourself unnecessary trouble, for I shall take the matter into my own hands now."

After this, the rector knew that there was nothing further to do at Hedeby; he therefore rode away as fast as he could, hoping to be able to send a message to the sheriff before nightfall.

Captain Löwensköld called all his men together, told them what had happened, and asked them if they were willing to accompany him next morning, at four o'clock, to hunt for the thief. There was not a man among them who refused to do such a service for the dead General and for his son; and the remainder of the evening was spent collecting all sorts of weapons, old blunderbusses, short hunting spears, long swords, cudgels, and scythes.

VI

NEXT morning, when the Captain started, at four o'clock, to hunt for the thief, he was accompanied by as many as fifteen men. They were all in the best possible humour. They had a just cause and the old General at their back, for if he had managed to carry the affair so far, he would certainly carry it to a successful conclusion.

They had some miles to go before reaching the real wilderness. On starting from Hedeby, they had first to traverse a wide valley, cultivated in parts, and studded with small farms. Here and there, on the surrounding ridges, there were fairly large villages. One of these was Olsby, where Bard Bardsson had lived before the General burned down his farm.

Farther on lay the great forest, spread over the earth like a thick pelt, tree after tree, without a break. But still there were signs of human activity. There were small paths which led through the forest to summer cottages and charcoal burners' clearings.

The Captain and his men seemed to take on a new mood, a new bearing, the farther they penetrated into the wood. They were out after game, and the hunting spirit sprang up within them. They cast sharp glances toward the thickets as they began to walk carefully and lightly, almost creeping as they went.

"We must arrange about one thing, boys," said the Captain. "None of you need worry about the thief— you can leave him to me. All you have to do, is to see that he doesn't escape."

This warning was not without its significance. These men who, on the previous day, had been peacefully occupied, spreading the hay on hurdles to dry, were now on fire with a longing to give Ingilbert, the thief, something by which he should remember them.

Meanwhile, they had reached a spot where great pine trees that had stood from all eternity grew so thickly packed that they spread above their heads, like an unbroken roof; the undergrowth had ceased, and only moss covered the ground. Suddenly, they saw three men coming toward them, carrying a stretcher made of boughs, on which lay a fourth man.

The Captain and his party hastened forward to meet them, and the bearers stopped on seeing such a crowd of people. They had laid large bracken leaves over the dead man's face so that no one could see who it was; but the men of Hedeby guessed, and a shudder ran through them.

They did not see the General beside the bier. No! Not even a glimpse of him. But, anyhow, they knew he was there! He had come from the forest with the dead man—he was pointing toward him with his finger.

The three men who bore the stretcher were well-known, respectable folk. There was Eric Ivarsson, who owned a large farm at Olsby, and his brother, Ivar Ivarsson, who had never married but remained on with his brother in the old home. They were both elderly, but the third was young. He also was known to them all. He was Paul Eliasson, and was the adopted son of the two old brothers.

The Captain went up to the Ivarssons, and they set down the stretcher in order to shake hands with him. But he appeared not to notice them, he seemed unable to take his eyes off the fern leaves which covered the face of him who lay on the bier.

"Is that Ingilbert Bardsson lying there?" he asked, in a strange, hard voice. He seemed to be speaking against his will.

"Yes," answered Eric, "but how did you know, Captain? Did you recognize him by his clothes?"

"No," said the Captain, "I did not recognize him by his clothes. I have not seen him for five years."

Both his own men and the strangers regarded the Captain curiously. There seemed to be something strange and mysterious in his manner that morning. He was unlike himself. As a rule, he was polite and friendly.

He began to question the Ivarssons. What were they doing out in the forest so early, where had they found Ingilbert? The Ivarssons were well-to-do farmers, and they resented being questioned in this manner; however, he managed to extract from them the chief facts. On the previous day, they had gone to visit some of their people on an outlying farm, some miles farther on, carrying meat and provisions with them, and had slept there overnight. Very early in the morning, they had started on their homeward journey, Ivar walking in front of the two others, for having been a soldier he had caught the trick of marching.

He was a good way on in front when he saw a man coming along the path toward him. The forest was fairly open just there, no shrubs, only bare tree-stems, so he could see the man a good way off. He had not recognized him immediately, for a thin mist hovered between the trees, looking like yellow smoke when the sunshine glinted athwart it, and this had prevented his seeing the other very clearly.

Ivar said that, as soon as the man caught sight of him through the mist, he stopped in terror, stretching out his hands toward him with a beseeching gesture. As Ivar continued to approach, he called out not to come any nearer. He seemed to be insane, and Ivar thought to try and quiet him, but the other immediately fled into the wood. He had run only a few steps when suddenly he fell forward and lay motionless. By the time Ivar got up to him he was dead, but he recognized him as Ingilbert, son of that Bard Bardsson who used formerly to live at Olsby, but had moved to a smaller place after his house was burned down and his wife had drowned herself. He could not understand why Ingilbert fell dead, for no one had touched him; and, though he had tried to shake some life into him, he could do no good. As soon as the others came up, they saw that he was dead. As Bardsson had been their neighbour, when he lived at Olsby, they could not leave Ingilbert lying there in the forest, so they had knocked together a stretcher and brought him with them.

The Captain listened with a dark frown. It sounded quite probable. There lay Ingilbert, equipped for a long journey—a knapsack on his back, thick shoes on his feet. The hunting spear lying on the stretcher was also his. Undoubtedly, he had been starting for some foreign country, where he could sell the ring, but on seeing Ivar through the mist he had thought he saw the General's ghost. Yes, that is what must have happened. Ivarsson was dressed in an old uniform and had the brim of his hat turned up in the Carolinian manner. The distance, the mist, and his evil conscience were enough to account for the mistake.

In spite, however, of this explanation, the Captain's displeasure grew; he worked himself up to a fury of bloodthirstiness. He would have liked to squeeze Ingilbert to death in his own strong arms. He craved for an outlet for his vengeance, but could find none. At the same time, he realized his own unreasonableness, and controlled himself sufficiently to explain to the Ivarssons why he and his men had come at that early hour to the forest; and added that he would like to search the dead man to see if the ring was in his possession.

His mood was such that he wished that the men would refuse to permit the search, so that he would have to fight for his rights. But they found his desire quite natural, and withdrew to one side while a couple of the Captain's own men searched the dead man's pockets, his shoes, his knapsack, even the seams in his clothing.

At first the Captain watched the examination with the greatest attention, but once he looked toward the farmers, and he thought they seemed to exchange spiteful glances with each other, as though expecting him to find nothing.

And indeed this was the case. The search had to be abandoned, for no ring could be found. The Captain's suspicions now fell on the three men, as did that of his followers. What had become of the ring? Ingilbert must certainly have had it on him when he fled. Where was it now? No one saw the General, but they left him standing in the middle of the group, pointing to the three Olsby men. They had it. It was more than probable that they had searched the dead man already and had found the ring. It was also probable that the story they had just heard was not true, and that the whole thing had happened quite differently. These men, who were from the same district as Bardsson, had probably known that he possessed the ring. They probably knew that Bardsson was dead, and on meeting his son in the forest, they understood that he intended to fly with the ring, and had therefore overpowered and killed him, in order to get possession of the treasure.

There was no wound upon him, except a contusion on his forehead. The Ivarssons had said that he struck his head against a stone as he fell; but might that contusion not also have been caused by the thick, knotted stick that Paul Eliasson was carrying in his hand?

The Captain stood staring on the ground. A great struggle was taking place in his mind. He had never heard anything but good spoken of these three men, and it went against him to think that they had robbed and murdered.

His men closed up round him. Some of them were already fingering their weapons; they never expected to leave that place without a fight.

But Eric Ivarsson stepped forward and said:

"Captain Löwensköld, my brother and I, as well as Paul Eliasson—who is our adopted son and is soon to be my son-in-law—know very well what you and your people are thinking about us. We consider that we ought not to part until you have searched our pockets and garments, also."

On hearing this offer, a ray of light stole into the blackness of the Captain's soul. He objected. Both the Ivarssons and Paul Eliasson were persons upon whom no suspicion could fall.

But the farmers wanted to put an end to the affair, and they began to take off their shoes and to turn out their pockets; so the Captain made a sign to his men to let them have their way.

No ring was to be seen; but in the wallet that Ivar

Ivarsson carried on his back there was found a little goatskin bag.

"Does this bag belong to you?" asked the Captain, after searching it and finding it empty.

Now had Ivar answered "yes," the matter would have ended, but, instead, he gave utterance to the most frightful lie.

"No, it was lying on the path, not far from the place where Ingilbert fell. I picked it up and threw it into my wallet, because it looked new and unused."

"But it was in just such a bag that the ring lay when the rector threw it to Ingilbert," said the Captain; and the anger reappeared, both in his face and in his voice.

"Now there is nothing for it but you three must come with me to the sheriff, unless you prefer to hand the ring over to me voluntarily."

But the patience of the Olsby men was exhausted.

"You, Captain Löwensköld, have no right to get us arrested," said Eric Ivarsson; whereupon, seizing the very spear which lay on the bier beside Ingilbert, he proceeded to force his way through the men, accompanied by his brother and his adopted son.

In their first astonishment, the Hedeby men fell back —all except the Captain, who laughed aloud with satisfaction at the chance of letting loose his wrath. Drawing his sword, he thrust aside the spear.

But that was the only feat of arms in the battle. The Captain felt himself suddenly pulled back by his own men and the weapon snatched from his hand. It happened that Carelius, the sheriff, had seen fit to walk into the forest that morning, accompanied by a constable, and he now appeared in the centre of the path in the very nick of time.

Then began fresh searchings and questionings, with the result that Eric Ivarsson, his brother Ivar, and Paul Eliasson were all arrested and led off to prison on the charge of having robbed and murdered.

VII

IT CANNOT be denied that in Varmland, in those
olden days, our forests were vast and our fields
narrow; our farms were large, but our houses were
small. Our roads, too, were narrow, and our hillsides
steep; the doors of our houses were not wide, but the
doorposts were tall; our churches were small, but our
services long! Added to this, the years of our life were
few, but our difficulties were beyond reckoning. Yet, in
spite of all, we folk in Varmland were neither grumblers
nor commonplace individuals.

It is true that the frost spoiled our crops, and that
wild beasts took our cattle, and that illness bereft us of
our children—yet we had the spirit to bear up to the
end. How, indeed, could we have carried on otherwise?

But one comforter was always to be found in every
home, and this may have been the secret of our courage.
This comforter was to be found near the poor as well as
the rich, and it was one that never failed and never
wearied.

But you must not imagine that it was anything solemn, or magnificent, such as the Bible, or peace of mind,
or even happy love! Neither was it anything base or

evil, such as drink or gambling! It was a perfectly harm-less and everyday thing—in fact, it was nothing other than a fire which burned cheerily on the hearth on a winter's evening!

Dear me! how snug and homely it made the tiniest cottage; it would joke with the inhabitants for an en-tire evening! It crackled and hissed as if trying to laugh; it spat and fizzed as if imitating some cross or angry being. Sometimes nothing would persuade it to consume some old, gnarled log; it filled the whole room with smoke and damp, as if protesting that it had not enough to eat. Then, perhaps, it would burn away quickly and sink down into a glowing heap, just when work was in full swing, and folks must sit with folded hands in lap until it chose to burn up again.

It was most roguish, though, when the mistress of the household came with her three-legged cooking pot and tried to coax it to cook the dinner! Sometimes it would be good and docile and do its work well and quickly; but oftener it would flit round and round—anywhere except under the pot! How it gladdened the eyes of the master when he came in wet and frozen out of the snow, filling him with a sense of warmth and com-fort. How pleasant to think of the watching light, streaming out into the winter's night, a guiding star to the wanderer and a warning to the prowling fox or lynx.

But there were other things the fire could do, besides give light and warmth and cook the food. It awakened a thirst for pleasure in the soul of man. For what is man's soul but a flame? It flickers in and around the body of a man as does the flame around the rough log.

Now, one winter's night, when the folk who sat round the fire had been silently gazing into the flames for a time, the fire began to speak to one and all, in their own language.

"Brother soul," it would say to one, "are you not a log, too? Why are you so sad and heavy?"

"Sister flame," would answer the human soul, "I have been chopping wood and minding the housework all day. I want nothing better than to sit still and watch you."

"I know," said the fire. "But, now it is evening, do as I do, shine and sparkle! Fun and warmth!"

And the souls obeyed the fire and began to play. They told stories, guessed riddles, they tuned the fiddles, and hung garlands on the tools and implements. Then they sang songs, played forfeits, and recalled old proverbs, thus thawing the ice out of their limbs, the peevishness out of their minds. They waked up and were merry, for the fire renewed in their hearts the wish to live out their humble and difficult lives.

One of the chief joys connected with the fire, however, was to sit round the hearth and tell stories of daring and adventure that pleased both young and old and seemed never to be exhausted, for, thank God, there have always been plenty of brave deeds to talk about.

The best-loved stories were those told about King

Charles's days; he was a warrior among warriors, and there was wealth of legend about him and his men. Instead of disappearing with him into the grave, the tales lived on and were his best legacy. The most popular were, of course, those about the King himself; but next best were those about old General Löwensköld of Hedeby, whom many of them had seen and could describe from head to foot.

The General was so strong that he could bend iron as others broke chips. It was related how there dwelt a blacksmith at Smedsby in Svartsjö who made the best horseshoes in all the district. One day, the General rode to Smedsby and told Michael to shoe his horse. Soon Michael came out of the smithy with a finished shoe, and the General took it in his hand to test it. The shoe was strong and well made, but the General laughed out loud and said, "Do you call this iron?" whereupon he bent the shoe till it broke in half.

The smith grew nervous; he thought his work must be bad.

"There must have been a flaw in the iron," he said, and hurried into the smithy to get another shoe.

But the same thing happened again, only that this time the shoe was doubled up like a pair of scissors before it broke.

Then Michael grew alarmed. "You must either be King Charles himself, or else you are Strong Bengt from Hedeby."

"That wasn't such a bad guess, Michael," said the

General, and then he paid the smith for shoeing his horse and for the two shoes he had broken.

Many and many were the stories told of the General, and there was not a man in the countryside who had not heard of him and who did not respect and admire him. They knew all about his ring too, and how it had been buried in his grave but had been stolen, owing to the avarice of man.

These things being so, we can understand that, if there was one thing that could excite the interest and curiosity of the people more than another, it was the news that the ring had been found and lost again; that Ingilbert Bardsson had met his death in the forest, and that the farmers at Olsby had been imprisoned on suspicion of appropriating the ring.

When the people returned from church on Sunday they hardly gave themselves time to take off their Sunday clothes and eat a mouthful of dinner, but began immediately to relate everything that had been seen and heard, and to discuss what punishment the accused would receive.

They could talk of nothing else. Every evening meetings were held around the hearth of every house, both great and small, and were attended by gentry as well as peasant.

It was a strange and dreadful case, and very difficult to get to the bottom of and to judge fairly; for it was hard, indeed almost impossible, to believe that the Ivarssons and their adopted son could have murdered a man, in order to get a ring, however valuable it might be.

To begin with, there was Eric Ivarsson. He was a rich man owning much land and several houses. If he had a fault, it was a certain arrogance and jealousy of his own honour, which made it hard to conceive that any jewel in the world could tempt him to a dishonourable action.

Even less could suspicion fall on his brother, Ivar. He was poor, it is true, but he lived with his brother and had everything he could possibly desire. He was so generous that he had given away nearly all he owned. Was it likely that such a man would steal and murder?

As for Paul Eliasson, it was well known that the brothers had the highest regard for him, and he was shortly to be married to Marit, Eric's daughter and heiress. He was the sole person of the three on whom suspicion might fall, for he was a Russian by birth; and, after all, people knew that Russians did not think it a sin to steal. Ivar had brought him back with him from Russia, where he found him in a prison. He was only three years old at that time, without father or mother, and had Ivar not rescued him, he would have starved to death there. He had been brought up honestly and uprightly, and had always been well behaved. Marit and he had grown up side by side, they had always loved each other, and it was hardly likely that a man with happiness and riches waiting for him in his future life would risk everything for the sake of a ring.

But, on the other hand, there was the General to be

considered; the General, about whom they had heard so many legends, ever since their childhood; the General, whom they knew as well as their own father; he was so big and reliable—he who was dead and had been bereft of his dearest possession.

The General knew that Ingilbert Bardsson had taken the ring with him when he fled; otherwise Ingilbert would have gone on his way in peace and would not have been killed. The General must also have known that the three Olsby men had taken the ring; otherwise they would not have met the Captain in the forest or have been arrested and sent to prison.

It was very difficult to get at the truth in such a case; but the people relied on the General almost more than on King Charles himself, and therefore the self-appointed courts of justice, sitting in the cottages, pronounced judgment.

Much astonishment, however, was aroused when they learned that the district judge of the real Court, which held its sittings in Broby Town Hall, had announced that, after the strictest examination, no proof of guilt could be found, nor could the accused be made to confess; he therefore felt himself compelled to acquit them of murder and robbery. They were not, however, set at liberty, for the decision of the District Court had to be revised by the Court of Appeal, and this latter decided that the Olsby men were guilty and would be hanged.

This sentence could not be carried out at once, since

the decision of the Court of Appeal must first be ratified by the King.

But when the King's decision was pronounced and made public, the churchgoers willingly postponed their dinners in order to relate the wonderful news to their home-keeping brethren.

To put it shortly. The King had decided that it was quite evident that one of the three accused men must be guilty; but that, as none of them would confess, the Judgment of God must decide between them. Therefore, at the next sitting of the Court, the three men were to cast lots in the presence of the judge, the jury, and the whole community. He who threw the lowest number would be considered guilty, and would be hanged for his crime; the other two would immediately be set at liberty and allowed to return to their daily life.

It was a wise decision and a just one. Everyone in Varmland was satisfied with it. Was it not splendid of the old King, who, instead of thinking himself wiser than everyone else, had appealed to the All-Knowing to decide. Now at last could they be certain that the truth would come to light.

There was certainly something very unusual in this trial. It was not a case of man against man, but a dead man was a party in the case—a dead man who desired to recover his own property. In any other case, one might have hesitated to resort to dice, but not in this. The General knew perfectly well who was withholding the ring; and the best thing about the King's decision was that it would give the old dead General an opportunity to show his knowledge. It seemed almost as though King Charles wished to leave the decision to the General. He had probably known him in the old war days, and knew that he was to be relied on. Perhaps that was the idea—it was difficult to know.

In any case, everyone was determined to be present at the meeting of the Court on the day when judgment was to be pronounced. Every person not too old to walk or too young to crawl set out for the Town Hall; for it was many years since anything so wonderful as this trial had taken place. No one was content to hear the news bit by bit—no! Each one must be present in person.

The farms lay at long distances apart, in many cases, and, as a rule, one might walk for miles without meeting a soul; but when all the inhabitants of the district had gathered together in one place, it was surprising how many there were. They stood closely packed in lines outside the Courthouse. They resembled a swarm of bees clinging to a beehive on a summer's day; they resembled the bees, also, in any other way, for they were not in their usual good humour. They were not silent and reverent, as when in church, nor cheerful and talkative, as when at market; they were excited and irritable and possessed by hatred and revenge.

Can anyone wonder at it? They had imbibed a dread of malefactors with their mothers' milk; they had been rocked to sleep with cradle songs of wandering outlaws. They regarded all thieves and murderers as abominations and changelings, they no longer considered them human. They did not think it necessary to show them any pity. And now, to-day, one of these horrible creatures was to be brought to judgment, one of these bloodthirsty devils was to die, and they rejoiced at the thought; he would no longer have a chance of doing any harm!

The Ordeal, as was fitting, was to take place, not in the Courthouse, but in the open air. The crowd resented the fact that a cordon of soldiers was formed round the open space in front of the Town Hall, so that no one could get close to the prisoners; and many angry glances, you can believe, were cast at those soldiers for blocking their view. Ordinarily, such a procedure would have raised no resentment, but now everyone had grown daring and pushing.

The work people had all received permission to leave home early, so as to get good places; they had, therefore, many dreary hours to wait pressed as near to the cordon as they could get, and there was little to divert their attention. Once an official brought out a great drum and placed it in the centre of the open space; this pleased the crowd, for it showed that those inside the Courthouse proposed to start business before nightfall. Presently the official appeared again, this time carrying a table, a chair, an inkstand, and a pen, and, finally, he brought out the dice box, in which the dice rolled about. He then proceeded to throw the dice several times on to the drum, in order to test whether they were correct, whether they fell this way and that, as dice should.

This finished, he hurried back to the Courthouse again, and this was hardly to be wondered at, for each time he appeared the crowd shouted jests and sarcasms at him. They would never have behaved thus at other times, but to-day they had lost their wits.

The judge and the jurymen slipped through the cordon, having ridden, or walked, up to the Town Hall; and as soon as they appeared the crowd woke up and called out greetings and remarks in loud tones. Nothing could be done to prevent this; it was a big crowd, and in the worst of humours. The gentry present now began to slip inside the cordon; there was Löwensköld from Hedeby, the rector of Bro, the owner of the works at Ekeby, the naval Captain from Helgesäter, besides many others. These fresh arrivals were promptly informed of their good fortune in not having to stand in the crowd, fighting for places—with many more remarks of a like nature!

When there were no more left to jeer at, the crowd turned its attention to a young girl who stood pressed as close to the soldiers as possible. She was short and slight, and time after time the young men tried to force her back and take her place; but on seeing this, some of those standing near shouted that she was Marit, the daughter of Eric Ivarsson, and then she would be left in peace for a time.

Then it would begin again, but, instead of pushing her, they showered down insulting questions. She was asked which she would prefer to see hanged, her father or her betrothed. They wondered why she, the daughter of a thief, should have the best place.

People at home far away in the forest had wondered how she had had courage to stand where she was, but they knew, oh, yes, they knew very well. She was no timid girl, she had been present all through the examination of the accused and had neither spoken nor wept. She had nodded to the prisoners as if she expected them to be released the next day. Her presence had inspired them with fresh courage. They knew that there was one, at least, who believed in their innocence, who knew that no gold ring could tempt them to crime.

Beautiful, gentle, patient, she had sat the whole time in Court, disturbing nobody; indeed, she had made friends of the judge, the jury, and the sheriff. They would not absolutely assert it, but it was believed that the district judge would not have pronounced the accused innocent, had Marit not been in Court. It was impossible to believe that anyone beloved by her, could be guilty of crime.

Now here she stood, so that the prisoners might see her, might gain confidence and strength from her presence. She would pray that God's Will might be fulfilled in them, throughout the Ordeal.

It was difficult to know the truth; yet, they say that the apple never falls far from the tree, and she certainly looked good and innocent. Besides she must surely have a loving heart, to be able to remain where she now stood.

She heard all the unkind things hurled at her, but she neither wept nor answered, nor did she try to escape. She knew that the unfortunate prisoners would be glad to see her. She was the only one, in that great crowd, who had a human heart to be touched by their sorrow.

She did not, however, stand there entirely in vain. Here and there was a man who had daughters of his own, equally innocent and sweet; and each one thought to himself, he would not wish a girl of his to stand where Marit stood now. And here and there a voice would be raised to defend her, or at least to try to silence the cruel, biting remarks thrown at her.

And so, at last, when the doors of the Town Hall were thrown open, and the Ordeal was about to commence, people rejoiced, not only because the long hours of waiting were ended, but also for Marit's sake. Walking in solemn procession, came first the constable, the sheriff, and the prisoners, the latter unfettered but with a soldier on either side. Next came the sexton, the rector, the jurymen, the clerk, and the judge. Last of all followed the gentry and several farmers, whose position entitled them to a seat within the cordon.

The sheriff and the prisoners took up their position to the left of the Courthouse, the judge and jury withdrew to the right, while the gentry were placed in the centre. The clerk seated himself at the table with his roll of papers. The great drum stood entirely alone in the centre of the open space, where everyone could see it.

As soon as the procession appeared, the people began to struggle and push; several big, strong youth tried to force their way into the first row, their object being to hustle Marit. But, terrified lest she should be prevented from seeing, she ducked down and, being small and slim, managed to creep through the legs of the soldiers and get within the cordon. This was, however, contrary to all discipline, and the sheriff made a sign to the constable to remove her. The constable went up to Marit and, putting his hand on her shoulder as though to arrest her, led her in the direction of the Courthouse. But, as soon as they reached the thick crowd standing there, he let her go. He had seen enough of her to know that, if only she were allowed to stay in the vicinity of the prisoners, she would never think of trying to escape, and if, later, the sheriff wanted her, he would easily find her.

But who had time now to think of Marit? The rector and the sexton had stepped forward and taken up a position in the centre of the circle. They took off their hats, and the sexton started a hymn. As soon as the crowd heard this, they realized that something greater and more solemn than they had ever known was about to take place. An appeal was being made to the Almighty to make His Will known to them.

They grew even more serious when the rector began to speak. He prayed to Christ, the Son of God, beseeching Him who had Himself once stood at Pilate's judgment seat to watch over the accused, that they might not be wrongly judged. He prayed Him to guide the judge that he might not condemn an innocent man to death. Lastly, he prayed Him to protect the crowd, in order that they might not be witnesses to so great an injustice as had been the Jews on Golgotha.

The crowd listened with bowed heads as the rector prayed; their earthly thoughts fell away from them; their mood changed. It was as though God Himself had been called down into their very midst.

It was a lovely autumn day; the blue sky flecked with little white clouds, the trees covered with yellow leaves. The birds flew high above, starting for their winter quarters in the south; it was unusual to see such numbers as appeared that day. It surely betokened something strange. Could it be a sign from God that He approved of what was taking place?

As soon as the rector had finished, the judge stood forth and read the King's decree. It was long, with many turns of phrase that made it hard to follow. But they understood that the earthly power had laid aside its sword and sceptre, its wisdom and knowledge, for the nonce, and now desired to be guided by God. And they prayed, all and earnestly, that God would guide and help them.

Next, the sheriff took up the dice and begged the judge and several persons standing near to test them and see if they were true. The people listened, as they fell on to the parchment, with a strange shudder. Were those little objects, which had been the ruin of so many, now reckoned worthy to point out the Will of God?

When the dice had been tested, the prisoners were led forward, and the dice box handed to Eric Ivarsson, as being the eldest. The sheriff explained to him that this was not the final throw; it was only to decide which of the three should begin. The result was that Paul Eliasson threw the highest and Ivar Ivarsson the lowest. The latter, therefore, had to start.

The three accused men still wore the clothes in which they were arrested after meeting Captain Löwensköld in the forest, on their way home from their little farm, and they presented an untidy, worn appearance. Of the three, Ivar looked the least tired; having been a soldier, he was hardened by his sufferings and imprisonment during the wars. He held himself upright, and appeared courageous and unafraid.

As he stepped forward to the drum and received the dice box from the sheriff, the latter proceeded to show him what to do, but the old man replied, with a little smile:

"It isn't the first time, Mr. Sheriff, that I have thrown the dice." He spoke loudly so that the crowd could hear him. "Strong Bengt of Hedeby and I have often amused ourselves with them, on the long winter evenings away on the Steppes; but I never thought I should have to throw against him once more."

The sheriff tried to hurry him, but the people wanted to listen to him; he was a brave man to be able to joke in such a position. He placed his hands together over the dice box, and they saw that he was praying, and when he had finished the Lord's Prayer, he said in a loud voice:

"Now I pray Thee, Lord Christ, Thou Who knowest my innocence, be gracious and let me throw low, for I have neither child nor lover to weep for me." So saying, he dashed the dice down on to the drum, so that they resounded.

At that moment, there was not a man in the crowd who did not wish that Ivar Ivarsson might go free. They knew now that he was brave and upright; they wondered how they had ever supposed him to be a criminal.

It was unbearable to be so far away and unable to know what number was thrown. The judge and the sheriff bent eagerly forward, even the jury and the gentry went nearer to see the cast. There was general astonishment. Many nodded to Ivar, some shook hands with him, but great numbers knew nothing. They grumbled and growled. Then the judge made a sign to the sheriff, who mounted the steps leading to the Courthouse, so as to be better seen and heard.

"Ivar Ivarsson has thrown double sixes! The highest throw of all!"

They knew now that Ivar was acquitted. They were delighted; many shouted, "Good luck to you, Ivar Ivarsson!"

But then something happened which filled everyone

with amazement. Paul Eliasson burst out in a wild hurrah, pulled off his woollen cap, and threw it into the air. It was so unexpected that his guards had not time to prevent him. Everyone wondered at him. It was true that Ivar had been like a father to him, but this was a question of his own life. Could he really be so glad that another man was acquitted?

Order was, however, quickly restored; the officials returned to their places on the right-hand side, the prisoners and their guard going, as before, to the left, the other spectators retiring toward the Courthouse, leaving the drum again exposed to view, in the centre of the ring.

It was now Eric Ivarsson's turn to undergo the Ordeal. People could scarcely recognize the broken, stumbling old man who now came forward. Could that possibly be Eric Ivarsson, he who had always been so steady and powerful? His sight was dim, and many persons thought that he seemed hardly conscious of what he was doing. But as he took the dice box into his hand he made an effort to straighten himself up and to say a few words.

"I thank God that my brother is acquitted," said he, "for though in this matter I am as innocent as he is, still he has always been the better man of us two. And now, I pray Our Lord Christ that He will give me a low throw, so that my daughter may marry the man she loves and live happily with him to her life's end."

As is the case with so many old people, all Eric's vanished strength seemed now to be concentrated in his voice. What he said could be heard by everyone, and it waked strong feeling. It was so unlike him to admit that anyone was better than himself and to wish for death in order to make another happy. No one could ever again think of him as a thief and a murderer. Tears came to the eyes of many standing around, and they prayed that God might send him a high throw. He barely shook the dice in the box, but just threw them out after moving it up and down once. His eyes were too dim for him to distinguish the black spots on the dice; indeed, he did not notice them, but stood staring out into the distance.

The judge and the others hurried forward. The same look of astonishment came over their faces as on the former occasion. The crowd seemed to understand what had happened, before the sheriff had had time to make his announcement, for a woman cried in a high voice: "God bless you, Eric Ivarsson!" and a man's voice added quickly: "God be blessed and praised for helping you, Ivarsson!"

Again Paul Eliasson's cap flew into the air, and again men wondered. Couldn't he understand what this second throw meant for himself?

Eric stood listless and indifferent; there was no light in his eyes; it seemed as though he were waiting for the sheriff to announce the result. But even after it was made known that he too, like his brother, had thrown double sixes, he remained unmoved. He made an effort to stagger back to his former place, but was so weak that the constable had to put his arm round him to support him.

Now came Paul Eliasson's turn to try his fortune at the drum, and every eye was turned toward him. They had now made up their minds that he alone could be the culprit, and his doom was a foregone conclusion, for there was no higher throw than double sixes.

They were not displeased, so far, with the result, but now they saw that Marit Ivarsson had crept close to Paul. He did not hold her in his arms, nor did any kiss or caress pass between them; she only stood close pressed to him, and he put his arm about her waist. No one knew how long they had stood thus together, for every eye had been riveted on the drum.

There, at all events, they stood now, pressed close together in an inscrutable manner, in spite of the guard, in spite of the menacing authorities and the crowd of spectators, in spite, above all, of the frightful game of life and death in which they were involved. It was love—a more than earthly love—which united them. Thus they might have stood at the garden gate on an early summer's morning, after having danced the whole night together and first agreed to take each other for man and wife. Thus might they have stood after their First Communion, with souls free from all taint of sin. And assuredly thus might they have stood when, the horror of death behind them, they had met to part no more, for all eternity.

She stood gazing at him with ineffable love, and there

was something in their souls that made the people sorry for Paul. He was like a young tree that would never blossom and bear fruit; like a cornfield, to be trampled down before it had had a chance to yield its rich crop.

He took his arm gently from Marit's waist, and went with the sheriff toward the drum. There was no sign of anxiety about him as he took the dice box in his hand. He did not pray, as had the others, but turning toward Marit he said:

"Don't be afraid! God knows I am as innocent as the others are." Thereupon he shook the dice playfully and sent them spinning round the drum as they fell.

He stood eagerly watching them, as they rolled, but when, at last, they stopped there was no need to wait for the sheriff to announce the number. Paul Eliasson himself cried out in a loud voice:

"I have thrown double sixes, Marit! I have thrown double sixes, like the others!"

It never occurred to him that he would not be acquitted at once, and he could hardly stand still for joy. He jumped, he threw his cap into the air, he even seized the soldier who guarded him in his arms and kissed him!

"That shows he is a Russian," thought the people, "had he been a Swede, he would never have rejoiced so soon!"

The judge, the sheriff, the jurymen, and the gentry

all went quietly and leisurely to the drum and looked at the dice. But there was no look of joy this time; they shook their heads, and no one congratulated Paul Eliasson on his throw.

For the third time the sheriff stood on the steps and announced:

"Paul Eliasson has thrown double sixes, which is the highest throw!"

Then arose a great commotion among the crowd, but no rejoicing. No one believed that there had been any fraud about the matter—that was impossible—but everyone was uneasy, for the judgment of God had not been clearly made manifest.

Were all the three prisoners equally innocent, or were they all equally guilty? Captain Löwensköld was seen to hurry excitedly toward the judge. He was trying to explain that nothing had been decided; but the judge turned brusquely away from him.

The judge and the jury retired within the Courthouse, to deliberate over the matter, and while they were absent there was not a movement in the crowd—scarcely even a whisper. Paul Eliasson stood perfectly still. He seemed to understand that the decision might be interpreted in more ways than one.

After a short deliberation, the officials returned, and the judge announced that the District Court felt bound to interpret the decision to mean that all three men should be acquitted. Once again Paul Eliasson shook himself free of his guard and cast his cap high into the air, with a great cheer. But his joy was premature, for the judge continued:

"The decision of the District Court must, however, be referred to the King by means of a courier, who will start for Stockholm to-day; the accused will, therefore, remain in custody until His Majesty's confirmation of the District Court's decision arrives."

ON A fine autumn day, thirty years after the wonderful ordeal by dice that took place in front of the Courthouse at Bro, Marit, daughter of Eric Ivarsson, sat on the steps outside the cottage, on the Big Farm at Olsby, where she lived. She was knitting a child's glove. She wanted to knit the gloves in a specially pretty pattern of diamonds and stripes, in order to please the child for whom she intended them, but she could not recall the pattern.

After sitting for a few minutes, trying patterns on the steps with the point of her knitting needle, she rose, went into the cottage, and opened a clothes chest to hunt for a good pattern. Near the bottom of the chest she came upon a woollen cap, artistically knitted in rows of various widths, and a good border; after hesitating for a few moments, she took it with her and went out again on to the steps.

While twisting it this way and that in her hand to study the pattern, Marit noticed that the moths had eaten little holes here and there in the cap. "Dear God," she said to herself, "it is hardly to be wondered at. For it is thirty years at least since it was in daily use. It is

fortunate that I saw it in the chest that I may do something with it."

The cap was ornamented with a fine, big tassel made
of many colours, and here the moths seemed to have
enjoyed themselves most for, as Marit shook the cap,
they flew out in every direction, and finally the tassel
itself fell off into her lap.

She took it up to see whether there was an end of
wool left by which she could sew it on to the cap again,
and, as she looked, she fancied she saw something bright
shining amid the strands. Hastily parting them, she
found a great gold signet ring with a red stone in the
centre, firmly sewn with coarse linen thread into the
very middle of the tassel.

Tassel and ring fell from her hands! She had never
seen the ring, but there was no need for her to stare
at the royal signature on the stone, or to read the in-
scription on the inner side, for her to recognize it and to
guess to whom it had belonged. She leaned against the
railing and, shutting her eyes, sat back white and still
as a dying woman. She felt her heart must break.

For the sake of that ring her father Eric, her
uncle Ivar, her betrothed Paul, had yielded up their
lives, and now she had found it here, sewn into Paul's
woollen cap!

How had it come there? When had it come there?
Had Paul known it was there? Never! she said immedi-
ately. It was impossible that he could have known it.
She remembered how joyfully he had thrown this very

cap into the air the day that he and the old Ivarssons
had been acquitted.

It all came back to her as if it had happened yesterday! Again she saw the crowd, who had at first been so
spiteful and unfriendly to her and her dearest ones, but
who, later, had come to believe in their innocence.
She recalled the lovely blue sky, the migrating birds
flying round and round and hovering over the Courthouse. Paul had seen them too, and as she had leaned
against him he had whispered that soon his soul would
be flying up into the heights like a poor little lost bird.
And he had asked whether he should come back to her
and dwell under the eaves at Olsby.

Impossible that Paul could have known that that
cap, which he threw so joyfully up into the lovely
autumn sky, could contain a stolen thing.

Then there came another day. Her heart shrank
within her whenever she remembered it, but now she
must think of it. Message had come from Stockholm
saying that God's judgment was to be interpreted to
mean that the three men were equally guilty, and were,
therefore, to be hanged.

She herself had been present when the sentence was
carried out, so that the men whom she loved should
know that there was at least one human being who believed in them, and grieved for them. But there was no
longer then any need for her to have gone to the gallows.
The people had all lately changed their point of view.
The crowd standing outside the Courthouse even had

been good to her; they had argued and debated among themselves, and they had come to the conclusion that the judgment ought to have been interpreted to mean that the three men were all innocent. The old General had allowed them each to have the highest throw—surely that could mean nothing but that none of them had taken the ring.

There had been universal lamentation when the three men were brought out. Women cried, the men stood with clenched fists and set teeth. They said that the parish of Bro would be destroyed as the city of Jerusalem had been, for putting innocent men to death. The crowd called out comforting words to the doomed men, and threatened the hangmen. Many curses were called down on Captain Löwensköld; they said that he was in Stockholm at the time, and that it was his fault that the judgment had been interpreted to the detriment of the accused.

However that may have been, it was a fact that all the people shared her belief and confidence; and that knowledge had helped her over that day—indeed, not only that day, but even up to the present time. Had the people among whom she lived considered her to be the daughter of a murderer, she could never have borne to go on living.

Paul Eliasson was the first to ascend the small platform under the gallows. He fell on his knees and prayed to God, he then turned to the priest, who stood beside him, and said something to him. Marit noticed that the priest immediately removed the woollen cap from Paul's head. When all was over he gave the cap to Marit with a message from Paul, saying that he sent it to her as a sign that she was in his thoughts during his last hour on earth.

Was it possible to believe that Paul would ever have done that had he known that the ring was hidden in the cap? Never! If there was one thing absolutely certain in this world, it was that Paul had no idea that the ring that had been on the finger of the dead man was hidden in the cap.

Marit suddenly bent down and, holding the cap close to her eyes, studied it attentively. "Where can Paul have got that from?" she thought. "He was rather fond of finery, and never liked us to weave him gray clothes; he always wanted a colour in the frieze. He liked a red cap with a big tassel. He must have been very fond of this one." . . .

She put the cap down, and leant back again against the railings, her mind going back into the past.

She remembered being in the forest the day that Ingilbert had been scared to his death. She saw how Paul, together with her father and her uncle, had stooped over the body. The two elder men had settled that Ingilbert must be carried down to the village and had gone to cut branches to make a bier. Paul had remained a moment to look at Ingilbert's cap, and had been so seized with a longing to possess it—for it was knitted in red, white, and blue wool in many patterns—

that, unperceived by anyone, he had exchanged it for his own cap. He had meant no harm; probably he had intended to keep it only a little while. His own was quite as good a cap as Ingilbert's, only not composed of so many colours or so well knitted.

Ingilbert had sewed the ring into his cap before leaving his home; he probably expected to be pursued, and had thus tried to conceal it. Since his death, no one had ever thought of searching in his cap—Paul least of anyone.

She felt she could swear to it that that was what had happened, and yet one could never be entirely certain. She put the ring back in her chest and, taking the cap in her hand, she went out to the byre to speak to the milkmaid.

"Come out into the sunshine, Martha," she called into the dark cowhouse, "and help me with a pattern I can't make out."

When the girl appeared, she held the cap out toward her. "I know you are good at knitting, Martha," she said. "I want to work this edge, but I can't understand it. You look at it, you are more at home with this sort of thing than I am."

The milkmaid took the cap and glanced at it. She seemed surprised, and came out of the shadow of the byre to look at it more closely.

"Where did you get this?" she asked.

"It has lain in my clothes chest for many years," said Marit. "Why do you ask?"

"Because I knitted this cap for my brother, Ingilbert, in the last summer of his life," said Martha. "I have never seen it since the morning he went away from home. How can it have come here?"

"It probably came off when he fell," said Marit. "Perhaps one of our farm hands found it in the forest and brought it here. But if it has such sad memories for you, perhaps you would rather not copy the pattern for me?"

"Leave it with me, you shall have the pattern to-morrow," said the girl.

She took the cap and went back to the cowhouse, but Marit had heard the tears in her voice.

"No! You sha'n't do it if it hurts you," she said.

"Nothing that I can do for you, Marit, ever hurts me."

It was Marit herself who had remembered Martha, Bard's daughter, sitting alone in the forest after the death of her father and her brother, and she had asked her to come and be the dairymaid at the Big Farm at Olsby. Martha had come, and had never failed to show her gratitude for being received back into the company of her fellow creatures again.

Marit returned to the steps in front of her cottage and took up her knitting, but she was too restless to work, so she leaned her head against the railings and tried to think what ought to be her next move.

If anyone on the farm at Olsby had understood the life lived by women who had left everything in the world to dwell in the cloister, he would certainly have said that Marit was one of these women. Her face was sallow and without a wrinkle. It was almost impossible for a stranger to say whether she was old or young. She had a gentle, peaceful expression, as of one who had laid aside all desires for herself. She never appeared to be very happy nor, on the other hand, to be deeply grieved about anything.

After the heavy blow she had received in her youth, she knew that life for her was ended. She had inherited the Big Farm from her father, but she knew that it was her duty to marry in order to carry on the farm and give it a master. To escape this, she had made over the whole property to one of her cousins, without any payment, on condition that she should have a cottage on the farm, and a pension for life.

She had been content and had never regretted her action. There was no chance for time to hang heavy on her hands for lack of work. Everyone relied on her wisdom and goodness; as soon as there was illness she was sent for; the children loved her—her cottage was constantly filled with young things—for they knew she always had time to adjust their little troubles.

As Marit sat wondering what she ought to do about the ring, a great wrath rose suddenly in her heart. She thought how easily it might have been found, how easily the old General might have arranged for its discovery; she understood now that he must have known where it was the whole time. Why had he not made them search

Ingilbert's cap? Instead of this, he had allowed three innocent men to die on account of the ring. He had had power to allow that, but not to bring the ring out into the light of day.

At first, Marit thought she would go to the rector, tell him the whole story, and give him the ring; but finally she decided not to do so. Wherever she appeared, in church or at a party, she was always treated with respect; the contempt usually felt for the children of criminals had never attached to her. The people were firmly convinced that a great injustice had been done to her, and they wished to atone for it. The gentry in the neighbourhood also would go to meet her when they saw her leaving the church, and would exchange a few words with her. Even the family at Hedeby—not the Captain, it is true—but his wife and daughter-in-law, had made several attempts to approach Marit, but she had always evaded them. Since the trial, she had never spoken a word to anyone from Hedeby.

Was she to come forward now and confess that the Hedeby folk had been right? The ring had been found in the possession of the men of Olsby. Perhaps people would say that they had known where it was, and that they had borne imprisonment and examination in hopes of being acquitted, and of so having a chance to sell the ring.

In any case, Marit realized that it would be regarded as a justification of Captain Löwensköld—and even of his father—if she were to show the ring now and say where it had been found—and Marit was determined that she would do nothing advantageous or good for the Löwenskölds.

The Captain was now eighty years old, rich and powerful, honoured and respected. The King had made him a Baron; no misfortune had ever touched him; he had sons who also were rich and well married. And this was the man who had bereft Marit of everything—everything—everything. She lived alone, without possessions, without husband, without children, entirely through his fault. She had expected, all through the long years, that punishment would strike him, but nothing had ever happened.

Marit woke out of her deep meditation. She had heard the sound of little feet running toward her, and she knew that she was wanted. She saw two boys—one of ten, the other of eleven—approaching. One was Nils, the son of her cousin; the other, she did not know; they had probably come to ask her to help them.

"Marit," said Nils, "this is Adrian, from Hedeby; we were rolling our hoops on the road when we quarrelled and I tore Adrian's cap."

Marit looked at Adrian, a handsome boy with a gentle, friendly expression. Her heart began to beat—she always felt hurt and frightened when she saw a Löwensköld.

"We have made friends again," said Nils, "and now I want you to mend Adrian's cap for him before he goes home."

"Yes," said Marit. "I will mend it."

She took the torn cap and went into the cottage.

"This must be a sign from God," she murmured. "Play out there for a little," she called out to the boys. "It will soon be ready."

She closed the door of her cottage and sat alone inside while she mended Adrian Löwensköld's woollen cap.

IX

SEVERAL more years had passed since the ring had last been heard of. Now it happened that Miss Malvina Spaak, in the year 1788, went to Hedeby as lady-housekeeper to the Löwenskölds. She was the daughter of a poor clergyman in Södermanland who had never before set foot over the border into Varmland. She had, therefore, no idea of the customs of the house where she was going to work.

On the day of her arrival at Hedeby, Baroness Löwensköld sent for her and gave her a remarkable proof of her confidence in her.

"I think it is only fair," said the lady, "that I should tell you at once that we have reason to believe that Hedeby is haunted. It is not unusual for us to meet on the stairs, in the passages—sometimes even in the rooms—a tall, strong man, dressed in long jack boots and a blue uniform resembling that of a Carolinian. He will appear suddenly in front of you, if you come out of a room or stop on the stairs; and, before you can detain him, he disappears. He does no harm—in fact, we think he likes us—but I must beg you, Miss Spaak, not to be frightened if you meet him."

Malvina Spaak was only twenty-one, slim and neat, yet extraordinarily clever at all kinds of household and domestic matters; she was also active and industrious, so that, wherever she went, the house was run with the regularity of clockwork. But she was terrified of ghosts, and had she known beforehand that Hedeby was haunted she would never have taken the situation. But now she was here, and beggars cannot afford to be choosers! She therefore thanked the Baroness for her warning, with a little bow, and said she did not intend to let herself be frightened.

"We have no idea why he haunts us," continued the Baroness. "My daughters think he resembles my husband's grandfather, old General Löwensköld, whose picture you can see over there; they always refer to him as the old General. You can understand, however, that does not mean that the old man himself—who was really an excellent person—walks here. So, if the servants come to you with any foolish tales, I am sure you will be wise enough not to listen to them."

Again Miss Spaak bowed slightly and assured her employer that she never listened to servants' gossip about their masters and mistresses and so the audience ended.

The girl was by no means an ordinary housekeeper, for she came of gentlefolk, and, consequently, she took her meals with the family, as did also the house steward and the girls' governess. As she was a spick and span little figure with fair hair and blooming cheeks, she made a pleasing addition to the family board. Everyone found her obliging and pleasant, and useful in many ways, so she soon became very popular.

It did not take her long to discover that the ghost spoken of by the Baroness was an ordinary topic of conversation at the dinner table. Either the governess or one of the young people was sure to remark, "I saw the General to-day," as though it were something to boast of. Hardly a day passed that she was not asked whether she had seen a ghost, but she had always to reply that she had not; and her answer seemed to cause a certain misgiving. It seemed to make her inferior to the steward and the governess, who had both frequently seen the General.

Malvina Spaak had never before come in contact with so jaunty a manner of treating a ghost, and from the very first she determined to try and conquer her terror. She told herself that if it was really a being from the other world who appeared, he must be unhappy and in need of help from the living, to enable him to rest in peace in his grave. She was one of those resolute characters who felt that, had she the power, she would make serious investigation and get to the bottom of the matter; she would not allow it to become a subject of conversation at meals.

But she recognized her own position and would never allow a word of blame to pass her lips concerning the behaviour of her employers; and she herself was careful never to joke on the subject of the ghost, but kept her own forebodings to herself.

Malvina had been a whole month at Hedeby before she saw the ghost. One forenoon she had been up to the attic to count the laundry; while on the stairs, she met an unknown man, who drew aside quickly to let her pass. It was bright daylight, and she was not thinking about ghosts, so she only wondered what a strange man could be doing up near the attics, and turned to ask him his business. There was no one there. She ran upstairs quickly, went into the attic, searched every dark corner in the box room—quite prepared to take the thief by the scruff of the neck. But at last, when no human being appeared, she suddenly realized what it must have been.

"What an idiot I am!" she exclaimed. "Of course, that could be no one but the General!"

Yes, of course! The man was dressed in the very same blue coat and enormous jack boots that the General wore in his portrait. She could not quite recognize the face, for there was a gray, misty appearance over the features.

She stood for some time in the attic trying to recover herself. Her teeth chattered and her knees shook under her. Had there been no dinner to think of, she would never have got down those stairs again. She determined, however, to keep what she had seen to herself, and not to let the others joke about it.

Meanwhile, she could not get the General out of her thoughts, and she must have looked unlike her usual self, for as soon as she sat down to dinner, the son of the house, a youth of about nineteen, home from Upsala for Christmas, turned toward her.

"You have seen the General to-day, Miss Spaak," he said.

She could not deny this abrupt announcement, and immediately found herself the most important person present. Unfortunately, she could not deny, either, that she had been a little frightened, and that made them very merry! Frightened of the General! Surely nobody could possibly be frightened of him!

Malvina had often remarked that neither the Baron nor his wife ever joked about the General themselves, though they did not restrain the others from doing so. She now noticed that their son took the matter far more seriously than the others did.

"Personally," he said, "I envy all you people who see the General. I want to help him, but he never appears to me."

He spoke feelingly and in so kind a tone that Malvina prayed in her heart to God that his wish might soon be fulfilled. The young Baron would certainly be merciful to the poor ghost, and would send him to rest eternally in his grave.

During the next few days, the ghost seemed to turn his attention more particularly to Miss Spaak than to any of the others. She saw him so often as almost to become accustomed to him. He would appear on the stairs, in the passages, or in some dark corner of the kitchen.

No reason could ever be discovered for these appearances. Malvina sometimes wondered whether the General might possibly be searching for something in the house; but as he vanished the moment he met the glance of a human eye, it was impossible to gain any clear idea of his intention.

Miss Spaak noticed, in confirmation of what the Baroness told her, that the young people were firmly persuaded that it was the General who haunted Hedeby.

"He is uncomfortable in his grave," said the girls, "and it interests him to see what we are doing here at Hedeby. We mustn't deny him that little pleasure!"

Each time she met the General, the housekeeper, who was obliged to retire to the pantry to hide her chattering teeth from the raillery of the girls, wished that he would interest himself a little less in the affairs of Hedeby. But, at the same time, she realized that the whole family would frankly miss him were he to stay away.

On the long winter evenings, for instance, they would sit with their needlework; one would spin, another, perhaps, would doze. At length, both reading and conversation would stop. Then, suddenly, one of the girls would give a little shriek—she had seen a face, perhaps only two rows of glistening teeth, pressed against a windowpane. Someone would hurry out to light a lantern, the door would be opened, and all the women, the

Baron at their head, would rush out to find the peace-breaker. Naturally, there would be no one. Then they would all come back again, bolt the windows, shrug their shoulders, and say it must have been the General!

But by this time everyone would be wide awake, and there was something interesting to think about; so the spinning wheel flew round with renewed vigour, and conversation began again.

It was the belief of the entire family that, as soon as they left the dining room at night, the General occupied it himself, and had anyone gone in they would have found him there. Malvina even believed that they found satisfaction in the thought that their restless ancestor was in a comfortable, warm room.

It was a peculiarity of the General that he should find the dining room tidied and arranged when he arrived. Every evening, the housekeeper noticed that the Baroness and her daughters gathered up their work and took it with them; even the spinning wheel and the embroidery frames were put into another room, not so much as an end of cotton was left on the floor.

One night Miss Spaak, who slept in a chamber near the dining room, was awakened by a loud thump on the wall near her bed, which caused her to roll out on to the floor. She had scarcely picked herself up before a fresh bang was heard, and again she rolled out. The same thing happened twice more.

"Good gracious! What is he doing in there?" she groaned, for she knew whence the noise proceeded. It was certainly not a pleasant neighbourhood. She lay the whole night sweating with terror lest the General should come in and give her a ghostly embrace.

Next morning, taking both the cook and the housemaid with her, she went into the dining room to see what had happened. Nothing was disturbed, everything was tidy, except that four apples lay in the centre of the floor. Dear, dear! They had sat eating apples in front of the fire the previous evening, and four apples had lain unperceived on the mantelshelf. But this had not pleased the General! Miss Spaak had had to pay for her carelessness with a sleepless night!

On the other hand, she had had a true proof of friendship to place to his credit.

There had been festivity at Hedeby—a big dinner party and many visitors. Malvina had been up to her eyes in work: joints on every spit, puff pastry and pies in the oven, soup kettles and saucepans on the fire and on the hearth. But this was not all. She had to see to the arrangement of the dining-room table, to receive the silver from the Baroness, who herself counted it over with her. There had been the beer and wine to be got up from the cellar, and the candles to be put into the chandeliers. When you consider that the kitchen at Hedeby was situated in a distant wing of the building, so that you had to cross the yard to reach it, and that, on these great occasions, the house was full of strange and inexperienced servants, you can understand that it needed a capable person at the head of affairs.

But all went well and as it should. No thumb marks on the tumblers, no soggy lumps in the pastry; the beer had frothed high, and the soup was flavoured to a turn, and, needless to say, the coffee was perfect. Miss Spaak had risen to the occasion, displaying her true worth, and the Baroness herself had complimented her, saying that nothing could have been better.

But there came a terrible reverse! When the moment arrived for handing the silver back to the Baroness, two spoons—one teaspoon and one tablespoon—were missing!

There was an uproar! In those days there could be no greater upset in a house than for any of the silver to be lost. There were fever and unrest at Hedeby. People did nothing but search and search; they remembered that an old beggar woman had been in the kitchen on the very day of the party, and they were prepared to go right away up to Finmark to catch her. People grew suspicious and unreasonable.. Ths mistress mistrusted the housekeeper, the housekeeper mistrusted the servants, the servants mistrusted each other and all the rest of the world! First one and then another appeared with eyes red from weeping, because she thought that the others thought that she had taken the spoons to bed with her!

This went on for days; no spoons were found, and Miss Spaak was almost in despair. She had been to the pigsty and had hunted in the pigs' feeding trough to see if the spoons might have got there. She had crept up

to the servants' clothes cupboard, and had surreptitiously searched in their little trunks, but all in vain, and
she was completely at a loss where next to hunt. She
could see that the Baroness, as well as the rest of the
household, suspected her, for she was a stranger. She
would be given notice to leave, she knew, unless she gave
notice first herself.

She stood bending over the kitchen fire, weeping, so
that her tears fell sizzling on to the hot iron of the
grate, when she had a feeling that she must turn round.
She did so, and there stood the General, by the kitchen
wall, pointing to a shelf that was so high up and so in-
conveniently placed that nothing was ever kept on it.

As usual, the General vanished the instant she saw
him, but Miss Spaak obeyed his gesture. She fetched the
stepladder from the pantry, placed it under the shelf,
and, stretching up her hand, took hold of a dirty old
dishcloth, in the middle of which lay the two silver
spoons rolled up.

How had they come there? It must certainly have
been done without the knowledge or consent of anyone.
During the hurry and endless work of a big party, anything might happen. The cloth had been thrown aside
because it was in the way, and the spoons had gone too,
without being noticed.

But now they were found, and Miss Spaak took them
to the Baroness beaming with joy, and immediately became again everyone's helper and right hand.

It is an ill wind that blows nobody good. When young

Baron Adrian came home in the spring, he heard how the General had shown Miss Spaak an unwonted favour, and forthwith he began to regard her in an entirely new light. As often as he could, he would go and talk to her in the dining room or out in the kitchen. He would make the excuse that he wanted a new line for his fishing rod; sometimes he said it was the delicious smell of newly baked buns that attracted him. On these occasions he always brought the conversation round to the subject of the supernatural. He led her to talk of the ghosts in the big houses in Södermanland—such as Julita and Eriksberg—and asked her what she thought of them.

But oftenest he wanted to talk about the General. He said he could not argue the matter with the others, for they only saw the amusing side of it. He himself felt only pity for the poor ghost, and wished to help him to rest. If only he could find out how it was to be done!

Miss Spaak said that, in her humble opinion, there was something in the house for which he was seeking.

The young Baron grew rather pale. He looked searchingly at the girl.

"*Ma foi!* That is an idea, Miss Spaak! But I can assure you that, if we possessed anything here, in Hedeby, which he wanted, we should not hesitate a moment to give it to him."

Malvina knew that he came after her simply and solely on account of the ghost, but all the same he was a charming young man, and so handsome! Yes, but she really meant that he was something more than handsome. He carried his head slightly bent forward; he had a thoughtful expression—indeed, many people thought him too serious. But that was only because they did not know him. Sometimes he would throw back his head and laugh, and play more roguish tricks than any of them. But whatever he did, there was an indescribable charm in his gestures, his voice, his smile.

On Sunday, Malvina had been to church and was walking home by a little short cut which ran through the rectory garden. Several members of the congregation were also walking along this path, when Malvina, being in a hurry, had to pass a woman who was going very slowly. Soon afterward, she came to a high and difficult stile. With her usual thoughtful consideration for others, she remembered the woman whom she had passed walking so slowly, and determined to stop and help her over the stile. When she put out her hand to help the woman, she noticed that she was not so old as she had thought her to be from the first glance. She was extraordinarily slight and pale, but the girl did not think she could be more than fifty. Apparently only a country woman, yet she had a certain dignity about her, as if she had undergone some experience that had raised her above her station.

After helping her over the stile, Malvina and she walked side by side along the narrow path.

"You are helping with the housekeeping at Hedeby, I think," said the woman.

"Yes, I am," said the girl.

"I wonder if you get on there?"

"Why should I not get on in so good a situation?" asked the girl, with a certain reserve.

"People say the place is haunted."

"We need not believe folks' gossip," said Malvina in a tone of reproof.

"No, certainly, we should not—I know—we should not," said the other.

They went on in silence for a little. She could see the woman knew something, and, as a matter of fact, she herself was burning with a desire to question her companion, but it was not right and fitting for her to do so. It was the woman who resumed the conversation.

"I think you look good," she said, "and I will therefore give you a piece of good advice. Do not stay too long at Hedeby, for he who walks there is not good to deal with. He never goes until he has got what he wants."

When the woman began to speak, Malvina determined to thank her haughtily for her warning; but her final words aroused her curiosity.

"What does he want? Do you know what he wants?"

"Have you no idea?" asked the woman. "Then I shall say no more. Perhaps it is best that you should not know."

Thereupon, giving her hand to Malvina, she stooped and, turning into another small path, soon disappeared out of sight.

At dinner, Malvina was careful not to refer to what

had happened, but when Adrian joined her in the dairy, during the afternoon, she told him what the stranger had said to her. He was very much surprised.

"It must have been Marit Ivarsson from Olsby," he said. "Do you know, that is the first friendly word she has spoken to anyone from Hedeby for the last thirty years. Once she mended my woollen cap, which was torn by one of the Olsby boys, but she looked at me then as if she would have liked to tear out my eyes."

"But does she know what the General is looking for?"

"She knows better than anyone else, Miss Spaak, and I know too. My father has often told me the story, but my parents do not want my sisters to know it, for they might be frightened then, perhaps, we should not be able to continue living in this house. I ought not to tell you the story either."

"God forbid!" said Malvina. "If the Baron has forbidden . . ."

"It hurts me not to," said Adrian, "because I believe you could help me."

"Ah! How I wish I could!"

"I repeat," said Adrian, "I want to help the poor ghost to rest. I am not afraid of him. I will follow him as soon as he calls me. Why should he show himself to everyone but me?"

X

ADRIAN LÖWENSKÖLD was lying asleep in a gable room at the top of the house, when he was awakened by a slight noise. He opened his eyes, and, as the shutters were not fastened up and it was a light summer night, he could plainly see the door open slowly. He thought it was the draught causing the movement until he caught sight of a dark form filling up the doorway and bending down as if searching for something inside the room.

Adrian plainly discerned an elderly man dressed in an old-fashioned cavalry uniform: a buff waistcoat of elks skin showed under his partially unbuttoned coat, the boots came above his knee, and he held up his long sword, as if to prevent its rattling.

"That is certainly the General," thought the young Baron. "What a good thing! Now he shall see that I am not afraid of him!"

All the others who had seen the General maintained that he vanished as soon as they fixed their eyes on him; but this did not happen now. The General remained standing in the doorway for some time after Adrian first saw him, and, after a few moments, when he had apparently satisfied himself that Adrian could endure his scrutiny, he held up one hand and signed to him.

Adrian immediately sat up in bed. "Now or never!" thought he. "At last he wants my help, and I shall go with him."

He seemed to have been expecting this moment for years; he had prepared himself for it, had tried to fortify his courage by thinking of it. He always knew he would have to undergo some ordeal. . . .

He would not keep the General waiting, but got straight out of bed and followed him just as he was, with only a sheet wrapped round him. For a moment, as he stood in the middle of the room, it occurred to him that it might be a dangerous experiment to trust himself to a being from the other world, and he recoiled from it. But he noticed that the General now stretched out both his hands toward him, as if in despairing supplication.

"What folly is this?" he thought. "Am I frightened already, before I am even out of the room?"

He went toward the door; the General slipped out in front of him and went in the direction of the attics, walking backward, as if to make sure that the young man was following him. As Adrian was about to cross the threshold of his room to follow the ghost toward the attics, a wave of fear again passed over him. Something told him to shut the door and hurry back to his bed. He began to discover that he had miscalculated his strength. He was not one of those who could pry into the secrets of the other world without danger to himself.

Still his courage did not entirely fail him. He tried to reason with himself that the General certainly would not want to lead him into any danger. He only wanted him to show him where the ring was. If he could only hold on for a few minutes more, he would accomplish that for which he had striven so long—he would send the tired wanderer back to his eternal rest.

The General was standing outside the room, waiting for him. It was darker there, but Adrian could yet see the dark form with the hands outstretched in supplication. Controlling himself, he stepped over the threshold, and the journey began again. The ghost turned toward the stairs, and when he saw that Adrian was following, he began to descend them. Still going backward, he seemed to stop on every step, as if to force the shrinking youth along by the power of his will.

It was a slow journey with many pauses, but continued relentlessly. Adrian tried to fortify himself with the thought of the many times he had boasted to his sisters that, whenever the General called, he would follow him. He also reminded himself how, from his very childhood, he had burned with a longing to investigate the unknown world and to get through to the other side. And now the great moment had arrived, now he was to follow a ghost out into the unknown. Was his wretched cowardice to prevent him from learning something at last?

Thus he forced himself to keep on, but he was careful not to approach too near the ghost. They walked about a couple of yards apart; when Adrian was halfway down the stairs the General had reached the bottom, and, as Adrian's foot touched the last step, the General stood in the hall.

But here Adrian stopped again. On his right, near the staircase, stood the door opening into his parents' bedroom, and he laid his fingers on the handle, not to turn it, but just to caress it lovingly. Imagine if his parents had known that he was just there, and in that company! He longed to throw himself into his mother's arms. He felt that the moment he let go the handle of the door, he would be completely in the General's power.

While he stood, still holding the handle, he saw the front door burst open and the General about to step out over the threshold.

The light had been very dim, both in Adrian's room and on the staircase; but now a bright light streamed through the open door, and, for the first time, the young Baron saw the General's features. It was the face of an old man—he recognized it at once from the portrait in the drawing room. But there was none of the peacefulness of death there—a furious greed shone in the eyes, and on the lips trembled an uncanny smile of triumph and of certainty of victory.

To see these earthly passions depicted on a dead man's face was terrifying. We like to picture our dead friends at rest, far removed and free from human lusts and sufferings. We would have them removed from earthly desires, rejoicing only in heavenly things. Adrian could see nothing in this being, fast bound by earthly passions, but a seducer—an evil spirit, dragging him to his destruction.

He was overwhelmed with terror. In unreflecting anguish, he dashed open the door of his parents' room and, stumbling over the threshold, cried out:

"Father! Mother! The General!" and fell on the floor in a dead swoon.

.   .   .   .

The pen drops from my fingers. Is it not bootless to try and write these things? This story was told me in the twilight sitting by the fire. I can still hear the compelling voice, I can feel the appropriate shiver running down my spine—that little tremor not so much of fear, as of expectation.

How breathlessly we listened to the story, for it seemed to lift a tiny corner of the veil hiding the unknown. What a strange sensation remained with us, as if a door had been opened, and now, at last, something would appear from out that great obscurity!

How much truth is there in it? Each narrator has inherited the story from his predecessor; one has added a little, another has taken away a little. But does it not contain, at least, a little germ of truth? Does it not give the impression of describing something that really happened?

Who and what was the ghost that wandered about in Hedeby, who was seen in broad daylight, who interfered in household affairs, who found lost possessions? Who was he? What was he?

Was there not something unusually clear and solid in his appearance? Can he be distinguished by any special peculiarity, from other family ghosts? Does it not seem as though Miss Spaak might really have heard him throw apples at the dining-room wall, and that the young Baron Adrian might really have followed him out of his own room and down the stairs?

Well, well! Anyhow, perhaps some of those who even here and now can see the reality that lies behind the reality in which we now live, may be able to solve the riddle.

XI

YOUNG Baron Adrian lay in his parents' great bed, white and motionless. On laying a finger on his wrist, one could just feel the blood pulsing, but with difficulty. He had never regained consciousness after his deep swoon, but life was not extinct.

There was no doctor in the parish of Bro, but a servant had ridden at four o'clock that morning to Karlstad to fetch one. It was a very long ride, and even should the doctor be at home and willing to come so far, he could not be expected for at least twelve hours. One must even be prepared to wait a whole day or even two, if he was detained over a case.

Baroness Löwensköld sat beside the bed and never took her eyes from her son's face. She seemed to think that the faint glimmer of life could not fade so long as she sat watching and waiting.

Occasionally, the Baron sat on the other side of the bed, but he could not keep still. He would take one of the limp hands between his own and feel the pulse, then he would go to the window and look out toward the road. Again he would take a little turn to consult the dining-room clock. He shook his head in answer to the eager questions that he could read in the anxious eyes of his daughters and their governess. And then he would return to the sick room.

Except the parents, no one was allowed in that room except Malvina Spaak; neither the daughters nor the servants—only the housekeeper. She had just the right step, the gentle voice—she suited a sick room.

Adrian's scream had waked Malvina in the middle of the night. On hearing the heavy fall, she had immediately jumped up and thrown on her clothes—she could never say how—but it was one of her unfailing maxims never to leave your room undressed, for then you could be of no possible use to anyone. She had met the Baroness coming from her room to call for help, and had helped the parents to get Adrian into bed. At first they thought he was dead, but Malvina noticed a frail movement of the pulse.

They used every effort to restore him, but the little spark of life was so frail, that it seemed to grow weaker in spite of all their efforts. After a time, they lost heart, and could do no more, but only sit and wait.

The Baroness liked to have the girl in the room, for she was so calm and so convinced that Adrian would soon wake up. She allowed Malvina to arrange her hair and put on her shoes; and, though she had to move to put on her clothes, she allowed the girl to fasten the buttons, so that she need not take her eyes from her son's face.

Presently she fetched a cup of coffee, and persuaded the Baroness, with friendly solicitation, to drink a little; and though her mistress had the impression that the girl was with her the whole time, as a matter of fact, Malvina went back and forth to the kitchen to see that the meals were prepared as usual. She forgot nothing. Her face was deadly pale but she went on with her work; breakfast was on the table at the proper time, and the boys who drove the cattle to pasture found their lunch packed in their knapsacks as usual.

The maids in the kitchen wanted to know what had happened to the young Baron; she told them that all that was known was, that he had burst into his parents' room, calling out something about the General, and had then fallen into a dead faint, from which it was impossible to rouse him.

"The General must certainly have appeared to him," said the cook.

"Isn't it funny he should be so unkind to his own people?" said the housemaid.

"Oh, he has lost patience with them. They do nothing but laugh at him. He wants his ring back."

"You don't suppose the ring is here in Hedeby," said the housemaid. "He would burn the house over our heads to get it, if it was here."

"It must be here in some corner," said the cook, "or else he wouldn't be wandering all over the place as he is."

That day Miss Spaak made an exception to her good rule of never listening to servants' tales about their employers.

"What is that you are saying about a ring?" she asked.

"Don't you know, miss, that the General wanders about here looking for his signet ring?" The cook was delighted to be asked the question. She and the housemaid lost no time in telling Miss Spaak the complete history of the robbery of the ring from the grave, and all about the ordeal of the dice; and when they had finished their tale, not a shadow of doubt remained in her mind. The ring somehow must have got to Hedeby, and was hidden in the house.

Now she was overtaken by a great trembling, such as she had experienced during her first encounter with the General on the attic stairs. She had gone in fear of him, the whole time; now she knew how cruel and merciless these ghosts could be. She saw one fact standing out clear and direct before her—unless the ring could be restored to the General, Baron Adrian would die.

Hardly had she reached this conclusion, however, before she knew precisely what she had to do, for she was a very resolute creature. If that horrible ring was really in Hedeby, it had got to be found.

She went back to the house and peeped into the sick room, where there was no change; she then ran upstairs and made Adrian's bed, so that it might be ready in case he got better and could be carried up to it. She finally went to find the governess and the girls, who were sitting about frightened and unhappy and not able to settle to anything, and told them what she had just heard from the servants about the ring. She impressed on them how important it was to find it, and begged them to help her look for it. They grew interested at once, and undertook to search inside the house—in all the rooms and in the box attics.

Malvina herself undertook the kitchen department, so she started all the women servants on the search there.

"The General appears in the kitchen as well as in the rest of the house," she thought to herself. "Something tells me the ring is about here somewhere."

They hunted everywhere. They turned out everything in the pantry, the kitchen, the bakehouse, the brewery. They searched in the cracks in the walls and in the fireplaces; they emptied all the spice boxes—they even tried the rat holes!

In spite of all her preoccupation, Malvina never omitted to run across and peep into the sick room, from time to time. On one of her visits she found the Baroness crying.

"He is worse," she said. "I think he is dying."

Malvina went up to Adrian, took his powerless hand in hers, and felt his pulse.

"Not worse, Baroness, surely a little better?"

She succeeded in reassuring the poor lady, but was very doubtful herself. Think, if he should die before she found the ring!

In her anxiety, she forgot to be as careful as usual;

and in laying Adrian's hand back upon the bed, she gave it a little caress. She was scarcely aware of her own gesture, but the Baroness noticed it.

"*Mon Dieu!*" she thought. "Poor child, is that what ails her? Perhaps I ought to tell her. . . . But if we are to lose him, it doesn't matter. The General is angry with him, and those who anger the General have got to die."

When Miss Spaak returned to the kitchen, she asked the servants whether there was anybody in the country-side who could be of use in this great trouble, or whether it was necessary to go on waiting till the doctor could come?

Yes, there was a woman called Marit Ivarsson, at Olsby, whom people always sent for when they were hurt. She could staunch the flow of blood and set bones; she might even be able to wake Baron Adrian from his death sleep—but she would certainly never come to Hedeby.

While the housemaid was telling Malvina about Marit Ivarsson, the cook had got up on to the stepladder and was feeling along the high shelf where the lost silver spoons had been found after the big dinner party.

"Ah!" she called out. "I have found something I've been looking for ever so long. Here it is! Baron Adrian's old woollen cap!"

The housekeeper was shocked! What possible kind of method could there have been in the housekeeping at Hedeby before she came? How could Baron Adrian's old cap have got there?

"It isn't so curious, after all," said the cook. "He had grown out of it, so he gave it to me to use as a dish cloth. I *am* glad I have come upon it again!"

Miss Spaak took the cap quickly out of her hand.

"It is a shame to cut it up," she said. "We can give it to some poor person."

Taking it with her, she went out into the yard, and began to beat the dust out of it. While thus employed, the Baroness came out toward her.

"We fear that Adrian is worse," she said.

"Is there no one about here who understands doctoring?" asked Malvina innocently. "The servants mentioned a woman named Marit Ivarsson."

The Baroness Löwensköld drew herself up stiffly.

"Of course, if it was a case of Adrian's life, I should not hesitate to send for my worst enemy. But it would be quite useless. Marit Ivarsson will never enter Hedeby."

Malvina dared not oppose her mistress after such a statement. She returned to her search for the ring; then she busied herself about the dinner and succeeded in persuading even the Baroness to eat something. But there was no sign of the ring, and Malvina repeated over and over again to herself: "We must find the ring. The General will let Adrian die if he doesn't get his ring back."

That afternoon she started off to Olsby. She went on her own responsibility, for the last time she had seen Adrian his pulse had grown slower and weaker, and she could no longer wait for the doctor from Karlstad. It was more than likely that this woman, Marit, would refuse, but Malvina would leave no stone unturned.

Marit was sitting in her usual place on the cottage steps when Miss Spaak arrived. She had no work in her hands, but sat leaning back with her eyes closed. She was not, however, asleep, and looked up as the other approached. She recognized her at once.

"Well?" she said. "So they have sent for me from Hedeby?"

"Have you heard of our great misfortune?" asked Malvina.

"Yes, I have heard of it," said Marit, "and I will not come."

The girl answered not a word. A great hopelessness fell upon her. Everything seemed to go against her, but this was surely the worst of all. She could see and hear that Marit was glad. She had been sitting there, on those steps, rejoicing at their misfortunes, rejoicing that Adrian Löwensköld was dying.

Hitherto, the girl had succeeded in keeping up her courage; she had neither cried out nor wept when Adrian lay helpless on the floor that night. Her one thought had been to help him and the others. But Marit's cruel opposition broke down her strength at last, and she began to weep violently and uncontrollably. Stumbling forward, she leant her forehead against the gray stone wall, and sobbed and cried.

Marit leant forward a little and sat for some time

gazing at the unhappy girl. "Ah, so that is what ails her," she said.

But as Marit sat watching this young creature, weeping tears of love over her beloved, something happened in her own soul. She had heard, a few hours before, how the General had appeared to Adrian and had frightened him almost to death, and she had said that now, at last, her hour of revenge had come. She had waited for it so many years, and all in vain. Captain Löwensköld had gone down to his grave untouched by punishment. It was true that the General had haunted Hedeby ever since she had sent the ring there; but apparently he had pursued his own family with his usual cruelty.

But now that misfortune had come upon them, they immediately sent to her for help! Why did they not go rather to the dead upon the gallows?

It did her good to say, "I will not." That was her method of revenge. But when Marit saw that young girl weeping with her head pressed against the wall, a memory rose within her.

"I, too, have leant against a hard wall and have wept with no one to comfort me or support me."

Thinking thus, the full tide of her girlhood's love welled up in the woman's heart and filled her with its warmth. She sat amazed, and said to herself, "That was how I too felt then; that is what it means to love some-one—so strong and sweet a feeling."

The sight of Paul Eliasson rose within her mind; she could see him as he used to look—young, bright and happy, and handsome. She could recall his look, his voice, his every gesture—her whole heart was filled with him.

She thought that she had loved him always, and so indeed she had; but now, alas, her feeling had cooled during the long years! But now, again, it rose and flooded her soul with light! Yet with her awakened love came the memory of her awful suffering, caused by the tragic death of her beloved.

Marit looked once more at Malvina Spaak, who still stood weeping by the wall; she understood now what the girl was suffering. Gradually, during the long years, her love had weakened, she had forgotten how the fire could burn. But now she remembered, and she determined she would never be the cause of suffering to another such as she herself had undergone. She rose from the steps and went to Malvina.

"Come," she said curtly, "I will go with you."

They walked back to Hedeby together. Marit uttered not a word during the journey. Malvina found, later, that she had been considering what means she should take to find the ring.

They entered the house together by the front door and went straight to the sick room. There was no change. Adrian lay there white and beautiful but still as death, and the Baroness sat motionless beside him, watching. Only when Marit came up to the bed did she look up.

The moment she recognized the figure who stood gazing at her son, she sank on her knees in front of her and laid her cheek against the woman's skirt.

"Marit! Marit!" she said. "Forget all the harm the Löwenskölds have done you! Save him, Marit, oh, save him!"

The countrywoman drew back a little, but the distracted mother crept after her on her knees.

"You don't know how terrified I have been since the General began to haunt us here again. I have been fearing and expecting something the whole time. I knew he would turn his anger against us."

Marit stood still. She shut her eyes and seemed to be pondering deeply within herself. Miss Spaak was certain that it pleased her to hear the Baroness speak of her suffering.

"I wanted to go to you, Marit, and kneel at your feet, as I am doing now, and entreat you to forgive the Löwenskölds. But I dared not, I thought it would be impossible for you to pardon us."

"It is no use your asking me, Baroness Löwensköld. I cannot forgive."

"But yet you have come here?"

"I have come for the young lady's sake, because she begged me to do so."

Marit then went round to the other side of the bed. Laying her hand on the sick man's breast, she murmured some words, at the same time knitting her brows over her half-closed eyes and pursing her lips. She reminded the girl of a fortune teller.

"He will certainly live," said Marit, "but you must remember, my lady, that I am here entirely for the girl's sake."

"Yes, Marit," answered the Baroness. "I shall never forget it."

It seemed to Miss Spaak as though her mistress had intended to add something, but she broke off suddenly, biting her lip.

"And now you must let me arrange everything."

"You must do whatever you wish, Marit. The Baron is away—I begged him to ride and meet the doctor and ask him to hasten."

Miss Spaak had expected that Marit Ivarsson would take some steps to wake the young Baron from his stupor, but to her great surprise, she did nothing of the sort. She ordered that a collection should be made of all Baron Adrian's clothes—both those in use and those set aside as worn out. She wished to see everything that had ever touched his body, socks and shirts—even his woollen gloves and caps.

The entire day was spent in searching at Hedeby. Although Malvina sighed at the thought that Marit was nothing better than an ordinary "wise woman," with the ordinary fortune teller's tricks, yet she hastened to get together everything from cupboards, drawers, chests in the attics, that had been worn by the sick man. His sisters, who remembered what Adrian had been in the habit of wearing, helped her; and soon she had collected a whole bundle, which she took to Marit.

The latter proceeded to lay them out on the kitchen table and went carefully through each article. She laid an old pair of shoes on one side, together with some little woollen gloves and a shirt, while she murmured incessantly, in a low voice, "A pair for the feet, a pair for the hands, one for the body, one for the head."

Suddenly she said, in her ordinary voice, "I must have something for the head, I must have something that is warm and soft."

The housekeeper pointed to the hats and a helmet which she had found.

"No, it must be something warm and soft," said Marit. "Hadn't Baron Adrian any woollen cap like other boys?"

The girl was on the point of saying that she had not seen one when the cook forestalled her.

"I did find his old woollen cap on the shelf up there, this morning, but Miss Spaak took it from me."

Miss Spaak was therefore obliged to produce the cap, which she had intended never to part with, but to treasure as a loved memento for the rest of her life.

As soon as Marit took the cap in her hands, she began again to murmur her incantation; but now there was a different tone in her voice—the tone of a cat purring with satisfaction.

After turning and twisting the cap and murmuring over it for a long time, she said at last: "Now, nothing more is necessary. All these things must be laid in the General's grave."

But Malvina was perfectly astounded at these words. "How do you suppose that the Baron will ever allow the grave to be opened to receive this old rubbish?" she asked.

Marit regarded her with a little smile; then, taking her by the hand, she led her toward a window, where they could stand with their back turned toward the others in the kitchen. There, holding Adrian's cap near to Malvina's eyes, she parted the strands of the woollen tassel. Neither of the women spoke a word, but the housekeeper's face was deathly white, and her hands shook as she turned back into the room.

Marit tied the clothes into a little bundle, and gave it to Miss Spaak.

"I have done my share," she said. "Now it is for others to do theirs and to see that these things are put into the grave."

And with that she went out.

. . . .

Soon after ten o'clock that same evening Malvina Spaak walked up to the churchyard. She carried Marit's little bundle in her hand; otherwise, she had only gone for a random stroll. She had not the faintest idea how she was to get the things into the General's grave.

Baron Löwensköld had come riding in accompanied by the doctor soon after Marit had left; and Miss Spaak had hoped that Adrian would be restored to consciousness without her having to do anything further in the matter. But the doctor had immediately pronounced that he could do nothing. He said that the young man had but a few hours more to live.

Then, taking the bundle under her arm, the girl had started on her walk. She knew that there was no earthly possibility of persuading Baron Löwensköld to open the grave merely to lay Adrian's old garments in it. If she could tell him what the bundle really contained, she was certain that he would immediately return the ring to its rightful owner; but then she would betray Marit Ivarsson, for she was convinced that Marit must, at some time, have conveyed the ring to Hedeby.

Adrian had told her that Marit had once mended his cap for him. No, she could not possibly let the Baron know the truth of the matter

Later on, it occurred to Malvina to wonder why she had felt no fear that night; but she simply stepped over the low wall of the churchyard and went straight to the Löwensköld's grave, without a thought of anything but getting the ring into the vault.

She sat down on the gravestone and joined her hands together in prayer. "If God does not help me," she thought, "the grave will be opened, not for the ring, but for one for whom I shall always grieve."

While praying, she noticed a slight movement in the grass clothing the mound on which the gravestone rested. A tiny head peeped out and disappeared the moment Malvina moved—she feared the rat as much as the rat feared her! The sight of the creature, however, gave her a swift inspiration. Running to a large lilac bush, she broke off a long dry branch. This she pushed down the rat hole. First, she tried pushing directly down, but immediately encountered an obstacle. Then she tried pushing it on the slant and succeeded in getting it in a good way toward the grave. She was surprised how far it penetrated—the whole twig disappeared—but she drew it out quickly and measured it with her arm. It was three feet long and had gone the whole length into the earth. It must have reached to the vault!

Malvina had never felt so clear-headed and collected in her whole life. She realized that the rats must have made a way into the vault—perhaps they had found a drain, or a brick might have crumbled away.

She lay down on the ground, dug up a sod, and, scattering the loose earth under it, inserted her arm. She encountered no obstacle, but did not touch the wall. Her arm was too short! She could not reach the vault!

Then, hastily untying the bundle, she took out the cap. Thrusting the branch through it, she tried slowly to push it into the hole, and soon it had disappeared. She continued to guide the branch, slowly and carefully, farther and farther in; then, suddenly, when almost the whole twig had disappeared in the ground, she felt it strongly jerked out of her hand. It fell into the hole and vanished.

It was possible that it had only fallen by its own weight, but she felt absolutely certain that it had been snatched from her.

Now, at last, she began to be frightened. Taking the contents of the bundle, she thrust them all into the hole; put back the sods and the earth as well as she could, and hurried away. She ran the whole distance back to Hedeby without stopping for a moment.

When she reached home, the Baron and Baroness were standing together on the steps. They came eagerly down to meet her.

"Where have you been?" they asked. "We have been waiting here for you."

"Is Baron Adrian dead?" she asked.

"No, he is not dead," said the Baron, "but tell us first where you have been."

Malvina was so breathless she could hardly speak; but she managed to tell them of the task put upon her by Marit, and of how she had managed to get at least one of the things into the vault by means of the rat hole.

"This is most extraordinary, Miss Spaak," said the Baron, "for Adrian is really better. He wakened up a little while ago, and his first words were: 'The General has got his ring now!'"

"His heart is beating quite normally," said the Baroness, "and he wants to speak to you. He says you are the person who has saved him."

They allowed Miss Spaak to go alone to see Adrian. As soon as he saw her, he sat up in bed and stretched out his arms toward her.

"I know it, I know it already!" he cried. "The General has got back his ring, and entirely through you!"

Malvina laughed and cried as she lay in his arms, and he kissed her on the forehead.

"I thank you for my life," he said. "Had it not been for you, I should now be a corpse. I can never be grateful enough to you."

The rapture with which Adrian greeted her had possibly caused poor Malvina to linger too long in his arms, for he hastened to add: "And not only I am grateful, but there is also another."

He showed her a locket, hanging on his breast. Miss Spaak could faintly distinguish the miniature of a young girl.

"You are the first person, besides my parents, who knows of this," he said. "When she comes to Hedeby in a few weeks' time, she will be able to thank you much better than I can."

The housekeeper, Miss Spaak, bowed to the young Baron Adrian Löwensköld and thanked him for his confidence. She longed to say that she did not intend to stay at Hedeby to meet his betrothed, but she remembered herself in time. And besides, beggars cannot be choosers!

CHARLOTTE LÖWENSKÖLD

CONTENTS

CONTENTS

CHARLOTTE LÖWENSKÖLD

CHAPTER I

THE BARONESS

BEATA EKENSTEDT, born Löwensköld and
baroness, was the quintessence of culture and
refinement, highly accomplished and delightfully agreeable. She could write verse quite as amusing
as Fru Lenngren's.[1]

Though short of stature, she had a good bearing, like
all the Löwenskölds, and an interesting face. She said
charming things to everyone, and those who had once
seen her never forgot her. She had exquisite taste in
dress, and her hair was always beautifully arranged.
Wherever she appeared, hers was the prettiest brooch,
hers the choicest bracelet, hers the most dazzling ring.
She had a neat little foot, and, whether it was the
fashion or not, she always wore dainty high-heeled shoes
of gold brocade.

She lived in the finest house in Karlstad, and it was
not wedged in among the jumble of dwellings on a
narrow street. Her house stood apart on the shore of the

---

[1] Anna Maria Lenngren, leading woman poet of Sweden, satirized the
social foibles of her time.

Daläven, and the Baroness from the window of her little cabinet could look right down into the shining river. She used to tell how on clear moonlit nights she had seen the Neckan sitting beneath her window, playing on a golden harp. And no one doubted it. Why should not the River-god, like so many others, serenade the Baroness Ekenstedt?

All the notables who visited Karlstad paid their respects to the Baroness. They were immediately captivated, and thought it a pity that so adorable a lady should be buried in a small city.

It was said that Bishop Tegnér had written a sonnet to her and that the Crown Prince had declared she had the charm of a Frenchwoman. Even General von Essen, among others of the Court of Gustavus III, had to concede that such perfect dinners as were given by the Baroness Ekenstedt he had never sat down to elsewhere—either as to the viands, the service, or the conversation.

The Baroness had two daughters, Eve and Jaquette. They were pretty and amiable girls who would have been admired almost anywhere. But in Karlstad no one even noticed them; they were completely overshadowed by their mother.

When the girls attended a ball, the young gentlemen all vied with each other for the privilege of dancing with the Baroness, while Eve and Jaquette had to sit as wallflowers. As already mentioned, it was not the Neckan alone who gave serenades outside the Ekenstedt

house! But no one ever sang beneath the daughters'
windows. Young poets composed madrigals to B. E.,
but never a strophe to E. E. or J. E. Persons a bit
maliciously inclined said that a young lieutenant who
had courted little Eve Ekenstedt was coolly dismissed
because the Baroness thought he had shown poor taste.

The lady had also a husband. Colonel Ekenstedt was
a splendid fellow who would have commanded respect
and admiration in any society outside his wife's world.
But when seen beside his brilliant spouse, with her lively
wit and playful vivaciousness, the Colonel looked like a
staid country squire. When he spoke, the guests in his
home scarcely listened; it was almost as if he were not
there at all. It cannot be said of the Colonel's wife that
she allowed those who swarmed about her any familiarities. Her conduct was unimpeachable. But it never
occurred to her mind to draw her husband out of the
shadow. She probably thought it suited him best to
remain somewhat in the background.

This charming Baroness, this much-fêted lady, had
not only a husband and two daughters, she had also a
son. The son she adored. He was pushed forward on all
occasions. It would not have done for any guest of the
Ekenstedt house to overlook or slight him—not if he
entertained any hope of being invited there again.

The Baroness, however, had reason to be proud of her
son. Karl Arthur was a talented youth with lovable
ways and attractive exterior; he had delicate features
and large dark eyes. He was not, as other spoiled chil-

dren, forward and brazen. As a schoolboy, he had never played truant, had never "put up any game" on his teachers. He was of a more romantic turn of mind than either of his sisters. Before his eighth year he had made up neat little rhymes. And he could tell mamma that he too had heard the Neckan play and seen the brownies dance on the meadows of Voxnäs. In fact, in every way, he was his mother's own son.

He filled her heart completely. Yet she could hardly be called a weak mother. At least Karl Arthur had to learn to work. True, his mother held him as something higher than all other beings; and for that very reason it would not have done for him to come home from the *gymnasium* with anything short of the highest marks. While Karl attended class, the Baroness never invited any of his instructors to the house. No, it should not be said that he received high marks because he was the son of the Baroness Ekenstedt, who gave such fine dinners. Ah, yes, the Baroness had quality!

Karl Arthur was graduated from the Karlstad *Gymnasium* with highest honours, as was Eric Gustaf Geijer[1] in his day; and to matriculate at Upsala University was just play for him, as it had been for Geijer. The Baroness had seen the tubby little professor many a time, and had had him as table companion. A markedly gifted man, to be sure; still, she could but think that her Karl Arthur had quite as good a mind; that

---

[1] A noted Swedish historian and professor of history; also a poet of distinction.

some day he, too, would be a famous professor who would draw to his lectures Crown Prince Oscar, Governor Järta,[1] Fru Silverstolpe[2], and all the other notables at Upsala.

Karl Arthur entered the University at the autumn semester, year 1826. All that term, and in fact throughout his college years, he wrote home regularly once a week. Not one of his precious letters was destroyed; his mother kept them all, reading them over again and again. At the Sunday dinners, when the relatives gathered round the board, she would read to them his latest epistle. This she could do with good grace, for these were letters she might well be proud of.

The Baroness surmised that the relatives expected Karl Arthur to be a paragon of all the virtues now that he was on his own, so to speak; and it was a triumph for her to be able to read out to them how he had taken inexpensive lodgings, did his own marketing, and prepared his simple meals; how he arose at five every morning and worked twelve hours a day. Then, too, there were the many deferential terms employed in his letters, and the fulsome praises bestowed upon his mother. The Baroness quite gratuitously imparted to Provost Sjöberg, who had married an Ekenstedt, and Alderman Ekenstedt, uncle of her husband, and the

---

[1]Governor of Dalecarlia; Jurist; Publicist; a Member of the Cabinet and a Member of the Swedish Academy.

[2]Writer: best known for her *Memoirs*. Her salon was a centre for the *literati* of Sweden.

cousins Stake, who lived in the great house on the square, that Karl Arthur, though now out in the world, still maintained that his mother might have been a poet of the first rank had she not lived solely for her husband and children. Ah, no, she had sought no reward; it had been a voluntary sacrifice. Accustomed as she was to laudation of every sort, her eyes always filled when she read these lines from her darling boy.

But her greatest triumph came just before Christmas, when Karl Arthur wrote that he had not used up all the money his father had given him for his expenses at Upsala, that he still had about half of it left to come home with.

This was most astounding news to the Provost, the Alderman, and the most distant of the cousins Stake. Such a thing, they averred, had never happened before and surely would never happen again. They all agreed that Karl Arthur was a wonder.

It was lonely for the poor Baroness with her boy away at college the greater part of the year; but she had so much joy of his letters she hardly could have wished it to be otherwise. When he had attended a lecture by the famous neo-romantic poet, Atterbom, he would discourse so interestingly on philosophy and poetry. And when such letters came, the Baroness would sit dreaming for hours of the wonderful things her Karl Arthur was going to do. She believed he would outrank even Professor Geijer. Perhaps he might be as great a man as Karl von Linné, and as world-renowned. Or, why not a great poet?—A second Tégner? Ah, what more delightful entertainment than to revel in one's thoughts!

Karl Arthur always came home for the Christmas and summer holidays; and every time his mother saw him again, she thought he had grown more handsome and manly. In other respects, he had not changed. He showed the old worshipful attitude toward his mother, the usual respect for his father, and teasing, playful way with his sisters.

Sometimes the Baroness felt a trifle impatient, as Karl Arthur, year after year, remained quietly at Upsala, and nothing much happened. Her friends all explained, that since Karl Arthur was to take his Master's examination it would be some time before he was through. She must consider what it meant to pass in all the subjects studied at the University—in astronomy, Hebrew, geometry, and the rest. He couldn't "get by" with less. The Baroness thought it a cruel examination, and so it was; but it couldn't be changed just for the sake of Karl Arthur.

In the late autumn of 1829, when Karl Arthur was in his seventh term at Upsala, he wrote home, to his mother's delight, that he had presented himself for the examination in Latin, which, though not a hard one, was prerequisite to the finals.

Karl Arthur made no to-do of the thing, but only said it would be nice to be through with it. He had never had any difficulty with his Latin; so he had reason to think that all would go well. He also said that this was the last letter his dear parents would receive from him that term. As soon as he knew the result of the examination, he would leave for home. Without doubt, on the last day of November, he would embrace his parents and his sisters.

No, Karl Arthur had not made any "noise" whatever about his Latin "exam." And he was glad afterward, for he failed lamentably. The Upsala dons had permitted themselves to "pluck" him, although he had taken highest honours in all his studies at the Karlstad *Gymnasium!*

He was more surprised than humiliated. He could not see but that his use of the Latin language was quite defensible. To come home as one beaten was certainly exasperating; but undoubtedly his parents—or his mother, at least—would understand that it must have been due to malice of some sort. The Upsala dons wished perhaps to show that they had higher standards than the Karlstad masters, or they may have thought, because he had not elected to take part in any of the seminars, that he had been too sure of himself.

It was several days' journey from Upsala to Karlstad, and when Karl Arthur drove in through the eastern tollgate at dusk on the thirtieth of November, he had forgotten the whole wretched affair. He was quite pleased with himself for arriving on the very day he had set in his letter. He pictured his mother standing at the salon window watching for him, and his sisters laying the coffee table.

Driving through the narrow, crooked streets of the

city, he was in fine spirits, till he glimpsed in the distance the Ekenstedt home. What in the world was going on there? The whole house was lit up like a church on a Christmas morning. Sledges full of fur-clad people skimmed past him—all apparently bound for his home.

"Mother must be giving a party," he thought with some vexation; for he was tired after his hard journey and wanted to rest. Now he'd have to change his clothes and sit gabbing with the guests until midnight.

Then, all at once, he became uneasy. Perhaps his mother was giving the party for him, to celebrate his Latin triumph.

He ordered the postboy to drive round to the kitchen entrance, and got out there so as to avoid meeting the guests. His mother was immediately notified of his arrival and requested to come to the housekeeper's room to speak with Karl Arthur.

The Baroness had been on pins and needles lest he should not arrive in time for dinner. She was overjoyed, and came hurrying out to welcome him.

Karl Arthur met his mother with a stern face. He did not notice her outstretched hands and made no move to greet her.

"What have you been up to, Mother?" he asked abruptly. "Why is the whole city invited here to-night?" This time there was no talk of "tender parents," and Karl Arthur seemed anything but glad to see his mother.

"Well," said the Baroness, "I thought we ought to

celebrate a little now that you have passed that dreadful examination."

"I suppose it never occurred to you that I might be plucked," said Karl Arthur; "but such is the case, at all events."

The Baroness stood dumbfounded. That her son would let himself be beaten had never entered her mind.

"Oh, that in itself is of no significance," Karl Arthur continued; "but now the whole town will know of it. I dare say all these people have been invited here to celebrate my success."

The Baroness was utterly crestfallen. She knew the way of the Karlstaders: They no doubt thought diligence and economy admirable things in a student, but these were not enough. They looked for prize awards from the Swedish Academy and brilliant disputations that would make all the old professors turn pale under their beards. They expected clever improvisations at the national festivals and entrée to exclusive literary circles—to Professor Geijer's, or Governor von Kraemer's, or Fru Silverstolpe's. Such things they could appreciate. But thus far Karl Arthur had shown no evidence of having any extraordinary gifts. His mother knew that people thought him lacking in such. And now, when at last he had proved his scholarship, she had felt there would be no harm in making a little ado over it. But this, that Karl Arthur had failed, seemed unbelievable.

"No one really knows anything for certain," she said;

"no one but the home folk. The others have only been told they were to have a pleasant surprise."

"Then you will have to invent some pleasant surprise for them," Karl Arthur retorted. "I'm going up to my room and shall not be down to the dinner. Not that I think the Karlstaders will take my failure to heart, but I don't want their commiseration."

"What in the world shall I do?" wailed the Baroness.

"That's for you to decide," Karl Arthur rapped out. "I'm going upstairs now. The guests need not know that I am at home."

But this was too painful! The Baroness, then, was to sit at table and play the amiable hostess with her son up in his room, unhappy and out of temper. She was not to have the pleasure of his company. It was hard on the poor Baroness.

"Dear Karl Arthur, you must come down to dinner! I'll hit upon something."

"What will it be, pray?"

"I don't know. . . . Ah, I have it! You'll be perfectly satisfied. No one will know that the party had been planned in your honour. Only promise me that you will dress and come down!"

The dinner was a great success. Of all the delightful feasts given at the Ekenstedt home, this was the most memorable.

When the roasts were brought in and the champagne was served, there came a veritable surprise. The Colonel stood up and asked those present to join him in a toast

to the happiness and prosperity of his daughter Eve
and Lieutenant Sten Arcker, whose engagement he was
pleased to announce.

There was general rejoicing.

Lieutenant Arcker was a poor man with no prospects
to speak of. They all knew that he had long been daft
about Eve Ekenstedt, and because the little Ekenstedt
girls so seldom had any admirers, the whole city had
been interested in this affair; but everyone had thought,
of course, that the Baroness would nip it in the bud.

Afterward it leaked out that the Baroness had allowed
Eve and Arcker to become engaged because there had
been some hitch to the surprise she had hoped to give
her guests.

But nobody thought any the less of the Baroness for
that. On the contrary, people said there was no one who
knew so well how to handle an embarrassing and difficult
situation as did Beata Ekenstedt.

*   *   *

The Baroness was one who expected an apology from
a person who had offended against her. That little amen-
ity discharged, she heartily forgave everything and was
as friendly and trusting as before the breach.

All through the Christmas holidays, she hoped Karl
Arthur would ask pardon for speaking so harshly to her
the evening of the party. It was quite clear to her that
he had forgotten himself in the heat of the moment, but
she could not understand why he was so silent about his
offence after he had had time for reflection.

But Karl Arthur let the holidays slip by without uttering a word of regret. He enjoyed himself as usual at dinner dances and sleighing parties, and was pleasant and attentive at home. Yet the few words his mother was waiting to hear remained unspoken. Only he and she noticed it, perhaps, but an invisible wall had risen between them which prevented their getting quite close to each other. There was no lack of love or tender expressions on either side, but the thing that separated them and kept them apart had not been removed.

When Karl was back at Upsala, he thought of nothing but to make up for his failure. If the Baroness expected a written apology from him, she was doomed to disappointment. He wrote only of his studies; he was reading Latin with two docents and attending Latin lectures every day. Besides, he had joined a seminar for practice in Latin disputation and oration. He was doing his level best to make good this time.

His letters home were most hopeful, and the Baroness answered them in the same spirit. Nevertheless, she felt anxious for him. He had been rude to his own mother and had made no apology. Now, for that, perhaps, he might be punished.

It was not that the Baroness wished to bring punishment upon her son; she had prayed God not to make note of the slight offence, but to let it be forgotten. She explained to our Lord that it was all her fault. "It was only my foolish vanity; I wanted to shine in the light of his success. It is I who deserve chastisement, and not he." But she continued to search his every letter for the missing words. Not finding them, her uneasiness increased. She had the feeling that it would not go well for Karl Arthur at the examination unless he was assured of her forgiveness.

Then, one day, toward the end of the term, the Baroness announced that she was going to Upsala to visit her good friend Malla Silverstolpe. They had met the previous summer in Kavlås, at the Gyllenhaals, and formed a pleasant friendship. Dear Malla had begged her to come to Upsala in the winter and meet her literary friends.

All Karlstad was surprised that the Baroness would set out upon such a long journey in the middle of the spring thaw. The Colonel, they thought, should have said no to this; but the Colonel assented, as usual.

She had a dreadful journey, as the Karlstaders had predicted. Several times her coach stuck in the mud and had to be lifted out on poles. Once a spring broke; another time it was the tongue. But the Baroness, frail little body that she was, struggled on bravely and merrily. Innkeepers and hostlers, blacksmiths and farmers she met along the way were ready to lay down their lives for her. They all seemed to know how very necessary it was that she should get to Upsala.

The Baroness, of course, had notified Fru Malla Silverstolpe of her coming, but not Karl Arthur, and she had requested her not to let him know of it, as she wanted to give him a surprise.

At Enköping there was another delay. It was only a few miles more to Upsala, but now a wheel band had come off, and until that had been repaired she could proceed no farther. The Baroness was panic-stricken. She had been such a long time on the way, and the Latin examination might take place at any hour. Her sole object in making this journey was to afford Karl Arthur an opportunity to apologize to her before the examination. She felt in her heart that if this were left undone, no docents or lectures would profit him. He would inevitably fail again.

She could not rest in her room at the inn. Every little while she would run down the stairs and out into the yard to see whether the wheel had come back from the smithy.

On one of these restless excursions, she saw a cart turn into the yard. Beside the driver sat a youth wearing a student's cap who suddenly jumped from the wagon. Why—she could hardly believe her eyes—it was Karl Arthur!

He rushed up to his mother, seized her hand, and pressed it to his heart, while his beautiful, dreamy child-eyes looked pleadingly into hers.

"Mother!" he cried, "forgive me for my rudeness to you last winter, when you gave that party for me."

It seemed almost too good to be true.

The Baroness freed her hand, flung her arms around Karl Arthur's neck, and nearly smothered him with kisses. Why he was there, she did not know, but she knew that she had got back her son, and this was the happiest moment of her life.

She drew him into the inn, and explanations followed.

No, there had been no examination as yet; it would take place on the morrow. But in spite of this he had set off for home, only to see her.

"What a madcap you are!" laughed the Baroness. "Did you think to drive to Karlstad and back in a day and a night?"

"No," he said; "I let everything go by the wind, for I knew this had to be done. It was useless to try until I had your forgiveness. I should only have failed."

"But, my boy, all that was necessary was the least little word in a letter."

"This thing has been hanging over me the whole term like some obscure, intangible menace. I have been troubled, have lost confidence in myself without knowing why. But last night it all became clear to me: I had wounded the heart that beats for me so tenderly. I knew that I could not work with any hope of success until I had made my peace with my mother."

The Baroness put a hand up to her brimming eyes, and the other went out to her son. "This is wonderful, Karl Arthur," she said. "Tell me more!"

"Across the hall from me rooms another Värmlander, Pontus Friman by name. He is a Pietist, and doesn't mingle with the other students; nor had I come in contact with him. But last night I felt impelled to go to his room and tell him how it was with me. 'I have the dearest little mother in the world,' I told him. 'I have hurt her feelings and have not asked her forgiveness. What must I do?'"

"And he said——?"

"'Go to your mother at once,' he said. I told him that that was what I wanted to do above everything; but to-morrow I was to write *pro exercitio*. Besides, my parents would not approve of my skipping exams. Friman wouldn't listen. 'Go at once!' he repeated. 'Don't think of anything now but to make your peace with your mother. God will help you.'"

"And you went?"

"Yes, Mother, I went to cast myself at your feet. But I was no sooner seated in the cart than it struck me that I had been inexcusably asinine. I felt strongly tempted to turn back, for I knew, of course, that even if I stayed at Upsala a few days more, your love would pardon all. Well, anyhow, I drove on. And God did help me, for I found you here. I don't know how you happen to be here, but it must have been He Who sent you."

Tears poured down the cheeks of both mother and son. For their sake had not a miracle been wrought? They felt that a kind Providence watched over them, and realized as never before how strong was the love that united them.

For an hour they sat together at the inn, whereupon the Baroness sent Karl Arthur back to Upsala, bidding him greet dear Malla Silverstolpe for her, and say that his mother was not coming to see her this time.

The Baroness did not care to go on to Upsala. The object of the journey had been accomplished. She could go home with her mind at ease, knowing that Karl Arthur would come through the ordeal with flying colours.

* * *

All Karlstad knew that the Baroness was religious. She went to church every Sunday as regularly as the pastor himself, and on weekdays she held a little devotional service, both morning and evening, with all her household. She had her poor, whom she remembered with gifts not only at Christmas but the whole year round. She provided midday meals for a number of needy schoolboys, and always gave a big coffee party to the old women of the poorhouse on Beata Day.

But no one in Karlstad, least of all the Baroness, had any idea it was displeasing to our Lord that she and the Provost, the Alderman, and the eldest of the cousins Stake indulged in a quiet game of boston after dinner on a Sunday. And little did they dream it was sinful of the young ladies and gentlemen who dropped in at the Colonel's on Sunday evenings to take a bit of a whirl in the grand salon. Neither the Baroness nor anyone else in Karlstad had ever heard of its being a mortal sin to serve a glass of good wine at a feast, or to strike up a table song—often composed by the hostess herself— before draining the glass. Nor were they aware that our Lord would not countenance novel-reading and playgoing. The Baroness liked to get up amateur theatricals and appear in them herself. It would have been a veritable sacrifice for her to abandon that pleasure, for she was a born actress. Karlstaders were wont to say that if Fru Torsslow were but half as good an actress as Beata Ekenstedt, it was no wonder the Stockholmers raved so about her.

Karl Arthur had stayed on at Upsala a whole month after having happily passed the bothersome Latin examination. Meantime, he had been much in the company of Pontus Friman. Friman was a strict and zealous adherent of the pietistic cult, and Karl Arthur evidently had imbibed some of his ideas. It was not a case of sudden conversion or spiritual awakening, but it had been enough to make Karl Arthur feel uneasy because of the worldly pleasures and diversions which prevailed in the home.

One can understand that, just then, there was an especially intimate and tender accord between mother and son, so that Karl Arthur talked to his mother quite freely of the things he found objectionable, while she met his wishes in every way possible. Since it grieved him to have her play at cards, she pleaded headache the next Sunday afternoon, and let the Colonel take her place at the card table. Of course, she could not think of depriving the Provost and the Alderman of their usual game.

As Karl Arthur disapproved of dancing, she gave up that pleasure also. To the young folk who came to the house that evening she said that she was getting on in years (she was fifty) and did not care to dance any more. But seeing how disappointed they all looked, she sat down at the piano and played dance music for them until midnight.

Karl Arthur gave her certain books he wished her to read. She accepted them with thanks, and found them rather edifying and constructive. But how could the Baroness be content to read only these solemn, pietistical works? She was a woman of culture and *au courant* with the world's literature. And one day, when Karl Arthur came upon her unexpectedly, he noticed that under the sacred book she sat reading lay a copy of Byron's *Don Juan*. He turned away without a word, and she thought it dear of him not to chide her. The next day she put all her secular books into a large packing case and had them removed to the attic.

The Baroness, indeed, tried to be as obliging as she knew how. She was wise as well as gifted, and understood that all this was only a passing zeal with Karl Arthur; that the less he was opposed the sooner he would get over it.

Fortunately, it was summertime and the leading families were out of town, so that there were no social festivities going on. People went in for such simple pastimes as tramping in the woods, rowing on the river, berrypicking, and running-games.

However, toward the end of August, Eve Ekenstedt and her lieutenant were to celebrate their nuptials. Then the Baroness was quite concerned as to how the event would pass off. She had to give them a grand wedding; otherwise the Karlstaders would again be saying that she had no heart for her daughters.

Happily, her complaisance had a soothing effect upon Karl Arthur. He raised no objections to the proposed twelve-course dinner, or the garnished wedding cake, or the confections; he did not even protest against the wine and other potables ordered from Göteborg. Nor had he anything to say against a wedding at the cathedral and hanging garlands along the streets where the bridal procession was to pass, nor did he mind the magic lanterns, the tar casks, and the fireworks along the river bank. To tell the truth, he took a hand in the preparations; he laboured in the sweat of his brow at binding wreaths and nailing up flags, like any common mortal.

There was one thing, though, on which he stood firm. There must be no dancing at the wedding. This the Baroness promised, pleased to let him have his way in that, since he had been so decent about everything else.

The Colonel and the girls protested a bit; they wondered what they could do with all the beaux and belles, especially the young officers, if they were not allowed to dance all night. The Baroness assured them it would be a jolly evening anyhow. The young people would go out into the garden and listen to the regimental band, watch the rockets rise to heaven, and see the reflection of the pretty coloured lanterns in the waters of the river. What better entertainment could one wish for? Surely, this was a more dignified and fitting way to celebrate a marriage than to hop round on a dance floor! The Colonel and the girls gave in, as always, and the harmony of house remained undisturbed.

On the day of the wedding the arrangements were perfect. The weather was propitious, the ceremony at the church impressive, and the numerous speeches and toasts at the wedding dinner went well. The Baroness had composed a charming marriage song, which was sung at the table, and the Värmland Regimental Band, stationed in the butler's pantry, struck up a march as each course was served. The guests, finding themselves generously regaled, were in festive mood.

But when they had risen from the table and had had their coffee, they were seized with an irresistible desire to dance.

The dinner had started at four o'clock and, well served as it had been by a special staff of butlers and waiters, it was over by seven. It seemed strange that the twelve courses, with the many toasts and fanfares and table songs, should have consumed but three hours! The Baroness had hoped the guests would remain seated at table till eight o'clock, and time to repair to the garden. Of course, there could be no talk of breaking up until midnight, and the guests grew restless as they thought of the long, dull hours before them.

"If only we might dance!" they sighed inwardly. (The Baroness had been thoughtful enough to let them know beforehand that there would be no dancing.)

"How shall we amuse ourselves?" they wondered. "It will be dreadfully tiresome to sit and grind out small talk hour after hour."

The young girls looked down at their sheer, light frocks and their white satin slippers. These were meant for dancing. Dressed like that, how could they think of anything else?

The young lieutenants of the Värmland Regiment were in great demand as dancing partners. During the winter season they had to attend so many balls they grew almost weary of dancing; and sometimes it was hard work to get them on to the floor. But all summer they had not been to a big dinner party; they were now thoroughly rested, and ready to dance all night and all day.

Rarely had they seen so many pretty girls as were gathered at this wedding. What kind of party was it, anyway? Fancy! inviting a lot of beaux and belles to the house and not allowing them to dance!

It was not only the young people who felt unhappy; their elders, too, thought it a pity the poor young things could not move about a bit so that they would have something to look at. Here were the best musicians in Värmland, and here, too, was the best ballroom; then, why in the world should one not take a little fling?

That Beata Ekenstedt, with all her amiability, had always been rather selfish, they thought. Because she herself was too old to dance, her young guests must sit about and adorn the walls.

The Baroness saw, heard, felt, and understood that her guests were displeased. Good hostess that she was, and accustomed to seeing everyone happy and gay at her parties, this situation was unspeakably trying. She knew that, next day and for many days thereafter, people would be talking about the Ekenstedt wedding and voting it the most tiresome affair they had ever attended.

To the older people, she made herself as agreeable as possible; she related her best anecdotes, came out with her wittiest sallies—but all in vain. They were in no mood to listen to her. The biggest old bore of a Fru at the wedding sat thinking to herself, if ever she were lucky enough to marry off a daughter of hers, she'd let the young folks dance, and the old folk, too.

To the younger ones she proposed running-games on the lawn. They simply stared at her. Running-games, forsooth, at a wedding! Had she been other than she was, they would have laughed in her face.

When the fireworks were to be touched off, the gentlemen offered an arm to the ladies for a stroll along the river bank. The young couples just dragged themselves on, hardly raising their eyes enough to follow the soaring rockets. They would accept no substitute for the pleasure they craved.

The harvest moon came rolling up, big and round and red, as if to heighten the brilliant spectacle. A wag remarked that it had swelled up with astonishment at seeing so many handsome young officers and lovely young damsels stand gazing into the river as if contemplating suicide.

Half Karlstad had gathered outside the garden wall to watch the "grand doings"; but seeing the young folk wander about, listless and indifferent, they all said it was the worst wedding they had ever beheld.

The regimental band did its utmost to lighten the gloom; but as the hostess had forbidden the playing of dance music, lest she find it impossible to hold the youths in leash, there were not many numbers on the programme. The same pieces had to be repeated again and again. It cannot be truthfully said that the hours dragged. Time stood still. The minute hand on all the clocks moved as slowly as the hour hand.

Out on the river, just beyond the Ekenstedt house, lay a couple of big barges, on one of which sat a music-loving sailor rasping out a peasant polka on a squeaky home-made fiddle.

And now all the poor souls who had suffered torment in the Ekenstedt garden brightened. This, at any rate, was dance music! They quickly stole out through the garden gate and, in a moment, were seen whirling round in a country polka on the tarry bottom of a river barge.

The Baroness soon noted the flight and the dancing. It would never do to let the best girls in Karlstad dance on a dirty freight boat. She immediately sent word to her young guests to come back to the house. Colonel's lady though she was, even the youngest subaltern made no move to obey orders.

Then she gave it up as a lost game. She had done all that could be asked to please Karl Arthur; now she would have to save the reputation of the Ekenstedt house. She ordered the band to repair to the grand ballroom and play a contra-dance.

Shortly afterward, the dance-hungry youths came bounding up the stairs. Ah, now there was dancing! It was a ball such as rarely was seen in Karlstad. All who had been waiting and longing for this moment tried to make up for time lost. They glided and whirled, pirouetted and kicked. No one felt tired or indisposed. The plainest and least interesting girl there did not lack a partner.

Nor did the older people merely sit looking on. The joke of it was that the Baroness herself, who had given up dancing and card-playing and had relegated all her worldly books to the attic—even she was on the floor, gliding forward with ease and abandon and looking as young, aye, younger, than the daughter who had stood a bride that day.

The Karlstaders were glad to have back their merry, their charming, their adorable Baroness. The delight was extreme. The night had become enchantingly lovely. In fine, all was as it should be.

But the crowning proof of how contagious was the joy that swept through the rooms was that Karl Arthur himself caught it. All at once it struck him that there was nothing evil or sinful in moving about in time to the music with other young, light-hearted folk. It appeared only natural to him now that youth and health and happiness should take this form of expression. Had he felt as before, that to dance was a sin, he would not have danced. But to-night it all seemed such childish, such harmless amusement.

Just as Karl Arthur was doing his neatest steps in a reel, he happened to glance toward the open salon door.

There appeared a pale face, framed with black hair and black whiskers. And the large mild eyes stared at him in pained amazement.

He stopped in the middle of the dance, thinking, at first, it was an apparition. Then, in a moment, he recognized his friend Pontus Friman, who had promised to pay him a call when passing through Karlstad on his way home.

Karl Arthur instantly quit the dance and hastened to greet the unexpected guest, who without a word led him down the stairs and out of the house.

CHAPTER II

THE PROPOSAL

SCHAGERSTRÖM had proposed!—Rich Schagerström of Stora Sjötorp!

No, but was it possible that Schagerström had proposed?

Oh, yes, it was very certain that Schagerström had proposed.

But how in the world came Schagerström to propose?

Well, it was like this: At Korskyrka Deanery there was a young girl named Charlotte Löwensköld, a distant relation of the Dean who acted as lady's-companion to his wife, and who was betrothed to his curate.

Then what had she to do with Schagerström?

Charlotte Löwensköld, you see, was vital, blithe, and outspoken. The moment she set foot inside the deanery, it was as if a freshening breeze had swept through the old house. The Dean and his wife were elderly folk who had moved about the place as mere shadows of themselves, until she came and put new life into them.

The Curate was thin as a rail, and so pious he hardly dared eat or drink. The whole long day he attended to his clerical tasks, and all night he knelt beside his bed, and wept for his sins. He was about ready to give up the ghost, when Charlotte appeared and stopped him from destroying himself altogether.

But what has all this got to do with Scha——

You must know that when the Curate first came to the deanery, some five years back, he had but just been ordained and was unfamiliar with the duties pertaining to his office. It was Charlotte Löwensköld who initiated him. She had lived all her life at a parsonage, and knew pretty well everything that went with it. She not only taught him how to baptize children, but even how to preside at a vestry meeting. It was then they fell in love; and now they had been engaged fully five years.

But we are getting away entirely from Schagerström!

—Charlotte Löwensköld, you see, was exceedingly clever at planning and managing for others. They had not been long engaged before she learned that her fiancé's parents did not like his being a cleric. They had wanted him to continue at the University until he had taken his master's degree and then study for the doctorate. He had spent five years at Upsala, and in the following year would have become a *magister*, when he suddenly decided to take, instead, the examination for Holy Orders.

His parents were rich and a bit covetous of honours. It was a great disappointment to them that their son had chosen so modest a career. Even after he had entered the Church, they implored him to return to the University; but he gave them a positive No. Now, Charlotte knew that his prospects for promotion would be better if he obtained a higher degree; so she sent him back to Upsala.

As he was the worst old grind imaginable, she had him finished in four years. By that time, he had not only taken his *licentiate*, but was a full-fledged Doctor of Philosophy.

But what of Schagerström?

—Charlotte Löwensköld had figured out that her fiancé, after his graduation, would seek an appointment as headmaster at a *gymnasium*, where the remuneration would be sufficient to enable them to marry. If he needs must be a cleric, then in a few years' time he could have a large benefice, as had been the case with Dean Forsius and others. But it did not turn out as Charlotte had expected. Her fiancé wished to enter the ministry at once and go the way of the ordinary cleric; so he came back to Korskyrka as stipendiary curate. Doctor of Philosophy though he was, his compensation was less than that of a stableman.

Yes, but Schagerström——

—You understand, of course, that Charlotte, who had already waited five years, could not be content with this. But she was glad her affianced had been sent to Korskyrka and was now living at the deanery, where she could see him every day.

But we are not hearing anything about Schagerström!

Neither Charlotte Löwensköld nor her fiancé had any affiliation with Schagerström, who moved in a different world from theirs. The son of a high official in Stockholm, he was himself a man of means. He had married the daughter of a Värmland ironmaster—heiress to so many foundries and ore fields that her dowry alone amounted to some two or three millions. The Schagerströms had resided in Stockholm and had spent only the summer months in Värmland. They had been married but three years when the wife died in childbirth and the widower removed to Stora Sjötorp, in Korskyrka. He mourned her loss so deeply he could not bear to stay at a place where she had lived. Schagerström was now rarely seen in society; but passed his time supervising the administration of his various estates and remodelling and beautifying Stora Sjötorp, so that it became the most magnificent place in Korskyrka. Alone as he was, he kept many servants and lived like a *grand seigneur*. Charlotte would as soon have thought she could take down the Seven Stars to set in her bridal crown as to marry Schagerström.

Charlotte Löwensköld, you see, was the sort who would say anything that came into her head. One day, when they had a coffee party at the deanery and there were many guests, it happened that Schagerström went driving by in his big open landau, drawn by four black horses, a liveried footman on the box beside the coachman. Naturally, they all rushed to the windows and stood gazing after him as far as their eyes could follow. When he was well out of sight, Charlotte turned to her betrothed, who was standing back in the room, and shouted out so that everyone could hear:

"I'm rather fond of you, Karl Arthur, but if Schagerström should propose I'd accept him."

The guests went into shrieks, quite certain that she
could never catch Schagerström. Karl Arthur laughed,
too, knowing she had said it merely for the amusement
of the company. The girl herself seemed horrified at
what had fallen from her lips. Yet, there may have been
a little thought back of her words; she had wished, perhaps, to frighten Karl Arthur a bit, to make him think
of the headmastership he should be seeking.

As for Schagerström—he was too utterly sunken in
grief to have any thoughts of matrimony. But going
about in the world of affairs, he made many friends and
acquaintances who advised him to marry again. To all,
he invariably excused himself with the plea that he was
so dull and mournful no one would have him. Nor would
he listen to any assurances to the contrary.

But once, at a fellowship dinner which Schagerström
had felt obliged to attend, the moot question was the
main topic of conversation. When he came out with his
usual retort, a neighbour from Korskyrka told about
the young girl who had said she would "sack" her
intended if Schagerström came a-wooing. Everyone
laughed heartily at the story, treating it as a huge joke,
just as they had done at the deanery.

To tell the truth, Schagerström had found it rather
hard to get along without a wife; but his heart was still
with the dear departed, and the mere idea of putting
another in her place seemed abhorrent to him.

Now, after hearing about Charlotte Löwensköld, his thoughts took a new turn. Supposing he were to contract a sensible marriage; if, for instance, he should marry a meek, humble, guileless young girl, who would not usurp the first wife's place in his heart nor aspire to the high social position which had been hers by reason of her wealth and family connections, then the idea of a second union would be no insult to the departed.

The next Sunday, Schagerström came to church to have a look at the young girl, who sat with the Dean's wife in the rectory pew. She was simply and modestly attired and there was nothing very striking about her appearance. But that was no detriment. Quite the reverse. Had she been a dazzling beauty, he would never have thought of choosing her for wife. The departed could rest assured that her successor in nowise filled her place.

As Schagerström sat gazing at Charlotte, he wondered what she would say if he called at the deanery and asked her to be mistress of Stora Sjötorp. Of course, she never expected, when saying what she did, that he would propose. Therefore it would be interesting to see what she would do if he took her at her word.

Driving home from church, he wondered how Charlotte Löwensköld would look in fine clothes. All at once he found a certain allure in the thought of a second marriage. The idea of coming quite unexpectedly to bring good fortune to a poor young girl had a touch of romance about it which was far from displeasing. The moment Schagerström realized this, he put it away from him as a temptation. He had always thought of his sainted wife as having left him only for a short time, and that some day they would be reunited. Meanwhile, he must be true to her memory.

That night, in his dreams, Schagerström saw his sainted wife. He awoke full of the old tenderness. The doubts and misgivings that had arisen in his mind on the way home from church seemed now to have been quite needless. His love still lived. There was no fear that the simple-hearted girl he thought of taking to wife would efface from his soul the image of the departed. He needed a wise and capable woman in the home; one who would be a companion and a comfort. Any regular house manageress suitable for the position he had not been able to find, or a female relative either. He saw no way but to marry.

That very day he set out in great state for the deanery. During the past few years he had led such a solitary life, he had made no calls even there. As may be imagined, there was no little excitement when the black four-span turned in at the Dean's gate. Schagerström was immediately conducted upstairs to the large salon, where he sat talking awhile with the Dean and his wife.

Charlotte Löwensköld had quietly stolen up to her room. In a few moments, the Dean's wife came and asked her to join them in the salon. Ironmaster Schagerström was calling, and it was rather tiresome for him having no one to talk to but two aged persons.

The old lady looked a bit flustered, but solemn. Charlotte opened her eyes wide with surprise, but asked no questions. She untied her apron, dipped her fingers in the wash basin, smoothed back her hair, put on a fresh collar, then followed after the Dean's wife. About to step out of the room, she turned back and put on her large apron again.

Charlotte had no sooner entered the salon and greeted Schagerström than she was requested to be seated. Whereupon the old Dean made her a little speech. He used many words, dilating upon the comfort and joy she had brought to the house. She had been as a dear daughter to him and his wife, and it would be hard for them to part with her. But now that a man like Ironmaster Gustaf Schagerström had come and asked for her hand in marriage, they must not think of themselves, but counsel her to accept an offer which was so much better than any she could have expected.

The Dean made no mention of the fact that she was already betrothed to his curate. Both he and his wife had been long opposed to this bond, and heartily wished it broken. A poor girl like Charlotte Löwensköld could not afford to tie herself up with a man who positively refused to seek a proper living.

Charlotte had listened without moving a muscle. The Dean, wishing to give her time to form a fitting reply, added a glowing eulogy of Schagerström. He spoke of his fine estates, his splendid achievements, his wonderful capabilities, his high ideals, and his kindness to his employees. He had heard so much good of Ironmaster Schagerström that, although this was his first visit to the deanery, he already regarded him as a friend into whose keeping he was glad to place the destiny of his young kinswoman.

All the while Schagerström sat regarding Charlotte, to see how she was taking his proposal. She suddenly straightened in her chair, threw back her head, her blue eyes turned almost black, and her lip curled in a scornful smile. Schagerström was struck with amazement. Charlotte Löwensköld was a beauty! And, moreover, a beauty who was neither meek nor humble.

Obviously, his offer had made a strong impression, but whether favourable or unfavourable, he hardly dared venture to guess.

However, he did not have to remain long in a state of uncertainty. The moment the Dean had finished, Charlotte Löwensköld spoke up:

"I wonder if Ironmaster Schagerström knows that I am engaged?"

"Oh, yes," said Schagerström. Before he could utter another word, Charlotte continued:

"Then how can Ironmaster Schagerström have the audacity to come and propose to me!"

That was what she said; she used such a word as *audacity* when speaking to the richest man in Korskyrka. She had forgotten that she was only a poor lady's-companion. Now she was the proud aristocrat, the Honourable Fröken Löwensköld.

The old Dean and his wife were so shocked they nearly fell off their chairs. Schagerström, too, looked somewhat surprised; but he was a man of the world and knew how to act in an embarrassing situation. He stepped up to Charlotte, took one of her small hands between his two, and pressed it warmly.

"My dear Fröken Löwensköld," he said, "your answer only increases my respect and admiration for you as an individual."

He bowed to the Dean and to the Dean's wife, and indicated by a gesture that they need not speak or see him to his carriage. They, as well as Charlotte, marvelled at the dignity of the rejected suitor as he withdrew from the room.

CHAPTER III

WISHES

I T IS of no consequence, surely, that a person sits wishing. If she does not lift so much as a finger to attain the object of her desire, what harm can there be in her wishing?

When a body knows that she is homely and poor and insignificant, while the one whom she covets has not a thought of her, then assuredly she may revel in her wishes as much as she likes.

If, in the bargain, she is married, and a virtuous wife, and has a little leaning toward pietism, and wouldn't for all the world do anything wrong, then what does it matter that she sits wishing?

If, moreover, she is all of thirty-two and the one she thinks of is but nine-and-twenty; if, besides, she is awkward and shy and has no social gifts, she might as well sit at home and wish from morning to night. There's nothing sinful in that, surely? It can't lead to anything.

Though she may regard the longings of others as light spring breezes and her own as powerful storm winds, that can move mountains and drive our planet out of its course, she knows these are but fancies which, in reality, have no effect.

She should be glad that she lives in the church town, right on the main street, where she can see him pass by her window almost every day; that she can hear him preach every Sunday; that she can come sometimes to the deanery, where she may sit in the same room with him, though her shyness prevents her from speaking.

Strangely enough, there was a slight bond between him and her. He was unaware of it, perhaps, and she had never thought to mention it. Her mother was a Malvina Spaak, sometime housekeeper at Hedeby Manor, the home of his maternal grandparents, Baron and Baroness Löwensköld. Malvina, when about thirty-five years of age, had married a poor farmer and afterward had toiled and slaved in her own home, at weaving and household tasks, as she had once done in the home of others. But she had always kept up her connection with the Löwenskölds. They had come to see her, and she had made long visits at Hedeby, giving a hand at the spring-cleaning and the autumn bakes. This had lent a little lustre to an otherwise dull existence.

She had often talked to her little daughter of the days when she was in service at Hedeby; of the dead general whose ghost had haunted the place, and of young Baron Adrian who had wanted to help his old grandfather find rest in his grave.

The daughter knew that the mother had been in love with young Adrian from the way in which she had spoken of him. How handsome he was! and how gentle! He had such a dreamy look in his eyes and such indescribable charm in his every movement. The girl had thought at the time that the mother was exaggerating. A young man such as she had pictured was not to be found on this earth.

Then one day she beheld him!

Shortly after her marriage to the organist and their removal to Korskyrka, she saw him one Sunday step into the pulpit. He was no baron, only a Pastor Ekenstedt; but he was the son of a sister to the Baron Adrian whom Malvina Spaak had loved, and was handsome and boyishly slender and lithe. She recognized the large dreamy eyes her mother had talked about, and the pleasant smile.

She thought, as she looked at him, that her wishing had brought him there. She had always longed to see a man who measured up to her mother's description of Adrian, and now at last she saw one! To be sure, she knew that wishes have no power; but it seemed strange, all the same, that he had come.

He did not appear to notice her, however, and toward the end of the summer he became engaged to Charlotte Löwensköld. In the autumn he returned to Upsala to continue his studies, and she thought he had gone out of her life forever. Wish as hard as she might, he would never come back to her.

Then, after an absence of five years, he appeared again in the pulpit, and again she thought he had come in answer to her wishes. He had given her no reason to think so. In fact, he was hardly aware of her existence, and he was still engaged to Charlotte Löwensköld.

She had never wished Charlotte any ill; she could lay her hand on the Bible and swear to that. Sometimes, though, she had wished that Charlotte would fall in love with somebody else, or that one of her rich relatives would invite her on a long journey to distant lands, so that she might be parted from young Ekenstedt in some pleasant and fortuitous way.

As wife of the organist, she was invited to the deanery now and then, and she chanced to be there the day Schagerström drove by and Charlotte said she would take him if he proposed. She had wished ever since that Schagerström would propose to Charlotte. Now, there was nothing wrong in that, surely? In any case, it had no significance.

If wishes had power, our world would be quite different from what it is. Only think how people have wished! Think how much good they have wished themselves! Think of the many who have wished themselves free from sin and sickness!—of all who have wished they might escape death! Aye, she could safely go on wishing, for wishes had no power.

But one bright Sunday that very summer, whom should she see walk into the church but Schagerström! She noticed that he chose a seat from where he could see Charlotte, and wished that he would think her pretty and alluring. With all her heart she wished it.

Now, what harm was she doing Charlotte in wishing her a rich husband?

All that day she had the feeling that something was going to happen, and all night she lay tossing in a fever of expectancy. It was the same with her next morning: she could not do a stroke of work, but sat by the window with her hands crossed in her lap, waiting to see Schagerström drive by. But something far more wonderful happened. Late in the forenoon, Pastor Ekenstedt came to call.

It need hardly be said that she was surprised and delighted, and, at the same time, quite overcome with embarrassment. How she managed to greet him she never knew. At all events, he was soon seated in the most comfortable chair in her snug little parlour, and she right opposite him, gazing into his face.

Never had he appeared so young to her as now, when she saw him near to. She was well informed on all matters concerning his family, and knew that he was then twenty-nine years of age, though he looked a mere boy.

He vouchsafed in his charmingly simple and earnest way that he had but recently learned, through a letter from his mother, that she was a daughter to the Malvina Spaak who had been a good friend and veritable godsend to all the Löwenskölds. He was sorry not to have known of this before, and thought she should have enlightened him.

She was happy to know just why he had never noticed

her till now; but she could not say anything, could not explain. She mumbled a few stupid, incoherent words, which he did not catch.

He looked surprised; it seemed almost incredible that a person of her age should be so bashful as to lose the power of speech. To give her time to collect herself, he began to speak of Hedeby and Malvina Spaak. He also went into the story of the ghost and the fatal ring. He said it was rather hard for him to believe most of the details, but that underlying it all was a profound truth. The ring, to his mind, symbolized the love of the things of this world, which held the soul in thrall and made it unfit to enter the Kingdom of God.

To think that he should be sitting there with her regarding her with his adorable smile, and talking to her as naturally and easily as to an old friend! It was happiness almost too great!

He was perhaps accustomed to receive no verbal response when visiting the poor and disconsolate, to bring comfort and cheer; and went on talking. He had pondered long Christ's words to the rich youth, and was convinced that the primary cause of humanity's many ills lay in this, that they loved more the things created than they loved the Creator.

Although she had not uttered a word, she had listened in a way that tempted him to go farther. He confessed to her that he had no wish to become either a dean or a vicar. He did not want any large parish, with spacious parsonage, extensive fields, and big church books—

many responsibilities. What he desired was a small charge, where he would have time to devote to the cure of souls. His parsonage should be only a little gray cottage beautifully situated in the heart of a birch grove, by the shore of a lake. And the salary must be no more than enough for him to live upon.

She understood that, in this way, he would show people the right road to happiness, and her whole soul went out to him in worship. Never had she seen anything so young, so pure! How the people would love him! Of a sudden it struck her that what he had just said did not accord with something she had recently heard, and she wished to be quite clear on this point.

Had she been misinformed? The last time she was at the deanery she had heard his betrothed say that he intended to seek a position as headmaster of a *gymnasium*.

He sprang to his feet and began to pace the floor of the little parlour.

Had Charlotte said that? Was she certain that Charlotte had said it? He spoke so sharply it frightened her; but she answered in all meekness that, to the best of her recollection, Charlotte had said just that.

The blood mounted to his face and his wrath rose. She was so distressed she could have fallen at his feet and implored his forgiveness. Never had she thought he would take so to heart what she had told him of Charlotte. What should she say to "make him good" again? What could she do to appease him?

In the midst of her tense anxiety, she heard the tramp of horses and the rumble of wheels, and from force of habit turned toward the window. It was Schagerström who drove by. But her mind was all taken up with Karl Arthur, and she had no time to wonder whither the other was faring. Karl Arthur did not see the farer-by; he was still pacing the floor, a grim look on his face.

Suddenly, he stepped up to her and put out his hand in farewell. It was a terrible disappointment that he should be leaving so soon. She could have bitten her tongue off for uttering the words that had put him in such bad humour. There was nothing to do but take his proffered hand. She must be silent and let him go. In sheer desperation, she bent down and kissed his hand. He quickly drew it away and looked at her in surprise.

"I only wanted to ask your pardon," she stammered.

He saw tears in her eyes, and felt moved to offer her some sort of explanation.

"Suppose, Fru Sundler, that for one reason or other you had placed a bandage before your eyes so that you saw nothing, and had put yourself into the hands of another, that she might lead you; how would you feel if the bandage were suddenly torn away and you found that your friend, your guide, whom you had trusted more than yourself, had drawn you to the edge of a precipice, and another step would have sent you over it? Would you not suffer the torments of hell?"

After this rhetorical outburst, he dashed out the door, never waiting for an answer. But on the porch he stopped. Fru Sundler wondered what made him. Perhaps he remembered how pleased and happy he had been when he entered her house—he who was now leaving it in anger and despair. She ran out to see whether he was still there.

He began talking the instant she appeared. The mental excitement had given new impetus to his thoughts, and he was glad to have a listener.

"I'm standing here looking at the pretty roses that border the path to your house, my dear Fru Sundler, and am asking myself if this is not the most beautiful summer I have ever known. Here we are now at the end of July, but is it not true that so far the weather has been perfect? Have not all the days been long and light? —longer and lighter than ever before? The heat, to be sure, has been rather intense, but never oppressive. Generally, there has been a freshening breeze to liven the air. Nor has the earth suffered drought as in other fair summers. Almost nightly we have had an hour or two of rain. The growing things have flourished beyond all expectation. Have you ever seen the trees so massed with foliage, or the flower beds in the gardens so gorgeously colourful? Ah! the raspberries were never so sweet, the bird-song never so clear, the people never so merry and pleasure loving as they are this year."

He paused for a moment to take breath. Thea Sundler was careful not to disturb him by so much as a word. She thought of her sainted mother, and understood how she must have felt when the young baron had come to her in the kitchen or the milk room and given her his confidence.

The young clergyman continued:

"When at five o'clock of a morning I draw up my shade I see only clouds and mists. The rain patters against the windowpane and gushes down the water spout. Grasses and flowers bend to the shower. The clouds are so heavy with rain they almost trail along the ground. 'To-day there's an end to the fine weather,' I say to myself, 'and perhaps 'tis well.'

"Though almost certain the rain will continue all day, I stand at the window awhile to see what it will do. At five minutes past five of the clock the patter on the windowpane ceases; the water spout gushes a moment more, then it, too, subsides. Just at that point in the sky where the sun should appear comes a rent in the curtain of cloud, and a cluster of rays shoots down through the earthly mists. Soon the heavy gray vapours that rise from the hills at the horizon are transformed into thin blue mists. The raindrops on the grass blades trickle slowly to the ground, and the flowers lift up their sadly drooping chalices. Our little lake, which until now has looked quite sombre, begins to glitter as if a school of goldfish had swum up on to the surface of the water. Transported by all this beauty, I open wide my window and inhale the moist, scent-laden air—a delight beyond the imagination. And I cry out: 'O God, Thou hast made Thy world too beautiful!'"

The young pastor smiled and gave a little shrug. He

probably thought Thea Sundler was a bit shocked at his last utterance, and hastened to explain:

"I meant what I said. I have been afraid that this beautiful summer would beguile me into a love of the earthly. How often have I not wished the fine weather would come to an end! that the summer would bring thunder and lightning, drought and humidity, rainy days and chilly nights, as in other years."

Thea Sundler fairly hung on his words. Whither was he leading? What would he say? She did not know, but she wished almost convulsively that he would continue and let her enjoy awhile longer the rich, mellow tones of his voice, his beautiful language, and expressive play of feature.

"Do you follow me?" he suddenly burst out. "But perhaps Nature has no power over you; does not speak to you in strong, mystic words; does not ask you why you do not accept her bounties thankfully; why you do not lay hold of happiness when it is within your reach; why you do not get you a home of your own and marry your heart's beloved, as others are doing this blessed summer?"

He raised his hat and passed a hand across his brow.

"This lovely summer has been as a confederate to Charlotte. All this opulence, this mildness, this perpetual smoothness has intoxicated me. I have gone about like a blind man. Charlotte has seen my love grow stronger day by day, and my ardent desire to possess her.

"Ah, you do not know!—Every morning at six o'clock I leave the little annex, where my quarters are, and go up to the main building for early coffee. Charlotte joins me in the light, spacious dining room, where the fresh morning air comes pouring in at the open windows. She is happy and twitters like a bird as we sit down to our coffee, just we two.

"You think, perhaps, that Charlotte takes advantage of the occasion to discuss with me our plans for the future. Ah, no! She talks to me of my sick; my poor; she speaks of the points in my sermon that have especially impressed her. In all respects she seems to be just what a clergyman's wife should be. Very rarely—and then only in jest and by the way—does she mention the headmastership. Every day she becomes more dear to me. When I'm back at my desk, I sit dreaming of Charlotte, and find it hard to do any work. I have already told you how I would order my life. I believe that my love will free Charlotte from her worldly shackles and that she will come with me to my little gray cottage."

At this Thea Sundler involuntarily emitted a cry.

"Yes, of course you were right," he said. "I have been blind. Charlotte has been leading me toward a pit. Hoping to draw from me, in a moment of weakness, the promise to seek a mastership, she wished to prepare you and others for the change, should I decide to enter upon a new field of activity. But God has protected me."

He went close up to Thea Sundler. He must have read in her face that she was enjoying his talk; that she was happy; enraptured. It irritated him that she should delight in this flow of rhetoric called forth by his suffering. A look of contempt spread over his face. "Don't imagine that I am thankful to you for what you have told me," he said.

Fru Sundler was terrified. He had doubled his fists and was shaking them at her.

"I don't thank you for snatching the bandage from before my eyes. You should not be pleased at what you have done. I hate you for not letting me fall into the pit! I wish never to see you again!"

He turned on his heel and walked rapidly down the narrow path between Fru Sundler's pretty rose borders out into the road.

Thea Sundler, utterly crushed, went back into her parlour. She cast herself upon the floor and wept as she had never wept in all her life.

CHAPTER IV

IN THE DEANERY GARDEN

IT WAS only five-minutes' walk from the church town to the deanery; but in those few minutes Karl Arthur thought of many stern and lordly things he would say to his betrothed.

"The time is come," he muttered to himself. "Nothing shall stop me now. To-day we must arrive at an understanding. She must know that, much as I love her, nothing will induce me to strive after the worldly advantages which she seeks. I must serve my God. I cannot do otherwise; rather would I tear her from my heart."

He felt proudly confident. Now, as never before, he had at his command words that would crush, stir, convince. His strong agitation had set up an inner shaking and thrown open the door to a chamber in his mind of which he had not, till then, been aware.

The walls of this room were covered with rich clusters and beautiful blooming vines. The clusters and vines were words—luscious, glorious, consummate words. He had only to come forth and take possession. All this wealth —an inconceivable wealth of words—was his.

He laughed at himself as he thought how he had had

to cudgel his brains for ideas, in making up his sermons, and dig for words; yet all the while this "wealth" had been within him.

As far as Charlotte was concerned, things would be quite different after this. She had tried to lord it over him; but now all that was changed. He would talk and she listen; he would lead and she follow. Hereafter she should hang upon his words as did that poor wife of the organist. It meant strife, but he would never give in to her. Sooner than that, he would tear her out of his heart; yes, tear her out of his heart!

Just as he reached the deanery, the gates swung open, and an elegant carriage, drawn by four black horses, came rolling out.

He understood, of course, that Ironmaster Schagerström had been calling at the house, and it put him in mind of the remark Charlotte had let drop at the coffee party. It struck him in a flash that Schagerström had proposed to his fiancée. He dismissed the thought at once as utterly absurd, but all the same his heart contracted.

Was it not a most peculiar look the rich man had given him in passing? Was there not a sinister curiosity and, at the same time, compassion in that look?

Without doubt, he had guessed rightly. His heart stood still, everything went black to his eyes; he could barely drag himself up to the gatepost.

Charlotte had answered Yes. He would lose her and die of despair. While in the throes of an overwhelming anguish, he saw his fiancée come out of the house and hasten toward him. He noted the high colour in her cheeks, the bright look of her eyes, and the expression of triumph about her mouth. She was coming to tell him that she was to marry the richest man in the parish.

Such shamelessness! He clenched his fists, stamped his foot, and shouted out: "Don't come near me!"

She stopped short. Was she really surprised, or only shamming?

"What is the matter with you?" she asked him coolly.

He quickly summoned his strength, and roared at her: "You know well enough! What was Schagerström doing here?"

When Charlotte grasped the fact that he had guessed Schagerström's errand, she went right up to him and raised her hand as if she could have struck him in the face.

"So you, too, think I would break my word for a bit of gold and goods!" She gave him a look of contempt, then turned and walked away.

Anyhow, her words had allayed his worst suspicions. His heart gave a bound, and he felt his strength returning; he was able to follow after her.

"But he has proposed to you, hasn't he?" he said.

She scorned to make reply. Now she squared her shoulders and held her head stiffly erect, as she walked on, past the house, down a narrow path which led to the garden.

Karl Arthur knew she had reason to be offended. If she had rejected Schagerström, she had done a splendid thing. He attempted to justify himself.

"You should have seen the face he put up as he drove past me. He didn't look as though he had been repulsed."

She held her proud head higher still, and quickened her steps. She did not have to speak, her bearing told him plainly enough that his company was not desired; that she was going this way because she wished to be alone.

He perceived more clearly now the devotion and self-sacrifice in her act, and so he continued to follow her.

"Charlotte!" he cried. "Darling Charlotte!"

She showed no sign of weakening, but swept on, down the garden path.

Alas, this garden, this deanery garden! Charlotte could not have directed her steps to a spot more rich in memories precious to both of them.

It was a garden laid out in the old French manner, with many intersecting walks bordered by thick, man-high hedges of lilac. Here and there in the hedge was a narrow opening, through which one passed either into a small bower containing a homely, moss-grown seat, or out upon an even grass plot encircling a solitary rose tree. Though not a spacious garden, nor perhaps a beautiful one, it was an ideal trysting place for lovers.

As Karl Arthur hastened on in the footsteps of Charlotte, who would not so much as give him a glance, poignant memories awoke in him—memories of the many happy hours she had walked here with him as his loving sweetheart.

"Charlotte!" he cried out again.

There was a note of anguish in his voice that made her stop. She did not turn around, but the tautness in her bearing vanished perceptibly. She bent backward, toward him, so that he almost saw her face. He sprang to her side, caught her in his arms, and kissed her. Then, drawing her into a bower, he went down on his knees before her, and poured himself out in rhapsodic praises of her love, her constancy, her heroic courage.

His sudden fervour of enthusiasm was so surprising that she listened almost with distrust. And he knew why. There had always been a certain restraint in his attitude toward her. To him, she had represented the world and its allurements, against which he must be ever on his guard.

But in that blessed moment, when he knew how she had withstood the temptation of great riches, he could give rein to his feelings. She tried to tell him about Schagerström's wooing, but he interrupted her continually with his kisses. When she had told him everything, he had to kiss her again, repeatedly. At last they sat in a long embrace.

Where were the strong, imperious words he had meant to say to her? Gone from the mind; swept out of memory. They were no longer necessary, now that he felt this dear girl could never be a menace to him. She was no slave of Mammon, she who on this day had scorned wealth to remain true to him.

As she rested in his arms, a sweet smile trembled on her lips. She looked happy, more happy than ever he had seen her. Of what was she thinking? Perhaps at that moment she was saying to herself that his love was the only thing that mattered? Perhaps she had given up all thought of the headmastership, which had come so near to parting them?

She did not speak; he was listening to her thoughts: "Let us soon be united. I make no conditions. I ask for nothing but your love."

But, should he allow her to outdo him in generosity? Ah, he would make her supremely happy; he would whisper to her, now that he understood her disposition, and dared, that he would find a proper living for them.

How blissful this stillness! Perhaps she heard what he said to himself—heard the promise he made her? He tried to put his thoughts into words.

"Ah, Charlotte," he said, "how can I ever repay you for what you have sacrificed to-day for my sake!"

She sat with her head resting against his shoulder, and he could not see her face.

"My love," he heard her say, "I have no fear but that you will compensate me richly."

"Compensate"—what did she mean? Did she mean that his love was the only compensation she desired, or had she something else in mind? Why was she holding her head down? Why didn't she look him in the eyes?

Did she think him such a poor catch that he needs must pay her for being faithful to him? But he was a clergyman and a Doctor of Philosophy—a man of good family. He had always tried to fulfil his duties, and was beginning to gain recognition as a preacher, and he had lived an exemplary life. Did she really think it a great sacrifice on her part to reject Schagerström?

No, no, she meant nothing of the sort. He must be calm; he must probe her thoughts with gentleness and patience.

"Just what do you mean by compensation? I have nothing whatever to offer you."

She moved closer and whispered into his ear:

"You think too poorly of yourself, my friend. You can become both provost and bishop."

He drew away from her so quickly she came near falling.

"Then it was because you hoped I would become a provost and a bishop that you rejected Schagerström!"

She stared at him—bewildered—as one who has just come out of a dream. Yes, of course she had been dreaming. She had talked in her sleep and revealed her secret thoughts.

Why was she silent? Did she think his question called for no answer?

"I ask you again, was it because you thought I would become a provost and a bishop that you rejected Schagerström?"

The colour mounted to her cheeks. The Löwensköld

blood was surging in her veins, yet she held her peace.

Ah, but he must, he must have an answer! "Didn't you hear me ask you if it was because you expect me to become a provost and a bishop that you said No to Schagerström?"

She flung her head back and her eyes flashed fire.

"Oh, certainly!" she threw at him in a tone of utter contempt.

He rose to his feet, not wishing to sit beside her any longer. Her answer pained him exceedingly, but he would not admit it before a creature like Charlotte. However, as he did not wish to have anything to reproach himself for, he again tried to speak gently, and in all kindness, to this lost child of the world.

"My dear Charlotte," he said, "I cannot thank you enough for being so honest with me. I understand now that to you externals are everything. A blameless life, a constant striving to follow in the footsteps of Christ, my Master, mean nothing to you." He waited in suspense for her answer.

"My dear Karl Arthur," she said, "I think I know your worth, although I do not fawn upon you like the ladies of the church town."

Her reply seemed to him a positive vulgarity. The unmasked woman was venting her chagrin.

Charlotte rose to go, but Karl Arthur seized her by the arm and made her stay. This talk had to be carried on to a conclusion. That about the ladies of the church town had put him in mind of Fru Sundler. Remembering what she had told him, his ire began to rise; he was fairly boiling inside. The pressure forced the door to the room in his mind which held the vines and clusters of strong, eloquent words. Now he took a stern, admonitory tone; he upbraided her for her love of the world; her pride; her vanity.

Charlotte did not listen long to such talk.

"Bad as I am," she reminded him, "I have nevertheless said No this day to Schagerström."

"Good God!" he exclaimed, "what is the woman made of? She has but just confessed to giving Schagerström No merely because she preferred a bishop to an ironmaster."

Through it all spoke a still, small voice in his heart. It told him to have a care. Had he not marked that Charlotte Löwensköld disdained to defend herself? If anyone thought ill of her, she never tried to disabuse him of his evil suspicions.

He did not listen to the small warning voice; he had no faith in it. Charlotte's every utterance only revealed to him new depths of depravity. And now he heard her say:

"My dear Karl Arthur, don't attach so much importance to what I said as to your attaining such high distinction. It was all a joke. I don't believe you can ever become either a provost or a bishop."

He was already overwrought and sorely offended, but after this fresh onslaught the still, small voice within was mute. The blood surged in his ears and his hands shook. The wretched woman had robbed him of his self-control and was driving him mad.

He was conscious of jumping up and down in front of her, of raising his voice to a shriek. He knew that his jaw was shaking and his hands were beating the air. His loathing of her was unspeakable; it could not be interpreted in words, but had to express itself in motions.

"All your vileness is plain to me now," he shouted. "I see you now as you are. Never, never will I marry a woman like you. You would be my destruction."

"Anyhow," said Charlotte, "I have been of some slight service to you. It is thanks to me, is it not, that you are now a licentiate and a doctor of philosophy?"

After that it was not he, himself, who spoke to her. He heard the things that fell from his lips, and approved them; but the words came as a surprise; they seemed to be put into his mouth by another.

"You see!" cried the voice. "Now she reminds me that she has waited for me five years and, consequently, I am compelled to marry her. But I shall marry only whom God chooses for me."

"Don't speak of God!" she said.

He turned his face upward and began to study the clouds.

"Yes, yes, yes, I shall let God choose for me. The first woman that crosses my path shall be my wife."

Charlotte gave a cry and sprang to his side.

"Oh, Karl Arthur, Karl Arthur!" She tried to draw down one of his uplifted arms.

"Don't touch me!" he yelled savagely.

She put her arms around his neck, not realizing the extent of his fury.

A howl of hate broke from his throat, he caught her arms in an iron grip and flung her back on to the bench, then fled from her sight.

CHAPTER V

THE DALAR GIRL

WHEN Karl Arthur Ekenstedt first saw Korskyrka Deanery, with its stately lindens, its
green privet hedge, its venerable gateposts
and white gate, through whose pickets could be seen the
big circular sward and gravelled walks, the wide red-
painted, two-story house, with its two equally large
wings—the curate's to the right, the tenant farmer's
to the left—he said to himself: "This is how a Swedish
parsonage should look, at once cosily inviting and rest-
ful, at the same time inspiring in the beholder a feeling
of reverence."

And afterward, as he noted the well-kept lawns, the
orderly arrangement of the flower beds, where the plants
were all of uniform height and at equal distances apart;
the decorative designs of the border beds along the nicely
raked walks; the carefully pruned wildgrape vines
around the small porch; and the long, rich curtains that
hung down in even, graceful folds at every window—
this, too, gave him a feeling of satisfaction and respect.
He knew instinctively that all who lived here must feel
in duty bound to behave in a proper and sensible way.

Little did he think that one day he—Karl Arthur

Ekenstedt—would be running toward the white gate, his hat poised on one ear, his arms battling the air, and short, ugly howls issuing from his mouth. Shutting the gate behind him, he gave a wild laugh; he fancied the old house and the flowers in their beds stared after him in astonishment.

"Did you ever see the like of it?" went the whisper from flower to flower. "What sort of creature can that be?"

Aye, and the trees wondered, the grass wondered, the whole place wondered. He could hear how surprised they all were.

Could this be the son of the charming Baroness Ekenstedt, the most cultivated lady in all Värmland, who was running away from the deanery as if fleeing the abode of sin and evil?

Could this be a clergyman of Korskyrka Deanery, which had housed so many circumspect and dignified servants of the Lord, who was now going out upon the highway with a fixed determination to propose to the first unmarried woman he met? Was it young Ekenstedt, who had been so delicately reared and had always associated with people of culture and refinement, who recklessly set out to take as companion for life the first female he chanced upon?

Did he not know that he might get a tittle-tattler or a lazybones, a silly goose or a harpy, a slattern or a wasp-tongue? Didn't he realize that he was faring forth on the most hazardous adventure of his life?

Karl Arthur stood at the gate a moment, listening to the murmurs that went from tree to tree, from flower to flower. Ah, yes, he knew it was a precarious venture, but he also knew that this summer at Korskyrka he had loved the world more than he had his God. Feeling that Charlotte Löwensköld had been a menace to his soul, he wished to raise a barrier between him and her, an impenetrable wall of separation.

He knew the instant he had thrust Charlotte out of his heart, it opened again to Christ. And now he would show his Saviour how boundless was his love for Him; how he trusted in Him above everything. Therefore, he was going to let the Lord choose a wife for him.

No doubts assailed him as he stood at the gate looking toward the road. He thought he showed the greatest courage a man could have by placing his fate wholly in the Hand of God.

The last thing before leaving the gate, he said an "Our Father." During the prayer, all became quiet within and he also regained his outward composure. The angry flush disappeared from his face, and his jaw no longer trembled.

And now, as he walked toward the village, which he needs must do, of course, if he wished to meet people, his mind was not wholly free from dread. He had gone no farther than to the end of the deanery hedge when he suddenly halted. It was the poor, timorous heart of the man that stopped him. Only an hour or so earlier, returning from the church town, he had met at this very spot the deaf beggar woman, Karin Johansdotter, in her patched kirtle and thread-worn shawl, and shouldering her long beggar's pack.

To be sure, she had been married once on a time, though now a widow these many years, and free to marry again. A sudden fear that she might be the one he would meet had made him pause. But he scoffed at the poor, frightened thing in his breast that tried to prevent him carrying out his purpose—and walked on.

A moment later, he heard the rumble of a moving vehicle, and shortly afterward a cart, drawn by a fine pacer, passed him in the road.

In the cart sat one of the proud, influential mine-owners of the district who was reputed to be rich as Schagerström. He had a daughter with him, and, had he come from the other direction, the young clergyman, in accordance with his avowal, would have been obliged to signal the arrogant man to stop so that he could propose to the daughter.

It was not easy to say what the sequence to such a rash act would have been. . . . A cut of the whip across the face most likely. Mine-owner Aaron Månsson was accustomed to marry off his daughters to counts and barons, and not to humble curates.

The old sinful self that dwelt in his heart was again afraid, and counselled him to turn back. This was a foolhardy venture, it told him. But the brave new man of God in him now raised a jubilant voice; he rejoiced in the opportunity to show how great were his faith and trust.

To the right of the road towered a steep, sandy ridge, its slopes overgrown with pine saplings, young birch trees, and hagberry bushes. In among the thickets a woman was singing. Karl Arthur did not see the singer, but he knew the voice well; it belonged to the tavern-keeper's giddy daughter—she who ran after all the fellows. She was not far away, and might appear in the road at any moment.

Karl Arthur stepped softly now, lest his footfalls be heard by the singer; he even looked about for some way of escape.

On the other side of the road lay a meadow where a herd of cows was grazing. The cows were not alone. A woman was there, milking. Her he knew also. She was the tenant farmer's cow girl, who was tall as a man and who had three illegitimate children. His whole being shrank in horror. Whispering a prayer to his Maker, he hastened on.

The tavern-keeper's daughter still yodelled in the bush, and the big cow girl, having finished her milking, was preparing to go home. Luckily, neither of them crossed his path.

The wretched old sinner in him now took a new tack. He said that perhaps our Lord had shown him these two loose women not so much to test his faith and courage as to warn him. Perhaps He wanted to let him see what a reckless, idiotic thing he was doing.

Karl Arthur immediately silenced the weak, wavering sinner in him, and continued his quest. Should he give up for a thing so trivial? Should he believe more in his own fears than in the power of God?

At last he saw a woman coming down the road. Her he could not avoid. Though she was still at some distance he recognized her. It was Crofter Matts's Elin, whose whole face was disfigured by a purple birthmark. For an instant he stood aghast. The girl was not only hideous to behold, she was also the poorest person in the parish. Her father and mother were both dead, and she had ten dependent younger brothers and sisters to care for.

He had visited her in her lowly hut, swarming with dirty, ragged youngsters whom the eldest sister vainly strove to feed and clothe. The perspiration of dread stood thick on his brow, but he folded his hands and advanced resolutely.

"It is for her sake, that she may receive help, all this has come to pass," he mumbled to himself as they were rapidly nearing each other.

A true martyrdom was opening up to him, and he would not turn aside for anything in that line. For this poor girl he had no such feeling of revulsion as the cow girl or the tavern-keeper's daughter had aroused in him. Of her he had heard only good.

A few strides more and they would have been face to face—when, happily, she turned off from the road. Someone had called to her from the wood, and she quickly disappeared among the tangle of thickets.

Now that Crofter Matts's Elin was out of the way

he felt that a heavy load had been lifted off his chest. With fresh assurance, he strode on, his head held high—proud as if he had actually walked on the water to prove the strength of his faith.

"The Lord is with me," he said. "Christ walks with me on this journey, holding over me His protecting shield." This thought sustained him, and filled his heart with gladness.

"The right one will soon appear. The Lord has been testing me; He has seen that I am in earnest. I shall not turn back. My bride-elect approaches."

He had just covered the short stretch of road between the deanery and the church town and was turning in on the village street, when a cottage door opened and a young girl came out. She crossed the small garden path that led from the house and stepped into the road almost in front of Karl Arthur.

She had appeared so suddenly he had not seen her until she was almost upon him. He stood stock-still. Instantly he thought: "Ah, here she is! Didn't I know it? I had the feeling just now that she was coming my way." Clasping his hands, he gave thanks to God for His great and wondrous mercy.

She who came toward him was a young woman from a parish in northern Dalarne who went about the country as house-to-house peddler. She was dressed in the picturesque red and green, black and white peasant costume of her home parish. Here at Korskyrka, where the old peasant dress had long been laid away, she shone like a rose of the wilderness.

The girl herself was even prettier than her clothes. Her hair curled softly around a fine forehead, which, otherwise, would have appeared rather high, and her features were perfect. Above all, it was the deep, brooding eyes and the fine black eyebrows that settled the matter. Such lovely eyes and brows would have lent beauty even to a plain face. Moreover, she was tall and well built. None could doubt for a moment that she was strong and healthy. Though shouldering a large leather bag full of merchandise, she held herself erect and moved with ease, as if quite unconscious of her burden.

Karl Arthur was entranced. It was summer incarnate coming toward him—the rich, warm, blooming summer of that year. Had he been an artist, he would have painted it just so.

But, if it was summer approaching, it was not a summer he need fear. Quite the contrary. God wanted him to open his heart to it and rejoice in its beauty. His lovely bride-elect had come from distant hill regions, from the home of poverty and lowliness. She did not know the lure of riches, the consuming passion for material things that caused the children of the plains to forget their Creator. This daughter of the people would not hesitate to marry a man because he wished to remain poor all his life.

Verily, the wisdom of God surpasseth all! The Lord knew what was needful for him and, by a turn of His Hand, had placed in his path the woman more suited to him than any other.

The young clergyman was so lost in his own musings that he made no move toward the beautiful Dalar girl. When she saw how he was devouring her with his eyes, she could not help laughing to herself.

"You stare as if it was a bear you'd met," said she.

Karl Arthur laughed, too. It was extraordinary how light-hearted he had become all at once!

"Oh, no, it was no bear I fancied I saw."

"Then it must have been the Wood Nymph. 'Tis said that folk get so cracky when they see her they can't move hand or foot." She smiled, showing the prettiest, the most dazzling teeth, and wished to pass on; but he quickly barred her way.

"You can't go," he said, firmly. "I must speak with you. Sit you down here at the side of the road!"

She was surprised at the imperative command; but thinking he wanted to purchase some of her wares, she said: "I can't open the bag out here on the highway."

Immediately, a light broke in upon her. "Aren't you the pastor of this parish? I thought I saw you in the pulpit yesterday."

Karl Arthur was glad she had heard him preach and knew who he was.

"Oh, yes," he affirmed, "it was I who preached; but I'm only an assistant pastor."

"Then you must be living at the deanery," she said. "I'm just on my way there. You come round to the kitchen, and I'll sell you the whole bagful of goods."

"But I do not wish to purchase your wares," the Curate replied. "I want to ask you to be my wife." He spoke in a choked voice, for he was deeply moved. It seemed to him that all Nature—the birds, the quivering leaves of the trees, the grazing kine—was aware of the solemn event, and awaited in breathless suspense the young woman's answer.

She turned quickly to see whether he was in earnest, but otherwise seemed quite indifferent. "We might meet here in the road at ten this evening. I have business of my own to think of now."

With that, she went on her way. He let her go, certain she would come back and give him a Yea. For was she not the bride God had chosen for him?

Karl Arthur, however, was in no mood to go home and settle down to work. He turned toward the heights, and when he had gone far enough into the wood not to be seen from the road, he flung himself down upon the ground.

What luck! What marvellous luck! What dangers he had escaped! How wonderful were the happenings of that day!

Now all his troubles were over. Never again could Charlotte Löwensköld tempt him to become a slave of Mammon. Hereafter, he would follow his own bent. The meek and lowly wife would let him walk in the footsteps of Jesus. He saw in his mind's eye the little gray cottage, the blessed simple life, the perfect harmony between his teaching and his mode of living.

He lay blinking up at the brushy greenery through which the sunbeams were trying to steal, and it seemed to him that, in the same way, a new, auspicious love was stealing into his harrowed, broken heart.

CHAPTER VI

THE MORNING COFFEE

THERE was one who could have righted it all had she cared to; but that was perhaps too much to ask of a person who year after year had filled her heart with vain desires and longings.

That mere wishes can in any way affect the main issues of life would be difficult to prove; but without doubt they can take possession of the mind, weaken the will, and stifle the conscience.

All Monday afternoon Fru Sundler had grieved over what she had said of Charlotte, because it had driven Karl Arthur away. To think that *he* had been there, under her roof, and had talked to her quite freely and been more charming than ever she had dreamed him! Yet she, by her stupidity and want of discretion, had offended him to such a degree as to make him declare he never wished to see her again.

She was angry at herself and at all the world, and when her husband suggested that they go over to the church and sing awhile, as they were wont to do on summer evenings, she turned upon him so sharply that he fled the house and took refuge at the tavern.

This caused her still further chagrin, for she wished to

appear, both in her own eyes and in the eyes of others, as one without fault or blemish. She knew that Organist Sundler had espoused her merely because he admired her singing voice so much that he wanted to hear it every day. And she had always honourably discharged her indebtedness to him for establishing her in a nice little home, thereby relieving her of the necessity of earning her bread as a nursery governess. But that evening she was unable to meet her payment. Had she attempted to lift up her voice in the House of God, no sweet tones or pious words would have poured from her throat, but only lamentation and blasphemy.

However, at about half-past eight, to her great and unspeakable delight, who should come but Karl Arthur! He stepped in, happy and unconcerned, and asked whether Fru Sundler could give him some supper. She must have appeared somewhat surprised at the request, for he hastened to explain that he had been lying in the woods the whole afternoon and had not only slept through the dinner hour, but had also missed the evening meal, which was always served punctually at eight at the deanery. Did Fru Sundler, perchance, have in the house a bit of bread and butter with which he might appease his gnawing hunger?

Thea Sundler was not daughter to that excellent housekeeper Malvina Spaak for nothing; nor could it be said that she herself was a poor housewife. She immediately brought forth from her cupboard not only bread and butter, but also ham, eggs, and milk.

In her joy over Karl Arthur's return, and his asking a favour of her, as of an old friend of the family, she found the courage to tell him how sorry she was for what she had said that morning. Surely he could never have thought that she had any desire to create ill feeling between him and his betrothed. She understood, to be sure, that teaching was also a noble calling; yet, she could but hope, aye, and pray to God that Dr. Ekenstedt might continue as pastor here at the countryside, where one had so few opportunities to hear a living Gospel.

Karl Arthur, of course, replied that if anyone should apologize it was he. She had no occasion to regret her words. He knew now that Providence had put them into her mouth; and they had been to him both a revelation and a help.

One word led to another, and Karl Arthur soon told her everything that had transpired since their meeting in the forenoon. He was so exuberantly happy, so filled with wonder at God's great mercy to him, he simply had to talk, had to tell it all to a fellow being. It was pure luck, his coming upon this Thea Sundler, who, through her mother, knew his people.

Fru Sundler must have known, when hearing about the broken troth and also the new one, that this would end in nothing but misery. She must have understood that it was only out of pique and contrariness his fiancée had answered in the affirmative his query as to whether she preferred a bishop. And she must have

known, too, that the covenant with the Dalar woman
was not as yet so binding but it could be broken.

But when one has been longing for years to meet a
charming young man and to become his friend and confidante (nothing more, of course), would one be likely
to reason with him the very first time he bared his soul
to one's vision? Nor was it possible for Thea Sundler to
be anything but all admiration and sympathy, and to
regard his tramp to the church town as a veritable act
of heroism. That she should try to clear Charlotte's
name—now, could one ask it? That she, for example,
should remind Karl Arthur that his fiancée had a rare
gift for planning and doing for others but seldom showed
any cleverness in matters that concerned herself alone—
ah, no, that was hardly to be expected of her!

In all probability Karl Arthur was not so sure of himself as he appeared to be. A slight hint might have made
him hesitate; an honest protest or a word of warning
would have been enough, perhaps, to make him relinquish
all thought of a new troth. But Fru Sundler said nothing to warn or frighten him; to her it was all perfectly
glorious.

Think of his placing his fate like that in the Hand of
God! Think of his tearing the loved one out of his heart
so that he might follow in the footsteps of Jesus! Karl
Arthur, indeed, received no discouragement; on the
contrary, he was encouraged to go on.

Who knows? Perhaps Fru Sundler was quite sincere.
She had both Almquist and Stagnelius on her parlour

table, and she was a romanticist from crown to toe. Here at last was an adventure! Here was something positively thrilling!

There was just one little point in Karl Arthur's story that troubled Fru Sundler: If Charlotte was as avid for worldly advantages as Karl Arthur maintained (and Thea Sundler was not inclined to dispute it), then why had she said No to Schagerström? What could she have hoped to gain by her rejection of the Ironmaster?

Of a sudden, it all became clear to her. Charlotte had played for high stakes. Ah, Thea Sundler knew her thoroughly!

Charlotte, of course, had immediately regretted her refusal of Schagerström and had wished herself free from Karl Arthur so that she could give the rich ironmaster a different answer. That was why she had made a scene and worked Karl Arthur up to such a pitch that he finally broke with her. Here was the explanation; this was the truth of the matter.

Fru Sundler imparted her conclusions to Karl Arthur, but he only flouted them. She argued and elucidated; still, he refused to believe her. She stuck to her point, however, and in this instance she had the temerity to contradict him.

They were still arguing when the clock struck the hour of ten and he should be off to meet the Dalar woman. Fru Sundler had only succeeded in creating a slight doubt in his mind. Her own assurance, however, was unshakable; she averred that by to-morrow, or at most within a few days, Charlotte would be engaged to Schagerström.

Indeed, Thea Sundler had not righted the mischief On the contrary, she had sent a fresh poison dart into the mind of Karl Arthur.

There was one who would have liked to make things right again; there was Charlotte herself. But what could she do just then? Karl Arthur had rooted her out of his heart as if she had been a noxious weed. She had come between him and his God; therefore she was nothing to him. Even if he had wished to listen to her, could one imagine Charlotte choosing her words with care? Had she, the high-spirited, impulsive young girl, the wisdom to put aside her pride and speak the soft, conciliatory words that would save the lover?

* * *

When Karl Arthur next morning took his customary stroll from the annex to the main building for morning coffee, he paused time and again to inhale great draughts of the bracing air, to admire the velvety sheen of the dewy grass, the gorgeous colour array of the perennials, and the cheery hum of the honeybees. He felt, with pleasurable satisfaction, that to-day, for the first time (inasmuch as he had freed himself from the temptations of the world), he could enjoy the beauties of nature with perfect comfort.

As he stepped into the dining room, there, to his amazement, stood Charlotte, waiting to greet him, as usual. His mellow mood instantly changed to petty resentment. He had thought himself free; thought the battle was over. Charlotte evidently did not understand that the break was final and conclusive. Not wishing to be pointedly uncivil, he said a curt "Good-morning" and, pretending not to see the hand she held out to him, he went straight over to the table and sat down.

Now, that should have been enough, he thought, to show her that she need trouble him no further with her presence; but Charlotte, obviously, did not wish to see, for she continued to keep him company.

He was careful not to raise his eyes, lest he should meet her gaze, but he had seen, at the one glance he had given her, that she was ashen pale and that her eyes were red and swollen. Her whole appearance indicated that she had passed a sleepless night, in anguish and mayhap qualms of conscience.

Oh, well—he had not slept, either. From ten until two he had sat on a wooded hill, conversing with the "God-elected" bride. The usual early morning shower had forced them to part company, and had sent him scurrying back to the deanery. But, with a new and happy love filling his heart, the hours had been too blissful to sleep away. He had passed the rest of the night at his desk, writing the good news to his parents; and had thus lived over again those few short hours of perfect bliss. Certainly, none could have told by his appearance that he had not had a wink of sleep! Never had he felt better or more full of life.

It was embarrassing to have Charlotte fussing around him as if nothing had occurred; she moved the cream pitcher and rusk basket nearer to him, went over to the pantry slide and fetched the hot coffee. As she filled his cup, she inquired in a casual tone, as if asking about something quite usual and commonplace:

"Well, how did it go for you?"

It was positively distasteful to have to make reply. An afterglow of sanctity still rested over the summer night he had passed in the company of the young Dalar girl. The hours had not been employed in demonstrations of tenderness, but in explaining to her how he would pattern his life after the example of Christ. Her quiet way of listening, her gentle, hesitating replies, her modest concurrence had given him the self-confidence he needed. But how would Charlotte understand the peace, the happiness, which he had found?

"The Lord helped me," was all he at last managed to reply.

Charlotte was pouring coffee for herself as the words fell; they must have startled her, for she sat down so suddenly, as if her knees had given way.

"Good heavens, Karl Arthur! Surely you can't have been off and done something foolish?"

"Didn't you hear what I said I would do when we parted yesterday?"

"Yes, of course I heard; but, dearest, I thought it was only a shot in the air to frighten me."

"You may be sure that when I say I place my fate in the Hand of God, I do it."

Charlotte helped herself to sugar and cream and crumbled a rusk. Karl Arthur inferred from her silence that she was playing for time to collect herself.

He was surprised that she should appear so distressed. He remembered what Fru Sundler had said about Charlotte's precipitating the break. But in that his new friend certainly had been mistaken; Charlotte evidently had no thought of engaging herself to Schagerström.

"So you actually rushed off and proposed to the first woman you met," she said in the casual tone in which she started the conversation.

"Yes, Charlotte, I let God choose for me."

"And, of course, it was a foolish choice!" she shrieked.

He recognized the old Charlotte in this irreverent utterance, and could not resist the pleasure of administering a fitting rebuke.

"To place one's reliance upon God has always been foolishness in your eyes, Charlotte."

Her hand shook perceptibly, and the spoon clinked against the cup, but she did not permit herself to make an angry retort.

"For pity's sake," she begged, "let us not carry on as we did yesterday!"

"Quite right, Charlotte, considering that I am happier now than I have been heretofore."

It was a brutal thrust, but he thought it imperative to

let her know that he had become reconciled to his God and that his mind was at rest.

"So you are happy," said Charlotte.

It was not easy to tell what lay behind her remark. . . . Was it bitter grief or derisive surprise?

"The way lies clear before me," pursued Karl Arthur. "All barriers to my living by the spirit of Christ have been swept away; the Lord has sent me the right woman." He stressed his present felicity more than was necessary; but there was something in her quiet demeanour that troubled him; she did not yet seem to comprehend that he was serious, that the matter had been settled for good and all.

"It must have gone better for you than I thought," said Charlotte, dropping back into an easy, conversational tone. "I shall say nothing until I hear to whom you are now engaged."

"Her name is Anna Svärd," he said. "Anna Svärd." He could not help repeating her name; the mere sound of it called up visions of the night's enchantment— young love's power of enchantment—and dispelled the unpleasantness of the moment.

"Anna Svärd," said Charlotte, but in what a different tone! "Do I know her?"

"I dare say you have seen her; she is from Dalarne." Charlotte looked blankly questioning.

"She is not one of your fine acquaintances, Charlotte; she is a poor and lowly person."

"It can't be——" she broke out with such vehemence

that he had to look at her. (Her sensitive face expressed
the utmost horror.)—"it can't be that Dalar woman who
came into the kitchen yesterday. God in heaven, Karl
Arthur, I seem to have heard that her name is Anna
Svärd!"

He could not doubt that her horror was genuine, but
that didn't make it any the pleasanter. The guardian-
ship she was assuming over him! And what lack of
understanding she evinced! She should have heard Thea
Sundler last evening!

He quickly moistened another hard rusk in his coffee,
thinking to hurry through his breakfast in order to
escape the lamentation that would be coming now. But,
strangely enough, none came. Charlotte merely turned
in her chair so that she could see his face. Though she
sat silent he knew that she was weeping.

He got up to go, though still half-hungry. So she was
taking it like that! It was impossible to hold to Fru
Sundler's hypothesis that Charlotte had wanted to
break off with him; he had to believe in her acute distress, and, since her distress caused him a slight twinge
of conscience, he would rather not witness it.

"Don't go!" Charlotte implored him without rising.
"We must speak further about this. It is such a dreadful
thing, it cannot, it must not happen."

"It grieves me to see that you take it so hard, but,
Charlotte, I assure you that we two were not made for
each other."

She sprang to her feet and stood facing him, her head

flung back. "Do you think I'm weeping on my own account?" she said, contemptuously dashing a tear from the corner of her eye. "Do you think I care whether I am unhappy? Don't you understand it is for you I weep? You are meant to rise high, but with such a wife everything will go to pot!"

"What an expression!"

"I say what I mean. If you are bent upon marrying a peasant woman, I advise you, my friend, to take someone from this part of the country—some person you know; but don't go marry a peddler woman who roams about the kingdom, alone and unprotected. You are not a child; you must know what such things mean."

He tried to stem the devastating torrent of words coming from this short-sighted being who did not understand what was in question.

"She is the bride God has appointed for me," he reminded her.

"She is not!" Charlotte perhaps would have said that the bride God had intended for him was herself. Perhaps it was the thought of this that sent the tears coursing down her cheeks. She strove to regain control of her voice.

"Think of your parents!" she said.

"I'm not afraid of my parents!" he coolly replied. "They are earnest Christians; they will understand."

"Baroness Beata Ekenstedt!" cried Charlotte, aghast —"will she understand? Ah, Karl Arthur, little you know your own mother if you think she would receive as her daughter-in-law a Dalecarlian peddler woman!"

Karl Arthur, who had been quite calm through it all, felt his temper rising.

"Let us drop this talk about my parents," he said in a stern voice.

Charlotte saw that she had gone too far. "No," she replied, "we'll say no more about your parents. Let us speak, instead, of the Dean and his wife here at Korskyrka, of the Bishop in Karlstad, and the whole Consistory. What do you think they will say when they hear of a clergyman's rushing out on the highway and proposing to the first woman he meets? And what will people say here in Korskyrka, where they exact from their clergy the strictest decorum? You may not even be allowed to remain in the parish. And how do you think the other clergymen in the diocese will regard your strange courtship? You may be sure they and everyone in Värmland will be horrified. People will lose respect for you. No one will come to church when you preach. You will be sent to some poor wilderness parish up in the northern forests, and you will be nothing but a stipendiary curate to the end of your days."

Charlotte was so worked up that she could have talked on and on; but she suddenly noticed that her vehement protests made no impression whatever upon Karl Arthur.

To tell the truth, he was surprised at himself; he was really a changed man. Only the day before he had attached significance to her slightest utterance, and now it was quite immaterial to him what she thought of his behaviour.

"Isn't it the truth I am telling you?" she put to him squarely. "Can you deny it?"

"I cannot discuss matters of this kind with you, Charlotte," he said with an air of superiority; for he felt that, since the previous day, he had become, in a sense, her superior. "You speak only of preferment and favour with the rich and powerful; but it is just this that I consider harmful to a clergyman. I hold that a life of poverty with a humble wife who herself bakes your bread and scrubs your floors is what makes a parson free and independent and exalts him."

Charlotte made no answer. Karl Arthur, turning his gaze on her, saw that she was standing with downcast eyes and moving the tips of her feet forward and back, like a child when it feels embarrassed.

"I do not wish to be the kind of pastor who merely points the way to others," Karl Arthur averred. "I would also tread the path myself."

Charlotte stood silent. A pink glow spread over her cheek and a smile of infinite tenderness trembled on her lips. At length she said something surprising:

"Don't you think that I, too, can bake and scrub?"

Was she jesting, or what? She had the innocent look of a young girl at her first Communion.

"I would not stand in your light, Karl Arthur. You shall serve Christ and I will serve you. I came down this morning just to tell you that all shall be as you wish. I will do anything for you, only don't turn me away!"

He came a step or two nearer, then stopped as if fearing a trap.

"My beloved," she said in a voice scarcely audible, but trembling with emotion, "you don't know what I went through last night! It must be that I had to come so near losing you to understand the depth of my love."

He came a step nearer, and looked at her, as if trying to read her mind.

"Don't you love me any more, Karl Arthur?" She lifted to him a face white as death with anguish.

He was about to say that he had cast her out of his heart when something told him it was untrue. Her words had moved him; had fanned the smouldering embers of his love.

"You are not playing with me, Charlotte?"

"Oh, Karl Arthur, don't you see that I am in earnest?"

And now all the old love in his heart flamed anew. The night in the wood, the new sweetheart faded as mists before the sun; they were forgotten as one forgets a dream.

"But I have already asked Anna Svärd to be my wife," he murmured haltingly.

"Oh, that little tangle can easily be straightened; to her you have been engaged only overnight."

He was drawn as by a magnet, nearer and nearer;

the love that went out from her was strong and irresistible.

She suddenly flung her arms about him and cried:
"I ask for nothing, nothing, only don't drive me
away!"

Still he wavered. It seemed almost unbelievable, her
yielding so completely.

"But you must allow me to go my own way," he
said.

"You shall be a true, a living way-shower, Karl
Arthur; you shall teach the people to walk in the footsteps of Jesus, and I will work for you and with you."

She spoke with the warmest, the fullest conviction;
and at last he believed her. The battle which for five
years had been going on between them was now at an
end, and he was the victor; he could afford to dismiss all
doubt. As he bent down to her to seal their new bond
with a kiss, the door from the hall opened. Charlotte's
face was turned in that direction, and a look of terror
suddenly froze her features. Karl Arthur wheeled
quickly to see what had frightened her.

On the threshold stood a maidservant holding out a
bouquet. "It is from the Ironmaster at Stora Sjötorp,"
the girl announced. "The head gardener brought it.
He is standing out in the kitchen, if Fröken would like
to thank him."

"This is a mistake," said Charlotte. "Why should I
receive flowers from Stora Sjötorp? Alma, go take the
flowers back to the gardener!"

Karl Arthur had followed the exchange of words with close attention. Here was a test. Now he would know to a certainty.

"The gardener says positively the flowers are for Fröken," declared the maid, who could not understand why one should not accept a few posies.

"Oh, well—put them over there," said Charlotte, pointing toward a side table.

Karl Arthur was breathing hard. So she had accepted the flowers! Now he knew enough.

When the maid had gone and Charlotte again turned to Karl Arthur, he had no desire to kiss her. The warning, fortunately, had come in time.

"I understand that Charlotte would like to go out to the gardener and send her thanks by him," he said; and with a bow of annihilating politeness, he left the room.

Charlotte did not follow him. A sense of weariness now crept upon her. Had she not humbled herself enough to save the man she loved? Why had the bouquet come at the critical moment? Did not God wish him to be saved?

She went over to the table where the flowers lay, dewy fresh and brilliant. Almost blinded by tears and scarcely conscious of what she did, she began to pluck the flowers to pieces. Before she could destroy them all, the maid reappeared with something else for her. It was a small envelope addressed to her in Karl Arthur's handwriting.

As she tore it open, a plain gold ring dropped out and slipped through her trembling hands on to the floor. She let it lie where it had fallen while she read the few lines Karl Arthur had scribbed on a half-sheet.

A certain person I met last evening, and with whom I had a confidential talk about my personal affairs, intimated to me that Charlotte had immediately regretted her rejection of Schagerström; that Charlotte had deliberately forced a quarrel to make me break with her so that she could give Schagerström a better reception next time. I refused to believe it possible; but I see now that such is the case, and return, herewith, Charlotte's ring.

I presume that Charlotte promptly notified Schagerström yesterday that our engagement was off. Charlotte, of course, became uneasy while waiting for his answer, and so wished to make up with me. The bouquet of flowers, I infer, was the token of agreement. Had not this been the case, Charlotte, in the then prevailing circumstances, could not have accepted it.

Charlotte read the letter several times, but could not make it out. "'A person I met last evening . . .' I don't understand," she said helplessly. "'A person I met last evening—a person I met . . .'"

At the same time she felt that something cold and slimy—something that was like a huge reptile, was winding its coils around her and would surely crush her.

It was the venomous serpent of slander that snared her in, and it held her captive a long, long time.

CHAPTER VII

THE SUGAR BASIN

IN HIS early days at Korskyrka, Karl Arthur Ekenstedt was a terribly strict Pietist, and regarded Charlotte Löwensköld as a lost child of the world, with whom he did not care to bandy words. Naturally, this nettled Charlotte, and she determined to make him show her proper respect.

She soon perceived how inexperienced he was in all practical things a clergyman is expected to know, and offered him some helpful suggestions. He was embarrassed at first, and repulsed her; but after a while he became more appreciative of her kindness and encroached almost too much at times upon her good nature.

He used to go on long tramps to visit the poor old men and old women who lived in little cabins out in the forest, and would always ask her to accompany him. He said that she understood much better than he how to comfort these aged people in their petty troubles and cheer them up.

It was during these trips together that Charlotte came to love Karl Arthur. Before, she had always fancied that she would marry a dashing, gallant military officer; and now she was hopelessly enamoured of the refined and sensitive young curate, who wouldn't kill a fly and who had never permitted a swear word to cross his lips.

For a time they were allowed to continue their walks and talks undisturbed. But, early in July, Karl Arthur's sister Jaquette came on a visit. The Dean's wife being an old friend of his mother, it was only natural that she should invite his sister to spend a few weeks at the deanery.

Charlotte shared her room with Jaquette, and the two girls immediately became fast friends. Jaquette was so devoted to Charlotte that one would have thought it was on her account she had come to Korskyrka rather than the brother's.

Shortly after Jaquette's return to her home, Fru Forsius received a letter from Baroness Ekenstedt, inviting Charlotte to come to Karlstad for a visit with Jaquette. Her daughter, wrote the Baroness, talked of nothing but the charming young girl she had met at the deanery. She longed to see her again and had spoken of her in such glowing terms as to make her dear mamma quite curious to see her.

The Baroness, on her part, was especially interested in Charlotte because of her being a Löwensköld. The girl undoubtedly belonged to the younger branch of the family, which had never been "baronetted," but at all events she was descended from the old Hedeby General, so that there was a bond of kinship between them.

Charlotte declared outright that she would not go. She was not so stupid but what she understood that the Dean's wife, in the first place, and now Jaquette, had informed the Baroness about her and Karl Arthur, and that she was to be sent to Karlstad so that the Baroness could see and judge for herself whether she would be a desirable daughter-in-law.

The Dean's wife and Karl Arthur, in particular, begged her to go. (Karl Arthur and Charlotte were at that time secretly engaged.) He would be everlastingly grateful if she would grant his mother's request. He who had entered the ministry against the wishes of his parents of course would never give her up, no matter what they thought. But he was sure that, did they but see her, they would be charmed. Never had he met a young girl who could get on so well with elderly persons. It was seeing how kind and helpful she was to the Dean and his wife, and to all old people, that had first attracted him to her. If she would only go to Karlstad, all would be well. She was finally persuaded to accept his mother's invitation.

It was a day's journey to Karlstad and, as it would not have done for Charlotte to travel alone, the Dean's wife arranged to have her go with Ironmaster Moberger and his wife, who were going to the city to attend a wedding. With many admonitions and much sage advice, the old lady sent her off, Charlotte having promised, of course, to be "sensible and dignified."

But to sit the whole long day on the narrow front seat

of a closed carriage, gazing at the Moberger couple, who sat dozing in their separate corners, was not the most auspicious preliminary to the Karlstad visit.

Fru Moberger thought she felt a draught, and on no condition would she have a window open at more than one side of the carriage, and sometimes not even on that. The hotter and closer it became in the coach, the better she slept. Charlotte tried at first to start conversation, but her travelling companions, having had much to attend to before leaving home, were tired and wanted to rest.

Charlotte's small feet tapped and tapped on the floor of the carriage without her being aware of it. Fru Moberger, wakened by the noise, kindly requested her to be quiet.

They stopped at several inns along the way, where the Mobergers opened their lunch bag, and of course they insisted upon Charlotte's sharing their fare. In fact, they were very kind to her during the entire journey. All the same, it was a wonder they ever got her to Karlstad; for, the longer she sat agonizing in the heat, the more despondent she became. She had taken this trip only on Karl Arthur's account, and now, of a sudden, it seemed as if all her love were gone. So, why should she go on to Karlstad to show herself? Several times she felt tempted to open the carriage door, leap out, and run home; she sat on simply because she was too weary and heartsick to move.

When, at length, she arrived at the Ekenstedt home,

she was hardly in a mood to be sensible and dignified. She wanted to shriek, or dance, or smash something; that would have restored the balance and put her in good humour. Jaquette Ekenstedt, pleased and happy, greeted her with open arms. The instant Charlotte saw her she became conscious of her own shabby attire; her clothes were ordinary and old-fashioned. Worst of all, there was something wrong with her shoes; they were new and had been made expressly for the occasion. The parish cobbler had done his level best; but the shoes squeaked and gave forth an odour of leather.

Jaquette conducted her friend through several beautiful rooms to the Baroness's cabinet; and as Charlotte, in passing, noted the smooth parquet floors, the great mirrors, and the decorative friezes above the doors, she gave it up for lost. She would never be accepted as daughter-in-law of this house. It was sheer stupidity, her coming here. Her first impression, of having jumped into the wrong barrel, by no means passed when she entered the Baroness's cabinet.

The Baroness was sitting in an easy chair over by the window, reading a French novel. Glancing up from her book, she said a few words to Charlotte in French. She was so absorbed in her reading that she was not conscious of speaking in a foreign tongue. Charlotte understood perfectly what the Baroness said, but felt vexed, thinking her ladyship wished to ascertain whether she had any linguistic accomplishments. Charlotte answered her in the broadest of Värmland dialects. It was not the Värmland speech of the gentry, which is easily understood, but the patois of serving folk and peasants.

The Baroness elevated her eyebrows a trifle, obviously amused as Charlotte went on to show her astounding command of Värmland argot. Since she couldn't shriek or dance or smash things, it was a comfort to take refuge in homely speech. The game was lost, in any case, but she could at least show these fine folk that she would not curry favour with them by pretending to be better than she was.

The family had already supped when Charlotte arrived and, after a little, the Baroness bade Jaquette take her young friend down to the dining room and see that she had something to eat before retiring.

With that, happily, the day was over.

The next day being a Sunday, immediately after breakfast they went to church, to hear Provost Sjöberg preach. After the service, which lasted two and a half hours, the Colonel, the Baroness, Jaquette, and Charlotte passed another wearisome hour, strolling in Karlstad Square. They met many of the Colonel's friends. Several men joined them, but they walked with the Baroness, and talked only to her. For Charlotte and Jaquette they had no word or glance.

Then came the dinner with the family and their kinsfolk—the Provost and his wife, the Alderman and his, the brothers Stake, Eve and her lieutenant.

During the repast, the Baroness carried on a refined

and intellectual conversation with the Provost and the Alderman. Eve and Jaquette said not a word, and Charlotte, too, was silent—understanding that it was the rule in this house for the young to be seen and not heard.

Charlotte, meanwhile, wished herself miles away. She lay in wait, so to speak, for a chance to prove to Karl Arthur's parents her utter unfitness to be daughter-in-law of theirs. Her Värmland argot, apparently, was not enough; she would have to hit upon something more drastic and conclusive.

After such a journey, and such a sermon, and such a promenade, and such a dinner, she must make it quite plain that she wished to terminate her visit at once.

A maid was passing round a bowl of raspberries, and Charlotte, like the others, helped herself; whereupon she reached for the sugar basin, which stood near to hand, and proceeded to sweeten her berries. She had no idea that she was taking more than the required amount until Jaquette quickly said in a whisper:

"Don't take so much sugar! Mamma won't like it."

Charlotte knew, to be sure, that many old persons thought it a sinful extravagance to sweeten one's food. At home in Korskyrka, if she but touched a sugar spoon she received a reprimand from the Dean; so she was not at all surprised. But, at the same time, she saw a way to give vent to the rebellious feelings that had been rising in her from the time she left home. Now she dug deep into the basin and heaped spoonful after spoonful of sugar on her plate, till it presently looked like a snow-drift in miniature.

There was an ominous silence. Everyone felt that such conduct could not be overlooked. Nor was it long before the Baroness remarked: "The raspberries at Korskyrka must be very tart. Here they are not so bad."

Charlotte went right on sugaring, thinking to herself the while: "If I keep it up I shall lose Karl Arthur and be unhappy ever after; but all the same I must."

The Baroness gave a slight shrug and turned to the Provost to continue their interrupted conversation.

The Colonel now came to his wife's aid. "You are spoiling the flavour of the berries, my dear Fröken Charlotte," he said.

The words were hardly out of his mouth when Charlotte laid down the spoon, picked up the sugar basin with both hands, and emptied all it contained on to her plate. Whereupon she put the basin back on the table and replaced the spoon. Then, settling herself comfortably in her seat, she glared at her table companions, ready to meet the storm.

"Jaquette," said the Colonel, "perhaps you would like to take your friend upstairs to your room?"

The Baroness put up a restraining hand. "No, no," she said, "not in that way!"

She sat quietly thinking a moment; suddenly a glint of merriment came into her beautiful eyes, and she turned, not to Charlotte, but to the Provost.

"Have you heard, Cousin, what happened when my Aunt Clementine was to marry Count Cronfelt? The fathers of both parties met at the Riksdag in Stockholm and arranged the match. When they had settled it all between them, the young Count protested that he must at least see his intended before committing himself. But Aunt Clementine was at home in Hedeby and, since it would have occasioned considerable remark had she been suddenly carried off to Stockholm, it was decided that the Count should go down to Bro Parish and see her at church. No, Cousin, my Aunt Clementine was not averse to marrying a handsome young nobleman; but she had heard that he was coming to the church to take a look at her; and she did not like being placed, as it were, on exhibition. On that particular Sunday she would have preferred not to attend Divine Service, but, in those days, for the young to go contrary to anything their parents had decided was unthinkable. The young girl had to make herself as presentable as possible and go sit in the Löwensköld pew so that Count Cronfelt and one of his friends could take stock of her. But, Cousin, do you know what she did? When the verger struck up the opening psalm, she began to sing in a loud voice and quite off key, and she did the same in every psalm all through the service. When she afterward came out on the church knoll, there stood Cronfelt bowing to her. 'I ask your gracious pardon,' he said. 'I understand that a Fröken Löwensköld cannot allow herself to be shown like a horse at a fair.' With that, he

went his way. But he came again, Cousin, and made the
young lady's acquaintance at her home. They married,
of course, and no doubt lived happily. But, I dare say,
my cousin has heard the story before?"

"Oh, yes, but never so well related," said the Provost,
not understanding.

But Charlotte understood. She sat there, her heart
filled with a great hope, her eyes fixed upon the speaker
in wonder and admiration. The Baroness glanced at her
and smiled, then turned once again to the Provost.

"As you see, Cousin, we have with us to-day a young
girl; she came here that my husband and I might look
her over and see whether she would do as wife for our
son. The young girl, Cousin, is a true Löwensköld, and
does not like being put on exhibition. Cousin, I assure
you that, ever since her arrival last evening, she has
been at pains to sing false, just like my Aunt Clementine.
And I now do as did Count Cronfelt—I ask her gracious
pardon, and say to her that I understand that a Fröken
Löwensköld cannot allow herself to be shown like a
horse at a fair."

The Baroness stood up and held out her arms. Charlotte fell on her neck and wept for joy, and wonder, and
gratitude.

From that moment she had loved Karl Arthur's
mother almost more than she loved Karl Arthur himself.
It was for his mother's sake, that her hopes might be
fulfilled, that she had persuaded Karl Arthur to return
to Upsala and continue his studies. It was for her sake

she had sought that summer to make a headmaster of him; that he might have a standing in the world, and be something more than a poor country parson. And it was for her sake that she had controlled and humbled herself that morning before Karl Arthur.

CHAPTER VIII

THE LETTER

CHARLOTTE LÖWENSKÖLD sat in her room
writing to her mother-in-law, or, properly
speaking, to the one whom she had regarded
until that day as her future mother-in-law—the Baroness Ekenstedt.

It was a long letter, for she was writing to the only
person in the world who had always understood her.

For the first, there was an account of Schagerström's
wooing and all that had happened afterward. She described the scene in the garden, and made out no brief
for herself. She confessed that she had been provoked
at Karl Arthur and had chaffed him, but such a thing as
breaking with him had never entered her mind.

Further, she related the morning's conversation in
the dining room; told of Karl Arthur's extraordinary
announcement, that he was now engaged to a Dalar
woman; of how she had tried to win him back and nearly
succeeded, when, suddenly, all was lost through the unfortunate arrival of the bouquet. She also mentioned the
crazy note Karl Arthur had sent her, and apprised the
Baroness of the decision she had come to, in consequence, and expressed the hope that her dear mother-

in-law would understand, since she had understood her from the very first.

There was but one course open to her. Someone—she knew not who—presumably one of the ladies in the village—had accused her of being double-faced, designing, and mercenary. This she could not let pass unchallenged. As she was a poor girl, eating the bread of others, and had neither father nor brother to come to her defense, she must seek justice herself.

But, then, she was quite able to settle this affair. She was not one of the usual meek womenfolk who only know how to ply a broom or a needle; she could also load a gun, and fire it, too. At the last autumn hunt it was she who had brought down the biggest stag.

Courage she lacked least of all. Once, at a fair, she had given a blackleg a sound box on the ear for maltreating his horse. Though expecting that he would draw his knife and slash her, she had whacked him.

The Baroness perhaps remembered how once, on a St. Stephen's Day, she had jeopardized her social standing by surreptitiously taking the Dean's precious horses out of the stable in order to drive in a race with the farmer's men. Not many would have ventured to do that.

Moreover, she had made an enemy for life of that sinister fellow, Captain Hammarberg, by refusing to sit next to him as his table companion at a dinner party. Nothing would have induced her to sit through a long function and talk to a man who, shortly before, had ruined a good friend at cards and driven him to suicide. When she had dared as much as that because of a thing which was none of her affair, surely she need not hesitate in a matter that concerned herself.

She had the feeling that the creature who had maligned her to Karl Arthur was so vile she must taint the very air she breathed, and work harm wherever she moved. Listening to her talk was like being stung by a venomous reptile. One could render one's fellows no greater service than to rid them of such a monster.

After she had read Karl Arthur's note and grasped its meaning, she knew what she must do. She must go up to her room at once and fetch her shotgun. The gun was loaded, she had only to take it down from the wall and shoulder it. No one at the deanery would hinder her. She would call her dog and go down toward the lake, as if to see whether the young ducks were grown. When far enough away not to be seen from the house, she would turn in the direction of the village; for it was there, of course, the "person" lived who had dripped the poison into Karl Arthur's ear. She would halt before the house where the creature lived and call her out; the moment the ogre appeared, she would aim straight at her heart and shoot her dead.

Had she only known which one among all the women in the village was the culprit, this punishment would have been administered already. Now she had to wait for certain knowledge. She had thought for a moment of doing as Karl Arthur had done—simply go out with her gun in the hope that Providence would send the right woman across her path; in which case the real criminal might have gone scot free. And she did not mean to let that happen.

Nor would it have profited her to go down to the wing and ask Karl Arthur with whom he had talked the previous evening. She had sense enough to know that he would not have enlightened her. Therefore, she had decided to use stratagem; she would assume a calm and indifferent demeanour, and by that means draw the secret from him.

She had immediately pulled herself together, gathered up the remnants of Schagerström's bouquet which, in her bewilderment, she had plucked to pieces, and cast them into the dustbin; she had also picked up the engagement ring Karl Arthur had returned, whereupon she had gone to her room.

It being then only half-past eight, and some little time until breakfast, when she would see Karl Arthur at table, she was writing to her dear mother-in-law.

By the time her letter reached Karlstad, all would be over. Though determined as ever to carry out her resolution, she was glad of the delay, since it afforded her an opportunity to explain matters to the one person whose judgment she valued, and to tell her that, in all the ups and downs of life, her heart was ever with her wonderful, her adorable mother. . . .

The letter was finished, and Charlotte was reading it over. Yes, it was quite clear and legible. She hoped the

Baroness would understand that she was innocent; that she had been unjustly accused and had a right to punish the offender.

While reading, she saw that, in her desire to establish her own innocence, she had shown Karl Arthur in a far from enviable light. She read on and on in a frenzy of nervous apprehension. Supposing that what she had written should make the Colonel and the Baroness wroth with Karl Arthur? Only a short while before, she had warned him not to incur the wrath of his parents, yet here she sat working them up against him!

She was extolling herself at his expense; she had been magnanimous and reasonable while he had acted like a wild lunatic. And this she had thought to send to his mother; to her who loved him! She, too, must be stark mad! Would she bring such sorrow upon her dear mother-in-law? Had she quite forgotten how indulgent his mother had been toward her at the time of their first meeting, and, indeed, ever since? Had she no compassion?

She tore the long letter in two, and sat down to indite another. Now she would take the blame on herself; she would whitewash Karl Arthur. It was only right for her to do so. Karl Arthur had a great work to do in the world, and she should be satisfied to be able to shield him. Though he had broken with her, he was as dear to her as ever, and she must protect and help him now, as always.

Charlotte began the letter to the Baroness:

"May my gracious mother-in-law think not too ill of me——" Here she stuck. What should she say? Lying had never come easy to her, and the truth would be difficult to gloss over. Before she could think what else to write, the breakfast bell rang, and there was no time for meditation. She signed her name below the single line she had penned, folded and sealed the note, and dropped it in the post bag downstairs, before going into the dining room.

It occurred to her, meanwhile, that she need not bother now to find out who the "person" was. If she wanted the Baroness to believe her, if she really wished to take the blame on herself, then she could not punish anyone.

CHAPTER IX

UP AMONG THE CLOUDS

BREAKFAST at the deanery, when one had fresh eggs with *smörgås*, gruel with whipped cream and light fancy biscuits to dip in one's coffee such as were not to be had anywhere else in the parish, was usually the jolliest meal of the day. Then the Dean and his wife, refreshed by their night's sleep, were lively as a pair of youngsters in their teens. The lethargy of old age, which crept upon them as the day wore on, was now as if dispelled, and they jested with the young folks and with each other.

But that morning there was no banter. Both old and young were in disgrace, so to speak. Charlotte had grieved the old couple sorely by the way in which she had answered Schagerström, while Karl Arthur had offended them by absenting himself from meals the previous day without giving the slightest excuse.

When Charlotte came dashing in to take her seat (the others being already in their places), she met with a stern rebuke from the Dean's wife.

"Do you mean to sit down to breakfast with such fingers?"

Charlotte looked at her hands, which were dreadfully inkstained.

"Oh, dear, no!" she said, laughing. "Please forgive me, Tante!"

She hurried out and returned shortly with clean hands. She was not at all huffed by the reproof, though it had been administered in the presence of Karl Arthur.

The Dean's wife looked at her and wondered what was in the air now. "One day she hisses like a snake and the next she coos like a dove. Ah, the young people nowadays, one can't make them out!"

Karl Arthur hastened to apologize for his remissness. He had gone out for a long walk and, having got rather tired, had lain down in the bush to rest awhile, and fallen asleep. On awaking, he had found, to his surprise, that he had missed both dinner and supper.

The Dean's wife was glad the young man had the good sense to offer an explanation.

"Karl Arthur needn't be so shy," she said graciously. "We could have brought in a bit of food, though we ourselves had supped."

"Tante Regina is much too kind," Karl Arthur replied.

"And now," said the old lady, "you must eat a hearty breakfast to make up for what you missed."

"I assure you, my dear Tante, that I did not faint by the wayside. I dropped in at the organist's, and Fru Sundler gave me a good supper."

A wee bit of a cry came from Charlotte. Karl Arthur shot her a swift glance; at the same time, his face went red as a beet. Now, thought he, she'll jump up and say that she knew it was Fru Sundler who had accused her, and make a row.

But Charlotte never moved. She looked quite serene. Had he not known how much shrewdness there lay behind that smooth white brow, he would have said it shone by some inner light.

However, it was not strange that Charlotte's table companions were surprised; for, in truth, an extraordinary change had taken place in her. Yet, it could scarcely be termed extraordinary, since it was nothing but what we have all experienced at times when endeavoring, to the best of our poor abilities, to perform an irksome duty or make a personal sacrifice. Probably we went about it with poor grace; without enthusiasm or even the faith that we were acting wisely and doing the right thing; when all we expected, in return for our kindness, was still further complaint and misery. And then, of a sudden, we felt the heart give a bound of gladness; it began to move with the lightness of a dancer, and a feeling of satisfaction permeated every fibre of our being. We rose, as by a miracle, above our ordinary, mundane self; we became sublimely indifferent to all unpleasantness, aye, we were quite certain that hereafter we should go through life untroubled; that nothing could disturb the blessed, tranquil joy that pervaded us.

It was something of this sort that had come to Charlotte as she sat at the breakfast table. All the hard feelings—anger, resentment, wounded pride, outraged love—had been swept away by the great joy in her soul over having sacrificed herself for the one she loved.

At that moment there was nothing in her heart but tender affection and sympathetic understanding. All human beings seemed wonderful to her; she could not love them enough.

She sat gazing at Dean Forsius, a dry, spare old man with shaven chin, bald pate, a huge forehead, and small, keen eyes. He looked more like an old professor than a clergyman. As a matter of fact, he had prepared himself to enter the field of science. Born in the Eighteenth Century, when the world still raved about Linnæus, he had specialized in botany and had just been appointed Professor in Botany at Lund University, when he was called to the pastorate of Korskyrka. The parish for untold years had been shepherded by clergymen bearing the name Forsius. The cure had passed from father to son, as an entailment, and Botany Professor Petrus Forsius, being the last to bear that name, had been importuned to take up the cure of souls, and leave the flowers to their fate.

All this had long been known to Charlotte, though she had never before understood what a sacrifice the old man had made in giving up his favourite study. To be sure, he had become a very good dean; in his veins flowed the blood of many generations of clerics, and it was self-evident that he would perform the duties of his office as one to the manner born. But from various little signs Charlotte had noted, she thought he still regretted that he had not been allowed to remain in his proper sphere, and carry on his legitimate work.

Now that he had an assistant clergyman, the seventy-five-year-old Dean had again taken up his botanical studies. He went about botanizing and worked in his herbarium. Meanwhile, he did not abandon the parish to the mercy of the winds. He was very particular to preserve peace and not let dissension creep in to embitter the minds of the people. This was why he had been so upset by Charlotte's brusque reply to Schager-ström. But yesterday Charlotte had been quite a different person. Then, she had thought the old Dean needlessly anxious and fearful; but now she saw him in a new light.

And the Dean's wife . . . Charlotte turned her gaze upon the tall, scrawny old Fru, who was utterly devoid of external attractions. Her hair, which would not turn gray though she was almost as old as her husband, was parted in the middle and drawn down over the ears; then it disappeared from sight under a black tulle cap. The cap also concealed a goodly portion of her face, and Charlotte surmised that such was the intention for the Dean's wife had not much beauty of feature to reveal. Perhaps she thought it enough to show the eyes, which were like two round peppercorns, the two small tufts of eyebrow, the tip of a stubby nose, with its flaring nostrils, the wide mouth, and the high cheekbones.

She looked rather severe, and if at times she was a bit hard on her servants, she never spared herself. They used to say in the parish, "To be body to the soul of Fru Forsius was not an easy lot." She would never have been content to sit quietly on a sofa, embroidering or crocheting. It had to be rough work to satisfy her. She had never in her life indulged in anything so useless as reading a novel or thrumming on a harpsichord.

Charlotte, who at times had thought the old lady needlessly work-frenzied, could not now admire her enough. Was it not a praiseworthy thing never to spare one's self but to be untiringly active even in one's old age? Was it not commendable in her, this desire to have her house always clean and in order, and to ask no other boon of life than to be allowed to work?

Besides, the old lady was far from prosy. What an eye she had for the ludicrous! She could say things in a way that made her hearers double over with laughter.

The Dean's wife and the Curate, meanwhile, were discussing Fru Sundler. He had looked her up, he said, because she was the daughter of an old friend of the family—Malvina Spaak.

"Why, of course, of course." The Fru Dean knew all Värmland, and especially those of it who amounted to anything in a domestic sense. "Ah, yes, Malvina Spaak was an upright and capable person."

Karl Arthur then asked Fru Forsius if she did not think the daughter as admirable in every respect as the mother.

"Well, I can't say that she doesn't attend to her

house," said the old lady, "but I'm afraid she's a bit light in the head."

"Do you mean that she's flighty?" questioned Karl Arthur doubtingly.

"Yes, flighty. No one likes her, and so I have tried to talk to her. What do you suppose she said to me one time, as she was taking leave? 'When Tante sees a silver cloud with a golden lining,' said she, rolling her eyes, 'then think of me.' Now whatever did she mean by that?"

As the Dean's wife was telling this, the muscles round her mouth twitched. It seemed so ridiculous that any sane person could think of asking her, Regina Forsius, to look for gold-lined clouds!

She tried hard to keep a straight face, for she had made up her mind to be sternly grave all through the breakfast. But suddenly her face began to work; the eyes contracted, the nostrils expanded, the mouth flew open, and out rolled the laughter. Her funny faces and body contortions set the whole table laughing. Charlotte thought to herself: "You had only to see Fru Forsius laugh to like her. Then you did not notice how homely she was; you just felt thankful to the one who had so much fun in her."

* * *

After breakfast, as soon as Karl Arthur had left the dining room, Fru Forsius informed Charlotte that the Dean was to make a call at Stora Sjötorp during the forenoon. Though the young girl was still in a beatific mood, she became a trifle uneasy. She wondered if that would not tend to strengthen Karl Arthur's suspicions, but instantly dismissed the thought. She was up among the clouds, what happened down here on the earth was of small consequence.

At half-past ten, the large covered carriage drew up before the door. The Dean, to be sure, did not drive four-in-hand, but his two grayish-white Norway clippers with their black tails and manes, and his tall, well-set-up coachman, who bore his black livery with much dignity, were not to be despised. Indeed, there was no fault to be found with the deanery turnout save that the horses were a bit too fat. The old Dean was so tender of the beasts that he hated to take them out even on an occasion like this. He would have preferred to set off in a one-horse shay. Fru Forsius and Charlotte had promised to attend an eleven o'clock coffee party in the village that morning, to celebrate the Name-day of the apothecary's wife, and, since the road to Stora Sjötorp ran past the village, they could ride most of the way. As the carriage swung out from the gate, Charlotte turned to the Dean and said, as if it had suddenly occurred to her:

"Ironmaster Schagerström sent me a bouquet of lovely roses this morning before Uncle and Tante were up. If you like, Uncle, you can give him a word of thanks."

Imagine the surprise and delight of the old couple!

This was a great relief to them. Now there would be no rift in the harmony of the parish. Schagerström was not offended, though he had cause enough to be.

"And you're only just telling us now!" gasped the Dean's wife. "Well, you certainly are a queer one!"

The old lady, however, was highly pleased. She wanted to know how the bouquet had come; whether it was prettily bound, and if, perchance, a note had been tucked in among the flowers, and much else of the same sort.

The Dean merely nodded and promised to convey Charlotte's message. At the same time, he straightened his back as one who has been relieved of a heavy burden.

Charlotte wondered if she had again said something indiscreet; but that morning she could not rest content until everyone was satisfied, in so far as it rested with her. She felt an ineffable need to sacrifice herself for the happiness of others.

The carriage stopped where the village street debouched into the main road, and the ladies got out. It was almost at the very spot where Karl Arthur, the previous day, had met the pretty Dalar girl.

Charlotte on her visits to the church town used always to stop here awhile, to enjoy the fine view. The little lake, which was the middle point in the landscape, could be seen much better from here than from the deanery, where the ground was rather flat. Here they had a survey of all four shores, with their varying scenery. On the west shore, where they now stood, stretched mile after mile of fertile fields. That the land was fruitful was evident from the numerous small villages that dotted the plain. To the north lay the deanery, also surrounded by even, well-tilled grain fields. And beyond, to northeastward, was a tract of woodland through which ran a turbulent river with a foaming rapid, and through the trees peered black roofs and tall chimneys. Up there lay two large iron mills, which contributed even more wealth to the district than did the fields and the woodlands. Looking southward, all one beheld was a wilderness of low, wooded hills. The eastern shore presented a similar aspect, and that side of the lake would have looked drear and monotonous but for a beautiful manor house that a rich ironmaster had built him high on the slope of a ridge, in the heart of the forest. The white mansion, rising amid the tall, dark fir trees, was an impressive sight. By a clever arrangement of the park trees, an illusion had been effected. One seemed to be looking at a castle, with towers and battlements. This place was the pearl of the whole landscape. One would not have had it removed from its setting at any price.

Charlotte, whose mind was far above the earth just then, did not cast a glance toward the shining lake or the beautiful manor. It was the old Fru of the deanery, who was not much given to contemplating the beauties of nature, who stood gazing in rapt wonder at the scene.

"Stop a moment, Charlotte, and take a look at Berghamra. Fancy! Stora Sjötorp is said to be even larger and more beautiful. Do you know what? If someone that I'm very fond of lived in a grand place like that, it would make me very happy." The Dean's wife wagged her old head and folded her sinewy old hands almost prayerfully.

Charlotte knew quite well what the old lady was hinting at, and glibly rejoined:

"Ah, yes, it must be delightful to live back there in the pine woods, where no one ever comes. It is quite different from living as we do, by a great thoroughfare."

The Dean's wife, who liked to see people faring to and fro in the road, shook a finger at the girl. "Aha, you!"

With that, she took Charlotte's arm and went on down the pleasant village street, lined on either side with almost palatial buildings. At the upper end, however, stood a few humble cottages. If there were any others, they lay tucked away along the wooded ridge, and could not be seen from the street. The old stave-church, with its tall, awl-like spire piercing the air, the courthouse, the parish hall, the large, gay tavern, the Doctor's residence, the Judge's house, which stood somewhat back from the street, two or three big farm-houses and the apothecary's place, at the bottom of the street—all bore witness that Korskyrka was a prosperous parish; that the people were enterprising and progressive.

Charlotte and the Dean's wife, walking arm-in-arm, thanked the Lord that they did not have to live here, where one had neighbours on all sides and where a person could not stick her nose outside the door without the whole town's knowing it and wondering where she was going. The moment they set foot on the street they wished themselves back at the deanery, where one was a free agent, and mistress of all one surveyed. They would be ill at ease, they said, until they were on their way home, and saw in the distance the sturdy deanery lindens.

When at length they stepped inside the door to the apothecary's house, they seemed to have arrived somewhat late. Mounting the creaky wooden stairs to the upper story, they heard a hum of voices over their heads like the droning from a beehive.

"Just listen to them!" said the Dean's wife. "To-day they're at it like a flock of magpies. Something must have happened."

Charlotte paused in the middle of the stairway. It had never for a moment occurred to her that Schagerström's suit, the broken troth, and Karl Arthur's engagement to the Dalecarlienne had already become common talk; but now she began to fear it was just this they were discussing so zealously and in such strident voices.

"That blessed wife of the organist has been gossiping," thought Charlotte. "Nice confidante Karl Arthur has acquired!"

But she had no thought of turning back. She would not stand aside for a lot of gossip mongers even under ordinary circumstances, much less to-day, when she was wholly insensitive to all tittle-tattle.

A sudden hush fell upon the room where the Name-day celebrants were gathered when the late guests entered. Only one old dame, with index finger poised in the air, still held forth.

"And more, my dear," she shrilled to her neighbour, "what do you think happened the other day?"

They all looked embarrassed. No one had expected the ladies from the deanery to appear.

The apothecary's wife, meanwhile, hastened to greet the newcomers. Fru Forsius, who knew nothing about the break between Charlotte and Karl Arthur, felt quite unconcerned, though she perceived that something was wrong. Old as she was, her knees were supple as a dancer's. She made a grand *révérence* to the whole company, then went about, greeting each person in turn, curtseying to one and all. Charlotte, following in her footsteps, met with ill-concealed disapproval. Her curtseys were not so deep as the old lady's; but at that art none could compete with the Dean's wife.

Charlotte soon noticed how everyone avoided her. When she had received her cup of coffee and taken a seat at a window table, nobody came to occupy the vacant chair opposite her. It was the same after coffee, when the women brought forth from reticules and work-bags their embroidery frames and crochet work: she had to sit there by herself, as if none was aware of her existence.

Round about her sat groups of women with their heads so close together that the laces and frills on their large tulle caps became entangled. And now they talked in low voices so as not to be heard by her; yet, now and again, she caught their incessant, "And more, my dear, and more—think what happened yesterday!"

And they said, one to another, that first she had given Schagerström No; then, regretting it, she had deliberately provoked a quarrel with her fiancé to make him break with her. Such subtle scheming! Such diabolical shrewdness! All the blame was to fall upon him. None should say of her that she had jilted a poor man to become mistress of Stora Sjötorp. And her fine plan would have worked out successfully and she would have escaped all censure had the organist's wife not divined her evil intent.

Chârlotte sat quietly listening to the babble with never a thought of rising to defend herself. The mental exaltation in which she had revelled since early morning was now at its zenith. She walked on air, so to speak—high above everything earthly.

All this venomous gossip would have been turned upon Karl Arthur had she not shielded him. From every quarter would have come: "And more, my dear— have you heard that young Ekenstedt has broken with his fiancée. . . ? Oh, one thing more! He rushed out into the road and proposed to the first woman he met. Do you think, my dear, that such a man should continue as pastor here at Korskyrka? [Buzz-buzz].—Oh, what will the Bishop say?"

Charlotte sat rejoicing in her heart that it was she

and not Karl Arthur who had to take it all, when a thin, pallid little Fru came over to her.

It was her sister, Marie Louise, wife of Dr. Romelius. She was the mother of six children and had a husband who drank. Marie Louise was ten years older than Charlotte, and there had never been any close bond of intimacy between them. She put no questions, but sat down opposite Charlotte and went to knitting at a child's stocking. There was a determined expression round her mouth. It was plain that she knew what she was about, when she took her place at the window table.

And there sat the two sisters hearing this interminable "And more, my dear."

Presently they noticed that Fru Sundler was sitting with the Dean's wife, and whispering to her.

"Now Tante Regina will know of it," said Marie Louise.

Charlotte half rose from her chair, then quickly sat down again. After a little she said:

"By the by, Marie Louise, what was that about Malvina Spaak? Wasn't there some sort of prognostication?"

"Why, yes," replied the sister, "but I don't remember just what it was, only that some dire misfortune would befall the Löwenskölds."

"Perhaps you could find out what it was supposed to be?"

"Yes. I have it written down somewhere. However, it doesn't concern us—only the Löwenskölds of Hedeby."

"Thank you!" said Charlotte.

Presently, Fru Romelius, to whom all this slanderous talk was becoming intolerable, leaned forward and whispered to Charlotte:

"I understand. You are silent for Karl Arthur's sake. Oh, I could tell them how it is."

"Don't, for mercy's sake!" Charlotte enjoined in alarm. "It doesn't matter what they say about me, but Karl Arthur is highly gifted."

The sister understood the situation. She loved her husband, though from the first he had made her unhappy by his tippling. Still, she had the faith that he would straighten up and accomplish wonders in the field of medicine.

When at last the Name-day party was over and the guests were taking leave, fat Fru Sundler quickly stepped out into the hall, where the ladies had left their wraps, and helped Fru Forsius on with her mantilla and tied her bonnet strings.

Charlotte, who usually claimed the right to assist her old friend, meanwhile stood looking on. She blanched a bit, but said nothing. When they came out on the village street, it was the organist's wife, again, who rushed forward and offered her arm to the Fru Dean.

There was no one who tried Charlotte's patience so much as Fru Sundler; the girl of course thought she would be rid of the woman when they reached her house, at the top of the street. But when they had come that far, Fru Sundler asked if she might accompany them all the way to the deanery. It did her so much good, she said, to have a little exercise after sitting still such a long while.

The Dean's wife made no objection, nor did Charlotte say a word. Now the girl quickened her steps, keeping well ahead of the others, in order to escape the sound of Fru Sundler's oily voice and her irritating drawl.

CHAPTER X

SCHAGERSTRÖM

ON THE homeward drive from his unsuccessful courting adventure, Schagerström sat back in the landau, chuckling to himself. But for the coachman and the footman, he would have roared. It seemed such a huge joke that he, who had fared forth to confer a great favour upon a poor young girl, had been so thoroughly snubbed and taken down.

"But the girl was right," he mumbled. "Gad! of course she was right. I can't understand why I didn't think about her being engaged before rushing off to propose to her. Ha! she was superb when she blazed out like that. Well, anyhow, I had this compensation for my trouble: the pleasure of looking upon beauty."

What though he had made a fool of himself, thought he, he had had the satisfaction of meeting a person who was not awed by his wealth. Certainly, the young girl had not tried to ingratiate herself; she had treated him as if he were no better than a common tramp.

"That little girl has character! I only hope she doesn't think too ill of me. Oh, I'll be careful not to propose to her again; but I'd like her to know that I'm not such an unmitigated ass as to feel offended at her for the lesson she gave me."

All afternoon he wondered what he could do to atone for his brashness. At length, he seemed to hit upon something feasible. This time, however, he was not going to rush ahead blindly; he would give thought to the matter, make the necessary inquiries, and not go blundering again.

Toward evening, it suddenly struck him that there would be no harm in his sending Charlotte now, at once, a little token of appreciation. It would be nice, he thought, to send her a few flowers. If she accepted them, it would be easier to get on a good footing with her. He immediately went out into the garden.

"Now, Ericcson," he said to the head gardener, "I want you to make me up a beautiful bouquet. Let's see what you have to offer!"

"The prettiest I have," said the gardener, "are these carnations. We could use those for the centre, with a border of gillyflowers, then mix in a bit of mignonette."

Schagerström turned up his nose. "Pinks and gilly-flowers and mignonette! Why, man, they are to be found in any garden. You might as well offer me daisies and bluebells."

It was the same with the snapdragon, the larkspur, and the forget-me-not—they were all too common.

Schagerström presently stopped before a small rose bush, thick with buds and full-blown flowers; the buds, in particular, were lovely.

"This I think rather pretty," he said.

"But, Ironmaster," protested the gardener, "it is

the moss rose! And this is its first bloom. It rarely thrives so far north. You will not find another bush like it in all Värmland."

"But that's the very thing I want. It is to be sent to Korskyrka Deanery. There, as you know, they have all the other kinds of flowers."

"Oh, to the deanery!" The gardener was delighted. "I'd like the Dean to see my moss roses, for he is a knower of flowers."

And of course the poor roses were cut and sent. The sorry reception they met with at the deanery has already been recorded. But the one who, on the contrary, met with a cordial reception when he came next day to Stora Sjötorp, was the Dean of Korskyrka.

At first the spare little clergyman was a bit diffuse and ceremonious, though he, like Schagerström, was at bottom straightforward and unassuming. They soon saw that apologies and compliments were superfluous, and fell to talking as naturally and freely as a couple of old comrades.

Schagerström took occasion to make some inquiries about Charlotte. He wanted to know about her family, her circumstances, and, above all, whether her fiancé had any plans for the future. A curate's stipend was hardly enough for them to live upon. Did the Dean know whether young Ekenstedt had any immediate prospects of promotion?

The old clergyman was astonished, but as the things Schagerström asked about were no secrets, he gave clear and direct answers. "The Ironmaster is a business man and goes straight to the point," thought he. "Well, I suppose that's the proper way nowadays."

Schagerström then said that, as chairman of a board of foundry directors in the province of Uppland, he had the right to appoint the chaplain to the works. The salary, to be sure, was not large, but the parsonage was comfortable. The last incumbent had been well content there. Did the Dean think it would be a suitable place for young Ekenstedt?

Dean Forsius was never more surprised; but, being a wise old gentleman, he took it as a matter of course. He drew out his snuffbox, filled his large nose with snuff, dusted it with a silk handkerchief, put the box back in his pocket, then made reply.

"Ironmaster, you couldn't find a more worthy young man."

"Then the matter is settled," said Schagerström.

The Dean was elated. This, indeed, was good news to bring home! Charlotte's future had been a source of anxiety to him. He had the greatest respect for his curate, but thought it deplorable that the young man took no steps to procure a living that would enable him to marry. The friendly old cleric suddenly turned to Schagerström and said:

"You like to make people happy, Ironmaster, and you don't do it by half measures. Come along to the deanery with me and tell the young lovers of the splendid thing you are doing for them. Come witness their joy. I envy you that pleasure, Ironmaster."

Schagerström beamed. Obviously, the proposition pleased him.

"But perhaps my coming would be inopportune?" he said.

"Inopportune! That's out of the question when one brings such tidings."

Schagerström, about to accept the invitation, suddenly clapped a hand to his brow. "No, I can't," he said. "I have to set out on a long journey to-day. The travelling carriage will be at the gate at two o'clock."

"Oh, Ironmaster, what a pity! But I understand that time is precious."

"Orders for relays of horses have been sent out to the posting stations," said Schagerström mournfully.

"Why not drive with me as far as the parsonage?" proposed the Dean. "My carriage is waiting, and we could start at once. Yours can pick you up at the deanery at any time you say."

This arrangement was agreeable, and Schagerström, after giving orders for the travelling coach to proceed to Korskyrka Deanery as soon as the food bag and the other luggage for the journey were ready, drove off with the Dean. The two men were merry as a couple of peasants driving to a country fair.

"I must say, Ironmaster, that Charlotte doesn't deserve all this after the way she treated you yesterday."

Schagerström burst out laughing.

"Now she'll find herself in a tight place," the Dean continued. "It will be fun to see how she gets out of it. You may be sure, Ironmaster, that she'll do something quite unexpected—something that never would occur to anyone else." The Dean chuckled with glee in anticipation.

It was a great disappointment to both of them when, on arriving at the deanery, they found that the Fru and the Fröken had not returned yet from the Name-day party. The Dean, knowing they would be at home soon, conducted Schagerström to his own quarters, on the ground floor.

Dean Forsius had two rooms for his special use. The outer, a bare-looking place, was his office. A large writing table, two desk chairs, a long leather-upholstered lounge, a wall shelf for the bulky parish registers, were the only furnishings, unless one included in that category some cactus plants, in a window, that looked as if they were aflame. The inner room the Dean's wife had fitted up herself for the comfort of her "dear hubby." The floor was covered with a home-woven carpet, and the furniture was both decorative and serviceable. There were upholstered sofas and easy chairs, a writing desk with many drawers and compartments, a rack for pipes, and rows upon rows of bookshelves. Besides, over both high and low, were bunches of pressed flowers in cap-paper wrappings.

It was in there, of course, the Dean intended to take

Schagerström; but when they stepped into the office they saw Karl Arthur at the writing table, entering births and deaths in a big ledger.

The young man arose and was presented to Schagerström.

"To-day the Ironmaster will not have to go away from here without effecting his errand," he said rather maliciously as he bowed to Schagerström.

And no wonder he was stirred on seeing the Ironmaster at the deanery! How could he help but think that the Dean, his wife, and Charlotte had conspired together to amend the hasty decision? Had there been a lingering doubt in his mind as to Charlotte's duplicity, the sight of the suitor, whom the Dean himself had brought to the house, would have been enough to confirm his suspicions. To be sure, it was no longer any concern of his whom Charlotte married, but he thought this haste rather indelicate and ruthless. That a clergyman should be so eager to procure a rich husband for a kinswoman was positively indecent.

The old Dean, unaware, of course, of the break with Charlotte, stared at Karl Arthur in surprise. He could not imagine what the young man meant by his remark, but inferring from his tone that he was inimically disposed toward Schagerström, he thought it best to let him know at once that the Ironmaster was not there to-day on any wooing errand.

He said: "It was to meet you the Ironmaster dropped in to-day. I don't know that I have a right to reveal his plan until Charlotte comes; but you will be pleased, my dear confrère, you will be pleased."

His friendly tone had no effect upon Karl Arthur, who stood there, stiff and frowning.

"If Ironmaster Schagerström has anything to say to me, he need not wait for Charlotte. We two have nothing more to do with each other." With that he put out his left hand to let Schagerström and the Dean see that he wore no betrothal ring now.

The old man wheeled round in his astonishment. "Look here, my fine confrère, is this something you two have decided to-day, during my absence?"

"Oh, no, Uncle; the matter was settled yesterday. At about twelve o'clock Ironmaster Schagerström proposed to Charlotte, an hour later our engagement was broken off."

"Your engagement broken?" gasped the astounded Dean. "But Charlotte hasn't said a word——"

"Pardon, Uncle!" Karl Arthur cut in, thinking the old man was trying to play the innocent, "but I see plainly that you have acted as Cupid's messenger."

The little old Dean drew himself up; he was now coldly reserved and formal. "Please step into my private office, gentlemen; we must go to the bottom of this."

Directly they had taken places—the Dean at the writing desk, Schagerström on a corner sofa at the far end of the room, and Karl Arthur in a rocking chair, near the door—the Dean turned to his curate and said:

"It is quite true, my fine confrère, that yesterday I

advised my sister's granddaughter to accept Ironmaster Schagerström's offer. She had waited for you five years, young man. One time this summer I asked you whether you were going to take any steps that would make it possible for you to be united in the bonds of matrimony, and you said 'No.' You remember, perhaps, that I then told you I would do all that lay in my power to induce Charlotte to break off with you. The girl hasn't a penny to her name, and when I pass away she will be homeless and friendless. You know my sentiments, and I make no bones about having advised her as I did. But when Charlotte followed her own sweet will and said No, the matter was closed. There has been no further talk between us on the subject, understand, my fine confrère!"

Schagerström, from his corner, was observing the Curate. There was something in the young man's manner that displeased him. The fellow leaned back in his chair and rocked all the while as if he wished to show his superior that he considered his remarks not worth noticing. Time after time, he tried to interrupt, but the Dean went on talking.

"You may speak when I have finished, young man; you may speak then as long as you like; but I have the floor now. When I left for Stora Sjötorp this morning, I did not know of your broken troth. My errand there was not as you think, to offer Charlotte to Herr Schagerström. I went because I wish to have peace and harmony in the parish and because I thought Ironmaster

Schagerström might reasonably feel cut up about Charlotte's curt answer. But the Ironmaster seemed to take a different view of the matter; he thought my ideas old-fashioned and that Charlotte had answered rightly. In fact, he was so well pleased with everything that he wanted to do something for your welfare. He proposes to offer you the post of chaplain to the iron works at the Örtofta mines of which he is advowson. It was to talk this over with you and Charlotte that he came here to-day. Perhaps you'll understand from this that neither Ironmaster Schagerström nor I knew that your engagement had been broken off. You have heard what I had to say, and now you may apologize to us for your base insinuations."

"Far be it from me to doubt the word of my noble uncle," said Karl Arthur, rising. Then, striking an oratorical posture of sorts—arms crossed over chest, back braced against bookcase—he continued:

"In view of Uncle's candour and honesty I now perceive that Charlotte never could have thought of taking Uncle into her confidence in connection with her shady schemes. I must also say that my worthy uncle is right in that I am not a suitable mate for Charlotte. Had she, like my noble uncle, told me so, openly and honestly, whatever my own sufferings, I would have understood, and forgiven her. But Charlotte has chosen to go about it in a different way. Fearful perhaps of losing in esteem in the eyes of others, she at first proudly rejects the Ironmaster (not intending of course to scare him away for good), then makes me break our troth. Knowing the extreme sensitiveness of my nature, she takes advantage of this, and says things that she knows must infuriate me. She attains her object: I break with her. Now she thinks the game in her hand. On me she would lay all the blame. Upon my head she would bring down the wrath of my noble uncle and everyone else. What, I break with her who for my sake has spurned a magnificent offer? What, I break with her who has waited five long years for me? Who could wonder if, after such behaviour on my part, she accepts Ironmaster Schagerström? Could anyone blame her?" He flung out both arms in a grand gesture.

The Dean gave a jerk to his chair and half turned away from Karl Arthur. In the middle of the old man's forehead there were five small wrinkles. During Karl Arthur's tirade, these wrinkles began to redden, and now they were crimson as a fresh wound. That was a sign that the gentle Dean of Korskyrka was highly incensed.

"My fine friend——"

"Pardon, good Uncle, but I have not finished yet. When for the salvation of my soul I was compelled to break with Charlotte, God sent me another woman, a simple, guileless woman of the people. Last evening she and I exchanged vows of eternal fidelity. I have been well rewarded. I am truly happy and do not stand here as one bemoaning his fate. But I see no reason why I should bear the hateful burden of public contempt Charlotte would cast upon me."

Schagerström suddenly looked up. He had become conscious during young Ekenstedt's last remarks, of a change in the atmosphere of the room, and now he saw that Charlotte Löwensköld was standing in the doorway, just behind Karl Arthur.

She had come in so quietly that no one had heard her. Karl Arthur, unaware of her presence, talked on. As he dilated upon her artfulness and treachery, she stood there, sweet as an angel, regarding him with eyes of pure compassion and tender affection. Schagerström many a time had seen just such a look on the face of his own wife; knew what it signified; knew it to be genuine. He did not notice now whether she was pretty. To him, she appeared as one who had passed through a great fire unseared and unblackened, but with all imperfections burned away.—A glorified being. He did not see how young Ekenstedt could help but feel the warmth of her glance and how her love enfolded him. It seemed as if the love she irradiated filled the whole room. Schagerström could feel the power of its rays far back in his corner; and it set his heart beating violently.

The thought of her standing there and hearing all these preposterous aspersions made him writhe. He was about to rise when Charlotte, directing her gaze toward the dusky corner where he sat, descried him. She must have sensed his impatience, for she gave him a faint smile of understanding and put a finger to her lips as if she would have said, "You mustn't betray me." Then she disappeared as silently as she had come. Neither the

Dean nor the Curate knew that she had been in the room. From that moment a terrible fear possessed Schagerström. He had paid little attention to Karl Arthur's ravings, thinking they had to do with a lovers' quarrel that would adjust itself as soon as the fiancé came to his senses; but, after seeing Charlotte, he knew that a veritable tragedy had been enacted at the deanery.

Inasmuch as it was he himself who, by his thoughtlessness, had caused the trouble, he began to cast about in his mind for a way to reconcile the lovers. It meant establishing Charlotte's innocence; which should not be very difficult, he thought.

As lord of a manor and chairman of various boards, he had had considerable practice at reconciling warring wills.

Karl Arthur had just come to the end of his jeremiad when the heavy footstep of an elderly person sounded in the outer room, and in a moment Fru Forsius appeared on the threshold. The instant she caught sight of Schagerström she exclaimed:

"For goodness' sake, are you here again, Ironmaster!" It came out so simply and naturally, before she had time to pull herself up to anything more formal and appropriate.

"Yes," said Schagerström, "but my luck is no better to-day than it was yesterday. Then, I came to proffer Stora Sjötorp, and now I'm here to offer a benefice."

The Dean seemed to take fresh courage when his wife came in. He rose to his feet (the five small wrinkles still glowed fiery red), and practically showed Karl Arthur the door.

"You'd better go to your room and think it over once more. Charlotte, I grant you, has her faults—the usual Löwensköld faults. She is quick-tempered and proud, but crafty or designing or mercenary she has never been. If you were not the son of my esteemed friend Colonel Ekenstedt——"

The Dean's wife interrupted: "Naturally, my husband and I would rather side with Charlotte; but I don't know that we can do so in this instance. There is so much that seems incomprehensible. In the first place, I can't make out why she has said nothing to us about this. Nor do I understand why she seemed so pleased when my husband went to Stora Sjötorp this morning, or why she sent greetings by him to Ironmaster Schagerström, and thanks for his roses, when she knew what Karl Arthur thought of her. But I wouldn't pass censure on her merely for that; there's something else."

"What else?" questioned the Dean irritably.

"Why is she silent?" countered the wife. "At the Name-day party, everyone knew of the broken troth and of Herr Schagerström's suit. Some drew away from her, others were positively hateful; yet she took it all without a protest. Had she dashed her coffee cup in the face of one of those tabby cats, I would have thanked my Lord and Maker; but she sat there, meek as a martyr, and let them be as cruel as ever they would."

"But, surely," said the Dean, "you wouldn't believe her guilty of a thing so despicable simply because she does not defend herself?"

"On our way home," vouchsafed the wife, "I decided to put her to the test. The one who had been the most zealous in her condemnation of Charlotte was the organist's wife, whom the girl never could abide. Well, I took Fru Sundler's arm and let her see me all the way to our gate. Now, I ask you, would Charlotte Löwensköld have been content to let another lead me if her conscience had been clear? I'm merely asking."

The three men were silent.

Finally, the Dean said in a toneless voice: "It doesn't look as if we would get any clear light on this matter now; but Time, no doubt, will show us."

"Pardon, Uncle!" said Karl Arthur, "but for my sake it will have to be cleared now. My actions must appear most unpriestly, most reprehensible, if people do not know it was Charlotte herself who brought about the break."

"We might question *her*," the Dean suggested.

"I require more trustworthy evidence," said Karl Arthur.

"If I may put in an oar," Schagerström now interposed, "I should like to suggest a way to clear this point. The important thing, I believe, is to ascertain whether or not Fröken Löwensköld wilfully tricked her fiancé into breaking with her so that she might accept me. That is the point, is it not?"

Yes, that was it.

"In my judgment," said Schagerström, "it was all a misunderstanding. And now I intend to propose to her again. I am certain that she will give me No."

"But will the Ironmaster take the consequences?" asked Karl Arthur. "What if she says Yes?"

"She will answer No," said Schagerström emphatically. "And since it is plainly my fault that this misunderstanding has arisen between you, Dr. Ekenstedt, and your fiancée, I will gladly do what lies in my power to restore good relations between you."

Karl Arthur smiled mistrustingly. "She will answer Yes, that is, unless she is forewarned in some way as to what is involved."

"I do not intend to ask her in person," said Schagerström. "I propose to write." He went over to the Dean's desk and scribbled these few lines:

Pardon me for troubling you again, Fröken; but having heard from your fiancé that your engagement is broken off, I now wish to renew my proposal of yesterday.

He let Karl Arthur see what he had written, and the young man bowed his head in approval.

"I would request that this be delivered to Fröken Löwensköld by one of the servants," said Schagerström.

The Dean pulled the bell cord, and the housemaid appeared.

"Alma, do you know where Fröken is?"

"Fröken is in her room, your Reverence."

"Then give her this from Ironmaster Schagerström and say that he expects an answer."

When the maid had gone, silence fell upon the room. And now were heard faint droning strains from an old spinet.

"She is right above us," said the Dean's wife. "It is she who is playing."

They were afraid to look at one another; they only listened. Now the maid's step sounded on the stair; now a door opened; the music ceased. "Charlotte is reading the note," they said to themselves.

The Dean's wife sat shaking in every limb. The Dean had folded his hands in prayer. Karl Arthur had flung himself into a rocker. His lips were curled in a cynical smile. Schagerström looked unconcerned, as was his habit when an important business transaction was being concluded.

Now someone with light footstep crossed the floor up there. "Charlotte is just sitting down to her desk," they thought. "What will she write?"

In a few moments light feet went trip-trip toward the door, which thereupon opened and closed. It was the maid who had just come out from Charlotte's room.

Strive as they would to preserve an appearance of calmness, they could not sit still. All four were standing in the outer room when the maid returned and handed Schagerström a note, which he quickly opened and read.

"She has accepted," he said in accents that plainly

betrayed disappointment. Then he read out to the others what Charlotte had written.

If the Ironmaster wants to marry me after all the bad things now being said of me, I cannot do otherwise than accept the offer.

"Allow me to offer my congratulations," said young Ekenstedt in his blandest tone of exasperation.

"But this was merely a test," the Dean's wife declared. "The Ironmaster is in nowise bound by it."

"Why, of course not," confirmed the Dean. "Charlotte herself would be the first . . ."

Schagerström was nonplussed.

Just then they heard the sound of wheels, and all looked out. It was the Ironmaster's travelling coach drawing up before the door.

Schagerström said quite formally: "Will the Herr Dean and the Fru Dean please convey my thanks to Fröken Löwensköld for her answer? A business tour, long planned, compels me to be away for a fortnight. Upon my return, I hope she will allow me to publish the banns and arrange for the wedding."

CHAPTER XI

THE LECTURE

"GINA, my love," said the old Dean to his spouse, "I cannot understand Charlotte. I shall have to ask her to explain."

"Why, of course," his wife promptly concurred. "Perhaps I'd better call her at once."

Schagerström had departed, and Karl Arthur had gone to his wing. The two old people were now alone in the Dean's study. If they wished to hold a little inquisition for Charlotte, the moment was especially opportune.

"The one day she rejects Schagerström, and the next she thankfully accepts him," said the old man. "Have you ever heard tell of such fickle-mindedness! Really, I must say a few admonitory words to her."

"She has never cared what folks said or thought of her," sighed the Dean's wife. "But this has gone beyond all bounds."

The old lady was moving toward the bell cord when the sight of her husband's face made her stop. The five small wrinkles in his forehead still glowed like live coals, while the rest of his face was gray as ashes.

"My dear, I wonder if you're quite prepared to talk to Charlotte now? She is not the easiest person in the

143

world to cope with. Suppose you wait until this afternoon; that would give you time to think out some forceful argument that would strike home."

The Fru Dean devoutly wished her dear lady's-companion to receive a proper wigging; but the husband was utterly exhausted from the long drive and the excitement he had just undergone, and she felt that he must not be subjected now to another unpleasant encounter.

Dinner was announced. This afforded them a good excuse for postponing the bout with Charlotte.

An oppressive silence prevailed throughout the meal. The appetite of the four table companions was no better than their humour. Platters and deep dishes were carried out as full almost as when placed on the table. The four sat at the board merely because it was the proper thing.

When, after the meal, Charlotte and Karl Arthur had gone their separate ways, the Dean's wife insisted upon her husband's taking his customary after-dinner nap. There was no special hurry about that lecture to Charlotte; she was in the house and he could talk to her at any time.

The Dean did not seem to require much coaxing. It would have been better, perhaps, had he taken up the fight at once; for he had no sooner finished his nap than a bridal couple appeared who wanted to be married by the Dean himself. That matter kept him occupied until tea time. Just after tea, the district bailiff dropped in for a game of backgammon, and the two old gentlemen sat rattling their dice till bedtime.

The next morning the Dean looked quite hale and fit. Now, surely, there was nothing to hinder his bringing Charlotte to book.

But, alas! in the middle of the forenoon the wife discovered that her husband had gone to weeding a garden patch where the thistles were getting control. She promptly hurried out to him.

"Yes, yes, I know you think I ought to talk to Charlotte," he said the instant he caught sight of his wife. "Well, I have it in mind all the while. Oh, I'll read her a lecture such as she has never heard in all her life!"

The Dean's wife, with a sigh of relief, went back to her kitchen. She had her hands full just then. It was the middle of July, and there were the spinach to be salted, the peas to be dried, and the raspberries to be boiled down for preserve and syrup.

"Oh, dear!" she said, "he is spinning out a long sermon. But that's the way of preachers; they waste altogether too much eloquence on us poor sinners."

Despite her multifarious duties, she kept a watchful eye on Charlotte, to see that the girl got into no mischief. But this policing was hardly necessary. Early on Monday, before Schagerström appeared at the deanery and caused all this trouble, she had set about cutting carpet rags. She and the Dean's wife had brought down from the attic a lot of old dresses and other useless garments that were only fit for rags, and taken them to the pantry, where all work that made litter, and therefore was not to be performed in any of the fine, dust-free rooms, was done. The whole afternoon of Tuesday and all day Wednesday Charlotte sat there, cutting, cutting. She never stepped outside the door. It was almost as if she had sentenced herself to penal servitude.

"She may as well sit there," thought the Dean's wife, "for she doesn't deserve anything better."

The old lady also kept an eye on her husband. He stuck to his garden patch, and did not send for Charlotte. "Petrus must be preparing a sermon that will last a couple of hours. Charlotte certainly has behaved badly; but now I'm beginning to feel almost sorry for her."

The forenoon passed and nothing had been done in the matter. Then followed, in their usual order, the dinner, the forty winks, tea, the game of backgammon, and bed.

That night, as the old couple lay side by side in their big four-poster, the Dean ventured an excuse for the delay.

"Indeed," said he, "it is not an easy thing, this business of lecturing Charlotte! So many memories crowd in upon one."

"Never mind about the past," said his wife. "I know you're thinking of the time when she and the stable boy rode your horses of nights because she thought they were getting too fat. Put all that out of your head.

Only see that we find out whether Charlotte induced Karl Arthur to break off the engagement. Everything hangs on that. You may as well know that already people have begun to wonder at our allowing Charlotte to remain in our house."

The Dean chuckled as he said: "Aye, Charlotte did me a real service that time when she went riding of nights, and when she wanted me to have the pleasure of seeing that my horses were as good runners as any."

"Ah!" sighed the wife, "we've had a deal to contend with in that girl. But it's all forgiven now, and forgotten."

"Of course, of course," said the Dean. "But there are some things that I cannot forget. Do you remember how it was with us seven years ago, when Charlotte lost both father and mother and we had to take her? Then, Gina, my love, you didn't look as you do now. You were like an old woman of eighty, so feeble you could scarcely drag yourself about. Every day I was afraid I might lose you."

She knew at once to what he referred. The day the Dean's wife turned sixty-five, she decided that she had been a household drudge long enough and would have a housekeeper. And an excellent person she found, too, who relieved her of all responsibility; the woman did not even want her to set foot in her own kitchen. The Dean's wife, meanwhile, was failing rapidly; she felt weak and tired and was strangely depressed and unhappy. She actually thought her time had come.

"Yes," said she, "it's the truth that I felt rather poorly when Charlotte came, although I was leading a lazy life. Charlotte couldn't get on with the housekeeper, and on Saint Lucia Day, at the height of the Christmas rush, what did she do but tweak the housekeeper's nose! The woman, of course, left in a huff, and I, sick as I was, had to go out to the brewhouse and put the dried stockfish to soak in lye. No, that I shall never forget!"

"Nor should you," laughed the Dean. "Gina, my love, you're an old work horse; you perked up as soon as you were back in harness. I can't deny that Charlotte has been rather daring and troublesome; but with that nose-tweak she saved your life."

"And what of yourself?" The old lady did not relish this talk about her being so fond of domestic drudgery that she could not live without it. "You would have been in your grave by this but for Charlotte's falling off the bench in church that Sunday."

The Dean understood. When Charlotte came to live at the deanery, he was performing all the pastoral duties himself and preaching, besides, every Sunday. The wife had nagged and nagged at him to get an assistant. She had seen how he was wearing himself out and how unhappy he was because he could not find time to devote to his beloved science. Charlotte, however, did not nag at him; she simply went to sleep one Sunday during his sermon, and slept so soundly, too, that she rolled off the bench, to the consternation of the whole church. Naturally, the Dean was shocked; but in that moment he knew that he was too old to preach. Then at last he took on a curate; was relieved of a lot of routine work, and got a new lease on life.

"Ah, yes," he said, "by that little ruse, Charlotte has given me quite a number of good years. It's just this that comes between when I want to scold her, and I can't get anywhere with that lecture."

The Dean's wife slyly brushed a tear from the corner of her eye, but made no answer. She felt, however, that this time it would not do to let Charlotte escape a reprimand. After a little, she said:

"That's all very well; but do you mean to say that you are not going to find out whether it was Charlotte who broke the engagement?"

"When one can't see one's way clearly, it is best to stand still and wait," said the old man. "That, I think, is what we must do in this case, you and I."

"But you can't stand for Schagerström's marrying Charlotte, if she's the sort people say she is."

"If Schagerström should come and question me, I know what I'd say to him."

"Now, what would you say?"

"I'd say to him that, if I were fifty years younger and unmarried——"

"What!" shrieked the wife, and sat bolt upright.

"Yes," said the Dean, unabashed, "I'd tell him that were I fifty years younger, and single, and I met a girl like Charlotte, so chock full of life and with a certain something about her that's different—I'd propose to her myself."

"Yi, yi! You and Charlotte!—Ha! but you'd have a merry time." With arms waving and face working, the old lady threw herself back on her pillow and laughed.

The Dean regarded her with slight indignation, but she went on laughing. Soon he was laughing, too. They laughed till the tears ran down their faces; it was long past midnight before they finally cuddled down to sleep.

CHAPTER XII

SHORN LOCKS

LATE in the evening of Thursday, Baroness Ekenstedt came to the deanery. She ordered her
coachman to pull up at the door, but did not
step out of the carriage. She bade the housemaid, who
had hastened out to assist her, ask her mistress to please
step to the porch; she merely wished to have a word
with her.

Fru Forsius immediately appeared, curtseying and
smiling a smile that went from ear to ear. This was indeed a pleasant surprise! Would not her dear Beata
come in and rest after her long, tiresome journey?

Oh, there was nothing the Baroness desired more,
but first she must know whether that dreadful person
was still in the house.

The Dean's wife appeared not to understand. "Do
you mean that poor cook we had last time you were
here? She left long ago. Now you shall have some *real*
food."

But the Baroness kept to her carriage. "Don't pretend
ignorance, Gina! You know well enough that I mean
that wicked baggage Karl Arthur has been engaged
to. I wish to know whether she is still in your house."

This the Dean's wife could not ignore. Whatever she may have thought of Charlotte deep down in her heart, she was ready to defend any member of her household against all the rest of the world.

"Pardon me, Beata," she said, "but one who for seven years has been as a daughter to Petrus and me, we do not throw to the wolves. For that matter, nobody knows what is at the bottom of it all."

"I have a letter from my son, a letter from Thea Sundler, and one from herself," said the Baroness. "To me, at least, it is all quite clear."

"If you have a letter from the girl herself that shows her to be at fault, then, by Gad, you shall not go from here until I've seen it!" The old lady was so astonished and excited that she actually swore. Now she advanced toward the stubborn little Baroness, who quickly shrank back under cover; for it looked as if the old lady meant to lift her bodily out of the vehicle.

"Drive on!" the Baroness shouted to the coachman. "For pity's sake, drive on!"

Just then Karl Arthur emerged from the wing; he had heard his mother's voice, and came running toward the main building.

It was a most affectionate meeting. The Baroness flung her arms about her son and kissed him violently, as if he had just rescued her from the peril of sudden death.

"But, Mother, aren't you going to step out?" said Karl Arthur, to whom this osculatory demonstration before the coachman and the groom was a trifle embarrassing.

"No!" declared the Baroness. "I cannot sleep under the same roof with the person who has so shamefully deceived you. Get in with me, and we'll drive to the inn."

"Now, don't be childish, Beata!" said the Dean's wife, who by this time had regained her composure. "If you will stop, I promise that you'll not see a sign of Charlotte."

"Still, I should feel that she was in the house."

"People have quite enough to chatter about already. Shall they also have this to spread abroad—that you would not stop with us?"

"Of course you'll stop here, Mother," Karl Arthur decided. "I see Charlotte every day, and it doesn't affect me in the least."

With this reassurance from her son, the Baroness looked about as if seeking a way out. Suddenly she pointed to the wing where the son had his quarters.

"May I stop down there with you, Karl Arthur? If I knew you were in the next room, perhaps I wouldn't be thinking of that terrible creature." Turning to the Dean's wife, she said: "My dear Regina, if you really wish me to stay, then put me in the wing. You needn't go to any trouble; a bed, just a bed, is all I require."

"I can't see why you wouldn't as soon occupy the guest room, as usual," grumbled the Fru Dean. "But anything rather than have you go." She felt quite put out. As the carriage rolled toward the wing, she muttered something to the effect that that Beata Ekenstedt, with all her fine airs, was no lady. Returning to the dining room, she saw Charlotte standing by the open window. The girl must have overheard it all.

"You heard, I suppose, that she does not wish to see you; that she won't sleep under the same roof with you?"

Charlotte, who had not been so happy in a long while as when she witnessed the affectionate meeting between mother and son, stood there pleased and smiling. She knew now that her sacrifice had not been in vain. She said with the utmost calmness: "I must keep out of her way, then," and left the room.

The Dean's wife, fairly choking with ire, rushed into her husband's study. "What do you think of this?" said she. "Karl Arthur and the organist's wife must be right, after all. She hears that Beata Ekenstedt won't sleep under the same roof with her, yet she smiles and looks as pleased as if she had just been crowned Queen of Spain."

"Now, now, my love!" soothed the Dean. "Rest easy a little longer! Forgiveness looms on the horizon. I'm sure the Baroness will help us out of our trouble."

The old lady was afraid her dear Petrus, who hitherto, by the grace of God, had retained his mental powers, was beginning to pass into his second childhood. That harebrained Beata Ekenstedt, how would she be able to help them?

The Dean's words had only made her the more dejected. She went out to the kitchen and ordered the maid to make up a bed in the wing for the Baroness, and sent her a supper tray; whereupon she went to her room.

"She'd better have her meals down there," thought the old lady, "where she can sit and baby her son to her heart's content. I thought she had come to give him a good dressing down for his new troth, but she only pets and humours him the more. If she thinks she'll have any joy of him by such indulgence . . ."

In the morning, both mother and son appeared at the breakfast table. Her ladyship was in excellent humour, and conversed with her hosts in a delightfully amiable way. But the Dean's wife, now seeing the Baroness in the full light of day, thought her faded and wraith-like. Though Fru Forsius was the older by many years, she looked hale and hardy by comparison.

"Poor soul! She is not so happy as she pretends to be."

When they had breakfasted, the Baroness sent Karl Arthur to the village to fetch Fru Sundler, with whom she wished to speak. The Dean went to his study, and the ladies were left to themselves. The Baroness immediately began to speak of her son.

"Ah! my dear Gina, I can't tell you how happy I am! I came away from home directly I received Karl Arthur's letter. I expected to find him in the depths of despair, and perhaps contemplating suicide, but I find him quite content and supremely happy. Wonderful, isn't it, after such a shock?"

"Aye, he quickly consoled himself," rejoined the Dean's wife drily.

"Yes, I know. . . that Dalar girl. . . . a passing fancy, nothing more, a lozenge one puts into one's mouth to take away a bad taste. How would a man of Karl Arthur's habits be able to endure a person of that sort for long?"

"I have seen her," said the Dean's wife, "and I can tell you, Beata, that she's a perfectly gorgeous female."

The Baroness blanched, but only for a second, whereupon she said: "The Colonel and I have decided to treat the matter as a bagatelle. We shall not refuse our consent. The poor boy has been so cruelly betrayed. Naturally, he was wild with grief. If we don't drive him on by opposition, he will soon forget that little plaything."

The Dean's wife for once had taken to knitting with a frenzy that set the needles rattling. It was the only way in which she could maintain her equanimity while listening to all this foolishness. "My dear friend Beata," she said in her mind, "aren't you supposed to be an intelligent and gifted person? Yet you fail to see that this is all wrong." Her nostrils dilated, the wrinkles round her eyes quivered, but she controlled her desire to laugh. Now she felt very sorry for the Baroness. Aloud she said: "Yes, children are like that nowadays; they can't tolerate any opposition from their parents."

"We have made mistakes before in respect to Karl Arthur," the Baroness confessed. "We were against his entering the ministry. It was futile, and only estranged him from us. We intend to take no stand against his engagement to the Dalar woman. You see, we don't want to lose him altogether."

The Dean's wife raised her eyebrows so that they nearly touched the edge of her hair. "Well, I must say, it is very sweet of you."

The Baroness then vouchsafed that she wished to consult with Thea Sundler on this matter, that was why she had sent for her. Thea seemed to be a sensible woman and very devoted to Karl Arthur.

The Dean's wife could hardly contain herself. The organist's wife, that poor, insignificant thing, and the Baroness Ekenstedt, a lady of quality, despite her eccentricities! She herself did not dare to reason with her son; that another must do—the organist's wife!

"Such little niceties no one bothered about when I was young," she said.

"After the break, Thea Sundler wrote me such a nice, comforting letter," said the Baroness.

At the mention of the word "letter" the Dean's wife jumped to her feet and struck her brow with the flat of her hand. "Oh, that reminds me! Would you care to tell me what Charlotte wrote concerning this unfortunate affair?"

"You may read her letter, I have it here in the reticule." The Baroness handed the Dean's wife a folded note which contained the one short line: "May my gracious mother-in-law think not too ill of me."

The old lady looked blank as she returned the scrap of a letter. "This leaves me no wiser than I was before," she said.

"To me it is perfectly clear," the Baroness rejoined conclusively.

It suddenly struck the Fru Dean that her guest had been speaking all the while in a singularly loud voice. This was not at all like her. But perhaps it was because she was all unstrung, and off her guard. At the same time it flashed upon her that, if Charlotte was still at her rag-cutting out in the pantry, she must have heard every word. That shutter in the wall through which the food was passed into the dining room was far from soundproof. The old lady had often complained that the slightest noise in the pantry could be heard in the dining room.

"What does Charlotte herself say?" asked the Baroness.

"Nothing. The Dean had thought to call her to account, but now he says it isn't necessary. I know nothing."

"Extraordinary!" exclaimed the Baroness. . . . "Most extraordinary!"

The Dean's wife then proposed that they go upstairs. How very neglectful of her not to have thought of it before! Such a distinguished guest should not be sitting in the dining room like folk that drop in every day.

But on no condition would the Baroness be shut up in any of the rooms above stairs; which, to tell the truth, were not nearly so pleasant as those in daily use. She went right on talking about Charlotte in the same loud voice. What was she doing now, and where was she pursuing her work? Did she seem to be pleased at the prospect of marrying Schagerström?

Of a sudden, the old lady in a tearful voice sobbed out: "I have loved her dearly! I would have expected anything but this of her! . . . Anything but this!"

A pair of shears went crashing on to the floor of the pantry. "Now, surely, she can't sit there listening to this any longer," thought the Dean's wife. "She'll come rushing in to defend herself." Charlotte, however, did not appear.

The painful situation was finally relieved by Karl Arthur's return from the village with Thea Sundler. The Baroness, her son, and Fru Sundler immediately repaired to the garden, while the Dean's wife went into the kitchen to grind coffee, crush sugar, and lay a tray; all of which might have been left to the maid; but she felt that it would rest her nerves.

She pondered, meanwhile, over the scrap of a note Charlotte had sent to Karl Arthur's mother. Why had she made it so brief? She remembered the girl's coming to breakfast one morning with inkstained fingers. Would she have daubed herself like that just scribbling the one line? She must have written another letter. And it was on Tuesday, the day after the Ironmaster had first proposed. Here was something she must ferret out. She sent the maid to lay the table in the lilac bower.

They were to have eleven o'clock coffee that day, in honour of the grand guest.

"Charlotte must have written a long letter," thought the old Fru. What had she done with it? Had she sent it or torn it up?

She was preoccupied with these speculations during the coffee hour and, contrary to her usual habit, she was silent. Fru Sundler, on the other hand, chattered incessantly. She reminded the Fru Dean of the inflated toad in the fable, so proud and important had she become, because these aristocrats sought advice from her. Heretofore, the old lady had thought her merely a harmless fool, but now she felt that there was something malicious about her. "She arches her neck and gloats while the rest of us are troubled and unhappy."

But, of course, she poured her not only a first, but a second cup of coffee, and pressed upon her her choicest cakes. The rules of hospitality must be observed though it be one's worst enemy that is within one's gates. After coffee, the Dean's wife went back to the kitchen. The Baroness was leaving at two o'clock and, before that, she must have dinner. The hostess wished to supervise its preparation herself.

At one o'clock, Fru Sundler came into the kitchen to say good-bye. The others were still in the arbour, she said, but she must go home and prepare dinner for her husband.

The Fru Dean, who stood bending over the soup kettle, now put down the skimming ladle and accompanied her to the outer hall. She curtseyed, asked to be remembered to the organist, and excused herself.

Thea Sundler, she thought, should have seen that she was busy; but there she stood for what seemed an eternity, holding her hostess's hand and saying how sorry she was for the poor Baroness on account of this new betrothal.

In that the Dean's wife accorded with her. Fru Sundler, pressing her hand hard, declared she could not go without asking how Charlotte was.

"She's right inside cutting rags," said the old lady. "You go ask her yourself!"

They were standing just outside the pantry. With sudden determination, the old Fru opened the door and pushed Thea Sundler across the threshold.

She thought: "It was this she wished. Charlotte has been stand-offish toward her, and she wants to see her now, humbled to the dust. The toad! I hope Charlotte gives her the reception she deserves. Ha, ha! I'd like to witness the greeting." She stole softly toward a door that led to the dining room, opened it gently, and, in a twinkling, she was over by the pantry wicket. By raising the slide a trifle, she had a good view of the small room where Charlotte sat, surrounded by piles of old dresses, some of which belonged to Fru Forsius; others had been left by the deanery ladies of former days. They had been sorted and cut according to colour—the greens by themselves, the blues by themselves, also those in figures and checks. On the floor lay mounds of narrow strips, and in a box were large balls of strips, already sewed together. Obviously, the girl had not been idling.

Charlotte was so seated that her back was turned to Thea Sundler, who stood down by the door as if hesitating.

"So she has got no farther," observed the Dean's wife from her point of vantage. "This is a good portent. She's going to have a pleasant moment!"

Fru Sundler put on a mien of condolence and, at the same time, encouragement, and said in the commiserating tone one employs when speaking to invalids, or convicts, or paupers:

"Good-day, Charlotte!"

The girl made no response. She sat with shears in hand, but had ceased cutting.

A faint sneer crossed the face of Fru Sundler baring for a second her pointed teeth. (That was enough for the Dean's wife to see what she was.) In an instant, she was all sweetness and sympathy again. She took a step forward, then said with benign forbearance, as if addressing an ignorant servant or a refractory child:

"Good-day, Charlotte!"

But Charlotte never moved.

Thea Sundler now bent over her to have a look at her face. Perhaps she thought Charlotte was weeping because Karl Arthur's mother would not see her. It happened that a couple of Fru Sundler's curls brushed

Charlotte's bare shoulder, from which the wimple had slipped down while she was working.

The moment those locks touched her shoulder Charlotte came alive. Like a hawk after a hen, she seized hold of a bunch of the nicely dressed curls, raised the shears and snipped.

It was no premeditated act. The moment it was done Charlotte rose to her feet, rather aghast at what had occurred. The other sent up a shriek of horror and rage. This was the worst that could have befallen her. The curls were her pride; her sole claim to beauty. She could never appear anywhere until she had grown new curls. Now followed a succession of frenetic howls.

In the kitchen, adjoining, there was a deafening noise of crackling firewood, pounding mortar pestles, and boiling pots, which deadened her cries. The Baroness and her son could not have heard her from the garden. No one came to her aid.

"Well, what business had you in here?" said Charlotte. "I am silent for Karl Arthur's sake. Do you think me such a fool as not to understand that it was you who created all the mischief?" With that she stepped to the door and flung it open. "Now go!" She made a clip at the air with her shears, which was enough for Thea Sundler to take to her heels.

The Dean's wife cautiously closed the wicket, then clasped her hands and chortled: "Lord, Lord, that I should have been permitted to see this! Now my old man will have something to laugh at."

Then, all at once, she became very serious. "The precious child!" she cooed. "There she has sat for days and allowed us to think evil of her! Now this must end."

A moment later, the Fru Dean quietly stole upstairs. Noiselessly as a thief she entered Charlotte's room and went straight over to the porcelain stove. There she found some torn and crumpled sheets of notepaper.

"Dear Lord, forgive me for this!" she said. "Thou knowest it is the first time in my life I have read another person's letter without leave." She took the closely written pages to her own room, hunted up her spectacles, and went to reading.

"Aye, aye," said she, "this is the real letter. It was just as I thought."

Document in hand, she went downstairs thinking to lay it before the Baroness; but coming out she saw her guest sitting with her son on a bench outside the wing. How tenderly she leant toward him. With what love, what adoration she looked up at him!

The Fru Dean paused. "Never in the world could I read this to her!" she thought, then turned and went inside, to her husband's room.

"Here's some pleasant reading for you, old boy," she said, spreading the letter before the Dean. "I found this in Charlotte's stove. It was thrown in to be burned, but the blessed child forgot to set fire to it. Read! It will do your old heart good."

The Dean noted that she looked quite a different woman from what she had been during these last distressing days. She probably felt that there would be no harm in his reading the letter also.

"This is how it was, of course," he remarked when he had read to the end. "But why was the letter not sent?"

"The Lord only knows!" sighed the wife. "I brought it down to show to Beata. But do you know, when I stepped out on the porch and saw how she sat gazing at her son with that worshipping look in her eyes, it seemed best to let you see the letter first."

The Dean arose, stepped to the window, and looked out at the Baroness.

"So it was," he said, and nodded approvingly. "You see, Gina, my love, Charlotte could not send this to such a mother. That was why she cast it into the stove. She would not justify herself. Nor must we do anything in the matter."

The old couple sighed heavily; for now there seemed to be no immediate possibility of their establishing Charlotte's innocence in the eyes of the world. But, all the same, they felt wonderfully relieved. When they met their guest at dinner, they were in the best of spirits.

Singularly enough, the Baroness, too, must have undergone a similar change. Her gaiety was not forced, as it had been at breakfast. She looked positively rejuvenated.

The Dean's wife wondered if Thea Sundler had wrought this change in her. And she had, though not precisely in the way the old lady supposed.

The Baroness and Karl Arthur were sitting on the

bench outside the wing when Fru Sundler came dashing out of the house, fleeing like a dove that has been in the talons of a hawk.

"What is the matter with your friend Thea?" the Baroness had asked her son. "Look! She is running and holding a hand to her cheek. For mercy's sake, Karl Arthur; run and intercept her at the gate! Perhaps she has been stung by a swarm of bees. Ask her if there is anything we can do for her."

Karl Arthur had hastened to do his mother's bidding. Though Fru Sundler had motioned to him frantically not to come near her, he had caught up with her at the gate. When he went back to his mother he was highly indignant. "Charlotte has been at it again," he said. "She is utterly ruthless. Fancy! When Fru Sundler went in to ask her how she was, Charlotte seized her by the hair and cut off the curls at one side of her face."

Whereupon, the Baroness had said with an impish smile: "What are you telling me?—Fru Sundler's lovely locks? Dear me, she must look a fright!"

"It was revenge, Mother," Karl Arthur declared. "Fru Sundler knows what Charlotte is; it was she who opened my eyes."

"I understand," the Baroness said. She sat quietly thinking for a moment, then turned to her son. "Let us not discuss Thea or Charlotte, Karl Arthur. We have only a few minutes left before my departure; so let us speak of you and your plans for the betterment of poor humanity."

Later, at the dinner table, the Baroness, as has been said, was her usual merry, entertaining self. She and the Dean's wife matched wits, they kept up a steady fire of quips and sallies and exchanged amusing anecdotes. Now and then, the Baroness would cast a glance toward the wicket in the wall. She wondered, perhaps, how Charlotte endured her solitude; whether the young girl who had lavished upon her an almost worshipful affection longed for her.

After dinner, when the travelling carriage was already at the door, it happened that the Baroness was alone in the dining room. In a second, she was over by the wicket, pushing it open. And there before her stood Charlotte; Charlotte, who all day had been sick with longing for just a glance from her eyes. Quick as a flash the Baroness caught the sweet face between her two soft hands, drew the girl to her and kissed her impulsively, whispering between kisses a few detached sentences.

"My precious child! Can you stand it to keep silence a few days, a few weeks more? It will all come right. Have I tortured you dreadfully? But I didn't know where I had you till you cut that woman's locks. The Colonel and I will manage this affair. Can you hold out awhile longer, for my sake and Karl Arthur's?"

There was a pull at the door, the slide went shut in a second. Shortly afterward, the Baroness was seated in her carriage.

CHAPTER XIII

A CHILD OF DESTINY

RICH Schagerström maintained that he would have been nothing but a lout and a rapscallion, except for a strange sort of luck that attended him throughout the early years of his life.

He, the son of wealthy and socially prominent parents, might have been reared in the lap of luxury and ease, as were his brothers and sisters; he might have slept every night in a soft bed; have worn fine clothes and fared sumptuously. But all that would have been fatal to one constituted as he was. Nobody understood this better than he, himself.

But, then, it had been his good fortune to be an ugly and awkward boy. His parents—the mother in particular—never could abide him. They could not imagine where they had got this child with the big head, the short neck, and the thickset body. They, themselves, were a stately, handsome couple, and their other children were perfect little cherubs. This Gustaf seemed to them a veritable changeling; and as such he was also treated.

To be the ugly duckling in a family of swans was no fun, and Schagerström readily conceded that many a time he had felt his position keenly; though in after years he regarded it as a blessing. If he, like the other children, had been coddled by a fond mother and told every day that he was a little angel, and had always had money in his pocket, it would have been his destruction. To be sure, his brothers and sisters grew up to be charming and estimable men and women. They, perhaps, had more character than he to start with, and were therefore better able to stand happiness; which in his case would have been harmful.

That he had been poor in Latin and backward in all his classes he counted as a special grace from the goddess Fortuna. Not at the time, perhaps, but afterward, since it had caused his father to take him out of school and apprentice him to an iron manufacturer in Värmland.

Here again Fortuna stepped in and so ordered it that he fell into the hands of a hard and parsimonious taskmaster who could give him the training he needed. Indeed, with him he had no downy bed to rest on; if there were a thin straw mattress over the hard plank bed bottom, it did well enough. With him he had to learn to eat porridge though burnt, and salt herring even when stale. With him he had to work from morning to night without compensation but with the positive assurance that a rap or two of the master's cane awaited him for the slightest negligence. Nor was all this pleasant while it lasted. But rich Schagerström could never be thankful enough to the Fates that taught him to sleep on straw and subsist on poorman's fare.

When he had served his years of apprenticeship, he was sent to a foundry estate near Filipstad known as Kronbäcken, where he became a clerk. Here he found a just and kindly employer. Here he ate at the family table, had good and bountiful fare, and received a small remuneration, enough to keep himself decently clothed.

He was now both pleasantly and comfortably situated. This might not have been well for him in the long run; but there was small chance of his being spoiled, for his old luck was still with him. Before he had been a month at Kronbäcken, he had fallen in love with a young girl, the foster daughter of his employer, Ironmaster Fröberg. That was indeed the worst that could have happened. The girl was not only ravishingly beautiful, talented, and popular, but she was also the heiress to foundries and mines valued at many millions of kronor. It would have been presumptuous in any foundry clerk to raise his eyes to her—especially in one who was ugly and taciturn; the "changeling" who never received a penny from home but had to shift for himself. Schagerström perceived from the first that the only thing for him was to keep well in the shadow, lest someone should see that he was in love. It was for him to sit still and look on when scores of young subalterns and young collegians came to Kronbäcken during the Christmas and summer holidays, to pay court to *her*. It was for him to clinch his teeth and control his fists when the others boasted that they had danced with her so and so many times in one evening; that they had received so and so many cotillion favours from her, and so and so many friendly glances and smiles.

He had small joy of his good position with this unfortunate love to worry him. It pursued him at his work on weekdays and at the hunts on Sundays. The only times he was at all free from the torments of love were when he sat reading about mines and the mining industry in a bulky tome he had found on the office shelf, which probably no one else would have thought to dip into.

Ah, well—long afterward he understood that this unhappy love had also been a discipline; though one to which he never became resigned: it had been too heavy to bear.

The young girl whom he worshipped was neither friendly to him, nor unfriendly. Since he did not dance and made no attempt to approach her, she had no occasion to speak to him.

But one summer evening, when there was a dance in the grand ballroom, Schagerström, as usual, stood down by the door following the loved one with his eyes. Never would he forget how astonished he was when, in an interval between dances, she came over to him, and said:

"Herr Schagerström, I think you ought to retire. It is now twelve o'clock, and you have to go to work at four. The rest of us can lie abed till noon if we like."

He promptly betook himself down to the office; for he understood that she was sick of seeing him hang round the door. She had looked pleasant, and spoken in a kindly tone; but to interpret that as a sign of good-will toward him and a feeling of pity that he should be tiring himself out needlessly, would not have occurred to him.

Another time, they were out on a fishing trip, she and a couple of the usual gallants, and he, Schagerström, sat at the oars. It was a hot day, and the boat was heavy pulling; but he felt happy because she was sitting in the stern, just opposite him, and he could gaze at her all the while.

Upon their return, as he helped her out of the boat, she thanked him kindly for the row; then she added, as if thinking that he might misconstrue her politeness:

"I can't understand, Herr Schagerström, why you do not go through the School of Mines at Falun. A man who is the son of a Chancellor surely cannot be satisfied to be only a foundry clerk?"

Naturally, she had noted how, during the row, he had devoured her with his eyes. She knew that he loved her, and wished of course to be rid of him. He never for a moment dreamed that she was interested in his future; that she had learned from her guardian that he would make an excellent mining engineer if he only had the proper schooling, aye, and that she had also thought of a way to remove the social barrier between him and her—between the foundry clerk and the foundry owner's daughter.

However, since she wished it, he wrote to his parents for financial assistance to enable him to study at the

School of Mines, and actually received what he had asked for. It would have been pleasanter, perhaps, to accept the money had his father not written that he hoped his son would do better than he had done at the Klara High School in Stockholm, or if he had not conveyed so plainly that the parents thought he would never be anything but a clerk, were he to go through fifteen schools. But later he understood that such things only showed that Old Fortuna was working all the while to make a man of him.

It must be said that he did well at the School of Mines, that he took to his studies almost voraciously. His instructors were pleased with his progress, and he would have felt perfectly satisfied with his world but for the fact that every moment when he was not absorbed in study he was thinking of her down there in Värmland, and those who swarmed about her.

When at last he had finished the two years' course (with honours to his credit, be it said), her guardian wrote and offered him the position of superintendent at Gammalhyttan, her largest and most beautiful foundry estate. It was an excellent position, better than a man of three-and-twenty could have expected. And Schagerström would have been overjoyed had he not known that she was back of the offer. He never supposed, of course, that she had faith in him, and wanted to give him an opportunity to distinguish himself. To him, it simply meant that she wished, in some nice way, to prevent his returning to Kronbäcken. She was not unkindly disposed toward him, for she stood ready and willing to help; only she could not stand his being anywhere near her, he thought.

He would have bowed to her will, and not shown his face to her again; but, before taking up his new duties, he was obliged to go to Kronbäcken for his instructions. When he appeared, Ironmaster Fröberg bade him go over to the house, where the ladies were, as his ward, too, had some instructions for him.

When he entered the small reception room where the ladies were wont to sit at their needlework, *she* immediately came toward him with outstretched hands, as if greeting a person for whom she had been fervently longing. He saw to his dismay that she was quite alone. It was the first time he and she had met when no one else was present.

That in itself made his heart beat violently; worse still, she said to him in her pleasant, forthright way, that at Gammalhyttan, where he was to be superintendent, there was a large, fine manor house, and that now, at any time, he could think of marrying.

He was too hurt to reply. So she was not satisfied with turning him away from Kronbäcken, but must also have him married. Ah! he did not deserve this; he had never been obtrusive.

She continued in the same straightforward way: "Gammalhyttan is the most desirable of my foundry estates. I have always thought I should like to live there when I marry."

That declaration would have been plain enough to anyone else; but Schagerström, who from early childhood had been under stern masters, turned to go. Before he could get to the door she was there, her hand on the latch.

"I have rejected many suitors in my day," she said; "so perhaps it is only fair that I should be rejected when I myself propose."

He brought his hand down hard on hers in order to pull the door open. "Don't trifle with me!" he said. "On my part it is serious."

"And so it is on mine," she answered, and looked him deep in the eyes.

In that moment Schagerström realized how well Old Fortuna had meant by him. All the loneliness, all the cruelty, all the privations which Life had hitherto brought him had been only that this divine happiness might enter his heart and find room there to spread so that It, and It alone, would be found there.

CHAPTER XIV

THE FORTUNE

WHEN Schagerström, in the third year of their happy union, lost his beloved wife, it was found that she had left a will to the effect that all her possessions, in case she died childless and before the husband, were to go to him. When the will had been probated and certain bequests to aged servitors and distant relatives had been paid, the administrators turned over to Schagerström his vast fortune.

That matter settled, there was a sigh of relief on all the Schagerström foundry estates. Everyone was glad that the property would not pass into strange hands. It seemed like an act of Providence that the numerous works were to be under the control of a capable foundry man.

But shortly after Schagerström had come into his inheritance, foundry directors, managers, supervisors, tenants, gamekeepers—in a word, all who had to do with the care of his estates—began to fear that the new régime would be anything but a blessing. Schagerström continued to reside at Stockholm, which was bad enough though it would not have mattered so very much had he only replied to letters. There was pig iron to be purchased, bar iron to be sold. There were contracts to be renewed for deliveries of coal and wood; vacancies to be filled; buildings in need of repairs, and accounts to be settled. But from Schagerström came neither instructions nor funds. Sometimes he would send a line to say that the communication had been received and instructions would follow; but they never did.

In just a few weeks' time, things were in a muddle. Some of the foundry managers sat idle; others undertook to act on their own responsibility, which was worse. Everyone now thought that Schagerström was not the proper person to handle this great wealth.

None was more displeased than Ironmaster Fröberg of Kronbäcken. Schagerström had been his protégé, and he had expected great things of him. Deep as had been his grief over the death of the happy, radiant young girl who had grown up in his home, it had been a comfort to him that her estates, which he had so long administered—these productive mines, these driving falls, . these beautiful manors, these vast woodlands, these wealth-producing smithies and smelting houses—had come into good hands.

He knew that Schagerström was well qualified to take up his responsibilities as owner of a large property. On the advice of the guardian, Schagerström and his wife had spent the first year of their union in foreign travel. From their letters to him, the old man gathered that they had not wasted the time running about to art galleries or visiting old monuments. These two sensible beings had studied mining in Germany, manufacturing in England, cattle breeding in Holland. They had been untiring in their quest for knowledge. Schagerström had sometimes lamented their having to pass by the most glorious places without stopping to view them. "We think only of acquiring useful knowledge," he had written. "It's Disa who is the driving force; I, poor wretch, would like to live for love alone."

The last two years they had resided in Stockholm, where they had purchased a fine mansion and entertained lavishly. This, too, had been done at the suggestion of the guardian. Schagerström was now a *matador*, so to speak, and associated with the highest in the land. He had acquired ease of manner, made the acquaintance of influential persons, and gained the confidence of those in power.

Naturally, the Squire of Kronbäcken, though having nothing more to do with Schagerström's affairs, felt aggrieved. It was imperative that he should talk with Schagerström, learn what was wrong with him, and persuade him to knuckle down to business.

One fine day, he summoned a clerk, a young man who had come to Kronbäcken at about the same time as Schagerström, and who had been his good friend and comrade.

"Look here, Nyman!" he said to the clerk. "There must be something the matter with Schagerström. You're to leave for Stockholm at once, to fetch him here. You may take my travelling coach. If you come back without him, I'll discharge you."

Bookkeeper Nyman stood shaking in his boots. He did not wish to lose his good position. He was a clever fellow, though rather lazy; but he had managed to make himself indispensable to the ladies at Kronbäcken, by which means he had been relieved almost entirely from office duty. He played whist with the old Fru, read aloud to the young Mamselles, traced patterns for them, accompanied them on their riding tours, and was their faithful and obedient cavalier. "Obliging" Nyman—an appellative the ladies had bestowed on him —had to be present on all occasions when there was a question of diversion. Indeed, he was quite content with his lot, and had no desire to change it.

Nyman set off in all haste for Stockholm to save both himself and Schagerström. He travelled day and night, and in the early morning of the third day he arrived at the capital. He put up at a tavern, ordered fresh horses for the return journey, ate a hurried break-fast, then went straight to Schagerström's house.

He was informed by the lackey who answered his ring that Herr Schagerström was out. He gave his name and bade the servant tell his master that he, Nyman, had been sent here by Ironmaster Fröberg on a matter of importance and would call again in an hour.

And within an hour he reappeared, having come this time in the Fröberg carriage, with fresh horses and a well-stocked food bag—all ready for the journey to Värmland.

But, as he stepped into the vestibule, the lackey gave

him greetings from Herr Schagerström, who, he said, would not be at home until later in the day. There was a conference keeping him.

The man's tone sounded forced, and he seemed embarrassed. Nyman began to suspect that the fellow was lying, and asked him where the conference was being held.

"The gentlemen," said the lackey, "are assembled in the grand salon."

Nyman now saw a long row of hats and overcoats hanging in the vestibule, so he removed his own hat and caped coat and handed them to the lackey.

"There must be some place here where I can sit and wait," he said. "I don't care to tramp the streets. I've been driving all night in order to get here in time."

It looked as if the servant were not going to admit him; but Herr Nyman insisted, and was presently ushered into a small anteroom just outside the salon.

In a moment, a couple of men passed through the room preceded by the lackey, who opened the door to the salon for them. Bookkeeper Nyman took advantage of his opportunity to peep into the conference hall. He saw quite a number of elderly gentlemen seated round a large table, covered with documents, which he noticed were written on stamped paper.

"What's all this?" he wondered. "Those papers look like contracts and title deeds. Schagerström must be engaged in some big transaction."

It suddenly struck him that he had not seen Schagerström himself at the conference table. If Schagerström took no part in the meeting, what was there to hinder his seeing him, Nyman?

A young man who was to attend the conference came into the anteroom. He was a secretary to the king whom the foundry clerk had met at Kronbäcken in the days when the secretary, like so many others, came a-courting. He rushed forward to speak to him.

"Well, well," said the secretary, if it isn't Obliging —I mean Bookkeeper Nyman! Glad to see you here in Stockholm. All's well at Kronbäcken, I hope."

"Will the Herr Secretary please see that I get a word with Schagerström? I have come all the way from Värmland on urgent business."

The man glanced at the clock. "I'm afraid Herr Nyman will have to exercise patience for a few hours, until the conference is over."

"What in the world is he doing?"

"I don't think I am at liberty to speak of it—yet."

The bookkeeper thought of his pleasant position at Kronbäcken as all-in-all to the Madam and the daughters, and ventured a bold guess. "I know, of course, that Schagerström intends to dispose of his property."

"Ah! then you have already got wind of it at the foundries."

"Yes, that much we know, though we have not yet heard who the purchasers are."

"Purchasers!" exclaimed the secretary. "There's no talk of purchase and sale. The whole fortune is going to charitable organizations: the Freemasons' Orphanage, widows' pension funds, and other causes of the same sort. But, good-bye for the present. It's I who must draw up the donation letters, when the gentlemen inside have agreed upon the terms."

The foundry clerk swallowed and swallowed like a fish cast upon the shore. If he came home with such tidings, old man Fröberg would be furious, and he, Nyman, would be turned out of his desirable place instantly. He must hit upon something—but what?

As the secretary was disappearing through the open door, Herr Nyman caught him by the arm and said: "Please tell Schagerström that I must speak with him. Tell him it's important! Tell him that Gammalhyttan is burned down!"

"Why, certainly. Oh, what a misfortune!"

In a moment there appeared in the doorway a pale, emaciated man with bloodshot eyes. Turning to the foundry clerk, he said curtly: "What do you wish?"

Nyman again stood swallowing. He was speechless. So this was Schagerström! Though the Ironmaster was never a stately or handsome man, there had been something indescribably good about him in the days when he went about at Kronbäcken, filled with his love longings. But now his old comrade was almost afraid of him.

"You said something about a fire?" Schagerström continued. "Has Gammalhyttan been destroyed?"

The clerk, who had resorted to the white lie simply

to catch the ear of Schagerström, thought it best not to show his hand for awhile.

"Yes," said he, "there has been a fire at Gammal-hyttan."

"What has burned?—the manor?"

The foundry clerk scrutinized Schagerström, whose eyes had a glassy stare and whose hair had begun to whiten at the temples.

"It isn't enough with the manor house," he thought. "A rousing shock is needed here."

"It's worse than that," he told Schagerström.

"The smithy?"

"Nor that either, but the big, wretched building where you had twenty families housed. Two women were burned to death and a hundred persons are without a roof over their heads. Those who were rescued haven't a rag to their backs or shoes to their feet. The distress down there is said to be appalling. I haven't seen it myself; I was sent to fetch you."

"The manager has not advised me of this," said Schagerström.

"It's useless writing to you. Börjesson appealed to Fröberg for aid, but the old man thought it was too much for him; that you should attend to this yourself."

Schagerström stepped to the door and rang for the lackey.

"I'm leaving for Värmland at once," he said. "Tell Lundman to get the carriage ready."

"Beg pardon," said Nyman, "but I have Ironmaster

Fröberg's travelling coach with a fresh span of horses waiting outside the gate. You've only to change to your travelling clothes, and we can be off at any moment."

Schagerström suddenly clapped his hand to his forehead. "The conference! It is really important. I can't leave for a half hour yet."

Nyman, however, did not propose to allow him time to give away his property; so he said:

"Oh, a half hour wouldn't matter to us; but to those who are lying outdoors on the bare ground in the chilly autumn weather, it may seem long enough!"

"Why are they lying on the bare ground? They have the manor house."

"Börjesson probably did not dare shelter them there."

Still Schagerström wavered. And now Nyman said:

"I wonder if Disa Landberg would have stopped to finish a conference had she received such tidings?"

Schagerström shot him an impatient glance, went into the salon, and was back in a moment.

"I have just notified the gentlemen that the meeting is adjourned for a week. Now come!" he said.

*　　*　　*

It would be a sin to say that Bookkeeper Nyman had a pleasant journey faring toward Värmland with Schagerström. That fib about the fire troubled him greatly. He wanted to confess that he had lied, but did not dare.

"If I tell him there has been no loss of life down there

and that none are homeless he'll turn round and go back to Stockholm. It's the only hook I have to hold him by."

Nyman wondered if Schagerström couldn't be persuaded to change his mind. And he let his tongue run. He recounted a lot of trivial incidents in connection with the foundries. There were old servants who had said amusing and apt things; there were wily coal haulers who had fooled green inspectors; there were rumours of rich finds of mineral deposits in the vicinity of Gammalhyttan, and there were graphic accounts of an auction at which great tracts of woodland had gone for a mere song. He talked as it were for his life. But Schagerström must have found Nyman's efforts to arouse his interest in the property too obvious, for he cut him short.

"I cannot hold these estates," he said. "I'm going to give them away. Disa would think I did not miss her were I to accept all that."

"You should accept it, not as a joy but as a cross," said Nyman.

"I can't carry it alone!" Schagerström cried out in a tone of such hopeless despair that Nyman was afraid to pursue the subject.

The next day it was no better. Nyman had hoped that Schagerström would pick himself up when he got out into the country and saw fields and woods on every side; but there had been no perceptible improvement. The foundry clerk was actually alarmed about his old comrade.

"He won't bear his cross long," he thought. "As soon as he disposes of his wealth, he'll lie down and die. The man is grieving himself to death." And now it was not only to save his own skin but also to save the life of his friend that he tried once more to make Schagerström change his mind about his property.

"You should consider those whose labour has produced this wealth," he said. "Do you think they have worked merely for their own profit? Oh, no! Their purpose in consolidating all this producing power was that great things might be accomplished which would benefit the whole province. But you want to cut up the property and give it away. Now, I call that conscienceless. In my opinion, you have no right to do it. You should take up your burden and attend to your business."

The admonishment seemed to have no effect upon Schagerström; all the same, Nyman went on courageously:

"Come and work with us in Värmland. You are too good a man to be wasting your winters in Stockholm in idle amusements and spending your summers at the works just to kill time. Come and see to your property. I assure you it is necessary."

The foundry clerk marvelled at his own eloquence. Schagerström smiled and said rather facetiously:

"Well, listen to Obliging Nyman!"

"Oh, I know I've no call to preach," said the clerk, reddening. "I haven't a penny to my name and can't get anywhere; but I feel that I've a right to make life as pleasant for myself as I can. If I owned as much as a pinch of earth, do you think I'd part with it? No, no!"

The third day, at about six in the morning, they arrived at Gammalhyttan Manor. The sun beamed on the yellow and russet crowns of the trees, the heavens were gloriously blue, and the little lake in the distance peeped through a light veil of mist—smooth and shining as a disk of steel.

No one came to receive them, and when the farmer driver went down to the barn to look for the stableman, Nyman seized the opportunity to make confession.

"Don't bother to question Börjesson about the fire. That was only a little ruse of mine to get you here. Fröberg said he would discharge me if I came back without you."

"But those burned to death and those without shelter?" said Schagerström, who could not change the current of his thoughts so rapidly.

"There are no such!" the foundry clerk blurted out in utter dismay. "I had to lie to you to stop you from giving away your possessions."

Schagerström eyed him coolly, as if the matter were of no interest whatever. He said: "No doubt you meant well, but it was all quite needless. I shall return to Stockholm as soon as I have ordered fresh horses."

Nyman sighed but said nothing. The game was up, so what was the use?

The driver meanwhile came back and reported that there was not a man on the place. He had met an old

woman who told him that the managers and all the
foundry men had gone deer hunting. "The beaters-up
went off at four this morning and, in the rush and confusion, the stableman forgot to feed the horses. The
gentlemen can hear how they're stomping."

And, in fact, it was a deafening noise that issued from
the stable, where the hungry horses were kicking up as
much of a row as they could.

Schagerström flushed slightly. He handed a coin to
the driver and asked him to give the animals some
fodder; then, looking about with suddenly awakened interest, he observed that there was no smoke rising from
the smelting house.

"The furnaces are blown out for the first time in
thirty years," Nyman elucidated. "There was no ore,
so what could one do? Börjesson, with all his men, goes
a-hunting, as you see, and I don't blame him."

Schagerström flushed a shade deeper. "The smithy
—is that idle, too?"

"Certainly. The smiths, like the beaters-up, are out.
But what's that to you? Aren't you going to give everything away?"

"Oh, yes," said Schagerström weakly. "To be sure,
it's none of my affair what they do here."

"It is the fine gentlemen directors of the Freemasons'
Orphan Asylum who'll buckle to down here, and not
you."

"Yes, of course."

"Do you care to go in?" Nyman asked him as they

walked toward the manor house. "There was an early breakfast for the huntsmen, and the ladies and maid-servants are having their sleep out after the pother."

"You needn't waken them," said Schagerström. "I'm leaving immediately."

"Hello!" shouted Nyman as a shot was heard. "Look!"

A stag came running from the park. It was wounded. One foreleg hung limp, dragging and flopping from side to side as the animal continued its flight.

In a second a hunter dashed out of the park and, with a well-aimed shot, brought down the game. The stag, roaring with agony, dropped a few feet from where Schagerström stood. The marksman, a tall man with a military bearing, approached slowly and as if with reluctance.

"It's Captain Hammarberg," said Nyman.

Schagerström instantly recognized the ruddy, fair-haired officer who exercised a strange power over wo-men, who all liked him though they knew him for a scoundrel and a blackguard.

He would never forget how the fellow had tried to make up to Disa Landberg when she was a young miss; how he had cast a kind of spell over her, so that she allowed him to walk with her, ride with her, dance with her.

"How dare that wretch come here!" he muttered.

"Well, you don't seem to be able to prevent him," Nyman retorted in a tone that was far from "obliging."

Memories crowded upon Schagerström. This captain, who must have surmised that Schagerström loved the young heiress, had tormented and ridiculed him; had boasted before him of his low intrigues, as if to make him suffer a double agony in the thought that Disa Landberg might get such a man for a husband.

"For God's sake, come on!" he roared at the Captain, "and put the animal out of its misery." Then, turning his back on the man, he went straight to the house and pounded on the door.

Manager Börjesson and the other hunters had now come back from the game park. The foundry manager, having recognized the Ironmaster, came rushing up on to the porch.

Schagerström gave him a withering look. "I'll say nothing about the furnaces being blown out, the smithy standing idle, and the animals not being fed; this is, perhaps, as much my fault as yours; but you alone are to blame for allowing that cur of a Captain Hammarberg to hunt on my grounds. And now, sir, you are discharged."

With these words Schagerström resumed control of his estates. And it was a long time before he thought again of disposing of his property.

CHAPTER XV

IN THE DILIGENCE

WHEN Schagerström left Korskyrka Deanery after his second proposal, he was in no mood for laughter. The previous day he had come away from there highly edified, thinking that he had met a proud, high-minded woman; and now, since Charlotte Löwensköld had proved to be a sordid and calculating person, he felt utterly disheartened.

He knew, from the way it affected him, that the young girl had made a stronger impression than he cared to admit. "Thousand devils!" he muttered. "Had she stood the test, I'm afraid I should have lost my heart to her." But that was out of the question now that she had revealed her true character. He must marry her, of course; but he knew that he could never love a designing, untrustworthy, and mercenary woman.

Schagerström suddenly lowered the leather shades at the windows of the small closed carriage which he always used when making long journeys. The sight of the perpetual sunshine and the grain fields flaunting their rich harvests was a torture to him that day.

As he sat in the darkened carriage, with nothing to attract his gaze, there appeared to his mind's eye a vision of Charlotte as she stood in the doorway bending toward young Ekenstedt and regarding him with tender compassion. If ever love shone in a face, it did in hers.

"To hell with you! There you stood looking like an angel from heaven, and only ten minutes afterward you accepted rich Schagerström!"

A wave of self-contempt swept over him as he thought of how badly he had conducted this affair. He had stood up and vouched for a person merely on account of her beautiful eyes. Such credulity! Such stupidity! The whole episode had been an almost unpardonable indiscretion. Had he quite lost his reason? Were his parents right after all in their estimate of him? Certainly, in this instance, he had been clumsy and witless enough!

After a little, he began to regard his failure as a punishment. He had been unfaithful to the memory of his sainted wife; therefore, he must espouse a woman he could neither love nor respect.

Suddenly, all the old grief reawoke in him. He felt that in this grief he lived and moved and had his being. Life, with its manifold duties and perplexities, was actually repellent to him.

This time Schagerström had set out on a tour of inspection. He was to examine the managers' accounts; see whether the smithies, with their gaping forges and iron-bound hammers, were in good condition, and determine how much coal and pig iron should be ordered for the winter's use. It was a regular business tour, such as he made every summer, and therefore must not be neglected.

In a few hours, he was at Gammalhyttan, where his good friend Henrik Nyman was now manager. Of course both Nyman and his wife, who was one of the nice Fröberg girls of Kronbäcken, welcomed him cordially. Here he was greeted, not as a feared master but as an old comrade.

Though Schagerström could not have fallen into better hands, the melancholy mood into which he had sunk during the drive did not pass. Gammalhyttan, indeed, was the last place he should have come to as a newly affianced man. Every path in the park, every tree in the avenue, every bench in the garden held precious memories of tender avowals and tokens of endearment which had passed between him and his late wife. Here she still lived, young and radiant. He could see her; could hear her voice. Was it possible that he had been untrue to her? Was there a woman on this earth worthy to take her place in his heart?

His hosts could not help noting how dejected he was, and wondered what had made him so; but since he vouchsafed no explanation, they would not intrude upon him by asking personal questions.

Korskyrka being only a few miles away, it was inevitable that the news of Schagerström's engagement and everything connected with it would reach Gammalhyttan before the Ironmaster was ready to leave. The foundry manager and his wife, therefore, soon learned the cause of his despondency.

"He regrets it," they said between themselves. "But that is unfortunate. Charlotte Löwensköld would be the very wife for him; she'd pull him out of these perpetual megrims and broodings."

"I should like to speak to him of her," said Fru Nyman. "I know Charlotte of old. All this talk about her perfidy and craftiness is untrue. She is the soul of honour."

"I wouldn't meddle in this affair if I were in your place," counselled the husband. "Schagerström has again that staring look he had when I fooled him away from Stockholm, six years ago. It might be harmful, you understand."

The little wife carefully refrained from alluding to the matter during the greater part of Schagerström's stay. But on Friday evening, when the books had been audited and the guest was to leave the next morning, she could no longer control her kind and sympathetic heart.

"It would be cruel to let him go away feeling so sad and rueful," she thought. "Why should he be unhappy when there's no reason for it?"

With rare delicacy, and as if quite incidentally, during the evening meal she brought the conversation round to Charlotte Löwensköld. She recounted a number of current stories of the young girl; she told of her tweaking the Dean's housekeeper's nose; of her falling off the bench in church; of her racing the Dean's horses, and other things that were typical of her. On the whole, she pictured for Schagerström's benefit a proud, high-spirited, daring, and, withal, remarkably sensible and steadfast person. She tried not to suggest that she knew he had become engaged to Charlotte.

While Fru Britta Nyman was most eloquently defending her friend, Schagerström suddenly sprang to his feet and pushed his chair far out into the room.

"It is well meant of you, Britta," he said. "I know that you wish to comfort me by gilding this wretched affair. But I prefer to face the unvarnished truth. It is only right that I who have been so heartless as to think of marrying again should have for wife a false and designing wench, than which there is nothing worse."

Having delivered himself of this, he rushed out of the room. Immediately after, his terrified hosts heard the front door open and shut with a bang.

Schagerström wandered about the great forest, east of Gammalhyttan. He had been tramping for two or three hours, not knowing exactly where he was. Meanwhile, old notions that had been laid away these six years recurred to his mind. This encumbering wealth, which was to him a plague and a torment, why not cast it off?

Britta Nyman was right in a certain degree, he thought. Charlotte was no worse than others. She had met with a temptation that proved too strong. Why should he go about tempting people with his riches? Since taking control of his property, he had had extraordinary success; he had nearly doubled the fortune. All the more reason why he should rid himself of the oppressive burden. By that means, perhaps, he would escape a new marriage bond. Fröken Löwensköld would not care to wed a poor man. As he went stumbling round in the darkness, sometimes falling, sometimes standing still, he had as much difficulty finding his way in the brambly wilderness as in his own mind.

At length he came out on a broad, gravelled thoroughfare. It was the Stockholm Road, which ran eastward from Gammalhyttan. He began to tramp it. Was not this a leading from On High? Was it not a significant thing, his happening upon the Stockholm Road the moment he decided to give away his fortune?

He quickened his steps. Indeed, he was not going back to Gammalhyttan to be drawn into a discussion of his plans. He had money with him, and could order horses at the nearest inn. While trudging up a steep hill, he heard from behind the clatter of an approaching vehicle. Glancing back, he saw a big coach drawn by three horses.

The Stockholm diligence!—Leading number two! By that he could get to Stockholm more quickly. Before anyone at home had the least suspicion, he could convene another meeting and send out the donation letters. He stood waiting for the diligence. When it was almost in front of him, he called out:

"Stop! Any room inside?"

"Oh, yes, but not for tramps," the postilion shouted as the diligence proceeded on its way. However, at the crest of the hill it stopped. When Schagerström came up, the postilion raised his cap.

"The driver says he recognized Ironmaster Schagerström by the voice."

"Quite right."

"Please step in and take a seat! There's no one inside but two women."

*　*　*

Any reasonable person must concede that it would be rather embarrassing for elderly persons who are jealous of their honour to confess to spying at wickets and searching stoves for discarded letters; so it was not surprising that the Dean's wife said nothing to Charlotte about her discovery.

On the other hand, neither she nor her husband could think of letting the young girl remain shut up in the pantry with her tiresome work. The Ekenstedt carriage was hardly outside the gate before the old lady poked her head in at the pantry door.

"I'll tell you what, my little duckling," she said, her old face shining with beneficence—"when I saw the Baroness drive off, I had a sudden inspiration. It would be nice, I thought, to take a journey while the weather was pleasant. I have an old sister at Örebro I haven't seen in ever so long. She would be glad if we paid her a visit."

Charlotte was a bit startled at first; but since seeing
the Baroness and hearing her whispered assurances,
the world had looked brighter to her. A journey to
almost any place at all she would love above everything.
That she had been taken back into favour by the Dean
and his wife was by no means the least of her joys. All
afternoon she was happy as a lark, and went about the
house singing and chattering. Her scorned love and the
hateful slander were quite forgotten. There were hurried
preparations for the journey, and at ten in the evening
they stood down by the garden gate, waiting for the
Stockholm diligence.

When the big yellow coach, with its three span of
horses, came into sight; when one heard the noisy rumble of wheels, the merry jingle of harness, the sharp
crack of the whip, and the cheery blasts from the
postilion's horn, it was enough to arouse the wander-
lust in anyone. Charlotte went into transports of delight.

"Just to travel, to travel!" she burst forth ecstatically.
"I'd like to travel day and night, around the world."

"Oh, you'd soon tire of it, my girl," said the Dean's
wife. "But who knows? That wish may be fulfilled
sooner than you think."

Reservations had been made from the inn, and the
diligence stopped at the deanery to pick up the two
passengers. The postilion, not daring to drop the reins,
shouted from the box a pleasant "Good-evening" to
the Fru and the Fröken, and asked them kindly to step

in. "There's plenty of room," he said. "I haven't a single passenger inside."

"Oh, dear!" sighed the old lady. "And you think we should be pleased at that? You should have had a couple of handsome cavaliers in the coach for us to flirt with."

Everyone—the postilion, the driver, and the whole deanery household, which, with the exception of Karl Arthur, had come out to see them off—had a good laugh. When the Dean's wife had settled herself comfortably in a corner seat, with Charlotte at her side, the postilion tooted the signal, and they were off.

The two ladies kept up their chatter and banter awhile, but presently the older one fell asleep. Charlotte, being in a talkative mood, tried in vain to waken her.

"She has had a hard day," thought the young girl. "No wonder she's tired. It's a pity, though, for we could have had such a jolly time. As for me, I could talk all night."

To tell the truth, she was a little afraid of being alone with her own thoughts. Night had fallen, and the road ran through dense forests. Doubt and Despair lay in wait, ready to fall upon her.

They had been driving about two hours when Charlotte heard a call to the diligence. When in a few moments the coach stopped and the new passenger stepped in, he took a seat just opposite Charlotte. For a while there was no sound in there except the quiet breathing of two sleepers. Charlotte had suddenly feigned sleep so that she would not have to speak to Schagerström. When she had got over her momentary astonishment, the imp of mischief flew into her. Such an opportunity she could not afford to let slip. Perhaps, in some artful way, she might be able to induce Schagerström to abandon his matrimonial plans. If, at the same time, she could chaff him a bit, it would do no harm.

Schagerström, who was still in the depths of despond, gave a start on hearing himself addressed by a voice from the opposite corner of the coach. He could not see the one who sat there; he could barely distinguish the light oval of a face.

"I beg pardon," said the voice, "but I think I heard the postilion speak the name Schagerström. Can this be Ironmaster Schagerström of whom I have heard so much?"

Schagerström felt slightly annoyed at being recognized, but could not deny facts. He raised his hat, and mumbled a few words apropos of nothing.

The voice out of the darkness was heard again.

"I wonder how it would feel to be so rich? I have never been in the company of a millionaire before. I don't know whether it is right of me to keep this seat and let the Ironmaster ride backward. I'll gladly exchange places."

The fellow passenger spoke in a meek and oily voice, and was afflicted, besides, with a slight lisp. If Schagerström had had any social intercourse with the people of

Korskyrka town he would have thought at once it was Thea Sundler, the organist's wife, who was speaking. Of one thing, however, he was certain: He had never listened to a more affected and irritating voice.

"By all means keep your seat, madam!" he said.

"Oh, I am so used to hardship and discomfort," drawled the voice, "that it doesn't matter to me whether I occupy a despised place. But the Ironmaster, no doubt, is accustomed to sit in a gilded chair and to eat with a golden fork from a plate of gold."

"Let me tell you, milady," Schagerström retorted, his ire rising, "that for a good part of my life I have slept on straw and eaten with a wooden spoon from a pewter dish. I once had a master who, when angry at me, tore from my head such quantities of hair that by gathering up the remnants I saved enough for a cushion. It was the only soft pillow I had."

"How romantic!" gushed the slithery voice. "How lovely and how romantic!"

"Beg pardon, madam! it was not at all romantic; but it was useful, for it saved me from becoming such a fool as your ladyship takes me for."

"Oh, Ironmaster! what are you saying?—A fool!— Could a person in my position regard a millionaire as a fool? It is so interesting to learn what an exalted being thinks and feels. Dare I ask how you felt when your luck finally turned? Did you not feel—how shall I put it?—did you not feel as if you had come to the Seventh Heaven?"

"The Seventh Heaven!" Schagerström exclaimed in disgust. "Had I only been allowed to, I should have given away the entire fortune."

He thought the person in the corner should have understood that he was annoyed and offended. But the oily voice ran on:

"How lovely that all this wealth has fallen into worthy hands! It is so gratifying to know that virtue has received its just reward."

Schagerström made no response, hoping thus to escape further discussion of himself and his riches. The lady in the corner, though aware that she had been rather bold, did not subside; she simply took a new tack.

"And to think that the Ironmaster is going to marry that stuck-up Charlotte Löwensköld!"

"That what?" cried Schagerström indignantly.

"Ah, forgive me!" The voice became even more meek and insinuating. "I am one of the lowly of this earth, and unaccustomed to associate with grand people. I express myself poorly, and can't help that the word 'stuck-up' always comes to the tip of my tongue when I speak of Charlotte. But if it is displeasing to the Ironmaster, I'll not use it again."

Schagerström emitted a grunt, which the person in the corner could take as his response if she wished.

"I understand, of course, that you made your choice after mature deliberation," pursued the voice. "It is said that all your doings are carefully planned and deliberated. I presume that this would also apply to affairs of the heart. In any case, I should very much like to hear whether you really know what sort of person this stuck-up—beg pardon!—this pretty and charming Charlotte Löwensköld is. It is said that you had never exchanged a word with her until you proposed; but, of course, you satisfied yourself by other means that she was fitted to be mistress of Stora Sjötorp."

"Milady seems to be well informed," said Schager-ström. "Is your ladyship one of Fröken Löwensköld's intimate friends?"

"I have the honour, Ironmaster, to be the confidante of Karl Arthur Ekenstedt."

"Ah!" said Schagerström.

"To come back to Charlotte—pardon my saying so, but you do not seem to be happy. I hear you sigh and groan. Can it be that you regret having promised to marry this—what shall I say?—this—ah—elusive young girl. That epithet, I hope, is not offensive to you! Elusive might mean—well, anything. I know that a Schagerström cannot take back his given word. The Dean and his wife are fair-minded persons, and ought to consider what they themselves have had to stand from Charlotte."

"The Dean and his wife are very much attached to their ward."

"Say, rather, that they are wonderfully patient. Yes, patient is the word for it. The Dean's wife at one time had an excellent housekeeper. Charlotte didn't like her, so she tweaked her nose one day, during the worst of the Christmas rush. Naturally, the poor thing was offended and left at once, and old Tante Gina, sick as she was, had to attend to all the work herself."

Schagerström had shortly before heard a different version of the story, but he did not bother to put in a protest.

"Fancy, Ironmaster, the Dean who so loves his horses——"

"I know about her exercising them," said Schagerström.

"But don't you think it was dreadful of her?"

"I have heard that the horses were ready to expire in their stalls for lack of motion."

"Perhaps the Ironmaster has also heard how she treated her former fiancé's mother?"

"When she emptied the sugar basin?"

"Yes; when she poured all its contents on to her plate. A person to be mistress at Stora Sjötorp certainly ought to have good table manners."

"Quite right, milady."

"Surely, you wouldn't care to have a wife who refused to receive your guests?"

"Why, no."

"But that is what may happen, Ironmaster, if you marry Charlotte. Only think how she behaved at Chamberlain Dunker's home! It had been arranged that she was to sit next to Captain Hammarberg at a grand banquet, but she positively declined, and said she would rather leave the house. As you may have heard, Ironmaster, Captain Hammarberg hasn't the best reputation in the world; nevertheless, he has many good qualities, and I who am now speaking to you have had intimate talks with the Captain, and know how unhappy he is in mind and heart because nobody understands or trusts him. However, Charlotte is not his judge. If the Chamberlain receives him in his home why should she express her disapproval?"

"As to that," said Schagerström, "I do not intend to invite Captain Hammarberg to my home."

"Oh—ah—h'm!" murmured the voice. "That is another matter. I note that the Ironmaster has greater sympathy for Charlotte than I had supposed. It is very kind and chivalrous. I believe you would spring to the defence of anyone subjected to slander. But, in your heart, I think you will agree with me that a union between a gentleman of your standing and an erratic person like Charlotte would be utterly preposterous."

"Milady means that, with the aid of the Dean and his wife, I—— No, no, impossible!"

"The impossible thing," said the oily voice in its smoothest accents, "is to marry a person who is in such disgrace."

"Disgrace?"

"Asking your pardon, Ironmaster, but you do not understand. You are too good-hearted. Karl Arthur Ekenstedt has told me how you stood up for Charlotte. Though you have now learned from sad experience that the accusations against her are true, still you defend her. But others are not like you, Ironmaster. Baroness Ekenstedt came to the deanery yesterday and left to-day. She would not see Charlotte, would not even sleep under the same roof with her."

"Really?"

"Yes," said the voice, "it's the plain truth. And do you know, Ironmaster, that some of the men in the church town were so incensed over Charlotte's behaviour that they decided to give her a whistle serenade, the way the students at Upsala do when they are displeased with a professor."

"Oh!" gasped Schagerström, horrified.

"Last evening the young men appeared at the deanery and started the din. Karl Arthur, however, dissuaded them from continuing. His mother was staying for the night in the wing, and she wouldn't tolerate anything of that sort."

"Otherwise, young Ekenstedt, no doubt, would have let it go on."

"I wouldn't like to venture an opinion as to that. But, in the interest of justice, I hope the men will come again another night, and I also hope that blind Kalle will long go about singing his comic song of her. The words are by Captain Hammarberg, and they're sung to the tune of *When the Moon Wanders*. When you have heard that ditty, Ironmaster Schagerström, you'll understand why it would never do for you to marry Charlotte Löwensköld."

Schagerström pounded on the wall of the coach as a signal to the driver to stop.

"Oh, I say, Ironmaster, are you getting out?"

"Yes, milady!" Schagerström was as furious now as he had been when, earlier in the evening, Britta Nyman had spoken in praise of Charlotte. "I see no other way to escape hearing further aspersions against a lady I hold in high regard and intend to marry."

"But, for goodness' sake, that was not the intention!"

Just then the diligence stopped. Schagerström flung the door open and sprang out.

"Oh, no, that was not the intention!" he shouted back, and quickly slammed the door after him. Then he stepped up to the postilion to pay his fare.

"Are you leaving us already, Ironmaster?" said the postilion. "Now the ladies will be unhappy. The Dean's wife berated me when she got in because there were no gentlemen in the coach."

"The Dean's wife?—What dean's wife?"

"The wife of the Dean of Korskyrka, of course. Haven't you talked enough with the fellow passengers to find out that it was Fru Forsius and Fröken Löwensköld who were seated in the coach?"

The postilion raised his cap and plied the whip; the diligence went on its way, and, for a good while, Schagerström stood gazing after it.

"Charlotte Löwensköld!" he gasped. "Was that Charlotte Löwensköld?"

It was long after midnight when he returned to Gammalhyttan.

Foundry Manager Nyman and his wife meanwhile had been anxiously awaiting his return, and wondering if they ought not to send out men to search for him. They were pacing up and down the avenue when Schagerström at last came in sight. They saw his powerful and rather settled figure outlined against the nocturnal sky. Though knowing it for Schagerström they could scarcely believe it was he.

The man who approached was singing an old ballad. As he met his hosts, he burst out laughing.

"For goodness' sake, go to bed!" said he. "In the morning, you shall hear the whole story. By the by, Nyman, you'll have to get ready to make that tour of inspection in my place. I must go down to Korskyrka again, to-morrow."

CHAPTER XVI

THE BANNS

ON SATURDAY morning, Schagerström appeared at the deanery. He had come to consult with the Dean as to what had best be done to stop the persecution of Charlotte that had been recently started.

As a matter of fact, he could not have arrived at a more fitting moment. The poor old clergyman was beside himself with fear and indignation; the five small wrinkles in his forehead flamed red as fire.

The same morning he had been visited by three men from the church town: the apothecary, the organist, and the high bailiff. They had come to express their desire, and that of the entire community, that he turn Charlotte out of his house. The apothecary and the high bailiff had been quite civil; they had shown plainly that to them it was most unpleasant business to come on an errand of this sort. The organist, on the other hand, had been highly incensed; had raised his voice, been overbearing and utterly unmindful of the respect he owed his superior.

He had given the old Dean to understand that he was lowering his prestige by allowing Charlotte to remain at the deanery. It was not only that she had shamefully deceived her fiancé, or that she had conducted herself on various occasions in an unseemly manner; she had also laid violent hands on his wife, who certainly did not expect to meet with any harm when coming to this honoured house as a guest.

The Dean had declared outright that his kinswoman Fröken Löwensköld would remain in his house as long as he was able to hold his old head up. And with that as their answer the men had been obliged to depart. But one can imagine how unpleasant all this must have been to a peace-loving old gentleman!

"There'll be no end to the clamour," he said to Schagerström. "It has been going on like this the whole week. You may be certain, Ironmaster, that the organist won't give up at the first attempt. The man himself is a very nice fellow, but his wife is goading him on."

Schagerström, who was in excellent humour that day, tried to calm him; but with slight success.

"Ironmaster, I assure you," the Dean continued, "that Charlotte is as innocent in this matter as a newborn child, and I couldn't think of sending her away. But the peace of the parish, the peace which for thirty-five years I have fostered and guarded, will now be broken."

Schagerström understood that that which the old Dean regarded as the most creditable achievement of his long pastorship was now in jeopardy. He doubted that the old man had the strength or the courage to resist further pressure from his parishioners.

"To tell the truth," he said, "I, too, have heard about the persecution of Fröken Löwensköld. My errand here to-day is to consult with your Reverence on ways and means to combat it."

"You are a clever man, Ironmaster, but I doubt that even you would be able to bridle the evil tongues. I suppose we'll have to keep silence, and prepare for the worst."

Schagerström began to protest, but the old man went on in the same doleful strain:

"We must be prepared for the worst. If only you were safely married! Or, if at least the banns had been published!"

Schagerström jumped to his feet. "Would it be any help, do you think, if we ordered the banns read?"

"Assuredly, it would be a help," said the old man, brightening. "If the people of the parish knew for certain that Charlotte was to be your wife, they would leave her in peace. In that case, she would be allowed to remain at the deanery till the day of the wedding, and no one would say a word. People are so constituted, Ironmaster, that they do not care to offend the rich and powerful."

"Then I would suggest that the banns be proclaimed from the pulpit to-morrow," said Schagerström.

"This is a very kind thought on your part, Ironmaster, but it can't be done. Charlotte is away from home at present, and you probably have not the necessary papers with you."

"The papers are at Stora Sjötorp," said Schagerström, "and can be fetched. As your Reverence knows, I have Fröken Löwensköld's definite promise and, besides, you are her guardian."

"No, no, Ironmaster—not quite so hurriedly!"

The old man began to talk of something else. He showed Schagerström a number of rare botanical specimens, and told him where he had found them. While discoursing on his pet subject, he grew animated and eloquent. It seemed as if he had quite forgotten his troubles. However, in a short while he came back to the subject under discussion.

"The reading of the banns is no nuptial ceremony," he said. "If Charlotte is dissatisfied, they can be revoked."

"This is merely a question of expediency," Schagerström elucidated, "in order to preserve peace and harmony in the community, and to put a stop to the slander and persecution. I have no intention of dragging Fröken Löwensköld to the altar against her will."

"Aye, who knows?" The Dean was thinking of a certain letter he had read. "Charlotte is very impulsive, let me tell you; for her sake, it would be best to put a stop to the gossip at once. Else, perhaps, she wouldn't rest content with merely cutting off a few curls."

They went on discussing the matter of the banns for

some little time, and became more and more convinced that it was the best way out of the difficulty.

"I'm sure that my wife would be with us in this," said the Dean, who now had become quite hopeful.

Schagerström was thinking to himself that the moment the banns of marriage for him and Charlotte had been published, he would have the right to appear as her protector. Then there would be no more whistle serenades or any lampooning.

For the rest, one must consider that Schagerström, since the conversation in the diligence, had become satisfied that Charlotte was disinterested, and had only the most tender feeling for her. There was something positively alluring about the step he wished to take; but this, naturally, he would not admit, even to himself. He was persuaded that he was acting purely from necessity. That is the way of people when they are in love, and one must overlook their stupidities.

It was finally decided that the banns should be published at church on the morrow. Schagerström hurried home to fetch the required papers, and the Dean himself wrote the license for the banns of marriage. When everything was in order, Schagerström felt greatly relieved. Indeed, he had no objection to his name being read out in church in connection with Charlotte's!

"Foundry Owner Gustaf Henrik Schagerström and the Honourable Charlotte Löwensköld" would sound well, he thought. He felt a keen desire to hear it himself, and decided to stop over at Korskyrka till after the Sunday service.

* * *

On the Sunday of the first reading of the banns, Karl Arthur Ekenstedt preached an extraordinary sermon; which was only to be expected after the harrowing experiences he had been through during the week.

The Scriptural lesson for the day was on the false prophets against which our Saviour warned His disciples. The subject, however, did not accord with the mood of the preacher; he would have preferred to discourse on the vanity of earthly things, the menace of riches, and the blessings of poverty. Above all, he felt the need to approach his hearers in a simpler and more intimate way than had been his wont; to make them understand how much he loved them, and thereby win their confidence.

Tormented by doubt and uncertainty, he had been unable, during the week, to prepare his sermon. All Saturday night he had sat up working, but to no avail, the sermon was still unfinished when it came time for him to leave for church. So as not to be utterly stranded, he tore from an old postil a few pages containing a sermon on the lesson for that day, and thrust them into his pocket.

While from the pulpit he stood reading the Gospel, a thought shaped itself in his mind. He seized upon it as though it had come straight from God.

"My dear friends," he began, "I stand here to-day to

warn you in the Name of Christ against false prophets. But perhaps in your hearts you are thinking: He who now speaks to us, is he a proper teacher? What do we know of him? What assurance have we that he, too, is not a thorn on which no grapes can grow, or a thistle, from which one cannot gather figs? Therefore, my friends, I should like to tell you something of the ways by which God led me when He willed to make me a proclaimer of His Word."

With deep feeling the young pastor then related the simple story of his life. He told his hearers how in his first years at college it had been his sole ambition to be a great and noted scientist. He told of how he had failed in his Latin; of his homecoming, when he had offended against his mother; of the reconciliation, and, finally, how it had all led to his making acquaintance with the Pietist Pontus Friman.

He spoke quietly and with rare modesty. None could doubt the sincerity of his every utterance. But perhaps it was mostly the vibrant note in his voice that charmed his hearers. After the first few sentences they listened in rapt stillness, with heads thrust forward and eyes riveted upon the preacher.

As always happens when a person speaks out freely and honestly, as man to man, they were drawn to him, and took him to their hearts. The poor from the forest cabins and the rich from the great mining estates, all understood that he was giving them his confidence in order to win theirs and restore their faith in him. They followed his sermon as never before; they were moved and rejoiced.

He went on to tell of his first faltering attempts to follow Jesus. He described the marriage feast in his home, when carried away by the joys of earth, he had become as it were intoxicated with its pleasures, and joined in the dance.

"After that night," he said, "for many weeks darkness reigned in my soul. I knew that I had betrayed my Master; that I had failed to watch and pray with Him. I was a slave of the world, conquered by its temptations. I felt that Heaven would never be my heritage."

As he pictured for the people his anguish of mind there were many in the church who wept. The man in the pulpit had them wholly in his power; they felt, and suffered, and strove with him.

He said further: "My friend Friman sought to comfort and help me. He assured me that in the love of Christ lay salvation. But I could not lift up my heart to our Saviour, for I loved the things created above their Creator.

"Then, one night, when my need was greatest I saw the Christ. I was not asleep; during those days and nights there was no sleep for me. But frequently visions, such as one sees in dreams, would pass before my eyes. I knew that they were called forth by my extreme physical weariness, and attached no significance to them.

"Suddenly came a vision that stood out, clear and distinct. It did not vanish at once like the others. I saw a lake of blue and shining waters, along the shore of which there was a great gathering of people. In the midst of this gathering sat a man with flowing locks and deep, sorrowful eyes, who seemed to be speaking to the multitude. The instant I beheld him, I knew that it was Jesus.

"And I saw a young man step up to Jesus, bow low before Him, and ask Him a question. I could not hear his words, but I knew that he was the rich young man of whom it is related in the Gospel of Saint Luke that he asked the Master what he must do to inherit eternal life.

"Jesus then spoke a few words to the youth, and I knew that He said to him that he should keep the Ten Commandments of God.

"The young man again bowed low before the Master, and smiled a self-satisfied smile. I knew that he answered, 'All these have I kept from my youth up.'

"Jesus looked at him long and searchingly, then He spoke again. And this time also I knew what He said. 'Yet lackest thou one thing: sell all that thou hast, and distribute unto the poor, and thou shalt have treasure in heaven; and come, follow me.'

"The young man now turned from Jesus and went his own way. And I saw that he was sorrowful, for he had great possessions. And for a long while Jesus sat looking after him. And in His look I read such infinite love and such infinite compassion! Oh, my friends, in that look there was something so heavenly it made my heart leap for joy, and light came again to my darkened soul! I sprang up. I wanted to rush over to Him and cry out that I loved Him above everything. The world was nothing to me now; my only desire was to be allowed to follow Him.

"But as I moved the vision passed, though not from memory, my friends, not from memory!

"The next day I went to my friend Pontus Friman, and asked him what he thought Christ required of me, for I had no possessions to offer Him. He said that Jesus surely wished me to sacrifice for His sake all glory and distinction that might come to me through my learning, and become His poor and lowly servant. And so I cast aside all thought of this other, and became an humble parson, that I might speak to the people of Christ and His love.

"But pray for me, my friends, for I, like you, must live in this world. The world would tempt me, and I am in fear and trembling lest it turn my desire away from Christ, and make of me one of the false prophets."

The preacher folded his hands. All at once he seemed to see the temptations and the anguish of soul that lay before him, and at the thought of his own frailty he burst into tears. Overcome by his emotions, and unable to continue, he pronounced a short "Amen," then sank to his knees in prayer.

Everywhere in the church people broke into audible sobs. By that one brief address, Karl Arthur had made himself the idol of all these people. They could have borne him in their arms; they could have sacrificed themselves for him as he had sacrificed himself for his Lord and Maker.

Whatever the effect produced by his sermon, it would not have been so consummate but for the reading of the banns, which immediately followed.

The young clergyman first read out a few indifferent names, to which no one gave any further thought. Suddenly he blanched perceptibly and bent down over the paper, to see whether his eyes had deceived him. Whereupon he read the banns in a low voice, as if not wishing them to be heard.

"I publish the banns of marriage between Foundry Owner Gustaf Henrik Schagerström of Stora Sjötorp and the Honourable Charlotte Adriana Löwensköld of the Rectory, both of this parish. This is the first time of reading.

"Wishing them happiness in this holy union and the blessing of God, Who instituted the Sacrament of Marriage."

It did not help that the young clergyman had lowered his voice almost to a whisper; in the funereal stillness of the church his every syllable carried.

It was dreadful!

Schagerström himself realized how dreadful it was. There stood the man who would renounce the world to become an humble follower of Christ, reading that the woman he had loved was to marry one of the richest men in the country.

Aye, it was positively shocking. There in the pulpit

stood the man who for five years had been Charlotte's affianced, and who only the Sunday before had worn on his finger her engagement ring! And now she was ready to wed another. The people blushed for shame. They dared not look at one another as they passed out after the service.

Schagerström felt it worse than anyone, though he maintained an appearance of calmness; but in his heart he thought: "I would not wonder at the people if they spat upon me or cast stones."

And this was what he had imagined would rehabilitate Charlotte! Many a time he had felt awkward and foolish, but never to such a degree as when on that Sunday he walked up the main aisle out of the church.

* * *

Schagerström at first thought of writing Charlotte a letter of explanation and apology; but he quickly found that to indite such a letter was too difficult a thing, and decided instead to order a conveyance and drive down to Örebro.

He had learned from Dean Forsius the name of the elderly Fru the ladies were visiting, and on Monday morning he called on Charlotte and asked if he might have a talk with her.

He immediately told her of his presumptuous act; he did not seek to justify himself, but simply stated how it had all come about.

Charlotte crumpled as if she had received a mortal

wound. To keep from falling, she sank into a low armchair, where she remained motionless. She did not break forth in reproaches; her agony was too great, too real.

Until then she had been able to say to herself that when Karl Arthur, with the help of his mother, had come to think differently; when he had renewed the old bond with her, her honour would be restored and her traducers would understand that the whole thing had been only a lovers' quarrel. But now that the banns for her and Schagerström had been read in church, everyone must think that she actually intended to marry the rich Ironmaster.

There was no help for it now. Nor was it possible for her to explain. She was forever disgraced. People would always think her false-hearted and mercenary.

She had the horrible sensation of being driven as a manacled captive toward some unknown goal. All that she wished to avoid she seemed to do; all that she tried to avert she only furthered.

It was like sorcery. Everything went wrong. From the day Schagerström first proposed to her, she had not been a free agent.

"Ironmaster, who are you?" she asked abruptly. "Why do you continually cross my path? Why can't I tear myself free from you?"

"Who am I?—Well," said Schagerström, "I'll tell you, Fröken Lowensköld: I am the stupidest ass on God's green earth."

And he said it with such honest conviction it brought a faint smile to Charlotte's face.

"From the time I first saw you at church, Fröken, I have wanted to be of service to you and to see you happy; but I have brought you only sorrow and suffering."

The ghost of a smile had already vanished. Charlotte now sat inert, her face deathly white, her arms hanging limp at her sides. The staring eyes seemed to see nothing but the dire misfortune he had brought upon her.

"Fröken Löwensköld," said Schagerström, "I give you my personal permission to forbid the banns next Sunday. You know, Fröken, that the banns are not valid in law until they have been read on three consecutive Sundays from the same pulpit."

Charlotte by a slight movement of her hand told him that this concession meant nothing now; her reputation was ruined and could not be saved.

"And I promise you, Fröken Löwensköld, not to cross your path again till you, yourself, call me."

Schagerström moved toward the door. There was one thing more he wished to say to her. It called for greater self-abnegation than anything that had preceded it.

"I should like to add," he said, "that I'm beginning to understand you, Fröken Löwensköld. I have wondered a little how you could love young Ekenstedt so greatly as to expose yourself, on his account, to all this calumny and persecution; for I comprehend, of course, that you think only of him. But now that I have heard him preach, I see why he must be shielded. He is destined for something big."

He felt rewarded, as she now looked up at him and he saw a little colour come into her cheek.

"Thank you, Ironmaster!" she said. "I thank you for understanding." And then she sank again into a lethargy of hopelessness. There was nothing more for him to do, so he bowed and went his way.

CHAPTER XVII

THE PAUPER AUCTION

IT IS said that misfortunes always bring a little good in their wake. And to Charlotte Löwensköld grief and humiliation had brought the very thing she had lacked to be truly charming.

The deep despond had driven away all that had been too boylike in her nature, and too audacious. It had given to her voice, her features, her bearing, a gentle dignity, and to the eyes, that shimmer of wistfulness, the appealing, fitful glow that bespeaks a lost happiness. This lovely, chastened young girl would awaken interest, sympathy, and affection wherever she appeared.

Charlotte and the Dean's wife had returned from Örebro in the forenoon of Tuesday, and in the afternoon a party of young people from the near-by foundry estate of Holma called at the deanery. Among these dear young persons Charlotte had friends who, like the Fru at Gammalhyttan, refused to believe any evil of her. And now they had only to see her to know that she had met with a great sorrow. They asked no questions and made no allusions to her prospective marriage; they simply tried to be as kind and considerate as they could.

As a matter of fact, they had not come to offer their congratulations on the banns, but on quite a different errand. Seeing how depressed Charlotte was, they scarcely knew whether to present the matter.

However, after a little, it crept out that they wished to speak of Crofter Matts's Elin, the girl with the purple birthmark and the ten brothers and sisters. Elin had been to Holma that morning and complained to their mother that her little brothers and sisters were to be auctioned off.

Crofter Matts's Elin and her brothers and sisters had lived by beggary. What else could the poor things have done? But people had grown tired of feeding this large brood of hungry mouths, and the parish authorities had decided to put the children out to board in various homes. An auction of sorts had been announced, where those wishing to take over one or more of the children could make their bids.

"Your ladyship probably knows how it's done," the girl had said. "The only thing the authorities want to know is, who will take the youngsters at the least possible cost to the parish. No one thinks of the children, whether they will have proper care and upbringing."

The poor girl, who had been as a mother to the younger children, was frantic with dread. She knew that people who bid in children at these auctions were poor crofters needing cheap labour: herders for their sheep and goats, and domestic help for toil-worn housewives. Her little brothers and sisters would have to work hard as regular servants, for nobody spared these auction youngsters; they had to earn such fare as was provided them. The youngest child, a little girl, was only three years of age, so that she, of course, could not go as herder or houseworker. Her they would surely starve to death, since she was too small to make herself useful.

Most of all, Elin had deplored that the children would be separated and scattered in different directions. There was now a very strong bond of unity and affection between them, but in a few years' time, they would be strangers to one another and to her. And hereafter, who would teach them to be upright and truth loving, which she had always tried to do?

The kindly lady of Holma had been deeply moved by the poor girl's plaint; but there were so many youngsters on the hillsides around Holma she had to do for, that she felt unable to take upon herself any additional responsibilities. However, she sent two of her daughters to the pauper auction, which was to be held later in the forenoon at the parish public room, as she wished to know who bid in the poor little things.

When the young ladies from Holma stepped into the public room, the auction had just begun. On a long bench, far forward, sat the pauper children—the eldest in the middle, with the three-year-old in her lap, the others ranged on either side of her. They made no outcry; only a low and continuous wailing was heard. Ragged and starved as the children looked, one would have thought they could not be worse off than they were already; yet, obviously, that which was in store seemed to them the acme of misery.

Over against the wall on all sides of the room sat the bidders—poor folk, as was to be expected at an auction of this kind. Only at the counsel table there were a few members of the Parish Council—some two or three rich farmers and a couple of mine-owners who were there to see that the auction was conducted in an orderly manner, and that the children were given over to reputable folk, well known in the parish.

The eldest boy, a thin, gaunt lad, was standing on the table, placed there for public inspection. The man who offered him was holding forth on his potentialities as herdboy and woodcutter, and a woman who, judging from her attire, must have been extremely poor, came forward to have a better look at the boy and see whether he was any good for work.

That was as far as they had got with the auction, when the door opened and Karl Arthur Ekenstedt came in. He paused a moment on the threshold, and looked round the room; then, raising his arms toward heaven, he cried out: "O God, turn Thine eyes away from us! Look not on what is happening here!" Whereupon he went up to the counsel table, and said to the authorities:

"My fellow Christians, I beg of you not to commit so great a sin! Let us not sell human beings into slavery!"

All present were aghast at the Curate's action. The shabby woman at the table quickly drew back and made for the door. The peasant councilmen, in their embarrassment, shifted uneasily on the bench. Obviously, it was the Curate's interference in the business of the parish they disapproved, rather than their own doings. At last one man rose.

"This auction is held in accordance with a resolution passed at a vestry meeting," he said.

The young clergyman stood there, handsome as a god, his head thrown back, his eyes blazing. He certainly did not look as if he meant to give way to any such vestry resolution.

"Mine-owner Aaron Månsson," he said, addressing the Chairman, "I request that the auction be suspended."

"Dr. Ekenstedt has heard that the auction is a decision of the vestry."

Karl Arthur, with a shrug, turned away from the man and placed his hand on the shoulder of the lad who was up for sale.

"I'll buy him," he said. "My bid is so low that none can underbid me. I offer to take charge of the boy without any compensation from the parish."

Mine-owner Aaron Månsson now rose again. Karl Arthur did not look at him, but said to the auctioneer:

"No need to cry out any more. I offer to take all the children on the same terms."

Now everyone stood up, except Crofter Matts's Elin and her brothers and sisters, who did not comprehend what had happened.

Mine-owner Aaron Månsson protested that it would

be the same old nuisance over again; that the auction had been called in order to have done with this perpetual beggary.

"The children will do no more begging," said Karl Arthur.

"Who will be sponsor for that?"

"Jesus Christ; He Who said, 'Let the children come unto me,' He will sponsor these little ones."

There was a commanding power and a noble dignity about the young clergyman as he said that, and the rich mine-owner could not find words to answer him.

Karl Arthur now went over to the children. "Go your way," he said to them. "Run back home! I have bidden you in."

They were still afraid to move. Karl Arthur then lifted up the littlest one, and, with her in his arms and the ten others following close behind, he left the parish public room.

No one attempted to stop them. Some of the bidders, shamed and abashed, had already departed.

When the two sisters went home and recounted it all to their mother, the latter declared that something must be done to help the young curate with the care of his numerous wards; she suggested that they start at once to raise funds for a home for orphans, and it was in order to speak of this that the girls had come to the deanery.

When Charlotte had heard all, she arose and went out of the room, weeping. She had to hurry upstairs to her own room so that she might go down on her knees and give thanks to God.

Her long-cherished dream had now come true: Karl Arthur had stepped forth as a leader of the people; a foregoer who led the people in the ways of God.

CHAPTER XVIII

THE TRIUMPH

"HUSBAND dear," said Fru Forsius, coming into the Dean's study a day or two after the auction, "find an excuse to go to the dining room if you want to see something lovely!"

The old man rose at once. As he stepped into the dining room he saw Charlotte seated at a small table over by the window with some needlework in her hand. She was not working, but sat gazing out toward the wing where Karl Arthur had his quarters. There was a constant stream of callers that day, passing between the gate and the wing, and it was this she sat watching.

The Dean pretended to be hunting for his spectacles, which he knew were safe in his own room. Meanwhile he cast sidelong glances at Charlotte who, with a happy smile, followed intently all that was happening down by the wing. A faint flush coloured her cheek, and her eyes shone with a rapt serenity. She really was lovely to look at.

When Charlotte became aware of the Dean's presence in the room, she said to him: "All day people pass in and out at Karl Arthur's."

"Yes," replied the old man drily. "They don't leave

him in peace for a second. I'll soon have to attend to my daybooks myself."

"She who has just gone in is a daughter to Aaron Månsson; she has brought a firkin of butter."

"That, of course, is a contribution for those children."

"Everyone loves him!" cried Charlotte ecstatically. "I knew it was bound to come."

"Oh, well, when one is young and good-looking," the Dean remarked laconically, "it isn't hard to fool the old women, and make them weep buckets of tears."

But Charlotte's ardour was not to be dampened.

"Awhile ago one of the smiths from Holma came seeking him—one of those Pietists who, as Uncle knows, never come to church and won't listen to any of the regular clergymen."

"What are you telling me?" The old Dean was really interested now. "Has he actually been able to move those blocks of stone? I verily believe, my girl, there's something in the fellow!"

"Think how happy his mother would be if she could see this!" said Charlotte.

"I don't know whether this was precisely the kind of success she wished for her son."

"He makes people better. Some come away from him weeping and drying their eyes. Marie Louise's husband has also been to see him. Think! If Karl Arthur could help *him*, wouldn't it be wonderful!"

"It would indeed, my girl. But the best of it all is that you like to sit here and see the people."

"I'm sitting here conjecturing what they talk to him about, and I seem to hear what he says to them."

"Aye, aye, that's right, my girl. Do you know—I think those spectacles must be somewhere in my study."

"If this had not come to pass," said Charlotte musingly, "the whole thing would have been unexplainable. Then I should have had no reward for trying to shield him. But now I understand the reason for it all."

The old Dean hurried out of the room. In a second, the girl would have had him weeping. "What in the world shall we do with her?" he mumbled to himself. "Surely, she can't be losing her mind!"

But if Charlotte gloried in Karl Arthur's triumph during the week, she had even greater cause for rejoicing when it came Sunday. The roads swarmed with people, just as when Royalty visited the parish. Carriages and pedestrians moved in unbroken procession. Evidently reports of the young clergyman's new kind of preaching, his piety and power, had spread throughout the parish.

"The church won't hold them all," observed the Dean's wife. "Everyone has come out to a man. I only hope that fires won't break out while their homes stand deserted!"

The old Dean was not altogether satisfied. He knew that a religious revival had begun, to which he would have had no objections had he only been certain that Karl Arthur was the right man to keep the sacred flame burning. But, rather than wound Charlotte, who was in ecstasies, he kept his doubts to himself.

Late in the week the girl had had a letter from the Baroness, begging her to be patient a few days more; consequently, she did not take advantage of Schagerström's permission to forbid a second reading of the banns.

The Dean and his wife, fearing that all these people who now fairly worshipped Karl Arthur might offer some insult to Charlotte, thought it best to leave her at home.

Their carriage had no sooner disappeared round the corner of the garden than Charlotte put on her hat and mantilla and set off for church on foot. She wanted to hear Karl Arthur preach in the new, compelling way by which he had won the hearts of his hearers; wanted to have the pleasure of witnessing the adoration that now centred about him.

Charlotte managed to squeeze herself into a pew far back in the church, where she sat in breathless suspense until Karl Arthur appeared in the pulpit.

She marvelled at the easy, natural tone of voice in which he addressed the congregation. It was as if he were conversing with a group of friends. Not one word did he use that was not easily understood by the simplest person there, and he told the people of his trials and his struggles as if seeking help and guidance from them.

Karl Arthur that Sunday had to speak on the parable of the unjust steward whom Jesus commended, and Charlotte felt uneasy as she thought of his having to expound a text so difficult and paradoxical. She had heard many clerics complain that the parable was obscure, and hard to interpret. The beginning and the end did not seem to belong together. It was, perhaps, because of the strictly condensed form in which the parable had been recorded that it was almost incomprehensible to people of our day. Charlotte had heard various preachers discourse on the first part and on the second, but never any who could give clarity and continuity to the parable as a whole.

Doubtless everyone in the church thought the same— that the text was too difficult for him; that he would stray from the subject as he had done on the previous Sunday.

With supreme courage and confidence the young curate took up the obscure Scriptural text and gave it meaning and significance. Led by a divine inspiration, he revealed the parable in all its pristine beauty and mystic depth. It was as when one washes away the dust of centuries from an old painting, and finds himself standing before a masterpiece.

Charlotte grew more and more astonished. "From where does he get all this? It is not himself speaking. It is God Who speaks through his mouth."

She saw how the Dean sat with a hand cupped to his ear so as not to miss a word; she noted that the attention seemed to be most marked among the older men, among those who liked profound and serious thought. After this, none could say of Karl Arthur that he preached for women only, or that it was his fine appearance that carried him through.

Everything was perfect. Charlotte was happy. She wondered if life ever again would be as rich and glorious as it was in that hour.

But perhaps the most noteworthy thing about Karl Arthur's preaching was the comfort and peace it gave to his hearers, making them forget their afflictions. They felt that they were being led by a good and wise shepherd. Many in that congregation made solemn promises in their hearts, which they afterward tried to live up to.

And yet, it was not the sermon, beautiful though it was, that made the greatest impression upon the people that Sunday. Nor was it the reading of the banns of marriage. The banns for Charlotte and Schagerström were followed, of course, by murmurs of disapproval; but, then, everyone knew beforehand that they were coming. No, it was something else.

Charlotte had tried to slip out immediately after the sermon; but, the church being crowded to the doors, she had to stay through the entire Altar Service.

When the people afterward began to move toward the exit, she again sought to hurry out ahead of the crowd. But in vain. No one stepped aside to let her pass; no one spoke to her.

She felt instantly that she was surrounded by enemies. Several of her old acquaintances drew away as she approached. Only one person came up to her—her brave

sister, Fru Romelius. When the two were at last outside the door, they stopped short.

On the walk leading from the church stood a group of
young men with bouquets of thistle, of yellowed leaves,
of dried grass which had been hastily gathered outside
the wall of the churchyard. Obviously it was their
intention to present these to Charlotte as offerings of
congratulation on the banns. In the forefront stood
the tall Captain Hammarberg, who was considered the
cleverest wit and the wickedest man in the parish. He
cleared his throat in preparation for the delivery of a
befitting congratulatory speech.

The church people had gathered round the young
men, and were waiting in gleeful expectation to hear
the young girl who had jilted her lover for goods and
gold held up to ridicule and scorn. They grinned in
anticipation. Hammarberg was not likely to spare her,
they thought to themselves.

Fru Romelius, trembling for her sister, tried to draw
her back into the church, but the latter would not go.

"It doesn't matter," said Charlotte. "Nothing matters now."

They were advancing slowly toward the waiting men,
who had assumed a mien of smiling friendliness, when
Karl Arthur came running toward them. Having noted
their dilemma in passing, he quickly turned back to go
to their aid. He offered an arm to the elder sister, raised
his hat to the felicitating gentlemen, gave them to
understand, by a gesture, that they must not carry out

their design, and conducted the two ladies safely through the crowd down to the highway.

That he, the supposedly injured party, had taken under his protection the one who had wronged him, that was something beautiful; something not to be seen every day! And it was this that made the greatest impression upon the people that Sunday.

CHAPTER XIX

ADMONISHING CUPID

CHARLOTTE went down to the village next
morning to consult her sister, Fru Romelius.
The sister, like most of the Löwenskölds, was
deeply interested in the supernatural. She would tell
of having seen the dead wander on the village street in
the full light of day, and there was no ghost story too
wild for her to believe. Charlotte, who was of a different
cast of mind and who had always laughed at the sister's
visions, now wanted to hear her interpretation of the
mystery which she, herself, had been unable to solve.

The young girl, after the unpleasant scene at the
church, again had become sensible of her unhappy plight.
Again she felt as when Schagerström had told her about
the banns—that she was bound and held in thrall by
strange powers. She had the feeling that she was being
pursued by some malevolent being, who had parted
her from Karl Arthur, and who was continually sending fresh misfortunes upon her.

Oppressed by an indescribable physical weariness,
the girl walked slowly toward the church town, keeping
her eyes the while to the ground. Persons who saw her
probably thought she was suffering from a bad con-

science, and dared not meet their gaze. It was only with great effort that she finally reached the village street.

She was just dragging herself along the high hedge enclosing the organist's garden, when the gate opened and someone came out into the road and started to walk in her direction. She involuntarily looked up. It was Karl Arthur! . . . She was so startled at seeing him here, and nobody else about, that she stopped dead. He had not gone many paces, however, when a voice from the garden called him back.

The weather was more fitful now than it had been earlier in the summer. Sudden, violent showers came pelting down at all hours of the day. Fru Sundler, having seen a dark cloud appear behind the forest ridge, came running down the garden path with her husband's long caped coat over her arm to offer to Karl Arthur.

As Charlotte slipped past the gate, she saw her help him on with the coat. The two were standing only a step or so away from the gate and she could not help seeing them. Fru Sundler was buttoning the coat for Karl Arthur, who laughed in his boyish way at her being so careful of him.

The woman looked happy and at ease. It was all very innocent apparently, but when Charlotte saw how she took thought for Karl Arthur like a mother or a wife, it struck her instantly that the woman was in love with him. The girl hastened on lest she might see more; but she said to herself, again and again, "She loves him. I should have understood it before. This explains every-thing; this is why she has parted us."

She knew at once that Karl Arthur had no suspicion of it; he was probably dreaming the whole time of his pretty Dalar girl. To be sure, he passed all his evenings now at the organist's house. But no doubt it was the good singing and playing that drew him there. Besides, he had to have someone to talk to, and Thea was an old friend of his family.

The girl was neither shocked nor distressed at her discovery. She raised her head, straightened her back, and walked now with her usual erectness and elasticity.

"It is Thea Sundler who has caused all the mischief," thought Charlotte, "but I'll surely be able to cope with her."

She felt like a sick person who has learned the nature of the illness from which he is suffering, and knows it to be curable. Her hope had been renewed, her confidence restored.

"Fancy my thinking it was the dead General's ugly old signet ring that was out witching again!" she laughed.

She had a vague recollection of once having heard her father say that a promise the Löwenskölds were sup-posed to have made to Thea Sundler's mother, Malvina Spaak, had not been kept, and that therefore a terrible punishment would be meted out to them. It was in order to find out the particulars that she was on her way to her sister's. She had thought until now that the things which had happened to her these last few weeks were linked with some inexorable fate from which there was no escape. But since it was nothing more serious than that Thea Sundler was in love with Karl Arthur, she could find a remedy.

She suddenly abandoned the idea of calling on her sister, and went back home. No, she did not want to believe herself the victim of some ancient curse; she would trust to her own common sense, her strength of will, her initiative, and banish from her thoughts such childish superstitions.

That night, as Charlotte undressed for bed, she stood a long time before a little porcelain Cupid that rested on her bureau.

"So it is *her* you have been protecting all the while," she said to the little image. "Your hand has been held over her and not over me. Then it was for her sake, because she loved Karl Arthur, that Schagerström had to propose to me, and that all these other things had to happen. So it was for her sake that Karl Arthur and I had to quarrel; for her sake that he had to propose to the Dalar girl; for her sake that Schagerström had to send me those flowers, which spoiled the chance of a reconciliation.

"O Cupid! why do you protect her love? Is it because it is secret? Is it true that you look with the greatest favour upon the kind of love that isn't sanctioned?

"My dear Cupid, you should blush for shame! I have

placed you here to watch over my love, and you—you only help the other one.

"Because Thea Sundler loves Karl Arthur, you have allowed me to suffer slander, lampooning, and whistle serenading without coming to my defence. Because Thea Sundler loves Karl Arthur you let me say Yes to Schagerström; you let the banns be proclaimed for us, and perhaps you also mean to lead us to the altar.

"Because Thea Sundler loves Karl Arthur, you have allowed us all to live in a state of misery and terror. You spare no one. The old couple here at the deanery, and his old parents at Karlstad, all must suffer because you protect that fat, fish-eyed wife of the organist!

"Because Thea Sundler loves Karl Arthur you have robbed me of my happiness. I thought it was some horrid troll that wanted to destroy me, and it was none other than you, Cupid, none other than you!"

She had begun in a bantering tone, but the recital of her many cruel experiences worked upon her feelings so that her voice shook as she continued:

"O thou god of lovers, have I not shown thee that I can love?

"Is her love more pleasing to thee than mine? Is she, then, more steadfast than I? Does her heart burn with a stronger, purer flame than mine? Wherefore, wingèd god of lovers, dost thou watch over her love and not over mine?

"What can I do to propitiate thee? O Cupid, Cupid, bethink! Thou art driving him I love to despair and

ruin! Dost thou also mean to give her his love? That is
the only thing thou hast so far denied her. Cupid!
Cupid! dost thou mean to give her his love?"

Then she questioned no more, wondered no more, but
went to bed weeping.

CHAPTER XX

THE FUNERAL FEAST

A FEW days after the Baroness Ekenstedt's return from her visit to Korskyrka Deanery there came to the city of Karlstad a very pretty Dalar girl, one of those itinerant peddlers who carry their wares in a big leather bag, slung across the shoulders. In the city, where there were regular merchants, she was not allowed to carry on her usual trade. Leaving the heavy bag at her lodgings, she fared forth with a small basket on her arm containing hair bracelets and watch chains made of hair—her own handiwork.

The young Dalar girl, in her house-to-house quest of purchasers for these trinkets, came also to the Ekenstedt home. The Baroness, charmed with the beautiful workmanship, invited the vendor to stop at the house a few days and make up some souvenirs from the long fair curls she had cut from her son's head in his childhood, and carefully treasured. The offer was most acceptable to the young wayfarer; and she set about the work the following morning.

Mamselle Jaquette Ekenstedt, who was rather clever with her hands, would often run over to the Dalar girl's room, at the back of the house, to see her at her work.

245

In this way, the two became acquainted and formed what might almost be termed a friendship. The rich city girl was attracted to the poor country lass by the latter's good looks, which were enhanced considerably by her picturesque costume. Jaquette admired the girl's deftness and skill and her good head, which manifested itself in her ability to give terse and pertinent answers.

She was surprised to find such keen intelligence in a person who could neither read nor write, and was somewhat taken aback when, on one or two occasions, she surprised her puffing at a small iron pipe; but, on the whole, there was nothing to mar their pleasant relations.

An amusing thing, too, was the Dalar girl's use of quaint words and expressions which Mamselle Ekenstedt did not understand. Once, when Jaquette was taking her new friend through the house to show her the many fine objects of art they had in the home, the poor girl could only express her wonder and delight by saying "That was gross." Mamselle Jaquette felt rather offended until she found, to her great amusement, that the word *gross* on the lips of a Dalar woman denoted something especially beautiful and grand.

The Baroness herself rarely looked in on the busy worker in hair. It seemed as if she had chosen to make her daughter the medium through whom she would investigate the character, the habits, and the capabilities of the girl, and so find out whether she could be thought of as a wife for her son. For that she had surmised from

the first that the young woman was her son's new
fiancée none could doubt who had any idea of the
Baroness's keenness of perception.

However, the Dalar girl's stay at the Ekenstedt house
was cut short by a sad event. The Colonel's sister, Fru
Elise Sjöberg, widow of the late Provost, who, since
the death of her husband, had made her home with her
brother, had suffered an apoplectic seizure, after which
she lived but a few hours. There were the funeral preparations, and the whole house was given over to seam-
stresses, bakewomen, and decorators, who were to drape
the rooms in black; and the Dalar girl, of course, was
immediately dismissed.

She was called to the Colonel's office to receive her
pay. The servants noted that the conference lasted
uncommonly long, and that when she came out her
eyes were red from weeping. The kind-hearted housekeeper, thinking the girl was unhappy at having to leave
this house where she had been so well treated, as a kind
of solace invited her to come to the kitchen on the day
of the funeral for a taste of the delicacies they would be
having then.

The day set for the burial was Thursday, August
13. The son of the house, Dr. Karl Arthur Ekenstedt,
who had been called home, arrived on Wednesday
evening. He received a hearty welcome, and passed
the hours until bedtime chatting with his parents and
his sister, telling them of the affectionate regard in
which he was now held by his parishioners.

It was not easy for the modest young clergyman to speak of his success; but the Baroness, who already knew something of this through letters from Charlotte, by persistent questioning drew from her son an account of the many expressions of love and gratitude which he had received from every quarter. One can imagine the joy this brought to her mother heart!

Very naturally, on this occasion there was no mention of the poor peddler girl who had been stopping at the house. And in the morning everyone was so preoccupied with preparations for the funeral that Karl Arthur was not informed then, either, of the pretty Dalar girl's visit at his home.

It was Colonel Ekenstedt's wish that his sister be laid away with all honours. Both the Bishop and the Governor had been requested to attend the funeral, as had also many of the first families of Karlstad—those who had had any social affiliation with the widow of the Provost. Among the guests was Ironmaster Schagerström of Stora Sjötorp. He had been invited because of his being related, through his deceased wife, to the sainted Provost. Touched by this recognition from persons who had every reason to feel ill-will toward him, he had thankfully accepted the invitation.

When to the chant of dirge and followed by a long procession of mourners, the body of the Widow Sjöberg had been borne to its last resting place, the funeral party returned to the house of mourning, where an elaborate feast awaited them. Needless to mention that the seriousness and solemnity befitting such an occasion were meticulously observed.

As a kinsman of the departed, Schagerström was placed near the hostess at table, which afforded him an opportunity to see and talk with this remarkable woman whom he had never met until then. The Baroness in her deep mourning made a poetic appeal, and though the sparkling gaiety and ready wit for which she was celebrated could not be brought into play now, her conversation was singularly entertaining and stimulating. Without the least hesitation Schagerström let himself be harnessed to the triumphal chariot of this enchantress. And he was glad to be able to afford her some slight pleasure by telling her about the sermon her son had preached on the Sunday of the week before, and the effect it produced upon his hearers.

In the course of the dinner, young Ekenstedt rose and delivered an impressive oration, which won the admiration of all present. Everyone marvelled at the charming simplicity and, withal, compelling fervour of his utterance, also at the clear portrayal he gave of the admirable qualities of the departed, who, it seemed, had been very much attached to him. Nevertheless, Schagerström's attention, like that of most of the guests, wandered at times from the speaker to the speaker's mother, who was lost in worshipful admiration and wonder. He was informed by a table companion that the Baroness was fifty-six or fifty-seven years of age, and though her face did not precisely belie her years, he doubted whether any young belle could boast such speaking eyes and a smile so fascinating.

Thus far everything had gone well. But when the guests had risen from table to repair to the drawing room, where coffee was to be served, a slight mishap occurred in the kitchen. The housemaid who was to carry in the heavy coffee tray chanced to break a glass and cut her hand so that it bled badly. No one out there seemed to know how to staunch the flow quickly, and, slight as the injury was, the girl could not carry the tray, with her hand dripping blood all the while.

The special waitresses refused to carry the heavy tray, and the housekeeper, in despair, turned to the buxom Dalar girl, who had duly appeared for the promised taste of the delectables, and bade her take in the tray. Without hesitation she picked it up; whereupon the housemaid bound a napkin round the injured hand and went along to see that the guests were served in their proper order.

A waitress with her tray does not ordinarily attract any special attention; but the instant the beautiful Dalar girl, in her colourful dress, appeared among the black-robed mourners, all eyes were drawn to her.

Karl Arthur Ekenstedt, like the others, turned to look. For a moment, he stared blankly, then he rushed up to her and seized hold of the tray.

"You shall not carry a tray in this house, Anna Svärd," he said, "you who are my affianced wife."

The beautiful girl looked at him—half-pleased, half-frightened.

"No, no!" She tried to fend him off. "Let me be till I'm through with this!"

By that time, all the guests were assembled in the drawing room. And now the Bishop and the Bishop's lady, the Governor and the Governor's wife, and everyone else saw the son of the house take the tray away from the girl and set it down on a near-by table.

"I repeat," he said, in a loud tone, "that my fiancée shall not carry a tray in this house!"

Whereupon a high, piercing voice rang out: "Karl Arthur, remember what day this is!"

It was the Baroness who had protested. She was seated at the far end of the room on a large sofa, before which stood a heavy divan table, and to right and left of her sat venerable and corpulent dowagers. She rose and began to thread her way across the floor, but all were so interested in what was going on at the other end of the room that they did not move to let her pass.

Karl Arthur had taken the Dalar girl by the hand and was drawing her forward. The girl was shy, and held a hand to her eyes like a bashful child; but all the same she looked happy. In a moment he stood with her before the Bishop.

"I was not aware until now of my fiancée's presence in my home," he said. "But since she is here, allow me to present her to my Bishop and Superior. And I beg the favour of my Lord Bishop's consent and blessing to my union with this young woman, who has promised to companion me on the path of duty and renunciation which it behooves a servant of Christ to tread."

It could not be denied that the young clergyman by this bold stand—even though, for obvious reasons, it was inexpedient—gained general sympathy. His courageous recognition of the lowly bride he had chosen, like his impassioned words, won favour with many. His pale, fine-featured, sensitive face was stamped on this occasion by a manly strength one would not have attributed to him, and some of the men present had to concede that he was now treading a path which they would have hesitated to take.

Karl Arthur was about to say more, when from behind came an agonizing shriek. The Baroness, in working her way toward the group round the Bishop, had caught her foot in her long frock and fallen, striking her head against the sharp corner of a table and sustaining an ugly bruise on the forehead.

There were cries and commiserations and perhaps a sigh of relief from the Bishop, who had just been saved from a rather awkward situation. Karl Arthur dropped the hand of his fiancée and ran to help his mother to her feet. But that was easier said than done! The Baroness had not lost consciousness, as many another woman in her plight would have done; but she had had a bad fall, and could not rise. The Colonel, with his son, his son-in-law, and the family physician, lifted her gently into an easy chair, and carried her to her room, where the daughters and the capable housekeeper took charge; they undressed her and put her to bed.

The funeral guests stood about the drawing room in grave concern, unwilling to leave before they knew whether the Baroness had been seriously hurt. They saw the Colonel, the daughters, and the maids with anxious faces rush from room to room in quest of linen for bandages, liniment, and a strip of lath that would serve as a splint. By questioning the servants, the guests learned that the bruise on the forehead, which had looked alarmingly bad, was nothing serious; that the left arm had been fractured and must be carried in a sling for a time, but that it, too, would soon be all right. With the knee, however, it was a grave matter. The knee pan had been cracked, and for that to mend the Baroness would have to lie perfectly still; but how long, none could say.

After what they had heard, the guests knew that their hosts had enough to think of without being bothered with them, and they began to troop off. While the gentlemen were out in the hall putting on their coats and hats, the Colonel came hurrying out; he glanced about anxiously till he caught sight of Schagerström, who was just drawing on his gloves.

"Ironmaster Schagerström, if there's nothing to prevent, I wish you would remain awhile."

Schagerström looked mildly surprised, but quickly removed his hat and coat, and followed his host into the now almost deserted drawing room.

"I'd like to have a word with you, Ironmaster," said the Colonel. "If time permits, please sit down till the worst confusion is over!"

Schagerström had rather a long wait. The son-in-law of the house, Lieutenant Arcker, meantime kept him company. The Lieutenant, who was all stirred up over what had happened, told the Ironmaster about the Dalar girl's coming to Karlstad early in the week and her visit at the house. The poor housekeeper, very sorry now that she had asked the Dalar girl to serve the coffee, explained to any and everyone who would listen how she came to invite the girl to be present on the funeral day, and thus the Ironmaster soon understood how it all hung together.

The Colonel at last reappeared.

"Praise God! the bandages have been applied," he said, "and Beata is now resting quietly. I hope she has passed through the worst of it."

He sat down, drew out his handkerchief, and dried his eyes. Colonel Ekenstedt was a tall, well-set-up man with a round head, a ruddy complexion, and a big moustache. He looked the jolly and valiant soldier, and Schagerström was surprised at his sensibility to suffering.

"Ironmaster, I suppose you think me a poor wretch; but that woman has been the joy of my life. When anything happens to her, it's all up with me!"

But Schagerström thought nothing of the kind. He who for nearly a fortnight had fought his unhappy love

for Charlotte in loneliness at Stora Sjötorp was in just
the right mood to understand the Colonel. He admired
the whole-hearted way in which the man spoke of his
love for his wife, and immediately felt a sympathy and
respect for him which he had never felt for the son,
though he conceded that the young man was gifted.

The Colonel, it seemed, wished to speak to Schagerström of Charlotte, that was why he had asked him to
stay.

"I hope you will pardon an old man for meddling in
your affairs," he said, "but I have heard, of course,
about your proposing to Charlotte, and I wish you to
know that we here in Karlstad——" He stopped short.
One of his daughters now stood in the doorway, peering
anxiously into the room. "What's the matter, Jaquette?
Is she worse?"

"No, Father dear. But Mother keeps asking for Karl
Arthur."

"Why," said the Colonel, "I thought he was still
with her."

"No, he hasn't been there for some little time. He
helped carry her in, since then we have not seen him."

"Go see if he's in his room!" said the Colonel. "He
must have gone up to change his clothes."

The instant she was gone, the Colonel again turned
to Schagerström. "Where did I leave off, Ironmaster?"

"You were saying, Colonel, that here in Karlstad
you——"

"Yes, to be sure. I wanted to tell you that we were

certain from the first that Karl Arthur had made a mistake. My wife went down to Korskyrka to learn how the matter stood, and she found that the whole thing——"

Just then the married daughter came to the door.

"Father, dear, have you seen Karl Arthur? Darling Mother is asking for him and can't rest."

"I must speak to Modig," said the Colonel.

The daughter vanished, and the father, too uneasy now to pay any attention to Schagerström, paced the floor until his orderly appeared.

"Modig," he said, "do you know whether that Dalar girl is still in the house?"

"Lord deliver us, Colonel! She came out of this room bawling and went off like a streak."

"And the boy—I mean Dr. Ekenstedt?"

"He came to the kitchen shortly afterward looking for her, and when he heard that she had gone, he, too, rushed out into the street."

"Modig, go down to the city at once and find him. Tell him that the Baroness is seriously ill and wants him!"

"All right, Colonel."

The man was off, and the Colonel immediately picked up the thread of his broken thought.

"As soon as we knew the facts in the case, we determined to effect a reconciliation between the lovers. But first we had to get that Dalar girl out of the way, and then——" He checked himself—afraid that he had said something rude.

"I express myself badly, Ironmaster. My wife should have talked with you; she would have gone about it in the right way."

Schagerström hastened to allay his fears. "The Herr Colonel expresses himself well enough. And I want to say that, as far as I'm concerned, I am already out of the way. Fröken Löwensköld has my consent to forbid the banns whenever she wishes."

The Colonel rose, gave Schagerström a warm handclasp and thanked him profusely.

"This will delight Beata," he said with fervour. "It is the best news that she could have."

Before Schagerström could respond, Fru Eve Arcker was back in the room.

"Father, dear," she said, "I don't know what to do! Karl Arthur has been home, and he didn't come in to see Mother!"

Fru Eve had stood at the bedroom window and seen her brother come up the street and had called back to the Baroness: "Ah! now I see Karl Arthur. He is uneasy about you, darling Mother, and comes running." She had expected her brother to appear in the sick room at any moment, when Jaquette, who was over by the window, suddenly cried out: "O Heavenly Father! Karl Arthur is running back to town. He has only been home to change his clothes."

At that the Baroness raised herself in bed. "No, no, Mother dear!" Fru Eve then cautioned her. "You must lie perfectly still, as the doctor said. I'll bring Karl

Arthur back, never fear!" She ran to the window to call to her brother; the mother protested, but all the same, Fru Eve opened the window, and was leaning out to call to Karl Arthur, when the Baroness, in a stern voice, ordered her to shut the window again. She said emphatically that neither the daughters nor anyone else was to call Karl Arthur home. And now she had sent for the Colonel, presumably to give him the same instructions.

Colonel Ekenstedt rose at once and went to his wife, and Schagerström took this opportunity to inquire about the Baroness's condition.

"Mother suffers some pain," Fru Eve told him, "but that wouldn't matter to her if only Karl Arthur were here. Ah! if one could run down to the city and fetch him!"

"The Fru Baroness, I understand, is very devoted to her son," Schagerström remarked.

"Ah, yes, Ironmaster! Darling Mother thinks of no one but him. And now she is brooding because her son, though he knows she is ill, does not come to her, but runs after that Dalar girl. It is very hard on poor Mother, yet she won't even let us look for him!"

To which Schagerström replied: "I can understand how the Fru Baroness feels; but since she has not forbidden me to search for her son, I shall try to find him."

He was just on his way out when the Colonel came back.

"My wife would like to say a few words to you,

Ironmaster; she wants to thank you." And with a certain ceremoniousness he took Schagerström by the hand, and led him into the sick room.

The Ironmaster, who but shortly before had so greatly admired the vivacious, fascinating woman of the world, was deeply affected as he saw her now a poor invalid, her head swathed in bandages, her face waxen pale and as if shrunken. She did not appear to be suffering, but over her features rested a stern, almost threatening look. A blow that hurt far more than the bodily injuries had kindled in her a proud, contemptuous wrath. Those about her, knowing what had called it forth, thought she could never forgive the son the lack of feeling he had shown that day. As Schagerström stepped to the bedside, she opened her eyes and gave him a long, searching look. Then she said, in a faint voice:

"Ironmaster, do you love Charlotte?"

Schagerström felt reluctant to bare his heart to a stranger. Nor could he lie to this sick and unhappy woman; so he said nothing.

The Baroness, however, did not seem to require an answer; she already knew what she needed to know. After a little she said:

"Ironmaster, do you think Charlotte still loves Karl Arthur?"

This time he could answer without hesitation that Charlotte loved her son with unfailing devotion.

As she looked at him now there were tears in her eyes.

"It is hard, Ironmaster," she said in the gentlest voice, "when the one you love has no love for you."

And Schagerström understood why she spoke thus to him: she knew how it felt to be spurned. Now she was no longer a stranger but a fellow sufferer; she felt for him, and he for her. To the lonely man, her sympathy was as balsam to a wound.

He slowly drew nearer and gently lifted the hand that rested on the coverlet, and kissed it reverently.

Once again she gave him a long look. Now it was not veiled by tears. That look penetrated the inmost recesses of his heart—searched and saw. And now she said to him, almost with affection: "Ironmaster, I wish you were my son!"

A slight tremor went through Schagerström. What had prompted the Baroness to say just that to him? Did she know, then, this woman whom he had met that day for the first time—did she know how, as a child, he had stood outside his mother's door and wept—hungry for a little love? Did she know with what agony of dread he had approached his parents, fearing their glances of disapproval? Did she know that he would have been proud had the humblest peasant woman said that she wished she had a son like him? Did she know that she could have paid him no higher tribute?

In his overwhelming gratefulness he threw himself down beside the bed, and wept. In a few broken sentences, he tried to express what he felt.

The others must have thought him very impressionable. But how should they understand what her words meant to him? It seemed as if all his ugliness, his awkwardness, his stupidity had suddenly dropped away; he had not felt like this since the day his deceased wife had first told him that she loved him.

But the Baroness understood all that was at work in his heart, and she said once more, as if to dispel any lingering doubt:

"It is the truth, Ironmaster, that I wish you were my son."

Then he knew that the only way in which he could repay her for the happiness she had given him was to bring her own son back to her. So he went out at once to seek for him.

The first person Schagerström met in the street was Lieutenant Arcker, who was out on the same errand; he also came upon the Colonel's orderly and, with their help, he proceeded to take the necessary steps. The house where the Dalar girl lodged was easily found; but neither she nor Karl Arthur was there. All the other places where Dalar folk were wont to stop were thoroughly searched, and the night watchman was ordered to keep an eye out for Karl Arthur.

Soon darkness came, and it seemed impossible to go on with the search. In a city where the streets were so narrow and poorly lighted; where the buildings were crowded together; where whipping posts and houses of the strangest sort stood huddled like cattle in a snowstorm; where every yard held any number of good hiding places, the chances of spying out anyone were slight indeed.

Schagerström, however, continued to tramp the streets for several hours. It was long past midnight when he heard quick footsteps and guessed whose they were. By the reddish glimmer of a street lamp he recognized the slender form of young Ekenstedt. Since Karl Arthur was going in the right direction, the Iron-master did not speak, he simply followed him up the street all the way to the Ekenstedt house.

When at last he saw him go in he felt that his services were no longer needed. But a great curiosity to learn the outcome of the meeting between mother and son spurred him on. A few moments after Karl Arthur had entered the house, Schagerström opened the front door and stepped into the hall.

There stood the son of the house surrounded by his own people. Everyone, it seemed, had sat up for him— too uneasy to go to bed. The Colonel came bearing a light, and held it up to his son as if asking, "Is it you or someone else?" The two sisters came running down the stairs with their hair in curl papers, but fully dressed. The housekeeper and the orderly rushed out from the kitchen.

Karl Arthur, no doubt, had meant to steal quietly up to his room, and had got halfway on the staircase when he was stopped by the onrushing household.

As Schagerström entered, he saw the two sisters seize

hold of the brother's hands and try to drag him along with them.

"Come to dear Mother!" they said. "You don't know how she has been pining for you!"

"Is it right and proper for you to be running about the town," roared the Colonel, "when you know that your mother is ill?"

Karl Arthur was still on the stair. His face was as if cut in stone; he showed neither embarrassment nor regret, but said quite coolly:

"Does Papa wish me to go to Mamma now, at once? Wouldn't it be better to wait till morning?"

"Gad, boy! you must go to her now. She has fretted herself into a high fever, lying there waiting for you!"

"Pardon me, Father, but it is no fault of mine." There was something downright hostile in the son's attitude, and the Colonel, wishing to avert a war of words, said in a mild, conciliatory tone:

"Just let her see that you are at home. Go in and kiss her, and by morning all will be well."

"I cannot kiss her," the son declared.

"You damned——" The Colonel checked himself. "Say straight out what you mean! No, wait a bit!— Come with me!"

He led him into his office and shut the door on the group of curious listeners. In a moment he came out again, went up to Schagerström, and said to him:

"I should be very glad, Ironmaster, if you would be present at our conference."

Schagerström followed him at once, and the door was closed again. The Colonel sat down at his writing table, then turned to the son. "Now, tell me quickly what has come over you!"

"Well, Father, since you say that Mother has fever, I suppose I must make my confession to you, though I very well know that she is the real offender."

"May we hear what you're driving at?" asked the father.

"What I want to say is that after to-day I shall never again set foot in my parents' house."

"Whew!" said the Colonel. "And the reason?"

"*This!*" Karl Arthur drew from his pocket a roll of bank notes and slapped it down on the table in front of the Colonel.

"Oho! So she couldn't hold her tongue."

"Oh, yes," said Karl Arthur, "she kept silence as long as it was possible for her to do so. We had been sitting in the cemetery for hours, she and I, and all she would tell me was that she must go away and would never see me again. It was not until I accused her of having found another sweetheart here in Karlstad that she finally told me how my parents had bribed her to give me up, and how my father, moreover, had threatened to disinherit me if I married her. What could the girl do? She had accepted the two hundred riksdalers you offered her. I was rather amused to find that my parents had set so high a price upon my person."

"Well," said the Colonel with a shrug, "we also

promised that she should have five times that amount to set up house when she married some other fellow."

Karl Arthur replied, with a slight laugh, that she had mentioned that also. Then he became serious and said with rising indignation:

"And it is my own father and my own mother who treat me thus! Two weeks ago my mother came to see me at Korskyrka and we talked of my prospective marriage and my plans for the future. I told her then that Providence had sent this young girl to me; that I counted upon her as a helpmate with whom I could lead a life in accordance with the will of God. She was my hope. My life's happiness depended upon my having her for wife. When I told my mother that, she seemed to be touched and said that I was right. And now, a fortnight after, I find that she has been trying to part us. What am I to think of such ruthlessness—such duplicity? Should I not shudder at having to call such a woman Mother?"

The Colonel shrugged his shoulders, as if insensible of any guilt and incapable of remorse. Then he said:

"Oh, Beata felt sorry for you because Charlotte had played you a mean trick, and she didn't want to rail at you about your new troth. Naturally, we knew that you had jumped from the frying pan into the fire, but thought it best to let matters take their course for a time. Then the heaven-sent one flew right into the mouth of us poor sinners! Beata engaged her in order to find out what sort she was. And, indeed, she's an excellent person in many respects, but she can't read or write; besides, she smokes a pipe and, as for cleanliness . . . Well, my boy, we tried to settle it in the best way. You would have been satisfied had you allowed yourself time to come to your senses. But the whole play was spoiled by that blessed person's appearing with the coffee tray."

"Father, can you not see what it was?"

"Certainly, I can see that it was damned unfortunate."

"I see in it the finger of God. This woman whom the Lord has chosen as a mate for me, He again sent across my path. And, moreover, I see His just retribution. When I asked the Bishop to bless our union, my mother rushed forward to prevent it. She thought that feigning to stagger and fall would be the most effective interruption. Her manœuvre succeeded all too well. . . . God intervened!"

The father's coolness now deserted him. "For shame, boy!" he cried. "How dare you accuse your mother of such craftiness!"

"Beg pardon, Father, but I have had occasion of late to prove woman's deceit. Charlotte and my mother have taught my heart a lesson it will not soon forget!"

The Colonel thrummed on the table a moment, then he said:

"I'm glad you mentioned Charlotte. I was just going to speak to you of her. You can never make me believe that she threw you over in order to marry a rich man.

She cares more for you than for all the wealth of the world. I believe that it was all your fault and that she shouldered the blame so that we, your parents, would not be angry at you, and that you might escape the condemnation of others. What have you to say to that?"

"She allowed the banns to be published."

"Reflect, Karl Arthur! Clear your mind of all delusions as to Charlotte's perfidy. Don't you understand that she blamed herself in order to protect you? She let the world think the engagement was broken at her behest. But think back! Search your heart! Was it not you who broke the troth?"

Karl Arthur stood silent awhile; he really seemed to be searching his heart, as his father had bidden him. Suddenly he turned to Schagerström, and said:

"Ironmaster, how came you to send that bouquet of flowers? Had you received any message from Charlotte on Monday afternoon? What was the Dean's errand to you?"

Schagerström answered the questions in their order. "The flowers were sent in token of my profound respect. I received no message from Fröken Löwensköld on Monday. The Dean's errand was to return my call of the previous day."

Again Karl Arthur was lost in thought. At length he said:

"In that case, it would appear that my father is right."

His two listeners drew a sigh of relief. It was a gracious admission of an error in judgment. No ordinary man would have done a thing like that.

"Well, Son, then—— But first I must tell you that Ironmaster Schagerström has promised to forego all claim——"

"Ironmaster Schagerström need make no sacrifice on my account," Karl Arthur interrupted. "Please understand, Father, that I shall never make up with Charlotte. I love another."

The Colonel brought his fist down on the table. "One can't get anywhere with you! So you attach no value whatever to such steadfast devotion and such noble sacrifice?"

"I regard it as a providence of God that the bond between Charlotte and me has been broken."

"I understand," said the Colonel bitterly. "At the same time, no doubt you thank God that the bond between you and your parents has also been broken."

The young man treated this with silence.

"Mark my words!" the Colonel continued. "You are on your way to destruction. And we are to blame. Beata humoured and spoiled you till you came to regard yourself as a demigod, and I allowed it simply because I couldn't bear to oppose her in any way. And now you are repaying her just as I thought you would. I have felt all the while that it would end like this; but it's hard, all the same, when it comes!"

He sighed heavily; then he said in a mild voice:

"Look here, Son! Now that you have foiled all our wicked designs, won't you go in and kiss your mother to ease her mind?"

"If, as you say, I have foiled your evil designs, am I therefore to forget the pernicious bent of mind which characterizes my nearest of kin? Wherever I turn, I find nothing but love of the world and all that pertains thereto: folly and deceit!"

"Don't worry about that, Karl Arthur! We are old-fashioned folk; we have our piety, as you have yours."

"Father, I cannot."

"Well," said the Colonel, "I've settled my account with you; but she, she—ah! you must know that she thinks you love her. I beg of you, Karl Arthur, for her sake, just for her sake. . . .!"

"The only kindness I can show my mother is to go away without telling her how my heart has been wounded by her perfidy."

The Colonel rose to his feet. "You—you don't know what love is!"

"I am a servant of the truth," Karl Arthur declared. "I cannot kiss my mother."

"Go to bed!" said the old man. "Sleep on the matter!"

"The conveyance is ordered for four o'clock, and we have only a quarter-hour till then."

"The conveyance can come back at ten," said the Colonel. "Do as I say—sleep on it."

Now for the first time Karl Arthur seemed to weaken a bit. "If my father and my mother will turn from their worldly ways, if they will live like humble folk; if my sisters will serve the poor and the sick——"

"None of your impertinent cant!"

"This cant, as you call it, is the word of God."

"Bosh!" said the Colonel.

Karl Arthur raised his arms toward heaven, like a preacher in the pulpit. "Then forgive me, O Lord, that I cast off these my fleshly parents! Let nothing that is theirs, neither their cares nor their love, their estates or their money, touch me! Help me, Lord! Deliver me from these creatures of sin, that I may live in Thy glorious freedom!"

The Colonel had listened impassively. Now he said: "The god you believe in is a merciless god, and he will surely grant your prayer. And when some day you come to my door, begging and pleading, you may be sure that I, too, will remember your prayer."

That was the last that was said between father and son. Karl Arthur now quietly left the room, and the Colonel was alone with Schagerström.

For a few moments the old man sat with his head bowed on his hands. Presently he turned to Schagerström.

"I wish you would tell Charlotte what has happened. I can't write about it. Tell her everything, Ironmaster, everything. I want her to know that we tried to help her, though we failed miserably. And say to her also that she is the only person in the world who can help my poor wife and my poor son."

CHAPTER XXI

SATURDAY MORNING

IT WAS on a Monday, just fourteen days after
Schagerström had proposed, that Charlotte by
chance discovered that Thea Sundler was in love
with Karl Arthur. The peculiar feeling that came to
her then, of at last having in her hands a weapon by
means of which she might regain her lost happiness—
that feeling persisted for several days. By Tuesday's
post she had a letter from the Baroness, telling her that
everything was going surprisingly well, and that very
soon the misunderstandings would be cleared away.
All that heartened her; which, indeed, was well.

On Wednesday she heard that Karl Arthur had gone
to Karlstad to attend his aunt's funeral, and felt that
she could count upon the Baroness to take advantage
of the opportunity to speak to him of her. Her innocence
of any intrigue would then be established. Perhaps he
would be touched by her sacrifice and come back to her.
She had no conception as to how the Baroness would
work the miracle, but she knew that the Colonel's wife
could find ways and means where things looked hopelessly black to others.

Despite her great faith in the Baroness, the days while
Karl Arthur was away at Karlstad were exceedingly

anxious ones. She was tossed between fear and hope, and wondered what the Baroness would do. Charlotte, who saw Karl Arthur every day, could not deny that his love for her was dead. Though they sat at the same table, he would look beyond her, as if she were not there. This was not a misunderstanding; this could not be explained away. With him it was over. His love was like a sawed-off branch; no power on earth could re-attach it to the tree and make it grow again.

Karl Arthur was expected home on Friday, and that, of course, was the most trying day of all. From early morning till late afternoon, Charlotte sat at the window of the dining room that gave on the wing—watching and waiting. For the thousandth time she went over in her mind all that had happened—searched and probed and was none the wiser. It looked as if she would be kept in suspense the whole day. However, at four o'clock, Karl Arthur returned. He went straight to the wing, came out in a moment, walked briskly toward the gate without casting a glance at the main dwelling, and set off on the road to the church town.

So it was Thea Sundler he wanted to see and not Charlotte. This, then, was the result of the Baroness's efforts! Charlotte could but say to herself that they had failed.

All hope seemed to die within her. She avowed that never again would she allow herself to be deluded into thinking that there was any help or salvation for her.

And yet, there must have been some hope left in her

heart; for when the housemaid came to her room at about six o'clock on Saturday morning with greetings from Dr. Ekenstedt, who asked if he might speak with her, Charlotte instantly interpreted the request to see her at the early breakfast as evidence that he still loved her; that he longed to resume the old happy relations; the old ways.

She felt confident now that the Baroness had kept her word, and that the miracle had been wrought. She ran down the stairs and into the dining room so fast that her curls flew about her ears. But one glance at Karl Arthur told her that she was wrong. He rose as she entered, but there were no embraces or kisses, no outpourings of gratitude for her shielding of him. He stood awkwardly silent for two or three minutes, as if she had come upon him so suddenly that he had not had time to collect his thoughts. Finally he said:

"It seems that you, Charlotte, out of sheer compassion, assumed the blame for the break between us; that you went so far as to accept Schagerström's proposal of marriage and to have the banns for you and him read in church in order to lend plausibility to the deception. You probably meant well, Charlotte, and thought you were doing me a great service. For my sake you have had to suffer much slander and revilement, and I understand that I owe you a debt of thanks."

Charlotte drew herself up and stiffened her neck as she had not done in weeks, and her face assumed a stony expression. She made no answer.

He continued: "Your mode of action, it appears, was prompted in the first place by a desire to shield me from the wrath of my parents. If such was your hope, I must tell you that your efforts were futile. During my recent visit to Karlstad, dissension arose between me and my parents over my matrimonial plans, which led to a complete break. I am no longer son of theirs, and they are no longer my parents."

"Why, Karl Arthur!" cried Charlotte, all fire and life now, "whatever are you saying? Your mother—have your broken with your own mother?"

"My dear Charlotte, my mother tried to bribe Anna Svärd to marry some man of her home town. By underhanded methods, she sought to wreck my life's happiness. She has no understanding whatever of the things that are vital to me. My mother wishes me to renew the bond with you. In fact, she went to the trouble of inviting Schagerström to the funeral that she might have opportunity to ask him to release you. But I need not go into all that, as you, of course, are already familiar with the details of my parents' plot. You bounded right merrily into the room, thinking, no doubt, that the pretty plan had worked out successfully."

"I know nothing about your mother's plans, Karl Arthur—nothing. The only thing she has told me is that she does not believe the lies Thea Sundler has been circulating about me. When I knew you had been to Karlstad, I thought that perhaps you had learned the truth. But let us not talk of me! Look here, Karl Arthur, you can't be angry at your mother! Won't you go back at once and make up with her? Ah, say you will!"

"How can I? To-morrow is Sunday, and I have to preach."

"Then write her a few lines and let me go. Remember that your mother is old. She has retained her youthful spirit because of her joy in you. You have been youth and health to her. The instant you desert her, she will become an old and broken woman. It would be the end of her gaiety, her delightful banter. She would become more dour, more bitter than anyone. Oh, Karl Arthur, I fear that this will kill her! You have been her god, you can give her life or death. Let me go to her with a word from you!"

"I know all that, Charlotte, but I do not wish to write. My mother was ill when I left Karlstad; my father begged me to make up with her, and I refused. She has lied and played the hypocrite."

"But, Karl Arthur, if she has dissembled, she has done so only for your sake. I don't know in what way your parents have offended you; but whatever they may have done, it was for your welfare. Such things one must forgive. Can't you think of your mother as she was when you were a little chap? What would your home have been without her? When you came home from school with good marks, what satisfaction would it have been to you if your mother had not been so pleased with them? And later, when you returned from college for the Easter and Christmas holidays, where would have been the joy had your mother not been there to welcome you? And when you sat down to the Christmas feast would you have had any pleasure if your mother had not thought out little surprises? It was she who frosted the Yule pudding and trimmed the Yule-buck. Think of these things, Karl Arthur!"

"I sat alone by the roadside all day yesterday, Charlotte, and thought of my mother. From a worldly standpoint, she has been a good mother. I concede that this is true according to the world's idea and your idea of goodness. But I cannot say the same of her according to God's way and mine of judging. I have asked myself what Christ would have said of such a mother."

"Christ—" Charlotte's throat suddenly tightened so that she could scarcely utter the words—"Christ would have looked beyond the outer and incidental. He would have seen that such a mother could have followed Him to the foot of the Cross, aye, and let herself be crucified in His stead. He would have judged accordingly."

"Perhaps you are right, Charlotte I dare say my mother would die for me, but she would never let me live my own life. Charlotte, my mother would not allow me to serve God; she would expect me to serve her and her world; therefore she and I must part."

"It is not Christ Who commands you to break with your mother!" Charlotte exclaimed indignantly. "It is Thea Sundler who makes you think that your mother and I——"

Karl Arthur stopped her with a gesture. "I knew," he said, "that this discussion was going to be an unpleasant one, and would have preferred to avoid it; but it was the very person whom you have just named and whom you choose to hate who prevailed upon me to tell you the result of my parents' efforts."

"Oh, really!" said Charlotte. "Well, I'm not surprised. She knew that I should feel unhappy enough to weep tears of blood."

"Construe her motive as you will, it was she, at all events, who intimated to me that I should thank you for what you had wished to do for me."

Charlotte, knowing that nothing would be gained by angry protests, controlled her feelings and went about it in a different way.

"Forgive me," she said, "for being so hasty! Indeed, I had no wish to hurt you; but you know that I have always loved your mother, and I think it is dreadful that she who lies sick and longs for a word from you does not get it. Really, Karl Arthur, wouldn't you like me to go? It would not imply that you wish to make up with me, too."

"Certainly you may go, Charlotte."

"But not without a message from you."

"Don't ask me again!" snapped Karl Arthur. "It's useless."

Into her pretty face came a dark, accusing look, and she regarded him fixedly. "That you would dare!"

"Dare? What do you mean, Charlotte?"

"You said awhile ago that you were going to preach to-morrow."

"Yes, of course."

"Do you remember the time at Upsala when you were afraid to take an examination because you had been rude to your mother?"

"I'll never forget it!"

"But you seem to have forgotten. And I say to you now, that never again will you preach as you have preached the last two Sundays until you make your peace with your mother."

Karl Arthur laughed. "Now, Charlotte, don't try to frighten me."

"I'm not trying to frighten you. I am only telling you how it will be: Every time you enter a pulpit you'll think of this, that you refused to be reconciled to your mother, and it will take from you all power, all inspiration."

"My dear Charlotte, do you think to frighten me as one frightens a child?"

"Remember my words!" said the young girl. "Think of them now, while there is time! By to-morrow or the day after, it may be too late."

She moved toward the door. Before he could answer, she was gone.

* * *

After breakfast the Dean asked Charlotte to come to his study.

"Schagerström must have driven by the house last evening," he said, "for his groom came to the kitchen with a large envelope addressed to me, which contained a lengthy epistle to you, Charlotte, also a short note to me, requesting that I prepare you for the sad news in his letter."

"I am not unprepared, Uncle," said Charlotte. "I have talked with Karl Arthur to-day, and already know that he has broken with his parents and that his mother is ill."

"What are you telling me, child?" The Dean was dumbfounded.

"I can't talk about it now, Uncle." Charlotte patted the old man's arm. "But let me have my letter." She took it from his hand and went up to her own room.

Schagerström's letter gave quite a full account of what had taken place recently, especially on the day of the funeral. From the hastily scribbled lines, Charlotte got a pretty clear conception of all that had transpired: The Dalar girl's visit to Karlstad; her unexpected appearance on the day of the funeral; the Baroness's unfortunate fall; her vain longing for her son; Schagerström's visit to the sick room; the search for the son; the heated altercation in the Colonel's office between father and son; and last, the writer mentioned the fact that the Colonel had requested him to tell Charlotte all this, and quoted, word for word, what the Colonel had said as to Charlotte's being the only person in the world who could help his poor wife and his poor son.

He wrote further:

I promised to carry out the Colonel's wishes; but on returning to my quarters it occurred to me at once that I ought not to intrude myself upon you, good Fröken, and therefore I decided to pass the short space still left of the night inditing these lines. I beg your indulgence for there being so many. Perhaps it was the certainty that they would be read by you that set the pen running. It is now well into the morning, and my travelling carriage has been waiting an hour or two; but I must add a few words more.

I have observed young Ekenstedt on various occasions, and at times have found him a gifted and noble soul who gives promise of future greatness. But sometimes, too, I have found him hard, almost cruel, credulous, irascible, and lacking in sound judgment. My own supposition is that the young man is open to an evil influence which, in some insidious way, is undermining his character.

You, dear Fröken, are now cleared in the eyes of your fiancé of all suspicion. As you and he see each other every day, he surely cannot remain insensitive to your great charm. Without a doubt, good feelings between you two will be restored. At all events, it is the sincere hope of your humble servant that your happiness, which through me has been blighted, may soon bloom anew. Permit a man who loves you and wishes you a perfect happiness to warn you against the *influence* to which I referred, and counsel you to remove it if possible.

And permit me one word more. I need not tell you that the Colonel's prayer is also mine. For the Baroness Ekenstedt I have a boundless affection, and if, to save her life, you should have need of my help, you may count upon me, even to the supreme sacrifice.

Your humble and devoted servant,

GUSTAF HENRIK SCHAGERSTRÖM.

When Charlotte had read the letter through twice, she sat for a long moment wondering what these two men, the Colonel and the Ironmaster, hoped from her. What did the Colonel mean by his message? and why had Schagerström taken the trouble to dash off in such haste this long letter to her?

Suddenly she remembered that the next day was the one for the third, and last, reading of the banns. Did Schagerström think that by his letting her know all this, she would allow their banns to be published once again, and thus make them legally binding?

However, she quickly absolved him from suspicion of any such intent. He had not thought of himself, or he would have written more guardedly. As it was, he had expressed himself quite freely about Karl Arthur; had unwittingly laid himself open to the suspicion that his communication had been prompted by desire to injure a rival.

What, then, did he and the Colonel think she could do? She knew well enough what they expected of her; they wanted her to bring the son back to his mother. But how could she? Did they suppose that she had any power over Karl Arthur? Had she not already tried to persuade him? Had she not exhausted every argument at her command—and all to no effect?

Closing her eyes, she saw, as it were before her, the Baroness lying with head bandaged and face ashen-pale and drawn. She saw the look of proud, contemptuous wrath; she heard her say to the man who, like herself, suffered from slighted love, "It is hard when the one you love has no love for you."

Charlotte suddenly rose, folded the letter, and slipped it into her pocket, thinking it might be a protection to her, and a help. In a few moments, she was on her way to the village.

When she came to the hedge enclosing the organist's garden, she paused a moment and prayed a silent prayer. She was going to try to persuade Thea Sundler to send Karl Arthur home to his mother; for Thea alone could do it. Charlotte prayed God to fill her heart with patience that she might soften this woman who hated her, and win her to her cause.

She had the good fortune to find Fru Sundler at home, and quite alone. She asked whether Thea could give her a few minutes of her time. They were soon sitting *vis-à-vis* in Fru Sundler's cosy parlour.

Charlotte, feeling that she ought to start conversation with an apology for having cut off those curls of Thea's, said:

"I was so distraught that day; but of course it was dreadful of me to do such a thing."

Fru Sundler was extremely affable. She understood Charlotte's feelings perfectly, she said; she, herself, she added, had still greater cause to ask forgiveness. She had believed Charlotte guilty and judged her harshly. But from this time forth she would do all that lay in her power to reëstablish Charlotte's honour.

Charlotte, with equal politeness, thanked her for the promise, and said that she had something on her mind just then more pressing than the righting of her own wrongs.

Whereupon she told Thea Sundler about the Baroness's accident. Karl Arthur, she said, probably was not aware that his mother had suffered such grave injuries, or surely he would not have left Karlstad without saying a kind word to her.

Thea now became very reserved. She had found that Karl Arthur, in the more important moves, was guided by some Divine inspiration. In all his doings, he walked in the ways of God.

Charlotte reddened slightly at this, but said nothing that might give offence. She merely stated that it was her firm conviction that the Baroness would never recover from Karl Arthur's break with her. Did not Thea think it dreadful that he would have his mother's death on his conscience?

Fru Sundler replied with condescending sweetness that she had the faith that God's protecting Hand would rest upon both mother and son; that Providence perhaps would lead dear Tante Ekenstedt into a more earnest Christianity.

Charlotte saw again the ashen-pale face with its look of scorn, and feared that this was hardly the way to make the Baroness a more devout Christian. However, she was careful not to offer any unwise comment. She had come, she said, simply to beg Fru Sundler to use her influence with Karl Arthur to bring about a reconciliation between him and his mother.

Fru Sundler now spoke in a low voice, more sibilant, more oilily meek than ever. Well, perhaps she had some little influence with Karl Arthur; but in a matter of such import she dared not use it. This he must decide himself.

"She does not want to do it," thought Charlotte. "It's useless trying to appeal to her sympathy; she will do nothing unless there's something to be gained."

Charlotte rose at once, said a most polite Good-bye, and went toward the door. Fru Sundler, of course, accompanied her, airily unfolding, meanwhile, her ideas as to the responsibility which rested with one who had the good fortune to be in the confidence of Karl Arthur.

Charlotte, her hand on the latch, now turned and cast a glance round the room.

"You really have a very pleasant parlour," she said. "I don't wonder that Karl Arthur likes it so well here!"

Fru Sundler, not understanding the drift, kept silence.

"I can picture how you pass your evenings here," Charlotte continued. "Your husband sits at the piano, you stand over there and sing, and Karl Arthur drops into one of these nice easy chairs and listens to the music."

"Yes," said Fru Sundler, still uncertain whither this was leading; "we have, as you say, very pleasant evenings."

"And sometimes perhaps Karl Arthur, too, contributes to the entertainment?" said Charlotte. "Reads a poem or talks about the little gray parsonage of his dreams?"

"Yes. My husband and I are very happy that Karl Arthur honours our humble home with his visits."

"If nothing comes between, this happiness may continue for many years, perhaps; Karl Arthur is not likely to marry his Dalar girl very soon. He will find it rather dull and lonely at the deanery, and may need a pleasant refuge like this."

Fru Sundler was all attention now. She felt that there was something back of the girl's remarks, but what, she could not make out.

"If I were to remain at the deanery," said Charlotte with a slight laugh, "then perhaps I could furnish him some diversion, now and then, for an idle hour. I know, to be sure, that he has ceased to love me, but we need not live a dog-and-cat life on that account. For instance, I might help him establish his orphanage. When people see each other every day, they have many interests in common."

"Naturally. But, Charlotte, do you really intend to leave the deanery?"

"It is hard to tell. You know, of course, that I have thought some of marrying Schagerström."

With that, Charlotte opened the door. When out in the hall, she noticed that a shoe lace had come undone and bent down to retie it. For safety's sake, she also retied the other string. "I must give her time to think it over," she said to herself. "If she loves him, she won't let me go. But if she doesn't . . . ?"

While she stood bending over her shoe Fru Sundler came out into the hall.

"Dear Charlotte, would you mind stepping inside again? It has just occurred to me that this is your first visit to my home. May I not offer you a glass of raspberry juice? You must not leave without having some refreshment. That would be robbing the house of the pleasure of hospitality, as the saying goes."

Charlotte, having finished with her shoe laces, straightened up and thanked the hostess kindly. Indeed, she had no objection to waiting in the cosy little parlour while Fru Sundler ran down to the cellar for the cordial. "Thea is no fool," thought Charlotte. That at all events was some consolation.

Fru Sundler was gone rather long. Charlotte took it as a good omen, and bided quietly and patiently. In her eyes was the look of a fisherman when he sees the fish circling round the baited hook.

However, in due time the hostess appeared with the cordial and some small cakes. Charlotte poured herself a little of the dark raspberry liquid, took a ginger cookie, and nibbled at it while listening to Fru Sundler's excuses for having been gone so long.

"What a delicious gingersnap!" Charlotte ejaculated. "It must have been made by your mother's recipe. She is said to have been a veritable wizard of the culinary art. It's fortunate for you, Thea, that you are such a good cook. Karl Arthur, I'm sure, has better fare here than at the deanery."

"No, indeed!" said Thea. "You must remember that we are poor folk. But, Charlotte, let us not talk of such trivial things! We must think of poor, dear Tante Ekenstedt. May I speak quite frankly to you?"

"It was for that I came, dear Thea," Charlotte replied in her blandest tone.

Neither of them raised her voice, but lowered it, rather. They sat quietly sipping their cordial and nibbling their cakes, but their hands trembled like those of eager chess players, when near the end of a long game.

"Then I'll tell you honestly, Charlotte, that I think Karl Arthur is a little afraid of his mother. Not so much of herself, perhaps; for she is too far away, and has few opportunities to influence him directly; but he has marked that she is striving to bring you and him together again. Pardon my saying so, but it is this he fears more than anything."

Charlotte smiled to herself. "So that's how we're to take it!—Ah, no, Thea is not stupid!"

"Then you really believe, Thea, that you could persuade Karl Arthur to go to Karlstad and make it right with his mother; that is, if he were assured that it would not entail any consequences as regards myself?"

Fru Sundler gave a shrug. "It is merely a supposition," she said. "Perhaps he is also a bit afraid of his own weakness. You are a very attractive woman, Charlotte, and I don't see how a young man would be able to resist one who is as beautiful as you are."

"You mean——"

"Ah, Charlotte, it's hard to say it, but I think that if Karl Arthur had something definite to hold to——"

"You mean that if to-morrow there is a third reading

of the banns for Schagerström and me, he would feel safe?"

"That, of course, would be a good thing. But, Charlotte, an announcement is not a fulfilment. The wedding might be postponed indefinitely, and you would continue to reside at the deanery year after year."

Charlotte set her glass back on the tray rather hastily. She knew when she came that she would have to pay a high price if Thea was to allow Karl Arthur to go to his mother, and thought it would be sufficient with the banns.

"I would suggest"—Fru Sundler spoke now in whispers—"that you go home at once and write a little note to Schagerström requesting that he come to the deanery to-morrow, immediately after Service, to be married, then——"

"Impossible!" It came out like a desperate cry for mercy. It was the only time during the entire conversation that the young girl had betrayed her sufferings.

Fru Sundler went right on, regardless of the other's protest. "I don't know what may or may not seem impossible to you. I'm only saying that, if you were to write such a letter and send it to Stora Sjötorp by a reliable messenger, we could have a reply within five or six hours. If the answer is satisfactory, I will do everything in my power to induce Karl Arthur to go."

"But if you should fail?"

"I have a warm affection for Tante Ekenstedt, Charlotte, and am really distressed about her. If I can only dispel Karl Arthur's fears in the matter already mentioned, I don't think that I shall fail. In fact, I'm confident that Karl Arthur will leave for Karlstad to-morrow as soon as the service is over. Before the marriage is solemnized, you will hear that he has gone."

It was a clear and carefully thought-out plan, with no escape gaps or loopholes. Charlotte sat looking down. Could she do it? It meant living a whole lifetime with a man whom she did not love. Could she? . . . Her hand fumbled over the letter in her skirt pocket. . . . Yes, she could!

She took up the glass again and drained it at one draught, in order to clear her throat.

"I will let you know what Schagerström answers as soon as possible," she said, and rose to go.

CHAPTER XXII

SATURDAY AFTERNOON AND EVENING

WHEN something difficult lies before one, it is well to be able to say: "This is a necessary thing. I know why I do it." The strong dread is allayed by the clear conviction that one cannot do otherwise. It is a true saying that when once a thing has been done, and there is no altering it, one finds it quite easy to bear.

Charlotte wrote to Schagerström immediately upon her return to the deanery. It was only a few lines, but they cost her a deal of effort. Here is what she finally managed to set down:

In consideration of the last lines in the Ironmaster's letter, I should like to know whether the Ironmaster can come to the deanery to-morrow at about two o'clock, to have the Dean pronounce us man and wife.

I beg for a word, in reply, by the bearer.

The Ironmaster's humble servant,
CHARLOTTE LÖWENSKÖLD.

After obtaining the Dean's permission to send the note by his coachman, she began to relate to the two old friends what had happened that morning, to prepare them for what the morrow might bring forth.

"Never mind!" said the Dean's wife. "You can tell us about it some other time. Go up to your room now and rest awhile. You look like a ghost!"

The old lady helped her upstairs, made her stretch out on a sofa, and spread a shawl over her. "Now don't be uneasy," she said. "I'll waken you in time for dinner."

For a while the thoughts churned in Charlotte's head faster and more furiously than ever; but gradually they quieted down, as if understanding at last that there was no need to bother further, that the matter had been settled once and for all. Before long, the poor girl dropped off to sleep.

When dinner was served, the Fru Dean looked in as she had promised; but finding the girl asleep, she did not disturb her; nor was she awakened until the coachman returned from Stora Sjötorp with Schagerström's answer.

The Ironmaster had written just the one line:

Your humble servant will be proud and happy to come.

The scrap of a note was immediately sent to Fru Sundler. Now Charlotte began once more to recount her experiences of the forenoon. And again she was interrupted. This time it was an urgent message from her sister, asking that Charlotte come to her at once, as she had had a severe hemorrhage that morning.

"Only misfortunes happen nowadays!" sighed the old lady. "It's consumption, I fear. She has had the look of it for a long time. Of course you must go to her, child. I only hope it won't be too great a strain on you!"

"No, indeed, Tante," said Charlotte, who hurriedly got ready to go to the village for the second time that day.

She found the sister sitting up in a straight-backed armchair in her parlour, with all the children about her. Two stood bending over her solicitously; two sat on a stool at her feet, and the two youngest, who knew nothing of sickness or peril, sprawled on the floor. The four who had arrived at some degree of understanding were anxious and fearful. It looked as if they had constituted themselves a guard round the mother, to protect her against a fresh attack. When Charlotte came, the eldest boy put up a warning hand and said in a whisper:

"Mother mustn't move or talk."

There was no fear that Charlotte would tempt the patient to speak; but the instant she entered the room her throat contracted; she had to struggle for breath to keep from crying.

Fru Romelius's parlour was a small, bare-looking room with a few fine old pieces of birchwood furniture, heirlooms she had brought from her parental home. But, as there was nothing else in the room, not a strip of carpet on the floor, nor a potted plant in the window, the place had always seemed dreadfully cheerless to Charlotte. On none of her visits to the sister had she been allowed to enter any of the other rooms; and she had suspected from the first that Marie Louise's living quarters were very poor and shabby, and that that was why they had always been closed to her.

Physicians were usually quite well off. But Dr. Romelius, who passed most of his time at the tavern, drinking, earned next to nothing, and let wife and children live in want. It was only natural that the doctor's wife, who loved her husband and feared the sister might censure him, had always kept her at a certain distance lest she should get an insight into the true state of affairs.

When Charlotte saw how Marie Louise, ill as she was, still received her in the parlour, she was deeply moved. It was for the sake of the husband; her one thought was to shield him.

Charlotte stepped softly over to the sister and kissed her on the forehead. "Ah, Marie Louise!" she whispered. "Dear Marie Louise!"

The sister looked up with a faint smile, inclined her head toward the children, then looked again at Charlotte.

"Yes, of course," said Charlotte, understanding. "See here, children." She spoke now in such a brisk and positive tone she wondered where it came from. "Fru Forsius has sent you some cakes. They are out in the hall, in my reticule. Come along and you shall see!"

Thus she tempted the children away from the room, divided the cakes among them, and sent them out into the yard to play. Whereupon she went back to the sister, sat down on the stool at her feet, took her thin, toil-calloused hands between her own, and laid them against her cheek.

"Now, dear heart, they are out of doors; so tell me what you would like me to do."

"If I should die——" The sick woman was afraid to go on lest she might start coughing.

"Ah, to be sure," said Charlotte, "you are not to talk! You were going to ask me to take care of your children in case you should pass away. That I promise you, Marie Louise."

The sister nodded, and thanked her with a smile. Her eyes filled, as she said in a voice so faint it was scarcely more than a whisper: "I knew that you would help me."

"She does not question how I am to take care of so many children," thought Charlotte, who in the presence of this acute misery had forgotten all that she herself had been through in the forenoon. Suddenly, it flashed across her mind that she could take care of the children; she would be well-to-do; she was going to marry Schagerström.

Immediately another thought arose in her mind: "Perhaps it was in order that I might be able to help Marie Louise that things have gone as they have?"

It was the first time Charlotte had thought of a union with Schagerström with any degree of satisfaction. Hitherto she had simply accepted her fate with meek resignation.

She offered to put the sister to bed. The sick woman

shook her head at this. There was something else she wished to say. "You mustn't let the children stay with Richard."

Charlotte fervently promised not to. At the same time she was quite surprised. Marie Louise, then, did not worship her husband so blindly as she had supposed. She saw that he was a derelict, and that the children should be removed from his influence.

Then the sister said, as it were in confidence: "I am afraid of love. I knew what Richard was, but love compelled me to marry him. I hate love!"

Charlotte knew that Marie Louise had said that only to comfort her; she wanted her to understand that even the strongest love could mislead one and make one commit terrible mistakes. It was best to be guided by one's reason.

She was about to reply that, for her part, she would be in love with love to the last moment of her life, and never be wroth with it, no matter how much suffering it brought her, when the sister was seized with a paroxysm of coughing. As soon as it had passed, Charlotte made haste to prepare the sister's bed and help her into it.

That evening Charlotte attended to all the housewife's duties: she prepared the children's supper, kept them company during the meal, and also put them to bed. While thus handling kitchen utensils and crockery, wearing apparel and bedding, she was shocked to find how chipped and cracked and worn everything was.

Such a lack of the most essential household furnishings! How careless and incompetent the servant girl had been! How patched and threadbare the children's clothes were! How badly tables and chairs had been used! Here a back-rest was missing, there a leg gone.

There were scalding tears behind Charlotte's eyelids, but they were not allowed to fall. Her heart ached for the sister who had endured such poverty with never a murmur or an appeal for aid.

Every little while, in the midst of her work, Charlotte would run in to see Marie Louise, who was now resting comfortably and seemed to enjoy being cared for.

"Now you shall hear something pleasant," said Charlotte. "You'll not have to wear yourself out like this any more. To-morrow I shall send you a good maid, and you can lie abed and play lazy until you're quite well."

The sick woman smiled wistfully, as if pleased at the prospect, but there was something, apparently, that weighed on her mind.

"All this comes too late," thought Charlotte. "She knows that she is dying."

When, in a few moments, Charlotte again stood by the sick bed, she talked of sending the sister to a health resort, where she could have proper care and attention. "You know that I shall have abundant means and that you can depend on me."

It went against her to speak, in that way, of Schagerström's wealth. But the sister liked it. The thought that

Charlotte would be well-to-do was the best medicine for her own ills.

She drew Charlotte's hands to her bosom and caressed them in thanks; still she did not appear to be wholly at ease.

Charlotte wondered what it was that troubled her. She had a faint suspicion, but would not entertain it. Did Marie Louise also wish to plead for her husband? She who lay there worn out, blotted out, and sick unto death!

When Charlotte had tucked all the children into their beds, she went again to the sister's room. "I think I'd better go now," she said. "But I'll drop in at the night nurse's house and ask her to stay with you to-night. In the morning, early, I'll be here again."

"I shall not need you to-morrow," said the sick woman, patting the sister's hand affectionately; "but come again on Monday."

Charlotte understood that Marie Louise expected her husband, who that evening was out on a professional call, to be at home over Sunday, and probably did not wish him and the sister to meet.

The sick woman still clung to her hand. Charlotte knew there was something else she wanted to ask of her. She bent down and brushed back a stray lock from the sister's forehead. As she did so, it seemed to her that she had touched death itself. In the sudden rush of feeling that this was perhaps the last time she would see her brave, loyal sister, she again met her unspoken wish.

"I promise you that Schagerström and I will take care of the Doctor."

Oh, the look of joy that lighted up the face of the sick woman! She pressed Charlotte's hand to her lips, and then sank back upon her pillow—happy and content. Her eyes closed, and in a little while she was sleeping peacefully.

"I knew it!" Charlotte said to herself. "It was of him she was thinking all the time. I knew that she could not hate love."

*　　*　　*

It was after ten o'clock when Charlotte returned from her sister's. She was about to open the back gate when she ran into the housemaid and the kitchen girl who had just come from a Pietist prayer-meeting at Holma.

The meeting, they said, had been held in an old smithy. Dr. Ekenstedt had spoken, and the place had been overcrowded. People had come, not only from the foundries and the church town, but from all parts of the parish.

Charlotte wanted to ask them whether Karl Arthur had been eloquent as usual, but the maids were so eager to relate what they had heard that she could not get a word in.

"Pastor Ekenstedt talked almost the whole evening about Fröken Charlotte," said the housemaid. "He told how he and everyone else had done Fröken a great wrong. Fröken had not been false and crafty, and he wanted the whole community to know it."

"And he told what Fröken had said and what he had said that time when you had the falling out," the kitchen girl reported. "He wanted us to know how it had all come about. But I didn't think it was very nice of him. A couple of boys who sat in front of me laughed till I thought they'd split their sides."

"There were others, of course, who laughed and made fun," vouchsafed the housemaid, "but they were the sort who haven't any sense. All the rest thought it was lovely. And last the pastor said that we should all unite in prayer for Fröken Charlotte; for Fröken was going to set out on a perilous journey; Fröken was going to marry a rich man. And then he reminded us of Jesus' words about it being so hard for the rich to get into heaven. . . . But where is Fröken?"

Charlotte had slipped away without a word. She ran to the house like one pursued—through the hall, up the stairs, and into her room. She did not stop to make a light, but tore off her clothes and got into bed. There she lay as if paralyzed, staring into the darkness.

"Now it is over," she muttered. "Karl Arthur has killed my love."

He had not succeeded before. Though he had wounded her love; despised it; insulted it; slandered it, yet it had lived on. But now it was dead.

She asked herself why that which he had just done was more unbearable than all the rest. She could not say why, but knew that it was.

Karl Arthur no doubt had meant well. In his desire

to clear her name, he must have followed the dictates of his conscience; but all the same he had given her love its death blow.

She felt so pitiably poor! Think of having no one to dream of! No one to long for! When she read a beautiful story, the hero would no more assume *his* form and features. When she listened to impassioned music, aglow with the fervour of love, it would find no response in her heart. Would she ever again see any beauty in flowers or birds or children now that her love was dead?

The marriage state she was to enter lay before her like some great desert waste. If only love were with her still, she would have something in her heart. But now she must dwell in a strange place, desolation within and without.

She thought of the Baroness, and knew now what had kindled her wrath, and why she had looked so stern and resentful; she, too, lay thinking that Karl Arthur had killed her love.

Charlotte's thoughts also turned to Schagerström. What had the Baroness seen in him that made her wish he were her son? She had not said it merely to pay him an empty compliment; she meant every word.

Charlotte did not have to ponder long to understand what the Baroness had seen in him; she had discovered that Schagerström could love. That was something Karl Arthur could not do; he could not love in the right way.

She smiled, a bit dubious. Could Schagerström love

in a better way than Karl Arthur? At all events, he had shown a lack of consideration in proposing to her, and he had been rather high-handed about the banns. But the Baroness was more intuitive than most people; she knew that Schagerström would never kill the love in one who loved him.

"It is such a dreadful thing to kill love!" sighed Charlotte.

Now she began to question whether Karl Arthur had done it of his own volition. He who for five years had been her fiancé must have known that nothing would wound her so deeply as his talking to a motley crowd about her and her love, and thereby making her a butt for ridicule and impertinent familiarities. Or, was it perhaps Thea Sundler who persuaded him in order to be done with Charlotte forever? Had the woman thought it was not enough with getting her married and out of Karl Arthur's way, that she must also offer her this deadly insult?

It mattered little which one of the two was to blame; at that moment Charlotte detested them both equally.

She lay for a while in an impotent rage. Now and then a tear trickled down her cheek on to the pillow.

In Charlotte's veins flowed the blood of Swedish peers, and in her soul lived the true Swedish will; the noble, proud will that remains undaunted in defeat and springs up with unbroken zeal to new struggles.

Of a sudden, she sat bolt-upright in bed, clenched her fists, and brought them together with a resounding blow.

"One thing is certain," she said: "They shall not have the satisfaction of seeing me unhappy in my marriage!"

With this good resolution firmly fixed in mind, she lay back on her pillow and went to sleep. Nor did she awake until the Dean's wife came in at eight o'clock on Sunday morning with a coffee-tray, bedecked with flowers, worthily to usher in the solemn day.

CHAPTER XXIII

THE WEDDING DAY

AT THE appointed hour on Sunday Schagerström appeared at the deanery. The Ironmaster came in his big landau, horses and trappings spick and shining; coachman and footman in gala livery, each with a nosegay tucked in his waistcoat. The dashboard had been removed so that their white buckskin breeches and varnished leather boots, which came almost to the knee, were in full view. The master's splendour was as nothing to that of his servants, though he, too, was in festal attire, having donned for the occasion a white frilled shirt, a white waistcoat, and a well-fitting gray frock coat, in the buttonhole of which was a rosebud. In short, all who saw his equipage must have thought to themselves, "Well, well, is rich Schagerström going off to be married?"

The Ironmaster was touched by the hearty welcome accorded him at the deanery. During the recent distressing weeks, the old place had presented a sombre and inhospitable aspect. It would be hard to explain in what way this had shown itself, but to a sensitive person the change was quite marked.

To-day, the white gate stood open, and also the front

doors. The Venetian blinds at the front windows of the upper story, which for weeks had been drawn, were now up again, and the strong sunshine could pour in and fade the colours in carpets and upholstery as much as it would. But the change did not consist in this alone. The flowers, that day, looked especially bright, while the twitter of the birds sounded merrier than common.

It was not only the trim housemaid who stood on the porch; the master and mistress also were there to welcome the bridegroom. The old couple, waiving all ceremony, embraced him, kissed him on each cheek, patted him, and called him by his Christian name. In fact, they treated him as a son. Schagerström, who had passed the night in anxious concern to find the right way, experienced a relief as distinct as when a bad tooth suddenly stops aching.

He was immediately conducted to the Dean's private study, where the bride awaited him. She looked charming in a gown of light changeable silk. The dress, to be sure, was of a style not then in vogue. (Charlotte had nothing of her own suitable for the occasion and the Dean's wife had found this in an old chest in the attic.) The dress was short and quite low at the neck, and it was fashioned in a way that made the wearer look as if her waist line were somewhere up around the armpits. However, the style was admirably suited to Charlotte. She had not bothered to procure any bridal crown or wreath, but the Dean's wife had caught up her curls with a high tortoiseshell comb, so that the coiffure har-

monized with the gown. Round the neck she had two or
three rows of pearl beads with a pretty locket, and there
were bracelets to match. Though these were things of no
intrinsic value, they were becoming to the wearer, who
looked as if she had stepped out of an old painting. As
Sehagerström bent down to kiss her hand, she said with
a tremulous smile:

"Karl Arthur left for Karlstad a few moments ago, to
make up with his mother."

"No one but you, good Fröken, could have brought
that about," said Schagerström. For he understood that,
by her consenting to marry him, she had induced young
Ekenstedt to go home. What was back of it all, he did not
know; but, to tell the truth, he was displeased with the
whole proceeding. Naturally, he admired the young
girl's self-sacrifice and wished to see the Baroness and
her son reconciled. All the same—well, to be more
explicit, he wished the young lady were marrying him
for his own sake and not on account of young Ekenstedt.

"It was the *Evil Influence* you wrote about," said
Charlotte. "The Evil Influence would not be satisfied
with less than my marriage and removal from Korskyrka Deanery. And it had to be done at once. No
respite was granted."

Schagerström noted the expression "no respite," and
thought it meant that Charlotte suffered unspeakable
qualms in having to give him her hand.

"My dear Fröken, I regret——"

"My name is Charlotte," the girl announced, with a curtsey, "and I'm going to call you Henrik."

Schagerström bowed in thanks for the concession.

"I'm going to call you Henrik," Charlotte reiterated, her voice now trembling a little. "Your late wife, I understand, called you Gustaf. I shall let her keep that name for her very own. One must leave to the dead what is theirs."

Schagerström was agreeably surprised. He judged from her remark that she no longer felt such aversion for him as she had shown when they met at Örebro. If humility and self-depreciation had not become second nature with him, he would have been highly elated.

Charlotte now asked him whether he would be satisfied to have the nuptial ceremony performed in the Dean's office, where so many bridal couples in the course of time had been united. "The Dean's wife would have liked us to be married in the grand salon, but to me it seems more solemn and churchlike down here."

As a matter of fact, Charlotte, having wished to pass the whole morning in close communion with her two dear old friends and guardians, had not allowed the Fru Dean to waste the precious moments in sweeping and dusting the now long unused salon.

The young Ironmaster had no objection, of course, to the marriage taking place in the Dean's office. The coachman and the footman from Stora Sjötorp, the deanery farmer-tenant, his wife and all the servitors on the place were called in to witness the solemn act.

While the Dean was reading the Marriage Service, outside the open window bullfinches and sparrows chirped right lustily and merrily; it seemed as if they knew what was happening and wished to celebrate the event by singing their best wedding hymns.

When it was over, Schagerström stood there looking rather awkward, not knowing what he should do; but Charlotte turned to him immediately and offered him her lips. She actually made him feel giddy. He had expected tears, stony grief, supercilious arrogance, in fact, anything but this complaisant submissiveness.

He remarked to himself: "All who see us must think it was I who was forced into this marriage, and not she."

He couldn't account for it in any way, except that Charlotte found it more consistent with her pride to appear happy and content. "But how well she does it," he thought, slightly vexed, but with a certain feeling of admiration.

And later, when they sat down to the wedding breakfast, the preparation of which, according to the Dean's wife, had been left to chance and Providence, Schagerström tried to cast off his gray-weather mood. The host and hostess, understanding that he found his position somewhat embarrassing, did their utmost to liven him, and were fairly successful.

At all events, they made him loosen his tongue. He spoke of his foreign travels, of his efforts to advance the Swedish iron industry by introducing certain methods he had learned in England and Germany. He noticed that Charlotte listened with rapt attention. She sat with head thrust forward and eyes wide open, following his every word. But that, he thought, was only play-acting. "She's doing it for the sake of the old people. It isn't likely that she would be interested in things of this sort, of which she has no understanding. She wants the Fru and Herr Dean to think she's in love with me, that's all."

Anyway, this was the better and more pleasing hypothesis. It did him good to see how devoted his wife was to this grand old couple.

Toward the end of the meal gloom settled over the spirits of the four. The old Dean and his wife sat thinking that in a few moments Charlotte would be leaving them. Charlotte, the radiant being, with her strange freaks, her drolleries, her ready tongue, her impetuosity; Charlotte, of whom they had so often disapproved but in whom they had forgiven everything because of her lovableness—she would be gone from their home. How empty and uninteresting life would be without her!

"It's well," said the old lady, "that you're coming back to-morrow to pack your belongings!"

Schagerström understood that they were trying to take comfort in the thought that Charlotte would not be so far away but they could see her, now and then. At the same time, he observed how shrunken and bent they suddenly became, and how the lines in their faces deepened. They had no one now to keep old age away!

"We are so happy, child of my heart," said the Dean, "that you have a good husband and are going to a lovely home! But you know that we shall miss you—we shall miss you dreadfully!"

He was on the verge of tears. But, happily, his wife saved the situation by telling Schagerström what her husband once said he would do if he were fifty years younger and a bachelor. This made them all laugh, and dispelled the sadness.

When the landau drew up before the door and Charlotte went over to the Dean's wife to say good-bye, the old lady led her into the adjoining room and whispered to her:

"Keep an eye on your husband this day, my dear! There's something he contemplates doing. Be watchful!"

Charlotte promised to do her best.

"He looks very well to-day," the old lady remarked. "Have you noticed it? Fine clothes are becoming to him." She was surprised when Charlotte rejoined:

"I have never thought him bad-looking. There is something forceful about the man; he's like Napoleon."

"Well, I declare!" said the old lady. "That never occurred to me. But I'm glad you think so."

When Charlotte came out on the porch, ready to depart, Schagerström noted that she had on the same bonnet and mantilla she had worn when he first saw her at church, and which he had then thought severely plain and unbecoming. Now he found them charming, and felt a sudden wild elation that this lovely young girl was his and was going home with him. While Charlotte was engaged in a leave-taking which he thought would never end, Schagerström stepped up to her, seized her in his strong arms, and lifted her into the carriage.

"See there! see there! That's as it should be," the deanery folk shouted after him as the carriage swung round the circular flower-bordered drive, and out through the gate.

*   *   *

It need hardly be said that the young Ironmaster immediately regretted his bold act. It was wrong to frighten Charlotte. If he behaved in that manner, she would think he regarded their union as something more than a sham marriage and would claim the rights of a husband.

Charlotte really looked a trifle uneasy. She had moved over into the corner of the carriage, as far away from him as she could get; but before they came to the church town she again sat close beside him, chatting and smiling.

It was self-evident that she would maintain her pleasant mien while they drove along the village street; but it would be a different matter, thought Schagerström, when once they were out on the lonely country road.

However, Charlotte continued to talk in her easy, animated way throughout the whole long drive. Her topics of conversation tended to show that she was taking her marriage seriously.

She began with his horses. For the first, she wanted to know something about the four drawing the landau. Where he had purchased them; how old they were; their names. Were they skittish and had they ever bolted with him? Then she asked him about the other horses at Stora Sjötorp. Were there, perchance, any riding horses there, any well broken-in mounts? And saddles? Had they really an English sidesaddle?

She gave a pitying thought to the poor deanery horses; they would be utterly ruined now that she was not there to exercise them.

At that, Schagerström could not resist making a thrust. "The other day I was told by a strange lady in a diligence how a certain Fröken mistreated her benefactor's innocent beasts."

"What!" cried Charlotte, aghast. Then, in a second, she knew to what he alluded, and broke into peals of laughter.

A good laugh is a wonderful thing. All at once the formal constraint was broken, and these newly wedded persons were like two old friends.

Charlotte went right on with her quizzing. What sort of works and contrivances had they at Stora Sjötorp? How many forges in the smithy? What were the names of the smiths, the smiths' wives and children? She seemed to have heard that he had also a sawmill. Ah! so there was a flour mill, too. How many stones in the mill, and what was the name of the miller?

It was a thorough examination. Schagerström became utterly befuddled from all this quizzing. To some of the questions he could give clear and correct answers, but he did not know how many sheep he had, nor was he certain as to the number of milch cows in the cow byre, or just how much milk they gave. "That is the overseer's affair," he said, laughing.

"You actually sound as if you didn't know anything," said Charlotte. "There must be a terrible lack of order at your home. It will mean a lot of work before things are as they should be."

The prospect, apparently, was not displeasing to her and Schagerström confessed that he had long wished for a regular domestic tyrant, just such a stern house-wife as Fru Forsius.

He had said something about an overseer, so she wanted to know how many men ate at the family table. What constituted the household. How many maid-servants there were; and how many menservants. Had he a housekeeper? Was she any good?

Nor did she forget to speak of the garden. On learning that there were both hothouse and vinery, her surprise was as great as when he had told her about the saddle horses.

Schagerström, indeed, did not find the time long. When the landau turned in on the forest road leading to his home, he thought that the twelve or thirteen English miles between the church town and Stora Sjötorp had been wonderfully short that day. Otherwise, he was careful not to entertain any illusions.

"I understand her quite well," he said to himself. "She is trying to make the best of a bad bargain, and talks to keep from thinking."

Meantime, they had had a busy day at Stora Sjötorp. The messenger from the deanery had come at about three o'clock on Saturday; but the Ironmaster had not said a word concerning his expectations until late in the evening, when it suddenly occurred to him that he must procure a wedding ring. Then one of the overseers was ordered to drive to the nearest city and to rouse the goldsmith from his sweetest slumber, if need be, in order to purchase a plain gold ring, and have the names engraved therein.

Happily, the overseer had notified as many as he could that a new mistress was coming to the Manor on the morrow. And, indeed, it was well he had! Else, how would the housekeeper have found time to air the grand suite, remove all the furniture coverings, and clear away the dust? Or how would the head gardener have managed to get all the walks raked and all the flower beds weeded? However else would they have had time to clean livery, polish boots and harness and even the landau itself? The Ironmaster had wandered about in a daze, unable to attend to anything. Johansson the footman had been obliged to select what he thought was the proper raiment for a bridegroom.

Fortunately, there were those on the estate who knew how to receive a young Fru. Both the housekeeper and the head gardener had been at Stora Sjötorp from the time Doomsman Oldencrona's lady had ruled there, and knew what the honour of the house demanded.

The housekeeper, for appearance' sake, had asked

the Ironmaster for instructions regarding the reception just before he set out on Sunday, and the head gardener had been equally punctilious. Any thought of a reception had not occurred to Schagerström, but if Fru Sällberg wished to prepare a little dinner of welcome and the gardener could manage to put up a gate of honour, it would be quite agreeable to him.

These capable servitors, having thus obtained a free hand, had only to await the master's departure in order to set about preparations for an almost royal welcome.

"Bear in mind, Fru Sällberg," said the gardener, "that she is a lady of quality and knows what is customary on a large estate like this."

"But she comes only from a parsonage," the housekeeper reminded him, "so I don't think she knows anything; but that's no reason why others shouldn't show that they've some wit."

"Oh, don't be so cocksure about that!" the gardener retorted. "I have seen her at church, and, indeed, she does not look like any ordinary parsonage mamselle. You should have seen how she carried herself! She reminded me of her venerable Grace of Stora Sjötorp. My heart warmed to her."

"Let be as it may with her aristocracy," said the housekeeper, "I'm glad we're to have a young Fru in the house. Now there'll be balls and parties here again, and one can show what one can do. It will be quite different from preparing meals, day after day, for a few menfolk, who bolt their food."

"Just so you don't have too much of a good thing!" laughed the gardener. "One who has lived with Fru Forsius for so many years knows how to manage a house."

With that he rushed out. There was no time to waste in talk, if four triumphal arches were to be erected and the entrance decorated in monograms of floral design.

Nor could the gardener have carried out so ambitious a programme but for his many zealous helpers. One must consider that all on the estate—the foundry workers, the tenantry, the foresters, the servants—had been fired with enthusiasm. They were to have a Fru again at the big manor house; someone to whom they could go with their troubles and ailments. A mistress meant so much more than a master. She stayed at home, and to her they could talk of the children and the cow. That she would be there that very day seemed almost too good to be true.

A couple of boys had carried the news to the tenantry, and on every croft and in every house the people put on their best and went up to the Manor to catch a glimpse of the bride. All and sundry, the moment they appeared, were set to work. The gates of honour were raised; old flags and standards that had done service under former owners were hoisted all along the sides of the road. A pair of small cannon had been dragged forth from somewhere, and mounted. It was a bustle and a rush of which one could scarcely form a conception.

But when the bride and groom drove in on Stora Sjötorp ground at about six o'clock, everything was in order.

At the first gate of honour, out in the woods, they were met by all the smiths from the foundries, who stood on guard with their sledge hammers held against the shoulder. By the second gate, at the edge of the wood, stood the farm workers, saluting with their spades. At the third gate, which marked the entrance to the avenue, they were greeted with huzzahs from the millers and the sawyers, while at the fourth gate, which led to the house grounds, the head gardener, with all his workmen about him, presented a gorgeous bouquet to the bride. And last, up at the house itself, the foundry manager, the overseers, the clerks, the housekeeper, and the maidservants stood bowing and curtseying.

However, it cannot be truthfully said that the people observed such perfect order as has here been described. They were all in high spirits; they shrieked and hurrahed at the top of their lungs, even after the carriage had passed through the gate where they stood guard. Besides, the children ran alongside the carriage in a far from mannerly way, and the cannon salutes went off at the most unexpected moments.

But, then, it was all so delightfully festive. Had the sainted Fru Oldencrona looked down from her heaven she would have been pleased to see that Stora Sjötorp and her old gardener had done themselves honour.

Schagerström, of course, had not expected this big demonstration, and felt rather indignant at his employees for taking such liberties. But, luckily, his displeasure vanished as he looked at Charlotte.

Her lips were smiling, at the same time tears glistened in her eyes, and her hands were clasped.

"How beautiful!" she whispered. "How beautiful!"

All this: the gates of honour, the flowers, the flags, the cheers, the friendly smiles, the salutes from the small swivel-guns—all this was for her, to wish her welcome to the place. She who for weeks had been an object of scorn; she from whom everyone had turned away; she whose slightest movement had been followed with suspicion and odium; she who had hardly dared venture outside the door lest she meet with insult, she was honoured now beyond deserts or merit. Ah! she was touched; she was grateful.

Here there were no lampoons, no bouquets of thorns and thistles, no ribald laughter; here she was welcomed with joy.

She put out her arms to the people. She loved the place from the first moment, and everyone on it. It was as if she had come to a new world. A happy world. Here she wished to live and die.

*　*　*

What happiness for a man to lead his young bride into a beautiful home! To hear her exclamations of delight as they go from room to room; to run ahead a step or two and throw open the doors to the adjoining one, then say: "This one, I think, is not half bad." And to see her flit about like a butterfly, now striking a few notes on the piano; now darting over to a painting; now casting a glance in a mirror to see whether the glass reflects a presentable image of herself; now flying to a window to look at a wonderful view.

But fancy his dismay when in the midst of it all she suddenly bursts into tears! With what anxious solicitude he asks her to tell him what troubles her, and how heartily he offers to alleviate her distress.

How glad he is to learn that it is nothing else than that she has a dear sister who lies ill in bare, ugly quarters while she herself, quite undeservedly, is permitted to enjoy all this beauty and grandeur. How pleased and proud he is to assure her that she may give the sister whatever help she needs. If she so wished, that very evening . . .

"No, not to-night. It will be time enough to-morrow."

Now that anxiety is over. She forgets it entirely, and the house inspection is resumed.

"This," she says, "is such a comfortable chair, and over there by the window is a suitable place for a sewing table."

Aye, to be sure. He thinks to himself, what a charming picture she will make seated at the sewing table. Then he remembers something he had almost forgotten: This was not a real marriage. All this was merely a play, though at moments it seemed as if she were taking it seriously. It was hard to tell just where he stood with her.

Anyhow, there was one comfort: He could let the play go on a few hours more, enjoy it as she was enjoying it, hide his anguish deep in his heart, and live in the happiness of the moment.

And thus, with the same delight, he continues to show her about until dinner is announced.

Oh, the wonder of it! To offer her his arm and lead her in to dinner! To seat her at a table beautifully laid with rare old china, glittering glass, and shining silver! To sit down with her to a royal feast of eight courses, with wine that glowed in the bottles like liquid jewels; with food that melted on the tongue so that one was scarcely conscious of eating!

Then the joy of having by your side a young woman who is everything you love most; who is clever and unaffected; who can hold her own; who fairly bubbles with mischief; who can laugh and cry in the same breath, and who at every moment reveals some new and charming trait.

And perhaps, too, it is a fortunate thing to be snatched away from it all just as one is about to lose one's head. For now the gardener, who that day is master of ceremonies at Stora Sjötorp, has come to announce that all is in order for the dance at the loft, but that no one will start dancing till the master and mistress appear. At a wedding, the bride and groom, of course, must open the ball.

What a delightful way to celebrate a wedding! Not among social equals, who perhaps would be envious and critical, but among these admiring, devoted servitors who regard you as something almost divine. For form's sake, the bridegroom dances just one round with the bride on the slippery loft floor, then retires to watch her whirl about with smiths and millers, with old men and young boys—always with the same good humour. How wonderful to sit there recalling old tales and legends of elves and fairies who join in the dance with mortals, and carry away handsome youths to the woods with them. For, as she moves among the toil-worn people, she does not seem to be made of common earthly clay but of some finer, better substance.

Aye, and to sit there watching the moments fly till one sees that the time is at hand, that the wedding day is over, and one must face again the old empty life, the old loneliness!

* * *

As for Charlotte, her ears had been ringing the whole time with the warning: "Keep an eye on your husband this day, my dear! There's something he contemplates doing. Be watchful!"

She noted his sudden changes of mood from gay to grave, and grave to gay, and always, before beginning a dance, she looked to see whether he was still in the loft, and the instant a partner left her, she ran over to her husband and sat down by him.

Charlotte being the sort who had her eyes about her, had observed when crossing the stable yard on her way to the loft that the small carriage Schagerström used on his long journeys had been drawn out of the coach house. That had aroused her suspicion and made her the more watchful. While dancing with the coachman she made a slight attempt to find out what was doing.

"I hope we are not dancing too long," she said. "At what time is the Ironmaster leaving?"

"The time has not been fixed yet, your ladyship. But I have the carriage outside and the horses harnessed. In half-a-jiffy, I can be ready to go."

Ah, now she knew what was in the air! But, as her husband was still sitting in the loft, calmly talking with some of his tenants, she thought it best to say nothing.

"Evidently, he had planned to leave to-night; but perhaps he has changed his mind, since he sees that I'm not so dangerous as he fancied."

A little later, just as she had finished a long polka, she suddenly missed him. Darkness had come, and the big loft, illumined only by a couple of lanterns, was now quite dim, yet she knew at once that he was not there. She looked about anxiously for the coachman and the groom; they, too, seemed to have disappeared.

She quickly threw her mantilla about her, joined a group of young people, who stood in the wide doorway of the loft cooling themselves after the dance, said a few words to them, then slipped out, unobserved.

Stranger that she was on the place, she did not know

which way to turn to get to the house; but seeing directly ahead the faint gleam from a lantern, she hastened in that direction. Coming nearer, she saw that the lantern stood on the ground outside the stable. The coachman had already led out the horses, and was putting them in the shafts.

Charlotte stole up to the carriage without making her presence known, thinking to open the door as soon as the coachman's back was turned, and hop in. Then, when the carriage pulled up at the house and Schager-ström came out to take his place, she would tell him what she thought of his attempting to run away. "Why doesn't he tell me what's on his mind?" she wondered. "He's like a bashful boy."

But before she could put her plan into effect the coachman was ready; he hung the reins over the guard, drew on his driving coat and was about to step up on to the box, when he happened to remember the lantern. He said a quieting "Whoa, there, Peter and Paul" to the horses, then blew out the light, and put the lantern in the stable.

He was quick about it, too, but someone not far away was quicker. He had just shut the barn door, when he heard the crack of a whip and a sharp command. The horses were off and out through the gate—which he had taken the precaution to open—and down the avenue. The vehicle disappeared in the night darkness, but he heard the rumble of wheels and the clop, clop of the horses' hoofs.

If ever a coachman ran faster than his horses to get to the house and notify the master that some accursed rascal of a boy had jumped into the driver's seat and driven off under his very nose, it was Coachman Lundman of Stora Sjötorp!

He found Schagerström in the entrance hall in earnest conversation with the housekeeper, who was telling him that the young Fru had disappeared. "Master bade me tell her ladyship he hadn't time to stay longer at the loft and that she was to go on dancing as long as she liked, and when I went to speak to her ladyship——"

The coachman could not wait to let her finish; he had more important news. "Ironmaster!" he broke in.

Schagerström turned to him and said: "What's the trouble, Lundman? You look as if someone had stolen your horses."

"That's exactly what somebody has done, Ironmaster." Then he told just when and how it happened. "But it wasn't the fault of the horses," he added. "They never would have gone off without me if some limb of Satan hadn't sneaked up on the box! If I only knew who had dared——"

He stopped short. The master in the presence of the coachman, the footman, and the housekeeper, had flung himself down in a chair and was guffawing at their dismay.

"So you don't know who has stolen my horses?" he chuckled.

The three servitors stared.

"We must catch the thief," said Schagerström when he was through laughing. "Lundman, make haste to saddle three horses! Johansson, you go along and help him! Fru Sällberg, for certainty's sake, you'd better run upstairs and see whether her ladyship is there."

The housekeeper vanished, but reappeared in a moment with the information that the gracious Fru was not upstairs.

"Lord of Mercy!" she exclaimed. "I hope nothing dreadful has happened."

"That depends on how one takes it, Fru Sällberg. Up to this we've had to worry along by ourselves here at Stora Sjötorp, but now we have someone to rule over us."

"Yes; and for that we ought to be thankful, Iron-master."

At which Schagerström, rich Schagerström, patted the old cook on her fat shoulders and danced her round the hall shouting: "Fru Sällberg accepts her fate with proper resignation. May I be able to do the same." Whereupon he rushed out to join the coachman and the footman in their hunt for the "thief."

In a short while the chase was over and the runaway sat incarcerated in a corner of the carriage, with Schagerström at her side. Lundman had mounted the box, and was driving slowly back to the manor, while Johansson the footman led the saddle horses.

Charlotte, it seemed, had cleared about three miles of

level road at a good rate of speed, and then there had been some stretches of steep uphill pulling. The animals, despite all her flourishes of the whip, had refused to take the hills at anything but a walking pace; so of course she was overtaken and had to surrender.

For a few minutes there was silence in the carriage. Suddenly, Charlotte asked:

"Well, how did it feel?"

"It was overwhelming!" said Schagerström. "Now I understand how a wife feels when her husband runs away from her."

"That was what I meant to do," Charlotte confessed.

Whereupon Schagerström felt a tight clutch at his shoulder.

"You are only putting on," said Charlotte. "You're laughing. You don't believe I meant to run away."

"My love, the one really gleeful moment I have had to-day," Schagerström declared, "was when Lundman came and told me that you had stolen my horses."

"And why so?" she asked in a monotone.

"Darling, I knew then that you would not let me go away."

"I wasn't thinking of you!" she burst forth. "The whole church town has been talking about me these last three weeks, and if you had gone away——"

"Yes, dear, I understand." Schagerström laughed now from pure joy. But after a while he said quite seriously:

"My beloved, let us for once speak frankly to each

other. Did you understand why I wished to leave to-night?"

"Yes, I understood," Charlotte answered, in a firm voice.

"Then why did you prevent me?"

She was silent. He waited a long while for an answer; but, receiving none, he went on to say:

"When we get home you will find in your room a letter from me, in which I say that I shall not take advantage of the circumstances which have thrown you into my arms; that I wish you to be perfectly free; that you need not regard our union as anything but a mock marriage."

Again he paused for an answer. None came.

"In that letter," he continued, "I say, further, that as an earnest of my affection and to make amends for the suffering I have brought upon you, I propose to deed to you Stora Sjötorp. When a legal divorce has been effected, I shall be happy to know that you are living here, where everyone already loves you."

Another long pause. Still no response from Charlotte.

"This little adventure in nowise affects what is stated in the letter. At first I misconstrued your motive, but I see now that you played me this trick so as not to be put to scorn again in the church town."

Charlotte moved a trifle nearer. He felt her warm breath on his cheek as she whispered into his ear: "The stupidest ass on God's green earth."

"What?"

"Shall I say it again?"

He quickly put his arm around her and drew her to him. "Charlotte, you must speak! I've got to know what I'm to do."

"Very well, then!" she said in a tone that was a bit sharp. "It is not a pleasant thing to relate, but perhaps you'll be glad to hear that yesterday, at about this time, Karl Arthur killed my love."

"Did he?"

"Yes, he put it to death. Probably he had grown tired of it. I almost believe he did it wilfully."

"Darling!" said Schagerström. "Never mind about Karl Arthur. Speak of me! Even if your love for him is dead, it doesn't necessarily follow——"

"No, of course not! Oh, dear! Why do you require such long explanations?"

"You know how stupid I am."

"It is most extraordinary," said Charlotte thoughtfully. "I don't love you, yet I feel at ease, and safe, with you. I can talk to you about all sorts of things; I can ask anything of you; I can laugh and jest with you; I feel as tranquil and comfortable as though we had been married thirty years."

"About like the old Dean and his wife," Schagerström flung back at her.

"Yes, about the same. Perhaps you are not satisfied with that? But I think it a very good result for the first day. I like your sitting here beside me in the carriage. I like the way you followed me with your eyes when I danced. I like to sit at table with you, and I like being in your home. I am thankful to you for taking me away from all the unpleasantness. Stora Sjötorp is charming, but I shouldn't care to live there a day if you were not there. I could never consent to your deserting me. Still, if that which I felt for Karl Arthur was love, then this is not love."

"It may become——" Schagerström spoke quietly, but his voice, nevertheless, betrayed his emotion.

"Perhaps it may," said Charlotte. "Do you know what? I don't think I'd mind it if you kissed me."

Schagerström's carriage was an excellent vehicle. It rolled along easily—no bumping, no shaking. The young Ironmaster could very comfortably avail himself of the permission.

ANNA SVÄRD

CONTENTS

PART ONE

PART TWO

CONTENTS

PART THREE

PART ONE

CHAPTER I

THE KARLSTAD JOURNEY

WHATEVER one may think of Thea Sundler it must be said that she understood better than anyone else how to approach Karl Arthur Ekenstedt. There was Charlotte Löwensköld who wanted him to go back to Karlstad and make his peace with his mother; but she reminded him of all that his mother had done for him and even tried to frighten him into the belief that he would never preach again as he had preached of late, if he showed no gratitude toward his mother. It actually looked as if she wished him to return like the Prodigal Son and beg to be taken back into favour. That was not for one in his state of mind, and he an eloquent preacher who was fairly idolized by the whole parish.

Thea Sundler, however, went about it in quite another way. She asked him if it was not true that dear Tante Ekenstedt expected a person who had offended her the least to beg her pardon, and that if she was so exacting with others, doubtless she, herself, would be ready and willing . . .

Oh, yes. He had to admit that his mother, the mo-

ment she saw that she had forgotten herself, was anxious
to make amends.

Thea then reminded him of the time when dear Tante
Ekenstedt had made the perilous journey to Upsala
during the spring thaw, in order to assure him of her
forgiveness, and she wondered how he, a Christian
clergyman, could be less forgiving than a common
worldly person.

Karl Arthur stared at her blankly, not understanding
the drift. Fru Sundler then went on to say that this
time it was dear Tante Ekenstedt who had offended
against him, and that if she were really as fair-minded
as he maintained, surely he must know that she was
sorry now and longed with all her heart to ask his forgiveness. But his mother was ill and could not come to
him, therefore it was his duty to go to her.

Ah, here was a different argument from the one Charlotte had presented! This did not mean his going home
as a prodigal but as a hero. He was not to sue for pardon
but to grant it. The idea appealed to him strongly, and
he was grateful to Thea for having put it into his head.

The next day, which was a Sunday, as soon as the
service was over and he had eaten a hasty meal at the
Sundlers', he set off again for Karlstad. So as not to lose
time, he drove all night, keeping awake by picturing to
himself a touchingly beautiful reconciliation with his
mother; for there was no one who could make an occasion of that sort more charming than she.

He reached Karlstad at about five on Monday morning. Instead of going straight home, he stopped off at the inn. There was no doubt in his mind regarding his mother's attitude toward him, but he was not so sure of his father. The Colonel might turn him away, and he did not care to expose himself to such an indignity in the presence of the driver.

The innkeeper, who came out on the porch when Karl Arthur drove up, recognized him as an old Karlstader. He had heard this and that about a break between the clergyman and his parents on account of the young man's betrothal to a girl of the peasant class, and addressed him guardedly, though not without a certain feeling of sympathy. Karl Arthur, however, looked so tranquil and satisfied and greeted the host in so cheerful a tone, it made the latter think the rumour of a quarrel utterly false.

Karl Arthur engaged a room so that he could wash up and change his clothes. When he reappeared he was dressed in a clergyman's coat, collar, and high black hat. He had donned the habit of his office in order to show his mother that he had come in a pious, ministerial mood.

To the host's inquiry as to whether he desired breakfast he said No. He would not delay the happy moment when he and his mother would fall into each other's arms.

He walked rapidly through the streets, directing his steps toward the banks of the Klar River with the pleasurable expectation which he had felt in his college years when coming home for the holidays.

But all at once he stopped, as if stunned by a blow in the face. He was near enough now to the Ekenstedt house to note that the shutters were drawn and the outer doors closed. In the consternation of the first moment he thought the innkeeper had notified his parents of his arrival and that they had barred the house to him. Flushing with chagrin, he faced about and walked away.

He had not gone many paces, however, when he began to laugh at himself. It was hardly six o'clock, and the house was never open at that early hour. How could he have imagined for a moment that the shutters and doors had been closed only to keep him out! He turned back, went in by the garden gate, and sat down on a rustic bench to wait for the house to awaken. Still, he thought it a bad sign that his home should be closed when he arrived. He felt quite uneasy now. The colossal self-assurance which had sustained him on the journey was gone.

He looked at the beautiful flowers, at the well kept lawns, at the fine big mansion, and thought of her who ruled over it all, and who was so highly esteemed and so fêted. There was small chance of his getting an apology from her! He couldn't understand himself or Thea. Back at Korskyrka it had seemed a natural and foregone conclusion that his mother was sorry for what she had done; but here he thought it a stupid assumption.

He got up to go, anxious to be off before anyone discovered him. But as he stood at the gate he happened to think that this was probably his last visit to the old home. When he went now it was never to return.

Then, leaving the gate half open, he began to walk about the grounds, to take a last farewell. Rounding the corner of the house, he came out beneath the towering trees along the riverside. Ah! here he would never stroll again to enjoy the lovely view. His gaze rested a long moment on the old rowboat drawn up on the bank. Of course no one bothered about the boat now, he thought, since he was no longer at home. But he found it tarred and painted exactly as when he had used it.

He now ran over to a small garden patch which he had cultivated in his boyhood. It too looked the same as of old, with the same kind of vegetables growing there that he used to raise. Evidently his mother had seen to the upkeep of his little play-garden. It must have been at least fifteen years since he had tended it himself. He searched under an astrakhan tree for apples and slipped one into his pocket, although it was too green to eat; and he tasted of the gooseberries and currants—now old and overripe.

Next he went down to the range of outbuildings, and hunted up the garden shed where he had kept his small spade and rake and a little wheelbarrow. He peeped in. And there, sure enough, were all three implements, just where he had left them.

It must be nearly seven now, he thought, and time to be going—if he wished to escape unobserved. But always there was something more he must see for the last time. Everything about the place had suddenly acquired a new value in his eyes. Yet, at the same time, he felt a little ashamed of being so childish. He would not have liked Thea Sundler to see him now!—Thea, who had admired his heroic stand of a few days back, when he renounced home and parents.

At last he began to suspect that what really held him here was a secret hope that someone would see him and let him in. The moment this became clear to his mind he resolved to hurry away.

He was already out of the garden and down by the gate when he heard a window open in the locked house. And of course he had to turn round. . . . It was the window of the Baroness's bedroom which had just been opened; and his sister Jacquette stood leaning out for a breath of the fresh morning air.

The instant she caught sight of her brother she nodded to him and beckoned. He nodded and beckoned back, then pointed toward the closed front door. Shortly afterward he heard the grating sounds of unbolting and unlocking; the door swung wide, and the sister appeared on the threshold holding out both hands to him.

He felt shamed before himself and Thea; for he knew now that his mother would never apologize. He had no business coming home, he thought. All the same he rushed up to Jacquette and, grasping her hands, drew her to him, tears of gratitude filling his eyes because she had opened the door to him.

The sister was overjoyed. Seeing him weep, she put

her arms around his neck and kissed him. "Oh, Karl Arthur!" she cried, "thank God you have come!"

He had fully persuaded himself that he would not be admitted to the house, and this hearty welcome was such a surprise it nearly knocked him speechless.

"I say, Jacquette," he stammered, "is Mother awake? May I speak to her?"

"Why, of course you may speak to dear Mother. She has been feeling better the past day or two. Last night she rested quite well."

Jacquette led the way up the stairs, Karl Arthur following slowly. Never had he dreamed that he would be so glad to be at home again. He let his hand glide lightly along the smooth banister, not for support but, rather, as a caress.

When he came to the upper hall he expected to be intercepted and driven out. However, nothing of the sort happened. And now a light broke upon him. . . . His father, evidently, had not informed the family of the break. . . . No, he couldn't speak of it on account of the mother's illness. Understanding this to be the case, Karl Arthur stepped with more confidence.

How beautiful the rooms were! He had always thought them so; but that morning they looked more beautiful to him than ever. The furniture was not placed against the wall, in that staid fashion one saw at other houses. There was an air of elegance and ease about the rooms; everything bore the stamp of her who was mistress here.

They had passed through the drawing room and the Baroness's cabinet and were now at the bedroom door. Jacquette gave him a sign to wait outside and let her go in first.

Karl Arthur stood stroking his brow in an effort to remember why he was there. But he had forgotten everything save that he was at home and would see his mother again. Presently Jacquette came out and ushered him into the room.

And now when Karl Arthur saw his mother lying there so deathly pale, her head and arm bound with bandages, he fell upon his knees beside the bed. The mother, with a cry of joy, flung her sound arm round his neck and drew him to her in a close embrace. As they looked into each other's eyes, all their grievances were forgotten. He had not expected to find his mother looking so frail and ill and could hardly control his emotion. He showed such tender concern for her state that she could not but see that he loved her. This was the best medicine for the patient. Again she drew him close.

"Everything is all right now," she said. "I have forgotten how it felt."

He knew from her answer that she was as fond of him as ever, and knew, also, that he had regained all that he had recently mourned as lost. He could again count himself a son of this great house. What more could he wish?

But in the midst of his elation a sudden fear gripped him. He had not yet attained the object of his visit. His mother had not begged his pardon. Nor did it look as if she meant to do so.

He felt tempted to dismiss all thought of the matter. Still, it was an important point with him. For, if the Baroness admitted that she had done him a wrong, he would have quite a different standing in the home, and his parents would be compelled to accept Anna Svärd as his future wife.

"It's best to have this question settled at once," he thought. "Mother may not be so amiable and sweet another day."

All this time he had been on his knees; but now he rose to his feet and took the chair by the bedside. It was a trifle embarrassing having to take one's own mother to task. But he had a bright idea. He remembered that in the old days, when he or his sisters had done something naughty for which the mother expected them to apologize, she invariably addressed the culprit in the following words: "Well, my child, have you nothing to say to me?"

So, in order to introduce this awkward subject in a light and easy way, he knitted his brows and held up his forefinger, smiling at the same time, so that his mother would understand that he wished to treat the matter playfully.

"Well, has my mamma nothing to say to me?"

The Baroness, apparently, did not understand, for her only response was a querying look. But poor Jacquette, who had stood by and witnessed with joy the happy meeting of mother and son, was horrified and raised a warning hand.

Karl Arthur—perfectly sure that his mother would be charmed with his whimsy and respond in kind when she caught the allusion—despite the warning, went right on:

"Surely you must understand, Mother, that I was rather cut up last Thursday, when you attempted to part me from my betrothed. I wouldn't have believed that my dear little mother could be so cruel. I was so hurt that I went away not wishing to see you again."

The mother lay very still; she showed no signs of anger or displeasure. But the sister, growing more and more uneasy, drew nearer and, from behind the bedpost, gave him a hard pinch on the arm.

He understood what she meant, but thinking he knew better than Jacquette how to take the Baroness, he continued in the same strain:

"When Father and I parted on Friday morning I told him that I would never set foot in this house again. Yet here I am. I wonder if the cleverest lady in Karlstad can guess why I have come?"

Having said that much, he paused—confident now that his mother would speak out. She drew herself a trifle higher on the pillow and fixed him with so steady a gaze he found it almost painful. Had the shock of the accident affected her mind? She could generally take a hint. Since she failed to do so now, he was obliged to speak more plainly.

"It was really my intention, Mother, never to see you again. But when I mentioned this to a friend, she asked me if it was not my mother who expected one to apologize for every trifling offense, and she wondered whether my mother herself——"

Now his sister fairly shook his arm.

"Don't bother him, Jacquette!" said the Baroness. "Let him continue."

Karl Arthur had a faint suspicion that his mother was not altogether pleased with him, but quickly dismissed the thought. Surely his mother couldn't think him harsh or unloving? He had touched on the matter so lightly. Greater forbearance on his part she could scarcely ask. But perhaps she merely wished to make Jacquette stop interrupting him. In any case, having gone so far, he thought he might as well continue.

"It was this friend, Mother, who sent me here. She said it was my duty to go to you since you could not come to me. Do you remember, Mother, how you once made the long journey to Upsala only to afford me an opportunity to ask your forgiveness? My friend moreover assured me that you would freely admit—that—that——" Oh, why was it so hard to bring one's own mother to rights! He stammered and coughed, but the words seemed to dry on his tongue.

A feeble smile trembled on the lips of the Baroness as she asked him who the friend was who had such a good opinion of her.

"It was Thea, Mother."

"Wasn't it Charlotte who thought I lay here yearning to beg your forgiveness?"

"No, Mother, not Charlotte, but Thea."

"I am glad it was not Charlotte!"

The Baroness raised herself still higher on the pillow, and lapsed again into silence. Nor did Karl Arthur speak. He had said what he had to say, though not so eloquently as he could have wished. There was nothing to do now but to wait.

Meanwhile he regarded his mother intently. She was having a hard battle with herself, he thought. To confess her fault to her own son would take no little courage.

Presently she observed that he was wearing his clerical coat.

"I wanted to show you, Mother, in what spirit I have come."

A strange smile overspread her features—a baleful, sardonic smile. Then, all at once, the face on the pillow looked as if turned to stone. The words Karl Arthur was waiting to hear did not come, and he began to fear that his mother was incapable of remorse or repentance.

"Mother!" he expostulated with all the exhortative power at his command.

Then came a change. The blood rushed to the face. The Baroness raised herself in the bed, then lifted her sound arm and, shaking it, cried:

"It is over! the patience of God is exhausted!"

The last word died away—indistinct and feeble. She sank back on the pillow, her eyes rolled upward so that only the whites were visible, and her hand fell limply on the coverlet.

Jacquette ran out calling loudly for help. Karl Arthur threw himself upon his mother. "Why, Mamma," he said, "what has come over you? Now, Mamma, don't take it so hard!"

He kissed her on the mouth and kissed her on the brow, as if trying to kiss life into her. Suddenly he felt a hard clutch at his neck. A strong hand gripped him by the coat collar and carried him out of the room, then flung him down on the floor of the hall. And he heard his father say in a dreadful voice:

"So you've come back! You couldn't rest satisfied until you had put an end to her!"

2

At half-past seven that morning Karl Arthur Ekenstedt stood at the door of the Burgomaster's house. The elderly serving woman who answered his ring thought to herself: "If I hadn't lived in Karlstad these many years and seen him both as boy and man, I'd never have known him again." He was purple in the face and his eyes were distended as if ready to fall out of their sockets.

The maid, who had been long in service at the Burgomaster's, having garnered no little knowledge in matters of this sort, thought young Ekenstedt had the look of a murderer. She would have liked to turn him away; but considering that he was the son of Colonel Ekenstedt and the charming Baroness, what could she do but ask him to step in and wait. The Burgomaster had gone out for his usual morning walk, she said, and would surely be back by eight o'clock, as he always breakfasted then.

But if the mere sight of young Ekenstedt had been enough to frighten her out of her wits, it did not make her feel any the easier when he brushed past her without a word or a look of recognition, as though she were not there.

It was plain, of course, that all was not right with him. The Baroness Ekenstedt's children were usually polite and friendly. This son, she thought, must be in great trouble.

Karl Arthur tore off his hat in the hall, then went straight into the Burgomaster's room, where he flung himself down in the rocking chair. It was not long, however, before he was up and over by the writing table, rummaging among the Burgomaster's papers.

The *jungfru* was obliged to go back to the kitchen and watch the clock, to see that the eggs for her master's breakfast did not boil too long. Besides, she had to lay the table and put the coffee pot on the fire. Meanwhile young Ekenstedt was on her mind. Every other minute she would run to the Burgomaster's room and cast an eye on him.

Now he was pacing the floor in there. One moment he

was over at the window, the next down by the door,
and all the while he was talking to himself.

No wonder the woman was afraid! The Burgomaster's
wife and children were in the country, visiting relatives,
and the other servants had been sent away. She was
alone in the house, and had all the responsibility.

What should she do with the man, who walked in
her master's room and who seemed to be out of his
mind? Supposing he were to destroy any of the Burgomaster's important papers? She could not drop her
work entirely to watch him. And then it occurred to the
wise old serving woman to ask Karl Arthur if he
wouldn't like to come to the dining room and have a
cup of coffee while waiting. She felt greatly relieved
when he followed her. For while she had him at the
breakfast table he couldn't be up to any mischief.

Karl Arthur seated himself in the Burgomaster's
place and gulped down the scalding hot coffee the jungfru had poured for him. Then, grasping the coffee pot,
which she had left on the table, he refilled his cup and
drained it. As he put down the empty cup he noticed
that the jungfru was standing at the other side of the
table, watching him. Turning to her, he said:

"It was very kind of you to make such good coffee
for me. This is probably the last coffee I shall ever get,"
he added in a low, confidential tone, as if imparting a
great secret.

"Sure, your Reverence must get good coffee at the
deanery in Korskyrka."

"Yes—there," he said with a foolish little laugh. "But, you see, Jungfru, it is doubtful that I shall ever go back there again."

The woman thought nothing of that, since it was the customary thing for the younger members of the clergy to be sent from place to place. "Oh, I'm sure they can make good coffee at any parsonage your Reverence comes to."

"But do you think, Jungfru, that they can make good coffee at the prison?" He spoke now in whispers. "There, I dare say, I shall have to do without both coffee and cakes."

"But why in the world would your Reverence be going to prison?"

"I don't care to answer that question," he said, turning his attention again to the breakfast table. He buttered a slice of bread, laid cheese on it, and ate as if he were famished. The jungfru began to think there was nothing wrong with the man, that he was only hungry. So she ran out to the kitchen for the eggs she had prepared for the Burgomaster.

Karl Arthur finished the two eggs in almost no time, and fell back upon bread and butter again. While eating, he remarked in a casual tone, as if he were saying it's a pleasant day: "There are many dead walking in Karlstad this morning."

Now the woman could not help being just a bit frightened.

Karl Arthur, noting it, said: "You think I talk

strangely, Jungfru? I think it strange myself that I should see the dead. They never appeared to me, so far as I know, until this morning—after the thing that happened to me about an hour ago."

"Oh!" said the woman.

"You see, Jungfru, as I was leaving home for the city I had a bad heart attack and had to stop and hold onto the paling round our garden. While standing there I saw the late Provost Sjöborg and his sainted wife come walking, arm in arm, the way they used when they came to dine with us on Sundays. They knew, of course, what I had done, and told me to go to the Burgomaster, confess my crime, and take my punishment. That was impossible, I said; but they insisted."

He poured himself a fresh cup of coffee and looked sharply at the serving woman to see how she was taking what he had told her.

"There are so many nowadays who see ghosts," she said quietly; "so your Reverence needn't feel at all uneasy."

"That is just what I think. . . . Apart from this one thing, I'm quite myself."

"Of course you are." She thought it best to humour him, but she wished the Burgomaster would come.

"I'm perfectly willing to carry out their wishes," Karl Arthur declared; "but I know the Burgomaster will only laugh at me. I cannot deny that I have a terrible sin on my conscience. However, it's nothing for which I could be arrested and punished."

With that he closed his eyes and bent backward in his chair. The morsel of bread fell from his hand; his features became distorted as if he were in great pain. The attack soon passed, however.

"It was the heart again," he said. "Strange how it takes me whenever I say I can't do it!"

He jumped up from the table, and began to pace the floor. "Yes, yes, I'll do it!" he cried, forgetting that the jungfru stood there listening. "I'll tell the Burgomaster that I have done something punishable. I'll tell him that I am responsible for another's death. I must say that I did it deliberately."

Then, stepping up to the serving woman, he said with a happy smile: "It's all over now; it passes if I but say that I'll suffer my punishment."

The sensible old jungfru was no longer afraid of Karl Arthur. Moved to sympathy, she took his hand and, patting it, said:

"But you understand, Dr. Ekenstedt, don't you, that you mustn't plead guilty to something you haven't done?"

"Yes, I understand. At the same time I know it's the right thing for me to do. Besides, I really wish to die. I want to show my mother that I loved her. It will be such joy to meet her on the Other Side, when I have atoned for it all with my life."

"But that must never happen! I'll speak to the Burgomaster myself."

"No, don't, Jungfru! Why shouldn't a judge condemn me? I have committed a murder, although I employed no gun or knife. Jacquette knows how it was done. Don't you think, Jungfru, that cruelty and lack of love are more deadly than steel or lead? My father knows about it too, and can testify. Ah, yes, I can be punished, for I'm not without guilt."

To that the jungfru did not have to reply; for just then, to her great relief, the street door opened, and she heard the familiar step.

She ran out into the hall to give the Burgomaster a cautioning word, but Karl Arthur was right at her heels. He intended to begin his confession at once—but lost his head.

"So you are back in town," the Burgomaster observed. "It is very sad about the Baroness," he said as he extended a hand in greeting.

Karl Arthur, holding his right hand behind him and fixing his eyes on the wall, said, in a shaky voice:

"Uncle, I have come to give myself up. It was I who killed my mother."

"Bosh!" said the Burgomaster. "The Baroness isn't dead. I met the doctor . . ."

Karl Arthur staggered back. Then, quickly regaining his balance, he snatched up his hat and dashed out.

The first person he saw in the street was the old family physician. Rushing up to him, he cried: "How is it with Mother?"

The doctor glared at him. "You miserable whelp!" he said. "It's well I happened upon you. Would you presume to go home again *now?*—What's the matter with you? The idea of your preaching a castigatory sermon to a sick person!"

That was enough to send Karl Arthur straight back to the parental home. When he was almost at the gate he saw his married sister, Eve Arcker, standing there.

"Eve!" he cried, "is it true?—Is Mother alive?"

"Yes," the sister answered quietly. "The doctor thinks she may survive the shock."

He wanted to rush in, cast himself at his mother's feet, and implore her to have pity; but Eve stopped him.

"You cannot enter, Karl Arthur. I have been waiting here for some little time to see you. Poor Mother has suffered a hard stroke and is not able to speak to you."

"I will wait as long as you say."

"It is not only on dear Mother's account that I cannot admit you," said Eve, with a perceptible lift of the eyebrows, "but for Father's sake as well. The doctor says that Mother will never be herself again. So, if Father were to find you here, there's no knowing what might happen. The best thing you can do is to go back to Korskyrka!"

The sister's remarks irritated Karl Arthur. He did not believe the father's wrath was so great as she made it out, or that it could do the mother any harm to see him.

"You and your husband have always wanted to eat

me out of my parental house and home," he flung at
her. "You two know how to take advantage of an auspicious occasion. . . . Help yourselves!"

With that, he turned on his heel and went his way.

3

Nobody likes to have things go to smash. If it is
nothing but a common stone jar or a china plate that
has been shattered, we pick up the pieces, lay them edge
to edge, cementing or gluing, to make them hold together.

It was something of the sort Karl Arthur Ekenstedt
was busy about on the drive back to Korskyrka. Not
the whole way, to be sure; for consider! he had not had
a wink of sleep the night before. In fact, owing to various distressing experiences, he had slept very little
during the previous week. But now the body claimed its
rights. And, despite the jolting wagon and the quantities of strong coffee which he had consumed at the Burgomaster's, he slept through most of the journey.

However, during the short waking intervals, he tried
to collect the broken parts of himself so that the Karl
Arthur who had traversed this road whole and sound
only a few hours earlier, and who had gone all to pieces
in Karlstad, might again become a useful vessel.

Some may think, perhaps, that the broken vessel
was only an ugly earthen thing and not worth expend-
ing time and labour upon. But one must pardon Karl
Arthur if he regarded it differently; if in his opinion

it was a choice porcelain vase, hand painted and richly gilded, that had come to grief.

Curiously enough, his thoughts of Sister Eve and her husband were quite helpful to him in the reparation work. Recalling to mind innumerable occasions when they had evinced envy and complained of the mother's unfairness put him in a fine frenzy. The more he thought of the old grudge which Eve harboured against him, the more certain he became that she had lied. The Baroness's condition was not so serious as she had pictured it. As for the Colonel being so wroth with him— that was just something Eve and Arcker had made up. They hoped to profit by his recent stupidity (he could not deny that it had been inconceivably great) and keep him out of his home for the future.

He had just arrived at the conclusion that all would have been well had not Eve turned him away—when sleep claimed him. And he slept until the chaise stopped at a posting station.

At another interval between naps his thoughts were of Jacquette. She was not envious like Eve. Jacquette was a nice girl, and devoted to him. But wasn't she rather simple-minded? Even if she had not interrupted his important talk with his mother, he would have said practically the same things, but in a different way. It is not easy to choose your words with care when someone stands at your back all the while, pulling at your sleeve and whispering that you must be careful.

It had helped him a lot to think of Jacquette as witless and dull. But he soon dozed away from her too.

It was with a certain reluctance, however, that he thought, now and then, of Thea Sundler in connection with this unfortunate affair. She was his dearest friend, and there was no one whom he could trust so implicitly. But perhaps she knew too little about the world and its ways to be a safe counsellor. Her supposition that the Baroness lay waiting for an opportunity to beg his pardon had been wrong. Her high estimation of him had blinded her judgment and made her the innocent cause of a great misfortune. The Baroness might have died, and he might have gone insane. Indeed, he had been well on the way!

But he hated to think of his visit to the Burgomaster and his talk with the serving woman, since it would only break him up again and the whole reconstruction work would have to be done over.

In one of his wakeful moments it occurred to him that perhaps the remorse and grief he had shown might be in his favour. The Baroness would be sure to hear of it and understand that he loved her. She would be touched, no doubt, and send for him, and all would be well between them.

He liked to think it would end in that way, and would pray God every day that it might.

It must be said that the Reverend Karl Arthur Ekenstedt was very nicely cemented together when he reached Korskyrka Deanery at about eleven o'clock in the evening. He was himself surprised at his having come through such a nerve-racking ordeal in fairly good form. When he had stepped out at the gate and had paid the driver, he thought: "It will be good to stretch out on a bed once more, and sleep, sleep, sleep!"

He was just going to his quarters in the wing when the housemaid came to tell him, with the compliments of her mistress, that a warm supper awaited him in the dining room. Naturally, he would have preferred to retire at once; but inasmuch as the Dean's wife had been kind enough to consider that he might need a substantial meal after an all-day journey, he went along in.

That, of course, he would never have done had he thought there was anyone round to question him about his journey. The venerable Dean and his wife had been abed this long while and Charlotte, he knew, had moved away. In the hall he nearly fell over a box, or whatever it was, that stood just inside the door.

"Oh, for goodness' sake be careful, Doctor!" said the maid. "Those are Fru Schagerström's things. We've been busy all day, packing 'em in straw."

But for all that it did not occur to him that Charlotte herself had come down from Stora Sjötorp and was stopping at the Deanery overnight. He went quietly into the dining room and sat down to the table. There being no one to bother him, he took plenty of time to eat a hearty supper. He was folding his hands for grace-after-meat when footsteps sounded on the stairs. They were heavy, shuffling steps. He thought it was the Dean's wife coming to hear about his trip, and would have run away had he dared. In a moment the door opened softly and someone came in. . . .

It would have been bad enough, he thought, had it been the Dean's wife; but worse—it was Charlotte! He had not been engaged to her five long years for nothing! He knew her! What a scene there would be when she heard that the Baroness had suffered a stroke! Oh, she'd read him a lecture! Tired as he was, he'd have to listen to her for hours.

He made a quick resolve to treat her with disdainful politeness—as had been his habit of late. It was always best, he thought, to keep her at a distance.

But before he could say a word Charlotte had come far enough into the dusky room for her face to be plainly visible in the light of the two tallow candles that stood on the table. She was deathly pale, and her eyes were red with weeping. Something dreadful must have happened to her, he thought.

He immediately jumped at the conclusion that she was unhappy with her husband. And yet, it was not like her to show her feelings so plainly. And certainly her old fiancé was the last person to whom she would reveal anything of that kind.—True, he had heard that her sister, Fru Romelius, was seriously ill, and thought he knew now what had happened.

Charlotte drew up a chair and sat down at the table.

"Captain Hammarberg was here about an hour ago," she said in the hard, expressionless voice of one who has determined not to give way to tears. She did not look at him, but talked as it were to herself. "He had been to Karlstad, and left there this morning shortly after you did. But he drove with two horses, and therefore arrived much earlier. He said he had passed you on the way."

Karl Arthur jerked his chair back from the table. He felt a stab as if a sharp instrument had been plunged through his head down into his heart.

"As the Captain was driving by," Charlotte continued in the same monotone and going into all the particulars, "he saw a light in the study. Thinking the Dean was still up, he stopped, that he might have the satisfaction of telling the Dean how his curate had behaved in Karlstad this morning. He loves to recount such things."

Stab on stab went through the head and cut into the heart of him. All that he had been at pains to gather up and put together was about to fall apart. Now he would hear how his fellow men judged his actions.

"We had left the front door open," said Charlotte, "as we thought you might be here at any moment; so there was nothing to hinder him walking right into the study. Uncle had just gone up to bed, so that it was not him he found there, but me. I sat there writing letters; for I couldn't think of retiring until I knew how it had gone with you at Karlstad. And now I have heard about it from Captain Hammarberg. I think he took greater delight in telling me than he would have telling Uncle."

"And you, of course, took no less delight in listening to him," Karl Arthur retorted.

That little thrust Charlotte thought not worth parrying. It was the sort of thing a person resorts to when in great trouble, yet wishing to present a bold front. She went on with her story.

"Captain Hammarberg did not stay long. He went soon after telling me that you had lectured your mother and that she had suffered a paralytic seizure in consequence. Ah, yes—and your visit to the Burgomaster, he mentioned that also. Oh, Karl Arthur, Karl Arthur!" Charlotte covered her face with her hands and burst into tears.

No one likes to have another weep over him. Nor does one like to think that another has been listening to a humorous account of one's asinine doings. Karl Arthur, therefore, had to say something to the effect that Charlotte, who was now another man's wife, need not concern herself so much about him or his people.

Charlotte ignored this too. She thought it only natural that he should resort to such means of defence, and nothing to feel hurt about. She choked back her tears so that she could say calmly what she had been wishing to tell him from the start.

"When I heard about it I decided at first not to speak to you to-night; for I understood, of course, that you wished to be alone. But this is something I have got to tell you now. I'll not be long."

He shrugged his shoulders and looked unhappy but resigned.

Charlotte said: "I want you to know that it was all my fault. It was I who persuaded Thea. . . . You did not want to go to Karlstad, and I wanted you to. If your mother should die now, it is I, not you——"

She broke down, her sense of guilt was too heavy! When she had recovered herself sufficiently to speak she said:

"I should have been more patient and not sent you off so soon. You still harboured resentment against your mother and had not forgiven her; that was why things went as they did. But I ought to have known that no good could come of it. I'm to blame for it all."

She walked to and fro, nervously plucking at her handkerchief. Suddenly, she stopped in front of Karl Arthur. "It was this I had to tell you."

He took her hand in both of his. "Charlotte," he said in a quiet, tender tone, "think how many talks we have had in this room and at this very table! Here we have argued and quarrelled, but we have also had many happy hours. And now it is for the last time."

She stood by his side, and he sat stroking her hand and speaking to her more kindly than he had spoken in years.

"You have always been magnanimous, Charlotte.

You have always wanted to help me. Charlotte there's no one so generous as you."

She was too astonished to protest.

"I have only repulsed your generosity," he continued. "I never wanted to understand . . . and yet, you come to me this evening and would have me think it was all your fault."

"So it was, Karl Arthur."

"No, Charlotte, it was not. Say no more! It was my self-righteousness, my intolerance. . . . You had only the best intentions."

He bowed his head on the table and wept, but did not release her hand. . . . She felt his tears trickle down upon it.

"Charlotte, I feel like a murderer! There's no hope for me!"

She stroked his hair with her free hand, but did not speak.

"I had such pain in the heart at Karlstad, Charlotte, and I think I was insane. Afterward, on the way home, I tried to put it all away from me, but now I know that it can't be done. There is no one to blame but myself."

"Tell me, Karl Arthur, just how it was and how it happened. I have only heard Captain Hammarberg's version."

When Charlotte spoke in that gentle, motherly way it was impossible to resist her. He told her everything; and felt somehow that he was doing penance by concealing nothing; excusing nothing.

"Oh, Charlotte, why was I so blind! Whatever possessed me to do it?"

She made no answer; but her compassion, like a soothing balm, eased his smarting wounds. Neither of them thought it strange their being together like this, and speaking to each other more trustfully than they had ever done before. He sat all the while at the table, and she stood bending over him. They talked about everything. He asked her whether she thought he could continue as a clergyman after this. To which she replied:

"Why should you be afraid of Captain Hammarberg or what he might say?"

"It is not Captain Hammarberg I'm thinking of, Charlotte. But I'm such a despicable, worthless wretch!"

"Karl Arthur, you must have a talk with Uncle Forsius to-morrow. He is so wise and understanding. Perhaps he will say that you are better fitted for the ministry now than you were before."

It was a good suggestion and a comforting thought. Indeed, everything she said did him good. His fears and misgivings had been allayed. And now he imprinted a light kiss upon her hand.

"Charlotte, I don't like to speak of that which is past and done; still, I must say that I can't understand what made me break with you. I'm not trying to justify myself; but it seems to me as though I were driven to do things against my own will. Why did I throw my mother into the arms of death? And why have I lost you?"

Charlotte moved to a dark corner of the room, lest her face might betray her agitation. Ah! she could have enlightened him as to the why and wherefore; but she wouldn't. This was a sacred hour, and nothing that might appear like revenge should intrude upon its sanctity.

"Dear Karl Arthur," she said, "I am going abroad in a week or so. My husband and I have planned to take my sister Marie Louise down to Italy, where we hope she may find healing for her lung trouble and so be spared to her little ones. Perhaps it was for this it all had to happen."

Now she went back to the man she loved, and, stroking his hair again, said to him:

"The patience of God is not exhausted. I know it to be lasting."

CHAPTER II

HORSE AND COW, MANSERVANT AND MAIDSERVANT

WHO was she that she should be raised above all the other poor peddler women, to fortune and distinction?

True, she was thrifty and knew how to turn every penny to account. Clever and artful she was too, so that she could persuade folks to buy not only things they needed but those they did not need. Yet she felt that she did not deserve to be raised to a station so far above that of her old comrades.

Aye, who was she that a man of high estate had cast eyes on her?

Every morning, on awaking, she would say to herself: "It's a miracle! Aye, it's a miracle as great as any the Bible tells of, and it ought to be preached about in the churches." Then she would fold her hands and imagine herself sitting in a pew at church, with people round about her, and a preacher in the pulpit. It was the regular Sunday service, only the pastor had chosen an unusual subject for a sermon. He talked of nothing but the poor Dalecarlian women who went about the country peddling their wares, and who had to endure many hardships and be exposed to peril at every turn.

He spoke as one who knew how badly the women fared in their wretched quarters, how small their profits were, and how they often went without food rather than touch the paltry coppers they wished to take home. But the pastor was happy to inform his beloved hearers that the Lord in His mercy had cared for one of these poor wanderers so that she would never have to tramp the highways and byways any more in snow and rain. She was going to marry a clergyman and live at a parsonage, where they had horse and cow, manservant and maidservant.

At that point in the sermon it became very light and bright in the church. Everyone was glad that the poor girl would be thus honoured and well provided for. Those who sat near Anna Svärd nodded to her and smiled. She flushed with embarrassment. But it was quite overwhelming when the pastor, turning toward her, directed a few remarks to her, personally.

"Anna Svärd, you have been favoured above all other poor peddler women. But bear in mind that it is through no merit of your own, but by the grace and mercy of God, that fortune and distinction have been bestowed upon you. And do not forget those who must go on toiling for their food and clothing."

That preacher talked so beautifully she could have stayed in bed all day listening to him. But when he came to that about the other poor Dalecarlian girls she burst into tears. At that, she threw off the quilt (if it was anything so fine as a quilt she'd had over her and not a gunny sack or an old rag of a floor mat), and leapt out of bed.

"Idiot!" she ejaculated, "to cry over things you're making up yourself!"

There was only one way in which she could help her former comrades—to start for home now, in mid-September, when the market fairs were already being held, here and there. It would be a sacrifice, but she resolved to make it, and leave the field to her old competitors. She would not stand in the way of those who could never hope to marry a gentleman. She thought of Ris Karin, who, like herself, was from Medstuby; of Annstu Lisa, and a host of others who would be glad she was not on the fair grounds, drawing all the trade to herself.

At home, everyone would wonder, of course, why she had been so foolish as to come away from all the autumn fairs; but she would never tell them how it happened. She had to do something for Our Lord—she who had received so much from Him!

Meanwhile there was nothing to hinder her getting a fresh supply of merchandise before leaving Karlstad. Nor was there any reason why she shouldn't stop at every house on her way north and try to make sales. But when the bargaining was over and the bag had been strapped to her shoulders, as she stood at the door with her hand on the latch, she would turn her face toward the room and testify to the wonderful thing which had come to her.

"Now I give you thanks, all of you here," she would say. "I'll not be coming this way again, for I'm going to be married."

Then, if the folks in the cottage hastened to offer her a few words of felicitation and asked her what sort of fellow she was getting, she would answer with great dignity:

"It is a miracle so great it ought to be preached about in the churches. I am going to marry a clergyman and live at a parsonage. I shall have a horse and a cow, a maidservant and a manservant."

She knew, to be sure, that they would make fun of her when she had gone, but she did not care. She had to express gratitude for the good that had come to her, otherwise it might be taken away.

Once she came to a place where the mistress could not be induced to buy anything, although the woman was a rich widow who held the purse strings herself. So she said: "To-day the dear missus can't refuse to buy something, for this is the last time I'll be here on an errand of this kind." Then she looked very mysterious.

The parsimonious widow became curious and wanted to know why Anna Svärd was giving up the trade.

The pretty Dalecarlian girl replied that it was on account of a great miracle, as great a miracle, indeed, as any the Bible tells of. But that was all the information she would give; and the widow had to question her further.

Anna pressed her lips together. She was so utterly the old Anna Svärd that the parsimonious widow had to treat herself to a silk shawl and a back comb before she learned that the Lord had looked with favour on the humble peddler girl and that she was to marry a clergyman and live at a manse, where they had horse and cow, maidservant and manservant!

"That was a good stroke," thought Anna, "and it worked like a charm." She'd try it again at other places. However, she did not repeat the experiment for fear it might bring harm to her. One should not misuse sacred things. So, instead, she would slip into the hands of the little girls at the various cottages a small breast pin, with a stone of coloured glass—as a gift. She had never before thought of giving anything; but this was just a little thank-offering to Our Lord.

Aye, who was she that Fortune should smile on her at every turn? Was it because she had stayed away from the market fairs, and left them to her old comrades, that the people in the cottages were so eager to buy? It was the same all along the Klarälven Valley—the moment she opened her bag children and adults, alike, crowded around her as if they thought she had sun, moon, and stars to offer them. Before she was halfway home, her stock ran low.

One day, when there was nothing left in her bag but a few horn combs and some rolls of ribbon belting, she met Ris Karin, coming from the North, her bag bulging with merchandise. The old woman was glum and sour, for she had not sold a penny's worth in two or three days.

Anna Svärd bought the whole bagful of goods the old woman had been dragging about for days, and gave her into the bargain the news of her own prospective marriage to a clergyman.

She would never forget the heath where they sat while transacting the business. This was to her the jolliest incident of the journey homeward. Ris Karin flushed purple as the heather, and she actually squeezed out a tear. Anna, seeing her weep, and remembering how she herself had been favoured above all other poor women venders—and through no merit of her own—gave Karin a bit more for the goods than the price they had agreed upon.

At times, as she stood far up on a hillside, leaning against a fence to ease the weight of her bag, she would watch the birds in their southward flight. If there was no one near to laugh at her, she would call to them to take her greetings to the one whom they knew she loved. And she wished that she too had wings and could fly to him.

Aye, who was she to be chosen above so many others; to have her heart opened so that it was beginning to speak the old, old language of Love and Longing?

2

Anna Svärd was at last so near home that she could see, in the distance, the little village of Medstuby.

She stood stock-still and looked. . . . Yes, there it lay, undisturbed, in its old place, along the Dal River. The low, gray houses on the closely built *gårds*[1] and the little white church on the Ness, to the south of the village, were all there as usual. Nor had the birch groves and the fir woods been swept from the earth during her absence.

But when she had satisfied herself as to this, it looked as if she, like many another, when near the goal, was too tired and spent to reach it. She broke off a stick from a wattle fence to use as a staff; but even with its aid she could barely drag herself along the road. The weight of the heavy bag on her back made her walk almost doubled over. She had to pause at every step and gasp for breath.

Slow as was her progress, she finally reached the village, where she hoped to meet her mother or some good friend who would help her with the bag. But not a soul appeared.

Some person or persons probably saw her and, noting her plight, wondered what would become of the poor mother if the daughter was returning as broken and ill as she appeared to be.

Mother Svärd was a soldier's widow without means or a cot of her own. She would never have been able to support herself and her two children had not her brother-in-law, Jobs Eric, a well-to-do man, allowed her to live rent-free on his gård, where she occupied a small room, between the stable and the byre. Berit

---

[1] Farms.

Svärd was clever at the loom and could turn her hand
to any number of things; she was one of those all-round
capable women that no community can do without.
But she had been in harness, so to speak, day and
night while bringing up the children, and had hoped
to have things easier now that her daughter had gone
into trade. It was a bad sign, thought the watchers,
Anna's coming home so early in the season. Ah, the
poor! There's nothing but trouble for them.

Anna Svärd threaded her way among woodstacks,
farm vehicles, and piles of timber crowded between the
many outbuildings on the Jobs gård—to the byre
room.

The mother, at home for once, sat at the spinning
wheel when Anna came in, all bent over and leaning
heavily on a stick. Needless to say, it was a terrible
shock to old Berit to see her daughter looking so ill
and broken. And Anna did nothing to allay her fears.
She said "Good-morning" in a weak voice, as if unable
to speak. Gasping and sighing, she turned her head so
as to avoid her mother's eyes.

What was old Berit to think? She was accustomed to
see her daughter erect of posture and moving as if
unaware of any burden. Fearing the worst, she pushed
the spinning wheel aside and stood up.

Anna Svärd, still breathing heavily, crossed to the
table over by the window and set the bag down. After
unbuckling the straps, she rubbed herself across the
loins and tried to straighten her back. Bent as when

she had entered the room, she went over to the fireplace and sat down on the edge of the hearth.

Aye, what was Mother Svärd to think? The bag was as full now as when her daughter had left home, in the spring. Had she sold nothing the whole summer? Had she been ill, or had she hurt herself in some way? She did not dare question the girl—afraid of what she might hear.

Now, Anna thought that before her mother could receive the great news in the proper spirit she would have to be more desperately unhappy than she had ever been in her life. So she asked her in a doleful voice if she would do her the favour of opening the bag.

Yes, indeed. Mother Svärd would do anything she could for her daughter. But her hands shook so hard that it was some little time before she mastered all the knots and clasps and could dig into the bag.

Old Berit had seen many strange things in her day, but nothing to equal this! Her head was in a whirl. She found no silk shawls, no crocheted buttons, no needle cases. The first thing her hand touched was a small ham. Under it lay a large sack of brown beans, and another, quite as large, of yellow peas. There was not a thimble nor a ribbon band nor a piece of cotton print—nothing, in fact, that a vender of notions should have in her bag. Instead, there were oatmeal, rice, coffee, sugar, butter, and cheese.

The hair on her old head rose. She knew that her

daughter was not one to come lugging home festival fare. What was wrong with the girl? Had she lost her wits?

She was about to go call her brother-in-law and have him look into the matter when, glancing in the direction of the fireplace, she saw that her daughter was laughing. Then she understood that Anna was making game of her and thought that, by rights, she should drive her out. But first she must know what was back of it all; for her daughter was as little given to play and banter as to prodigality.

"Is it for the hawk you've brought all this home?"

"No, for you."

Mother Svärd thought that one of the women neighbours had asked Anna to carry home for her these fine provisions. "Pooh!" said she. "I can't believe you'd strain yourself carrying such a load for me."

"I sold out on the way home. It seemed queer to be walking with nothing in the bag, so I filled it with whatever I could pick up."

But old Berit, who was accustomed to mix straw and bark with her meal and who could seldom afford the luxury of milk with her porridge, was not satisfied with the explanation. She went over to the daughter and sat down beside her. Taking her hand, she said:

"You must tell me, child, what has happened to you."

Now at last Anna thought her mother sufficiently prepared, and imparted the glad tidings.

"Well, you see, Mother, it's a miracle. Aye, as great a miracle as any the Bible tells of; and it ought to be preached about in the churches."

3

Mother and daughter decided that Jobs Eric should be the first to hear the good news. Not only was he their next of kin, but Anna had always stood well with him. Many a time he had said that if his brother's daughter would only furnish the bridegroom he would give her a grand wedding.

In the early afternoon they went over to the house. They found him seated in the fireplace, knocking from his pipe the ashes of the wretched maidenhair moss, which he smoked now instead of tobacco. At this time of the year, when the young men were still in the South at work, there was not a packet of smoking tobacco to be found anywhere in Medstuby.

Anna Svärd saw at a glance that her uncle was in a bad humour, but she was not at all concerned. "Oh, he'll be happy," she thought, "when he hears the good news."

Jobs Eric was a man of towering height, dark haired, with regular features and deep blue eyes. Anna was enough like him to be his own daughter. Jobs Eric had also gone about the country in his youth as a house-to-house peddler. He had been shrewd and resourceful, just as she was, and had made quite a bit of money. When his own children were grown he had wanted

them to take up the same line of work; but they had
shown no bent toward trade. Anna Svärd, on the contrary, had evinced the proper zest and the requisite
aptitude. The uncle had often bragged about her and
lauded her to the skies, at the expense of his own
children. But this time, when Anna appeared before
him, he had no word of praise for her.

"Are you clean daft?" he roared. "Have you run
away from all the big market fairs?"

But she who had been raised by a miracle of God
to fortune and distinction felt that it would never
do to announce her betrothal in the direct manner in
which one says "thanks for the fare" after a meal.
She would have to prepare the way, so to speak, for
the news to be received on its merits. Therefore she
made no mention of her glorious adventure, but merely
said that she had grown tired of wandering and longed
for home.

"One must never tire," Jobs Eric retorted. Whereupon he told her how he had stuck to the business and
how it had profited him.

Anna listened quietly until her uncle had finished
his long story, before making the next move. Then she
went down in her kirtle pocket and drew forth a packet
of smoking tobacco, which she begged him to be good
enough to accept.

It so happened that Jobs Eric had lent Anna a little
money some three years back, to start her on the road.
Before, upon her return at autumn, she had told him at

once how much she had earned and had made a payment on the loan. But this time, instead of money, she handed him tobacco. To be sure, it was something he craved. Just the same, he looked rather glum as he took it.

Anna Svärd knew her uncle as she knew herself, and saw that he became uneasy when she gave him the tobacco. She had never before presented him with anything. Perhaps business had been poor with her, he thought. Was she giving him tobacco because she had no money for him?

He sat dangling the pouch by the string and never said so much as "Thank you."

"Just for once I thought I'd give you something for helping me," said Anna, in another move toward the sacred point. "And now I'm giving up the trade."

Jobs Eric weighed the pouch in his hand as if he would throw it in her face. So she was not going on with the business. All he could make of it was that she had no money for him now and never would have.

"Well, you see, Uncle," Anna continued, "the fact is, I'm going to be married. We thought, Mother and I, that you should be the first to hear the good news."

Jobs Eric put down the packet of tobacco. Now there was not the faintest hope, he thought, that the debt would be liquidated. And what was worse, he might have to give a wedding party for his niece. He cleared his throat, about to speak his mind—then bethought himself.

Mother Svärd felt sorry for her brother-in-law; for

he looked as if all the troubles of the world had suddenly fallen upon him.

"Who would have thought," said old Berit, "when you sent her out three years ago with the peddler's pack, that she was to meet with such good fortune! She's going to marry a clergyman down in Värmland, and she is to live at a parsonage, where they've a horse and a cow, a manservant and a maidservant."

"Aye," said Anna, modestly dropping her eyes. "It's a great miracle, and it looks as if poor little me would be even better off than Uncle Jobs Eric himself."

But the uncle did not appear to be greatly impressed. He glanced from mother to daughter with a smile of amusement.

"Oh, a parson—nothing better? When my brother's daughter came in so high and mighty and presented me with tobacco, I thought 'twas nothing less than a prince she'd caught."

"But, my dear brother," protested Mother Svärd, "surely you don't think she's fooling you?"

The old man rose to his full majestic height.

"No," he said, "I don't think she's fooling. But the folks down country are always chaffing and joking, as everyone knows who's had any dealings with them, and I'm not surprised at a young girl like her being caught with chaff. But, Berit, you and I mustn't lose our heads Now you go out to the kitchen and tell the womenfolk to prepare some good fare for that daughter of yours, to have on the way, and send her off to-morrow morning. Two months from now she can come back, but not a day sooner."

Berit and Anna sprang up, aghast, and hastened toward the door. Anna stood there a moment. Then she turned to her uncle and said, haltingly:

"The money I owe you I've got with me to-day. But maybe you'd rather not have it until some time in December?"

Jobs Eric gave her a look that went right to the marrow of her bones.

"Asch!" he said. "Are you so far gone that you'd poke fun at your old uncle? Don't go and get married, girl! Stick to the trade, and perhaps some day you'll be rich enough to buy the whole village of Medstuby."

4

Anna Svärd proposed that she and her mother should go over to Ris Gård and tell Mother Ingborg of the great miracle. But old Berit wouldn't hear of it.

The Ris gård lay close by the Jobs gård, and while there had been no open break between the neighbours, they were none too friendly.

Mother Ingborg, owner of Ris Gård, was a widow, and hers was the best farm in Medstuby. But there being no man on the place and the outdoor work having to be done by hired labour, her cares and responsibilities were heavy. Her sole ambition was to keep the gård until her sons were grown, when all difficulties would adjust themselves. And the one who helped her was her sister, Ris Karin. The whole village knew it was Karin who furnished the money for wages and taxes. But she had not done so well on the road since Anna Svärd began to go about with the peddler's pack. Consequently, the Ris gård folk felt ill-disposed toward their neighbours on the Jobs gård, and especially toward Anna and her mother.

Anna Svärd thought it high time to have done with such unfriendliness. It was with this end in view that she wished to call on Ris Ingborg. Her mother could stay at home if she liked, Anna would go in any case. So, in the end, she had it her own way. Mother Svärd went along, thinking she might be of some little use.

She had not been at the Ris gård in several years, and had quite forgotten how attractive the place really was. Every inch of wall space in the living room that was not hidden by the decorative cupboard, the grandfather clock, and the canopied bed, was covered with mural paintings of Biblical subjects. On the main wall, in a four-span calèche, with coachman and groom on the box, sat Joseph on his way to meet Father Jacob. And above the wide, low window appeared a little Virgin Mary, curtseying to an Angel of the Lord in a gold-trimmed uniform and tri-cornered hat.

Anna regarded both the one and the other as good premonitory tokens. She liked being reminded of humble folk who had been raised from their lowly estate by a miracle of God.

Mother Ingborg of Ris Gård was a comely woman of

a quiet disposition, who loved pretty things, and who knew how to make her home attractive. She was generally occupied with some fancy work; and now she sat at the table, embroidering flowers and leaves on a white mitten, drawn over her left hand.

She received old Berit and her daughter in the customary way, though her manner was noticeably reserved. After shaking hands, she bade them be seated on the bench under the window; then, going back to her seat, she went on with her work.

There was an awkward silence. Anna thought: Ris Ingborg must be wondering if these womenfolk expected her to treat them to coffee. But of course she had no such intention. Should she offer refreshment to those who were taking the trade away from her sister?

When a reasonable time had elapsed, Anna said that she had come with greetings from Karin, whom she had met on the road, and to tell Mother Ingborg that her sister was hale and hearty.

"I'm glad to hear that she's hale," said Ris Ingborg; "for the main thing is to have one's health."

"Aye," Mother Svärd quickly assented. "And it's needful too for all of us, but most for one who must tramp the country roads in all weathers."

"You're right, Berit," agreed Ris Ingborg.

Pause.

Mother Ingborg must be wondering again if she need offer these womenfolk coffee, thought Anna.

They had only come with greetings from her sister. It would take more than that for her go to any bother on their account.

Anna Svärd then said, apologetically, that she would not have come over like this, in the middle of the afternoon, and interrupted Mother Ingborg at her work merely to convey a greeting. When she had met Karin, the latter was going South with a bagful of merchandise, while she, Anna, was coming North, having sold all her wares. Therefore Anna had bought from Karin her entire stock. When they parted, Karin had to hurry on to Karlstad for a fresh supply of goods before going to the autumn fairs.

There was one thing peculiar to those sisters: When they were moved or excited, they went purple in the face. And Ris Ingborg now sat listening—purple as heatherbloom. Otherwise, she gave no indication of being particularly thrilled by the news. She merely remarked that it was well Karin had met Anna so that she could sell.

"And indeed it was lucky for Anna," old Berit put in, "that she met Karin, and could get a fresh supply of goods to sell on her way home."

There was another lull.—Perhaps Ris Ingborg was wondering if, after all, she ought not to treat them to coffee. No doubt she thought the artful young wench from the Jobs gård had simply come over to brag of the help she had given the older girl of the Ris gård.

No, Ingborg was not going to put the coffee pot on the fire for her!

Anna Svärd now declared it was not just to tell Mother Ingborg of this that she had come over to the Ris gård. It so happened that with the purchase she had got something that was not in the bargain. When transferring the goods from Karin's bag to hers, they had not taken time to examine the things carefully. But when Anna next day spread out her wares at a farmhouse, she found, tucked away in a silk shawl, a five-riksdaler note.

With that, she took from her pocket a folded bank note and laid it on the table before Ris Ingborg.

Mother Ingborg purpled deeper than ever. "But how is it possible that my sister could be so careless with money? Surely she would not leave a five-riksdaler note lying loose in the bag? Perhaps it isn't hers at all?"

"Perhaps it isn't," shrugged Anna. "The five-riksdaler note may have been in the shawl when she bought it. I too am almost sure she never knew it was there."

Ris Ingborg at last put her work aside and regarded Anna Svärd with amazement. "But if you really think Karin didn't know of the note you could have kept the money. You bought of her everything she had in the bag."

"Anyhow," said Anna, "the money is not mine. And now I must ask you to take charge of it until Karin comes home."

Mother Ingborg made no reply. She thought now that

she really must give her guests some refreshment, little as she loved them.

"I should have liked so much to offer the ladies some coffee," she said, "but, shame to say! there's no genuine coffee in the house, and it will have to be only rye-and-chicory."

She arose and went out to the kitchen. In due time she reappeared with the coffee tray. There was a first and a second pouring, then a wee drop more. Ris Ingborg still seemed a bit constrained. Although she treated them well, they felt all the while that she did so with reluctance. When they had finished their rye-and-chicory Anna gave her mother a slight nudge.

"My Anna, here, feels kind o' shy about telling it herself, but something wonderful has happened to her. She's going to be married to a clergyman down in Värmland."

"Well, I declare!" exclaimed Ris Ingborg. "So she's going to be married! Then, of course, she'll not——" She checked herself, for she would not let it appear that she immediately thought of this as boon to herself.

But Mother Svärd filled out the partially stifled measure. "No, my Anna will not go about any more with the peddler's bag. She is going to live at a parsonage, and she'll have a horse and a cow, a maidservant and a manservant."

Mother Ingborg was all smiles now. This was indeed glorious news! She stood up and made a deep curtsey.

"Goodness gracious!" she cried. "Why didn't you tell me sooner? Is it a prospective parsonage fru I'm treating to rye coffee? Wait, till I see if I haven't a bag of genuine coffee lying about somewhere. Oh, I say, do sit down! Oh, please, sit down!"

CHAPTER III

THE BAILIFF'S WIFE

ANNA SVÄRD had been at home about a fort-night when she and her mother one day went up to Bailiff Ryen's gård, just north of Med-stuby, to have a talk with the Bailiff's wife. Jobs Eric and Ris Ingborg both knew and approved the nature of their errand. Ris Ingborg, who was now their best friend and adviser, had been quite eager to have them go; if the idea had not actually originated with her.

They went in by the kitchen way, as that was old Berit's wish, though Anna no doubt thought that a prospective parsonage lady should have entered at the front door. They were immediately shown into a room off the kitchen where the Bailiff's wife stood at a large table, covered with freshly laundered linen, counting the wash.

Fru Ryen arched her eyebrows a trifle on seeing who her callers were, and did not appear to be especially pleased. She had already heard the story of Anna Svärd's engagement to a clergyman, and guessed at once what the two women wished of her. To be sure, she received them well, and bade them be seated so that they might convey their wishes with perfect ease.

It had been arranged that Mother Svärd should do the talking. Ris Ingborg had said it was the proper thing, and she had also cautioned Berit not to beat about the bush but to go straight to the point.

Mother Svärd therefore stated at once that they had come over to ask Fru Ryen whether Anna might come to the Bailiff's gård for a few months' training. The girl was going to marry a clergyman down in Värmland, and it was necessary that she should learn the ways and customs of gentlefolk.

Fru Ryen was an active little lady, and quite good-looking, except for her small, sharp eyes. There was so much life in her little body she could never be still for a moment. The whole time that Berit was talking Fru Ryen stood sorting and counting towels—dozen after dozen—without once losing the count and although she listened with but half an ear, she had a ready answer.

"I have heard about the match," she said, "and disapprove of it. I will have nothing whatever to do with the matter."

Berit and Anna were too astonished for words. And no wonder! Ever since Anna's return they had gone from house to house recounting over the coffee cups the story of the courtship and the troth. And everywhere people had said it was the best news they had heard in many a day, and all thought it an honour to Medstuby that one of their girls should rise to a position of distinction like that of a clergyman's wife. Some had told Anna right out that before this they had found her unbearable because she, like Jobs Eric, had thought only of money. But now she was as a young girl should be—light-hearted and gay. Others had said the best of it was that old Berit would have a good home with her daughter in her declining years. The same feeling of satisfaction had prevailed everywhere. And yet the Bailiff's wife had just declared that she would not countenance the marriage!

Fru Ryen, seeing how crestfallen they were, thought it best to give a reason for her stand.

"Pretty Dalecarlian girls have been known to marry noblemen before," she said. "But these unions never turn out well. I think, Berit, that you should advise Anna to give up all thought of the marriage."

Anna Svärd felt as if she had suddenly come out of a beautiful dream. During the last few days the young folks had been coming back from their summer's labour. As for the girls—some had been doing garden work; others had ferried passengers across the Norrström in Stockholm; while many had been employed in breweries at bottle washing. But with them it had been all work and no play. And now that they had heard of wonders that could happen out in the world their eyes shone with hope. Anna had been obliged to tell them over and over again how the handsome young minister had come toward her in the road, what he had said and what she had said. The men, however, had taken it all in different way. They had made no ado of

Anna before, and now they wondered where their eyes had been. The moment any one of them chanced to be alone with her, he would blurt out that in case that preacher fellow in Värmland went back on her, she needn't grieve, for he who walked by her side in the village street was ready to give her full compensation for the loss. And yet the Bailiff's wife thought that she ought not to marry a gentleman. Well, perhaps she was too lowly for him.

Anna Svärd and her mother rose without a word. Fru Ryen shook hands, as when they came, and saw them out. Whether it was because she did not want the servants to see them go away looking so dejected, or whatever her reason, she took them through the drawing room to the entrance hall and let them out the front way.

To be rejected by the Bailiff's wife was the worst that could have happened, they thought. Had it been the wife of the Pastor who had given them such advice, it would not have mattered so much. But everyone in Medstuby looked up to the Bailiff's wife, and folks were guided by her in all their affairs. If she saw a man and a maid who suited each other she would have them united in marriage, and that settled it. And if the men on adjoining farms got into a squabble and threatened to air their grievances in court, she was there in a flash, making them adjust their differences.

Fru Ryen had no authority whatever over Anna Svärd or her mother. Nevertheless, Anna felt that, because the Bailiff's wife did not wish her to marry a high-born gentleman, it was all off.

The blank despondency of her hard childhood years threatened to close over her again. But, happily, it soon receded. That very day came a letter. She could not read it, but knew who it was from. She carried the letter in her pocket and thought of the writer. His own parents had also considered her not good enough for him. Yet he had stood out manfully against them; so, surely, he would be able to hold his own with the Bailiff's wife, too.

Next day she did what everyone else in Medstuby did when they received a letter: she went to Sexton Medberg and asked him to read it to her.

The sexton, who was also the village schoolmaster, held forth in the schoolroom, which adjoined the kitchen of his cottage. Seated round a large table, which took up half the room, were a number of small boys, who were just learning to read in a book.

Taking the letter, he broke the seal carefully and glanced at the handwriting, which was neat and legible. Then he read it in a loud voice. It never occurred to him to send the children out; and there they sat listening to the tender avowals of love the fiancé had indited. Sexton Medberg perhaps thought it would profit the boys to hear how easily he read script. It would not have done to ask him to wait and read the letter some other time. Very likely he would have told her to clear out and read the letter herself.

Anna tried to follow the sexton closely; but at the
same time she could not help watching the boys. Needless to say they were having fun. They sat there, with
flushed faces and cheeks puffed out, trying to hold in
the laughter.

Since her visit to the Bailiff's house Anna had been
perturbed. All the joy and self-confidence had gone out
of her. She did not wonder at the boys' amusement,
for she was unworthy of such a beautiful letter from
him.

For several days she wondered how she should reply.
She wanted to tell him that she had come to think
that his parents were right—that she was not good
enough for him, and that he must put her out of his
mind. When at last she had formulated a lengthy answer she went again to Sexton Medberg. This time,
however, she was careful to come after school hours.
The sexton immediately sat down at the big table to
write at her dictation. There being no boys in the room
now to laugh at her, she could say what she wished
without fear of interruption. The sexton wielded the pen
with vigour and purpose, and it seemed no time at all
until the letter was finished.

But when he read her what he had written Anna was
dumbfounded. Sexton Medberg had indited many love
letters in his day, and knew better than a young girl,
who had only got as far as her first, what should be
conveyed in a letter of that kind. So of course he had
not bothered to write what such an inexperienced child

had dictated. He began by saying that the writer was pleased to hear that her fiancé was well; for health was the greatest of blessings. On this theme he spread himself over a whole side of the paper. Whereupon he said that she missed him so dreadfully that every day away from him was as a month, and every month was as a year. This he also embroidered. And lastly, he assured the fiancé of her fidelity and besought him never to desert her. For, otherwise, she would have as many nights of anguish as there were leaves on the linden and nuts on the hazel tree. Aye, their number would be countless as the sands of the sea and the stars in the heavens.

When she asked the sexton why he had not written according to her dictation, he wondered if she thought he did not know how to write a love letter. It would never do, he said, to put down on paper such piffle as she had made up. She must remember it was a clergyman she was writing to.

Anna had to be satisfied with that. The letter was folded, sealed, and sent just as it was. What would her betrothed think when he read it? She felt more insignificant and more unworthy of him than ever.

The third time she called on Sexton Medberg she asked him if he would teach her to read and write. He told her in plain words that she was too old to learn such hard tricks; but she persuaded him to let her try. She might come to him in the morning, he said, at the same hour as the boys.

And that was how it happened that Anna Svärd, some weeks later, sat at the sexton's big table, with goose quill in hand and paper before her, writing from copy: "The morning hours are golden."

It was a desperate task. She held the slender quill in a tight clutch and pressed the nib so hard against the paper it spattered tiny drops of ink all over the paper as she formed large, queer-looking curlycues instead of letters.

It was a desperate labour in another sense too. Her sole purpose in striving to learn this difficult art was to write to *him* down there at Korskyrka that she was unworthy of him and that he must forget her.

Although the end in view was such a sad one she did her utmost—straining every muscle as if she were lifting a barrel of rye. Each word cost her so much effort that she had to lay the pen down and puff hard before going on to the next.

"The pen should be held lightly, with the fingers straight," said the sexton.

But Anna felt that the goose quill would not stay in her hand unless it were held in so firm a grip it whitened the knuckles. The boys sniggered all the while and made fun, until Anna, sick and tired of the whole thing, was about to give it up, when the door opened and the Bailiff's wife came into the schoolroom.

Fru Ryen, keen-eyed and alert as usual, had come to discuss some village business with Sexton Medberg;

but when she saw Anna Svärd sitting among the small boys writing, her interest was aroused.

"So you have not yet abandoned the idea of becoming a parsonage fru, I see."

Anna made no answer. The sexton muttered something to the effect that if Anna couldn't become a parson's fru short of learning to write, she would have to forego the distinction.

The boys sniggered again. But the look they got from the Bailiff's wife sobered them instantly. Fru Ryen now leaned over Anna's shoulder and glanced at her paper, on which the scrawls pointed in every direction like the wattles of a broken-down fence.

"What are you writing? Let me see the copy.—'The morning hours are golden.'—Lend me your pen!" Smiling, she bent down to the table, pondered a moment, pressing the quill to her lips, then said: "What is the name of your intended?"

"Karl Arthur."

"Watch now, and you'll see!" She printed the name in large, round letters. "Can you read what I have written? It spells Karl Arthur. Now try to write that name. You'll find that you can if you love him."

She handed the pen back to Anna. Whereupon she and the sexton repaired to the kitchen, so that she could speak to him in private.

Anna Svärd sat gazing at the beautiful name Fru Ryen had printed, and wished she could write it in the same way. It was no use trying, so she threw the pen down.

When in an hour the sexton and the Bailiff's wife returned to the schoolroom, it was silent as the grave in there. The boys were not laughing now, nor were they engrossed in their primers. They were all leaning across the table, watching something Anna Svärd was doing.

She sat there, happy and smiling, her deft fingers busy at a bit of fancy work, which she quickly hid under the table when the sexton and the Bailiff's wife reappeared.

"Out with it, Anna!" Fru Ryen commanded.

And what she beheld was a work of art. Instead of labouring with pen and ink, Anna had taken from her outer pocket needle and twist and a small white clout, on which she had embroidered the name. The letters were neat and well formed as those Fru Ryen had printed. In her joy at being able to stitch the name, she had worked around it a dainty wreath of flowers.

Fru Ryen studied the work, her forefinger on her nose, as was her habit when contemplating an important move.

"Well, well," she said, "do you love him as much as that? I didn't know it, you see. I supposed you thought only of the parsonage and the title of fru. You may come to me to-morrow, and I'll try to make a lady of you."

CHAPTER IV

THE WEDDING

ONE Saturday afternoon Anna Svärd stood on the porch of the Bailiff's house watching a sleigh that came slowly up the avenue. It was a bitter winter's day, but she did not feel the cold. Her heart beat fast, and her cheeks were burning. She knew that in the sleigh sat he to whom she had sent greetings by the birds.

Anna had been at the Bailiff's gård about four months, and had received some good schooling. She had been taught to mind how she stood and how she walked, how she ate and how she drank, how she spoke and how she answered when addressed, how she greeted people and bade farewell, how she laughed, coughed, sneezed, yawned, and a thousand other things. Of course it was not to be expected that Anna Svärd should be transformed into a fine lady in so short a time; but at least she had learned to detect her own faults and shortcomings. And now, as she saw the sleigh bearing her beloved draw nearer and nearer, her joy was not unmixed with fear. Perhaps he would not care for her at all when he saw her among folk of his own class. The Bailiff and his wife had two daughters. The girls,

to be sure, were snub-nosed and tow-haired, but they
had such nice manners, and they walked with such
light, easy tread, and their speech sounded so sweet
to her ears. And then what pretty clothes they wore!
If she could only afford to dress like a lady! But she,
alas, was still wearing the traditional parochial peasant costume! Surely, the wife of a clergyman of Värmland couldn't go round looking gaudy as a green wood-
pecker?

It troubled her, moreover, not to know why her fiancé
was coming. Was it perhaps in order to break the
troth? Shortly after Christmas he had sent certain letters and papers so that the banns could be published
in church. She had often heard that when once the banns
for a couple had been read they were as good as married. But she took no comfort in that.

Everyone in Medstuby had been glad of the banns.
Jobs Eric, who had been quite sceptical about the
marriage, after the third reading, solemnly announced
that he would give his niece a grand wedding. It was
to be a three-day celebration the like of which had never
been seen in Medstuby, with plenty of food and drink,
music and dancing, and the young folks all sleeping in a
common bed on the floor. For, since his niece was making such an advantageous marriage, the wedding must
be in accordance. One of the Ryen girls meanwhile had
written to the prospective bridegroom for Anna, in-
forming him of Jobs Eric's plan. Strangely enough, in
reply to that letter he had merely said that he was

coming to see her. Perhaps he rued his bargain when he heard that there was talk of a big wedding?

She had no time to ponder over that, for the sleigh had already turned in on the drive. Now she would meet him again, and that was a consolation. Whatever the outcome, it would be good to see him once more, she thought.

When he stepped out of the sleigh not only Anna but Bailiff and Fru Ryen stood on the steps to receive him. After shaking hands with his host and hostess, he came over to Anna, put his arms around her, and was about to kiss her, when she drew away, abashed. She could not let him kiss her with folks standing there looking on. Suddenly she remembered that it was customary among the gentry to kiss in the presence of others and felt vexed with herself for having acted so foolishly.

As soon as Karl Arthur had removed his pelts they all went into the dining room, where the table had been laid with Fru Ryen's finest coffee set, her choicest copper, and silver cake baskets, heaped with delicious small-cakes.

Anna was placed next to her fiancé. She had drunk afternoon coffee with the Bailiff's family every day for months, and knew what was proper. But of a sudden she forgot all her teaching, and filled her cup to overflowing. Instead of sweetening her coffee, she put a lump of sugar in her mouth, and drank out of the saucer as if she were having coffee with Mother Svärd and Ris Ingborg. A sharp look from the Bailiff's wife made her gulp so hard that sugar and all nearly went down the wrong lane.

Again she was provoked at herself, but took comfort in the thought that nothing mattered now. She felt that something was wrong. Her betrothed had not been so indifferent toward her the last time they met. He had surely come to break off with her, she thought.

During the coffee hour he talked only with the Bailiff's folk. It was so easy for him and for them to say nice things. He thanked them for all they had done for his fiancée and Fru Ryen replied that he owed them no thanks; that Anna was such a clever girl and had made herself so useful in the home, it was they who were indebted to her and not she to them.

The Bailiff's wife, the daughters, and even the Bailiff himself had been so bright-faced and soft-spoken since he had come. Of course they had not expected to find him the sort of man he was. Perhaps they had pictured him as a hunchback or a one-eyed man. Anyhow, they must have thought there was something defective about him since he wanted to marry a poor Dalecarlian girl.

Well, she could forgive them for that, for she, herself, had almost forgotten how handsome he was and how perfect in every way. She wondered if they saw the shimmer round his smooth white brow, and thought it a mercy his eyelids were heavy and inclined to droop, or they could have done nothing but sit and gaze into his deep, marvellous eyes.

Her intended, apparently, felt quite at home with the Ryens. The coffee table had been cleared, but he still sat there, chatting with them. It was not only the host and hostess who conversed with him, but the daughters too had their say. She thought they were taking him away from her, and she felt strange and forlorn.

"It's with them he belongs," she said to herself. "He doesn't care for me any more. He sees now that I'm not fit for him. I haven't a word to say, and neither he nor anyone else remembers that I exist."

Just then he turned to Anna and, raising his heavy lids, gave her a look which she felt as one feels the sun when it breaks through a cloud. He would like to make a call at the parsonage, he said, if it was not too far away.

No, it was not very far. He had only to go through the village, then turn to the left; it lay just north of the church. She spoke so gruffly that they all noted it and looked at her in surprise and disapproval.

"I thought that you would show me the way," he said.

"Oh, that I can do, of course." She understood that he wished to speak to her alone in order to have done with her forever. But how could she be expected to look happy and pleased when her heart felt so heavy in her breast? How unlike himself he was in every way, she thought. The others, who had never seen him before, did not know how changed he was.

When they were out on the country road Anna and her fiancé walked as far apart as possible. It was near the end of February, and the sun had done no damage as yet to the high snowbanks on either side. The roadway was quite narrow, and Anna had some difficulty keeping as far away from her betrothed as she wished.

The days were getting longer so that it was still quite light. A crescent moon appeared in the pale sky. It looked terribly sharp and menacing hanging there, she thought—like a sickle that would cut her off from happiness.

She was used to being out in all kinds of weather and had never minded the cold; but anything so bitter as that evening she had never experienced. Every time they put down a foot the snow sent up a squeak. "No wonder it wails," she thought; "for the feet that trample it are heavy with sorrow."

They had walked the whole way in silence; but when they stood at the door of the parsonage Karl Arthur said:

"Now, Anna, I expect you to raise no objections to what I shall ask of the Pastor. You understand, of course, that I'm trying to arrange matters in a way that is best for both of us."

"Indeed I'll not thwart you, be sure of that. Everything shall be as you wish."

"Thank you for the assurance," he said, after which they went into the Rector's study.

They found the Rector seated at his writing table.

It being a Saturday evening, he was making up his sermon. It was no friendly look he gave the two intruders who had come and disturbed him.

Karl Arthur stepped forward and introduced himself. The Rector showed a different mien on learning that the caller was a brother cleric. Anna Svärd stood quietly down by the door while the two colleagues exchanged a few words on matters pertinent to them. After a little Karl Arthur went over to her and, taking her by the hand, brought her forward. Standing with her before the Rector, he said:

"I see that your Reverence is pressed for time and I will therefore state the errand on which I have come without further delay. Your Reverence, I'm sure, can readily understand the feelings and desires of a young lover. It occurred to me only the day before I left Korskyrka how delightful it would be if I were not obliged to return alone. The idea appealed to me, and I wondered if it could be carried out. The little home which I have procured for myself and bride was then nearly ready for occupancy. Kind friends had promised to make the painters and carpenters rush the work so that we might move in by the end of next week."

The Rector showed plainly that he disapproved; but before he could put in a word, Karl Arthur continued:

"I left home last Tuesday and should have reached Medstuby on Thursday, or Friday at the latest; but unfortunate circumstances upset all my calculations. Overdriven horses, tipsy drivers, and ice-blocked rivers prevented my arriving here until this afternoon. But, Herr Rector, should that necessarily affect the plan on which I have set my heart? The only reasonable objection might be that my fiancée has been looking forward with pleasure to the festivities which her uncle had planned in honour of our nuptials; but I have no doubt that she would relinquish all thought of a marriage feast in order to come with me now. Therefore I would ask your Reverence to be good enough to marry us at church to-morrow, immediately after the Service."

The Pastor reflected a long moment. He knew his parishioners; knew with what joy many of them were looking forward to a three-day celebration, and was afraid they would censure him if he acquiesced.

"My dear young friends," he said, "won't you take an old man's advice and give up this notion? You know, Dr. Ekenstedt, that there has been considerable talk of this marriage among us, and our people are unprepared for a wedding so unceremonious and hasty. They expect a grand celebration."

Karl Arthur waved the thought aside. "Let us discuss this matter frankly, Herr Rector," he said. "You know as well as I do what a big wedding means: Drunkenness, gormandizing, fighting, and lewdness. I cannot be a party to a thing of that sort. My object in making this journey was primarily in order to forestall the possibility of such entertainment. I can think of no better or more effective means of settling the matter than by the plan which I have had the honour to unfold to your Reverence."

The Pastor glanced up and down the room as if seeking some means of escape from his persistent colleague. Finally his eye fell upon Anna Svärd. He brightened at once, thinking he had found a way out of his difficulty.

"Dr. Ekenstedt," he said, "you have not yet told me how your fiancée regards this proposition, which in my opinion seems a bit brash."

Karl Arthur, without the least hesitation, replied:

"Before I stepped into this room my betrothed agreed to accept my arrangements."

Anna Svärd made a slight movement of surprise, which did not escape the keen eyes of the Rector. Turning to her, he said:

"But, Anna, are you fully aware of the nature of these arrangements?"

She blushed to the roots of her hair. One thing had become clear to her in the course of the conversation: Karl Arthur wished to marry her. She had no cause for anxiety. He did not find her too lowly and uncouth, but intended all the while to make her his wife. At the same time she felt displeased and hurt. Why had he not asked her out in the road if she was ready to marry him on the morrow?

"He doesn't love me as I love him," she thought. "If he loved me he'd've asked me first how I'd like to have it."

However, offended and hurt though she was deep down in her heart, she would not take her fiancé to task before the Rector.

"Sure, you must know, Church-father, that I'm ready to go with him wherever in the world he wants to take me."

"Oh, in that case," said the Rector, "I am at the Herr Doctor's service."

2

The Bailiff's wife sat in her drawing room with a finger on her nose, trying to solve a difficult problem. She had learned to know and to like Anna Svärd, and thought it a pity the young girl was not to have the grand wedding she had been counting upon. So on Saturday evening Fru Ryen had set everyone in the village and in her own home astir in order to give the girl a wedding of sorts. The bridal things, which were kept at the Ris gård, had been overhauled and freshened, and on Sunday morning Ris Ingborg and her sister had come to the Bailiff's gård to dress the bride. The procession, which formed on the church knoll, was both long and impressive, thanks to the efforts of Fru Ryen. Two fiddlers led the march into the church. Behind the bride and groom, in the following order, marched Bailiff and Fru Ryen, Sexton Medberg and Jobs Eric, the church-wardens with their wives, the parish councillors with theirs. And last came the young peasants—Dal men and Dal women in gala attire. It was all quite charming and effective. Even with long preparation the result could scarcely have been better.

True, there were no festivities at the Jobs gård, but Fru Ryen was giving a little wedding supper at her home for the bride and groom. Fortunately, she had already made preparations for a party in honour of the fiancé and his new relatives, so that it was an easy matter to make it a nuptial celebration instead. Moreover, the guests were sensible folk, who understood that any lavish entertainment was out of the question.

But if she had known what a dreary affair it was going to be, she would never have carried out her good intentions. All who came were usually voluble enough, but that evening they had nothing to say. The hostess tried her best to enliven the company, as did also her husband and her daughters; even the bridegroom made special effort to keep up a flow of talk. But there was a heaviness in the air which nothing could dispel. Perhaps they were all thinking of the big wedding with the grand doings of which they had been deprived.

As for the bride—she sat there the whole evening with her heavy dark eyebrows knotted—staring straight before her like a prisoner in the dock awaiting her doom.

"This is not a good beginning to the marriage," thought the Bailiff's wife. "I should like to know what Anna is brooding over. Is it because she could not have the big wedding at Jobs Gård that she looks so dejected?"

Fru Ryen turned to Karl Arthur and asked him to

say a few words to them. (This was merely for something to pass the time.) He spoke easily and well, but she could not deny that his remarks frightened her. "The young man surely intends to venture out upon ice too thin to bear him."

She grew more and more alarmed. What did it all mean? As a follower of Christ, would he live all his life in poverty? Was it simply in order to carry out this idea that he had chosen a lowly woman for wife; one whom he thought was of the same mind, and who, like himself, would scorn riches and believed that happiness was only to be found in doing God's work among one's fellow men?

Fru Ryen, knowing that the young bride during the betrothal period had dreamed all the while of a parsonage with maidservant and manservant, horses and cows, was dumbfounded.

"What a terrible misunderstanding!" she thought. "Anna knew nothing of this. Where will it lead to?"

The longer she listened the better she understood what manner of man she had before her. "Poor Anna Svärd is tied to a religious fanatic, who has married a woman of the peasant class only to have by his side a person who is used to hard toil and will do her own housework. He is one of those young aristocrats who would live like the peasants. It is not the fashion nowadays to be a gentleman."

She glanced from one to another of his hearers. . . . What did Jobs Eric think—he who never gave out a

penny needlessly? What did old Berit think, who had
had a life-and-death struggle with poverty? What
thought Ris Ingborg, who never went to sleep a night
free from anxiety for her farm? And the young wife
herself, who for three years had tramped about the
country with the peddler's pack, what did she think of
this revelation?

"They ought to feel as distressed as I do," thought
Fru Ryen, "yet they sit there, calm and unconcerned
as if it were nothing at all."

She saw, of course, that they did not take the young
clergyman seriously, that they regarded his talk about
the blessings of poverty as something peculiar to his
calling. It was good preaching and edifying, but none of
them believed for a moment that he meant to practice
what he preached. They knew that there were impecunious parsons, and were not surprised that so young a
man had not as yet come into a large benefice; still they
thought that he would be able to give his wife more
comforts than she had been accustomed to having. He
was the child of upper-class folk, and such never died of
starvation in Sweden.

Fru Ryen, who, on the contrary, felt that he was in
earnest and knew that the life before Anna would be
one of hardship and trial, wondered whether she could
stand it. "These two young persons have barely met,
and as Anna can neither read nor write they have not
learned to know each other through letters. They are
no better acquainted now than they were at their first

meeting on the highway. Perhaps it would be well to open her eyes. She is a splendid girl, but her virtues do not lie along the path of renunciation. I have really grown fond of the girl. Can I let her enter upon her marital duties without telling her what she will have to meet?" However, upon reflection, she decided not to interfere. Had they not already become man and wife, she would have felt in duty bound to speak; but, in the circumstances, it seemed best to leave them alone.

After supper, when the guests had departed and the daughters of the house had conducted the bride upstairs to the guest chamber, where the marriage bed stood ready, the husband asked if he might have a word with the hostess.

Fru Ryen, after their talk, which lasted about half an hour, went into her bedroom to fetch her Bible. With the Book under her arm, she repaired to the guest chamber, where the two daughters had just relieved the bride of her wedding finery and put her to bed.

Anna's brows were still knit, and her deep, brooding eyes continued to stare as it were toward some impending doom. Seeing the Bailiff's wife come in with the Bible under her arm, Anna nodded her head as much as to say: "I was right after all! This is what I've been expecting the whole evening."

Fru Ryen was in no haste. She trimmed the candles, sent her daughters to bed, adjusted her spectacles, and opened the Bible, leisurely turning the leaves until she found the right place. Whereupon she said that there were certain passages of Scripture she wished to read to Anna, now that she was launching out upon the sea of matrimony.

Anna Svärd raised herself to a sitting position and folded her hands. She understood, of course, that the Bible reading was only an introduction to something unpleasant and would have preferred not to be kept in suspense.

Fru Ryen read from the thirteenth chapter of the First Epistle to the Corinthians:

"*Love suffereth long, and is kind; love envieth not; love vaunteth not itself, is not puffed up. Doth not behave itself unseemly, seeketh not her own, is not easily provoked, thinketh no evil. It rejoiceth not in iniquity, but rejoiceth in the truth.*

"*Love beareth all things, believeth all things, hopeth all things, endureth all things.*"

The Bailiff's wife, thinking perhaps of her own nuptial night, read the beautiful verses with deep feeling. As Anna listened, it seemed to her as if the words came from her own heart. Never had she heard anything read from the Bible that sounded so right and so true! At the close of the reading Anna repeated the last verse to herself.

"Would you like to hear it again?" Fru Ryen asked her.

"Yes," said Anna, so moved she could only whisper the word. Her brow was smoother now, and her eyes had lost their fixed stare.

Fru Ryen felt more hopeful now of carrying out her mission without arousing violent protests.

"Anna Svärd is far from stupid. She heard what her husband said a while ago and perhaps already understands the situation." When she had read once more the beautiful verses on love, she closed the Bible.

"If you should find that everything is not as you had expected," she said, "then think on this!"

The deep, brooding eyes were turned upon the speaker. That last remark of hers might be only a friendly admonition to a newly wedded wife; but it might also be the introduction to the dreadful thing that was to come.

Fru Ryen hastened to elucidate:

"I mean, you see, that if one really and truly loves somebody, one does not mind how one fares in a worldly way. It is not for horses and cows, menservants and maidservants that one marries."

Fru Ryen thought Anna's behaviour most extraordinary. Surely such a broad hint should have made her feel terribly uneasy. But the girl did not move or say a word. Fru Ryen saw that she would have to be more explicit.

"You mustn't think, child, that I am meddling in your affairs gratuitously. After you had gone upstairs your husband came and told me quite frankly how you and he were to live. When I asked him whether you knew of this, he said that you had known it from the first."

"What should I have known?" said Anna in a tone of utter indifference. Evidently this was not the dreadful thing she was waiting to hear.

"Don't you remember his telling you," Fru Ryen continued, raising her voice as if speaking to one who was not fully awake, "that he wanted to live as Jesus had lived? He said the same to me this evening."

"Yes, but . . ."

"I suspected at once that you did not understand what he meant by that; and when I told him so he requested me to inform you that he has no parsonage, that he is only a curate, with a yearly stipend of one hundred and fifty riksdalers. Up to this he has lived at the Deanery. Now that he is married he will receive a certain allowance of meal, butter, and milk—probably enough for your needs. But since you have entertained such great expectations . . ."

Anna Svärd asked Fru Ryen, merely out of politeness, where they were to live.

"Your husband received a small legacy last autumn —about a thousand riksdalers and some pieces of furniture—enough to furnish one room. With this money he has purchased a small cottage of one room and kitchen; which will do well enough for the two of you. But there are no outbuildings, you understand; no fields or meadows. You will have to prepare your own meals, make the fires, do the baking, the scouring, the washing —everything, in fact."

Fru Ryen wondered if Anna was merely feigning indifference and if the tempest that should be raging in her would break upon the husband when he appeared. Still, there were no indications to that effect. The strong, vigorous young peasant woman saw all her hopes crushed without evincing the least sign of regret or disappointment.

"I'm sorry I put you to the trouble of giving me the training," was all she said.

"Oh, that was no trouble," Fru Ryen assured her. "It has been a pleasure to teach so apt a pupil. You know, child, that we all love you. This is the first unhappy moment I have had on your account."

Anna gave her no word of appreciation for all her kindness, and Fru Ryen felt almost vexed with the girl.

"I daresay you are comforting yourself with the thought that your husband will soon have a better living. But you mustn't count on that. At least he says that he wishes to remain a poor man to the end of his days. If you are thinking of his rich parents, I must tell you that he has quarrelled with them on your account and can expect no pecuniary assistance from home. Moreover, he has been disinherited."

"Poor Mother!" said Anna Svärd. "And she thought she'd have a home with us in her old age."

"If the Dean of Korskyrka should die," Fru Ryen went on regardlessly, "your husband will be sent as curate to some other parish. The worst of it is that he cannot take you with him, and you will be left alone in your house. The Dean is now seventy-six years of age and not likely to be here much longer."

"I understand that it'll be hard sledding for us," said Anna, unconcerned as ever.

"And since your future is rather uncertain," Fru Ryen pursued, "I think your husband is right in what he proposes to do. He bade me ask you—as he could not do it himself—he wished me to tell you——"

An abrupt movement cut her short. Anna had turned right round and now sat facing her interlocutor. Her lethargy was gone; she was now wide awake.

The Bailiff's wife coloured a bit. "My dear girl," she said, "don't look at me like that! You almost frighten me. But I really think your husband's objections are well taken. It would surely be unwise of you two to raise a family. You understand, of course, what I mean."

Anna sank back on her pillow. She did not weep, but wrung her hands, and her features were distorted with anguish. "I knew it," she said. "It is just as I expected, he doesn't love me any more."

"Dear child, don't take it in that way! Your husband is not like the rest of us; he is of a totally different stamp, you understand. I know that he loves you, but he is one of those zealots who think they serve God by renouncing the things they most desire."

"If he loved me would he send me such a message?" shrieked Anna. "Hasn't he shown in every way that he's tired of me? And now he'll not have to be bothered with me any more."

With that she flung off the bed covers, snatched up her shoes and stockings, and began to dress.

"My dear child, you are wrong, I assure you. Your husband has told me himself that he loves you passionately. From the moment he came and saw you again he has been fighting his desires. That is why he has hardly spoken to you."

"Stuff!" cried Anna, throwing on her clothes as if dressing to flee from a fire. "If he loved me, do you think he'd be satisfied with such a marriage? What he wants of me I don't know."

Fru Ryen, noting the frantic movements of the girl's hands, the wild look of her eyes, and the ghastly pallor of her face, ran out of the room and down the stairs to call the husband.

She found him in the dusky dining room, down on his knees, lost in prayer. She rushed over to him and shook him by the arm. Flushing with embarrassment, he rose to his feet.

"I have prayed God to grant that Anna might receive the message in the right spirit," he said.

"There's no time now for prayers," Fru Ryen shouted, shaking his arm again. "Unless you go to Anna at once and show her that you love her as a man should love his wife, we'll have to search for her to-morrow in some ice hole in the river."

CHAPTER V

THE NEW HOME

ANNA SVÄRD was by nature a vender. She had a correct eye for the things that would appeal to her customers, and never carried in her bag an unsalable article. If she came to a place where the folks did not wish to buy she was not disagreeably insistent, but went her way at once. If she happened upon the sort who liked to higgle she let them have their own way and looked just unhappy enough to make them think they were getting a good bargain. Moreover, she was strictly honest. She had never been known to offer a piece of cloth that was moth-eaten or water-damaged. If a silk shawl had lain in her bag so long that there were breaks in the creases, she would point out the flaws and sell the article for almost nothing.

Without doubt Anna Svärd would have made a small fortune had she continued with the business. But from the day she first met Karl Arthur Ekenstedt a great change had come over her. True, she was just as clever, resourceful, and alert as before, only the good attributes which had enabled her to earn her living, were now put to the service of love. She often wondered how she could have been so eager to make money. Was it really herself who had stood in the market place and rejoiced over every customer that approached her stall? Was it actually she, Anna Svärd, who had gone about the country with no other thought in her mind than to put penny to penny? It seemed incredible. But, then, she did not know at that time what was the important thing in life.

The newly married couple had stayed in Medstuby a few days, leaving there early on Wednesday. They arrived at Korskyrka Friday afternoon, happy and pleased, to take possession of their humble home on the hill above the churchtown.

Karl Arthur, who had received some friendly advice from the Bailiff's wife, did not keep Anna in ignorance of what was in store for her. He asked her whether she had seen, during her stay at Korskyrka the previous summer, two small cottages that stood on the hill, just behind Dr. Romelius's garden. And she, who for three consecutive summers had travelled the length and breadth of the parish, saw as it were before her eyes two dilapidated huts which looked ready to collapse. She had never been inside either of them; for a vender of merchandise does not visit such hovels, where the occupants are too poor to mend their broken windowpanes. But, as a matter of course, she had ascertained who the owners were and knew that in the one dwelt an old soldier, who lived on a pension of twenty riksdalers a year, and in the other a poor girl, known as Crofter

Matts's Elin, with her ten younger sisters and brothers, for whom she toiled and slaved.

That Karl Arthur had bidden in all ten children at a pauper auction, from which they were to have been sent out to nurse, was news to her. Nor had she heard of the fortunate change in their circumstances which followed upon his merciful act. Several of the influential ladies of the parish had formed a benevolent society, which had taken charge of the orphans, repaired their cottage, and provided them with food and clothing. All would have been well had not the oldest sister taken to her bed and died.

It almost looked as if the poor worn-out girl, when seeing the children decently clad, the cellar filled with potatoes, the cupboard full of flour and herring, the floor mended so that the rats could no longer come up through the cracks, new panes at the windows, so that they did not have to be stopped with rags—felt that there were no further duties in life for her to perform, and that she could at last take a long, much-needed rest.

The kind protectresses of the children soon found a new nurse in an elderly spinster, who had once been in service at the Deanery. In certain respects she took excellent care of the children; but she was too old to exercise much control over ten unruly youngsters. Karl Arthur would have been glad to help her keep order among his wards, but it was impossible for him so long as he lived at the Deanery. Therefore, upon receipt of his legacy, he had purchased the old soldier's cottage, which was close by the children's house, and had had it put in repair.

It was there they were to live. The young minister assured his bride that the house had been so thoroughly done over she wouldn't know it again. On the whole he had made an advantageous deal, he thought, in getting a modest little home, well situated, from where he could keep watch of the large family of children.

Anna Svärd, to whom nothing mattered so long as her husband loved her, took it all good-naturedly. What else could she do? She had promised to take him for better or for worse. But she had faith in her own ability, and knew that if things went too badly she was able to earn a living for both of them.

As they were approaching Korskyrka Anna told her husband that in her part of the country it was customary for newly married folk, when entering their house for the first time, to kneel on the threshold and ask God to bless their home and their life within its walls. Karl Arthur thought it a beautiful custom, which they too should observe.

But when they arrived they forgot. It was not that Anna was struck with wonder at sight of the house, for to her, it looked about the same as of old. It was by no means transformed into a manse! The workmen had not even put up a porch, and the wobbly stone that had done service as doorstep in the old soldier's time was still there. She was as certain as ever that she would think twice before going into such a hovel with a view to soliciting trade, and said as much to her husband—chaffingly, of course. They were both in high spirits and laughed heartily.

There was nothing about the house itself that made them forget to kneel and ask a blessing on their new home. But the moment the sleigh stopped before the entrance, the door opened and a tubby little woman stepped out upon the wobbly stone to receive them.

Anna Svärd, who had spent three summers at Korskyrka and knew every person in the parish both by sight and name, did not remember having seen the woman before. Then, all at once it struck her that it must be Fru Sundler, the wife of the organist. The last time she had seen her she had had long, pretty curls, but now her hair was cut short as a boy's, which accounted for her changed appearance.

"Of course it was Fru Sundler," thought Anna. Karl Arthur had talked of her continually on the journey. It was she who had helped him purchase the house; she who had hired the workmen and supervised the work. In fact, everything relating to their marriage was her doing. They would not be sitting in the sleigh so blissfully happy but for Fru Sundler. It was only natural, therefore, that she should have come to the house to make up a fire in the rooms and to welcome the bride and groom—she who had been so active in their behalf.

Fru Sundler clasped them both in a warm embrace. She was so happy to see them, she said, quite moved.

Her fondest wish had been fulfilled. Karl Arthur's dream of a little gray cottage and a lowly wife had now come true.—How wonderful!

It was while the organist's wife was making her little speech that all thought of asking a blessing on the home passed out of mind. The young couple were wholly taken up by her.

When she finally let them out of her arms, she opened the door and ushered them into a narrow hallway, which ran the whole length of the house, dividing it into two sections. While they were taking off their wraps and hanging them up she averred that something had told her they would arrive that evening. So she had taken the coffee pot under her arm and come over to the little sparrows'-nest, as she was wont to call Karl Arthur's cottage. There was barely time to lay the supper table before the tinkle of sleigh bells sounded in the road. She could not begin to tell them how happy she was to be there to receive them, so that they did not have to come to a cold and empty house.

The great change that came over Karl Arthur the moment he saw the woman gave Anna food for thought. He was no longer the intrepid, light-hearted man he had been on the journey, but seemed overanxious to please Fru Sundler.

The young bride felt that her husband would rather not have seen Fru Sundler just as they were to take possession of their home. But perhaps his conscience smote him at the thought of her many kind services,

for he proceeded to tell his wife all over again how helpful Thea had been to him in every way. It was she who
had put up the hooks in the hall so that they would have
a place to hang their clothes. Fancy, her being so
thoughtful! He opened the door to the right and bade
her step in and behold!

If she had not known that this was her own kitchen,
where she was to live and rule, she would not have believed it. Karl Arthur seemed to show her in only to
elicit praise and admiration for Thea and her arrangements.

The kitchen took up one half of the cottage. It was
thrice as large as the byre room at Jobs Gård. The walls,
as in all new houses, smelt of lime and plaster. It was
perhaps this unpleasant odour that gave the room such
an air of discomfort. Besides, the place looked rather
bare. Indeed, it was not what she had expected. She
was thinking of the living room at Ris Gård with its
large wall-cupboard in blue and brown; its tall grandfather clock with the pretty hand-painted roses on the
case, and the four-poster bed with its bright home-woven
hangings. And of course she would have liked to find a
Joseph in a golden chariot on the wall, between the
cupboard and the bedstead, and a little Virgin Mary,
curtseying to a gold-laced angel, above the window.
But it was vain and foolish of her to expect such grandeur; she must be satisfied with things as they were.

At all events, they sufficed for her needs, and they
had been ordered by Fru Sundler. The table by the

window, the chairs before it, the water barrel down by the door, the wood-bins on the hearth—all had been selected by her. To hear the husband talk, one would have thought that Fru Sundler was the only person in the world who knew that a kitchen should have pots and pans, whisks and ladles, coffee boilers, tubs, knives, forks and spoons. Even if Fru Sundler herself had not partitioned off a corner for the small pantry or put up the shelf for kitchen utensils, it was thanks to her that they were there.

The first object that caught Anna's eye was a narrow sofa-bed, which stood far back in a corner of the room as if ashamed of being there at all. The wooden seat had been removed and placed against the wall, and the sofa made and turned down for the night. It looked quite neat and proper. But the bed was no wider than a coffin. If a person once squeezed himself into it, he would be pinned in so tight he'd lie there all night in fear and trembling lest he should never be able to get up in the morning.

She tried to listen to her husband's account of what Thea had done for them, but her mind was on the sofa. Thea, it seemed, had attended several auctions and bidden in the house furnishings at a very low figure. But he had told her all that on the journey. . . . Since the sofa was bedded, it was plain that one of them was to lie in it; and there were not many to choose from.

Fru Sundler had provided a light supper, consisting of eggs, bread, butter, cheese, coffee, and small-cakes.

Anna could not deny that the food tasted good; but Karl Arthur went on as if it was the first decent meal he had had since he last sat at Fru Sundler's hospitable board. The Bailiff's wife at Medstuby was famed for her excellent table. Karl Arthur, apparently, had forgotten everything, including his wife, to curry favour with Thea Sundler. It seemed as though he had wronged her in some way, and was trying to get back on her good books.

After he had partaken of everything Fru Sundler had provided and done cringing and praising enough, he got up from the table to go into the other room. As he passed right by the sofa-bed, Anna wondered whether he would go into raptures over that too, but he made no comment whatever.

They crossed the narrow hall into a room which, though not so large as the kitchen, was quite spacious. As the wife looked in she instinctively drew back. What she beheld was a room for grand folk only. The kitchen looked dreadfully bare, but here there was plenty of furniture: writing table, bookcase, divan-table, sofa, bureau, bed, and much besides. These, then, were the things he had inherited from his paternal aunt. The furniture was of some dark fine-grained wood, highly polished. The sofa and the chairs were upholstered in satin. Wherever she looked her eyes caught the gleam of mountings and beautiful inlays.

In this room the walls were papered and hung with tapestries, and there were long curtains at the windows.

Above the sofa hung a large mirror in a gilt frame; from the ceiling depended a crystal chandelier, and on the writing table there were silver candlesticks. The room would have been more in keeping with the Eken- stedt mansion at Karlstad.

The bed in here, like the kitchen sofa, had been turned down for the night. It was a single bed, and rather nar- row at that.

One thing was clear to the wife: her husband was to occupy this room. Here he would both work and rest, and she must keep to the kitchen, day and night. He was to live like a gentleman, and she would be merely his servant.

Karl Arthur continued his rhapsodizing. When he went away to be married the porcelain stove in the room was not quite finished and the furniture had not been moved in; but during his absence Thea had put every- thing in order. How charming, how attractive she had made the room! "Now would you ever think," he said to his wife, "that you were in a little backwoods cabin?" A more elegant room was not to be found in the whole churchtown.

He wished his wife would join in the praises of Fru Sundler; but she was pursuing her own train of thought. Thea and Karl Arthur were so busy examining the va- rious drawers and compartments of the writing table that they did not see her slip out of the room and go back to the kitchen.

She took a light from the kitchen table and went out

into the hall to find her fur coat and hood. She was quite calm and had no thought of doing away with herself. She was only going to some folk in the churchtown with whom she had lodged in the summer, while plying her trade at Korskyrka—to spend the night. For she had to do something to show him and his Thea that she would have a wife's place in the home and not that of a servitor.

While searching for her wraps she saw that there was still another door in the hall. It was locked, however, and the key had been removed. Taking the key out of the kitchen door she inserted it carefully into the lock of the other. It yielded.

She found herself peering into a small room, which was hardly more than a cubbyhole. On one side was a narrow window, but there was no fireplace. Still, it was not cold in there, as the back of the Dutch stove in the husband's room projected into the one corner. The walls were whitewashed and bare, except for a few hangers. The room was evidently intended for a clothes closet.

Far back, to her surprise and delight, stood a complete bed of state. It had a beautiful red canopy, billowing bolsters of down, sheets of fine damask with a wide border of lace—in a word, it was all that she could have wished for.

The young bride stood a while regarding this wonder of wonders, whereupon she took off her hood and coat, restored the purloined key to its proper place, and went back into the kitchen.

She had been there but a few moments when the others, aware at last that she had left them, came rushing out to her.

"Why did you run away?" queried Karl Arthur. "Are you tired after the long journey? Would you like to go to bed?"

"I came out here to try the bed I'm to lie in," Anna replied. "I was afraid, you see, that I'd not find room in it." She was a bit vexed; but at the same time she was laughing.

Karl Arthur laughed too. "Well, how did it work?"

"It was like putting a cow in a calf-pen—too small both lengthwise and crosswise. It might do, perhaps, if I lie on my side. But that would be bothersome too, for I'd have to throw off the quilt and step out on the floor every time I wanted to turn over."

She spoke without resentment, and the husband went on laughing. She saw that he was slightly embarrassed and was trying to cover his confusion with laughter.

"Oh, you can laugh, Husband! But you must consider that I've been sitting in a sleigh for three days and I'm both cramped and stiff in the joints."

Karl Arthur came over and looked at the sofa.

"You go sleep in the bed in my room," he said, "and I'll see if I can't squeeze into this box."

"Oh, fiddlededee! Sure, you didn't get married to lie on edge all night, with your feet outside the bed! I think I'll sleep on the floor. It wouldn't be the first time for me. All the same, I'm a little afraid to risk it. It'll be cold here along in the night, when the fire's gone out, and I'd hate to catch my death just as I've come to my own."

The husband seemed utterly helpless. He looked appealingly at Fru Sundler. His dear friend sat thrumming on the table, as if not caring to listen when husband and wife discussed their personal affairs.

"One should have pelts both under and over, if one is to sleep on the floor on a cold winter's night," said Anna; "and as we've but the one, I must ask you, Husband, to let me go down to some folks in the churchtown who lodged me last summer and beg them to house me for the night. You can ask Fru Sundler, who has ordered everything else so nicely for us, if this is not the best way out."

They both turned to Fru Sundler for advice, but she would not be drawn into this.

"Well, good-bye, then," said Anna, holding out her hand to the husband.

Karl Arthur went red in the face and the glance he shot Fru Sundler was none too friendly.

"This is preposterous!" he said. "Thea, can't you give me a helpful suggestion? Why, I could sleep on the sofa in my room—I have slept on it many a night during my visits at the Provost's—and let Anna have the bed. We must accommodate ourselves to the circumstances. The sofa which you have procured for Anna's use is really impossible. We'll take the bedding into my room."

Fru Sundler shifted uneasily in her chair when Karl Arthur addressed her thus sharply,. but not a word could he get out of her. Anna, however, spoke up at once.

"How you talk! Do you think you'll be allowed to lie on that costly satin? And there's only loose straw under the sheets of this sofa. It won't do to drag that into the grand room Fru Sundler has fixed up so prettily for you. I'd better go."

She put out her hand again in farewell. He brushed it away; at the same time he seemed to be so timid and uncertain of himself that she actually felt sorry for him.

"It's good of you to say that I may sleep in there with you. But it would never do, you know. At home in Medstuby and at the hostels it was all right for us to sleep in the same room. Down here in Korskyrka, where everyone knows that you're much finer than me, I'll have to sleep in the kitchen like any other servant girl."

"Why, Anna!" he exclaimed, once again waving away her proffered hand. That was as far as he went. Although she would have liked to see whether he really meant to let her go, she thought it best not to force his hand. Knowing that she held the winning card, she felt more inclined to laugh than to rage.

Now she went right up to Fru Sundler. "It seems very strange," she said, "that I should go and you should stay. In a little churchtown like this everyone knows what goes on; so perhaps you'd better give up this monkey game."

Fru Sundler was at last aroused.

"What do you mean, Fru Ekenstedt?" she said.

"I never thought I'd find out so soon that my uncle was right when he said the folks down here were great for fooling and playing jokes. You hear that my husband and I are near to quarrelling and parting bad friends, because there's no sleeping place here for me. Yet you know there's a spare bed in this house, with feather bolsters and pillows—the best one could have. Now I call that a good joke."

Karl Arthur, turning to Fru Sundler, demanded an explanation. She knew how to clear herself!

"I've been in such a quandary!" she said. "A bed came last evening—a wedding gift from the Deanery folk. I thought the Dean's wife might wish to present it herself; so it seemed only right to lock it away. But since Fru Ekenstedt has already seen the bed . . ." She fished out a key from her skirt pocket, and gave it to Anna.

Along in the night Anna awoke with the feeling that she had forgotten something important. She remembered now that she and her husband had neglected to ask a blessing on their home.

"Our Lord will have to forgive us," she said. "It was Fru Sundler's fault." Then she turned over and went to sleep again.

CHAPTER VI

MORNING

ANNA awoke at dawn in her best morning humour. Instead of rising at once, as was her habit, she lay musing awhile.

"Is the new parsonage Fru perhaps waiting for her nice maid to come in with coffee and freshly baked bread?" she murmured laughingly. Every little while she would raise herself in the bed and look toward the door.

"Strange there's no one astir in the kitchen, and it must be going on six o'clock! Well, I suppose I'll have to dress and go see what's the matter out there."

The husband was still asleep in his room, and Anna dressed very quietly so as not to disturb him. She stole out in her stockinged feet and went into the kitchen, where she put on her shoes. That done, she looked about with wide-eyed amazement.

"I've had to put up with a lot in my day, but this beats all!—Both the cook and the parlourmaid have overslept. You'd think they'd be on hand the first morning, at least. Regular lazybones, that's what they are! There's no wood here and no water. What's worse, they've let the fire go out. You may be sure it was Fru

Sundler who hired the servants, just as she has ordered everything else on the place; so what can you expect?"

In the middle of her song of woe she clapped a hand to her forehead. "Oh, but you're stupid, Anna! They're down at the byre, of course, milking the cows."

She went out into the hall, opened the front door, and stepped down on the wobbly stone to view the surroundings.

"H-m——" she said, measuring with her eye a small enclosure containing a woodshed, a cellar, and a well. "I wonder what the parson's Fru will say when she sees all these fine outbuildings? That must be the barnyard over yonder. The new parsonage folk won't find it easy to get cows enough to fill such a large byre."

She went down into the yard and stood there a moment, rubbing her eyes. "If I only knew where to look for the manservant's room!" she mumbled. "There's not a stick of kindling in the wood-box; but the man no doubt is in the stable, currying the horses. Oh, I say, it's well Anna Svärd came along on this honeymoon, or the new parsonage lady would be in a tight fix!"

Some seconds later she was standing in the woodshed wielding the axe with might and main. After a few happy strokes the blade stuck in a tough billet, and she had to twist and pull a good while to get it out. While tugging at this she heard footsteps approaching; and, suddenly, in the doorway, appeared a lanky boy.

"What's that youngster doing around here, I wonder? Now the whole churchtown will know that the parson's wife has to cut her own wood. How can one make a little fellow like him understand that it is not the Fru herself who's chopping, but only Anna Svärd?"

She had just worked the axe loose and was raising it for a fresh blow, when the boy stepped up to her.

"I'll chop for you," he said.

She gave him a quick glance, saw that he was thin and sallow, and shook her head.

"What, you?" she laughed. "Sure, you're not more than nine, are you?"

"I'm fourteen," said the boy, "and I have chopped wood all my life. I've just been chopping for us."— He pointed to the near-by cottage, where a thin spiral of smoke was rising from the chimney.

The offer was certainly tempting, but Anna Svärd did not forget to exercise her usual prudence.

"You'll want to be paid, I suppose."

"Y-e-s," said the boy with a grin that exposed every tooth in his head. "And I want to be well paid," he added. "But what I'm going to ask I'll not tell you beforehand."

"In that case, I'll have to do the chopping myself."

All went well for a time. Then, as luck would have it, the axe stuck again.

"It isn't money I'm after," the boy assured her.

Anna glanced at him again. He had a tight-lipped mouth and small, shrewd eyes. The boy looked old and canny for his age, but not at all malicious. Then, all at once it struck her that he was one of her husband's ten wards.

"In a sense, he's one of our own; so there'll be no trouble about the pay.

"You may chop, then," she said. "Come in when you're through, and I'll give you a sandwich."

"Thanks," said the boy, "but we've got food at home. We've almost more than we can eat."

"Then what in the world can I offer such a grand gentleman?"

The boy had already seized the axe. No longer able to keep up his air of mystery, he blurted out: "You brought the bag with you, of course? Do you think you can come over to our house and let me and my brothers and sisters see what you have in it?"

"Are you clean crazy, boy? Do you suppose that one who is married to a clergyman can go around with the peddler's pack?"

Just then she heard a light step behind her. A little girl had come into the shed. She too had a sallow complexion, and her face wore an anxious look. It was obvious that the two children were brother and sister. The girl went straight up to the boy and queried eagerly: "What does she say? May we peek in the bag?"

It was a well laid plan. The poor little youngsters at Crofter Matts's cabin, never having been honoured by a visit from a trades person, felt a burning desire to see the pretty things which Anna had displayed at other houses.

"She says she can't go around with the peddler's bag now," the boy explained, "because she's married to a preacher."

The little girl looked ready to cry. "I'll fetch water and milk for you," she said coaxingly. "And I'll make a fire in your stove."

Anna had to think quickly. The bag, to be sure, had come with the other luggage, but it contained only her personal things. She would have to find some way to pacify the children; it was most imperative, for the sake of good neighbourship.

"As I said before, the lady of the parsonage can't go about with the peddler's pack, but if you will cut plenty of firewood and carry it into the kitchen, and then go fetch me a brand from your own hearth, I'll see that a person named Anna Svärd comes over to you with the bag."

And, sure enough, that very morning, at about eleven o'clock, a beautiful Dalecarlian girl, bearing on her back a large black leather bag, stepped into Crofter Matts's cabin.

She stopped just inside the door, curtseyed, and asked if anyone was there who would like to see what she had to offer.

In a twinkling she was surrounded by ten children. The two oldest, recognizing her, jumped up and down for very joy as they tried to tell the others who she was. The elderly nurse, who sat on the bench under the window, spinning yarn, looked up when the Dalecarlian girl came in, and said: "In this house live only some children who are too poor to buy anything." Anna gave her an understanding look.

"It was the children themselves who bade me come," she said, "as they have no end of money to spend."

She stepped up to the table and, turning her back, rested her bag on it and undid the shoulder straps. Then she went over to the old serving woman and shook hands with her.

"You remember me—Anna Svärd—Jungfru? You bought a thimble and a comb of me last summer."

The old woman batted her eyes. She arose and made a deep curtsey that would have done credit to the Dean's wife herself.

The beautiful Dalecarlian girl, returning to her bag, proceeded to unfasten the buckles and clasps. The children meanwhile stood by in breathless expectation. Imagine their disappointment when she opened the bag!—it was filled with straw!

No one was more surprised or distressed than the poor Dalecarlian girl herself. She struck her hands together and groaned. She had not opened the bag since the previous evening, and during the night someone had stolen all her pretty silk shawls, her cotton prints, her ribbons, her buttons, and filled the bag with this horrid straw! She had thought, when strapping the bag to her shoulders that morning, that it felt remarkably light, but she had no suspicion of anything like this; for the people with whom she had lived were honest and good as gold.

The children stood there crest-fallen—cheated of their pleasure, and the beautiful Dalecarlian girl went on deploring that anyone could be so mean as to carry off all her pretty things, and fill her bag with this miserable straw.

She stirred about in the straw, thrust it to this side and that, to see if there was not something of hers still left in the bag. And down at the very bottom she found a little silk shawl, a woolen scarf, and a small box, containing a dozen scarf pins, with a head of coloured glass. She was so sorry there was nothing more. Since all the other things were gone, these, she said, were not worth keeping. But if the oldest girl would like the shawl, she could have it, and the boy could take the scarf. The scarf pins, the smaller children might divide among themselves, and if the Jungfru would accept the box in which the pins had lain she would be glad, as she had no use for it herself.

And now there was joy in the little cabin.

CHAPTER VII

THE VISION IN CHURCH

ANNA SVÄRD came into her kitchen, trolling out an old shepherd's song. She suddenly broke off. . . . On the narrow sofa bed sat Fru Sundler, waiting.

The woman had come while Anna was over at the children's cottage. To say that she was a welcome visitor would be a gross exaggeration. Irrespective of the little clash of the previous evening, the young wife had much to do that day. A cartload of things had come a while ago—her clothing, her wedding presents from friends and relatives at Medstuby, her loom and her spinning wheel—and she had to unpack and put everything in place.

Unfortunately, she could not call upon her husband to entertain the guest, as he had gone to the Deanery immediately after breakfast to take up again his sadly neglected work and would not be back before two o'clock.

The moment Anna set eyes on Fru Sundler she became the crude rustic in manner and speech. All the little refinements which she had acquired during her four months with the Bailiff's family were as if forgotten.

Perhaps she knew instinctively that fine manners were of no use on this occasion, and perhaps, too, it amused her to let the woman think her ignorant and stupid.

Fru Sundler approached her with eager solicitude. She said that while sitting at home that morning it had occurred to her that it would be hard on Fru Ekenstedt, who surely had many things to attend to the first day in her new home, if, in addition, she were obliged to prepare dinner for her husband. Now Karl Arthur might just as well dine that day at the organist's, and every day, for that matter, until they were quite settled and had time to get in some provisions from the farmers. She would be very happy indeed to help them out in this way. Wouldn't Fru Ekenstedt like to send Karl Arthur over to her to-day?

While Fru Sundler was delivering this effusion Anna began to unwrap a bolt of linen—a wedding present from Ris Karin. Coming upon a refractory knot, she loosened it with her teeth. It gave Fru Sundler the shivers; but she made no comment.

"It is only for the very first," she hastened to assure the wife.

Anna put down the bolt of linen and walked over to Fru Sundler. Standing before her with feet wide apart and arms akimbo, she said:

"Sure, I'll tell him you're expecting him, but I'll also tell him that if he can't eat the food his wife cooks for him she's not too grand to go out with the peddler's bag and fend for herself."

Fru Sundler put up her hands as if to ward off a blow.

"It won't do, I see, to talk straight out like this to a lady," said Anna.

"Oh, my dear Fru Ekenstedt, I'm sure that you prepare just such dishes as Karl Arthur likes! My suggestion was offered with the best intentions.—Now, we'll say no more about it."

Anna proceeded to measure the web, using her left arm as yardstick. She could not have shown the woman more plainly that she had no time for her.

"I had thought, dear Fru Ekenstedt, that we two should be great friends," Fru Sundler went on, now speaking in her mellowest accents. "But I'm afraid you think I consider myself your superior in a worldly sense. Such is not the case, however. I too come of poor and humble folk. My mother had to work and slave from morning to night. As for me—I should have been forced to go out as a common servant but for the kindness of Baron Löwensköld of Hedeby, to whom I owe the little schooling which enabled me to qualify as governess. Mother had been in service with his parents for fifteen years and had once rendered the young Baron a great service, which he wished to requite. Karl Arthur is the son of a sister of my benefactor. Mother always told me that I must stand by the Löwenskölds and try to serve them wherever I chanced to meet them; and Karl Arthur and wife are one to me."

"Twenty-seven, twenty-eight, twenty-nine, thirty

. . ." Anna counted, then paused to direct a remark to Fru Sundler.

"If it's true that you hold us as one you'd have asked me to dinner when you asked him."

Fru Sundler turned her eyes toward the ceiling as if there were someone up there who could bear witness to her goodness and piety.

"You are too severe, Fru Ekenstedt," she protested in a half-deprecatory, half-bantering tone. "You put the worst construction on everything. No offence was meant, I assure you, though it might so appear. This is Saturday, you know, and we have the usual Saturday fare: ale soup, salt herring, and boiled turnips. It doesn't matter so much about Karl Arthur, for he's in and out at our place as it pleases him; but I couldn't offer Fru Ekenstedt such plain fare on her first visit to my humble home."

The woman looked suspiciously grovelling. Anna thought her slippery as a snake. Try as one would to corner her, she managed to wriggle out.

"This is really too distressing!" sighed Fru Sundler. "There is something which I think that you should know. Until this matter becomes clear to you there can be no real understanding between us. At the same time it is with great reluctance that I speak. Oh, I wish Karl Arthur had told you of this unpleasant matter himself! But he has not done so, apparently."

Anna had measured the web once and was going over it again. Because of the interruptions, she was uncertain as to the exact number of yards. Lest she might lose the count again she made no retort to Fru Sundler's innuendoes.

"I presume you disapprove of my mixing in your affairs like this," the woman continued, undaunted; "but I think it my duty. Ah, Fru Ekenstedt, if you would only meet me with confidence! I do not even know whether Karl Arthur has spoken to you of his mother and the strong bond of affection which existed between him and her. At all events, you know that dear Tante Ekenstedt did not approve of the match. Shortly after the death of his paternal aunt strong words passed between Karl Arthur and his mother on your account. Perhaps he went at her a bit too hard. She was weak and—well, it ended in her having a stroke. Karl Arthur now reproaches himself as the one responsible for her sad plight. I believe that at one time he thought seriously of breaking with you simply to please his mother. But he soon learned that it would have been of no avail. Although dear Tante Ekenstedt has now recovered her physical health, her memory is gone. Any sacrifice that Karl Arthur might make for her now would be futile. What's done is done."

From the moment Fru Sundler said that the Baroness Ekenstedt had suffered a paralytic seizure she could not complain of a lack of attention. The bolt of linen had dropped to the floor, and was left lying where it had fallen. Anna now sat opposite the woman, staring her in the face.

"It is as I feared: Karl Arthur has not told you of the terrible thing he is brooding over. He has wished to spare you as long as possible, and perhaps I shouldn't speak of it either. You looked so happy a while ago; so it's best, perhaps, that you know nothing."

"Now that you've got me so well scared," said the wife, "I think you'd better lay out all the bad cards you have up your sleeve."

Fru Sundler winced every time Anna said *du* to her. True, it was common usage among the peasants of Dalecarlia; but now that Anna was the wife of a clergyman she should not permit herself such a liberty. "Karl Arthur ought to break her of the obnoxious habit of *du*-ing people," thought Fru Sundler.

"How shall I begin?—Ah! first I must tell you that Karl Arthur one Sunday in September saw his mother at church. She was seated in a pew under the gallery, and although it was not so light there as in other parts of the church, he saw her distinctly. She had on the familiar small bonnet that tied under the chin. She had loosened the ribbons and pushed them to either side in order to hear better. He had often seen her sitting just so in the church at Karlstad, with that upward, slightly oblique turn of the head and the happy, expectant look on her face with which she had always welcomed an opportunity to hear him lecture or preach.

"Naturally, he marvelled that she had been able to make the long journey so soon after her hard stroke, but he did not doubt for a moment that it was she. He was so overjoyed he could hardly go on with his sermon. 'Mother is well again,' he thought. 'She has come because she knows how unhappy I am.' And he said to himself: 'To-day I must preach better than ever.'

"That he failed is not surprising. He did not look at her again, lest it might disconcert him, but he could not forget that she was there. Consequently his sermon was short and disconnected. When he had finished, before stepping down from the pulpit, he cast a glance toward the place where he had seen her, . . . but now she was not there. She must have tired of listening to the long prayers, he thought, and was waiting for him outside.

"Fru Ekenstedt, you must pardon my going into such minute particulars, but I want you to know that Karl Arthur was sure he had seen his mother. He was so certain of it that, not seeing her on the church knoll, he went about asking this one and that one in which direction the Baroness had gone. No one had seen her, of course, yet he did not despair of finding her. He thought then that she had driven down to the Rectory. But when he did not find her there, either, he began to wonder if his eyes had deceived him. He was disappointed, of course, but it never occurred to him that there was anything peculiar about it."

"But the Baroness isn't dead, is she?" said Anna, who had been sitting all this while with her gaze fixed upon the speaker.

"I know what you think, and I'll come back to that

later. But first I must tell you that Karl Arthur is in great favour at the Deanery; which has not always been the case. Last summer, before that dreadful thing happened to his mother, he had preached such inspiring, such gripping sermons. He had brought about a great religious revival. The people here fairly worshipped him and were ready to give up all their earthly possessions for a home in Heaven. The old Dean and his wife, however, were not in sympathy with the movement. They are advanced in years, you know, and old people dislike innovations of any sort. But after that experience with the mother, Karl Arthur was afraid to rely on his powers of inspiration and turned to the Dean for advice and guidance. Although he continued to preach good sermons, the old fire and enthusiasm were gone. It was a source of grief to many, but the old Dean and his wife were pleased. Karl Arthur has become as a son to them. I have heard the Dean's wife say that they never could have got over the loss of Charlotte Löwensköld, who had lived with them for many years, but for Karl Arthur, who had so lovingly filled the void. I question whether this was good for Karl Arthur. For my part, I'm glad he has come away from the Deanery influences and has a wife now, and a home of his own. I do not say this to gain favour with you but that you may understand the hopes which Karl Arthur's true friends have placed upon you."

This was almost too much for the young wife. She

strove hard to follow the speaker through all these
verbal ramifications, but it was a terrible strain.

"Weren't you going to tell me what it was he saw in
church?" she queried.

"Yes, to be sure," said Fru Sundler. "I shall not
stress further his relations with the Deanery folk. It
is enough for you to know that they love Karl Arthur
and wish him well. He did not tell these good friends,
however, that he thought he had seen his mother at
church. He does not like to speak of her. Then, too,
he had a faint hope that she had stopped at our house
—to see me, you understand. So, immediately after
dinner, he came over to the house. Nor did he find her
with us.

"But I must say, Fru Ekenstedt, that my husband
and I were very glad to see Karl Arthur again. The
autumn, alas, is such a busy time with the clergy. What
with all the catechetical meetings and recordings, we
had seen nothing of Karl Arthur in weeks. I think he
enjoyed being with us, for he stayed the whole afternoon. We three passed the time in such innocent amusements as playing, singing, and reading from the poets.
There's no harm I suppose in my saying that they have
no understanding of such things at the Deanery and
that Karl Arthur felt repaid, in some measure, for his
disappointment regarding his mother. After supper we
talked of the intangible things of the other side of existence—you understand, of course, to what I refer.

It was then Karl Arthur told me that he had seen his mother that day in church. We discussed this phenomenon at length and wondered what it could have been. It was nearly midnight when he finally went home.

"Next day he had to set out again on his catechetical mission, and we did not see him for a week. If he had a free evening he probably felt that he must devote it to the old folks at the Deanery. Karl Arthur is the most considerate, the most thoughtful person in the world."

Anna Svärd was nonplussed, but she let the woman continue without interrupting her.

"As I said before, we did not see Karl Arthur again the whole week, and I gave no further thought to what he had told me about his mother. But on Sunday morning, as we met on the road to church, I said— merely in jest—that I hoped dear Tante Ekenstedt would not appear to him in church that Sunday and distract him from his sermon. And do you know, Fru Ekenstedt, I had the feeling that he resented my remark, for he answered rather curtly that he had come to the conclusion that it was some traveller—a lady who resembled his mother—who had been in the church a while the previous Sunday. Anything else, he said, was unthinkable.

"Before I could reply we met others who were on their way to church, and there was the usual exchange of commonplaces. Afterwards, during the service, I was afraid I had said something indiscreet and tried to quiet my fears by thinking that Karl Arthur couldn't attach any importance to my facetious remark. Imagine my horror when he stopped in the middle of the sermon and gazed in the direction of the gallery! And when, in a moment, he went on with the sermon he was strangely confused and unintelligible. He had started on a fascinating subject and suddenly lost the thread. I can't tell you how distressed I was!

"In the afternoon he came to me in utter despair. He averred it was what I had said that made him see his mother again. Now one can't be certain of such things, and I thought him very unfair. In that case, I said, I must be to blame also for her appearing to him the other time, and then I had not seen him in several weeks."

Anna sat tracing with her thumb nail the stripes in her apron, following the lines down and up, down and up. "But how could he believe that his mother appeared to him when she isn't dead?" she questioned.

"That was just what I said to him," Fru Sundler replied. "I assured him that his eyes had played him a trick this time as well as the last, and that dear Tante Ekenstedt, who from all accounts was alive and well, couldn't appear to him. Still, he maintained that it was none other than his mother he had seen. He had recognized her and she had nodded to him.

"He was distracted, you understand. He said, if these appearances were to continue he would have to give up the ministry at once, for the sight of his mother put him in such a state that he did not know what he was saying. He thought now that his mother's appearing to him was an act of vengeance; and he remembered what his former fiancée had once told him—that he would never be able to preach again until he had made his peace with his mother. Her prediction was now coming true."

It cannot be denied that the young wife paid close attention to everything that was said. Sensible person that she was, she mistrusted the woman, and feared that she might persuade her to believe something that was not so. But as Fru Sundler got deeper into her story, it had stupefying effect upon Anna—not to the point of drowsiness, however; but she became less sceptical, less wary. "It must be true," she said to herself. "The woman can't be making up all this."

"Ah, Fru Ekenstedt, what was I to think or say? I could but regard it as pure imagination. And I said to him: 'How could dear Tante Ekenstedt appear at the church in Korskyrka when she was miles away? And, above all things, how could he think that so loving a mother would wish to do him harm?' By reasoning with him in this way, I finally succeeded in quieting him somewhat. Fortunately, my husband had gone out for a walk, so that we had time before his return to thrash out this difficult and delicate question. Afterward, we had some beautiful music, which always does Karl Arthur good. You must remember that, Fru Ekenstedt. The following week he came to see me several times, and he always wanted me to assure him that the vision in the church was an optical illusion. I thought he was fully convinced of this when we parted on Sunday morning. But that day he saw his mother again.

"And then, Fru Ekenstedt, I was really concerned about him. People were saying that his preaching was much poorer than it had been during the summer. They thought his utterances not only constrained and guarded, but involved and meaningless as well. Oh, that was a trying time, Fru Ekenstedt! Think of such retrogression in a truly gifted man! The large congregations of the summer had dwindled to a scattered few. And he, himself—think how unhappy he must have felt! A man of his education and culture could not believe there was anything supernatural behind it all, nor could he doubt the evidence of his senses. He began to fear that he was losing his mind."

Fru Sundler showed genuine feeling, and there were tears in her eyes. Without doubt she had been deeply concerned. Anna, meanwhile, was being more and more ensnared. The multiplicity of words wound themselves about her like fine, imperceptible cords. She saw the matter now only from Fru Sundler's viewpoint. She could not raise a question or be rude, as at first—something held her bound.

"Then what do you think it was?" she asked meekly.

"To tell the truth, Fru Ekenstedt, I don't know. Perhaps it was the qualms of conscience that took this form of expression, or it may have been his mother's thoughts that created the illusion. But to him it is all so humiliating; so dreadful. He feels that he is no longer master of himself. He has prayed God to free him of these hallucinations, and yet they return. His mother appeared to him the fourth Sunday also."

The young wife was terror stricken. She seemed to see the Baroness emerging from a dark corner of the room.

"In the afternoon," Fru Sundler continued, "he came to tell me that he would write to the Bishop requesting his immediate release from the ministry. But I suggested that he write his sermons hereafter, which he has been doing of late. You can't imagine what a difference it makes when Karl Arthur reads his sermons! You would hardly know it was he that was speaking. Anyhow, it has been a help, for the 'apparition' has not troubled him since. That is why he feels more at ease. Still, one never knows. . . ."

"But don't you think that he'll get over the hallucination?" Anna interrupted.

"That is just what you must help him do, Fru Ekenstedt. Karl Arthur came to the house one day at Christmastide and told me about a legacy he had received from his aunt, the late Fru Sjöborg—she who died when you were in Karlstad last autumn. It was only a thousand riksdalers and some pieces of furniture. Now that he had something to live upon, he said, he was ready to leave the ministry. After hearing about the legacy, I urged him to carry out his original plan—to live the simple life of the common labourer. I urged him also to take advantage of this opportunity and become united in marriage to the bride whom God had chosen for him. You see, Fru Ekenstedt, I felt that he should take up some big, inspiring work; that he should become a shining example to the rest of us, and point the way to a good and holy life. If he could do something to bring the Kingdom of Heaven down to us while we are still on this earth, then perhaps our Lord would preserve him from these delusions, which threaten to destroy him utterly.

"He seemed doubtful at first, but I talked and talked, till at last he became as enthusiastic about the idea as I was. I'm almost certain that he went to see the old soldier that very evening and offered to buy his cottage. And ever since, he has been happy in the thought that he could now live as a true follower of Christ. He has said to me, time and again, that if you and he were only married and settled in his humble home, he would venture to preach once more in the old way. For then the 'visions' would trouble him no more, he thought.

"There is one thing, my dear Fru Ekenstedt, that I have got to speak to you about. It is a very delicate matter—but perhaps you already understand that Karl Arthur must not be dragged down into anything earthly. I know that he has looked forward with joy to having you here with him, in this little cottage. He looks upon you as the guardian spirit who will protect him from all evil. It was a source of regret to him that he could not write to you about these matters, but such things cannot be said in a letter which others must read to you. Therefore, it was only to me that he could speak of the blissful warmth that permeated his whole being when he thought of the young bride from the Far North who would be by his side, and help him to show mankind the right way to live."

Fru Sundler's voice had grown mystically compelling, and Anna sat motionless, as if under a spell.

"Aye, Fru Ekenstedt, when Karl Arthur went to Medstuby it was with the idea that you and he were to be united in a bond of holiness, that you were to live like brother and sister. He was afraid the hallucinations would return if any pleasures of a fleshly nature were to touch your lives. Is that clear to you, Fru Ekenstedt? Do you comprehend now that it is no ordinary man you have married, but one of God's elect? And do you now understand me and my doings? I did not know, of course, that Karl Arthur had altered his mind. I arranged these rooms according to his instructions."

The woman's accents were no longer mellow and ingratiating; her tone had become magisterial and accusative. Anna, remembering her wedding night, suffered veritable pangs of remorse.

"But I never knew about this that you've just been telling me. I was only told that he was poor."

"Which is quite true, my dear Fru Ekenstedt; but

this other was the underlying motive. Karl Arthur knew you so slightly and perhaps had no opportunity, at the Bailiff's house, to speak to you in private; so he pleaded poverty. That I can well understand. Now I think you see the matter in a different light. Ah, Fru Ekenstedt, it is most important that Karl Arthur be spared! The hallucinations must not return."

The young wife was now so completely ensnared that Fru Sundler could have carried her wherever she wished. She opened her mouth to take the vow the woman demanded.

"I promise——" She stopped short.

Fru Sundler had suddenly risen and stood looking out of the window. A flush of joy overspread her ugly features, which made her almost beautiful.

Anna arose, too. So it was Karl Arthur Fru Sundler had seen coming toward the house. Then, all at once, it dawned upon her that it was not our Lord who wanted her to make that vow, but only Fru Sundler.

CHAPTER VIII

THE SUNDAY BONNET

WHO was she to think herself wiser than a man of such eminent learning as Karl Arthur; she, who could not read and who had gone to Sexton Medberg's school a whole autumn without learning to write so simple a sentence as "The morning hours are golden"?

Aye, who was she that she would dare assert that all this mystery about Karl Arthur was hocus-pocus? No, it was not the qualms of conscience nor any form of punishment: it was simply nothing.

While Anna sat listening to Fru Sundler she was perplexed and troubled; but before the woman was out of the house she understood what was back of it all.

But dear, dear, she knew what a poor, ignorant creature she was! So of course she never breathed a word to her husband about her conjectures. When he had gone to his room to work on the sermon he was to preach next day, she took out of the cupboard a small covered basket, put into it a few of his used clerical collars, and went down to the organist's house.

Nor did she tell Fru Sundler of her suspicions. The organist's wife was the last person to whom she would impart her thoughts. Anna had as much respect for Thea's erudition as for Karl Arthur's. She merely asked whether Fru Sundler would help her a bit with the collars. Her husband had bidden her starch and iron a few for him, and she had made a sorry botch of it. After trying her best for several hours, one collar was crooked and another was full of wrinkles. What she needed was a little instruction.

Fru Sundler was glad that Fru Ekenstedt had turned to her in this little difficulty. Ironing clerical collars was a fine art, and she was not sure that she, herself, was sufficiently at home in it; but, anyhow, she would do her best. They went out to the kitchen and practised at laundering clerical collars until Anna had got the proper knack.

When they had finished Fru Sundler asked if she might offer her guest some coffee. Anna declined, saying that she must hurry home. Fru Sundler then proposed a glass of nice cold fruit juice. She had some excellent raspberry syrup, which had been commended by no less a person than the rich Fru Schagerström. It would be so refreshing, she said, after the tiring work. When the hostess had gone down to the cellar for the syrup her guest stole into the hall, took down from its peg Fru Sundler's fine Sunday bonnet, carried it out to the kitchen, and stuffed it into a large kettle that stood on a high shelf.

It did not occur to Fru Sundler, when seeing Anna out, to look and see whether her bonnet was still in its place. In a community where people were so honest that it was considered unnecessary to lock one's door when going out, no one ever thought that anything might be stolen, or even hidden away.

Anna went home, well pleased with her achievement. She knew that Fru Sundler would have a long search for her Sunday bonnet. Like a good wife, she had done what she could to help her husband so that he might preach in peace next day and not be frightened out of his wits.

When on Sunday morning Anna accompanied her husband to church it was with a sense of satisfaction and relief. She felt as little compunction in the matter of the bonnet as a hunter in trapping a wolf. She had not been reared in Korskyrka, where the people were literate and enlightened. She was Anna Svärd of Medstuby, and the things which were held as verities in the lowly gray cottages of her native heath, in these she was well grounded, and it was that wisdom she went by now.

Her husband led her into the church through the sacristy. There the Dean's wife took her in hand and let her sit with her in the Rectory pew, up in the chancel. Anna wished some of the home folks could see her now. Neither Ris Karin nor the Bailiff's wife could ever hope to sit in the high place which she now occupied.

She looked to see whether Fru Sundler was in the church. Happily, she was not. Having satisfied herself of this, she, like the Dean's wife and everyone else, bowed her head in prayer. She implored God to stand by her and not let the organist's wife think to look in the big kettle for her bonnet. Anna felt quite sure that, unless the woman found the hat, she would not come to church. It wasn't likely that the wife of a poor organist had more than one Sunday bonnet, and with that gone, she'd have to stay at home.

Afterward, as she watched the people come straggling in, she felt quite provoked because the church was not full. There were vacant places in every pew. But in a moment she was laughing at herself. "Why, Anna, you're behaving like a regular parsonage Fru!"

She thought of all the ministers' wives who before her day had sat in this very pew, waiting for their husbands to step into the pulpit. What had been their thoughts and feelings? Had they too gone all cold and shivery when their man had to stand up there and preach the Word of God? Aye, she knew how inferior she was to the others, yet she dared to breathe a prayer to the old ministers' wives: "Help me, you who know what it means to sit here in fear and trembling! Don't let her come to church to-day!"

During the Altar Service, as time for the sermon drew near, she grew more and more nervous. Every time the door was opened by some latecomer she gave a start. "Oh, dear!" she thought, "it's the organist's wife!"

But Fru Sundler had not appeared. The Altar Service was over, the hymn before the sermon was being sung, and Karl Arthur entered the pulpit.

It was Quinquagesima Sunday, and the Epistle for
the day was the beautiful chapter on Love that Fru
Ryen had read to Anna on the evening of her wedding
day. That, she thought, could be only a good token.
And when Karl Arthur, after a fine preamble, began to
expound the text, she was certain that our Lord and
the sainted wives of her husband's predecessors had
heard her prayer. Now she could hear, in peace and
comfort, the man she loved speak the praises of Love.

She did not know what would be regarded as good
preaching, but—and this she could swear to—anything
so beautiful she had never heard before. Nor was she
the only one who listened to him with joy. She saw how
the people all turned their heads and looked up at the
preacher; some moved closer to the neighbour on the
bench and nudged him, as much as to say: "Listen to
that! That's real preaching."

And so it was. Had man ever been heard to speak like
that! She who sat in the chancel could see the faces in
the pews brighten as by some inner radiance. The eyes
of two or three young girls shone like stars.

Suddenly there was a slight commotion in the church.
Fru Sundler had just come stealing in. Embarrassed at
being so late, she tiptoed down the aisle, pressing close
to the doors of the pews so as not to attract attention;
but, all the same, everyone turned and glared at her.

It was no fine bonnet she had on her head, but the
shabby old poke she wore on weekdays. She had tacked
a large ribbon bow in front to brighten it up a bit.

In a moment, however, Fru Sundler was forgotten. The people turned their faces toward the pulpit again and listened to the beautiful words that came pouring out from there.

"He's doing so well," thought Anna, "that now perhaps she'll have no power over him."

But Fru Sundler had not been in the church more than five minutes when Karl Arthur stopped in the middle of a sentence and, leaning far out of the pulpit, looked off toward a dark corner of the church. What he saw frightened him so that he went white as a sheet.

Anna, thinking he might fall into a swoon, half rose to rush to his aid and help him down from the pulpit. But he quickly recovered himself and went on with his sermon.

It was no longer a pleasure to hear him. The young preacher had got entirely away from his subject. He said a few words which had no bearing upon the preceding thought, stopped, and went on to something else, equally irrelevant. The congregation shifted impatiently in the pews. The majority looked either distressed or bored; which added to the discomfiture of the man in the pulpit. He took out his handkerchief and mopped his brow, then raised his hands above his head as if in a desperate prayer for help.

Anna had never seen anything so pitiful. Must she sit there and see her husband suffer? About to rise, she cast a sidelong glance at the Dean's wife. The old lady sat motionless, her folded hands resting in her lap, her countenance serene. No one could have told from her expression that all was not right in the church.

"That was how a minister's wife should conduct herself," thought Anna. "She should sit quietly, with her hands folded and her face serene, whatever happened." So Anna remained quietly in her seat until the recessional hymn had been sung and the Dean's wife arose to go. Meanwhile she had had time to compose herself and consider that she was only a poor ignorant peasant.

At home in Medstuby every man and woman believed there were many wicked trolls in the world who could distort people's vision and make them see things that were not real. But here in Korskyrka perhaps they had never heard of such things.

Now in her parish they could tell you of Finn-Lotta, a wicked old witch who had been condemned to be burned. She was borne, blindfolded, to the place of execution, but she begged the executioner to let her look once more at the earth and the sky before he bound her to the stake. When he removed the bandage from her eyes they all saw the Court House in flames, and rushed off to put out the fire and save the records—leaving Finn-Lotta unguarded. The old witch freed her shackled hands and feet and disappeared. And of course the Court House was not on fire, the witch had simply distorted the vision of the populace.

And indeed they knew much more than that, back in her province. They could tell you how Jobs Eric once stood at the market fair, his stand full of wares, and couldn't sell a thing because a sorcerer in the next stall —one of those fellows who swallow flint and spit fire— had distorted the vision of folk who came to the fair. That sorcerer had somehow contrived to make Jobs Eric's bright steel knives, sharp-toothed saws, and keen-edged scythes look like rusty old junk. Not so much as a threepenny nail could he sell until he discovered the trick the sorcerer had played him and drove him off the fair grounds.

Every man and woman in her parish would have understood at once that it was Fru Sundler who distorted Karl Arthur's vision and made him see his mother in church when she wasn't there at all. Had anyone from Medstuby been at the service and seen what occurred, he'd have been as sure of it as she was.

But Korskyrka was not Medstuby, and Anna had to consider who her husband was, who Fru Sundler was, and who she, herself, was, and keep her thoughts and beliefs to herself.

On the way home the husband never said a word; he walked by her side as though unaware of her existence. She knew that many eyes were following her, and tried to carry herself as a clergyman's Fru should. When they reached home he went straight to his room and shut himself in. Usually, he liked to help her lay the table or prepare a meal and thought it great fun; but that day he did not give her a hand.

At dinner he sat opposite her and did not look at her

or speak. It made her feel as though she had committed some heinous sin, for which she was being punished. Karl Arthur thought he had preached badly because he had not followed Fru Sundler's instructions. Anna, at the suggestion of the Bailiff's wife, had roasted a few hazel hens and other game birds which abounded in the woods round Medstuby, so that she would have something ready to put on the table for the first few days. But maybe hazel hens were not considered a great delicacy down here? Her husband had eaten only a tiny morsel, when he put down his knife and fork.

Not once during the meal did she dare open her mouth to speak. The moment they rose from the table Karl Arthur mumbled something about a headache and said he must go for a walk—leaving her alone with her sad thoughts.

2

Strange, that it should be such a difficult thing to get what one wants above everything. If one wished for something that was not right and proper, it would be another matter; but when all one asks is that the man for whose company one longs would drop in of an afternoon for a little chat, or to listen to a bit of music, surely such a wish ought to be granted. If one wanted him all to one's self, that, too, would be a different matter. But the organist was quite welcome to be present, for she and Karl Arthur had nothing to conceal.

If she had sent his old fiancée away in some heartless

manner; if, for instance, the girl had been forced to earn her own living as a humble governess or housekeeper, then she might have expected to suffer punitory neglect. But when she had brought her the best "catch" in the country—wealth, social position, and a good husband— why should she be deprived of the little happiness she desired for herself? Why had the Dean's wife turned against her for no reason whatever? Karl Arthur had pleaded catechetical meetings and all sorts of excuses, but the Dean's wife, of course, had whispered into his ear that people had begun to wonder at the close friendship between Karl Arthur and herself. It was on account of the gossip that he did not come near her for weeks on end last autumn.

If she were in any way responsible for his delusion about his mother appearing to him in church; if she had frightened him afterward in order to bring about a renewal of the old friendly relations, there would have been some reason for all this unpleasantness. But since she had only tried to comfort him and talk him out of his fears, why should her husband become jealous all at once and kick up a row, making it almost impossible for her to receive Karl Arthur in her home? Never had Karl Arthur needed a friend and confidante so much as he did then, and all she asked was to be allowed to help him.

And what if she did advise him to marry in order to allay her husband's jealous suspicions—was that anything reprehensible? To be sure, she had not told Karl

Arthur the real reason for her wishing him to marry; he was too unworldly minded to understand such things. Anyhow, where was the harm in her helping him to realize the fondest dream of his life? That lowly peasant girl from the Northern wilds should have been satisfied just to live in his house and be fed and clothed by him.

Who would have thought he could be charmed with a person of no education or breeding; that he would return from the wedding trip so enamoured of his wife as to have no eyes for anyone but her?

It had been a pleasure to help him put his little home in order; to consult with him about the repairs and the furnishings. Should one be punished for that and be made to feel superfluous the moment his wife stepped into the house? Who was it that made a clergyman's Fru of that common creature? Who was it that gave her the noblest, the most gifted and most spiritual of men? But did the girl show any gratitude? When one entered the little house one had made ready for them, one felt that they only wished one would go.

She could not help taking a slightly malignant delight in the recurrence of the "vision." What could he expect after disregarding her advice? Goodness knows, she had not wished it to happen! Just the same, she couldn't feel sorry for him.

And it was most provoking that her Sunday bonnet had been carried off. It wasn't likely that anyone had stolen it. Some practical joker must have spirited it away to keep her from going to church. But who could have done it? Had her husband perhaps taken it into his head to hide the hat?

She knew that Karl Arthur would come to unburden his troubles, and thought he would be along soon after dinner. However, he did not appear until late in the afternoon. By that time she had already persuaded herself that he had turned to his wife for advice and consolation even in this matter, which hitherto had been something strictly between themselves. Meanwhile, she had recalled to memory all her disappointments and unsatisfied longings, and was in no temper to receive him when he finally appeared. She showed him into the living room and then seated herself on the corner sofa to listen to his plaint. She had to clench her teeth to keep from shrieking that she was weary, weary, weary, that she could not be amiable and submissive always, that there were limits to her patience, and that she was not a person who could be taken up and cast aside at will.

He had been for a long walk, he said, in the hope of arriving at a calm decision; but he was still wandering in a daze. Then came all the old talk about his being unable to stand the persecution and would have to resign from the ministry, since that was what his mother demanded of him.

Another time she would have done her utmost to comfort and reassure him, but that day she was hardly in a mood to bear with the man. Her fingers twitched nervously. She could have dug her nails into his skin and clawed his face. She was not sure whether it was him or herself she wanted to claw, but it would have been a great relief to do something of the sort.

He talked on and on. At last he noted that she did not respond; did not accord him the usual sympathy. He was surprised, and asked her if she were ill.

She was quite well, she answered curtly. But why should he come to her with his troubles now that he had a wife?

That was the most stupid remark she could have made. Perhaps she hoped he would say that his wife was too ignorant and inexperienced, that he needed to talk to a woman of education and culture, who could follow his thoughts. Instead, he merely arched his brows and said he regretted that his visit had been ill timed, then rose to go.

She heard the front door open, but could not believe that he was really going. He'll surely come back, she thought. But when he shut the door behind him she sprang up with a cry. She called to him. . . . Oh, what had she done? Had he gone forever? No, no, impossible! He was here, and she had turned him away. She wouldn't listen to his plaint. She had told him to go to his wife for help and consolation. And to-day of all days, when so much was at stake and she might have won him for good and all!

3

Karl Arthur walked home in the dusk of the evening, after his call on Fru Sundler. He wished he never had married, never had bought the old shack, never had let himself be drawn into this miserable adventure.

"It's dreadful," he muttered, "that I can't be alone when I'm feeling so wretched! But I have a wife who's had a dull afternoon, and I must try to cheer her up a bit. She'll be cross, no doubt, and say hard things; and, indeed, she has a right to. But how can I stand her wailing?"

He stepped up on the rickety door stone, reluctantly put out a hand to open the door, and quickly drew it back. From within came strains of a hymn sung by children's voices.

Immediately he felt a sense of relief. The awful pressure round the heart which, since the morning service, had made him feel but half alive, now lightened considerably. Something told him that he could enter his house with an easy mind, for within awaited him what he had not dared even to hope.

He quietly opened the door to the kitchen and looked in. The room was mostly in darkness, but a few firebrands still glowed on the hearth. Before the dying embers sat his wife with all the children from Crofter Matts's cabin gathered about her.

Despite the feeble illumination, or perhaps thanks to it, the little group made a charming picture. The youngest child lay sleeping in his wife's arms, the other children, standing close to her, their gaze fixed on her beautiful face, sang: "So from our time another day is passing."

Karl Arthur closed the door softly and stopped within the shadow of the wall. Into his heart, torn by anguish and remorse, stole anew the healing thought that here was the woman sent of God for his salvation. She was not, perhaps, as he had at first pictured her; but, then, what did he know? Ah, see! Instead of fretting over his absence, she had gone and fetched the children he had once befriended, and passed the time teaching them hymns. "Why not turn to her, in all sincerity, and ask her to help me?"

As soon as they had finished the Evening Hymn she sent the children home. She may not have marked that the husband had come; but, in any case, she left him in peace. Humming the song which she had just sung with the children, she went to the cupboard and brought out milk and unfermented beer; she freshened the fire, set the pot of milk on the coals to warm for the beer posset, then laid the table and placed two chairs before it.

It was a pleasure to watch her as she moved about the dusky room. The bright colours of her peasant dress, which in daylight were rather garish, had now toned down to a soft, warm colour effect. The stout homespun cloth looked like heavy brocade. All at once Karl Arthur saw that there was a reason for the various parochial peasant costumes. It was the peasant woman's way of copying the silk and satin dresses worn by queens and ladies of the nobility in olden times. The figured front breadth, the puffed sleeves, the hood, which concealed most of the hair—these, or something very like them, had been worn once upon a time by the finest ladies in the land.

It seemed as if his wife, in some magical way, had become invested with the authority and dignity associated with burghers' wives of old. What others regarded as her crudities were simply old-fashioned habits and customs from the time when queens lighted the fires on their hearths and princesses washed their own linen on the banks of the river.

The wife poured the beer posset into two cups. Then she lit a tallow candle and placed it at the centre of the table, after which she sat down and folded her hands for the grace before meat. As the soft candlelight fell upon her face, her features in some way became ennobled. A mature woman's wisdom and poise had superseded the youthful assertiveness and self-assurance.

"As she is now," thought the husband, "one might safely initiate her into the deepest and most profound mysteries. It was childish of me to think that she would not understand. Her innate nobility of character will guide her aright."

Before his wife had finished the grace Karl Arthur was seated at the table, his hands folded like hers in prayer. They ate their frugal meal in silence. He liked her habit of not speaking during meals, as if the consumption of food were a holy act ordained of God for the maintenance of life.

When they were through supper Karl Arthur drew

his chair around to her side and put his arms about her.

"You must forgive me," he said, "for being so cross and impatient at dinner. But you know how unhappy I felt."

"Don't you be sad about that, Husband! You never need think of how you are with me. I like you, man, no matter what you do."

On this occasion, which to Anna was a sacred one, she dropped her Dalecarlian accent and spoke pure Swedish. That no doubt made her sentiments especially gratifying to Karl Arthur. He thanked her with a kiss.

But that kiss proved rather disconcerting. He would have liked to continue the kissing and forget everything else.

"I love her to distraction," he said to himself. "She's mine and I'm hers. The 'vision' will probably appear to me every time I stand in a pulpit. I'll never be a good preacher, but that needn't prevent me from being happy with my wife in my own home."

"Now, Husband, let me tell you something," said Anna. "You're not going to be frightened in church any more, I'll answer for that!"

Karl Arthur smiled at her confident assurance, although he knew very well that his illiterate wife could not help him in that matter. But the sympathy which her words conveyed was comforting and reassuring.

"I know that you love me and would bear all my burdens," he said, and kissed her again.

It was a happy moment. Love filled the young man's

heart with joy and courage. He saw into a future where he and his wife, ever united in bonds of love, would make their little home a paradise on earth.

"Wife," he whispered, "we'll help one another; we are going to be very happy. . . ."

The outer door opened with a jerk, and noisy stamping was heard in the hall. Anna jumped up at once and began to clear the table. Karl Arthur, still seated, muttered: "Strange that people would break in upon us at this late hour!"

But when he saw that the intruders were Organist Sundler and wife, he arose to greet them.

The organist was a large elderly man with a shock of white hair that stood straight up above a face that was always red and bloated. But that evening his face looked redder and more bloated than ever. He marched himself into the room with his wife on his arm, leaving the door wide open, bitterly cold though the night was.

It was quite obvious that his blood was up. Anna thought him a doughty fellow, while his wife, who clung to his arm, reminded her of an old dish rag. "The woman has a good husband, but she has wallowed in too much dirt ever to be clean again."

Suddenly she noticed that Fru Sundler had on her Sunday bonnet. "Ah, now I'll catch it!"

As she went to shut the door she wondered if it wouldn't be wisest to run away from it all. But she stayed to face the music.

The organist offered no compliments or apologies,

but went straight to the attack. When his wife was about to go to church that morning she had discovered that her bonnet was missing and thought it had been stolen. But this evening, after he and she had been searching for hours, they found it stowed away in a copper kettle on the top shelf of the kitchen. His wife had accused him of hiding the bonnet, of which offense he was quite innocent—unless he had done it in his sleep. He had heard, however, that Karl Arthur's wife had been at the house the previous day, and he had come to put a straight question and to get a straight answer.

Anna came forward at once and told him that his supposition was correct. When his wife had gone down to the cellar for the syrup she, Anna, had stolen out into the hall, taken the hat, and hidden it in the kettle.

While making her confession she felt herself going down, down. She went down in the organist's estimation and in Karl Arthur's as well. But Fru Sundler, narrowing her eyes, regarded her with patent interest.

The organist was astounded. "But, for goodness' sake, Fru Ekenstedt, why did you do such a thing?"

"Yes—why,. why?" Karl Arthur roared at her. "What were you thinking of? What did you mean?"

Anna realized afterward that it would have been better for her had she made some excuse, and not told the truth. But at the moment she was glad of an opportunity to explain the whole affair. She forgot that she was not in Medstuby, talking to Mother Svärd and Jobs Eric. Ah! she was going to crush that designing woman. "I didn't want *her*"—she pointed at Fru Sundler—"to come to church to-day."

"But why not?" the organist wanted to know.

"Because she distorts my husband's vision so that he sees something in church that isn't there."

The three stared at her as if she had been dead and had risen from her grave.

"What did she say?"—"How could she think it?"—"How could she imagine it?"

Anna went close up to Fru Sundler. "Would you deny that you distort my husband's vision?" she said. "Ask the Dean's wife, ask anyone who was in church this morning if they have ever heard a better sermon than he preached to-day. But as soon as you came in it was all up with him."

"But, my dear Fru Ekenstedt, how could I do such a thing? And even if I could, would I wish to harm Karl Arthur—my husband's and my best friend?"

"One never knows what the likes of you may be up to," said Anna.

Karl Arthur seized his wife by the arm and pulled her away, lest she should fall upon Thea and beat her.

"Hush!" he shouted. "Not another word from you!"

The organist, now facing her with clenched fists, roared: "Mind what you say, peasant woman!"

Fru Sundler was the only one who maintained her

composure. She began to laugh. "For pity's sake, don't take it so seriously! Fru Ekenstedt seems to be a bit superstitious; but what can you expect?"

"Why, Thea," said Herr Sundler, "don't you understand that she fancies you're a witch of sorts?"

"Naturally. I told her yesterday that Karl Arthur at times imagines he sees his mother in church, and this is simply her way of accounting for it. She tried to protect her husband to the best of her understanding. Every woman in Medstuby would have done as she did."

"Thea, you're great!" Karl Arthur ejaculated.

Fru Sundler modestly disclaimed any title to greatness; but she was glad the little muddle had been so quickly and easily cleared. Now that this was done, there was no reason why she and her husband should not go at once and leave the young couple to themselves.

She bade Karl Arthur and Anna a pleasant goodnight. Her husband, still furious, grumbled because he had not been allowed to give full vent to his wrath.

Karl Arthur saw them to the door. Then, going over to his wife, he folded his arms and stood regarding her with silent contempt and disgust.

"He looks as if someone had promised him cream and given him whey," thought Anna. Unable to stand his silence any longer, she said meekly:

"Will you never care for me again?"

"Can you restore my faith in you as the woman whom

God Himself had chosen for me?" he queried in a broken voice.

He gave her a long, aggrieved look, then turned and walked out of the kitchen. She heard him cross the hall and go into his room; heard him lock and bolt his door.

CHAPTER IX

THE VISIT

THE old couple at the Deanery knew that the days of their happy companionship were numbered. And so, to make good use of the precious time, they were together more now than they had ever been. The old lady would come into her husband's study in the middle of the forenoon, drop down on the sofa, and sit there quietly for hours at a time, knitting or spinning, while the old man, sucking at his long-stemmed pipe, worked on, undisturbed, at his herbarium.

It was thus Karl Arthur found them the day he brought his wife to the Deanery to pay the initial call. The Dean's wife sat working at a ribbon loom and above the huge piles of cap papers on the Dean's table rose light clouds of tobacco smoke, which gave an added touch of homeliness to the room.

Karl Arthur made a graceful little speech in which he thanked the old couple for all the kindness which he had met with in their home, and thanked them, in particular, for the grand wedding present. The Dean responded with a few hearty words, and the Dean's wife, quickly pushing the loom into a corner, bade the young bride come and sit with her, on the sofa.

The Fru Dean, who was given to paying compliments herself, wiped a tear from the corner of her eye as she listened to Karl Arthur's pretty speech. But if anyone thought she approved of his marriage he was greatly mistaken. An old lady of her experience and knowledge of life, could but think it deplorable that an impecunious curate should marry. And the fact that he had espoused a poor, illiterate peasant girl made matters all the worse. Fru Forsius, indeed, had tried her best to dissuade him from this madness; but as Fru Sundler had wanted Karl Arthur married, all arguments against it were futile.

The old lady regarded the former peddler girl with a certain curiosity. The poor thing looked quite lost, she thought. To the few queries addressed to her she gave halting and timorous answers. That was to be expected, of course. But the surprising thing was Karl Arthur's attitude toward his wife. He was more like a crusty old schoolmaster with a particularly dull pupil than a newly wedded man with his bride.

Karl Arthur corrected his wife every time she opened her mouth. "My good tante must pardon Anna," he said repeatedly, "for she does not know any better. Medstuby is a nice town, to be sure, but, compared with Korskyrka, it is a hundred years behind the times."

The young wife made no retort. The big, strong-looking woman was so conscious of her inferiority to the husband, it was truly pitiful!

"Aye, aye," mused the old lady, "it is just as I expected. It will be all right as long as she holds her tongue; but there'll come a time when she will rebel."

Karl Arthur talked at great length of his visit to Medstuby, of the wedding and the new kinsfolk. His descriptions were all very humorous, and some things he said must have wounded his wife. Once she ventured to take exceptions.

"How you talk!—Now you don't believe, do you, Priest-mother——"

"Anna!" Karl Arthur cut in sharply. Then, turning to the Dean's wife, he said:

"My good tante will have to pardon Anna. I have told her repeatedly that she must not say '*du*' or 'Priest-mother,' that we cannot conform to the manners and customs of Medstuby down here."

As Karl Arthur went on with his recital, the Dean's wife wondered what would come of this. She had hoped that he would get a wife who could help him out of his difficulties.

The old lady was thinking in particular of his relations with Fru Sundler. She felt very certain that there was nothing improper between them, but evil reports were being circulated about her husband's assistant. She had tried to convince the gossips in the churchtown that Fru Sundler was too wise a woman to throw herself away, and that all she asked was to be allowed to sing to Karl Arthur and walk with him up Raven Ridge at sundown, to look for gold-lined clouds. But what good had it done! Because she was Regina Forsius, and mistress of Korskyrka Deanery for half a century, they listened respectfully to whatever she said; but the moment she finished, their tongues were wagging again. "Oh, we understand, my dear, why Thea arranged this marriage. It was to pacify the organist. Do you know, my dear, that the wife is to sleep in the kitchen like a hired girl? And, my dear, have you seen the sofa-bed? It's as narrow as a coffin. Now, my dear, what kind of a marriage do you call that?"

She had heard so much talk about the sofa-bed that she decided to dress up an old bed of state that had been standing in the guest chamber for years and send it over to Karl Arthur's new home. By that means she had put a stop to some of the gossip. But if Karl Arthur had loved his wife and shown that he loved her, that would have been the most effective medicine for the bad tongues.

"I wonder what the Dean thinks of it all? When Karl Arthur was here on Saturday he spoke of his wife in the most glowing terms. Oh, I hope Thea Sundler has not been making trouble!"

Her heart went out to the poor Dalecarlian girl, and she wondered how she might help her. The girl, however, had now overcome her timidity—at least to the extent that she dared raise her eyes and look round the room. The bookcases and the Dean's herbarium, apparently, did not interest her, but the instant she saw the ribbon loom a smile of delight overspread her countenance.

"Oh, look!" she cried, "a ribbon loom!" She was so
pleased she could have hugged it.

The attraction which this simple object had for her
was irresistible. She left her comfortable seat on the sofa
and went over to the corner where the loom stood. She
looked at it wishfully, and felt of the web.

"I've woven many a roll of ribbon belting in my day,
I can tell you," she said to the husband, as an excuse
for her conduct.

The loom had given Anna a feeling of self-confidence.
The Dean's wife, thinking that a pleasant occupation
would make the girl feel more at home, asked her if she
wouldn't like to do a few rows on the narrow web.

"My good tante is too indulgent," Karl Arthur protested. "My wife would only spoil the work. Therefore,
I cannot allow her to accept your kind offer."

"Nonsense, Karl Arthur! Certainly she may weave if
she wants to."

The young minister's bride immediately sat down to
the ribbon loom and fell to weaving in a way that surprised the old lady. She and the two husbands gathered
round the weaver, whose deft fingers moved swiftly as a
conjurer's; it was impossible for the eye to follow their
movements.

"Gina, my love," said the Dean to his wife, "you
thought yourself an adept in the art of ribbon weaving;
but here you see how far you must advance before you
can be ranked as an expert."

There was a happy smile on the lips of the young

bride. She suddenly felt herself transported to her old home. Round about her were familiar objects. She saw her mother pottering round the hearth and glimpsed through the window long ranges of gray buildings. She heard words spoken in the inflected accents of the Dalecarlian dialect.

After a few minutes of this rapid weaving there was no yarn left on the spool. The happy weaver looked up with a sigh. Her eyes sought the eyes of her husband. Was he displeased? Had she acted foolishly now, again?

Karl Arthur stood aloof. The Dean's wife, bending forward, felt of the web and nodded approvingly. Turning to the husband, she made a deep reverence. "I must say that I am struck with admiration. Ah, to be able to use one's hands like that! Permit me to offer you my heartiest congratulations. I am sure, Karl Arthur, that you have found the very wife for you."

The young clergyman made a wry face. "My dear tante——" he began but the old lady cut him short.

"I know what I'm saying, Karl Arthur. Now don't let anyone persuade you that you could have made a better choice."

Shortly afterward, when the callers had gone, the old lady arose and went over to the writing table, to hear what the Dean's impressions of this visit had been.

The old gentleman had moved the piles of cap papers to one side, and, with goose quill in hand, was rapidly covering a large sheet of paper with ornate script. His

wife, leaning over his shoulder, saw that he was inditing
a letter to his Lordship, the Bishop of Karlstad.

"Why, Petrus Forsius!" she exclaimed, "whatever
are you doing?"

The Dean paused in his writing, plunged the pen into
a small jar of birdshot, and turned to his wife.

"Gina, my love, I'm writing to the Bishop, requesting him to transfer Karl Arthur to some other parish
and to send me a new curate. I promised Charlotte that
I would try to put up with young Ekenstedt, and I have
stood by him as long as possible; but now he must go.
Consider, my dear, the whole parish maintains that he
is so enamoured of the organist's wife that he loses his
head whenever she appears in church."

The Dean's wife was shocked. "But, Petrus, Karl
Arthur is a married man. He has established his home in
the parish and thinks he is to remain here—at least
as long as you are alive. Have you no consideration for
his wife?"

"Dear heart, I have the greatest respect for that
excellent young woman, who has left her native heath
to follow her husband hither. It is for her sake that I am
writing to the Bishop to-day. If Karl Arthur were permitted to remain in the churchtown much longer you
may be sure that he would repudiate his wife as he has
repudiated Charlotte and his own mother."

PART TWO

CHAPTER I

PARADISE

KARL ARTHUR EKENSTEDT had been sent from parish to parish. He had been gone some eighteen months when, one bleak autumn day, he came driving back to Korskyrka. The old Dean of Korskyrka had recently passed away, and the Dean's widow, who had a soft spot in her heart for Karl Arthur, had appealed to the Bishop and the Consistory to let him officiate until a new rector had been appointed to the charge. They had granted the request, though with some reluctance, for Colonel Ekenstedt's son was *non persona grata* with his superiors.

The young curate's thoughts turned back to the time when he, as a newly married man, had been sent away from wife and home. True, he had not been sorry to go. The contempt and aversion engendered in him by the discovery that his wife's mind was filled with crude superstition would have embittered their life had they remained together. But now, after the long separation, he had only love and admiration for her.

"At last the time has come," he thought, "when we can create the little paradise of my dreams."

He had gleaned some useful knowledge from his experiences at various parsonages, and felt more confident than ever that his original plan was the right one and should be carried out. It was man's foolish attachment to the things of this world that was the cause of most of his ills. To live simply, freed from the bondage of desire, raised above all petty ambitions to outshine one's fellows—that was the way to attain true happiness in this life and bliss in the life to come.

But admonitions and exhortations were not enough to bring these simple truths home to the people. An example was needed—a living example which would be far more effective than eloquent words.

At this stage of his reverie Karl Arthur closed his eyes. A vision of his wife rose before his mind and he felt a thrill of rapture.

Before leaving home he had advised his wife to go back to Medstuby, as he could not take her with him. He had to live at the Rectory in the place to which he was being sent, he had said. But he would send her his small stipend, which amounted to one hundred and fifty riksdalers a year, on which he thought she could live better among her own people than here in Korskyrka. Besides, he had felt that it would not do for her to stay in their little house alone and unprotected.

But the wife would not go. "Sure it's no worse for me than for any other woman whose man is away at work," she had said. "And you must have a hearth and a bed to come to when you're free."

He thought it sweet of her to stop at home, to wait for him—despite the loneliness and poverty. Still, it was only what many another would have done in like circumstances. But she had done more than that.

Shortly after his departure the old serving woman who kept house for Crofter Matts's children gave notice. The benevolent ladies who provided for the orphans, having sought in vain to replace her, saw no other course than to put the children out to nurse. This time, of course, there was no talk of a pauper auction; the children were to be placed in well known and decent homes. But when the poor youngsters learned that they would no longer be together they set up a terrible wail, and when the appointed foster parents came for their wards they found a deserted house.

The new guardians, not knowing where to look for the lawless youngsters, stepped into the neighbouring cottage to make inquiries. It was there all ten children had taken refuge. They had gathered round Karl Arthur's wife, the humble Dalecarlian woman. She informed the strangers that her husband had bidden in these children at auction and that therefore they belonged to him. As they were now in their proper home, no one could take them away without her husband's consent.

Karl Arthur liked to picture this scene, of which he had read graphic descriptions in letters from the Dean's wife and Fru Sundler. There had been a rather animated exchange of words. Several ladies of the benevolent

society had been called in, and they had given his wife
to understand that the children would receive no further
aid from them unless they were turned over to the appointed guardians. But Anna Svärd of Medstuby had
simply laughed at their threats. Where was the need for
aid? The children could earn their own living, as she,
herself, had done all her life. These children, whom her
man had taken over, were not going to be sent out
among strangers—not while she was alive!

The husband could almost hear the ringing tones of
her voice and see her sweeping gestures. His wife stood
out to his imagination as a heroine, a protector of
helpless little children, and he was proud of her.

She had carried her cause to victory. The children
were allowed to remain with her. But she had assumed
a heavy responsibility. To be sure, the threat of the
ladies bountiful had not been seriously meant; but Karl
Arthur's wife would not allow his wards to accept
charity. It was a point of honour with her that she and
they should support themselves by the work of their
hands.

He longed to get home to thank her; to surround her
with loving attentions, and so make amends for the
presumptuous contempt which he had once shown
her.

Karl Arthur was suddenly awakened from his reverie.
His driver had swerved abruptly to make way for a large
carriage drawn by four black horses.

He instantly recognized the vehicle and its occupants.

How extraordinary that he should meet them just as he arrived at Korskyrka!

Charlotte was seated on the box, proudly driving the four-span, the coachman was sitting beside her, his arms folded over his chest, and back in the carriage sat Schagerström and Fru Forsius.

Charlotte, whose attention was centred upon the horses, did not see him, but Fru Forsius and Schagerström bowed. The sight of his old sweetheart affected him strangely, and he nearly forgot to return the salutation. He was no longer in love with Charlotte, yet his heart leapt with joy at this fleeting glimpse of the woman.

Then, remembering their last meeting, he understood his feelings better. It was his wife whom he really loved; Charlotte was his good friend, his guardian angel—that was why he was so glad to see her. Somehow he felt that his hopes for the future had been strengthened by his seeing her.

2

Nothing has ever been said about Adam and Eve having any children while they were still in paradise. There are no old legends that tell how the small sons of our First Parents played catch-as-catch-can with the lion's cubs or bestraddled Leviathan and Behemoth.

The children must have come to the world after the banishment. Or perhaps it was due to them more than to the serpent or the fine apples on the Tree of Knowledge, that the Parents were driven out from the beautiful garden. That sort of thing may be witnessed to this very day.

One need go no farther back than to the time of Karl Arthur Ekenstedt—he who came home with such fine notions about creating a new paradise in his little hill cottage, behind the doctor's garden. There was no doubt in his mind that he could carry out his plan, but he had failed to take the ten children into his calculations.

It had never occurred to him that the youngsters would be in his home night and day. He had thought that at least they would sleep at their own house. But when he asked his wife to send them home to sleep, she laughed:

"Why, man, you must think we've a gold mine to dig from! Sure you wouldn't want the children to lie in unheated rooms? And wood costs money."

He had to put up with the discomforts of the kitchen, once so well arranged by Fru Sundler, but now cluttered with a long settle-bed, two sofa-beds, a large loom, two ribbon looms, three spinning wheels, a reel, a lace-maker's pillow, and a small table, at which his wife did hair work. In fact, there were so many implements of labour crowded into the room, he could barely thread his way among them. But they were all necessary tools, as Anna and the children had to support themselves by weaving, lace-making and doing fancy hair work— making bracelets, watch chains, etc. Besides, they had to make their own clothes.

At every stroke of the batten the little house shook to its foundations. When looms and spinning wheels and reels were all going at the same time, there was a deafening whirr that made Karl Arthur think, as he sat writing in his room, that he was sitting in a mill house. When he went to the kitchen for his meals he found the food set out on a table leaf laid over the long settle-bed, in which some of the children had slept. If he suggested that the door be opened a trifle to let in a little fresh air, his wife would tell him that the door had been standing open a long time in the morning, while she was sweeping. They couldn't afford to chill the house more than once a day, for they had no gold mine to dig from.

Since all ten children were now living with him, their Sunday clothes—jackets, coats, trousers, and skirts— hung in the hall, in plain sight of everyone who called at the little parsonage. That was not the custom at Korskyrka, and he ordered the children's clothes removed to the garret. Then he was told that the garret was infested with rats and moths; up there the clothes would be utterly destroyed in a couple of months. His wife knew of no way to repair such a loss, as she had no gold mine to dig from.

The wife was more beautiful than ever. She adored her husband and was happy and proud to have him at home. And he was fond of her. Without doubt he and she would have been happy together if the children had not been there.

He had to admit that his wife was a wonderful hand

with children. She never coddled them, nor did she beat them. But scold—that she could do, and properly. If anything went wrong, she could be rather crusty. But whatever she said or did, the children always thought her lovely. It was not only Crofter Matts's orphans who loved her: all the children in the churchtown would have come into her kitchen, had there been room enough. They would have sat there for hours, watching her every movement and waiting for just a smile from her, or a pleasant word.

Wasn't it a marvel, her transforming ten of the laziest of lazybones into veritable ants of industry? Although the children worked from morning to night, they had grown plump and rosy-cheeked. It was the happiness of being with her that made them blossom out.

When Karl Arthur first came home, the children were ready to give him the same devotion they gave to his wife. The youngest child, in particular, took a great fancy to him. She climbed up into his lap and patted his cheek. The little girl did not know that her hands were dirty and that her nose needed attention; so, when he set her down on the floor, far from gently, she burst out crying.

Then you should have seen his wife! She came rushing like a whirlwind, caught up the child and hugged it to her bosom as if shielding it from a brute. And she shot her husband a glance that fairly staggered him.

His wife, though comely as ever, had changed in some respects. Since she had got all these children to rule over she had become dictatorial as an alderman's wife. The old submissive Anna Svärd was no more.

3

It cannot be said of Karl Arthur that he was spoiled. He worked the whole long day and was satisfied with the plainest of fare. He never complained when forced to ride in jolting carts or preach in icy cold churches. But what he missed sorely, on the other hand, was a certain orderliness, neatness, peace and quiet for work. And these, alas, were not to be found in his home so long as the children were there.

One morning, as he came out to breakfast, he found the parish cobbler in the kitchen. The man had set up his work bench by the window, in the very place where Karl Arthur liked to sit. The room reeked of leather and shoemaker's wax.

His wife had placed on the table—now drawn into the middle of the room—two plates of gruel and two large pewter bowls filled with gruel. The individual dishes were for himself and the cobbler, of course; the wife and the children were to spoon their food, as usual, from the bowls.

This was something which he had already commented upon. He had begged his wife to let each child have an individual dish, and suggested that it would be good for the children to be taught a little table etiquette.

"Are you crazy?" she had asked him. "Do you think I have time to stand and wash ten plates three times a day?" But he could have a plate to himself, as he was used to having.

However, he had to admit that the children behaved very well at table. They said their grace without having to be reminded; they ate what was set before them and never squabbled over the porridge bowl. He did not find it unpleasant to eat with them. But to sit at table with the cobbler—that went against the grain. One glance at the bezum-stained fingers was enough to take away his appetite.

Before he realized what he was doing he took up his plate, a spoon, and a slice of bread and went to his own room. There he could sit in peace and comfort, for the air was pure and the room clear of dust. He felt a bit ashamed of his flight. At the same time he had to confess that his food tasted better to him now than it had in a long time.

But when he took the dish back to the kitchen there was an ominous silence. The cobbler, who was still eating, had a dark frown on his face, while the wife and the children sat with their eyes cast down, as if ashamed of his conduct.

Home was not a pleasant place for him that day; so he put on his hat and went out. He tramped the country road, not knowing where to go. He could not call on Fru Sundler, as her husband had been ill all winter and she had to nurse him day and night. Nor could he go to the Deanery for a chat with Fru Forsius. Charlotte, not wishing her old friend to be there alone in her bereavement, had invited her to spend the winter at Stora Sjötorp.

But all the same, as he walked by the Deanery, a strange longing for the old home swept over him. He opened the gate, crossed the house yard and went down to the garden. While wandering about among the tall, trimmed hedges, he thought of his last walk here with Charlotte; of their quarrel; his break with her, and how he had told her that he would marry none but the woman whom God Himself should choose for him.

And now he was married to the woman whom Providence had sent across his path. He felt sure that she was the proper wife for him and that he and she, together, could create a new paradise on earth. Were all his grand plans to be frustrated simply because he had got this band of young ones on his neck? Charlotte would have a right to laugh him to scorn, he thought, if he failed because he couldn't get along with a few little children.

He came back to the house at dinner time; but before he could show his face in the kitchen his wife brought a nicely laid tray to his room. She was pleasant as ever.

"You see, Husband, I thought you wanted to eat with us," she said. "If you had only told me at first, you could have had all your meals in here."

Karl Arthur hastened to assure her that he had no objections to eating with her and the children. It was the sight of the cobbler's black fists that frightened him away from the table. And now he proposed that she too should eat in his room. Wouldn't it be jolly to dine by themselves just for once?

It would never do, she said. She had to sit at table with the children, to keep order; but she would be glad to stay while he ate his dinner.

She sat down in his desk chair and talked to him. He soon learned that the journeyman cobbler would give them but the one day. His time was engaged until well after New Year, so the children would not have the new shoes which she had promised them for Christmas matins.

Karl Arthur understood, of course, that the cobbler was offended and that he was to blame. But what could he do?

Just then the face of Charlotte loomed before his vision. He could see her laugh at him for his inability to adjust a thing so trivial.

When his wife had removed the tray he sat pondering a while. Of a sudden he saw clearly what he must do. He went out to the kitchen with a pair of shoes in need of half-soling and sat down at the shoemaker's bench. He asked the cobbler to show him how to go about it, so that he could mend these shoes himself. The man was quite willing to oblige him; so Karl Arthur borrowed a large apron of his wife and sat at the work bench until nightfall, taking instructions in cobbling.

However, as he couldn't master the craft in a single afternoon, he proposed that the shoemaker continue the instructions the following day. The old man, who was really a kindly, helpful fellow, having passed a pleasant afternoon, agreed to come.

4

They had a happy Christmas Eve at the little parsonage. The kitchen had been cleared of work tools, the floor scoured and strewn with fragrant yellow straw, and there was a white linen tablecloth on the large table, which now occupied the centre of the room. The children bathed and combed, in new shoes and new suits, were in high glee because Christmas had come at last. From almost every house in the churchtown had come gifts of spiced bread, butter, sausage, cheese, and Christmas candles. Since one could not refuse to accept anything sent at Christmas-tide, the little cupboard was full, to say nothing of the twelve mounds of buns, Yule cakes, wreaths, and apples that were stacked upon the table.

Karl Arthur made a short prayer, after which they all sang Christmas carols. Later, as the wife stood by the fire stirring the Yule porridge, he and the children tumbled about in the straw.

Toward the end of the evening Karl Arthur distributed a few presents. The children received skates and a sled which he had ordered for them, and the wife an antique shawl pin which had once belonged to his mother. All were pleased with their presents, and the joy rose high.

Karl Arthur, of course, did not expect to receive anything for himself; but when, after supper, the two oldest children came dragging a large bolt of cloth, with the other children and his wife forming a solemn procession, he knew that his turn had come.

The wife said: "The children have been so happy in the thought that they could give you something. They have been working on this cloth the whole autumn."

But what they were giving him was only a piece of gray wadmal. He bent down and felt of the cloth. Now everyone knows that such homespun, hand-woven wadmal is the softest, warmest and most durable cloth to be had. But it is heavy, of a coarse texture and of a dull greenish-gray colour. All his life Karl Arthur had worn only garments of fine, smooth material; he never would have thought of putting on a jacket of wadmal.

He was positively unhappy about his Christmas present, and wondered how he could escape having the cloth made up; for he did not care to go about garbed like a peasant.

There stood the wife and the children, anxiously waiting for some word of appreciation or praise from him. As none seemed forthcoming, they were disappointed and hurt.

Karl Arthur could understand how they had worked to gather the wool and card it, to spin the yarn and weave the cloth. There was no doubt that it had been a labour of months. And the children, while carding, spooling, and weaving, must have talked of how pleased he would be and how he would praise their wadmal.

He would marvel at their giving him anything so costly and he would say that he'd never have to suffer from the cold any more, either indoors or out, now that he had homespun clothes. It was this they expected of him.

"Oh, what shall I do? I must say something nice, or their Christmas joy will be spoiled."

Karl Arthur had inherited from his mother a certain ability to meet difficult situations and knew very well what he ought to say; but it cost him no little effort to come out with it.

"I wonder if Anders the tailor will be free during the Christmas holidays?" he said. "I've a notion to go ask him now. Perhaps he would make up the cloth for me between now and New Year's so that I could have something warm to put on when the hard winter weather sets in."

They all brightened—all eleven. And they thought now it was only his surprise at their cleverness that made him look so shocked at first.

5

Karl Arthur had never ventured to preach without notes since the Shrove Sunday when he stuck dead in his sermon on Love. He wrote all his sermons now, and insisted upon having quiet around him while he worked.

One morning, when he had a sermon to write, he made his wife and the children promise not to talk or sing. For a good half hour there was silence in the kitchen. Then of a sudden wild laughter rent the air.

He waited about two minutes, then stepped to the kitchen door to see what was up.

"Now, Husband, don't be angry at us," said Anna, laughing so hard the tears rolled down her cheeks. "It was the kitten's antics. We tried so hard to hold in the laughter, that's why it was worse than ever when it broke out."

But there was an end to all laughter when Karl Arthur in stern tones declared that they were spoiling everything for him, that he would rather go away than have to listen to this everlasting noise.

"Now, see that you keep quiet!" he said. "I'm not to be disturbed until dinner time, understand!"

With that he slammed the door shut and went back to his room.

And, indeed, his wishes were respected: he worked in peace and comfort the whole forenoon. When he came out to dinner his wife informed him that Fru Romelius and Fru Schagerström had been at the house a short while before and had ordered watch chains and bracelets of her. It was a large order. The sisters had both been very pleasant and friendly, and she was happy about their visit.

Karl Arthur knew that the doctor's wife had recently come home from Italy, restored to health. It was not strange that Charlotte, after calling on her sister, had dropped in at his house to see how he was getting on; but to him it was such surprising news it fairly took his breath away. Charlotte had been here! She had stood beneath his roof, and he had not been told of it till now!

He inquired with forced indifference if the ladies had wished to see him.

Oh, yes. They had asked after him several times; but he had given strict orders that he was not to be disturbed.

There was nothing to be said and no one to blame. But he thought it very strange that he had not heard them and recognized their voices. He bit his lips and kept silence.

The wife looked at him searchingly. "You understand, of course, that I'd rather have asked such fine folk to step into your room. I was sorry they had to stand in the kitchen in all the clutter and clatter; but I didn't dare to speak to you."

Disappointment lay upon him like a leaden weight. He had lost all desire for food and scarcely touched his plate.

Immediately after dinner he went to his room and threw himself down on the sofa. But he could not lie still for the seething ferment within. Regret and longing surged through every fibre of his being. Presently he put on his things and went out. He wanted to yell, fight, fence. Being in no condition to go for a quiet stroll, he turned into the woodshed, picked up the axe and fooled with it a while. Suddenly he began to hack at the wood-pile—not with the idea of performing a helpful service, but merely as an outlet for his pent-up emotions.

After a few swings of the axe he felt easier; so he went

on chopping for some two hours. Meanwhile, the agony passed, and he became quite calm. Warm and perspiring he stood resting on his axe when one of the children appeared in the doorway.

"Mother wants to know if you'll please come in now for afternoon coffee."

He went along into the house. So his wife was treating him to coffee in honour of his wood cutting.

It struck him at once that there was a changed atmosphere about the house. It was not merely that the kitchen had been aired and a place cleared in the middle of the room for the table—a real table this time, all set for coffee—but his wife and the children now regarded him in a new light. He was able to cut wood and therefore could contribute like the others to the upkeep of the household. He was a regular man.

All at once he had become the master of the house, the head of the family, to whom they all looked up.

CHAPTER II

THE FALL

ONE morning, as Karl Arthur stood in the shed, chopping firewood, he saw a flitting shadow. Glancing up, he thought he recognized Fru Sundler, whom he had not met the whole winter. He dropped the axe and ran out. . . . Yes, it was she. But she was already out of the gate and hurrying down the road. He called to her, but she did not stop; instead, she hastened her steps. He quickly drew on his coat, for he had been working in his shirt sleeves, and ran after her.

The organist had been troubled with the gout all winter, and hardly able to move. In order that he might perform the duties of his office, the beadle and the organ blower helped him up the narrow stairs to the organ loft. Thea always accompanied him and sat by his side during the entire service. She never appeared now in the nave or the sacristy

Karl Arthur had begun to suspect that Thea had some reason besides the husband's illness for keeping away from him; and he who held her in high regard was not going to lose this opportunity to obtain an explanation. He caught up to her before she reached the foot of the hill and could turn into the village street.

"Stop, Thea!" he cried, and laid a hand on her shoulder. "What's the matter? Are you afraid of me?"

She tried to shake herself free from his hand, but did not look at him. "Let me go!" she mumbled weakly. But Karl Arthur blocked her way.

He noted the dark circles around her eyes and saw that she had fallen away. She looked as though she, like the husband, had been through a hard siege of illness. He told her that she could not pass until he knew why his faithful friend and adviser of other days no longer wished to meet him. "What have I done?" he said. "In what have I offended you?"

"You!" she cried out in a tone of unspeakable anguish. "You have never offended me."

"Then why do you shun me?"

She turned to him a face ravaged by suffering. Karl Arthur regarded her with astonishment. Thea could never be called a pretty woman, but suffering had rendered her plain features sensitive and appealing.

"Let me go!" she begged. "Fru Forsius has exacted a promise of me, and I have sworn to keep away from you. It was on that condition that you were allowed to come back to your wife and your home."

She pushed him aside and turned in on the village street. He let her go. She had given him plenty of food for reflection, and he stood aghast.

Next day he saw her again. One of the children had
been taken ill, and he had gone to fetch Dr. Romelius.
The doctor had a patient in his office, so Karl Arthur
was shown into the waiting room. There, before him,
sat Fru Sundler, in animated conversation with an
elderly peasant woman.

Thea got up as if to go; then sat down again. Karl
Arthur bowed but did not speak. Thea, however, immediately addressed herself to him.

"Mother Per-Ers and I were just speaking of you,
and we felt a bit embarrassed when you came in. But,
really, we had no reason to be, for we had only good to
say of you. Eh, Mother Per-Ers?"

The big, stolid peasant woman beamed with satisfaction. "Your Reverence could well have heard every
word we said."

"Yes, indeed," Fru Sundler assured him. "We said
we couldn't understand how you endure it, with ten
shrieking young ones around you day and night and
never a moment's peace. We also said that you were
created for something higher than shoemaker and
wood chopper to Crofter Matts's offspring. Therefore, it seems all the more remarkable that you don't
tire."

"His Reverence doesn't appear to be any the worse
for the wear," the peasant woman observed. "I never
saw him looking so hale and fit."

"We think it very sensible of you to wear homespun
clothes," said Thea. "It proves that you have definitely

broken with the past, and wish to lead the simple life; you even avoid the appearance of being the gentleman you are."

"At first," said Mother Per-Ers, "we all thought the talk about the little cabin and the poverty was only foolery, but now we know better."

Karl Arthur felt the blood flush up into his face. Thea was utterly ruthless. She had no consideration for his feelings. He shook his head at her, hoping she would change the subject.

But Thea harped on: "What matter if you don't preach so well now as formerly? Your whole life is a sermon, as I said to Mother Per-Ers."

"Aye, both he and his wife are a lesson to all of us." came added testimony from the older woman. "When the wife comes to church of a Sunday with her flock of children, all of them rosy cheeked, well clad, and behaving so nice and proper, we old peasant mothers have to stand and look at them. And to think how those children used to run about the country—ragged and dirty and wild! It's a grand work the parson's folks are doing."

"Ah, so it is," Thea agreed. "Even if one knew of a way to relieve them of all bother with the children, one would hesitate to come forward. It would be a pity to break up a beautiful work which arouses such unqualified admiration."

Karl Arthur suddenly looked at Thea, a ray of hope lighting up his face.

"You don't mean, Fru Sundler," questioned Mother Per-Ers, "that there's someone who'd like to take the children? Here in Korskyrka we've never heard of their having any kinfolk but an uncle on the father's side, and he was as poor as their father."

"But supposing the uncle had married well and had his own farm and a good wife, wouldn't he be likely to want the children if he knew that his brother was dead?"

"Oh, in that case . . ." Just then the door of the doctor's office opened, a patient came out, and it was the old woman's turn to step in.

There was a tense moment of silence when Thea and Karl Arthur found themselves alone. After a little, Thea began to speak, but in a different tone from the one she had used before. Now she was all tremulous solicitude:

"I have sat at home and prayed God to help you. I knew, of course, that you wished to live humbly, but I never thought you would peg shoes and split wood. If you keep on like that you're bound to go under. I feel that I am responsible for this and that I ought to watch over you, but I'm not even allowed to invite you to my house. It's dreadful, dreadful!"

Karl Arthur waved his hand to show that he had heard enough. Thea, however, was not to be silenced. She came closer. And now she said, stressing her words to impress them upon his mind:

"My husband's brother, who is the organist at Ekshärad, is now visiting us. Yesterday, as we sat talking, the conversation turned upon you and the ten children. He said there was a man from Korskyrka at Ekshärad who must be a brother of Crofter Matts. The man, at all events, had spoken to him several times about a brother who was very poor and who had many children; but he does not know that his brother is dead. My brother-in-law is leaving for Ekshärad this afternoon. Shall I request him to inform the children's uncle that they are living upon the charity of yourself and your wife, or shall I ask him not to speak of it?"

Karl Arthur straightened his back, squared his shoulders, and drew a deep breath. All that he had suffered that winter on account of those children came vividly back to mind. To be relieved of them! To be relieved of them in a decent and honourable way!

"You have no peace, no quiet for work," Thea zealously continued. "Your sermons are so poor a schoolboy would be ashamed of them. Once you could speak like an angel who knew all the mysteries of the kingdom of God—now you know nothing."

He kept silent. Of late he had become more accustomed to his lowly surroundings; he and the children were now on good terms. It would be rather cowardly, he thought, to send them away and give up the struggle.

"Say something, Karl Arthur! I must know what to do. Mother Per-Ers may be here again at any moment. Just give me the least little sign."

He gave a laugh.

While Thea had been speaking he had felt bonds loosening, seen ice melting, and heard songs of freedom.

Now he did a thing he had never done before: he threw his arms around Thea, and from sheer gratitude and joy kissed the ugly little creature right on the mouth.

2

Who was Anna that she should sit in judgment on her husband—he who knew so much more than she; he who could preach the Word of God and warn poor sinners who had fallen upon evil ways? She must believe that he did right to give the children up. What else could he do, when their own uncle came for them? If the uncle were a poor man, it would have been another matter; but since he was well-to-do, had a large farm, a good wife, and no children of his own, Karl Arthur couldn't refuse to let him take his brother's children.

At first she had thought the man an impostor, but the two oldest children remembered him, as did others in the village, though no one had ever heard that he had prospered. When he left Korskyrka he was as poor as his brother.

The parish in which he lived lay far up North; so it was not strange that he had not heard that Crofter Matts was dead and that the children had been taken in by strangers. However, as soon as he heard of it he came down to Korskyrka to offer the children a home with him.

That was kind of him, to be sure, and she must try to think him a good man. Surely, no one could blame her husband for letting the children go with their uncle.

Karl Arthur had not been at all insistent. He had talked beautifully to her, had told her that it was a special dispensation of God, the man's coming to lighten the heavy burden which rested upon them, but mostly upon her, of course. He had said, moreover, that since she was expecting a little one of her own soon she could not go on toiling for the others.

In that she had thought he was right; but she had become uncertain as to what she really wished. His mention of God in connection with the children had confused her. They were such good children that God perhaps wanted them to have a better home than they had with her. And it had been hard upon Karl Arthur with the children around, harder than she had realized. But now she understood—now that he had talked so beautifully about their going.

And the children showed little regret at leaving her. But then they were going to see something new. Their uncle had horses and cows and pigs and chickens which they would be allowed to feed and tend. And he had a dog that could say thanks for meat and could imitate the verger, when he led the hymns in church. The children had never heard of anything so wonderful as a psalm-singing dog.

When they had gone Anna sank down on the worn

door stone, utterly listless. She had not sat thus, with idle hands, in two or three years, except on Sundays, and rarely then. She ought to be glad that at last she could rest awhile, she said to herself.

Her husband came out and sat down beside her. Taking her hand in his, he said that they were going to be very happy now. The children, he thought, had been sent to them as a discipline, and their being taken away was a sign that God was well pleased with what they had done for His little ones.

She knew that she was nothing beside her husband, that the ways of God were beyond her understanding, but, all the same, she was furious at Karl Arthur. She declared that to her the children had been a godsend, and that she did not know what she had done that they should be taken from her.

Karl Arthur got up and walked away. Anna did not call him back, nor did she regret her words. She was like a vessel full of bitter gall; if one went near her the bitterness flowed over.

She knew that she should go in and clear up after the children, but she dreaded to face the emptiness that would meet her. Now she would be as lonely and forlorn as she had been during the first months of her marriage, before she had taken in the children. With them she had been happy and content. Oh, why had she been such a fool as to let them go!

It had seemed easy for the children to tell her good-bye. They had not shed a tear; she had not wept either. Their only regret had been that the kitten would not come with them. They had thought of nothing but the horse and wagon and what they were to take along.

She saw before her the old farm wagon as it bore them off. The children had put into it their bundles of clothing and other things for the journey. The smaller children were allowed to ride, but the others and the uncle walked beside the wagon. He had laughed and said that it looked as if he were travelling with a band of gipsies—with the youngsters and all the bundles.

As she thought of the uncle's face she became uneasy. She was not so sure that the man was as good-humoured and kindly as he had made it appear. He was perhaps a smooth-tongued villain, a mean, bad fellow. The children might fare ill with him.

This possibility became to her mind a certainty. She wanted to run after the children and bring them back. Why hadn't she done it while there was yet time? Now she could not rest for the thought that the little ones would suffer hunger and cold.

Spring had come, the snow was gone, and a friendly sun beamed down upon her as she sat there. In a few days the children could have moved back into their own cottage and made it easier for Karl Arthur.

She tried to take comfort in the thought that there was only one to cook for now, and that she would not have to sit up half the night darning stockings.

If she were only sure the children would get their

stockings mended where they were going! If she only knew that they would continue to say their prayers at night! The smallest child was afraid of the dark—she was afraid to go to sleep unless someone sat at her bed and held her hand.

CHAPTER III

THE CUPBOARD

FOR several days after the children had gone Anna was too unhappy and listless to clear up after them. She was sure that they would be ill-treated by their relatives, and that she and her husband would be held to strict account for letting them go to such wicked people.

This came upon her without her volition. It was like a fever sickness: she could not throw it off. She had no special reason to worry like that, but she could not banish the thought that the uncle had a bad face; and she pictured his wife, of whom she knew nothing, as a regular hell kite. She feared, too, that the punishment would also be visited upon the child she was carrying: it would come to the world malformed and perhaps blind and deaf. Or she, herself, might die in childbirth and leave her little one motherless.

It was useless to speak of such things to Karl Arthur. He would not listen when she said the children suffered want and he and she would be punished. He was gentle with her, but he thought her fears and apprehensions not worth noticing. She had to fight them alone.

One morning she thought of a remedy. She set

about to clear the kitchen of looms, spinning wheels, and other implements. The settle-bed and the sofa, which where the children's property, she carried over to their cottage and closed their house. Then she white-washed the walls of her kitchen, scrubbed the floor, and scoured all the pots and pans. And she soon found her-self sitting in a kitchen as clean and tidy and bare-looking as it had been when she first stepped into it. Hav-ing removed every object that could draw her thoughts to the children, she resolved to act as if everything were the same as in the early days of her marriage. The children were never there—she had only been dreaming. If she could put them out of her mind all would be well. No one went about anxious and troubled over a dream.

"You know, Anna," she said to herself, "that a young newly married wife thinks only of her husband. Now bring out your knitting needles and yarn and start a pair of mittens for your man! Think of nothing but the wonder that you are a minister's wife, and raised above all other peddler women."

She began the mittens with a will. She had knitted but a few rows, when she saw at the end of the table before her some figures that had been cut with a sharp instrument.

"One of the small boys must have done that," she thought. "The little rascals know it's forbidden to scratch the furniture. But it seems impossible to break them of the habit of whittling at everything in the way of wood."

She raised her head to deliver her usual lecture, but there were no little flaxen-haired heads to pour vials of wrath upon—only the bare white walls stared at her blankly.

Anna quickly got up and went for a knife. With one sharp stroke, she cut away the markings on the table. Then she sat down to her knitting again, her face distorted with pain as if she had cut into her own flesh.

"What a fool I am!" she muttered. "It was Karl Arthur, of course, who did it. He always eats at this end of the table. We've never had any children in this house. How could poor folk like us afford to take in a lot of youngsters? We may be glad if we're able to feed and clothe ourselves and the little one that's coming."

Pressing her lips together and fixing her eyes on her work, she wondered whether everything associated with the children had now been stowed away. She heard a slight noise, then a thud. The kitten, the children's special pet, had awakened from his sweet slumbers on the hearth and jumped up onto the table, to play with her ball of yarn.

She quickly seized the cat. Nothing could bring the children so sharply back to her mind as this playfellow of theirs. Her first impulse was to throw the kitten out of the house; but feeling the soft, warm little body beneath her hand she had to caress it.

With that, the ball of yarn rolled off the table, and the cat went after it like a streak. He tried to stop it with his paws, but it kept rolling away. Anna also tried to capture the ball, fearing that her yarn would be ruined. It was a wild chase. The kitten darted from corner to corner, and the ball behaved as if it had life. Anna had to laugh at her futile efforts to check its speed.

"Now the children are having fun," she thought, and let the play go on longer than was necessary—just for their amusement. "Oh, children," she cried, "come and help me!"

But the words were hardly out before she remembered. Now she caught up the kitten, gave it a slap, and flung it out the door.

"Will I never get those children off my mind!" she said as she rewound the yarn. "Sure, I must be going mad."

She walked the floor, wringing her hands, and moaning as if in pain. After a little she sat down to her work again. And it was well she did, for presently the door opened and in came old Ris Karin of Medstuby.

Ris Karin had brought Anna greetings from home both that year and the year before. But on her previous visits the kitchen had been crowded with children and implements and alive with the hum of work.

"Well, in all my born days!" Karin ejaculated, her eyes widening as she looked round the room.

A perfect torrent of questions fell upon Ris Karin. She had to tell how it was with Mother Svärd and Uncle Jobs Eric; with Ris Ingborg and Sexton Medberg; with the Bailiff's folk and the Pastor's folk—collectively and individually. There was not a soul in Medstuby of whom she was not obliged to give a full account.

Her first curiosity satisfied, Anna hastened to make coffee. She ran out to the shed for wood and to the well for water. She blew on the fire to coax it up; she ground coffee, she cut bread and laid the table. She seemed in a terrible rush and made a noisy clatter with everything her hands touched. Ris Karin saw that she would have to wait until Anna sat down to the table before asking her about the children.

But they were no sooner comfortably seated, each with a lump of sugar in her mouth and the steaming hot coffee poured out into their saucers to cool, than a fresh torrent of questions rained upon Karin. Now they concerned old comrades, both menfolk and women-folk. Was old Annstu Lisa still on the road, and was she as daft about card playing as ever?

Now, Annstu Lisa was Ris Karin's most intimate friend and her most formidable competitor. Her queer tricks and misdoings gave them enough to talk about over the first, and the second, cup. Karin thought that such a creature should not be let loose on the country-side to carry on trade. It was a shame that the other venders, who tried to do straight business, must have a person like her among them.

When they had finished their coffee it was time for the old woman to be going. She was not so stupid but she could understand that Anna did not wish to tell her what had become of the children. Knowing that she could find out at the next place, she asked no questions. But when she had adjusted the peddler's bag to her bent old back and said good-bye, as she stood at the door, with a hand on the latch, she looked back at Anna.

"Oh, I mustn't forget my errand here!" She dug into her kirtle bag for her purse. "You don't ask me if I've made any money for you," she said, and held out a fifty-riksdaler bank note.

When Karin was at Korskyrka the previous spring Anna had given her a bundle of ribbon belting and a few yards of lace which the children had made and asked her to sell these for her. Anna had not forgotten about it, but she would not bring up any matter in which the children were concerned.

Fifty riksdalers was ever so much more than the things were worth. Didn't Karin have a smaller bill? Anna had no money, so she couldn't make the change.

"There's no change coming to me," said Karin. "The money is yours—all of it. I sold what you gave me, then I traded with your money, and now, you see, it's up to fifty. You'll need every penny, with all the mouths you have to feed!"

Old as she was, Ris Karin was brisk in all her movements. Not wishing to be thanked, she shut the door behind her, then walked rapidly down the hill. She had not gone far, however, before Anna came running after her. Anna was more like her old self now. She thanked

Karin extravagantly and walked with her all the way to the doctor's house, where Karin hoped to do good business, now that the doctor's wife was getting plenty of money from her rich sister and didn't have to turn the pennies over so many times.

Anna sat in her kitchen looking at the bank note in her hand, a happy smile on her lips. She was glad to have money, as she always had been. But this time her delight was not in the profit from sales but in something greater—a sign—a wonder! She had expected punishment for giving the children up, and now she received from them this generous gift. Never had she dreamed of anything so wonderful! This was the very opposite to the thing she had feared would happen.

Anna could not keep her joy all to herself, but wanted to share it with her husband. He was sitting at the writing table in his luxurious room when she came and showed him the bank note. She asked him to keep it for her, as there were no safe nooks or crannies in the kitchen.

Karl Arthur glanced up from his work a trifle distrait. He could hardly follow her when she told him that this was pay for little things the children had made, and that they had sent it as a thank offering, and a token that he and she would not be punished for sending them away.

He made no comment, although her train of thought seemed rather vague. His wife had regained her assurance and good-humour—that was enough for him. He proposed that she use this money, which had come so unexpectedly, to purchase something for herself—something that she would really enjoy.

It was a good suggestion, and Anna went back to her kitchen to consider for what she should spend this money which had come to her right out of the blue. Nor was it long before she knew what she wanted. From the first she had wanted a large cupboard in her kitchen—one that went from floor to ceiling, with bottom drawers and shelves and doors. Such a cupboard was not only useful, but it also lent a certain dignity to a room.

Anna could think of nothing they needed more, and since her husband was with her in this and the money lay to hand in a drawer of his desk, there was nothing to hinder her going at once to the village carpenter, who was a clever mechanic, and ordering the cupboard.

The carpenter's shop was on the main street, a few doors beyond the organist's house. And as Anna was on her way to the shop, she met Fru Sundler, who had been out gathering wild flowers and had in her hand a few small anemones.

Anna was surprised to see Thea without a coat, for she had not noticed how warm it had grown. She had been oblivious of weather conditions as of everything else since the day the children had left her. But now she saw that the sun was shining, that the heavens were high and blue and speckled with wooly little puffs of white cloud. It all seemed part of the joy that filled her heart that day. And when Fru Sundler extended a greeting hand Anna did not hurry by, as she would have done at any other time. "It won't hurt me to speak to the woman," she thought. "I can't go on forever at odds with a woman living in the same village."

"I feel like a released prisoner," said Fru Sundler, "now that my husband is able to go about by himself. I have been in the woods for two or three hours, and I can't begin to tell you how lovely it is up there. I have thawed out, and new life has sprung up in me, as in nature."

For the first time Anna felt a kind of sympathy for Thea Sundler. "It has been a hard winter for you," she said, then turned to go on her way.

"Oh, don't go yet!" said Thea. "When one has been shut in for months it is a joy to meet an old friend, for as such I have always regarded the wife of Karl Arthur. Won't you come in with me and chat awhile? We're only a step from my house."

"No," said Anna bluntly. She was not going to let anything keep her from ordering her cupboard now, at once. Never quite sure of herself with gentlefolk, she thought Fru Sundler might feel hurt unless she gave a reason for not wishing to go in; so she told her that she had received some money quite unexpectedly and was on her way to the carpenter's to order a cupboard.

Fru Sundler brightened at this. She did not wonder

that Fru Ekenstedt was in a hurry, and congratulated
her on being able to get herself something so useful and
decorative as a cupboard. Then she actually let her go.

Anna was in no haste when she presently stood in
the carpenter's shop. She gave herself plenty of time to
transact her business. It was an hour or more before she
and the carpenter had everything decided as to style
and design, wood, height, number of drawers, colour,
fittings, and other ornamentations. Fixing the price was
none too easy, but they finally agreed on a figure satisfactory to both.

When Anna came home with the carpenter's promise
that the cupboard would be ready in a month and
would come to no more than forty riksdalers, she was
jubilant and had to tell Karl Arthur about it at once.

He seemed to be anything but pleased.

"I wouldn't have thought you'd be so expeditious,"
he said. "You should have asked me to go with you.
I should have liked to talk to the carpenter."

"I didn't know you'd give any time to such things,"
said Anna.

"Not ordinarily, but this——" He checked himself
and nervously bit his lips.

Anna regarded him searchingly. He flushed like an
embarrassed youth. "You must say what you mean,
Husband."

"What I mean—well, I think, since you yourself
maintain that this money has come to us in a miraculous

way, that we should not spend it on ourselves but should do some good with it."

"Oh, have you given my money away?" said Anna, not suspecting that such might be the case.

Karl Arthur coughed nervously and cleared his throat several times. Then it came out that Organist Sundler had called. He had been so glad to be up and about again after the long winter's confinement, and Karl Arthur had advised him to take care of himself this summer so that he would not have to go through another winter of misery. Whereupon the organist had said that he would like above everything to go to Loka Springs to take the baths for his gout, but he had no money.

"You haven't given him what the children sent us!" Anna exclaimed reproachfully.

"My good woman," said Karl Arthur, his manner now very distant and superior, "do you know of any better way that one could use a gift from God than in an act of mercy?"

Anna came close up to him, her dark eyes flaming in her pale face like balls of fire. "But didn't you understand, man, that the note was a greeting and a token from the children? Have you forgotten how the fellow treated me the last time he was at our house?"

"Perhaps it was of that very thing I was thinking," said Karl Arthur.

She suddenly burst out laughing. He impatiently turned upon her.

"Do you think it so very amusing?" he said.

"What, *that?* No! I was thinking of something else. Just when was the organist here?"

"He—oh, about half an hour ago. He didn't stay long. You must have met him on your way home."

"He was not very anxious to meet me, I trow."

Again she went into shrieks of laughter. It was uncanny! Awful! Karl Arthur drew himself up to his full dignity.

"Will you be good enough to tell me at what you are laughing?"

"I'm not laughing at you. I'm laughing at myself for being such a fool as to tell that Thea about the fifty riksdalers. I might have known she'd wheedle it out of you."

Now he became a trifle alarmed. There was a malevolent gleam in his wife's eyes, and he feared that there was something back of it all that he did not know. He brought his fist down hard upon the table to command respectful attention.

"Now, tell me properly what it is you are laughing at!"

When he finally learned what it was he wouldn't believe that Fru Sundler had sent her husband here to "wheedle" the money out of him. It was a mere coincidence, he thought. "No," he said aloud, "it isn't possible. Why, that would be a knavish trick. Would Thea have sent her husband here the moment she heard that we had received some money—Thea, who is so high-minded, so upright, so conscientious?"

"I don't know how it happened," said Anna; "but it seems kind of queer, his coming to borrow money to-day."

Although Karl Arthur defended Fru Sundler, Anna could see that he was as astonished as if the heavens had fallen. She thought of the Sunday evening some two years back when Thea and the organist had come to bring her to book for hiding the bonnet. Perhaps it was worth the fifty riksdalers to see her husband's disappointment now.

Her satisfaction, however, was of short duration. Footsteps were heard in the hall, then a light, cautious tap at Karl Arthur's door—and in walked Thea.

Karl Arthur quickly turned to his desk and began to rummage among his papers. Fru Sundler, taking no notice of him, addressed her remarks exclusively to his wife.

"Oh, my dear Fru Ekenstedt, I'm so sorry! When my husband informed me that your husband had kindly lent him fifty riksdalers I told him that in all probability that was the money which Fru Ekenstedt herself had earned and therefore we could not accept it. Fru Ekenstedt was to have this for a cupboard—something she badly needed. As it was, she had to put up with the discomfort of having her dishes and utensils standing out on the kitchen shelves to catch the dust. So I asked him to let me have the bank note while I ran over to your house to find out how the matter stood. If the money belonged to Fru Ekenstedt, rather than take it, he'd better endure his gout. But in case it was Karl Arthur's own money we could accept it, of course. Oh, Fru Ekenstedt, I really felt sorry for him! He came home so happy at the prospect of going to Loka to take the cure for his gout; but he saw at once that I was right."

She drew the bank note from her pocket and held it out to Anna, just as Ris Karin had done a few hours before.

Anna hardly noticed the money. She was not looking at Fru Sundler—her eyes were on her husband. He was still over by the writing table, where he had stood silent during Fru Sundler's lengthy explanation. But for every word that Thea had uttered he had become straighter and taller, and had gradually turned toward her. When she had finished her speech he stood facing her with clear brow and eyelids lifted. The little woman of the fish eyes got a look from him which his wife could have envied her. Then, as he turned to Anna, who had just put out her hand to take the money, his brow darkened, his eyelids dropped, and he folded his arms over his chest.

There was nothing else for it: rather than have Thea appear in his sight as a paragon of all the virtues, Anna must sacrifice her fifty riksdalers.

"You keep the note," she said to Fru Sundler. "That's not the one I told you about this morning; that one is Karl Arthur's."

"Is it? Is it really?" Thea was too happy and thankful to say very much. She left almost immediately, as if afraid lest something might happen that would compel her to return the money.

Anna wondered why Karl Arthur, who was such a stickler for facts, did not tell Thea the truth of it; but this time he seemed quite satisfied to let the lie pass. When he came back, after seeing Thea out, he wanted to give Anna a big hug.

"Ah, my dear!" he said, "I don't know when I have witnessed anything so great!—Both you and Thea. I don't know which is the greater—you or she!"

As he started to put his arms around her, Anna pushed him back. She stood there clenching her hands, her face livid with wrath.

"And you let that woman take the note from me!— I could have forgiven you anything but this," she said, and walked out of his room.

CHAPTER IV

THE CARDS

SHE had not made herself and could not help that she was as she was. She was the sort who cannot speak when angry at a person. They usually find their tongue in a day or two; but she had suffered a great injustice and had to grit her teeth on it and not say a word for a week.

Nor could she take up any work. All day she sat on the hearthstone, huddled close to the fire, her face buried in her hands—rocking backward and forward, backward and forward. A small tri-legged coffee pot which she had carried at the bottom of her peddler's bag during her wander years was now always on the fire, and she would pour for herself cup after cup of coffee.

She pottered a bit about the house and prepared her husband's meals, that was all. The moment she had placed his food on the table she went back to the fireplace and never looked in his direction.

Oh, that husband, that husband! If she had only married a Dal man from Medstuby, he would have seen how helpless she was and known what to do for her. At least he would have thrown the coffee pot out and made her take up some handiwork. Now, that would have done her good.

But this one—he just looked in on her now and then, asked her how she was feeling, and begged her sweetly to say a word. Then, receiving no response, he patted her gently on the shoulder and assured her that she would soon feel better.

That was all the help she got from him! She knew, to be sure, what was passing in his mind. He had heard someone say that women when with child were a bit peculiar, and probably thought this was just one of those queer "spells."

But, indeed, it was nothing of the kind, and he, with all his learning, should have known what ailed her. Anna was very sure that he knew but pretended he didn't. He disliked the children, and rather than have them back he'd let her sit there and suffer.

No, she had not made herself and could not help that she was as she was. Her fears for the children had returned and were now ever with her. Up North, where they had gone, there were many old hags who went about the parishes, begging, and who always had a lot of children with them. If they had not enough of their own they would borrow others. Anna felt certain that the six youngest children had been hired out to such a hag. The poor little things must dress in rags and carry bags on their backs; they had to go barefoot, though the snow was still on the ground up there; they were starved, they were beaten and ill-treated in every way; for it wouldn't do for beggar brats to look well nourished and happy.

The moment she could see the children well and happy she would be herself again. But she couldn't speak of this to Karl Arthur; he ought to think of it himself.

Why, any man in Medstuby would have guessed what was troubling her: he would have hitched up and started for Ekshärad the very next morning to fetch the children. Or, if he had not cared to help her in that way, he would have dragged her away from the fireplace by the hair of her head. That, too, would have been good for her. But this one just gave her a few kind words and a pat on the shoulder. She was sick of him. Before, he had been the apple of her eye, but now she could hardly bear to have him come near her.

One day, when he came out to dinner he found his wife sitting on the hearthstone with a small black pipe between her lips—sending out thick clouds of tobacco smoke. Anna knew very well that this was unseemly in a clergyman's wife, but something had told her to do it; and she was curious to see how he would take it when he found his wife smoking like an old Finn-woman.

He was horrified, of course, and said that he would not tolerate a wife who smoked.

She looked at him expectantly. "Now, at last, perhaps he sees that he must help me," she thought.

"If you fill the room with tobacco smoke I cannot

eat out here. So, if you intend to keep this up, you'll have to serve my meals in my room."

He had spoken in his usual tone of kindly forbearance. And when she saw that he was not even ruffled it was quite clear to her that she could expect no help from him.

After that he had his meals in his room. He did not forget, however, to come out to see her. Each time he gave her a pat on the shoulder and a soft word.

Many times in the course of the day she heard the front door open and then loud, earnest talking in her husband's room. As Karl Arthur had charge of a large parish he had many callers, some who called to see him on official business, and others who came to talk with him about their souls.

"Huh! he's a fine one to turn to," thought Anna. "How can he advise anyone? He can't even help his poor wife."

Things had gone on like this for about a week, when one morning she found herself sitting with a knife concealed under her apron. A voice had commanded her to get the knife. She saw nothing strange in that, though she could see no sense in it, since it was only a common table knife. She couldn't hurt herself or anyone else with that.

In the middle of the forenoon Karl Arthur came to tell her that he had been called to the bedside of a dying man in a remote section of the parish—a journey of some twelve miles. She needn't bother to get dinner for him, he said, but he would be thankful if she had a bite of something ready when he came home, at about six o'clock.

She made no response. But when he said, "I think you look a little better to-day than you did yesterday, and you will soon be yourself again," she pulled at her apron a trifle. As he put out his hand to pat her on the shoulder she quickly drew the apron to one side, and he caught the gleam of a knife blade.

He sprang back, as if it were an adder she held in her lap. For a long moment he stood there shaking his head—at a loss to know what to do. At last he said:

"Oh, Anna, Anna, you must be very, very ill! We shall have to do something about it. As soon as I return this evening I'll ask the doctor to see how it is with you."

Then he went. But she had found out what she wanted to know: it had been proved to her beyond a shadow of doubt that that man was incapable of helping her out of her trouble.

2

What a blessed relief it was to come away from home, even though one had to travel in a jolting farm wagon in order to escape for a little from the everyday cares and worries! The wife's indisposition was only a temporary thing, and it would pass when the expected child arrived. His patience had been sorely tried of late, and it was a salutary thing to come out a bit and see that Life had something more to offer one than sulkiness and ill-will.

Karl Arthur had only to drive past the doctor's garden and turn in on the main street to meet with joy and gladness. Red, white, and yellow canvas signs fluttered in the breeze, and along both sides of the street were stands filled with merchandise, while in the roadway itself was a milling crowd of people. The horse had to edge its way through the crowd step by step.

There was, in brief, a market fair at Korskyrka. Though not so important as the autumn fair, when people had to lay in their supplies for the winter, it was nevertheless quite acceptable and well attended. The West Gothlanders were there offering their cotton prints and linens suitable for the approaching summer season. The Dalecarlians were selling ploughshares and scythes, needed for ploughing and reaping; the basket makers threaded their way, literally behung with baskets, handy to have when folks went berrying. Makers of weavers' combs were on hand, their backs laden with great bundles of combs. They did a brisk trade, for now during the long, light summer days was the best time for setting up a loom.

Karl Arthur thought it a good exhibition; but what appealed to him above all were the happy faces. Rich merchants from Kristinehamn, Karlstad, and Örebro who were not too proud to go about the country with their own goods, stood in their booths garbed in their fine fur coats and sealskin caps, greeting their customers with friendly smiles. The Dalecarlian women, picturesque and jolly, stood behind the plain stands on which their wares were spread, while the local inhabitants hailed friends and acquaintances with the spontaneous cheer that comes with the spring, when the cold winter days are over and they can be out of doors again. The corn brandy, no doubt, had contributed somewhat to the general good spirits; but thus early in the day there were no intoxicated persons to be seen; at the most, people were just a bit cocky and in laughing mood.

At two or three points the crowds were so dense that vehicles could not get by. Karl Arthur did not mind the delay. He liked to watch the amusing little scenes that were being enacted in the market place. Before a stall where there were fine hand-woven linens on sale, stood a toil-worn, shabby old crofter, holding by the hand a pretty young girl. The old man probably had had a nip or two, and the warm spring sun had done the rest. He was suddenly seized by a blissful audaciousness.

"Bonander, Bonander!" he shouted to the merchant at the top of his lungs. "What's the price of the red cap? Ho! Bonander! what's the price of the red cap?"

The "red cap" was a fine straw bonnet with a pink satin lining and long ribbon streamers, also of pink satin. The merchant had hung it outside his booth in order to attract to his stand the grand ladies of the gentry, and when the old crofter wanted to buy it he

turned a deaf ear. Consequently, the would-be pur-
chaser shouted all the louder his "Bonander, Bonander,
what's the price of the red cap?"

The crowd roared, and the small boys began to mimic
the poor old fellow; but to Karl Arthur there was something touching about the old man's thinking the finest
hat at the fair was none too good for his daughter.

Karl Arthur's conveyance had started to move again
when there came another halt. This time it was a miner,
a stalwart middle-aged man—well dressed—with a fine,
intelligent face, who had drawn a big crowd around him.
He stood in their midst, looking very grave and dignified. All of a sudden he gave a jump and snapped his
fingers. "Now I'm tipsy," he said. "Oh, how funny I
feel!"

The next moment he was serious again, and stood
there silent; then quite unexpectedly he repeated the
jump, the finger snapping, and the words: "Now I'm
tipsy. Oh, how funny I feel! "

The people seemed to think this very amusing, but
Karl Arthur, to whom all forms of intemperance were
abhorrent, kept his eyes averted until his driver told
him it was only foolery. "The man's no more drunk
than I am. He does the same at every fair he goes to,
just to make folks laugh."

Karl Arthur felt sorry for Anna, sitting at home,
huddled in the fireplace, unaware of the jolly doings just
around the corner. "What a pity she isn't here, where
she might meet some of her old companions, of whom

she cherishes such pleasant memories! She needs to be shaken out of her sulks!"

His thoughts, however, were soon diverted. As is always the case at country fairs, there were a good many fakers here—blacklegs and tricksters who make a living at trading horses and watches. One of these merry rogues came driving along the street at top speed, evidently to show off the speed of his horse to some prospective victim. Karl Arthur first descried him at a distance—a slim, swarthy man who stood upon the seat of his cart brandishing his whip over a little yellow scrub of a horse. The man ranted and swore, and the horse, mad with fright, dashed wildly on, the crowds meanwhile falling back lest they be run over. Karl Arthur's driver tried to swerve aside, but the crush was too great; for a second it looked as if the two vehicles would collide.

At the last moment the scalawag said a quieting word to his horse and drew rein. Then, as he drove slowly past the young clergyman he politely raised his cap, from which half the brim had been torn away, and shouted out:

"Your humble servant, Cousin. Gad, but you look moth-eaten! Cast off the black coat and come along with me! This is the life worth living." With a lash of the whip he put his horse to the trot, and Karl Arthur, to whom the incident had been extremely embarrassing, ordered the farmer-driver by all means to get out of this crowded market place.

When well out on the highway, he sat thinking of his cousin Göran Löwensköld of Hedeby, who when a mere lad had run away from home and joined the gipsies and other folk of the open road, and who had never shown the least desire to return to a regular mode of life.

Karl Arthur had always regarded his cousin as a reprobate, a failure, and a disgrace to the family, but now he was less disposed to pass the usual harsh judgment upon him. A vagabond's life was perhaps not without charm. There was freedom in it, and the unexpected. At every turn of the road loomed an adventure. For such a man there were no sermons to prepare for a set day, no tiresome records to keep, and no tedious vestry meetings. His cousin, perhaps, had not chosen badly when he exchanged the manorial halls for the highway.

The young clergyman had had considerable experience on the road himself. In his college days, when he had made the journey between Karlstad and Upsala four times a year, he had come to know the road quite intimately and had passed many happy days there. He remembered with joy the banks of bright flowers that bordered it, the fine views from the hilltops, the basket lunches at the pleasant wayside inns, the chats with genial farmer-drivers, who, in the course of the years, had come to know him, and who used to ask him, with awe and wonder, if he meant to stay in college until he was wise as King Solomon.

He, who always had been a lover of nature, enjoyed

these drives on the country roads. When others complained of the discomforts of travel he couldn't understand what they were wailing about. To him, the highway had always been friendly. He loved the steep hills that gave variety to his journeys, and the sombre, monotonous forests that had a power of their own to stimulate the imagination. Nor did he find bad roads wholly disagreeable. A broken axle once brought him a whole village of friends. And one time a snowstorm made him a guest at a ducal palace.

While deep in these recollections, which the sight of his cousin had called forth, an idea suddenly struck him. It came like a flash of lightning, straight down from the sky, and it startled him so that he stood up in the wagon and gave a shout.

The driver drew rein and glanced up at him. "Did your Reverence forget to bring the gown, maybe?"

Karl Arthur sat down again. No, he had not forgotten anything, he assured the man. On the contrary, he had recovered something which had been lost.

During the remainder of the long drive he sat with his hands clasped, his eyes shining by the light of his brilliant new idea.

However, as he had told the driver, it was no new discovery. Hundreds, nay, thousands of times, he had read in the Gospel according to St. Matthew the words of Jesus when He sent His disciples forth to proclaim the tidings that the Kingdom of Heaven would soon be established upon earth. Never before had he grasped the full import of the words, but now it was clear to him that Jesus had commanded His apostles to fare forth as poor pilgrims, without scrip or staff, and bear the glorious message to the homes along the way—to hovels and palaces alike. They were to appear in the market place and preach to the people; they were to accost wayfarers during their rests at the inns; they were to enter into converse with other pilgrims and everywhere proclaim the coming of the Kingdom.

How was it that he had not thought to obey this command, so plainly set forth? He, like other clergymen, had stood in the pulpit expecting the people to come to him. That was not as Jesus would have it. He wished His disciples to go out into the highways and byways in order to reach the people.

He had had his own plan—a self-made plan; he had tried to create an earthly paradise that would serve as a model for all mankind. He knew now why he had failed; why he had met with so much opposition; why he had been bereft of his oratorical powers, and why he had wrought so much harm. God had wished to show him that he had chosen badly. Christ did not wish His servant to have a fixed abiding place. A true servant of the Lord must be as a bird on the wing, a free pilgrim whose home is the great lap of Nature. He should accept food and drink as a grace from Heaven, or go hungry and cold, according as it pleased the Lord. He could rest in a bed whenever God so willed it, and if some morning he were found dead in a snowdrift, it would simply mean that God had called the weary pilgrim home to glory.

"Ah! this is the path of perfect freedom," he thought—in a transport of bliss. "I thank Thee, Lord, for helping me find it before it is too late!

"When I get home," he mumbled, "I'll write to the Bishop and ask to be released from the charge at Korskyrka. I shall withdraw from the Established Church of Sweden. A preacher I would continue to be, of course, but I shall preach no new doctrine. I can no longer be under canonical law, under bishops and consistories. I would expound the teachings of Christ in the way He, Himself, has appointed. I want to be a vagabond of the Lord, a mendicant priest, a God's fool."

Entranced, lost in these reveries, life had acquired a new meaning for him; it had again become rich and enchanting.

"My wife may remain at my house. She'll be happy there when I am out of the way. She will then call the ten children home. I need have no anxiety about her; she's well able to support herself."

Now, at last, he was free from his troubles and annoyances. His heart beat lightly, with a dancing rhythm that filled him with ineffable delight.

3

It was nearly eight o'clock in the evening when Karl Arthur stepped out of the wagon in front of his house. And when, in a moment, he opened the door of the kitchen (it was a long time since he had opened that door in so happy a frame of mind) he stopped, aghast at the scene that met his eyes.

His wife had abandoned her seat in the fireplace and was sitting at the table, over by the window, playing at cards with two strange men. And just as he came in she threw a card down on the table and cried in a loud jubilant tone, "Spades! Nobody there?"

"Oh, yes, Anna, my king is there and takes the trick," said one of her fellow players, throwing down his card.

The players caught sight of Karl Arthur, standing in the doorway with a horrified look on his face.

"These are two old comrades of my wander years," said Anna. "We're amusing ourselves in the way we used when we met at the inn, after a market day."

The men arose as Karl Arthur approached. One of them, a rubicund, bald-headed, jovial, prosperous-looking fellow in a black velvet waistcoat, buttoned up to the neck, and long-tailed coat of black duffle, he recognized as the tradesman who had the fine pink bonnet hanging outside his stall. The other man was a Dalecarlian, a good-looking chap with regular features who wore his hair in a short fringe across the forehead and long at the sides.

"This," said Anna, pointing a thumb at the merchant, "is Agust Bonander from Mark. He's one of those nabobs who stand in covered stalls at the fairs and, between times, drive around with their goods in wagons.

It's a wonder he'd look at poor Dal folk like me and Korp Matts here, who've always had to tramp the country with the goods-bag on our back."

The West Gothlander dismissed the implication with a polite gesture, as though he were rejecting a business proposition too absurd to haggle over. He had always felt honoured, he said, in associating with such an ornament to the trade as Anna Svärd.

"My wife's friends are always welcome," said Karl Arthur. "But I must tell you at once that card playing is forbidden in my home."

He had spoken gently but with great dignity. The visitors went a bit red in the face and glanced about timidly.

"Phoo!" said Anna. "You'd better not try to spoil our pleasure. Go to your room, where your supper is waiting, and leave us in peace!"

She had never addressed her husband in that tone before, and Karl Arthur was both shocked and hurt. He controlled himself, however, and said in a quiet, courteous tone:

"Wouldn't it do just as well to sit and chat? Old friends, of course, have many pleasant recollections to talk about."

"Go on with the game, Agust!" said Anna. "It's your lead. That one—he's the kind that won't let up till he's taken away from you everything you care about."

"Anna!" Karl Arthur cried in a sharp tone of rebuke.

"Well, didn't you rob me of the three-day wedding? Didn't you trick me out of the parsonage that I should have had? Didn't you take the children away from me, and the fifty riksdalers they sent me? And now you want to take away my pack of cards. Play, Agust!"

But the West Gothlander did not obey the command. Both he and the Dalecarlian sat quietly waiting for husband and wife to end their tilt. The men had not been drinking and Karl Arthur, no doubt, could have persuaded them to leave off playing had he kept his temper; but he was furious at his wife for daring to oppose him—and in the presence of company too—so he put out his hand to snatch up her cards.

At that Korp Matts, who used to go about the country shouldering a huge sack of hardware, moved his arm a trifle, as if brushing away a bothersome fly. It was a scarcely perceptible movement, but it sent Karl Arthur spinning across the floor; he would have fallen but for an arresting chair, into which he dropped. He sat panting a moment, after the surprise attack; but as he had been chopping wood a couple of hours every day for several weeks his own muscles were not exactly flabby. He was about to rush at his assailant, when a pair of hands with a firm grip pinned his arms down to his sides, then picked him up and carried him to his room. It was all done quietly and without haste; so it could hardly be termed an assault. The doors opened at a kick and he was carefully deposited upon his bed and left there without a word.

He lay grinding his teeth, in impotent rage and humiliation, but what could he do? That Dalecarlian had the strength of an ox! Unless he wished to run for the sheriff and get a posse to throw the men out of his house, there was nothing to be done.

Hour after hour he lay waiting for the men to go. Meanwhile the laughter, the chatter, and the thumping on the table when a high card was played, could be heard through the thin walls. An insane hatred of his wife took possession of him, and he made up wild plans of vengeance to be carried out when the men had gone.

At last he heard them go. When his wife had gone to her room and all was quiet, he arose and stole out into the hall, groping his way to her door. It was locked. He rapped hard once, and again. There was no response. He went back to his room for a light, and then ran out to the kitchen to look for a tool with which to prize open his wife's door.

The first thing his eyes fell upon was the pack of cards, which had been left upon the kitchen table. It struck him at once that here was his chance to destroy this enemy. "I'll attend to Anna later," he thought. "I've got her where she can't escape me."

In the drawer of the table he found a pair of scissors. He proceeded at once to destroy the cards. One by one, he cut them up in small triangular scraps—clipping methodically and well but with frenzied zeal. The whole pack of fifty-two cards gave him no little work, and he

was not through until the morning sun came peeping
at the window.

But meantime he had worked off his rage, and now he
felt cold, seedy and sleepy.

"It can go till to-morrow." He was thinking of
Anna. "But a little greeting from me she shall have, at
any rate."

He gathered up the pile of card scraps before him and,
chuckling, scattered them round the room, throwing
them out by handfuls, as a husbandman sows his seed,
taking pains to have them fall on every spot. When he
had finished, the floor looked like the ground after a
light fall of snow.

The flooring was old and rough, with wide cracks
between the boards. "The housewife will have a nice
job," he thought, "sweeping out all these sharp-edged
scraps that catch in every splinter and every crack."

CHAPTER V

THE MEETING

AT LAST the day had come when they were to meet again—these two who had been sweethearts in the old days at the Deanery. She was now a grand lady and at the same time a practical person who spread happiness wherever she appeared, and he a poor parson who was always striving to make his way on untrodden paths, and who seemed destined by the fates to bring misery and ruin upon all who loved him.

And where should they meet but in the Deanery garden, the scene not only of their love but of the deplorable quarrel which had parted them. The garden was not yet in its summer bloom. It lay on a shady site, and the spring was at least a month late there. The brown autumn leaves had not been raked away from the walks, and here and there on the turf seats lay antimacassars of dust-gray snow. And hither they were both drawn by the power of surviving memories associated with the place.

Charlotte had come to Korskyrka with Fru Forsius the day of the market fair at the churchtown. She would have liked to keep her dear foster mother at

Stora Sjötorp also through the summer, but felt it would be a pity to hinder this confirmed old house drudge from returning to the Deanery now that the mild season was approaching, with its tempting opportunities for scouring and cleaning. The old lady had told Charlotte that she longed to step into her husband's room once more, to sink down on his sofa and contemplate the piles of cap papers on his writing table, his swivel chair and pipe rack—all of which called back to mind the image of her dear departed. But Charlotte knew that it was something besides this that drew the old lady home. As her husband's successor had not been appointed, the late Dean's widow had obtained permission to remain another year at the Deanery. It was a matter of pride with her to keep up the place; to see that the flower beds were well tended, the wild grapevines properly pruned, the gravelled walks carefully raked, and the lawns evenly cut and green as they had been in her husband's time.

Charlotte had planned to stay at the Rectory for a few days, until the old lady had accustomed herself to her lonely estate. She had the pleasure of occupying her old room. She wanted to cry out to the old walls, "Look! Here I am again—I—Charlotte! You don't recognize me, of course. Look at my frock, at my shoes, and, above all, at my face. Behold a happy woman!"

She ran over to the mirror, which had hung there since her girlhood days, and scrutinized her reflection.

"All the world says that I am three times as pretty now as I used to be, and I think all the world is right."

Suddenly, she saw behind this radiant image a pale young face, lighted by a pair of sombre, burning eyes. Instantly she became very serious. "Ah!" she said, "I thought we should meet again, here. Poor little girl, how unhappy you were at that time! Oh, that love, that consuming love!"

She quickly turned away from the looking-glass; she had not come here to call up memories of that dreadful time, when her engagement to Karl Arthur was broken off. As to that, she was by no means certain that she regarded what had happened to her that summer as solely a misfortune. The rich Fru Charlotte Schager-ström knew very well that that which constituted her greatest charm was this look of unsatisfied longing, as if life had passed her by—this poetic wistfulness that made every man wonder if he were not the man to give her the unattained happiness. This characteristic was her heritage from the poor, scorned Charlotte Löwensköld.

But this wistfulness, this yearning which her face re-vealed in repose, what did it signify? Was this radiant, merry, courageous, pleasure-loving Charlotte Schager-ström then unhappy? Did she still bear love in her heart for the lover of her youth? These were questions she could not have answered herself. She was happy with her husband; but in the three years of her married life she had never felt that strong, passionate sympathy for him that she had felt for Karl Arthur Ekenstedt.

Since she had come out in the world her standards had changed. She was more critical now of things as well as persons. She no longer admired the red parsonage or the Fru Dean's prim parlour, and perhaps the poor country parson who had married a peddler woman, and who lived in a two-room cottage, was no longer a man to her taste. She had made but one attempt to see him after his return to Korskyrka, and when he did not appear, she was rather pleased. She would not have wanted the meeting to be a disappointment. And if it had not been, she would have desired it less.

Although she did not wish to meet Karl Arthur, she took a kind of motherly interest in his welfare. The Dean's wife kept her informed as to his outward circumstances: his marriage, his home life, Thea's baneful influence, and his wife's capabilities. No one was more pleased than she that he had regained the respect and affection of the parishioners, who wished he had the necessary years and qualifications to succeed the late revered Dean Forsius, as Pastor of Korskyrka.

Charlotte, who since her marriage had acquired the habit of rising late, did not appear next morning until breakfast time. The Dean's wife had already been on her feet a couple of hours. She had made a tour of the garden, had stood awhile at the gate and chatted with passers-by, gathering the latest news.

"Can you imagine it, Charlotte!" she exclaimed.

"Oh, that Karl Arthur! I can't help liking the fellow, but I must say that he's just the old Karl Arthur."

Whereupon she related what he had done. "Fancy his doing such a stupid thing as to send those children away!"

Charlotte threw up her hands. She felt now as she had often felt in the past, that it was useless to do anything for Karl Arthur. Some inexorable power was driving him on to destruction.

"Aye, isn't it unfortunate?" the Dean's wife continued. "Do you know, I would have gone to prison rather than let anyone take those children away from me!"

"I daresay he couldn't stand it," said Charlotte, remembering her visit to Karl Arthur's kitchen—the stuffy air, the clatter, the dust, the room overcrowded with work things, beds, and youngsters.

"Stand it!" the Dean's wife said with a look of contempt. "As if folks couldn't get used to worse than that! Bad as he has made things for himself, it looked as though our Lord meant to help him. I'm sure, if he had kept those children he would have ended his days as Dean of Korskyrka."

"But his wife—did she also wish to be rid of the children?"

"No, indeed! She wished above everything to keep them. I talked with Mother Per-Ers down by the gate, and she declared it was all Thea's doings."

"Thea! But you have forbidden――"

"Ah, forbidden—well, they may not have met at his home or hers; but in a little place like this they could hardly avoid meeting. Mother Per-Ers once sat in the doctor's waiting room with Thea when Karl Arthur came in, and Thea immediately began to talk to him about sending the children away."

Charlotte and the old lady looked at each other, aghast. A well laid plan was about to go to pieces.

That very morning some of the most influential men of the parish were to hold a meeting at the inn. Important matters were to be brought up. There had been talk of establishing a folk school at Korskyrka. Owing to the increase in population it was no longer possible for one man to do all the pastoral work. They proposed to install an assistant pastor, who would have an official residence and a salary. In order that this might not place too heavy a financial burden upon the parish, it was proposed that the perpetual curate should also be a person who could take charge of the school, and the one they had in mind was Karl Arthur Ekenstedt.

These matters, of course, would be decided at the vestry meeting; but as they would entail a large expenditure of money, a preliminary meeting had been called to ascertain whether those who had any suggestions to offer were willing to coöperate. .

No one had any suspicion that the whole idea had originated in Charlotte's clever brain. She had brought the matter about by very tactfully "playing up" the common people's great devotion to Karl

Arthur, without bringing herself into it. Of course everyone understood that he was too young a man to be made rector of so large a cure, but it seemed most fitting that these new posts should be created so that they might keep him among them.

It was no wonder, therefore, that the news which the Dean's wife had imparted made Charlotte almost frantic. She had nearly succeeded in providing for Karl Arthur a permanent berth, with a decent competence, and now Thea had to come and spoil it all! Thea, who loved him, should have understood that it was the wonder of seeing a poor clergyman take upon himself the care of all of those orphan children that had given him his present high standing in the community.

She glanced at the grandfather clock in the dining room and gave a sigh.

"It is now ten minutes to ten," she said, "and the meeting will soon begin."

She knew the effort it had cost her, and how she had to exercise her wits to bring about this meeting. Not the least of her difficulties had been to persuade her husband to be present, and to give his support to the plan.

"Ah, the meeting!" sighed the Dean's wife. "It wouldn't surprise me if the whole thing fell through. Persons who have been at Karl Arthur's say that his wife sits in the fireplace all day and doesn't say a word. She's jealous of Thea, you see. Such folk never seem to know how to control themselves. They are said to meet by appointment here, in my garden, but I'll soon put a stop to that!"

"Oh, that Mother Per-Ers has always been a gossip monger!" said Charlotte hotly.

At the same time she was surprised to find her hatred of Thea as strong as it was the day she cut off the woman's curls.

When they had finished breakfast Charlotte, shocked and aggrieved, threw a shawl around her and went out into the garden.

She kept her eyes to the ground, looking for tracks of the two who were said to have their love trysts here. The spot was well chosen, she thought. Karl Arthur knew of old what good hiding places there were among the hedges and the bushes.

"He was not in love with her in the old days," she remembered, "but naturally, it has now come to that. The poor Dalecarlian girl bores him to death, and he seeks consolation with Thea. As the organist is jealous, they can only meet outside."

Although it seemed to her quite natural, nevertheless she regarded it as an outrageous insult that these lovers should have chosen this place for their clandestine meetings.

"That they would dare!" she thought. "The hedges are not yet in leafage, and any passer-by could see them from the road."

She stopped and pondered over this. Through the brown tangle of hedge she saw a small summerhouse.

"There's where they've hidden!" she thought, and ran toward a building, badly ravaged by the tooth of Time —expecting to find the guilty pair inside.

The summerhouse was closed, and Charlotte, with a slight jerk at the rusty old lock, pulled the door open. Inside, she encountered all the usual discomforts of such houses in the spring: The musty smell, the broken window panes, the loosened wall paper. On the bed of dried leaves, which the autumn storms had blown in, lay something black and shiny. It was the guardian spirit of the garden—a big black snake, sleeping its winter sleep.

"Ah, no," thought Charlotte, "they have not been here! Our old snake would have sent Thea into hysterics."

Charlotte did not mind the presence of the harmless reptile. She walked right over to the broken window, opened it, and seated herself on the window sill.

From there she had a good view of the tangle of hedges, which now that their branches were swollen with sap showed the softest shades of colour, and from the greening turf peeped little patches of cowslips, daisies, and daffodils.

"This is not the first time," murmured Charlotte, "that I've sat here waiting for someone who didn't come."

The words were hardly out of her mouth when she saw a man walking among the hedges; he was coming toward the summerhouse, and would soon be near enough for her to recognize him. It was Karl Arthur.

Charlotte sat motionless. "He is not alone, of course; Thea will soon appear."

Karl Arthur suddenly stopped. He had seen Charlotte and involuntarily passed a hand across his eyes, as if it were a vision he had seen.

He stood now within a few feet of her. She noticed that he was very pale but that he still had his fine, smooth boyish complexion. He had aged a trifle, his features were sharper, but the refinement which had always distinguished the son of the Baroness Ekenstedt had not been lost. Standing there in his gray homespun clothes, he was like a modern Per Swineherd—a prince in disguise.

In a second it became clear to Karl Arthur that it was Charlotte herself who sat in the window. With outstretched arms he ran up the little incline to the summerhouse.

"Charlotte, Charlotte!" he cried. He seized her hands and covered them with kisses, the tears gushing from his eyes.

Obviously, the unexpected meeting had unnerved him; but whether it was joy or anguish she could not tell. He continued to weep violently, as if the pent-up tears of years had suddenly burst their dam. But all the while he held her hands, kissing and caressing them. She knew now that the talk of his love affair with Thea was a lie. It was not Thea who reigned in his heart, it was someone else.

Who was this other? Surely it couldn't be anyone but herself, the once spurned Charlotte, he was again in love with. No declaration of love could have conveyed it plainer than this impassioned weeping.

When this dawned upon Charlotte she felt as if a long-endured hunger had been appeased, or a lingering pain in the region of the heart had passed. She closed her eyes with a swooning sensation of happiness. But in a moment she came to her senses.

"This sort of thing will never do," she reasoned. "I'm a married woman and he's a married man; besides, he is a clergyman. I must try to quiet him.

"Come, come, Karl Arthur, you mustn't cry like that! It's only I—Charlotte. Fru Forsius wanted to come back for the summer, and I'm staying here for a few days to help her, until she can get things in running order."

She spoke in the most matter-of-fact tone, to make him stop crying; but he sobbed all the harder.

"Poor boy!" she mused. "I understand that you're not weeping only for me. You are pining for the beauties and refinements of life; for friends with whom you can exchange ideas; for your mother and your old home. But now we must be sensible and not think of things that can't be helped."

She let her eyes wander, for a moment, over the garden before she continued.

"Do you know, it is really a pleasure to be back at the dear old Rectory. Only this morning, I was thinking how delightful it was to be out here in the garden, before the tall lindens are in full leafage and prevent the sunshine from reaching the ground. It is a joy to see how greedily the herbs and the grass drink in the light."

As he still continued to weep, Charlotte went on in the same strain, thinking that it would have a soothing effect upon him.

"There's something unique in the way the sunshine gropes its way through the maze of branches to reach the ground. It is so modest and mild, and the flowers it calls forth never display any dazzling colours; they are all either white, or pale yellow, or pale blue. If they did not appear so early in the spring, and in such profusion, no one would notice them.."

Karl Arthur lifted up a tear-stained face and, with extreme effort, managed to gasp out a few words:

"I have longed—longed the whole winter——"

Naturally, he did not want to hear her talk of flowers and sunshine; he wanted her to feel the power of the storm that was raging in him.. But Charlotte, knowing there were many things that had better be left unsaid, persisted like a determined nursemaid who would lull an excited child to sleep.

"There must be an extraordinary power in the spring sun, for wherever its light falls it awakens new life. It works like magic. Cool as its rays are, they have far greater potency than those of summer, which are too scorchingly hot, or those of autumn, which bring only blight and death. Have you never observed that the pale sunshine of spring has the same effect upon one as the first love?"

At that word Karl Arthur became more interested. She quickly continued:

"I daresay you don't remember such trivial things, but I often think of an evening in spring when you first came to Korskyrka. You and I had been to visit some poor folk who lived in a little cabin back in the woods. We had stayed a bit too long, and before we reached home the sun went down and the mists gathered in the dells."

Karl Arthur suddenly looked up. The flood of tears had apparently been stemmed. He stopped kissing her hands so that he could drink in every word that fell from her pretty lips.

"Do you remember how we tramped? The way led from hill to hill. As soon as we came to the top of a hill the sun lighted our way. But down in the dells we were enveloped by mists, and the world round about us vanished."

The man who loved her let her carry him along with her on this journey among the sunlit hills.

"And what a wonderful journey it was!" Charlotte went on. "The mild, rose-coloured sun and the soft shimmering mist transformed everything around us. I saw, to my astonishment, the woods near by turn light blue, while the distant hills stood out in the clearest purple. We walked in a mystic land; we dared not speak of its beauties lest the enchantment be broken."

Charlotte paused a moment, thinking Karl Arthur would say something, but he did not wish to interrupt, so she continued:

"On the heights we walked quite slowly and sedately, but when we came down in the mist-veiled dells we danced—not you, perhaps, but only I. I danced along the road for sheer joy at the beauty of the evening. At least I thought that was why I had to dance."

Karl Arthur's face broke into a smile. Charlotte smiled back. She knew that his emotional paroxysm had passed and he was again master of himself.

"Then we wandered over another hill," she said. "You were silent. I wondered if the Herr Pastor disapproved of my dancing in the roadway. I was almost afraid to walk by your side. And then——"

"And then," Karl Arthur interrupted, "I kissed you."

Just then he saw a man standing outside the opposite window. He could not make out who he was, for he disappeared the instant Karl Arthur's eyes fell upon him. So he was not certain that he had really seen someone. In any case, he thought it best not to mention it, lest Charlotte should become uneasy. If one of the tenant farmer's folk or the gardener's man had seen them, what matter? Why dispel the moment's happiness?

"Yes," said Charlotte, "you kissed me, and then all at once I understood why the woods were so blue and why I had to dance in the mist. Ah! Karl Arthur, at that moment my whole life was changed. I seemed to be looking into my own soul, and I saw vast fields of wild flowers. Everywhere grew the light blue, light yellow and white flowers of spring. I saw millions of them spring up through the soil. I don't think I have ever seen anything so beautiful!"

She had talked herself into an emotional state. For a moment, her voice shook and her eyes filled, but she immediately regained her composure.

"My friend," she said, "do you understand now why these spring flowers remind me of my first love?"

He grasped her hand. "Oh, Charlotte——" he began. She arose.

"You see, we women never wholly forget the one who first let the sun of Love shine upon us. No, him we can never forget! There are a few among us—oh, a very, very few—who remain in the land of spring flowers. Most of us pass on to something stronger and bigger."

She gave him a nod, half roguish, half tender, and signed to him not to follow her—then disappeared.

2

When Karl Arthur awakened that morning the sun was directly opposite his window, by which token he knew that he had slept far into the morning. He got up at once. Still a bit heavy with sleep, he wondered why he had slept so late. Then he remembered that he had been up until sunrise, cutting into bits a pack of cards.

With that, all the happenings of the previous evening came back to mind; they filled him with horror and disgust, not only of his wife but of himself mostly.

Was it he who had become so enraged at his wife that he wanted to kill her? Was it really he, himself, who had done such a dastardly thing as to cut up her cards and strew them over the floor? What were these evil forces within him? Was he a monster?

He had not eaten anything the previous evening and the supper which his wife had laid for him was still untouched. He hurriedly ate the cold porridge and milk, then put on his hat and went for a long walk—glad to put off for a few hours more the necessary explanations to his wife. So he had taken the road to the Deanery, opened the gate, and gone in to the old-fashioned garden where, during the past winter, he had often sought refuge from the noise and confusion of the overcrowded cottage.

And there he had found Charlotte, more beautiful, more bewitching than ever. It was no wonder he was overcome. At first he wanted to cry out that his love for her had returned and clasp to his heart the woman for whom he had been fervently longing.

But, fortunately, his weeping had rendered him inarticulate, and Charlotte, wise, kindly woman that she was, had time to bring him to his senses. He understood quite well what she had wished to convey by calling up those pictures of the days of their first love. She wanted him to know that she loved the memory of those days but that her heart now belonged to another.

For some moments after Charlotte had gone, darkness and desolation reigned in his soul; but there was none of the impotent hatred of slighted love. He knew only too well it was his own fault that he had lost her.

It was not long, however, before a faint ray of light penetrated the darkness. Yesterday's thoughts, the blissful visions of the future, which had been driven away by the discord at home, now came back—vivid and irresistible. More glorious than any earthly love was the alluring prospect of serving his Saviour as an apostle of the open road; a bird on the wing that comes bringing the living word to the languishing; a mendicant of God who, in his poverty, distributes treasures which neither rust nor moth can corrupt.

He walked slowly back to the churchtown—thinking: First he would make his peace with his wife. What would happen afterward he did not know, to be sure, but he was blissfully untroubled. God had taken him under His wing, so that he had no need to worry.

When he came to the first little house in the churchtown, the one from which Anna Svärd had come the first time he met her, the owner of the place hailed him. She was a Dalecarlian by birth, and it was with her Anna had lodged when she peddled her wares in this region.

"Now, parson, you mustn't be angry at me," she said, "for coming to you with bad news; but Anna bade me tell you she was going away."

Karl Arthur stared at the woman—uncomprehending.

"Aye," she continued, "she's gone home to Med-stuby. I says to her, 'Sure you're not thinking of going home now, are you? You've only a few weeks till you'll be lying in childbirth.'

"'I have to go,' says she, and she was most partic'lar for me to tell you where she was going. 'He needn't think I'm making away with myself,' says she, 'I'm only going home.'"

Karl Arthur caught hold of the gatepost to steady himself. Although he no longer loved his wife, they had lived together so long that it seemed as if a part of himself had been torn away. And besides, it was most unfortunate. Now all the world would know that his wife had been unhappy and that she had left him of her own accord.

But in the midst of this fresh torment came the comforting thought of the new freedom. Wife, home, the respect of the community—all these meant nothing to him on the path he had chosen to tread. His heart beat lightly despite all that had happened. God had freed him from the cares and responsibilities that beset common mortals.

When a few minutes later he got back to his home and stepped into his room, he was surprised to find everything in order. His bed had been made and the tray removed. He ran out to the kitchen—there, too, everything was in perfect order.

A woman was down on her knees picking up the tiny

scraps of cards which had not yielded to the broom. She hummed and sang as she detached the stubborn scraps from the splinters and cracks in the rough floor. She looked up as he came in and he saw that it was Thea.

"Ah, Karl Arthur, I hurried over as soon as I heard your wife had left you. I thought I might be of help. I hope you don't mind my coming?"

"Not at all. On the contrary, I think it very kind of you. But don't bother about those wretched card scraps! They can just as well lie where they are."

But Thea went right on with her self-appointed task.

"I'm collecting them as a memento. When I came in, about an hour ago, I saw that she—you know who I mean—had taken a few strokes with the broom to sweep them up, but when she found that they stuck, she threw down the broom and went her way."

Thea laughed and hummed. Karl Arthur regarded her now almost with aversion.

She held up to him a bowl in which she had gathered quite a mound of these tiny bits of paper. "She's gone," said she, "and these were what drove her away; so why shouldn't I gather them up and keep them?"

"Thea, are you mad?"

There was a note of scorn in his voice and almost hatred. Thea, glancing up, saw him frown, but she only laughed.

"Oh, that might frighten the others, but not me. Beat me, kick me, still I'll come back. You will never be rid of me. That which frightens the others is the thing that holds me."

She began to sing again, first low, then louder, higher, until her voice rang out like a march of triumph.

Karl Arthur, to whom this hysterical outburst was a positive torture, fled to his room. As soon as he was alone the happy sense of freedom returned. He began at once his letter of resignation to the Bishop.

CHAPTER VI

THE ACCIDENT

SCHAGERSTRÖM had left home at an early hour to attend the meeting at the inn. The meeting began promptly at ten and lasted an unusually short time. By eleven o'clock he was on his way to the Deanery for a little visit with Fru Forsius and Charlotte. He missed his wife dreadfully. Although she had been away from him only a day, he wondered if he couldn't persuade her to return with him now.

"I really ought to go back at once and attend to my saw, which is out of order. But perhaps that would be too abrupt a departure. I might stay till afternoon—say, about five or six o'clock—then, surely, she could come home with me without any qualms of conscience."

He was received by the Dean's wife, who immediately began to question him about the conference. Of course, she had expected that nothing would come of it, for she had heard that Karl Arthur had sent the children away, which was awfully stupid of him.

Schagerström hastened to assure her that that had played no part. In fact, they had been ready to grant appropriations for both the school and the curate's house, when mine-owner Aaron Månsson arose and questioned whether it was worth while for the parish to assume these heavy responsibilities in order to retain a preacher whose conduct was such that his wife had been compelled to leave him.

"What!" exclaimed the old lady. "That excellent wife—has she gone? Then who will keep him in check?"

As a matter of fact, all who were present at the meeting had asked themselves the same question. They had all counted upon her. It looked as if it were she, and not the husband, who was to be chosen to fill the posts of schoolmaster and curate. For as soon as they heard that she was out of it, the whole project was postponed indefinitely.

Fru Forsius, who was both provoked and sorry about the outcome, let drop an indiscreet remark.

"It's useless to try to help Karl Arthur, as I have always told Charlotte."

His countenance fell instantly. He never liked to hear that his wife interested herself in her former fiancé. Fru Forsius, seeing that she had been indiscreet, tried to divert his mind by telling him that Charlotte had gone out into the garden.

Nor did she have to tell him twice. He betook himself at once into the labyrinth of hedges, in quest of his wife. Hearing her voice in the old summerhouse, he looked in through one of the windows and saw her sitting in the opposite window in earnest conversation with young

Ekenstedt. Without stopping to catch a word they said, he went back to the house and stood on the front porch to await her.

What he had seen had reduced him to that state of insensibility where one does not seem to be thinking one's self, but the thoughts come from without. Someone —he knew not who—reminded him of a conversation he had once heard. They had been speaking of Fru Dr. Romelius and had marvelled that she continued to love her husband, though he had become such a sot. "Oh, don't wonder at that," came the retort, "she is a Löwensköld, and the Löwenskölds never abandon their first love."

He did not remember where he had heard the remark or who had made it; he thought it must have been long before he knew Charlotte. But the words had come up from somewhere to frighten him out of his senses.

After a while he realized that he was standing there holding his head with both hands, as if to keep consciousness and reason from flying away. He dropped his hands at once and pulled himself together.

"I must appear quite composed when Charlotte comes; she may be here at any moment."

Presently, he saw her coming. She walked with lagging footsteps; her brows were knotted as if she were trying to solve a difficult and involved problem. But the instant she caught sight of her husband her countenance cleared.

"Oh, are you here already?" she cried, fairly beaming. She ran up to him, threw her arms about his neck and kissed him. He could hardly have wished for a more affectionate greeting.

"How well she does it," he thought. "It is no wonder that I have let myself be fooled into thinking that she really cares for me!"

He expected that Charlotte would tell him, in her usual straightforward way, that she had seen young Ekenstedt; but she never mentioned it. Nor did she ask him about the outcome of the meeting. She seemed to have forgotten the whole affair.

From her silence, Schagerström naturally drew his own conclusions. The feeling that she had deceived him became stronger and stronger. His only thought was to get away as quickly as possible so that he might quietly ponder the meaning of his discovery. He abandoned all thought of asking her to go home with him.

That which helped him to come away without betraying his suspicions was the old saw at Stora Sjötorp. He hastened to tell his wife that the saw had stopped the previous day, shortly after she and Fru Forsius had left. The foreman, the superintendent and the inspectors had all tried in vain to find the cause. They had turned to him, and he, too, had been puzzled.

Charlotte knew that her husband prided himself on being a good mechanical engineer and that nothing gave him greater pleasure than to prove his skill in that line; so she took it as a matter of course.

"I know those old saws," she said; "sometimes they

take a notion to rest for a few days, and all at once they start up again of their own accord."

While they stood talking the Dean's wife came out, made a grand reverence, and asked if she might have the honour of Ironmaster Schagerström's company at dinner. But Schagerström excused himself on the plea of the saw. He explained to the Fru Dean that it was no ordinary saw. Its mechanism was unique and intricate. Old workmen at Stora Sjötorp maintained that it had been built a hundred years ago, by the great inventor Polhem. And he could well believe it. For one had to be a mechanical genius to put together a thing so intricate. The previous day he had really despaired of putting it to rights, but on the way here he had got an idea. He believed he knew now what was wrong and must go home at once, of course.

Since he seemed to have no thought for anything but the mysterious old saw and its strange mechanism, Fru Forsius and his wife both concluded it was best to let him go.

But he was no sooner seated in the carriage than his mind began to work at the hopeless task of trying to explain away, or, rather, put out of his mind what he had seen through the summerhouse window. But, unfortunately, the eyes have an uncanny faculty for catching certain scenes sharply and imprinting them indelibly upon the mind.

He had to admit that Charlotte and Karl Arthur had not kissed, or even exchanged a caress. He might have thought they were merely engaged in an ordinary conversation, had he not seen the young clergyman's tearstained face and the look of adoration with which he regarded Charlotte, to say nothing of the tender sympathy in her gaze as she looked at him.

In addition, there was that remark of Fru Forsius, from which he gathered that his wife was always trying to help Karl Arthur. And then her own reticence—was not that proof enough?

He tried to reason with himself that Charlotte and he were very happy together, that she had never shown by so much as a glance that she longed for another; but all that was swept aside as he remembered how she and Karl Arthur looked at each other that morning.

"She may have thought the old love was dead, but when she saw him again it flamed anew."

And so, little by little, he succeeded in persuading himself that Charlotte's heart belonged to Karl Arthur. Then he began to consider what steps and measures he must take.

Charlotte could never be tempted to be untrue, which was a good thing to know. But was that enough? Would any real man be satisfied to have his wife go about sighing for another? No! A thousand times rather divorce!

But the mere thought of it darkened his entire world. What, live apart from Charlotte? Never again to hear her merry laughter or her sallies of wit or see her lovely face? He shivered from head to foot as if he were wading through icy waters.

When he arrived at Stora Sjötorp, without stopping to eat his dinner, he called the superintendent and asked him to go down to the mill with him.

"An idea came to me on the way," he said. "I think I know now where the fault lies."

They went into the big engine room, where the ingenious master builder had thrown together, as if in sheer deviltry, an indescribable jumble of wheels, pistons, and levers. Schagerström got a firm grip on a lever and gave it a jerk.

Evidently, he had not expected an immediate effect, or perhaps his thoughts were elsewhere; before there was time to step back, the powerful machine had started going, and he was carried along with it, toward the saw.

2

When Schagerström regained consciousness he felt himself being shaken to and fro in a way that was unbearably torturesome. He noticed that he was being carried on a stretcher, and although the bearers moved very slowly and carefully, this shaking at every step caused him such excruciating agony that he moaned.

One of the bearers, seeing that he had come to, signed to the others to stop.

"Does it hurt so very much, Ironmaster?" he said, as if speaking to a little child. "Shall we stop where we are?"

"We'll soon be there now," said another reassuringly.

"It'll be better, Ironmaster, when you can rest in your own bed."

With that they went on, and the terrible pains set in again.

"It was a lucky escape," said one of the men. "I thought sure he'd be cloven like a timber-log."

"Aye, 'twas a narrow escape," said another, "but the ironmaster still has his arms and legs."

"It may be that some of the ribs are broken," a third remarked, "and you can't wonder at that."

Schagerström knew that the men were trying to comfort him, and he was deeply touched and grateful for their kindness. He tried to be brave and not complain; but at the same time, he felt a bit displeased because no one had said a word about his remarkable achievement in setting the saw going. He wanted to be commended for that.

The men had borne him but a few steps farther, when he became utterly exhausted. If this jolting continued he would surely die, he thought. Had he only been able to speak he would have ordered them to stop. And now he felt one part of his body after the other becoming insensitive, as if dying away. It moved quickly, from his feet upward toward the head. . . .

When he came to again he smelt a faint odour of old rose leaves, from which he inferred that he was in the guest chamber. "They must have brought me in here to avoid the stairs," he thought. His own room was one flight up.

Someone was tugging at his boots, but he moaned so pitifully that the person had to leave off.

"We'll have to let it go until the doctor comes." Schagerström recognized the superintendent's voice.

"Yes," said another voice, which he thought must be the groom's, but it sounded so choked that he was not quite sure. "The ankle is badly sprained, I fear."

Schagerström opened his eyes to let them see that he was conscious. He lay on the broad guest-room sofa. The housekeeper and two maids were preparing the bed while the superintendent and the groom were trying to undress him.

He begged them to leave him in peace, but the sounds that issued from his throat had no semblance to the human voice; they were more like the wheezing gasps of an animal that has received a death shot. But, at all events, he made himself understood.

The men let him lie in his clothes and the women stopped fussing with the bed. The housekeeper brought a quilt to spread over him, but he couldn't bear the weight. Then she wanted to slide a cushion under his head; he wouldn't have that, either.

Meantime, it vexed him to think that the superintendent, who knew what an intricate contrivance the old Polhem machine was, did not utter a word in his praise. The saw might have stood idle goodness knows how long but for him!

He blinked his eyes at the superintendent, who came closer so that he could hear what was wanted. Schagerström whispered a request that the kind men who had carried him home be rewarded for their trouble. The superintendent, understanding, nodded his head, then asked whether there was anything else the iron-master wished.

Yes, there was something else, but he would prefer not to speak of it himself. He knew that the others would think him very childish, but the words burned on his tongue and had to come out.

"At any rate, I got the saw running."

"Yes, by God, you certainly did!"

Schagerström thought it provoking that the man should break down just then and begin to blubber. He had expected a more fulsome acknowledgment of his achievement.

He found it extremely unpleasant to hear sobbing and wailing around him and hissed out that he wished to be alone. Whereupon the housekeeper and the maidservants, as well as the superintendent, withdrew from the room, and only the groom remained in attendance.

Schagerström felt better for the quiet. He seemed to be more composed now and less irritable and captious.

"I'm not a helpless child," he said to himself. "When I command people obey. If I can lie still, perfectly still, I suffer no pain."

It was clear to his mind that he was dying, and the thought of it was not at all unpleasant. He only hoped that death would come creeping on like this, imper-

ceptibly, and that he could meet it quietly, without anyone's making a special affair of its advent.

He began to blink rapidly at Johansson. It had just
occurred to him what a lucky thing it was that his wife
was away from home. She would never let him die like
this, in his clothes, and lying on a sofa. He whispered a
command to Johansson that no one was to call her
ladyship. "She must not be alarmed," he said. They
were to send for the doctor and the jurist, but under no
circumstances must they tell her ladyship.

Johansson looked distressed, but Schagerström was
well pleased. His face did not betray it, but he was smiling inwardly. Didn't it sound well that her ladyship
was not to be alarmed? He was proud of having hit upon
that as an excuse. Think, if he should succeed in fooling
Charlotte! If he should die before she knew of it!

He heard the noise as the men drove off to fetch the
doctor and the jurist and glanced at the wall clock.
It was then half-past three, and, praise the Lord! it was
a good fourteen miles to the churchtown. Lundman, of
course, would drive like mad; but, anyhow, it would be
four hours before the doctor arrived. Quiet, unbroken
quiet, until half-past seven!

A boyish freak came over him. It seemed to him as if
he were up to some kind of deviltry, in dying by
stealth, so to speak—without medical attention. He
gloried in it. Ha! it would soon be over with rich
Schagerström. For the short time left to him he was
going to be his own master.

Charlotte would be displeased, of course, and angry, but it didn't matter. He had a good idea—he would leave her all his property as a recompense for her not being allowed to fuss over him while he lay at the point of death.

He thought it very strange that he did not think of any great or solemn thing when he had only a few hours to live. But his sole desire now was to escape pain and questioning and lamentation and every other unpleasantness and have peace. He was like a boy who expected a thrashing from the schoolmaster and who wished he could sneak away into a big black forest to hide.

He remembered what had happened in the morning, but it had ceased to trouble him. Such states of mental anguish seemed now ridiculously unimportant. It was not because Charlotte looked tenderly at Karl Arthur that he did not wish to see her, but because she was the only person who would pay no heed to his protests. He could control the superintendent, the housekeeper, and the groom, but not Charlotte. The doctor, too, he felt sure would listen to reason, but Charlotte— never! She would show neither mercy nor respect.

It was a little before half-past seven when he heard the sound of wheels. How quickly the time had passed, he thought—sorry that the doctor had come so soon. He had hoped he would be busy elsewhere, and couldn't come before nine or thereabout. Lundman must have driven like the wind, to bring aid to him. It was impossible to make anyone understand that he wished to be left alone.

Johansson slipped out of the room to receive the doctor. Now there'd be a pother! The doctor would feel, and squeeze, and pull his joints into place. He could see from where he lay that the foot was twisted, the toes pointed toward the sofa and the heel in the air. But what did it matter to a dying man? He hoped the doctor would not set it while he was still alive.

Dr. Romelius came into the room with a firm tread and a good bearing. Schagerström, expecting to see him drunk, as usual, was a trifle disappointed.

"Oy, oy! If he is sober he may think it his duty to do something." Anyhow, he would try to persuade the physician to leave him in peace. "You see, Brother-in-law, there's nothing to be done here. In a couple of hours it will all be over, in any case."

The doctor was bending over him. Schagerström saw the bloodshot, expressionless eyes and smelled the strong alcoholic breath. "He is probably just as full as ever, but he thinks the solemnity of the occasion demands that he keep up. He won't be troublesome."

"Yes, dear Brother Schagerström, it certainly looks as if you are right," said the doctor. "There isn't much that I can do here."

Romelius was not so stupefied with drink but that he could preserve an air of professional authority and make a feint at diagnosis. He felt of the patient's pulse, sent the servant after ice water and bandages so that he could lay a cold compress on Schagerström's fore-head, passed his hand very carefully along the wrenched ankle, and shrugged his shoulders.

"So my dear brother-in-law wants to rest in peace. Hm—yes—that's the best thing for you. But wouldn't you like to rest in bed?—No?—It's just as well as it is."

The doctor dropped into a chair, and sat there a moment, thinking; then he got up, went over to the patient, and gravely announced that he would remain all night so as to be on hand in case his dear brother-in-law should change his mind.

He sat down again and tried to think whether there was anything further required of him. Nor was it long before he was again at the patient's side.

"I have always made it a rule, Brother Schagerström, when it comes to a question of amputation never to operate without the consent of the patient. Are you quite sure, Brother Schagerström, that you do not wish surgical treatment?"

"Yes, yes, yes!" said Schagerström. "You can rest easy on that score, Brother."

The poor doctor went back to his chair with the same measured dignity and sat down once more.

Schagerström gave Johansson a look, which he understood, of course. The doctor, with polite compulsion, was led out of the room. When the servant came back he told Schagerström he had shown Dr. Romelius into the office, where he now sat dozing in a sofa corner.

Johansson was more dejected than ever. He had expected the doctor to perform wonders and was dreadfully disappointed. Schagerström, though glad to have peace and quiet in the room, felt almost sorry for the fellow.

"Now, wouldn't that good man be happy," he thought, "if I were to let that boozer operate on me!"

Fru Sällberg the housekeeper came in very softly and whispered something to Johansson, who went over to the master and said:

"Fru Sällberg wonders what she shall tell the people. They've been standing outside the whole afternoon and won't go till they know what the doctor thinks."

Schagerström understood that all these employees, who were dependent on him for their livelihood, felt deeply concerned lest he should pass away. They, too, would like nothing better than to have him put on the rack.

"Tell Fru Sällberg," he said, "to ask the doctor, himself."

All this disturbance had a bad effect on the injured man. He was suffering acute pain. The blood surged and pounded unmercifully—now here, now there—his respiration became increasingly difficult, and his head felt as if it were on fire.

"The end is near," he thought.

Again he heard the crunching noise of wheels and guessed that the jurist and his scrivener had arrived.

Shortly afterwards, the two gentlemen were ushered in. Paper, pen, and ink were now placed upon the table, and Schagerström began to dictate his will.

The jurist stood bending over him to catch the slowly whispered words, which he repeated to his scrivener. The wife, of course, was to be the principal heir, but there were a lot of workmen in the various foundries and many poor folk—widows and fatherless children—who were to be remembered.

It was a terrible strain upon the injured man. He could feel the sweat running down his cheeks and clenched his teeth so as not to give way to pain or weakness.

"Couldn't we leave it to Fru Schagerström to make the proper donations?" suggested the man of the law, who saw how his client was suffering.

Why, to be sure. But there was also another matter—his parents, his brothers and sisters—they should have some assurance that he remembered them in his last hour.

He strove in vain to make himself understood and had to stop lest he should lose consciousness again.

The jurists proceeded to draw up the will in legal form, after which it was to be read to him and he was to declare before they called in witnesses, that this was his last will and testament. How would he ever be able to go through with it!

Meantime, darkness had fallen, and lights had been brought. But to him the room seemed dark and the lights gave out no illumination. He lay in the shadow of death, he thought.

Now he must make a final effort, then all his duties would be fulfilled and he could die content. Anyhow, the worst had not happened—Charlotte had not come!

But, hark! What was that? The rumble of wheels now, again? Someone drove up to the house.

The front door was pushed open with a haste that only one person allowed herself. A thrill of life and hope swept through the whole house. A clear, commanding voice was heard to question the servants out in the hall. Johansson the groom raised his head, his face lighting up as he hurried to the door, which the housekeeper had opened a little to announce what the whole house already knew. "The Mistress has come!"

No; he must not give in. Now the hardest battle was about to begin.

When Charlotte came into the room her first thought should have been to go over to him—Schagerström—and ask how he felt; but she turned, instead, to the jurist and firmly but politely requested him and his clerk to leave the room.

"My husband has been lying here for hours with no attention whatever. He must be undressed as quickly as possible. The Herr Jurist no doubt sees that this is the most urgent need just now."

The man of the law then told Charlotte, in a low voice, that Dr. Romelius had said nothing could be done for the patient.

Charlotte controlled her feelings, but Schagerström knew that she was furiously angry and hoped the jurist would be on his guard.

"Must I repeat my request that you permit me to take charge of my husband?"

"But, Fru Schagerström," he protested, "the iron-master, himself, has ordered me to draw up this testament." Then he added in whispers: "Fru Schagerström will not suffer by the terms of this will."

R-rasch—— Charlotte had torn up the will.

"But, Fru Schagerström, this is——"

"If the will was for my benefit," she cut in, "then it needn't have been written. I should not have accepted a shilling."

"Well, in that case there is no more to be said."

Schagerström knew that the lawyer was highly offended, and thought it a good thing that this wealth was not going to her. He bowed himself out of the room, leaving her to her fate.

Nor did Charlotte come over to Schagerström's sofa now, either, but ordered Johansson to fetch the doctor at once.

While he was gone she talked with the housekeeper, who told her how distressed they had all been because her ladyship was not to be called home.

"It was my sister, Fru Romelius, who let me know," she said. "I came in the Dean's old cariole, behind one of his Norway ponies."

Schagerström, meanwhile, lay silent and motionless.

He did not like to admit that his pain had decreased since Charlotte had come. No; it was just as acute as ever, only he thought less about it. When Charlotte was in the room one could not think of anything but what she was doing.

The doctor came in. The moment he crossed the threshold she shouted at him:

"How dare you sit down to sleep when my husband is dying!"

"Dare——" Schagerström could have laughed. That was what she said to him the first time he proposed to her. He could not see her from where he lay but he could very well picture the look on her face.

The doctor answered her with the quiet dignity which he had maintained from the first.

"My good sister-in-law, it is contrary to my principles to perform an operation on a patient against his will."

"In the first place, will you help us to get him undressed?"

But Romelius was unwilling. "Brother Schagerström and I have already discussed this matter. He does not wish to be disturbed, and, in my judgment, he is right, my dear sister-in-law."

Schagerström waited in the greatest suspense. What would Charlotte do next? Would she give the doctor a box on the ear, or would she throw him into a tub of cold water?

"Johansson," she said, "fetch a bottle of champagne and two glasses!"

While the servant was gone on this errand, Charlotte said nothing more to the doctor, but Schagerström heard her whisper to the housekeeper.

Johansson came back. The pop of a champagne cork was heard, the effervescent liquid was being poured out into the glasses. "Fru Sällberg, have Johansson help you get everything ready, as we decided."

"Now, Brother-in-law," she said when the two servitors had left the room, "I propose that we drink a health to Ironmaster Gustaf Henrik Schagerström. I assure you, he is a veritable Polhem. He has not only succeeded in setting the old saw going again, but he has even managed to get into it himself. And of course no one thinks it was anything but an accident.—A *skål*, Brother-in-law, to Gustaf Henrik!"

Schagerström let her remarks pass without showing the least sign of life. "She doesn't believe that herself; she only wants to frighten that ass of a doctor."

He heard the doctor gulp his drink and set the glass down. Then, clearing his throat, he said in a voice that was neither thick nor toneless:

"What is my gracious sister-in-law telling me? But whatever made him do it?"

Schagerström heard again the slight effervescent sound and knew that Charlotte was refilling the doctor's glass.

"With your permission, Brother-in-law, we will now drink to me. This morning I chanced to meet my old fiancé in the garden at the Deanery, and I heard him declare that he loved me now as ardently as I once loved him. And I liked to hear it, which was perhaps not very nice of one who is now living happily with another man. But what say you, Brother-in-law? Wasn't it humanly natural in one who has been scorned and jilted? Let us suppose, Brother-in-law, that Henrik was passing through the garden and saw Karl Arthur and me together. Now wouldn't you think he'd stop to find out what I was saying to my old sweetheart before rushing home to throw himself into the sawmill?"

"Gad! I should say so," said the doctor. "Oh, I'll get after him, the villain! And he thought he would escape my knife. . . . *Skål*, Charlotte!"

Schagerström lay panting with suspense. Would Charlotte win?

The doctor's glass was refilled a third time, and then Charlotte made another little speech.

"We will drink now to Dr. Richard Romelius. Two-and-a-half years ago the doctor's wife lay sick unto death, his home was broken, and his children ran about like wild colts. Now, all that is changed, but to-day the doctor refuses——"

He set his glass down hard upon the table and his voice rang out:

"To-day, Richard Romelius will save the life of the man who restored his wife and home and is helping his children. No, thanks, no more champagne, Sister-in-law. By God, I'll save that man with or against his will!"

The doctor quickly arose and went out of the room to fetch his satchel. Schagerström knew that Charlotte and the champagne had conquered. He must undergo an operation no matter how hard he fought against it.

And now Charlotte came over to the sofa. She stood just back of the arm rest bending over him. He closed his eyes.

"Henrik," she said, "do you understand what I say?"

A little twitch of the eyelid was his only response.

"I must tell you that Organist Sundler came to the Deanery this afternoon and complained that his wife was leaving him. Karl Arthur, you see, has decided not to continue as a priest of the Established Church or to preach from any pulpit. He means to follow Christ's command and go forth as one of His apostles—without scrip or staff. He would preach on the highway and at market fairs; at hostels and posting stations, and Thea intends to forsake her husband to follow him. My poor dear husband, do you understand now that Karl Arthur, in resorting to such extremes, must have received an answer from one whom he loves that has driven him to desperation?"

Schagerström never moved. No, these were not the right words. Charlotte gave a little sigh of impatience.

"Oh, but you're stupid! Must I tell you that it's you I love—you, you, you, and no one else?"

Schagerström opened his eyes. He met his wife's tender, anxious, tear-dimmed gaze, and all the irritability and childish faint-heartedness which had possessed him since the accident, vanished. The will to live returned. He did not want to die. No, indeed, he was not afraid of pain. He would like nothing better than to put himself under treatment and be saved.

CHAPTER VII

MAMSELLE JACQUETTE

MAMSELLE JACQUETTE EKENSTEDT sat by the corner window of the cabinet, reading aloud to her mother from the letters her brother had written during his college days.

She read distinctly and carefully, emphasizing strongly such expressions as "My adorable mother," "My loving parents," "My filial respect and gratitude"; but most of all she stressed the passages in which Karl Arthur expressed his admiration for the mother's talents —especially for her gift as a verse writer. Such passages she usually read twice, for they always brought a pretty pink flush to the mother's pale cheeks.

Mamselle Jacquette showed no signs of impatience or weariness; but sometimes she would raise her eyes from a letter and recite long passages, for she knew them all by heart.

She sat looking out at the Klar River, flowing on— broad and majestic—past the cabinet window, and watching the constant stream of people coming and going across the western bridge. Market farmers from Grava and Storakil, having disposed of their garden truck, were driving home. Schoolboys were rushing to their lodgings during the morning recess, their books dangling from a strap slung across the shoulder. Now and then an elegant carriage, with prancing horses and liveried coachman, came rolling into the capital of the province.

That day Mamselle Jacquette was in a melancholy mood. She saw her life ebbing away in a changeless tide, without having known any of the joys or sorrows of really living beings. Such thoughts did not trouble her every day, but at times she could not help despairing at the tameness and emptiness of her existence.

The Baroness was intent upon her knitting and did not observe that her daughter was watching the moving stream of humanity on the bridge. All went well as long as Mamselle Jacquette did not lose the thread. But, all at once, she happened to be reading from another letter than the one she held in her hand. She had skipped from the autumn semester to the spring term, and as the letters were all very much alike she went on reading with the same clear enunciation and careful emphasis until the Baroness suddenly burst into tears and declared she would read them herself. Jacquette had again skipped some seven or eight letters. She did not want to read them, the Baroness said, which was not surprising, considering that she had never had any special love for her brother. For that matter, neither had her daughter Eve, nor her husband, nor even his own father.

The Baroness wept bitterly over the family's lack of love. Jacquette did not bother to defend herself or the others. She rang for the chambermaid and ordered her to bring in some fresh biscuits and preserve, which pleased the Baroness, and she forgot her grievance.

But she had no sooner put down her spoon than she begged Jacquette to do her the favour of reading a little from Karl Arthur's letters. They were so beautiful, she said, and it was such a long time since anyone had read them to her.

Mamselle Jacquette then took up the bundle of letters again and read from them carefully and with expression, while the Baroness sat listening, as she had listened every day for nearly three years to the reading of the same letters.

She was faultlessly attired, her hair was nicely dressed, and on her small feet she wore, as usual, dainty shoes of gold brocade. But she was a sallow, shrunken, and feeble old lady. There was scarcely a trace left of the beauty and charm that had once animated her features, and the sparkle in her lovely eyes was gone. She was like a faded rose: the last petals still clung, but the least puff of wind would make them fall.

Mamselle Jacquette was not a very satisfactory reader that morning. The Baroness had just become interested in a citation from a lecture by Atterbom and was trying to grasp the philosophy of romanticism when she noticed that her daughter stammered and stumbled over the words as if her thoughts were on something else.

She was distressed and begged to be allowed to read herself, since her daughter showed no interest in her brother's studies, but would rather gaze at the young fellows loafing on the bridge.

True, her eyes were fixed on the bridge, but she was not looking at any young men. What attracted her attention was a tall, handsome Dalecarlian peasant woman with a black leather bag on her back, who stood leaning over the railing and looking down at the water.

"No, it can't be she," thought Jacquette, "and yet the dress is the same. Oh, why does she stand there, hanging over the river!"

Despite the mother's complaining of her wretched reading, she had to cast a glance, now and then, at the woman who stood gazing at the Klar River. The big river, which now, after the spring thaw was at its best, was a magnificent sight as it went rolling on under the arches of the bridge. But who had ever seen a poor peddler woman take time to watch the lively play of the waves?

"I don't like the looks of this," Mamselle Jacquette remarked to herself. "Someone ought to speak to her and find out why she's standing there."

She was about to ask her mother if she might stop reading now and go for a stroll; but when she looked out again the woman was gone.

Almost against her will she scanned the surface of the water to see whether anything red and green was swirling about in the white foam. Happily, nothing of the kind appeared, and to the Baroness's great delight her reading for some moments was faultless.

But alas! The stuttering and stammering suddenly began again. Jacquette was utterly unbearable that day, thought the Baroness. Her mind had been distracted by the sound of voices coming from the Colonel's office, which was directly below the Baroness's cabinet. She could hear plainly her father's thundering bass, but could not tell whether it was surprise or anger that made it sound so much deeper than usual. She also distinguished a woman's voice, that rose and fell in strange accents.

To the amazement of the Baroness, Jacquette suddenly stopped reading without offering any apology or explanation. She simply rang for the maid and bade her stay with the mother awhile, then left the room.

A moment later she stepped into the Colonel's office. She found him talking to his daughter-in-law, the former peddler woman, a person whose name had never been spoken in the Ekenstedt house since the unhappy day of the funeral, when Karl Arthur had publicly announced his engagement to the woman.

The Colonel sat with his back half turned to his son's wife. Obviously, the visit was not welcome. Anna Svärd stood just behind his chair. She had removed the bag from her shoulders and was undoing the knots and straps. Apparently neither of them was disturbed by Jacquette's coming in, for they went right on talking.

"At first I intended to go straight home to Medstuby," said Anna Svärd. "But I didn't want to come home to Mother without a shilling in my pocket; so I took the roundabout way and came to Karlstad to see if Merchant Hoving would let me have some goods on credit—just what I could carry in this bag. I thought he might do it for old friendship's sake, but he was unwilling."

Mamselle Jacquette, whose mind was full of what she had seen from the cabinet window and also of the contents of a letter which she had received that morning from Fru Forsius, regarded her sister-in-law with the greatest curiosity. She saw at a glance that Anna was big with child, but, large, fine-looking woman that she was, her condition was not noticeably disfiguring. The face was as beautiful as ever, but the eyebrows were drawn together so that they formed an unbroken black line and the deep blue eyes under them flashed defiantly; they looked positively wicked.

The Colonel did not answer his daughter-in-law but addressed himself to Jacquette.

"Your sister-in-law," he said drily, "has come to inform us that she has tired of living with your brother and wants to take up her old occupation."

Anna Svärd had finished unstrapping her bag, which contained nothing but straw, and thrust it under the Colonel's nose.

"Do you see now that I've nothing in it? I hated to go round with an empty bag, so I put in a sheaf of straw."

The Colonel drew back his head and pushed the bag away. Anna then appealed to Jacquette.

"You were kind to me once, Jacquette. Put in a good word for me with your father. I want him to lend me two hundred riksdalers. I'll pay him back next year come Michaelmas."

Mamselle Jacquette, who had just been lamenting the tameness and futility of her life, was quite embarrassed on being asked to intercede in behalf of her sister-in-law and could not say a word. The Colonel, however, spoke up.

"She'd better not!" he roared. "We know very well who sent you here. He did not dare to come himself, and so we have the pleasure of a visit from you."

"But, Father dear——"

"Nothing of the kind!" said Anna Svärd, indignant at the Colonel's accusation. "You couldn't put up with him as a son, so you must know that another might be sick and tired of having him for a husband."

"Father dear, I had a letter from Fru Forsius to-day, and it is quite true that Anna and Karl Arthur have parted."

"Well, it's not surprising," said the Colonel, "but that doesn't make it any the pleasanter to have your daughter-in-law going about with a peddler's pack."

"Oh, I understand, of course, that you think it degrading," said Anna. "But if you don't care to help me in that way, then think of a better way. Now, if you were to give me three thousand riksdalers so that I could buy a small farm, where I'd have a horse and a cow and wouldn't have to run about the country but could stay at home with my child, you may be sure that I'd have no objections."

Having offered the Colonel this suggestion, she stood silent a moment, waiting for his answer. As none seemed forthcoming, she added:

"You couldn't think of doing that either?"

"No!" said the Colonel positively.

"Oh, well, if you won't," said the daughter-in-law, "there are others who'll lend me the money to start me in trade again. I know Agust Bonander is in town, and, although I've never wanted to have any business dealings with him, for he's a regular sharper, I'll go to him now."

She waited once more for an answer. Receiving none, she bent down and began to strap her bag. Her fingers worked with desperate haste, but there were so many buckles and clasps that Jacquette, if she wished to say or do anything to soften her father's heart, had time.

Ah, yes, Mamselle Jacquette was willing, but she had not the least idea as to how she should go about it. There was so much that stood in the way!

The Colonel was not like his wife, broken and prematurely old. He was still hale and strong, but there were deep lines graven on his forehead, and his eyes burned with a steady glow, as if fed by an unquenchable inner fire. Mamselle Jacquette often felt more sorry for her father than for her mother. Memory is a precious gift, but perhaps it were better to lose it than to let it nurse an undying hate.

There was just one key that would open the door to her father's heart. She knew what that key was, but how should she apply it?

She hurriedly left the room, as if she had grown tired of the whole thing and was leaving them both to their fate. But when Anna stood at the door, with her bag on her back, ready to go, Jacquette reappeared; this time with her hat and coat on. She went up to her father and held out her hand to him.

"Good-bye for the present, Father dear!"

The Colonel glanced up from his papers. "What's the matter? Where are you going?"

"I'm going with Anna, Father dear."

"Girl, are you mad?"

"No, indeed, dear Father! Last month, on my thirtieth birthday, you generously presented me with your beautiful country home, just outside Karlstad. I understand, dear Father, that it is your wish that I should live there when you are gone. The house is in good condition, very comfortable and cozy, there is even a little livestock on the place, and a garden. One couldn't wish for a better home. As for me, I can very well do without it; therefore, with your permission, Father dear, I propose to give the place to my sister-in-law. I am going to take her there now, and shall stay for some time—at least until her child is born."

The Colonel jumped to his feet. He looked anything but pleased.

"Well, upon my soul!" he gasped.

There had always been a strong bond of sympathy and trust between the Colonel and his daughters, and Jacquette was not at all afraid of him. But she was unaccustomed to assert her will; to make decisions and arrangements. Never in all her life had she been obliged to do anything of the sort.

"You gave me the property, dear Father, with a recorded deed of gift; so you cannot take it back. Anna will manage the place much better than I could do it. You would never allow us to speak of Karl Arthur; so you don't know what a capable wife he has. Eve and I have often wished we could show her some kindness, but we didn't dare on your account, dear Father."

A pretty flush overspread her slightly faded cheek as she unfolded her plan with fervid enthusiasm.

"In the summer Mother and you can row down to Älvsnäs to see your grandchild. It will be such a joy to have you there. Dear Mother will renew her youth."

The Colonel winced. He had not thought of it before, but what would he do about the Baroness if Jacquette were to leave home?

"Will you be gone so long?" he said. "Then who will read to Mother?"

"You will have to get Eve to come and read for a few hours every morning and afternoon. Or perhaps it would be better to engage a new nurse?"

The Colonel thrust his hands into his waistcoat pockets and whistled. He knew what a hue and cry there had always been whenever Eve had to read to her mother, and he also knew that no nurse in the world would stand having to read Karl Arthur's student letters, day in, day out. Jacquette was the only one who had the patience.

"I say, Jacquette, what will it take to make you give up this crazy notion?"

"Three thousand riksdalers, Father dear."

The Colonel opened a drawer of his writing table, quickly counted out three large rolls of bank notes, and handed them to Mamselle Jacquette, who, in turn, put them into her sister-in-law's pocket.

"Dear Anna," she said, "I know that someone has behaved very badly toward you. But when you come home and are sitting in quietude in your own village, then think of this: You have had proof that life gives as well as takes."

Then she saw her sister-in-law to the garden gate, and when they parted she noticed that Anna looked a little less resentful and hard.

Mamselle Jacquette, returning to the house, took off her hat and coat and went upstairs. She sat down again by the cabinet window, opposite her mother, and taking the bundle of letters in her lap, resumed her reading. Her usual habit of skipping a letter, now and then, still prevailed. But the moving throngs on the western bridge no longer distracted her mind. She sat dreaming that she and the sister-in-law had removed to the country house, that her brother's child had come to the world, and that she, herself, was now living and working for something young and growing, and not only for the old and withered.

CHAPTER VIII

ANNSTU LISA

MAMSELLE JACQUETTE'S kindness had really made a great impression upon her poor sister-in-law.

"You see now, Anna, there's still justice and honour in the world," she said to herself. "You don't have to go all the way to Medstuby to find good people."

As a matter of fact, upon further reflection, she was not especially eager to go back to her home town and be subjected to ridicule and scorn. "Now what did I tell you? She wasn't fit to be a clergyman's wife," would come from every quarter—from the Bailiff's wife to the small boys who were learning to read at the big table in Sexton Medberg's schoolroom.

She had always loved money, and to go with three thousand riksdalers in her pocket probably lightened the journey considerably. Besides, she had something pleasant to think of as she walked.

On the whole she had been very happy in the little cottage behind the doctor's garden, and she wondered if it wouldn't be foolish of her to abandon the place. Perhaps it would be wiser to buy a few acres of land, put up a byre, and procure some live stock. In a few years, God willing, she would have a flourishing farm.

So, instead of going northward, through the Klar Valley, which was the shortest way to Medstuby, she took the road along the eastern shore of Lake Vänern, which led to Korskyrka.

As to her husband—she took for granted that he would be at home, as usual, sitting at the writing desk in his luxurious room. And she supposed he would have no objections to their resuming the old domestic relations.

"He'll have to have someone to cook for him and keep his house in order. It's to be hoped he'd as soon have me as anyone else."

It had done her good to be astir in the fresh spring air; but above all, it was the thought of Mamselle Jacquette's kindness. Now that her mind was at peace, she could see things in their right proportions and no longer made mountains out of molehills.

She walked mile after mile through the rich farming country to the east of the Karlstad, and saw, scattered over the plains, many little villages and manorial estates. Here the fields could spread out, unbroken by mountain ridges, and the woods were away off toward the horizon. With the three thousand riksdalers in her pocket, she regarded these farms with a new interest.

"Perhaps it would be better to settle here," she thought. "I've never seen such good land for ploughing."

You may be sure that she looked at every place along the way, and everywhere there was something to learn and ponder over. Her eyes had been opened to the outer world; her thought no longer moved in a narrow circle round the ten children, Thea, Karl Arthur, and her fear of punishment.

She had just passed by one of the many little white churches in this region when she came to a small market fair. The hawkers, the wares, and the stands, with their flapping canvas signs, were about the same as had been seen at Korskyrka the week before. But as it was drawing on toward evening and the crowds had imbibed pretty freely of corn brandy, the conviviality was wilder and coarser. Rowing and quarrelling were heard on every side. The horse traders and gamblers in particular were in fighting humour. At any moment they might come to blows. Anna Svärd, who knew what that meant, quickened her steps so as to be out of the way before the strife began.

But suddenly she heard something that made her stop and listen. Above the human chatter, the bellowing of the cattle, and the rattle of the wagons—above all the deafening noises of the market fair rose a woman's voice in song. The voice was high and sweet and wonderfully clear, it could be heard throughout the fair grounds. Everyone must have wondered if it were not by some heavenly miracle that that glorious voice rose above the coarse, vulgar, raucous noises.

The people were struck with astonishment. They stopped higgling and trading; they broke off in the middle of a conversation; they waited with brandy flask in hand without raising it to their lips.

The singer had mounted a wagon, a common vehicle with no seat or hood, so as to be above the heads of the crowd. She was a short, stout woman, and had on a plain black cloak. Her features were homely, her eyes prominent and watery. She had drawn a large crowd around her, and the people looked a bit disappointed because she was so unattractive, but they were held by the sheer beauty of her voice.

"If it isn't——" Anna was staring at the singer. . . . "No, it can't be, my eyes must be deceiving me."

Something lovely had come into the woman's face while she sang—something pure and holy. She had never seen anything like that in the woman whom the singer resembled.

The hymn was finished, the woman stepped down from the wagon, and a man, who had been standing among the listeners, took her place.

He was dressed in gray wadmal and wore a broad-brimmed hat, which he took off at once and threw down on the bottom of the wagon. He stood for a moment with folded hands and eyes closed, in silent prayer. The wind played in his dark hair and tossed it over his forehead, thus emphasizing the clear pallor of his face. As he stood there a ray of sunshine cast a shimmer over

him, making the delicate features almost transparent
and framing the face, for a moment, with a nimbus.
It looked as if the sun had wished to help draw all eyes
toward him.

Anna Svärd, who of course recognized her own husband, thought she had never seen him look so handsome.
The people, who at the close of the song intended to go
back to their trading and their drinking, stood quietly
waiting to hear what this man had to say.

Nor was it long before he began to speak. Raising his
heavy eyelids, he let his dark eyes travel over the people,
but otherwise remained motionless. In the devotional
stillness which prevailed throughout the fair grounds
his voice could be heard distinctly.

His wife felt the blood mount to her head. She could
not grasp a word her husband was saying, but she kept
asking herself the meaning of it all. What were Karl
Arthur and Thea doing here? she'd like to know.

After a little, she was able to catch a few sentences.
She heard Karl Arthur tell the people that he would
follow Christ's command and go out on the highways
and byways to preach the gospel of the Kingdom of
God, that he would speak no more from a pulpit, for
he had resigned from the ministry.

The people, to whom it was all so surprising and beautiful, listened with bated breath. Now and then the
stillness was broken by some half-drunken rowdy who
shouted out that he was tired of hearing that prater on
the gipsy wagon; that this was a fair, where folk came

to amuse themselves and not to be bored by sermons. But these disturbers were promptly silenced, since those who wished to listen were in the majority.

Probably no one but Anna was highly incensed. Was her husband, then, no longer a clergyman? Were he and Thea to roam the country like gipsies? His wife would have something to say about that! She intended to work her way through the crowd to the wagon. Aye! she'd soon put a stop to his pretty talk. She would cry out what sort Thea and Karl Arthur were—whore and whore master, that's what they were. Both of them married to someone else—and they posing as saints and preaching the word of God!

She was about to push forward, when a restraining hand was laid upon her shoulder. Glancing round, she saw old Annstu Lisa standing beside her—the oldest and best of the women venders, a tall, scraggy woman, with inscrutable eyes, her face tanned and toughened by wind and weather, heavy and imperturbable as a block of granite.

Annstu Lisa was noted for her shrewdness and her inordinate love of tobacco, coffee, and card playing, but the old woman had certain gifts which folks did not care to talk about. Anna had heard whispers to the effect that she was both clear visioned and far-seeing, that she had a way of making people buy at her stall and pay whatever she asked. Anna knew, as she felt the strong hand on her shoulder, that it had been placed there for a certain purpose.

The old woman did not utter a word. Anna could easily have brushed her hand away, but, strange to say, she let it rest there. She stood quietly, like the others, and listened to the speaker.

Only once before had she heard Karl Arthur speak as he spoke that evening at the market fair, and that was the Sunday at Korskyrka, soon after they were married, when he preached the wonderful sermon on Love.

It all came back to her now, how she had sat in the church, hoping and praying that Thea would not come and frighten him with her tricks, and how distressed she had been when Thea suddenly appeared and he lost the thread of his sermon.

Now she could understand how happy he must be to think his inspirational powers had come back to him. If she were to step forward now he would lose his head again, as he did the other time, and that would be the worst harm she could do him.

But as she pondered how she could hurt him the most, it seemed to her that Fru Forsius, and not Annstu Lisa, was by her side. She stood there, calm and respectful, showing her how a clergyman's wife should conduct herself when her husband was preaching.

Of a sudden Anna began to move, not toward Karl Arthur, however, but in the opposite direction. She wanted to get away from the crowded market place as quickly as possible, and Annstu Lisa went before and opened a path for her.

They were hardly out on the road before Anna felt her wrath rise once again. She turned upon the old woman and rated her roundly.

"What right had you to meddle in this? Why couldn't you let me tell them what they were?"

"I saw that you were about to cast yourself into a sea of trouble," said old Annstu Lisa, in her hard, dry voice, "and I wanted to stop you for what you did for me and Ris Karin and other poor peddler women the time you gave up the autumn fairs to make room for us. You know that this late in the day folks are so crazy with drink there's no telling what they would do if you got them started."

Anna looked at the old woman in astonishment. She had never breathed a word to a living soul about her staying away from the autumn fairs for the sake of her old comrades.

"You're as blind as a new-born babe," the old woman continued. "You've been married to that man nigh on to three years, and yet you don't see that your way and his draw apart, while her way and his run together. You mustn't think that you can escape what has been predestined for you."

When Annstu Lisa said that, something very old and half-forgotten came back to Anna. She remembered having heard that somewhere in God's Heaven all that she would pass through stood recorded, and that that which was written no power on earth or in Heaven could change, not even our Lord Himself. So believed

Mother Svärd and Jobs Eric; so believed everyone in Medstuby, and in that belief they lived and died—fearless and happy.

After a little, she turned to the calm, patient old woman who walked by her side and said to her:

"Now I want to think you, Lisa. Sure, I'm not such a fool that I'd set myself against what is meant for me."

Annstu Lisa suddenly stopped and held out her hand —an enormous hand which never gave anything but the slightest pressure.

"I must go back to my stand now," she said.

Before they parted Anna put a query: "Since you know so much, Lisa, can you tell me where I should direct my steps?"

She answered without the least hesitation:

"You've only to go straight ahead, for that which you are to meet will come to you this evening."

Annstu Lisa then turned abruptly and went back to the fair, and Anna Svärd stood for a long moment looking after her. She, like Mamselle Jacquette, had been of great help.

Anna wandered on in the mild spring evening, hoping that that which she was to meet would be something pleasant and good. She tramped on and on, yet nothing happened. At last, hungry and tired, she sat down at the edge of a ditch and opened her lunch bag.

Then, just as she raised a sandwich to her mouth she saw two beggar women coming up the road—ragged,

filthy creatures with a long line of dirty young ones trail-
ing after.

"They'll come and snatch the food out of my mouth,"
thought Anna. She moved back a trifle and hid behind
a rock, hoping they would pass by without seeing her.

What those women and children had on was indescribable! They had old rags tied around their heads.
In place of skirts and jackets they wore gunny sacks
that looked as if they had been hanging on a scarecrow
a whole summer, and their shoes were made from scraps
of old birch bark, pieced together.

The two beggar women seemed quite happy in their
rags and filth. Their laughter and chatter could he
heard a long way off.

"I never thought it would be such fun to go around
begging," said one of the women.

"But think of the luck you've had," said the other;
"to get ten young 'uns without having to pay out a
penny!"

Anna began to suspect that all was not right here.
She had heard that sometimes well-to-do peasant
women from northern Värmland went begging in the
spring, when their granaries were empty, to get corn
for bread and for sowing. These two had not gone out
in vain; the youngsters as well as the women came
bearing well filled bags on their backs.

"If we only weren't so far from home," said the first
beggar woman, laughing. "I think we'll have to hire a
coach to take us back to Ekshärad."

At the mention of that place, Anna Svärd sprang out into the road. She looked at the beggar women sharply. Under the dirt and the wisps of hair that hung down over their eyes she recognized their faces. One of them lived at a backwoods croft and was probably so poor that she was forced to beg; but the other, when Anna had last seen her, was a well-to-do widow. The woman had treated her to coffee and cakes and had bought a neck comb and a silk shawl of her.

The moment the women saw Anna they began to beg.

"Haven't you got some old things in the bag you could give us for the children?"

"Well, I declare, if it isn't the mistress of Norrviken!" said Anna, half chaffingly. "How can you be so poor that you have to go round with the begging bag?"

"My farm's burned down, my cows are dead, the frosts killed my corn and——"

That was as far as she got when a wild shriek went up from the children. Ten beggar young ones came rushing up to Anna and in their excitement and joy almost knocked her off her feet.

For the moment, Anna Svärd took no notice of them, but laid a heavy hand on the shoulder of one of the women.

"So it's you that's married to the uncle of these children," she said. "And now you'll come with me to the Bailiff, and you can ride back to Ekshärad in the prison van—both you and the children."

At that, the woman gave a shriek, threw down her

bag, and took to her heels. The other woman did the same, as did all the children that belonged to her.

And there, on the highway, stood Anna Svärd with the ten children around her and peace and joy in her heart.

She thought that, before asking the children how they had fared at their uncle's, she and they should give thanks to God for bringing them together again. And she led them in the Evensong, the first she had taught them to sing.

> "So, from our time another day is passing,
>   And cometh not again.
>   Another night of heavenly peace descending
>   Broods o'er the sons of men."

PART THREE

CHAPTER I

THE VAGABOND BARON

THE gentlemen who had inherited the old foundry estates and manors on the shores of Lake Löven—these men who could tell of gallant exploits, who ruled like overlords on their estates, who decided all matters that came up at the parish meetings and were fêted like kings on their birthdays—how they must have grieved because no sons came to bless their marriage. Their wives, who in all other respects were obedient and subservient, seemed to have entered into a malicious conspiracy to bring only daughters into the world.

During the years that the many daughters were born into the families the husbands must often have brooded on the enigma of life and the decrees of Providence. They must have wondered if this were, perchance, a new way in which the Eternal Powers would show their displeasure with mankind. Was it perhaps their intention to send a deluge of women over the earth—an overflow that would annihilate the sinning human race more effectively than was possible in Noah's day?

And indeed they had good cause for their apprehensions. To be sure, there was no immediate danger of the extinction of the entire race of men, but the continuation of a number of old families was seriously affected. It might mean the dying out of the Sinclair family of ironmasters or the extinction of the proud Hedenfelt line of majors and colonels. Moreover it would wipe out the revered hereditary deans, who for more than a century had ruled the parish of Bro, and it might also prevent another descendant of the famous old German organist, Faber, from manipulating, with dexterous fingers, the bellowing and trumpeting organs of the old Värmland churches.

Although there was cause for alarm, most of the gentlemen of Bro Parish were able to enjoy life in peace and comfort. Only one man was so constituted that he longed for sons day and night. He would rather be a humble day labourer than a Baron Löwensköld of high degree, if he must live in the certainty that his line would die with him.

Adrian Löwensköld, this splendid lord of Hedeby Hall, who was continually improving his property and adding to the beauty of his house—this just master, who tried to make all his dependents happy, felt that he had failed in his duty to his country, his forebears, and all mankind, by giving the world five daughters but no sons. No sons to carry on the work of the loyal, able men who, in former times, had raised Sweden to greatness and power! He tried to be just and not lay the blame for his misfortunes on the innocent, but having to spend his life in the company of only women went against him. He knew, of course, that neither his wife nor his elderly aunt nor his five daughters nor their governess were responsible for his unhappiness; yet, every time he joined their circle he threw a wet blanket over them. He was always lamenting that he had not a score of noisy, prankish, big-eating rascals of boys around him, instead of these quiet, sedate womenfolk.

This perpetual discontent made him prematurely old. There was very little of the merry young "Knight Sunshine," who had married the famous beauty, Marianne Sinclair, left in him. When Marianne died, a year after their marriage, he lost much of his old gay humour. His second marriage, to the rich Fröken Wachthausen of Kymmelsta, had been a prudential match. This wife could not make him forget his consuming grief. But the old strong zest of life would have come back to him if he'd only had a son. With him, he could have gone hunting, or on long fishing cruises. As in his merry youth, he would have set out on a journey of days, just to dance for a night. Now, on the contrary, he went about the house, bored to extinction by all these sensitive, small-minded females he had around him continually.

It was just at the time when Baron Adrian's heart was becoming incurably hard that his brother Göran, the miserable, despised vagabond, who was at enmity with all his family, came driving to Hedeby.

This was something unheard of. At the other manors in the vicinity this strange reprobate, who consorted with gipsies and horse cadgers and had married a gipsy girl, frequently appeared. He would come in his dirty wagon, full of shrieking youngsters, old rags, and evil smelling bundles, to trade horses or buy junk; but never before had he dared go up to his brother's house.

A blinding snowstorm had been raging for days, and while his small, yellow scrub of a horse slowly ploughed through the drifts in the avenue, the poor vagabond baron dreamed himself back in his youth. He fancied he was a boy again, coming home from the school at Karlstad. His parents were standing at the door to welcome him. The servants came running out to the sleigh to unbutton the apron and relieve him of his robes. Eager hands pulled off his overcoat and cap and unbuttoned his bootees, while his mother could hardly wait until he was out of his wraps to embrace him and lead him up to a crackling log fire, give him a cup of steaming hot coffee, then sit her down to devour him with her eyes.

In the wintertime, when blizzards rage for days on end and all the roads are blocked with snow, people do not venture out on journeys. At lonely country houses the windows are always occupied by curious inmates, looking for something new, something improbable, to happen, they care not what. On such days even the arrival of a gipsy sledge was a great event, which was reported from room to room. So, when the little yellow horse came crawling along the avenue, Baron Adrian was informed as to who was approaching.

When the Baron, with a most forbidding mien, stepped to the door, prepared to give his brother a frigid reception, he saw that the despised ne'er-do-well, the prodigal son, who had brought misery and shame upon himself, did not come this time with any black-eyed gipsy young ones or loathsome beggar women, but with that which had been denied the faithful and righteous brother.

And it was no changeling the vagabond baron with the gallows-bird face lifted from the piles of rags in his sledge, it was too much like the portrait of his father for that. He recognized the delicate, sensitive face and the large, dreamy eyes, which he had so often admired. This beggar brat had inherited the beauty of his female ancestors, which none of the brother's daughters could boast.

For the moment there was not much life in the last of the Löwenskölds. When the father had lifted him out of the sledge he lay in his arms, almost insensible; his eyes drooped, and his hands and face were blue with the cold.

Baron Adrian did not utter the strong words with which he had meant to turn his erring brother away; for when Göran came bearing the child and he read in his eyes a diffident appeal he forgot all that he had suffered on account of this brother; forgot, too, all the sorrow this brother had caused his parents—and flung wide the door to his house.

But Göran Löwensköld went no farther than the entrance hall. When his brother also threw open the door to the drawing room and he saw the blazing fire on the hearth, the furniture and tapestries which he remembered from his boyhood, he shook his head.

"No, thanks," he said; "I'll stop where I am. But perhaps you will take care of the child for me?"

Baron Adrian received the child as a precious trust. He immediately began to rub and stroke warmth into the little body. He did not call upon any of the women-folk to help him, but knew, of course, that he must do so later. For the first few moments he wanted to have the child all to himself. Suddenly, he laid his bristly cheek against the cold, dirty cheek of the vagabond's child, in a shy caress.

"He is so much like Father," he said in a voice that was a trifle unsteady. "You are fortunate, Göran, to have a son."

Baron Göran, seeing his brother press the child to his heart, knew that the owner of Hedeby Hall would have given him food and shelter as long as he lived, simply because he happened to have a son. He knew also that his brother would put up with his indolence, his buffoon-ery, his card playing, and his drinking without giving him a word of reproach. Nevertheless, he had no desire to stay.

"You understand, of course, that I would not have

come here unless I was forced to," he said. "We had been driving round in the storm so long that the child was nearly frozen to death. I had to bring him here, or he would have perished. There's work waiting for me at the Deanery, and I'm going there now. I shall come back for him as soon as the storm is over."

As he said that his hand was on the latch. Baron Adrian did not hear what his brother said, as he was wholly taken up with the child.

"I say, Göran, his little hands are frost-bitten. We must rub him with snow. Go fetch me some, will you?"

Göran Löwensköld mumbled something that sounded like thanks and farewell. His brother thought he had gone out for the snow, as requested. But when, in a few moments, he heard the tinkle of a sleigh bell and looked out, he saw his brother drive away. He whipped up his yellow horse so that it set off at full speed, the snow whirling about it like a cloud of dust.

Baron Adrian could well understand that there were many things about the house which were painful for the brother to see again, and was not surprised at his flight. But his mind was on the child. He, himself, brought in the snow with which to rub life into the frozen little hands and face. And while he worked over the child he made plans for the future. Never would he allow the last of the Löwenskölds to be turned over to his father again, to grow up among his lawless companions.

It would be hard to say what Göran Löwensköld had

in mind when he left Hedeby. Probably he intended to
come back for the child in a few hours, and, at the same
time, to have the satisfaction of gloating over his
brother's rage for allowing himself to be fooled again.
As he drove away he roared with laughter at the thought
of his brother laying his cheek against the beggar youngster's and the pride with which he took into his arms
this new preserver of the family name.

But the laughter soon died on his lips. He sat in the
old sledge with his bare-worn fur cap drawn over his
eyes, driving without thinking of where he was going.
Strange, dark thoughts were at work in him; thoughts
that must be carried into immediate effect.

He did not drive to Bro Deanery, where he had said
he was going. Next morning, when a messenger from
Hedeby came to inquire for him, no one there could give
the desired information. But later in the morning a
couple of peasants, who had been ploughing a passage
in the snowlocked road, came to Hedeby to notify the
Baron that they had found his vagabond brother dead
in a roadside ditch. He had gone down in the darkness
and the sledge had turned over on him. Being too weak
to extricate himself, he had lain there all night and
frozen to death.

Nowhere could one so easily lose one's bearings as in
the flat country around Bro Church, on a dark night
in a blinding snowstorm. Therefore, it seemed quite
probable that Göran Löwensköld had lost his life
through an accident. They had no reason to suspect

that he had deliberately sought death in order that his child might remain in the good home which he had procured for it in one of his jocular moods.

He was almost a madman, this vagabond baron, and not accountable for his actions. But he was known to have loved his youngest child with a love that was quite touching. In its little face he had found again the Löwensköld features, and he had felt that this child belonged to him in quite another sense than did its black-eyed gipsy brothers and sisters. So, it might be that he sacrificed his life in order to protect this beloved child from misery and want.

When he came to Hedeby his only thought had been to play a joke on a good brother, who was pining for a son. But when he stepped into the old home and felt that comfort, security, and good-will came pouring out toward him, he must have said to himself:

"I wish my youngest child, the only one that is truly my very own, could stay here, and I must plan my journey so that I need never come back for the child."

In any case, life was not such a precious thing to him that he need hesitate to throw it away. It may have been a long-nourished wish that at last had been fulfilled. Perhaps he was glad to have found a definite excuse for an act which had been put off until now, either from indifference or apathy.

Who knows? Perhaps it afforded him a certain pleasure, even in the moment of death, to have a good joke on his brother, who always had kept on the right side of life? His lips were perhaps drawn in a last smile of amusement at the thought that the child he had placed in his brother's arms was only a girl in boy's clothes, and that it was only the disguise that had opened the doors of the ancestral home to the poor gipsy girl.

CHAPTER II

BARON ADRIAN'S WIFE

T HE day the vagabond baron had left his child
at Hedeby his brother came in to dinner in a
radiant humour.

"To-day I do not have to sit at table with only
women-folk; to-day there's a boy amongst them." He
thought there was a different atmosphere about the
dining room that day; he felt young, gay, and full of life.
He was going to suggest to his wife that she have some
wine brought in so that they could drink a health to the
newcomer.

He went straight to his place at the table, folded his
hands, and bowed his head while his youngest daughter
said grace. When she had finished he cast a beaming
glance around the table for his brother's son. But there
was no little boy in jacket and breeches, he saw only
skirts and close-fitting bodices at the table now, as
always.

He knitted his heavy eyebrows and gave a snort. He
had taken the child to the nursery to be bathed and
put into proper clothes. Was his wife really so foolish as

not to allow his nephew to come to the family table? The boy, to be sure, was a little vagabond with the manners and ways of Vagabondia, but all five well-brought-up daughters were not worth the boy's little finger.

Before he had time to express his disappointment the Baroness, with a slight motion of her hand, directed his attention to a nicely combed, well dressed little girl, who sat by his side. He did some rapid counting and found that there were six small girls that day at table instead of five. "They have dressed the boy in girl's clothes," he thought. "Naturally, he couldn't sit down to the table in the filthy rags he came in, and at Hedeby they had only girls' things. But the hair—the curly golden hair—they needn't have braided it in two pigtails that dangled about the ears like his own daughters'.

"Couldn't you have borrowed a pair of trousers at the farm bailiff's," said the Baron, "so that the child wouldn't look like a scarecrow?"

"I daresay we could," the Baroness replied in a casual tone; "but now she is clad in the proper raiment for her."

Baron Adrian looked at his wife and at the child by his side, then turned his gaze upon his wife again.

"I'm afraid Göran has played you another trick," said the Baroness. There was not a nuance in the voice or a glint in her eye that betrayed that she was not of the same mind as her husband. She thought, of course, that Göran had behaved shamefully and given another proof of his spite. If in the depths of her heart she had any other feeling she was careful to conceal it.

But if a person is made to be a doormat and is trampled upon every day, she cannot help but feel a little quiver of satisfaction, when the one who tramples the hardest tumbles heels over head.

And when she saw her husband frown and wave aside the platter of roast the maid was passing round, as if his chagrin had taken away his appetite, her body began to shake, although she managed to keep a straight face.

She wondered afterwards what would have happened to herself and the old aunt, the governess and the six girls, if he had not jumped up from the table just then and, with an ugly oath, rushed out of the room, for they couldn't have controlled their risibilities another minute. They suddenly threw themselves back in their chairs and burst out laughing.

They laughed loud and jubilantly—the one harder than the other. At the same time, they felt a bit ashamed to be laughing at their lord and master, husband and father, because he had been fooled. They were well bred people, who disapproved of such behaviour. But this laughter came from the very depths of their nature; it would have strangled them had they tried to hold it back.

For a few moments they cast off all restraint, all that oppressed and stifled them, and felt free and superior to it all. Never again would they be cowed or terrorized, they thought, for now they could laugh at the oppressor. And while they laughed at him, he lost his formidable greatness and became an ordinary petty mortal like themselves.

The Baroness, who had always spoken of Baron Adrian as though he were the best husband in the world and of herself as the happiest of wives, who would never permit anyone, not even his own aunt, to make the slightest remark about her husband's behaviour, vowed to herself that if ever Göran Löwensköld came her way she would try to do something for him in return for this moment of joy.

But when on the following day the vagabond baron was found dead in a ditch and his body was brought to Hedeby, she did not lift a finger to show the sympathy she had felt for him for a few passing moments. She let her husband attend to the obsequies without a protest from her. He arranged with the clergy at Bro about the day for the interment, and he alone, with a few servitors, drove to the cemetery with the body.

He would not allow them to put up white sheets at the windows or strew the road with spruce twigs. The Baroness and her daughters were not allowed to dress in black. He had not invited any of the gentlemen in the parish to attend the funeral nor ordered any funeral meats.

There was not a person in the whole parish of Bro that was sorry Göran Löwensköld was dead. Never again would he accost a gentleman at the market fair, pat him on the shoulder and call him "dear old pal" because once on a time they had been schoolmates at Karlstad. It was a relief for all and sundry to know he would never again try to exchange a battered old silver turnip for a fine gold watch, or an old jade for a good four-year-old mare. Indeed, it was well he was gone, for while he was alive there was no knowing what revenge he might take if one refused to trade with him.

But, nevertheless, everyone thought Baron Adrian had evinced too great a thirst for revenge. They maintained that, since Baron Göran had lost his life, his brother should have forgotten old grudges and conducted him to his grave with pomp and state.

They blamed the Baroness even more than they did her husband, for they expected more compassion in a woman. Not a flower had she placed on his coffin! The big calla that stood in the dining room at Hedeby was known to bloom at this time of year, and nothing could be more appropriate to give to the dead on his last journey than the calla lily; but even this mark of respect had not been accorded him. What was one to think of such wanton neglect? It was almost inhuman not to give her brother-in-law even a flower.

Many persons also thought that Baron Göran's wife should have been notified of her husband's death, and they wondered why the Baroness had not done so. And the girl—Göran Löwensköld's favourite child—should have had a mourning frock made up for her! She could hardly be so subservient and so afraid of her husband as not to dare take a sempstress into the house, and provide suitable clothes for the fatherless child.

The mistress of Hedeby, as everyone knew, was a sensible person who understood well enough what was proper. She should have talked her husband to rights when he failed in his duty. But, apparently, she had not done so in this case.

The dirty gipsy sledge, with its piles of rags and bundles, its tinning tools, its rum cask and packs of greasy cards, had been placed in a shed, and the little horse, which had stood by its master's body until people came and dug it out of the drifts, had been stabled. No one bothered about this survivor of the vagabond baron, either, except to give it fodder and water.

But the day after the burial Baron Adrian gave orders to have the horse re-shod and to give it an extra ration of fodder; so it was understood that he intended to send it out on a long journey.

At that time there was a farm bailiff at Hedeby who had been born and brought up in one of the northern parishes of Värmland where wandering gipsy bands had their winter quarters. He knew the tribe into which Baron Göran had married, and knew its whereabouts. So he was ordered to drive the horse and sledge, with all it contained, home, and to notify Baron Göran's wife of her husband's death.

It was Baron Adrian's intention also to send his brother's daughter home. She had no right to be at

Hedeby. She must go back to the people from which she had come.

The day after the funeral the Baron informed his wife that the girl was to be sent home the following morning. At the same time he told her that the girl must be dressed in the rags she had on when she came and added that he presumed his wife would be glad to be rid of the gipsy young one.

The Baroness made no protest against sending the child away. Without a word, she arose and went into the nursery to give instructions to the nursemaid.

But all day the Baroness was noticeably restless. She went from task to task, her lips moving continually, though not a sound crossed them. She appeared in the nursery oftener that day than usual, and sat for hours observing the child. The little girl stood at the window, looking down the avenue, as long as there was a glimmer of daylight. Thus she had stood every day, since she came to Hedeby, watching for her father to come and fetch her. She felt strange and shy and did not care to play with the other children. Ah, she would not be sorry to go home!

That night, as the Baroness lay beside her husband, she was too troubled to sleep. She had reached the limit of her endurance. It was time she took a stand against her husband. What he now proposed to do must not take place.

It was clear to her that Baron Göran had killed himself so that his child might stay at Hedeby; that he loved her and had been seized with a desire to have her brought up in a good home and become a real person. He had thought she would be reared according to her proper station and would eventually marry a gentleman. She was not to become a shrieking, cursing vagabond woman, driving round the country in a gipsy wagon with a pack of screaming, swearing gipsy young ones!

To attain this wish he had sacrificed his own life. He knew what it would cost him, and willingly paid the price. Did her husband understand what his brother had wanted him to do? Probably he did; but he seemed to take pleasure in denying him that which he had paid for with his life.

She must forbid it. She must assert her power and authority and tell him in a way that he would heed. He must not send his niece away. It would be wrong. Such an act, she knew, would bring punishment. She had kept silence and let him have his own way about the funeral arrangements, but this was another matter.

She remembered how her brother-in-law had sat cowering in the sledge as he drove away, and tried to imagine his sombre death thoughts when driving round in the lashing snowstorm. Could one think that such a man would find rest in his grave if he were denied what he had hoped to gain by his sacrifice? Here at Hedeby they knew, indeed, that the dead had the power to wreak vengeance.

She must speak. It would never do to defy the last

wishes of the dead. Whatever he had been in life, he had now gained the right to command obedience.

Clenching her hands, she beat her own body for her cowardice. Why did she not rouse her husband? Why did she not speak to him?

She had surmised what he had in mind, and had taken a slight counter measure. The day Göran's body was found she took his daughter on a visit to a lowly cabin, where the children were down with the measles. Her own daughters had had the illness. Whether their cousin had also had it she did not know, but she fervently hoped she had not. Every day she looked for symptoms; as yet none had appeared. However, she knew that the rash did not break out until the eleventh day, and this was only the eighth.

Minute after minute, hour after hour went by, yet she put off speaking. At last she began to fear that she would never muster the courage to speak. But she was his wife. Then why was she so miserably weak? Nothing could happen to her if she spoke to him. Her husband would not beat her, of that she was certain; but he had a habit of looking past her and ignoring what she said. Talking to him was like preaching to a block of ice.

There was another matter that troubled her greatly. The previous year, at a dinner party in Karlstad, her husband had met Charlotte Löwensköld, a distant rela-tion of his, who was married to Commerce Commissioner Schagerström. Baron Adrian had known Charlotte from the time that she was engaged to his cousin, Karl Arthur

Ekenstedt, and she had once visited Hedeby with her fiancé. That evening at the party, she and the Baron had an intimate talk, in which he lamented having no sons but only a lot of daughters. Charlotte had then asked him if he would not let her take one of the daughters, as there were no children in her home. She had had a little daughter, but had lost her.

The Baron, of course, was more than willing. So Charlotte said she would talk with her husband and see what he thought of the idea. Shortly afterwards came a letter of inquiry as to whether the Baron and his wife were willing to give one of their daughters to the Schagerströms to bring up as their own. The Baron, without consulting his wife's wishes, promptly answered in the affirmative. Such an offer from the wealthiest family in Värmland was not to be rejected. The girl would be reared like a princess, and incalculable advantages might be gained by one's entering into such a close bond with a powerful man.

The Baroness made no protest then, either; she merely begged for time. Charlotte wished to come down to Hedeby herself, to see which one of the small girls suited her best. But the journey was postponed from time to time, for about half a year. These postponements were mostly due to the Baroness. Once, she had written to say that she had a dress web on the loom and would like to have it off and some frocks made up for the girls, so that they would have something decent to wear when Charlotte came to inspect them. Another time when she wanted to come, the children had the measles; so of course the visit had to be put off again. And now the Baroness had not heard from Charlotte in a long time and hoped in her heart that the rich lady, who had so much to do in her great house, had forgotten the whole proposition.

After the death of Baron Göran, however, she wrote to Charlotte, asking her to come. Now she would let her have one of her daughters. She thought that by making this sacrifice she could induce her husband to let her keep his niece in their home.

But her sacrifice had been useless. Her husband had been too quick for her. The measles had not as yet broken out, and Charlotte had not come. In a few hours the child would be sent away.

She lay reckoning the number of miles from Hedeby to Stora Sjötorp. Her letter must have barely arrived. After the blizzard it had grown bitterly cold. It was unthinkable that Charlotte would set out in such weather. The walls had been creaking all night, as if someone were pounding on them with a heavy club.

She could hear that they were already astir in the kitchen. The scullery maid was laying firewood on the hearth and there was a banging of pots and kettles. There was a slight noise in the nursery. Nurse must be getting up, she thought, to dress the vagabond's child in the old rags she came in.

Once or twice she spoke her husband's name, not loud, but distinctly. He moved a trifle but did not awaken. Had he only awakened she would have talked to him, but to try again to arouse him, that was beyond her strength.

She heard the kitchen door open. It must be frightfully cold outside. The creaking noise, as the door turned on its hinges, could be heard throughout the house. She knew that the farm bailiff, who was to take the child away, had come for her.

Shortly afterwards the chambermaid came to the door and asked if the Baron and Baroness were awake.

"What's wanted?" said the Baron, sitting bolt upright in the bed.

"The farm bailiff bade me tell the Baron it's so cold to-day he wouldn't dare set out. He says, when he touched the key to the stable it took the skin off his hand. At his house the bread and the butter were frozen this morning, and the ice in the water barrel was so thick he had to break it with an axe. And he says, when it's that cold here, it must be even worse up North, where he's to go."

"Come here with your wax taper," said the Baron, "so that I may have a light."

The girl came into the room and lit the candle on the night table. The Baron got up, threw on his dressing gown, and went over to the window to look at the thermometer.

The windowpanes were covered with a thick coat of white frost, but in front of the thermometer there was a small strip of clear glass. The Baron looked for the column. It had dropped out of sight and crept down into the bulb.

"It must be over forty degrees below zero," he muttered.

"The farm bailiff says if the Baron really must get the load off to-day, he'll manage somehow, but he'll take no child with him in such weather."

"Tell him to go to hell!" the Baron roared, and drew the covers over his ears.

"The Baron means," his wife explained, "that you are to tell the farm bailiff that he need not set out until the cold spell is broken. You can also step into the nursery and tell Martha that the child is not going away from here."

The Baroness spoke in her usual quiet voice without betraying her intense relief.

The cold weather continued that day and the next. But toward evening of the second day came a decided change, and the Baron immediately said that the girl must be out of his house in the morning.

His wife did not oppose him, she merely said that there had been a strange look about the child that day and the day before. She was afraid the little one was not well.

The Baron looked at her coldly. "It's of no avail," he said. "That child shall not remain in my house. Do you think I am so fond of girls that I want one more to support?"

When, after supper, she went up to the nursery to see

how her children were, the little girl was red and fever-
ish and coughed continually. "Do you know, Baroness,"
said the nursemaid, "I believe she's coming down with
the measles." The Baroness remembered that the illness
had come in the same way when her daughters had it.

"It is too bad about this," she said. "The Baron has
just given orders to send her home to-morrow morning."
She thought a moment, whereupon she told the nurse
to ask Baron Adrian to come to the nursery for a second,
to see what ailed the child.

The Baron came. Though he knew very little about
sickness, he had to admit that all was not right with his
brother's child. Nor did he doubt for a moment that she
had the measles. It began to look as though he would
never be rid of that gipsy brat!

Whether the Baron suspected or not that his wife
had deliberately exposed the child to the measles, he
was obliged to keep the little one in his house, at least
another week, which put him in a dreadful humour.
Luckily, for the peace of Hedeby House, there came a
letter from Charlotte Schagerström that took him out
of his megrims. She wrote that, if the good driving continued, she would start for Hedeby by the middle of
March and would arrive about the sixteenth or seven-
teenth.

Every day the Baron went to the nursery to see
whether the girl was still in bed, and judged of her condition accordingly. The Baroness, knowing that the
child had a very mild form of the measles and that the

peeling was already over, had great difficulty keeping the child in bed. The nurse said that the patient was well enough now to be up and dressed, and the Baroness found it hard to convince her that the child should be kept in bed a few days longer.

It was a great relief to her, therefore, when in the afternoon of the sixteenth of March she saw Charlotte's sleigh drive into the yard. She welcomed the guest with open arms, hugged and kissed her. Charlotte was quite surprised, for she had begun to suspect, on account of the continual postponements, that the Baroness regarded her as a thief who was coming to rob the house of its dearest treasure.

The five small Frökens Löwensköld were soaped and scrubbed until their round, pink faces shone, and they were combed till every hair lay straight and smooth against the scalp, and the tight little braids stood out like rings about their ears. Then they were dressed in their new home-sewn, home-spun frocks and new, stout home-made shoes. The Baroness regarded them with maternal pride as she led them into the drawing room. She thought they were the sweetest little girls to be found anywhere on this side of the globe.

They were healthy girls, well formed and well brought up, and it was not without a certain expectation that their mother brought them into the drawing room for Charlotte to see.

Charlotte gave them a quick appraising glance and masked her disappointment completely. She was all sweetness and light when she shook hands with the little Löwensköld girls and asked each girl, in turn, her name and her age. But she was not so charmed with them as the Baroness had expected. She had in mind the delicate, spiritual beauty of the Baroness Ekenstedt, of her sister, Marie Louise, and of her own little girl; therefore she could scarcely realize that these little girls also were Löwenskölds.

She could see that they were good children, healthy and of a happy disposition. They would grow up to be excellent women and good housewives like their mother. Like her, they were red haired, undersized, overplump, and had short stubby fingers. All five were cast in the same mould; they all had round faces, snub noses, and pale-blue eyes. When they had got their full growth and were not, as now, of different shortnesses, it would be hard to tell one from another.

Charlotte, who was then thirty years of age, still retained her full beauty. The Baroness thought her more beautiful now than when she had last visited Hedeby as a young affianced girl. She was a grand lady now, and moved in the best society. The Baroness doubtless perceived that her daughters would not fit into Charlotte's present environment, but quickly put the thought out of her mind. She knew that in whatever station in life her daughters might be placed, they would fill it humbly and well.

Charlotte, for her part, thought the same. She wondered how she could ever get used to having a plain, awkward little country girl around her all the time, even if she were a paragon of all the virtues.

She was not the least bit snobbish or puffed up. No one could say that of her! She knew how to value goodness in people. If she were to adopt one of these nice little carrot-haired girls and win her affection, she would have a friend for life—one who would never think of herself but would be with her even in old age. For, of course, she would never marry—ugly as she was.

Suddenly, she resolved to take the common-sense view of it, and congratulated herself upon getting a plain-looking foster daughter. It was a veritable grace from God. Had the choice rested wholly with her, she would have picked out a little beauty, who would have become captious and spoiled and thought only of her self.

Charlotte easily made friends with both old and young, and it was not long before she had the five small Löwensköld girls at her feet, so to speak. Five pairs of pale-blue eyes looked up at her adoringly, and five little hands slipped into hers as soon as they were near enough. She could have chosen any one among them; they would have gone with her without a murmur or regret.

She liked their quaint way of answering questions. They were really amusing little dears.

Everything went well as could be. Baron Adrian passed the evening in the drawing room, making himself agreeable to the guest, and the Baroness, too, tried to be cheerful, for it looked as if her sacrifice would be accepted.

The five Frökens Löwensköld kept close to Charlotte the whole evening—fairly devouring her with their eyes and waiting for her to give them just a nod or a smile.

Charlotte was glad that they liked her, but she had no feeling of kinship with them.

During supper, when she had the five red-heads facing her and the five pairs of pale-blue eyes staring at her, she was seized by a covert fear. What if she should burden herself with something too heavy to bear? Supposing that she had to send the child back to its parents because it was too ugly? She knew that her fears were greatly exaggerated, but all the same she thought it best to be a bit careful and not to make her choice the first day. She would wait until to-morrow.

They had just finished supper when loud peals of laughter were heard from the kitchen. Charlotte looked surprised. The Baroness hastened to explain that the kitchen was now in the main building and not in the wing, where it had been when Charlotte was here last. It was a great convenience, she said, but unfortunately, any noises out there could be heard in the dining room.

There was more talk about this, and when they arose from the table, the Baron offered his arm to Charlotte to show her the changes and improvements he had made.

They first went into a small room off the dining hall.

Here he had torn down a wall; there, raised a partition. Charlotte listened with keen interest, for these were things which she understood.

While they stood there, discussing the changes, the laughter in the kitchen grew louder and more hilarious. Now they all became curious. The small girls ran to the kitchen door and threw it wide open.

On the kitchen table stood a little girl of four in her chemise and under vest. In her hand was a whip made of a porridge stick and a spindle cord. On the floor, before her, were two spinning wheels, at which she clacked her tongue and lashed. It was understood, of course, they were a team of horses, and it was also understood that this was a race at a crowded market fair. The horses were running at a furious pace, maddened by shouts and lashings, and the people had to stand aside or they'd be run over.

"Det out of my way, Pey Olsa! Back wiv you, countwy bumpkins!

"Here comes one who's not afwaid of bailiff or police!

"Here comes the wag'bon' bawon.

"Heigh-ho, heigh-ho! It's ma'ket day in Bwo!

"Heigh-ho, heigh-ho! Now it's fun to be alive!"

The kitchen resounded with the merry peals of laughter, while all eyes followed the movements of the child, who stood there with sparkling eyes and cheeks aflame. She was so completely lost in her play that the spectators could almost see her curly golden hair tossing in the breeze. The table became a jolting, swaying gipsy wagon, racing through the milling throngs of a market fair.

The child was supple and wild as a young savage; she was full of mockery and fun. Everyone in the kitchen, from the housekeeper to the stable boy, was simply carried away. They had all turned from their tasks to follow the child's perilous drive.

It was the same with those who stood in the doorway: they too saw the child standing not upon the table but in a high wagon, and they could see the people dart to one side as the horses, with manes flying, came dashing on between market stalls and vehicles.

The first one to cast off the witch's spell was Baron Adrian. He and his wife had agreed not to mention his brother's fate to Charlotte or let her see his child. The Baroness had assured him that, since the child had not yet fully recovered from the measles, she would be kept in the nursery. The Baron quickly stepped to the kitchen door and closed it, and then offered an arm to Charlotte to escort her back to the family quarters.

But Charlotte stood still, as if she did not see his proffered arm.

"Whose child is that?" she asked him. "That face. . . . She must be one of our kinsfolk." She gripped the Baron's arm, and her voice shook as she continued:

"Cousin, you must tell me if the child is a relation of ours. I feel a close kinship with her."

Baron Adrian turned away without answering. The Baroness, however, informed her that the girl was a daughter of Göran Löwensköld. "The child has been sick in bed with the measles, and the nursemaid has allowed her to come down to the kitchen without permission."

"I daresay my cousin has heard of my brother, the vagabond baron," Baron Adrian said in a hard voice. "The girl's mother is a gipsy wench."

Charlotte moved toward the kitchen door as if walking in her sleep, opened it, and crossed over to the table with outstretched arms. The little girl standing up there playing horse trader cast a glance at Charlotte, and seeing something about her that she liked, threw down her whip and, with a handspring, leapt into Charlotte's arms.

Charlotte caught the child to her breast and kissed her.

"It is you I want," she cried, "you, you, you!"

Here was her deliverance. She breathed a sigh of relief.

The ugliness, the awful ugliness which she had struggled against the whole evening, the ugliness which she had tried to find useful and good, she could now let pass for what it was worth. What the Baron would say or the Baroness would say she did not know or care, but she knew this was the child she had gone out to find.

Of a sudden she shrank back. Baron Adrian had come right upon her with clenched fists and blood in his eye.

"He looks like a mad bull, ready to gore me," she thought.

Just then the Baroness stepped between her husband and Charlotte and said in her quiet way:

"Charlotte, if you take this child home with you my husband and I will be everlastingly grateful."

"What, I?" said the Baron with a sardonic laugh.

The Baroness followed up her advantage with fervour.

"I shall be thankful to you because I do not have to part with any of my dear little daughters, and Adrian will owe you still greater thanks for preventing him from doing a thing which he would have regretted all his life."

The Baron was speechless. Perhaps it was the truth that lay back of his wife's words that struck home, or it may have been sheer amazement at her daring to oppose him. At all events, he turned round and walked out of the kitchen in silence.

CHAPTER III

THE MARKET PREACHER

WHAT could be more delightful, thought Charlotte, than to be awakened in the morning by the patter of little feet as the maid comes into your room to light the fire? Or what could be more fun than to shut your eyes and lie quite still, while a little child, despite the whispered warning not to disturb the sleeper, persists in pulling at the cover to clamber up into your bed? And then what shrieks of delight as you put out your hands to help her and she lands right on top of you! She smacks you on the cheeks, kicks, pinches, and kisses you. What can you do but laugh and rejoice with her? You begin to talk some kind of baby prattle and suddenly remember a lot of foolish pet names. The maid really needn't apologize for letting the child come in. The little thing, she said, had begged and coaxed her all the morning to let her see the pretty lady she had seen the night before, and she promised to be very quiet so as not to disturb the lady.

The maid wants to take the child out with her when she leaves the room. The little one, fearing something of the sort may happen, has crept in under the covers and pretends to be asleep. The moment she hears the door close she is wide awake and begins to chatter. She is relating something about her father, but she speaks so fast and so slovenly that Charlotte cannot follow her. But what does it matter? Anyhow, it is the sweet little voice of the child that charms her.

Just as the fire blazes at its best the door opens again, and the maid comes in with the coffee tray, followed by the lady of the house. The plump little Baroness, after asking how her guest has slept, serves the coffee. Then, pouring out a few drops for herself, she sits down by the fire to chat with the guest.

The child has ceased talking, but keeps a tight grip on her bedfellow's hand, lest she be taken away. After a little she falls asleep, and Charlotte, quite enraptured, lies regarding the rosy face; for she has fallen a willing victim to this vagabond youngster who has taken a fancy to her.

The Baroness hopes Charlotte will remain at Hedeby a few days longer. She and her household would be so happy if she would stay to brighten their loneliness. Besides, she must allow her to provide the child with proper clothing before she leaves. She should have a couple of mourning frocks made up, and a few changes of underwear, so as not to be too shabbily dressed when she comes to Stor Sjötorp.

It is a new and delightful experience to Charlotte to be called to the nursery a dozen times a day by a despotic little tyrant who wants her. Children must have a wonderfully good guessing ability, thought she. This child has guessed at once that Charlotte, like herself, is a good horsewoman. She has found out that none of the others can trot so well before the upturned stool that represents the wagon, or bear the reins with such true horse instinct, or mind so well her whoas and giddaps. There is something decidedly tragi-comic in being initiated into the mysteries of vagabond life by a little child; to play that the one chair is Ekeby and the other Björne; to drive up to those two chairs and ask for work, only to be turned away with a curt refusal, and then to discuss from actual experience the prospects of this or that place.

But the most touching of all is to see the child suddenly stop playing, drop her whip, and run over to the window to watch for the father, who has left his child forever. She stands there for hours, deaf to all inducements and coaxings. Charlotte could almost weep to see her stand there with her little face pressed against the pane, her little hands shutting out all distracting sights. "Ah, that child, whatever her faults, knows how to love!"

To judge from her wealth of games and pranks the child must be well endowed with brains, too. It is due to her that the days at Hedeby do not seem long or monotonous. For undeniably a spirit of gloom pervades the old place.

It is entirely the fault of Baron Adrian. He is sullen

and morose and has a depressing effect upon the whole family, who otherwise would be rather pleasant folk.

The day after Charlotte's arrival the Baron ordered the farm bailiff to take Göran Löwensköld's horse and sledge, with all its contents, back to northern Värmland. He was to turn the husband's property over to the widow and to inform her that the vagabond baron had been found dead in a roadside ditch and that relatives were caring for his child. Upon the messenger's return Baron Adrian told Charlotte, from what he could gather, that the mother was glad to be rid of the girl. Therefore he thought that she could now regard the child as hers. At the same time he cautioned her against taking any immediate steps toward a legal adoption. After all, he said, the child was only a little vagabond, with a poor heritage, and he wouldn't be surprised if, in a month or two, she were obliged to send her back to her mother.

On this occasion the Baron did the right thing, but otherwise he made no effort to control his irascibility. Fortunately, he rarely appeared save at mealtime. Then it was hard to find a topic of conversation that he would not break up with a cynical laugh or a cutting remark.

To one whose married life is supremely happy, and who, moreover, has a natural tendency to help, it is hard not to interfere. But Charlotte had to admit her inability in this case. It was too cruel a joke Göran Löwensköld had played on his brother at their last meeting, and Baron Adrian could not forgive him for having snatched from his hand the power to retaliate.

Since Charlotte felt powerless to help Baron Adrian, she devoted herself all the more zealously to his wife and his little daughters—lightening the burden of oppression that rested upon them. The mere fact that Charlotte was in the house seemed to give the poor Baroness more courage and confidence. So, little by little, Charlotte managed to call forth laughter and banter at table, anecdotes and stories round the fire at dusk. She arranged sleighing parties and invited all the ladies at Hedeby on long drives behind her own fine horses; she persuaded the Baroness to play some beautiful selections from Handel and Bach on her small piano, and discovering that the five carrot-heads had nice singing voices, she inspired them with the courage to stand up at the piano and sing, to their mother's accompaniment: "Come, lovely May, look down on us with smiling eyes."

By the time the child had been supplied with a sufficient number of dresses, petticoats, and other things, the Baroness saw that Charlotte had better be going. The snowdrifts in the avenue were beginning to sink, and already there were bare spots showing, here and there, in the road. Out on Lake Löven the ice was still thick and firm, but pools of water were visible on the surface, and the heavy traffic, which heretofore had been seen crossing the ice-bound lake in all directions, had ceased. Charlotte must leave before the ice route was closed.

The day before the departure the Baroness proposed that they take a stroll over to Bro churchyard to see the Löwensköld family tomb, about which there had been so much talk. It was only a short walk, but the road was slippery and difficult on account of the thaw. However, this disagreeable feature was overbalanced by the pleasure of walking in the bright sunshine, of feeling once again a warm, gentle breeze caressing the cheek, and the joy of hearing the first lark's trill across the still snowclad meadows.

On the way the Baroness touched upon a delicate subject: she spoke of Karl Arthur Ekenstedt. Although she saw that Charlotte winced at the mention of that name, she continued, hoping to arouse her sympathy. Wouldn't Charlotte do something for him—Charlotte who was so rich and whose husband granted her every wish?

Charlotte gave a shrug. True, no one had a kinder or more indulgent husband, and for that very reason she would take no chances. The old Polhem saw was still at Stora Sjötorp! For the last four years she had not permitted herself to think of Karl Arthur, much less to help him.

She tried to draw the speaker away from her subject; but the Baroness, contrary to her usual habit, did not take the hint. When they came to the grave where rests the huge sarcophagus, she pointed out to Charlotte the place where Malvina Spaak once on a time dropped the General's stolen ring back into the grave. Whereupon she remarked:

"The woman who travels about with Karl Arthur is said to be a daughter of Malvina Spaak."

"Yes," said Charlotte. "And that is why Karl Arthur has such unbounded faith in her. But let us say no more about those persons, I've had trouble enough on their account."

The little Baroness obeyed instantly. And now Charlotte was touched. "Well, I declare, I'm as bad as her husband," she thought, "not to let her finish what she has to say." Aloud she said: "I understand that you have something on your mind which you think I should know."

The Baroness then related that one day, the previous autumn, while visiting the big market fair at Broby, as she was making her purchases a woman's voice suddenly burst into song. It sounded strange amid all the noises of the fair, and she stopped to listen. The voice was far from beautiful, and the hymn was screeched out with such gusto it was enough to deafen you. She did not know who the singer was, but she had heard enough of the awful screeching and turned to go to another part of the fair grounds. But that was easier said than done. For at the sound of this dreadful voice people came running from all directions—eager and laughing—as if it were the introduction to some uncommonly jolly entertainment. The Baroness was caught in the crush and pushed forward until she stood right in front of the singer. The woman was standing in a common wagon, on the bottom of which were a lot of grimy bundles. She was obese and ugly, but whether she was young or old was impossible to tell. She wore a long wadded cloak, patched in several places, and her head was covered with a heavy woolen shawl crossed over the chest and tied at the back. She looked like a huckster in a market stall. It was obvious that she had no desire to make herself attractive or pleasing.

Before she could finish the hymn the listeners shouted at her to stop that caterwauling, but she went on singing until some convivial youths began to mimic her. At that, she broke off instantly and sat down among the bundles in the wagon, with her back to the crowd. She sat rocking her body from side to side and shivering with the cold, or anguish, perhaps.

A man now mounted the wagon. He had a heavy dark beard streaked with gray, and as he removed his wide-rimmed black hat he exposed to view a head that was almost bald. The Baroness recognized the man, nevertheless, as Karl Arthur Ekenstedt. He had grown thin to the point of emaciation, and there was not a trace of his former pulchritude left, but she knew him by his voice and a way he had of lifting his heavy eyelids. Besides, she had heard that he went about preaching at market fairs and other places where many people gather.

But Charlotte was not to think that Karl Arthur delivered any serious or constructive lecture. He opened with a reading from the Scripture, but afterward he did nothing but scold. He seemed incensed from the start, and railed at the crowds for coming only to laugh at him.

He turned upon a peasant woman and berated her for being well dressed, and pointed a finger of scorn at a small boy because he was fat and rosy. There was no conceivable reason for his attacking the one or the other—none save that within him burned an unquenchable wrath against everything and everybody.

All through his harangue he kept his hands clenched and hurled out his words with such force that they came down upon you like a shower of hailstones. The Baroness could not deny that he had a certain kind of success. People thronged round him and laughed at everything he said, as if he were talking for their amusement.

But the most surprising thing was to hear him rail against poverty, which in former days he could not praise enough. The Baroness had seen him show the people the patches on his clothes and had heard him curse those who he thought were responsible for his poverty. Most of all he blamed his father and his sisters. His mother was dead, and he should have had his share of her fortune and been a rich man now, had not his hypocritical, grasping, thievish sisters withheld from him his portion.

"Impossible!" said Charlotte. "The man couldn't have been Karl Arthur."

"But, my dear, he mentioned them by name! There is no doubt as to who he was."

"Is he insane?"

"No, for he expressed himself with a certain clearness; but I should say that he is a changed man. There is nothing of the old Karl Arthur about him. Fancy! He boasted that he could have become a bishop had he so wished; that there was no one in the whole country who could preach as he had preached. He said he might have been Archbishop by now, if designing persons had not brought about his ruin. You can understand how ludicrous it sounded to the people when that poor gaunt wreck of a man declared that he could have been a bishop; they were simply convulsed with laughter. For me, however, it was no laughing matter; I only wished I could get away from it all."

The Baroness cast a sidelong glance at Charlotte to see how she reacted; she frowned and turned half away, as if the story did not interest her.

"There is not much more to tell," the Baroness continued. "I merely wish to state that when he declared that he could have become the Archbishop of all Sweden there came a short derisive laugh from the woman squatting on the floor of the wagon. He heard it, of course, and from that moment his fury was vented upon her. How dared she laugh at him—she, who was the cause of all his misery; she who had parted him from his betrothed, from his mother, from his wife; she who had made him resign from the ministry so that he could no longer preach in a church. She was the noose around his neck, the venomous reptile that dripped poison into his wounds every day; she would never cease torturing him until he stuck a knife into her.

The Baroness paused again to see whether this had made any impression upon Charlotte. Neither by word nor gesture did she evince the slightest interest. The Baroness, in despair at this indifference, spoke now with furious rapidity.

"His high-sounding phrases apparently had no effect upon the woman; she sat quietly through it all. Then he said something to which she retorted, and they fell to quarrelling. Oh, I couldn't repeat the things they said to each other! They went into the most intimate personal matters. It looked as if they were about to spring at each other's throats. I was afraid I might have to witness such a spectacle; so I broke through the crowd, pushing and shoving the people out of my way. But, Charlotte, I can't forget those unhappy wretches! I suppose they are going about like that, even to this day. And his father and his sisters are living, and you, Charlotte——"

"I don't understand," Charlotte interrupted, as though she thought the whole description a gross exaggeration, if not an invention. "I saw Karl Arthur four years ago; he was dressed like a peasant but looked a prince in disguise. How, then, can he have become so degraded, so utterly unlike himself, in a few short years?"

"But suffering, dear Charlotte—think what he has suffered! Think of all he has passed through—the defeats, the disillusionment, the humiliation! Think of living with that woman! Imagine his hopelessness, his self-condemnation! Remember, he has had to lead about the same kind of life as that of my brother-in-law, the vagabond baron. What if he should end his days as a murderer? If you have ever loved him——"

"If——" Charlotte bit her lips to keep from shrieking. Without glancing round, she hastened away from the churchyard and turned down the road which led to Hedeby. She had thought she was through with that man forever, and now he comes again, unhappy and a reprobate, forcing himself upon her through his degradation and his appalling plight!

The two ladies walked apart most of the way back. Neither of them spoke. But at the beginning of the avenue Charlotte stopped to wait for the Baroness. She smiled rather wistfully and shook her head, but carefully avoided any mention of the subject they had just been discussing.

"Do you know that we've been gone scarcely an hour?" she said with forced gaiety. "Yet I'm really glad to get back. Can you understand the power that child has over me? I'm actually longing to see my little girl again."

As they walked along the avenue Charlotte looked up at the nursery window to see if there was not a little face pressed against the pane. When they came into the house yard she expected to see the front door flung open and a child come bounding out through the puddles and slush to greet her. But instead it was Baron Adrian who came hurrying toward them.

He had on his heavy wolfskin coat and long travelling belt, which was bound round his waist several times, and his high, wide riding boots that looked as though they had been patterned after the cavalry boots of Charles XII, as seen in his great-grandfather's portrait. It was obvious that he was going on a journey and was coming to tell them the reason.

The Baroness suspected at once that something dreadful had occurred in their absence. "Oh, dear, dear," she sighed, "what's the matter now?"

It did not appear to be anything alarming, however, but quite the reverse. Baron Adrian had suddenly cast off his sullenness and become friendly and affable. "Now you shall hear some surprising news," he said. "You had scarcely been gone an hour when a gipsy sledge with a man and a woman of the usual sort drove up to the house. The woman remained in the sledge, but the man got out, walked into the house and straight to my room. And what do you think the nature of this errand was? Well, merely to demand, in my honourable sister-in-law's behalf, remuneration for allowing us to take care of her child."

"But that was to be expected," said Charlotte.

"Naturally. There was nothing extraordinary in that," the Baron conceded. "The man who came in to see me was poorly clad and looked as fellows of that ilk generally look. I took him at first for a common vagabond. But there was something about his voice that sounded familiar, and while he was talking I wondered where I had seen him before. Besides, his manner of approach was not quite what one would expect in a fellow of that sort."

"Oh, my God!"

"I see that Cousin Charlotte has already guessed who the man was. But my wits were not so keen. I tried to recall to memory the various gipsy physiognomies one sees at the Broby fairs, while, at the same time, berating him for his impudence in making such a demand. I indulged rather freely in invective and profanity, as that seems to be the only talk those people understand. Had he been just a common vagabond he would have taken the abuse and not said a word, for those fellows usually have some respect for a gentleman. This man, however, gave me tit for tat; he let me know what he thought of me. I was told that I had treated my brother shamefully, that I should have asked my sister-in-law to attend the funeral, and much more of the same sort. At last I brought my fist down upon the table and told him to clear out. But he would not go."

"Did you tell him, Cousin——"

"——That it was the rich Fru Schagerström who was going to take the child? Oh, no, Cousin, I took good care not to mention that! It would only have brought increased demands. The fellow, however, kept on bullying me, as if it afforded him special pleasure. He went finally, but not until he had got me so infuriated that I was ready to throw him out. He said that unless I paid for the child I could not keep her."

Charlotte had listened with great uneasiness. On the way home from the churchyard she had come to the conclusion that she neither could nor dared do anything more for Karl Arthur. Was the struggle to begin all over again?

"Just as he slammed the door behind him," the Baron continued, "it flashed in upon me that the man I had had the honour of talking with was my cousin Karl Arthur Ekenstedt. He is said to have been much in the company of my late brother, the vagabond baron, and drives about the country in a gipsy sledge, the same as he did. He spends his winters up North, where these wandering tribes hold forth; so it was quite natural that he should try to squeeze money out of me for that gipsy wench my brother had married."

"But then, when you recognized him, Cousin, did you let him go?"

"Naturally, when I realized who the man was I ran out at once to have another word with him. But by that time he was already in the sledge and out of the gate. I called to him as loud as I could, but he drove right on."

"And now you intend to follow him?"

"Yes, Cousin, that is my intention. Do you know what has happened? Karl Arthur had gone but a short distance down the avenue when he suddenly stopped. Our nursemaid was walking there with the children—

presumably to meet you. The woman in the sledge, recognizing my brother's daughter, called to her. When the child ran over to her, the woman bent down and drew her up into the sledge. Karl Arthur plied the whip, and the horse set off. They carried the child away right before my eyes!"

"Is my little girl gone?"

"I stood there helpless. I couldn't pursue them, as my horses are all up in the forest, hauling firewood."

"But my horses——"

"Yes, to be sure, I remembered that they were here, and as this was a matter which concerned you, Cousin Charlotte, as well as myself, I took the liberty of asking your coachman to hitch up. I was waiting for him to drive round when I saw you and Amelie coming. You need not be at all uneasy, the child will soon be here again. Ah! here we have the horses."

He was just going to jump into the sleigh when Charlotte caught him by the arm.

"Wait a moment, Cousin Adrian—I would like to go with you."

He flushed all over his face. With the frank openheartedness which had characterized him in his youth, he turned to her and said:

"Have no fear, Cousin Charlotte, I'll bring the child back if it costs me my life! I've been going about here the whole week feeling rather ashamed of myself, and I should like to do something to show my gratitude to you for not letting me turn the poor child away."

"Ah, Cousin Adrian, I assure you that is not my reason for wishing to accompany you. But I am so constituted that it's hard for me to believe the worst. It is only now, since he has stolen my little girl, that I understand how bad things are with Karl Arthur. Therefore I want to go with you so that I may talk to him."

CHAPTER IV

THE PURSUIT

IT WAS not so easy to overtake the runaways as Baron Adrian had supposed, partly because they had a good start of their pursuers, but mostly because the going was bad. Charlotte's excellent horses strained to their utmost to pull the heavy touring sleigh, and where the road was entirely clear of snow, they could only walk their horses. Charlotte felt as if she were held in a vise, and glared angrily at the tracks of the narrow gipsy sledge, which could take advantage of every inch of snow along the edge of the road and cut across fields that were still snow covered.

But the farther they got away from the flat country around Bro the better the roads. Charlotte became more hopeful now of getting back her little girl. She and Baron Adrian had suddenly become the best of friends. They had each discovered in the other an honourable and upright person—a bit unreasonable perhaps, but nevertheless the sort with whom it is a pleasure to associate. The Baron declared outright that he was glad Charlotte had not left Hedeby before he had learned to know her. Charlotte, however, expressed herself with more reserve; but as she despaired of being able to persuade her husband to come to Karl Arthur's aid she asked Baron Adrian if he would not take Karl Arthur in hand.

"You are his cousin, and for you it must be most embarrassing to have a near relative going about the country like a common tramp."

"No, no, Cousin Charlotte," he said laughingly, "that won't go down with me! I will have nothing to do with those persons, and it would be best for you to follow my example."

She was surprised at his curt reply, but thought she knew the reason. "You think it shocking that Karl Arthur, who is a married man, goes about with another man's wife?"

"Ha, ha! So my cousin takes me for such a model of virtue! I wasn't thinking of that, though it is a deplorable thing to be sure. What could have possessed Cousin Karl Arthur that he did not see that travelling in such company would make all his preaching an abomination?"

"I think the first thing to be done is to separate them."

"What, them?" Baron Adrian laid a thickly gloved hand upon her shoulder. "Those two, Cousin Charlotte, you will never be able to part save at the block or the gallows."

Charlotte, who sat well tied in under a big carriage

robe, tried in vain to see her companion's face. "You're jesting, of course," she said.

The Baron made no direct reply. Removing his hand from her shoulder, he settled back in the sleigh and went on talking in the same light, half-jocular tone that he had used before.

"May I venture to ask whether my cousin Charlotte has heard of a curse that hangs over the Löwenskölds?"

"Oh, yes, I have heard of it, Cousin Adrian, but I must confess that I have forgotten what it hinges upon."

"You who live in the great world must regard all such things as crude superstition."

"Worse than that, Cousin. The supernatural has no appeal for me; it is a sense I'm lacking in. Sister Marie Louise, on the contrary——"

The Baron gave a light laugh. "If you are not a believer, so much the better. I wanted to tell you about the curse, but was afraid it would frighten you."

"You may be quite easy as to that."

"Well, then," he began—but suddenly checked himself and pointed at the coachman, who sat directly in front of them, thinking he might hear every word he said. "Perhaps I'd better wait till another time."

Charlotte tried again to see the Baron's face. There was a note of raillery in his voice, as if he were making fun of the old family myth. At the same time he was very particular not to have the coachman overhear him. Charlotte hastened to dispel his fears.

"Little you know my husband if you think that he would hire a coachman without first having assured himself that the man was deaf enough to permit the riders to carry on a conversation undisturbed."

"Admirable, Cousin! I'll go and do likewise. What I wished to say was that we Löwensölds once had a bitter enemy in a certain Marit Eriksdotter, a peasant woman whose father, uncle, and sweetheart were accused, though innocent, of robbing our ancestor's grave of a ring and, in consequence, lost their lives on the gallows. Naturally, the poor woman sought revenge, and that with the aid of the ring. My own father came near being the first victim. But, happily, he was saved by the intervention of Malvina Spaak, who had won the affection of Marit Eriksdotter and with her aid was enabled to restore the fatal ring to the Löwensköld grave."

"For goodness' sake, Cousin Adrian, don't think me a benighted heathen! The story of the Löwensköld ring I have heard from beginning to end."

"But I daresay you have not heard that Marit Eriksdotter, upon my father's recovery from the terrible shock, called upon my paternal grandmother, the Baroness Augusta Löwensköld, and demanded of her that she permit her son to marry Jungfru Spaak. She maintained that my grandmother had promised, the previous evening, to do so, and that it was only because of that promise she had refrained from carrying out her threat. My grandmother said that she could not have made any such promise, knowing her son was betrothed to someone else. She would gladly reward Malvina Spaak to any extent in her power, but that which Marit demanded of her was impossible."

"Now that you speak of it," said Charlotte, "I remember having heard something of the sort. But it seems to me the most natural thing in the world that Marit would not rest content with what had already occurred."

"Nor did she, Cousin. As she continued to press the matter, Grandmother sent for Jungfru Malvina, who corroborated her statement, that no promise of marriage with the son of the house had been made to her. In fact, Jungfru Malvina confirmed everything her mistress said. This infuriated Marit Eriksdotter, who felt that nothing had been gained by refraining from avenging the great wrong her kinsmen had suffered. She told my grandmother that the work of vengeance would be resumed.

"'Three of mine,' she shouted, 'have suffered a violent death. Three of yours shall also come to a sudden, cruel end because you have failed to keep your word.'"

"But, Cousin Adrian——"

"I think I know what you would say, Cousin Charlotte. My grandmother thought as you do, that the poor woman was harmless. And she answered quietly: 'You are too old now, Marit, to take the lives of three Barons Löwensköld.'

"'Aye, I am old and my days are numbered,' Marit

was said to have answered; 'but whether I am over the sod or under the sod I shall have the power to send an avenger.'"

Charlotte gave the sleigh robe a violent jerk so that she could look the Baron in the face.

"But you don't mean that you attach any significance to that kind of talk from a poor, ignorant peasant woman?" she said with all the assurance in the world. "As a matter of fact, I know the story very well. My dear friend the Baroness Ekenstedt used to tell it, only to show how little there was to such predictions. She regarded it as of no importance whatever."

"I'm not so sure that my aunt was right that time," said the Baron rising to cast a glance down the road. "It doesn't look as if we should overtake them very soon," he said, and sat down again. "If you will permit me, I should like to tell you of an extraordinary thing that happened at Hedeby in my parents' time."

"Oh, do, Cousin Adrian! The time will pass so much the faster."

"It was in the summer of 1816," the Baron began. "We were to have a big celebration at Hedeby in honour of my mother's birthday. As was usual on such occasions, my parents sent for Malvina Spaak some days before the party, to help with the preparations. At that time she was married, and her name was Thorbergsson, but we always called her by the name she had borne during the fifteen years she was in service at Hedeby as housekeeper, which name I think she, herself, preferred.

It was Fru Malvina's supreme delight to come to Hedeby and give a helping hand at a dinner party or some other important function. Her husband was a poor tenant farmer, and she had no opportunity at home to demonstrate her skill in the art of fine cookery. It was only at Hedeby she could shine in her specialty."

"Was there not also some other attraction that drew her there?" queried Charlotte, recalling to memory an episode in the family history.

"Yes, Cousin, there was. I was just going to touch upon that. Fru Malvina's old master and mistress, Grandfather Bengt Göran Löwensköld and Grandmother Augusta, had died, and my father, who was then master of Hedeby, had been the fancy of her youth. Although the first hot love had cooled, she still had a weakness for my father. It seemed to us children as if Father and Mother had a deep affection for Malvina Spaak. They always received her with marked pleasure, they let her sit with them at the family table and talked freely to her of their joys and sorrows. We boys never suspected that pity and remorse were at the bottom of their friendship."

"The Baroness Ekenstedt had often spoken of Fru Malvina's devotion to the family," said Charlotte.

"And her devotion to our parents was also extended to us boys—Brother Göran and me. She would prepare our favourite dishes and always had some tidbit to give us when we visited her in the kitchen, and she could tell the most hair-raising ghost stories. Göran, because of his personal appearance, was her favourite. I, who was a red-cheeked, flaxen-haired lad and who looked like the average country boy, could not awaken in her any tender recollections. But Göran, on the contrary, was a handsome lad, with large dark eyes and a creamy complexion. He was said to favour Father. When Fru Malvina looked up from the dough trough or roasting pot she must have fancied that time had stood still and that the idol of her youth had come back to ask her what one must do to make a dead man rest quietly in his grave."

A tinge of sadness had come into Charlotte's face. "I know those eyes," she said as it were to herself.

"The friendly relations between Fru Malvina and us boys," the Baron continued, "lasted until the summer of 1816, when she made the grave mistake of bringing her daughter Thea to Hedeby. The girl was only thirteen years of age, and as I was eighteen and Göran sixteen, we considered ourselves much too old to play with her. It would have taken a very high order of amiability to make us forget the difference in our ages. Besides, little Thea had a short clumsy body, protruding eyes, and a lisp. We found her detestable and avoided her. Fru Malvina, who thought her little Thea a remarkably clever child, felt a bit hurt."

"To think that I should be thitting bethide a Baron Löwensköld," said Charlotte, imitating her lisp and her drawl, "a thon of the Baron Adrian Löwensköld whom my thainted mother loved——"

She checked herself. "Ah! forgive me, Cousin! I forgot how it was with her now. It was wrong of me to make fun of the poor unfortunate creature."

The Baron laughed. "What a pity you have scruples, Cousin Charlotte, for you have a great talent. I thought it was little Thea, herself, I had beside me in the sleigh. . . . But before I go on with the story, please tell me if it bores you. It isn't every day that I meet a relation of mine, and, somehow, it makes me feel young again. All the past comes back to me."

Charlotte, who had followed with the keenest interest, quickly reassured him, and he continued:

"You would have been more lenient with us for our rudeness to little Thea than our parents were. My mother, noting that Fru Malvina was not in her usual good humour, guessed the reason why. She sternly commanded us to be polite to little Thea. My father also laid down the law. As we were accustomed to obey our parents, we took the girl along with us a few times, when we went rowing, and shook down pippins for her from the apple trees. Fru Malvina, the good soul, brightened, and all went smoothly until the day of the party."

"What a pity you didn't drown her!"

"Ah, Cousin, you can understand our feelings! All the gentry in the parish had come to the house. We met young boys and girls we knew well and liked; so we saw no reason why we should dance attendance on little Thea on this occasion. Mother had told us pointedly that she was to be at the party and, to the best of my recollection, she was appropriately dressed. But as no one there knew her, and as her appearance, moreover, was repellent, no one paid her any attention. We did not include her in our outdoor games and, in the evening, when there was dancing in the ballroom, she was not asked to dance. Mother was busy, entertaining her guests, and forgot to see how little Thea was faring. It was not until we sat down to supper that she suddenly thought of her. Then the mischief had already been done. She asked the maid what had become of the girl and learned that she was out in the kitchen with her mother crying. No one had spoken to her, she said, and she had not been asked to dance or to join in the games. Dear Mother of course felt rather distressed about it, but she couldn't leave her guests to go comfort a spoiled child. I'm quite sure that she thought little Thea as detestable as we boys did."

"Thea has always had an amazing faculty for creating trouble," Charlotte observed.

"You're right, Cousin. Fru Malvina, of course, was highly offended on her daughter's account, and next morning, before Mother had got the sleep out of her eyes, the maid came to her room and announced that Malvina was going home and wished to know if she could have a conveyance. Mother was surprised, for Malvina had arranged to stay a few days after the party, to rest. She hurried out to see her but found her inflexible. So she sent for Father. He told her that he had observed little Thea the previous evening and thought she conducted herself very well. Fru Malvina was immediately assuaged, and the journey home was postponed. It was decided that she should stay another week in order that the children might get better acquainted and become good friends."

"That was almost too cruel a punishment, Cousin."

"When that had been settled," the Baron continued, "Father summoned us boys to his room. 'How dare you disobey my orders!' he said, and dealt us each a sound box on the ear. Father had always been a patient and kindly man and never raised a hand to us before. So you can imagine our astonishment. We couldn't understand why Father should be so indulgent toward little Thea. He gave us to understand that we were to treat her with the utmost consideration and kindness. Then he informed us that she was to stay another week so that we children would learn to love her."

"And that, of course, was more than you could stand."

"I managed to keep silent, but Göran, who was of a more fiery temperament, incensed by the box on the ear, shouted out: 'Why should we be charmed with little Thea just because you've been in love with Malvina Spaak?' I thought Father would turn him out of the house. But instead, he sat down in his big armchair and bade us boys come closer and stand at either side of him. Taking our hands in his, he said that a great wrong had once been done Malvina Spaak. At one time, when his life hung in the balance (he was sure we knew to what he referred), he surmised that his mother had in some way led her to believe that she was to become her daughter-in-law if she succeeded in saving the life of her son. This promise, of course, could not be fulfilled, and Malvina accepted the situation with rare tact. Father felt that he owed her a debt of gratitude that could never be repaid, and he begged us boys always to treat Fru Malvina and her daughter with the greatest consideration and respect."

"It was a very touching appeal, Cousin."

"I must say that we boys thought it more ludicrous than touching."

Just then the coachman turned to them and said that he had sighted a vehicle at the top of the nearest hill.

The Baron stood up. He too saw a vehicle, but as the next hill was nearly two miles away he couldn't tell whether the vehicle was the right one. However, he told Lundman to drive as fast as he could and quickly made up a plan of attack. "When we come alongside their sledge you take the reins, Charlotte, and, Lundman, you jump down and hold their horse while I step up to their sleigh and move the child over into ours."

"We'll fall upon them like regular highway robbers," laughed Charlotte.

"That's the proper grease for such hide," the Baron rejoined.

He leaned over the side of the sleigh and looked down

the road. The zest of the chase was upon him, and he thought no more of the old tale he had been so eager to relate.

"It will be a half hour before we overtake them," said Charlotte, "so do let me hear the outcome of the episode."

"With pleasure, Cousin. Well, the upshot was that Göran couldn't stand the society of little Thea another week, so he hit upon the idea of making a large signet ring of beeswax, gilt paper, and a bit of red sealing wax. He showed it to the girl and told her it was the famous Löwensköld ring. He said that he had found it in the churchyard, and that now the General's ghost might haunt Hedeby at any time, to demand the return of his trinket. Little Thea was terrified, and Fru Malvina threatened to leave at once. There was an investigation, at which brother Göran produced the wax ring and confessed. Father gave him an awful flogging. After that, Göran ran away. For twenty-six years he never set foot in Hedeby again, but roamed the country as a common vagabond—to the great grief of his parents and the disgrace of all his kith and kin."

"Oh, Cousin Adrian, I never knew that his misfortunes began in that way!"

"Yes, Cousin, that was the way of it. All things considered, one might truthfully say it was little Thea who sent him to his death in the gutter. So, she has disposed of one of us. . . . Look, there we have them!"

Again the Baron leaned over the side of the sleigh;

but the sledge they were pursuing was soon out of sight. He turned again to Charlotte.

"I came near forgetting why I made you listen to this tale. It was to warn you against any attempt to separate Karl Arthur from Thea. You see, Cousin, I believe that Malvina Spaak's daughter has a duty to perform of which she, herself, is not aware. Remember, Marit Eriksdotter said that she would send an avenger."

With that he turned to Charlotte and looked into her eyes. On his face was an expression of impending doom. She saw, in a flash of intuition, that this morbid dreamer who had no one at home in whom he could confide in his hours of loneliness had brooded over the old tale of retribution until it had become a fixed idea with him, that Thea Sundler had been appointed to carry out the doom.

She remembered the unhappy time when her engagement to Karl Arthur was broken off. She too had had the feeling that some sinister and irresistible power had stood by Thea and opposed all her own efforts to save the man she loved. This she did not mention to the Baron, but met his questioning look with feigned surprise.

"I don t see how this can apply to Karl Arthur," she said. "He is not a Löwensköld."

"It was not specified in the prediction that all three victims should bear the name of Löwensköld, but only that they should be descendants of my paternal grandmother."

"And you think, because of that horrid old wives' tale, that I should not speak to Karl Arthur if I meet him this evening—that I should not try to part him from Thea or do anything at all to bring him back to a more decent way of living?"

Baron Adrian's troubled gaze still rested upon Charlotte, and his voice betrayed his utter hopelessness.

"I would not forbid you to try, Cousin Charlotte, I merely said it was useless. As you know, I saw Karl Arthur a few hours ago, and I assure you he will soon be ripe for death in the gutter—the way my brother went. A sudden cruel end, Cousin, right in the prime of his life!"

"How can you imagine anything so absurd!"

The Baron let his gloomy gaze wander over the landscape. "What do we know of the things that happen around us—why one person fares well and another ill? There are so many kinds of unpaid debts that must be met!"

Charlotte was losing patience, despite her sympathy for the man. "And after Thea has finished with Karl Arthur, I suppose it will be your turn next."

"Yes, then it will be my turn. But it is of no consequence, Cousin. If I had a son I would gladly give my own life to pay the debt that hangs over the Löwenskölds. My son, you see, could lead a happy life. He could bring honour to our name. There would be nothing to hinder him from being a useful and respected man. We three, Karl Arthur, my brother, and I, have been unable to achieve anything because of the curse laid upon us, but my son, Cousin, would not have that to bear."

Lundman, turning to them, saluted with his whip and pointed down the road.

Baron Adrian had settled back in his corner and showed no interest in the pursuit. Charlotte could see only his profile, but thought he looked sullen and morose—as he had earlier in the week.

"Now he is brooding again. What shall I do?"

This continued for some little time. The road they were traversing was crooked and hilly, now running along the lake shore, now losing itself in a dense forest, now winding its way between the closely built houses of a rural village. At no point did it present an open vista. The sledge they were pursuing came into view one moment and disappeared the next. Charlotte, little as she believed in the Baron's brain spectres, felt a stronger and stronger sympathy for him. She suddenly resolved to do the only thing that might perchance comfort him, though without much hope of success. But she felt an irresistible urge to do something.

"Cousin Adrian."

"What can I do for you?"

"I have something to tell you."

"I'm at your command, Cousin. You have shown unlimited patience in listening to my stupid tale."

His tone was unpleasant and sarcastic, but Charlotte was thankful that he spoke.

"May God forgive me if I do wrong! But I must tell you that the man whom you sent up North to the gipsy quarters, upon his return to Hedeby asked if he might speak to the Baroness in private, as he wished her to know that your brother Göran had left a son."

Once more the Baron laid a heavy hand on Charlotte's shoulder. "Cousin, is this something you are making up?"

"I'd be a monster to lie to you in a matter like this! Yes, Cousin Adrian, there is a boy up there. He is six years old, large for his age, and well built. He is not so good-looking as his sister, but more like old Bengt of the portrait. The farmer bailiff wanted to know whether he ought to tell you about the lad. There's something wrong with him."

"Is he an idiot?"

"No, indeed. He is a fine, bright boy, but—" her voice suddenly failed her under the strain, and she could only whisper the words—"he is blind."

"How was that?"

"He is blind!" Charlotte reiterated—almost shriekingly. "That was why the old man didn't tell you. Amelie cautioned him to keep silence. She thought it was not the proper time to impart such information. She would tell you herself, she said, when your temper was more equable."

"Amelie is a cautious fool and will never be anything else."

"He has been blind from his birth; so it's not anything curable."

The Baron actually proceeded to shake Charlotte, as if he would shake the truth out of her.

"Tell me, is it true? Can you swear to there being a boy up there?"

"Why, of course there is. His name is Bengt Adrian. The little girl has often spoken of her brother. What's the matter, Cousin?"

The Baron, beside himself with joy, had thrown his arms around Charlotte and was kissing her, both on the cheeks and mouth. When he released her he was laughing heartily.

"Forgive me, Cousin! Oh, I say, you're a crown of jewels! No shoddy about you. You have the courage of a man. Next time you come to Hedeby I promise you that it will be a different place."

"I'm so glad, Cousin—glad beyond words! But don't forget that he is blind."

"Blind! I have five daughters at home with nothing to do but lead him and feed him, if necessary. I shall continue northward this evening, after we have got the girl. Ho! Lundman, can you see them?"

"They are not far away, Baron."

"Speed up, then. Now we'll get them. . . . Oh, *herregud*, what did you say his name was?"

"Bengt Adrian."

"Anyhow, brother Göran still had a heart for the old family. What was it, Cousin, that you wished me to do for Karl Arthur?"

"But he is doomed to destruction."

"Nonsense! Surely, you do not take seriously the vapourings of a splenetic old baron? That was only talk. I'll take charge of Karl Arthur. But what shall we do with Thea?"

"She has a husband living who is pining for her."

"He shall have her back, Cousin. And Karl Arthur must come to Hedeby—in the first place, to put some flesh on his bones. Amelie will take good care of him. That's the kind of thing she loves to do.—Look! There they are! We'll take them on the next hill."

They both leaned out of the sleigh in order to see better. They were now driving down a steep road, leading to the lake shore, after which they had a short stretch of even road to traverse, and then another hill. It was there the Baron expected to overtake the runaways.

The runaways evidently knew they would be overtaken on that hill, which rose, almost perpendicular, before them; so Karl Arthur swung his horse right around and, turning off the road, drove out on the lake.

"Now," said the Baron, elated, "we'll catch them all the easier."

Lundman, who by this time had passed the slope, without thinking, drove out on the ice, which though covered with a blending of water and snow, was apparently quite firm. They had not gone very far out, however, when the Baron shouted, "Stop, Lundman! Hold your horses! What are those people thinking of, to be driving out on the ice at that point? The river is just beyond."

From Charlotte's high sleigh they could see plainly that the ice straight ahead showed dark, which indicated that it had been thinned by a turbulent stream that came rushing down from the forest.

The Baron leapt out of the sleigh, put his hands to his mouth like a crier, and cried out a warning. Charlotte pulled and tore at the sleigh robe bindings until she too was free to move.

In a few seconds they heard a crash. Karl Arthur's horse had gone down, the sledge following.

The moment the ice broke Karl Arthur and the woman jumped out of the sledge and saved themselves. The three in Charlotte's sleigh saw them standing safe at the edge of the ice.

The Baron, in his heavy fur coat and his big driving boots, ran toward the open hole crying, "The child! The child!" Charlotte hurried after, and the coachman threw down his reins and ran too. The Baron was almost up to the hole when Charlotte heard him shout: "I see the child!" But just then the ice under him broke.

Charlotte was now so near the loosened ice it was almost at her feet. She rushed on, thinking only of bringing help—when Lundman caught her from behind.

"Don't run, mistress! Creep, for God's sake, creep!"

They both went down on their hands and knees and crept over to the hole. But they saw nothing.

"There is a strong current here," said Lundman. "They are already under the ice."

CHAPTER V

THE RETURN

CHARLOTTE drives back in utter darkness, and all the while she is weeping. The handkerchief with which she wipes her eyes gradually becomes wet with tears. It has turned cold in the night, and the handkerchief stiffens with frost. She tucks it under the rug to thaw it out.

Whatever she does, whether she weeps or dries her tears or puts her handkerchief away, it is all done unconsciously; for she is listening for the answer to a prayer which she says over and over again.

She has not Baron Adrian by her side now. There is no one near who can be of any help or comfort except the coachman. Lundman and she are very good friends, and he considers it his duty to turn round on the box, now and then, to give her a word of sympathy.

"Do you know, mistress, this is the most dreadful thing I have ever witnessed!"

This is undoubtedly so, but Charlotte does not allow herself time to reply. She is still praying the same prayer and listening for the answer.

The sleigh glides noiselessly on. Lundman has removed the bell collars from the horses and laid them
away in the drawer under the seat. At every uneven-
ness in the road they send forth a muffled ring, which
sounds hollow and uncanny, but it is in keeping with
the whole journey.

The horses seem to know they are on the home stretch
and want to run; but Lundman, thinking it would be
unseemly to let them run, keeps a tight rein. Although
no one sees them, he drives as slowly as if he were riding
in a funeral cortège.

"He was a fine man, that Baron Löwensköld," Lundman remarks, "and he died a hero's death."

Nor does this call for any response from Charlotte.
She is thinking of something else, and prays, prays
without ceasing, and listens for the answer.

Charlotte and Lundman are not alone in the sleigh.
By turning her head a trifle, she can see beside her on
the seat a large bundle which contains a human form.
It is not the body of Baron Adrian, nor that of the little
girl. In fact, it is not a dead person. No word comes
from that quarter, nor any perceptible movement. But
they are faring so noiselessly, and all is so quiet around
them that she can hear the faint snoring which sometimes accompanies breathing.

She tries to turn her thoughts to Baron Adrian and
the child. It would be a relief. They are dead and gone,
but no sense of fear comes with the memory of them—
only grief. She must go on with her prayers until they

reach the very Throne of God. She must pray that some good may come out of all the terrible things that have happened this day.

When Charlotte and Lundman had crept up to the hole in the ice and looked in vain for a trace of the drowning, Karl Arthur had called out to them that he would run ashore for help; which he did, and Thea went with him. There was a small iron foundry near by, run by the same stream that had caused the disaster. From there men had come rushing out on the lake with grappling hooks, and poked far under the ice crust. But it had been hopeless from the start; the strong current had carried them away. The men would have had to break up the ice in the whole lake to find them.

Charlotte had seen nothing more of Thea, but Karl Arthur had come back. He had been one of the most zealous helpers, often at the risk of his own life. He had not gone near Charlotte until the men, disheartened by their futile efforts, had given up the search and were turning back.

Then he had approached very slowly and hesitatingly, keeping his eyes lowered, as was his habit. When he had come quite close to her he raised his eyes a trifle, just enough to see her dress and cloak but not her face. Standing thus, he said as an excuse or perhaps a consolation:

"Göran, you see, wanted to get back his young one,

and perhaps he also wished to thank his rich brother for the fine funeral he gave him."

"Karl Arthur!"

He looked up, aghast. Obviously, he had not expected to see Charlotte, but thought that the lady who had accompanied Baron Adrian was his wife. He stood there, speechless, looking into her face and she into his. All the pain and horror which she had felt over his degradation and coarseness were depicted on her countenance, and he could not help reading what was written there.

But with that a change had come over him, which Charlotte knew of old as one of his heart attacks: The wild staring eyes, the mouth open for a shriek and both hands pressed hard against his breast. He stood like that for a moment, and then he began to stagger, and would have fallen if Charlotte had not caught him in her arms. She quickly called for help. Two men came forward and carried him to her sleigh. When they laid him down on the seat he was unconscious.

Then she had driven over to the foundry, where she stopped for several hours, as Karl Arthur needed attention. Besides, Lundman and she, after crawling on the wet ice, had to dry their clothes, and the horses had to be rested and fed. But Charlotte did not remember anything that had occurred during those hours. She had prayed God all the while that she might be able to save Karl Arthur and free him from the woman who

was wrecking his life. They had been unable to revive
him before leaving; but as he showed marked signs of
life, Charlotte had rolled him into one of her carriage
robes and taken him with her in the sleigh.

It is a silent, murky, starless night. Charlotte sighs
at the thought of the great silence in which the Almighty
enwraps Himself. Never in all her life has she so longed
for an answer to prayer!

She suddenly notes a slight movement in the bundle.

"Karl Arthur," she says in a whisper, "how are you?"

He makes no reply. But now that she sees he is coming out of his swoon she is filled with a new fear. How
will he be? Will he be rude and cynical, as he was on the
ice? She must bear in mind that he is a changed man.

Presently, she hears him ask, in a faint voice: "Whom
have I beside me in the sleigh? Is it Charlotte?"

"Yes, Karl Arthur, it is Charlotte."

"I might have known it was Charlotte." His voice,
though beautiful as ever, sounds affected and almost
mawkish. "There is always something so fresh and vital
about you, Charlotte, that just sitting beside you makes
me whole again."

"You are feeling better, then?"

"I'm perfectly well, Charlotte, there's nothing wrong
with my heart at present. I suffer no pain. Not in many
a year have I felt so well!"

"You have been very ill, Karl Arthur."

"Yes, Charlotte, very ill."

He says no more for a while, and she sits quietly waiting. But he soon begins to speak again in the same effeminate, mawkish tone.

"Fancy! I'm sitting here, amusing myself by holding a funeral service over my remains."

"A funeral service, did you say?"

"Yes, that is what I said. Have you never wondered what the parson would say at your grave when you are dead?"

"Never, Karl Arthur. I'm not thinking of dying."

"Charlotte, wouldn't you like to tell the parson who is to speak at my funeral to say to the mourners: Here lies the rich young man who, in obedience to Jesus' command, went and sold all his possessions, and became a poor man?"

"Yes, yes, Karl Arthur; but you're not going to die now."

"Not yet, perhaps. I never felt better. But, anyhow, you might bear it in mind. And I also wish the parson to remind the mourners that I was the apostle who went out upon the highways and byways to carry the message of the Kingdom of God to the people in the midst of their work and their play."

Charlotte wonders if he is making fun of her, but says nothing.

He continues to speak in the same affected voice. "I think too it would be well if the parson said something about my humility; how I, like the Lord Christ, have eaten and drunk with publicans and sinners."

"Hush, Karl Arthur! You and Christ!—That is blasphemy."

He waits a moment before he answers her. "I don't quite like your interpolation. But perhaps it's just as well not to mention the publicans. It might be misunderstood. The other may be enough to explain why I have confined my activities to the highway, amongst the folk of the road. Certainly it has not been for lack of opportunity to extend my activities in other directions."

Charlotte is dumbfounded. Does he mean it seriously, or is he only talking for effect?

"Perhaps you recollect, Charlotte, that I have a friend who became a missionary."

"Pontus Friman?"

"Correct. He sends me letter after letter, urging me to come out to Africa and work with him. I feel strongly tempted to go. I'm rather fond of travel, and language studies interest me. It has always been easy for me to absorb knowledge. What do you think of it, Charlotte?"

"I think it is an excellent idea. But you are not chaffing me, are you?"

"I? Would I indulge in chaff? You should know of old that I always speak seriously. You seem to be rather undiscerning, Charlotte. I had not expected this, after our long separation. I'm afraid this meeting will be a disappointment."

"That would be a great pity, Karl Arthur." Charlotte

is appalled at this poor ragamuffin's presumption and conceit.

"I know that you are very rich, Charlotte, and rich people easily become superficial and judge according to the appearance. You don't seem to understand that my poverty is voluntary. I have a wife——"

At the mention of his wife Charlotte interrupts to tell him something she hopes will arouse his interest.

"Now, listen to me a moment, Karl Arthur! Do you know that your mother, during the last years of her life, would hear no other reading than your student letters? Day in and day out, Jacquette read them aloud to her. Then, at last, she grew weary, and what do you think she did? She went down to Korskyrka to see your wife and your little son, and brought them back with her to Karlstad so that your mother might see your child."

"Very sweet and touching, Charlotte."

"After that Jacquette did not have to read any more from your letters. Your mother wanted to have the boy with her always. She played with him, adored him, and thought of nothing else. She wouldn't part with the child, so your wife had to move to Karlstad. Anna has come into great favour with the whole family, especially with your father. After your mother's death, Anna went back to Korskyrka. She and her numerous foster children have converted your little cottage into a regular farmhouse. But your son stays most of the time with Jacquette, who lives now at Älvsnäs. Karl Arthur, wouldn't you like to see your son?"

"I know well enough that my wife and the others are pining to death for me. But it's useless, Charlotte, your trying to plead their cause. I prefer my freedom. I love the life of the road and its little adventures."

"He has no feeling left for anything good," Charlotte thinks to herself. "He only slips farther and farther away. I can't get a grip on him." But nevertheless she makes another attempt.

"You sound so satisfied, Karl Arthur."

"Should I not be satisfied now that I have found Charlotte again?"

"Don't you feel sorry that you stole the little child? At all events, it led to the death of two persons."

"Two persons, two persons—you make such queer remarks, Charlotte. Why should I care if two persons die? I hate all mankind! It is my supreme delight to gather people around me and tell them what miserable swine they are."

"Stop, Karl Arthur! You are dreadful!"

"I, dreadful? You think me dreadful? Oh, well, that's natural in a woman scorned. Anyhow, you must admit that one who has been able to call forth such devotion as I . . . Charlotte, I can't understand how she puts up with it! I expect her to appear at any moment and snatch me from your arms."

"For pity's sake, shut up, Karl Arthur!"

"But why? It is a pleasure to talk to you."

"You disturb my prayers. I have been praying to God ever since I met you this afternoon."

"A most praiseworthy occupation. May I ask for what you are praying?"

"That I may be able to save you from that woman."

"From her! It's futile, Charlotte. No power on earth can affect her devotion." He leans over and whispers into Charlotte's ear: "I have tried in every conceivable way, but there's no help for it—none save death. *Nemo nisi mors.*"

"Then I shall pray for your death, Karl Arthur."

"You have always been so unpleasantly honest, Charlotte. It is not very gratifying to know that you are praying for my death; but, of course, I shall not interrupt your devotions."

They ride a long while in silence. Charlotte wonders what she shall do with a man who is so utterly debased, when Lundman suddenly turns to her.

"Do you hear, mistress? There's someone following us. They're driving like fury. I can hear them lashing their horses and shouting to each other, 'Now we'll get 'em.' Mistress, shall I drive faster?"

"No, Lundman; we'll stop instead. They are welcome."

A few seconds later a couple of small sledges come alongside their sleigh. Dark figures appear in the road, two dash forward and seize the horses by the bit, and two, a man and a woman, step up to Charlotte.

"Isn't this Charlotte, wife of Commerce Commissioner Schagerström?" lisps the woman. "I should like to know if you can tell us what has become of Karl Arthur.

Before he went out on the ice we arranged to meet at one of the smithies, and I sat there waiting for him for several hours. Finally I made inquiries at the foundry office and learned that he had become ill and that Fru Schagerström had taken him into her sleigh. That was very kind and thoughtful of you. 'Old love,' as the saying goes, 'never rusts.'"

"You come well attended, Thea," Charlotte observes calmly.

"I was fortunate enough to meet some of our good friends on the road, who volunteered to help me find Karl Arthur. Ah! Fru Schagerström, you don't know how much good he has done among the folk of the road, and how much the people think of him!"

"I understand that you mean to take him by force if I refuse to give him up."

"Not by force, Fru Schagerström, that was not our intention. We merely wished to assure ourselves that Karl Arthur could act of his own free will and come back to us if he so wishes."

"There is no doubt, Thea, as to his wishes. He has been carrying on a polite conversation with me for the past hour, and he is bored to extinction. He's very glad that you have come. Certainly I shall not hinder his going. You may tell your friends that the drawn knives I see gleaming about me are not needed. You can have him."

Thea Sundler, who had expected strong opposition, is too astonished to answer.

"Take him, Thea!" Charlotte has raised her voice. "Take him and finish him! I thought that I might be able to help him, but I cannot. He has no feeling, no wit. Here he sits with the death of two people on his conscience, and he's hardly aware of it. Away with him! Take him back into misery and crime. Let him wallow in the gutter! He is pleased with what he has done to-day and has no desire to change his manner of living. Away with him!"

She leans over toward Karl Arthur's side, unbuttons the apron, and draws aside the robes so that he can step out.

"Go back to her who has made you the thing you are! I'm through with you!"

Karl Arthur stands up. Thea, without a word, goes around to his side. As she puts out her hand to help him down he pushes it away and, turning to Charlotte, falls at her feet.

"Help me! Save me!" he cries, and now his voice rings true and sincere.

"It is too late, Karl Arthur."

He clasps her round the knees and clings tightly.

"Charlotte, save me from her! No one but you can help me!"

Charlotte bends down to him and tries to look into his eyes. "You know what it will cost you," she says gravely.

"Yes, I know," he answers just as gravely, and meets her eyes with a steady gaze.

"Lundman," she says with a glad shout, "use the whip and drive on!"

Coachman Lundman, big bearded and brawny, swings his long whip forward and backward and to either side. The dark figures, cursing and swearing, run out of the way, the horses rise on their hind legs and set off. The men who were to hold them are dragged along a short stretch, but lash upon lash of the whip catches them, and they let go their hold. Charlotte and Karl Arthur drive at a mad gallop toward Hedeby.

CHAPTER VI

THE WEDDING RING

WHO was she that she should remember what everyone else had forgotten? Why should she always be thinking of the time when he went about from fair to fair like any mountebank? Why must she continually see, as if she were before her, the woman in whose company he had travelled?

She was quite certain it was the year 1842 he had gone out as missionary, and it was now 1850. He had been abroad but eight years; yet everyone thought that all should be forgiven and forgotten. But she, who was his wife, had her own thoughts about that.

Fancy! Now that he had come back to Korskyrka for a time and was stopping with the Schagerströms at Stora Sjötorp, all the neighbours in the churchtown came and asked her if she was not going back with him to Africa.

But the folks down here were easy-going and change-able; they ran up and down, like water in a trough. Should she go with him—she who was comfortably settled on her own farm? Was she to leave her home now when the foster children were grown up and self-supporting, when she could have peace and comfort and could give her mother a good home in her old age?

She had not seen him, although he had been in Korskyrka some two or three days. Well, at least he had sense enough not to come near her!

She did not want to go to church that Sunday lest he might think she was anxious to see him again. But Fru Schagerström had called for her, and to her it was not easy to say No. But who was she that she should always be thinking of what he had been in the past? Fru Schagerström had told her of the good work he was doing out there among the heathen. He had now found his proper place in life, she said. Our Lord had hunted and driven him until he was caught like a wild beast in a trap. All ways had been closed to him save this alone, and it had proved to be the right one—the one he should have chosen from the first.

Fru Schagerström had not said in plain words that she ought to give up everything and go with him; but she had intimated that he fared rather badly out there, and it would be well if he had someone with him who could prepare proper food for him. Herr Schagerström, who furnished the funds for his maintenance, would be glad to pay a helper, if one could be found.

She had said, moreover, that he had now learned to love his fellow men, which was the most important thing. It was in that he had been lacking. He had loved Christ and had shown that he could sacrifice all the things of this world to follow Him. But any real love of humanity he had never had; and he who would be a follower of Christ without loving his brother man can bring only misery upon himself and others.

And then Fru Schagerström had said that if she would only come with her to church and hear him, she would see how greatly he had changed. She would hear then that he loved the black people he was seeking to Christianize, and that it was this love that had made a new man of him. So she was persuaded to come to church.

When he appeared in the pulpit she did not recognize him at first. His head had grown quite bald, and his face was furrowed by much suffering. He came so quietly and humbly. She felt such a strange desire to weep when she saw him. Yet he did not appear at all sad. There was a smile of serenity on his countenance that seemed to light up the whole church.

She would not say that he preached a remarkable sermon. To her mind, there was too little of the Word of God in it. He spoke only of how the people lived out there in the land of the heathen, but then it was not intended as anything but a missionary lecture. She could understand that he loved the people, since he wanted to go back to them. The poverty and privation in Medstuby were hard enough, but they were nothing in comparison to this. These people had neither window nor floor in their huts.

While she sat regarding his benign countenance and listening to his words, every one of which came straight

from the heart, she suddenly remembered that he was
the man who had railed at the people at the market
fairs and been laughed at. For, as it happened, she was
not a native of Korskyrka; she was from Medstuby
and a niece of Jobs Eric, and she, like her uncle, was
stubborn and not easily convinced.

Coming out from church, she saw that a table had
been placed outside the gate, and on it was a brass
salver, into which people dropped whatever they felt
they could give toward the conversion of the heathen.

Two gentlemen of the churchtown stood guarding
the salver. She thought they stared at her as she went
by. She had brought no money along; for it had never
occurred to her that that preacher could coax her to
give anything. Having nothing else to contribute, she
hastily drew off her wedding ring and tossed it into the
salver. This he had given her, and he might as well have
it back.

She sat alone in her kitchen, wondering what effect
the ring would have on him. He could take it as a sign
that she considered their union dissolved and never
wished to see him again. In that case, she knew he
would not come near her. Then he would go away without further ado.

But he might also take it as a reminder that he had a
wife here in Korskyrka who was waiting for him.

Well, she would see how he took it. Whether in the
first or the second way depended on his mood.

But supposing he came to her, how should she answer him? What did she want to do? Did she know what she wanted?

Her heart palpitated a bit, and she felt so peculiar! Somehow, she couldn't forget that he was the man to whom she had once sent greetings by the birds.

Someone just passed by the window. Was it he? . . . It was!

And now she hears his step in the hall. Now he is at the door. . . .

How shall she answer him?

THE END